Jordan

KAYLA KATHAWA

Copyright © 2022 Kayla Kathawa
All rights reserved. No part of this publication may be reproduced, distributed, or transmitted in any form or by any means, including photocopying, recording, or other electronic or mechanical methods, without the prior written permission of the publisher, except in the case of brief quotations embodied in critical reviews and certain other noncommercial uses permitted by copyright law.

*For every Chaldean girl and woman in the world.
You are not invisible.*

The story, characters, and cities in this novel are entirely fictitious. Certain institutions and agencies, and events tied to them, are mentioned. However, the characters' experiences with these institutions, agencies, and events are wholly imaginary. Any resemblance to locations or actual persons, living or dead, is purely coincidental.

This novel explores violence on the "Dark Web" and contains content some readers may find disturbing. Please use discretion.

January

JORDAN

Get to work.
It was library time. There were novels to outline, goals to reach, and no excuses.
Living at home was driving me mad. My goal was to make enough income to move away from the dysfunction woven into my life. And, at twenty-four, perhaps a little too hard on myself, I was feeling the pressure to be fully independent.
So, after work on a Friday night, I went to the library. The plan was to brainstorm ideas for my next book. Create lists of possible themes, plots, characters. I loved lists. If there was a lot to do, and there usually was, I needed to organize it.
I had always been a perfectionist. How much of that was due to crippling anxiety growing up? The fear of failure, of making a fool of myself? I wasn't sure.
Probably a lot of it. Maybe all of it.
The anxiety was under control now, but I still loved my lists.
Laptop in hand, messenger bag loaded with colorful pens, highlighters, and a small journal on my hip, I walked through the library, searching for the night's seating arrangement.
I liked skimming the shelves along the way, always enjoyed taking in the thousands of books, all the information to which I had access. The possibilities for learning were endless.
I love books.
I found a soft sofa near some windows, sat down and opened up a blank document on my laptop. I'd decided this morning that the current outline I was working on was driving me mad. I needed a break from it, perhaps to explore new storylines. I was losing creativity, and I wondered if I really just hated the story I'd created.

I quickly realized that trying to think of something new right now was impossible. I sat there, staring at the screen, repeatedly typing the start of a word and then erasing it, not liking any of the sparse ideas I had.

I grabbed my notebook and a few colored pens. The author in me loved writing supplies, perhaps the creative part of me loved colors, and the perfectionist in me loved organization.

Maybe, if I wrote out my ideas in different colors, I'd be more inspired.

It sometimes worked for me. It didn't tonight.

Forcing creativity was exhausting, and I'd woken up at four that morning; I was tired.

I couldn't leave, however. There was always work to be done.

I let myself quit the brainstorming and do some research instead.

I got up and began my hunt for information. I needed a book on something particular: marketing as an author. This subject was *too* particular for me to expect to find anything relevant, but I hoped I'd come across something.

I perused, trying to take my mind off the guilt I felt for not working on the novel outline or new story ideas. *Take it easy on yourself, Nina.*

But easy didn't pay the bills.

I ignored that compulsive urge to force myself to work as I passed various books, some old, some new. I liked the wear and tear of the older books. They must have been touched by many, and perhaps that meant they held substance.

Throughout the stomach of the library, along the edges, were bookshelves, ten to fifteen feet long, parallel to each other. One after another, author surnames labeled alphabetically, underneath the subjects or genres for that section. *Biology a-l* on one side of a shelf, *m-z* on the other. Some shelves had one subject on a side and a different one on the opposite. *Textbooks* on one side and *Cookbooks* on the other. *Languages*, *Literature*, *Music*, *Business* and so on.

Finally, I found the word *Writing*. Brilliant.

Stepping between the two short shelves, I assessed the one to the left without reading its sign and discovered it was about accounting. *Ew.*

Turning to the right, I saw a few I hoped contained some gold, amidst the aging pages and shiny covers shoved together. I began pulling them off the shelf, one by one.

Flipping through the pages of one, facing the center of the library, I sensed in front of me a person passing by slowly. There was the fleeting thought that I should step out of the middle of the aisle, in case they came to peruse for themselves. But when they didn't stop, I focused once more on what I was reading.

All six books I grabbed were disappointing.

I decided to try my luck on the other side of the shelf. I rounded the corner and barely avoided a collision.

The person that had passed by a few moments prior had stopped there, unbeknownst to me. He was quiet, despite the silent nature of the library.

He was at the end, pulling a book off the shelf across from his face.

All five foot four of me would've had to reach up far above my head to get that book.

Well, hellooooo, Mr. Six-Three.

I could see his eyes clearly for the few seconds they met mine, before I stepped around him. They were not the type of eyes I was used to seeing.

They were powder blue, too pale to be sky blue, cerulean, cobalt blue, or any other blue I'd seen. They were like the bright eyes you saw on the Internet, but never in real life. *Ever* in real life.

They were shocking. What's more, his skin was the color of caramel, the darkness of it making his winter eyes glow so brightly that I noticed them in those few seconds it took me to pass him.

"Excuse me," I murmured, locking eyes with him and smiling a small smile.

"I'm sorry," he said quietly, words clear. His voice was deep, his words a gentle speed. He was completely unrushed and calm.

I always admired a person who was cool and collected. I wanted to be that way myself.

He wasn't in the way and didn't need to apologize, so I noted with intrigue that he did. And though it didn't seem to come out of shyness or nerves, I smiled reassuringly.

"That's alright," I replied quietly.

I glanced up at the books he was facing, then skimmed to the ones next to them. Lowering my glance, I dropped down into a low squat, trying to take in every book on the shelf. When I got down low enough, I shifted my eyes to the left to see the books in front of his knees. I was quick, so he wouldn't think I was trying to make him move.

There was nothing there for me, anyway. I moved down the aisle slowly, skimming the shelves up and down. This section wasn't about writing but computer technology. *Ridiculous.*

I sighed quietly and turned around to look at the other shelf, deciding to just explore what was there. More books about information technology and computers. One of few types of jargon that I could not bear to read.

"Is there something in particular you're looking for?" the low voice said. I turned around, surprised, and my jaw nearly fell off my head.

Wow.

"Oh, no," I replied, smiling a little. "I found what I was looking for; I just wish there were more of it." Despite my surprise, I knew my face was tired; it had been a long week and even longer day. I tried not to look so openly frustrated or disgusted. The poor stranger *was*, after all, searching through this section, and I didn't want to be offensive. I forced myself to make eye contact.

Oh wow, I thought, *those eyes.* My heart skipped.

He was *gorgeous*.

Apart from his smooth, tan skin and the stunning color of his irises that sent a jolt through me, his eyes were big, bordered by long, heavy black lashes, over which draped relaxed eyelids; his lips were full and shapely.
His nose was straight and narrow, cheekbones defined, but not in a way that made his face look rigid.
Then there was the silky smooth, dark caramel skin; he bore no shadow on his cheeks or chin. On his head sat a bed of thick, full black hair, three and half, maybe four inches long, sticking up smoothly, brushed slightly off to the side, a few tufts curling in and out. Though he had a lot, it looked silky, not coarse. And natural.
I envied a natural beauty.
The stranger was tall, lean but not thin nor lanky. I could tell through his pale green, fitted sweater that there was definition underneath. His waist was narrow, his torso long. He wore dark gray jeans.
The smooth skin and lack of facial hair made him look almost...boyish. But those vicious eyes and that very much adult body said otherwise.
He was Middle Eastern, like me. Except we looked nothing alike.
His cheek turned up slightly, as if he were going to smile but just barely did.
"Do you mind my asking what it is?"
What the—
Goodness gracious.
I felt a wave of surprise. It was unnerving to see such a gorgeous face when it was looking at you so intensely. Shamelessly.
I found it odd that he even spoke to me; most people were silent and kept to themselves in the library. And I didn't give off the most welcoming vibe. The word *intimidating* had been used once or twice.
I was introverted with little interest in making friends. For the most part, I focused on what I was doing when out and moved on.
He was intimidating. Something about him screamed, *Smarter than you and everyone else in the room.* He was comfortable, perhaps self-assured. It was in the way he looked at me so shamelessly, so observantly, unconcerned about what I'd think.
When I was intimidated myself, that was when my guard went up. Stoicism masked that intimidation well.
Maybe he just wants to help, I thought.
"I don't mind," I said, smiling, bringing all of my hair to one side of my face, letting it fall down my chest.
"I'm just looking for books on writing."
He nodded once, outrightly staring at my face. "I see. I'm sorry." He thought for a moment. "The library I usually go to has a lot of books on writing. But that one's not nearby."
I nodded politely. "Where is it?" I asked, tilting my head to the side. He had stopped looking at the spines of books and had turned to half face me.
"Cuttingham."

My eyebrows knitted together in confusion. I stopped looking at books as well, but stayed in my little crouch. "Where is that?"

"About an hour north of here." His expression barely changed at all. There was a subtle, kind smile on his face. Just barely there.

"Oh," I said, unsurprised. I'd never heard of it. "Do you live there?"

"Yes," he murmured.

Oooo, bummer. It was rare to see such a handsome face around here. Or, at least, one that *I* considered handsome. I should've known an oddity like him wasn't from around here.

I, not wanting to end the conversation regardless, replied, "Is it a big city? I've never heard of it."

It was nerve-wracking to talk to a beautiful stranger.

He nodded just a little. "Yes. Mostly large office buildings."

"Oh." I looked off to the side. "Well, maybe I should drive up there and go to that library. Thank you." Thinking I'd ended the conversation, I looked at his face and smiled another small smile, preparing to look away.

"Maybe." He looked at me curiously. "I've been to a few other libraries in the area. They have more. East Hills, Red Tree. I've seen wide writing selections at those." He lifted his eyebrows up suggestively.

"I'll have to go look." Since he wanted to continue the conversation, I stood and faced him directly. "Do you work around here?"

"No." He paused. "My parents live nearby. I visit them often."

His eyes were ridiculous. It made it less frustrating that he hadn't given me a full smile.

I simply nodded, expecting him to cut the conversation any moment.

"Do you live around here?" he asked.

"Yeah," I said, smiling. "Hampton. Five minutes." I cocked my head to the side. "I take it you go to the library a lot, then. Since you've been to the different ones here, as well."

He looked away for the first time for a second, then made direct eye contact again. "Yeah. There're too many books to peruse one library. But you know that." His smile grew, just a little.

This was *far* from casual conversation with a stranger. Everything about this man was intense. He stared a little too hard, looked away too infrequently. And that tiny smile, so natural and sincere…he was looking at me as though there was an inside joke between us. I just didn't know what it was.

I smiled a little bigger in return. "Yeah. Definitely." I paused. "Do your parents live in Hampton, East Hills…?"

"East Hills."

"Oh, wow, so close to me. Did you grow up here? Decided you didn't like it when you grew up?"

"No, East Hills is a nice city. I traveled a lot when I finished high school, though, and kinda lost any attachment I had to it. Eventually work took me north, and I settled down."

I liked that this was turning into a real conversation. I wanted to ask where he traveled, but when he said *settled down*, I knew I couldn't miss my chance to find out if he had a wife and kids.

"So, you don't have family up there?"

"No."

Not detailed enough. "You live alone?" I raised my eyebrows.

He tilted his head a little bit. "Yes."

I nodded, taking this information in. *But are you* single?

"Do you live alone?"

"No. I live with my parents." I smiled, trying to look unashamed and resisting the urge to justify it, the details teasing the tip of my tongue.

I'm twenty-four, I work full-time and pay all my bills except rent. I'm still just as much an adult as the rest of you. My community is just fond of staying at home until marriage. It's cultural.

I pressed my lips together. *Less is more.*

"Siblings?" The one-word question surprised me again. I wasn't the only one keeping the conversation going.

"Yes. Two. We all live there still." I shrugged. "I'd like to get away. I admire…your situation." I smiled again.

Finally! A small, closed-mouth smile appeared on his face. It made my heart skip.

His eyes did not light up to match it, remaining solemn. "I imagine a household of five gets pretty loud." He stared at me a moment. "You're Chaldean." He stated it confidently but not arrogantly.

I raised my eyebrows. My lips slid up slightly at the corners.

"How can you tell?" My voice became subdued.

"I know the look." His smile may have been small, but the way his face shaped around it, no wrinkles or crow's feet, just lips turning up at the corners, made my fingers on one hand twitch. Such a youthful look contrasting with eyes and an air that were both a million years old.

"Oh," I replied, playing along, nodding and smiling as though there *was* an inside joke between us. I stared at his eyes. "And what are you?"

"I don't know. I was raised with Arabic and Chaldean parents."

My eyebrows knitted together. "What do you mean, you don't know?"

"I was adopted." Even tone, quiet voice. No emotion. Just casual.

I tilted my head to one side, kept it there and stared at him for a moment. Matching his stare. Not letting his eyes chase mine away.

"What's your name?" I asked quietly.

His eyes opened up slightly, and his eyebrows moved a fraction of an inch upward.

"Jordan." He stared. "And yours?"

"Nina."

He lifted his chin slightly and opened his eyes more. After a long moment, he said, "I'm happy to meet you."

I smiled a small smile. Felt my eyelids getting heavy. "I'm happy to meet you, as well."

Then I sighed, trying to accept that I'd likely never see this stranger again. I made myself end the conversation. "Well," I said, smiling kindly up at him, "Maybe I'll see you around here some time, when you drive down."

His eyelids sat comfortably, but his eyes remained intense as he stared.

"Do you come to this library a lot?" he asked.

"I like to come after work, so I guess, yeah."

He nodded, that small smile making me crazy. "Then I'm sure I'll see you again." He paused, the intense look in his eyes sending a thrill through me. "I like this library. They have a lot of what I need. And my parents have been asking me to come down more."

That was nice to hear.

"Well, I'd like it if you did. So…" I paused a moment. "Come down more." Not really believing I'd ever seen him again, I smiled, told him goodnight, and walked back to get my stuff and leave.

JORDAN

Meeting the stranger that night at the library was odd. I couldn't forget about it as I drove home.

I wanted to ask him out, but I chose to just hope.

Teeter-tottering between confidence and insecurity was a difficult way to live.

I was hoping he would ask to see me. If I was wanting to see him after such a brief interaction, then maybe he was intrigued, too.

Alas, he did not. But he did say he would be around.

I went to the library the next night around five. I was hoping a little that he would be there.

I tried not to be disappointed when he wasn't. I studied social media marketing and the concept of cover reveals, mind flickering now and again to pale blue eyes and caramel skin.

Man, what's wrong with me?

I skipped the library on Sunday and Monday, instead choosing Marinette's Blend, the most popular coffee shop in the state. This time, I'd use the good old worldwide web.

After getting myself what I considered my defeated mocha, still bummed about not seeing the handsome stranger again, I sat down and researched trending storylines and genres. I *needed* to put another book out. The itch to say I was done with my second was getting worse.

My first novel was picked up by a small publisher. It was surprisingly easy to catch their eye. I was grateful.

I believed in my story. Who didn't want to read an action novel about a Middle Eastern, female assassin? The idea was fresh, in my opinion, and the novel sold decently every month. Not nearly enough to quit my job and write full-time.

I'd copyedit until then.

The rest of the week was busy at work, which kept me focused and made the days fly. Working at a successful marketing firm meant there were rarely slow days.

Friday came, and my typical stress was showing its ugly face more boldly. I'd argued with my mother last night, then my father, then went to bed; it dampened my whole day today. I wanted to move out of my parents' house, but I didn't get paid enough to take on a mortgage payment or rent.

These books needed to be written, and I needed to learn how to be my own advertiser.

The company I worked for marketed sports teams. That was quite different from marketing books, so I had little advantage there. I wasn't on the marketing side, anyway. I copyedited their work.

There was no time to waste.

I resisted the urge to go out to dinner with my sister and went back to the library. My household was too loud. A sister, a brother, my parents, constant arguing, the TV on, cellphones blaring videos or music. I was easily overstimulated. The library was my haven.

I found an armchair and opened my laptop. It was time to outline my next novel.

Deciding on the general storyline was difficult. I could write about anything. Five-hundred-page novels had been written about a single *day*.

Then, there were the genres I had to pick from. I enjoyed reading or writing nothing but horror, romance, crime or mystery novels. Everything else bored me. I loved horror, but I didn't think I had the ability to conjure up something terrifying. I'd written a few short horror stories for my blog, but the thought of writing an entire novel was daunting.

That left crime, mysteries and romance novels.

As intimidating as the thought of writing it was, mystery was my favorite genre; I told myself that I could write anything if I put my mind to it.

There'd be a lot of research and time spent. That was alright. I had few close friends, no boyfriend or hobbies other than running, which I did in the morning before work. I liked shopping for clothes, but that depended on how I was feeling about my body and how much cash I was willing to drop on myself. Which wasn't much.

So what was occupying my time? Right. Nothing.

Research it was.

I thought about romance. I thought maybe I could lace that in. Everybody, whether they admitted it or not, loved a little love.

And I wanted people to love my stories.

Keeping all of this in mind while I wrote, I ended up frustrated by my inability to conjure up anything unique or interesting. My creative juices were suddenly lacking. Again.

I put my face in my hands and sighed hard.

Take it easy, Nina. Do something else.

Disheartened, I continued my marketing research.

Twenty articles later, I tilted the laptop lid down and threw my head back against the couch, staring up at the ceiling.

It was seven-thirty. I liked to be in bed, ready for sleep, no later than eight-thirty during the week. But today was Friday, and though I liked to, I didn't have to be up early on Saturday. So I guilted myself into finding some other productive thing to do. A short story for my blog, another go at novel ideas, maybe tackling my existing outline again. I knew realistically I didn't have enough brainpower left for any of those things.

Maybe I should just call it a night.

I lifted my head back up and stretched my arms up into the air, feeling some tension release from my back. The stretch made me dizzy, sending a warm, grainy feeling throughout my head and body.

I sensed someone walking in my direction. After my vision cleared up, I gave a quick, fleeting glance, anticipating a stranger, maybe an old man or a lanky teenager in need of studying. Just as soon as my eyes returned to my laptop, they flickered back up.

Walking towards me was none other than the stranger from the week before.

Jordan.

Donning a beige sweater under a long, black hooded parka, paired with dark blue jeans, Jordan immediately had my heart beating fast. He carried nothing with him other than car keys and a cell phone. He looked unbelievably handsome as he approached.

I was so surprised to see him that I couldn't think of something to say. I just stared.

"Hi," he said, cheerier than anything he'd said during our first meeting.

My eyes went a little less wide, and I smiled at him. "Hi."

"How are you?" he asked, standing next to the armchair across from mine with his hands in his jacket pockets. The smile on his face was still small but bigger than he'd given me before. His eyes twinkled. He seemed happier than last time.

I was too thrilled for my own liking.

I opened my mouth, but no sound came out. I shook my head and tried again. "Surprised," I replied finally.

He smiled a little bigger. "About what?"

I let out a short, laughing sigh. "I truly didn't expect to see you again, if I'm being honest."

Now, Jordan smiled a tilted, half-smile. I again noted the tan color of his skin and lack of facial hair or any shadow. "Well, I do like this library." He looked me in my eyes and smiled again. The corners of his lips were getting higher by the millimeter. I wondered when I would see his teeth.

"It's clear to me I'm not the only one who likes to go to the library on a Friday night," he continued.

A breathy laugh escaped my lips. I smiled shyly and looked down to my left, trying to concentrate on a reply. I lifted my head back up, still smiling.

"Yeah, well, I'm not much of a partier and I...don't really have the patience for a movie or dinner right now."

"Not a partier, huh?" He smiled, looking at me with softer eyes than before; curious, pensive.

"No," I murmured. After a moment of hesitation, I leapt off the little gleam of courage that the softness in his eyes gave me. "Do you want to sit down?" I asked, gesturing to the armchair at his side.

Jordan blinked his relaxed eyelids lightly. "I don't want to disturb you."

I shook my head, forcing myself to speak at a normal pace and keep my voice even. "You aren't."

I thought of telling him how I was tired of working and that it was nice to look at something other than the screen. Especially his flawless face.

I said nothing more.

After a brief moment's thought, Jordan sat down across from me. I tried not to smile.

"I'll admit," he said, "I really only need to return the book from last week and was contemplating even stopping on my way home."

"You were at your parents'?"

He nodded.

"So..." I continued slowly. "What made you decide to stop?"

I tried not to hope that I was the reason. I prepared myself for him to exit just as soon as he'd arrived.

He looked off to the side for a moment. "Well, I remembered the book after I left my parents, and knew I would forget about it if I didn't come now. And I haven't been down here since the last time I saw you."

I nodded slowly. I still didn't understand why he mentioned his internal debate about stopping. *You didn't want the book to become overdue. Gotcha.*

Something told me he wouldn't care about a fine and would return it when he got around to it. I wasn't buying his bad memory excuse. If he didn't want to come for something else, he wouldn't have.

Wishful thinki—

Wait.

"There's the drop off outside," I noted curiously, pretending to be confused and not suspicious.

His lips turned up. He hadn't thought I'd further question him. But instead of appearing flustered by the crack in his cover, he seemed impressed. And satisfied.

I'd just given him the invitation to say what he was unsure he should say, if only to not appear weird or creepy.

He'd wanted me to catch him in his little lie, so he would have no choice but to tell the truth or another lie. He chose the truth, because that's what he'd wanted to say the whole time. He just needed the push. I'd given it to him without realizing it.

And he gave me the words I was dying for.

"I was curious to see if you were here."
I couldn't help it. My lips turned up. I blinked slowly, just watching him. *What should I say?*
I wanted him to just say it over and over again.
"I was wondering if I would ever see you again," I admitted quietly, blissful.
"Were you?"
I nodded.
"I'm glad you stopped by," I said quietly, offering him a small smile. "Do you have other plans tonight?"
A part of me wanted to tell him to leave, just so he wouldn't say it himself. That he was going to go.
"No, I have no plans." He settled into the couch a little more. He was almost too large for it, his height making the seat look smaller than it was.
"Not even on a Friday night?"
"Not much of a partier myself." His lips just barely turned up at the corners, but politely. I didn't feel mocked.
"Oh, no?" I replied, raising an eyebrow.
His eyes were quizzical as he watched me, and I wanted to know so badly what he was thinking. He took his time responding, unafraid of silence. I allowed myself to be at ease. It didn't bother me how he blatantly observed. I understood his curiosity.
"No," he said quietly, finally.
"Well," I murmured. "I'm glad I'm not the only one, then." I glanced down at my laptop for a moment, just to be able to break eyes with him for a second. Feeling diffident under his stare, I clicked a few buttons to shut it down. It took its time, as it always did, affording Jordan the opportunity to stare at me and *me* the opportunity to look away for a moment.
"Do you mind if I ask what you're working on?"
"Uh, no. I don't mind. Tonight," I sighed, "was research." I finally glanced up at him as my screen went black. Closing my laptop, I added, "I wanted to write but am lacking creativity." I smiled small. "What a waste," I breathed, gesturing to my little bag of supplies.
"Pens?" He seemed the slightest bit amused.
"All kinds of writing supplies. They're crack for a nerd like me," I teased. Jordan's lips turned up at my joke, and my heart skipped.
"Nerd isn't what comes to mind," he murmured.
I didn't speak for a moment. "Regarding me?"
He nodded. My heart picked up its pace. I was about to ask what did come to mind, but I figured the answer would be underwhelming, since we were strangers to one another.
"What were you wanting to write?"
"Mostly new ideas. There's an outline I'm halfway done with but avoiding at all costs."
"For an essay?"

I tilted my head to the side curiously. "No, a novel."
Now Jordan's eyebrows shot up. "A novel?"
I simply nodded slowly, not breaking my eyes from his.
But Jordan was able to handle the silence longer than I could. "Why did you say 'essay'?"
After a moment, he murmured, "I assumed you were in school. I shouldn't have." Then one of his eyebrows went up again. "Are you?"
I smiled a small smile. "No."
Jordan simply looked at me for a few more moments, so I asked, "Why did you assume that?"
"Because you're young," he replied immediately. "And you're spending Friday night at the library."
I scoffed slightly. "Well, I guess I'm just lamer than you thought."
He just barely narrowed his eyes. "I don't think poorly of it. I'm intrigued. When you said you weren't a partier…"
"I meant that I don't drink, don't go to clubs, don't dance. Not that I was skipping out on those things to study." One corner of my lips turned up.
"*You're* at the library on a Friday night as well. And, I suppose *I* shouldn't assume, but I'm guessing you aren't in school, either."
"What influenced that guess?"
I smiled. "You look older than the typical college student."
His face didn't move besides *one* eyebrow slightly shifting upward. Man, this guy could *stare*.
"Your assumption is correct."
"*Did* you go to school?"
He nodded. "And you?"
I looked at him for a few seconds, mimicking his observant behavior. He was *so* nice to look at. "Yeah."
"Are you a full-time author?"
"No, no, I wish." I smiled at him tiredly. "I work for a marketing company." He nodded, that focused stare that would make most other people uncomfortable back on his face.
"What do you do?"
His curiosity made me feel insecure; he could've admired what I said, or thought I was a loser.
"I'm a copy editor."
"Editor? Not a writer?"
I shook my head slightly, curious why he was surprised.
"So, the novel outline," he gestured to my laptop, "that's your own work?"
"Yeah."
"So you're a part-time author."
I chuckled. "There's what I call my daytime job, and then this." I tilted my chin down towards my computer.
"What genre?"
"Uh, this is gonna be a crime novel, I think. A mystery."

He nodded slowly, his crystal blue eyes burning into me.
"And you?" I piped up. "What do you do?"
He calmly looked down at his hand for a moment, thinking. "I work in computer technology." His words were relaxed and quiet. He radiated confidence, security.
So beautiful, and *smart?*
"IT?" I asked.
He paused. "Something like that, yes."
Odd answer. "What degree do you have?"
"Computer Science."
"Bachelor's?" I pressed.
He paused a moment, seeming apprehensive. He didn't want to answer. "Master's."
Master's? It gets better and better.
His lack of arrogance or feigned humility interested me the most.
"I admire that."
His eyes opened more. I sensed some surprise. "My degree?" He said it more like a statement, as he'd done with most of his questions. The lack of intonation contributed to his maddeningly level demeanor.
"No." I contemplated for a second. Then, "You."
Jordan sat back a little in his chair, regarded me. "Thank you. I don't quite understand."
His voice was honest, eyes sincere. I blinked slow, tired blinks and softly smiled. "I'm horrible with science. I'm fine with computers, but not like the stuff I'm sure you work with. I'm talking basic troubleshooting. You have to be very smart to be good at what you do, whatever that is."
He bit his bottom lip as he contemplated a response. "You aren't unsmart because you don't know about IT or computers."
"Well, yes, but I still admire you and the people that *do*. I wish I was good at stuff like that, or had the patience for it, anyway. You can make good money with those skills."
A flash of amusement flickered in his eyes. "That was the topic of discussion for many of my classmates."
I let out an amused "Hm" and smiled at him. "Where did you go?"
"A couple different schools. I finished up in the States."
Oh. Wow. "Did you travel a lot, then?"
"Some." He nodded. "I did a year in China," he added when I made a confused face. "I spent some time in the Middle East."
"Studying?"
He paused. "Yes."
"Have you traveled?" he asked.
I shook my head. "Not much. My parents didn't have a lot of money when I was growing up. I've been to a couple states, not out of the country."
"Is there somewhere you'd like to go?"

I shrugged. "Don't care too much about it right now. Just trying to focus on work at the moment."

"Your book, for example?" he murmured, gesturing to my laptop.

"Yes, exactly." I exhaled. "Man, it's late."

Realizing how nerdy I sounded, I added, "For me, anyway. I wake up early."

He nodded, no judgment on his face. "I understand. I won't keep you."

I tried to give him a smile, but I was so tired. I felt my eyelids getting heavy.

I didn't want to leave, in fear I would never see him again, but I suddenly realized the exhaustion in me.

"I actually would love to stay and talk to you," I said quietly, not bothering to mask my frown. "But I am exhausted."

He stared at me for a few moments, thinking. Taking me off guard, he murmured,

"Would you see me again?"

I stopped moving and looked at him. Face smooth, eyes waiting.

YES!

"Oh." A breathy laugh escaped me. In what reality was I going to say no?

"Yeah," I replied, adding some cheeriness to the sleepiness in my voice as I forced the surprise out of it. "Yeah. I'd like that."

I grabbed my jacket and stuck one arm in, just to have something to do. "Where should we go? You don't live here." I smiled.

At that, his lips curved upward slightly. "I'll drive down. Tomorrow? Dinner?"

No, no. I couldn't eat in front of a stranger so soon. I almost said that, but then decided I would just joke about it later.

"Can we do coffee instead? Earlier in the day? Maybe go somewhere and walk around? I don't want to talk inside a coffeeshop."

"Do you dislike restaurants?"

"No, I love them. But if I'm being honest, I really don't want to wait until nighttime." I decided to mask the truth with more truth.

Jordan's lips teased upward at the corners.

"I'll buy you dinner anyway. I might keep you all day."

If my heart hadn't picked up the pace before, it definitely did then. From any other man, that would've made me scoff and roll my eyes. But his words made me dizzy.

I couldn't believe he asked to see me again. I was nervous and elated, and he was so beautiful it made it hard to see straight.

"That's okay with me," I murmured through a shy smile.

He smiled once more, lips closed. "Is Tommy's Coffee on Seventh and Elm too far from you?"

"No, it's perfect."

"Does noon work for you?"

I smiled, suddenly feeling wide awake. "It sure does."

JORDAN

To say I was antsy Friday night would've been an understatement.
It took three and a half hours of rolling around in bed just to get sleepy.
I woke up at eight in the morning and couldn't go back to sleep. I tried to avoid looking at myself in the mirror. It was difficult.
There had always been things about me that were hard to accept. Some days, I was completely fine with myself. Other days, I panicked, because something on me seemed hideous.
I knew I had to face myself today, because that was what Jordan would see. And I had to make sure it was acceptable.
As I stepped away from the mirror to turn the shower on, I thought about the fact that I knew nearly nothing about this stranger. In fact, it was wise to be in a public place during the day with him. I didn't know if he was a human trafficker, serial rapist, murderer.
I was feeling an odd mix of excitement and apprehension.
I knew he was quiet, reserved. Confident. I didn't think I'd ever seen a man so secure in my life.
I undressed quickly and stepped into the shower. The warm water hit me, and I got to shampooing my hair. When I finished, I wrung it out in the shower and then wrapped my towel around myself, heading to my bedroom.
Closing the door and locking it, I dropped the towel off my body and used it to wring out my hair some more. I was dripping and cold. It was early January in the Midwest, which meant a freezing winter. I quickly looked around for what to wear.
We're going to a coffee shop. Be casual but cute. I grabbed a pair of black leggings and a silvery white sweater with a low but modest neckline. I would wear tall black boots.

I stayed in my bra until my makeup was done, so as not to ruin the white shirt. Once my eyelashes were satisfactorily cloaked in mascara and face smoothed with foundation, I was satisfied.

It was only nine-thirty by the time I'd finished my makeup, so I decided I would let my hair air dry and see if I liked it. I forced myself to eat an apple and a piece of wheat toast so that I wouldn't pass out.

But I wasn't hungry. I was excited and antsy. I just wanted it to be noon.

I sat down and thought about the unborn novel again.

I knew it would be hard to be productive at that moment, so I didn't even bother trying to write anything. I just contemplated how I could make a love story full of mystery and thrills that *wasn't* like every other book of its type.

My mother was the only one awake. "Where you goin'?" she asked me, after noticing my outfit and makeup. I regarded her for just a second, her brown hair pulled back into a bun, face bare. My mom had lovely features. Perfectly shaped little lips, a small nose and clear skin.

"Just meeting up with a friend," I replied. I knew she would get upset if she found out I was meeting with a stranger. My mother worried to the point of near paranoia. The way this made her behave was a cause of my extreme frustration over the years.

"Who?" Suspicion immediately crept into her tone. I didn't go out often. I saw my two closest friends once in a while. My mother was not used to seeing me leave to meet up with people. I was usually alone or with family.

"You don't know him," I said casually, as if it was nothing new or out of the ordinary. "His name is Jordan."

"Where do you know him from?"

Crap. I didn't want to lie, but she forced my hand. I was hoping she wouldn't ask too many questions, because if I told her the truth, she would start a fight, telling me to not be stupid, use common sense, a stranger doesn't randomly just ask you out, he could be a sex trafficker, he could kidnap you, this is a trap.

Well, mom, I thought, as though she'd actually said those things. *I guess we'll find out.*

"School. We've been messaging for a few weeks. I told him we should go out for coffee."

"Where are you going?"

I stayed calm. I loved her, but I wished she would stop talking. I informed her of the name of the coffee shop where we were meeting.

"When are you going?" she pressed.

"Um, I'm gonna leave around eleven forty-five. We're meeting at twelve."

"Okay." She sat back in the sofa where she'd been reading, coffee cup in her hand. "When will you be home?"

"Um, I'm not sure. I might spend the day out. I don't really go over there that often, and I've been working so much." Before she could object about my staying out alone, I told her, "I'll text you though. Wherever I go, I'll let you know."

"Nina, don't walk around outside alone," she warned.

I looked at her in her eyes, remaining calm. "I'm not, ma. I'll probably just bring my laptop into Tommy's when Jordan leaves and work. I just don't want to be home." I couldn't be. The house was exhausting, especially on a Saturday when no one was at work.

With that, I walked away. I didn't want to discuss further.

I sat down in my room with my laptop and tried to focus once more on the unborn novel.

Think, Nina.

What did people like in a love story? Who read them?

Middle-aged women? Teenage girls? What about women in their mid-twenties like me? The women in between?

I wanted my character to be Middle Eastern, like in my last novel. I'd *never* read any fiction about Chaldeans.

Chaldeans were a minority. A lot of people didn't know who we were, especially if they weren't from the few places where my people had congregated. Last I'd checked, less than a million Chaldeans lived in the United States. It was no wonder that there weren't any books about us.

I aimed to change that.

After spending some time making a list of different names, because that was all I was mentally capable of at that moment, I looked at the clock. It was finally eleven-forty. *I can leave now*, I told myself.

I wasn't antsy due to excitement alone. Part of me just wanted to get there. Going was the hardest part.

I was anxious and terrified I'd make a fool of myself.

Relax.

I put my jacket on, grabbed my purse, phone, and makeup that I brought for touch ups, said goodbye to my mother and headed out the door.

"Be careful!" she shouted after me. "Text me everywhere you go!"

It required a lot of effort to remain calm and feel a shred of confidence. I put on some gentle music, trying to soothe my nerves.

The drive felt shorter than I'd expected it to. My heart was already beating fast as I spotted the parking garage. I fortunately found a spot close to the exit. The shop was just a short walk away.

I checked my hair and makeup in the rearview mirror, looked under my unzipped jacket to make sure there was nothing on my white shirt and no lint on my leggings. When all was satisfactory, I looked at the time on my phone. It was eleven fifty-eight.

I slid out of the car and tried to walk at a normal pace to the coffee shop. It was frigid outside. I thanked God I'd thought to bring gloves and wear a sweater under a decent jacket.

When I stepped inside, I glanced around but didn't see Jordan. I'd expected him to be there already.

I stepped off to the side to wait for him; after three steps I heard a voice right behind me say, "Can I order for you?"
I spun around. Standing there was none other than the beautiful man I'd chatted with the night before, sporting a dark gray pea coat this time, black jeans that looked expensive, and black Oxford shoes.
GOODNESS, I thought. He looked so good. Not overdone but not sloppy.
"Oh, I had no idea you were right there." I exhaled, slightly out of breath from the surprise. I smiled. He smiled back. It was warm.
"I apologize. I didn't mean to startle you." His level volume was oddly soothing.
"No, no, that's okay. Let's go up together," I suggested.
As we walked, I asked, "What do you like?"
He squinted, thinking. "Not much. I drink tea. Don't drink coffee regularly but will have it, now and then." I dropped my jaw, teasing.
"You don't drink coffee?" I shook my head. "I don't think I trust people that don't drink coffee, Jordan." I smiled. I made myself say his name, to break the ice.
His lingering small smile grew. "No?" he asked. "Does that mean you love it?"
I nodded. "Oh, yeah. Absolutely."
I ordered a small cappuccino, two sugars, and a cup of water.
I gracefully turned and gestured to him. He looked at me and then at the barista and said, "I'll have the same."
I wanted to raise my eyebrow at him for that, but I was waiting for the credit card reader to tell me to insert my card. I'd had it out and ready before he even stepped inside. A twenty-dollar bill landed on the counter in front of me.
"Please keep the change," he told the barista politely.
I looked at him with the same appalled look on my face as when he'd said he wasn't much of a coffee drinker. "How dare you."
He smiled a small smile as we walked to the side of the counter to wait for our drinks. "You will not pay for anything today."
Before I could snap back, his cool, confident tone became soft. "Please. Let me."
As I looked into his eyes, my knees got a little weak.
I smiled shyly and tried to decide how to respond. Finally, I calmly replied, "Okay. Thank you."
We stared at each other for a moment, eyes locked.
"It's nothing at all," he said quietly.
I looked down for a second. I had to end the moment before I embarrassed myself somehow.
But wow, it was a nice moment.
I leaned against the counter. As we waited for our drinks, I looked back up at him. "How was your drive?" I asked.

He hadn't taken his eyes off me. There was that unsmiling sincerity on his face, the way he looked at me with soft but smooth, unreadable features. Serious and observant eyes. His attentiveness flattered me.

"It was fine," he said lightly.

"Thank you for driving all this way. I really wouldn't have minded at least meeting you halfway."

"You don't have to thank me," he murmured kindly. "It's really nothing on my part. Just a drive."

I shrugged and looked at the barista making our drinks. "Yeah, but, it's gas and time. All that for someone you don't really know. So…I appreciate it."

"Well," he replied, same kind tone as before, "I appreciate you meeting me." He looked behind the counter as he continued. "I know it's not—" He paused. "—or at least, it shouldn't be—the most comfortable thing, meeting up with somebody you don't really know. Especially alone."

"You mean, safety-wise?"

Jordan nodded.

"Yeah, you're right." I smiled up at him and said quietly, "I don't know if you're a serial killer."

His smile was small, and I could sense the seriousness in him. It surprised me.

"I know you're kidding, but it is a valid thing to be wary of. I'm glad you are."

He seemed hyperaware of the dangers of the real world. If he were, that would explain his solemn nature a little.

"Of course," I emphasized quietly. "It's dangerous for anybody."

The male barista place our prepared drinks side by side on the counter and said, "Two small cappuccinos and waters." We thanked him.

I looked up at him again. "Would you like to walk outside or sit here?"

"Whatever you prefer."

I knew you were going to say that. He was awfully accommodating.

"Let's walk," I decided, not overthinking it. "We can sit at some point later, if you want." I grinned. "Once we're sufficiently frozen."

An amused look on his handsome face, he replied, "I'm happy you wore a jacket. I'm worried it won't keep you warm. That's my only reservation about walking."

Perhaps my disbelief showed on my face. I was surprised by the concern in his voice, and the consideration.

"I have gloves in my pockets," I assured him. "I'm wearing a sweater, too. But you, your hands are going to freeze."

He smiled and reached into his pockets, pulling out black gloves.

Once our hands were cloaked, we stepped outside.

"I'm sorry if asking you to dinner was uncomfortable. I didn't realize until after that you probably wouldn't want to go out with a stranger at night."

I wasn't expecting those words. "Oh. Well, thank you for being thoughtful, but…" After a moment, I admitted, "I just don't like eating in front of strangers."
"Why not?"
"I dunno." I shrugged.
When he looked at me again, he still seemed the slightest bit dismayed. "It's okay," I said, kind of alarmed at how serious he was. "I'm being serious. Don't worry, I don't think you're here to traffic me. I am curious, though. What made you want to see me again?"
That seemed like the first question he didn't have an answer ready for, because Jordan thought for a few moments before responding.
"If I'm being completely sincere, I'm just…curious about you." He looked up, breaking his eyes from the cement. "I was when I first saw you. I don't know why. I know that sounds odd." He made a slightly disheartened face. "Or creepy."
"No," I reassured him, voicing my thoughts on it at an easy pace. "I know what you mean. It's okay," I said, leaning in front of him a little bit to look up at his lowered eyes. He still seemed unsure.
"Listen," I began. "I don't really…go out with strangers. I don't really know how people…meet people. Not even to date but just…if you're not at work or in a class, how do you meet people? Do you just walk up to a stranger at the store and talk to them, until one of you is comfortable enough to ask the other to hang out?" My voice was skeptical.
"My point is," I said, forcing myself to look up at him. I'd looked away while I was speaking, trying to coherently express my thoughts. "I don't think you're creepy. I was just as interested in you when I saw you." I smiled, adding the last part quietly.
He stared at me for a few moments, and finally, his lips turned up at the corners.
"Thank you," he murmured.
I wondered what had made him so empathetic to another person's fears. What made him hate so much the thought of making someone uncomfortable. Most people would, but he seemed perturbed by it.
There was something about him that was calming. I didn't know him well, but I felt safe around him. It was his quiet confidence and self-security that made me believe that Jordan could be unreserved, if need be. But I didn't feel threatened myself.
That was attractive to me.
"So," I started, as we strolled down the street, picking a less crowded strip. The air was clear, the sun was peeking out from behind light clouds.
"You told me you work in computer technology. What does that entail? Because that's a very large industry."
He paused a moment. "It is. I work in cybercrime."
Right away, I thought of one thing. The heinous "Dark Web."

Maybe Jordan was a cop who hunted creeps who used the Internet to prey on innocent people.

I made a milder guess. "Hacking?" I asked, disturbed by where my thoughts had gone.

"It involves that, yes." Now his eyebrows knitted together in confusion. He looked concerned.

"Are you a cop?"

Jordan shook his head slightly. "No."

"Okay," I said slowly. "Who do you work for?"

After a moment, he murmured, "A private company."

"That just works cybercrime?" He nodded.

"Okay. So, besides hacking...what else does it involve? Do you track criminals down by their devices? Help the cops find them?"

"Sometimes." I looked at him with encouraging eyes, asking for more. He received the message and continued.

"I work with a team of investigators trained in computer technology. We find and stop crime done or shown on the Internet." He was watching me carefully with each word. His elementary explanation made wonder if he thought I was stupid.

He could definitely tell I had something bad in my head.

"Okay," I repeated, drawing out the word. I didn't have the patience for generalities. "What they call the 'Dark Web'?" I anticipated a quick *no* and another slow, hesitant explanation about identity theft.

Jordan stared at me, not moving his head, facial expression unchanging. "Yes."

"Oh." *No way!*

I nodded slowly, trying to think of which question to ask next. I wanted to know if the movies, urban legend videos and stories about the Dark Web were accurate representation.

But I didn't want to say something stupid, like "I've seen that one movie about that; it was fake, but it still messed me up." I wanted him to know I was aware of it. "That sounds scary," I said quietly.

"It is." His voice was low and soft. "We stop as much of it as we can."

Thoughts of people doing evil things on camera ran through my head. Then, Jordan's role in stopping them did, and I looked at him in wonder. He was on the good side. A real hero.

I laced my fingers together and put them to my lips, nodding. Finally, I murmured, "That's very admirable."

"Thank you," he returned quietly. Then he changed the subject.

"How old are you?" he requested.

I looked ahead at a man leaning against the wall of the upcoming building. He was older, with a graying beard and dirty hands, smoking a cigarette. I was closest to him. He gave me a creepy smile; I braced myself for the embarrassment from whatever sleazy thing he was about to say.

Then he noticed Jordan for the first time. They locked eyes for a few seconds.
And I knew then that my earlier suspicion was right.
Jordan's eyes alone turned so menacing it raised goosebumps along my arms, even though I was already cold. The smile vanished off of the creepy man's face, and he mumbled something to himself, dismayed.
Jordan looked at me as though nothing had happened, waiting for my answer.
"Twenty-four." Even though I was startled, I was glad he asked. I wanted to know how old he was. "And you?"
"Thirty."
We were at a crosswalk, waiting for the green light to flash. I took a sip of my cappuccino.
"You're young," he murmured.
It was our turn to cross the street. Seeing how crowded the sidewalk was ahead, I gestured for us to turn left, cross the intersection and go back the way we came. We had to wait for our turn again.
"Sure," I replied. "So are you."
He smiled. It made my fingers twitch.
"When's your birthday?" I inquired.
Jordan's eyes were content. "October first."
"Oh. I love October. How fun."
"Yeah? What do you love about it?'
"I love fall."
"Do you?"
"Yes. I love to decorate."
Jordan's eyes opened up a little. He looked endeared.
"Your house?" he asked softly, the small smile on his face and his soft tone making me feel shy.
"Yeah," I replied, just as softly. I couldn't look at him for too long. We'd oddly just entered a sweet moment. He stared at me with what I thought to be wonder in his eyes.
Geesh, all over a season.
"Do you like the holidays?"
He tilted his head to the side a little. "Yeah. I like Christmas a lot."
"Are you Christian?" I asked, surprised. I was hoping so.
He nodded. "Catholic."
I smiled big. *No way.*
There were times I thought I'd never find a man I was attracted to.
Let alone a Catholic one.
"Me too," I said quietly, humbly. "It's nice to meet someone else who is. I feel like I never do."
"Most of our community is, though."

Our. I remembered then that one of his parents was Chaldean, the other Arabic. Even though Jordan was adopted and may or may not have been Iraqi, he was still a part of our community. It made me smile.

"Are both your parents Catholic?"

"Yes. That's how I was raised."

"Hm," I murmured to myself, thinking. I wondered how different than his parents he looked.

"So you're around Catholics all the time, right?" he continued with his earlier point.

I looked up and smiled. "Right, right, but I haven't really met anyone I was into."

"In the community?"

"At all."

"Why is that, you think?" He was pensive, looking at me with intrigued eyes.

"I don't know. I just…I'm rarely attracted to people. Honestly, I just haven't really…dated."

"No?"

I sighed. "Well, I have. Once. But he…" I shook my head. "He looked okay." I made a slight face.

Jordan laughed.

I glanced up at him. His eyes were gleaming in the daylight. "Just okay?"

It took me a moment to even process his question after hearing his laugh.

A wave of joy washed over me. It was lovely.

"Um," I let out a breathy laugh, trying to concentrate. "Yeah."

"Why'd you date him if he only looked okay to you?"

I chuckled. His laugh nearly had my head spinning. "It was different back then. I hadn't met many attractive people. He was the best I'd seen." I was grinning.

"But you don't even look like anyone I've ever met, so you don't count," I added, my eyebrows suddenly knitting together. "You're hot."

He laughed, a full laugh that I was expecting as much as he was expecting my comment. Not at all.

I shrugged, a little bounce in my step. I was more comfortable with him as the moments passed. I couldn't help but feel giddy after making him laugh.

I smiled a big smile up at him. His lingered.

"Thank you," he said, amused, the words genuine.

"You're welcome," I said cheerily. I couldn't picture Jordan calling anyone hot. I knew my language, mannerisms and just about everything else contradicted his own. I didn't care.

It made being around one another interesting.

I skipped in front of him, whirled around suddenly and stopped, facing him. "Jordan," I said, stress in my voice. I pulled out my phone and looked at the time.

"It's nearly one." I looked up at him, eyebrows climbing to the top of my forehead, eyes wide, as though something very serious had happened. "Are you hungry?" I asked gravely.

The humor in his eyes pleased me. There weren't many people that enjoyed my idiotic moods.

"A bit," he replied, trying to match my seriousness and play along but was just a little too amused. Then he got serious. "Are you?"

"Ummmm." I didn't have too much of an appetite, but I hadn't eaten and didn't want to get tired. "Not really, but I haven't eaten, and I'm kind of worried that you have to eat."

He laughed again. I was thrilled. "Why?"

I brought my serious tone back. "Because you're large." I reached up to the top of his head to emphasize his height. I was cheery.

Jordan smiled a small, fond smile. I probably would've started jumping up and down if I didn't have the right mind to calm myself. The complete lack of judgment on his face and the subtle sweetness thrilled me.

I felt so comfortable with him, as though we'd been friends for a long, long time.

I can definitely eat with him.

"I appreciate your concern, very much." His smile grew as he said it. Then, "We'll go wherever you want to go."

Oh, no. He had to learn fast. "Jordan, if we're going to hang out, I need you to know something about me." I looked him dead in the eye, face grave. "I cannot make decisions."

His smile turned up slowly, and his eyes narrowed a little with it. It was downright beautiful.

"Okay," he said, nodding, looking around, determined. "Don't worry."

Finally, he declared, "We'll go down the block to Bezzing's. Is American food okay with you?" Before I could even answer, he said, "Tell me what you like, and I'll pick something."

I shook my head. "It's perfect. I've never been there, but I trust you." I smiled.

"My mom likes it," he told me. "My brother brings her here all the time."

"That's sweet," I said. "Where is it?"

"It's down the block. Is a little bit more of a walk okay?"

"Yeah, yeah, that's fine. It's no big deal." I kept my voice soft, the corners of my lips refusing to fall back in place.

And so we walked to the restaurant and got a table for two.

Once we'd ordered two bowls of soup and a plate of fries to share, he mentioned how glad he was that I felt comfortable enough to eat in front of him.

I laughed. "It's funny that you mentioned that now. I thought for sure you were going to say something when I asked if you were hungry."

"Well, I didn't want to remind you. I was worried you'd get apprehensive again and change your mind. So, I decided to wait, at least until after you'd

ordered." He smiled small, staring into my eyes again inquisitively. "Please don't change your mind."
I smiled back. "I won't. I love fries."

JORDAN

Jordan and I had a date.
After lunch last Saturday, we'd exchanged phone numbers. He asked me if I would see him again and said it was lovely spending time with me. I was thrilled.
Preparing to shower, I undressed down to my underwear and looked myself up and down carefully, envisioning how he saw me, how anyone would see me.
Lean. My biceps and triceps would peek out if flexed, and my upper and middle abs showed; my waist was small, torso long, hips narrow.
Working out was compulsive. At one time, I had to constantly remind myself that skipping a workout wouldn't make me fat or knock me off of my regimen. If I didn't do it, I'd be anxious and full of dread. It wasn't as pressing of a fear now.
I stared at my solid abdomen, getting lost in the memories, as I always seemed to do when someone brought back those insecurities. He didn't mean to, but Jordan made me second guess myself. He just seemed perfect. The nightmare of my eating issues during my preteen years, peaking simultaneously with my unhealthy fixation on exercise, flashed through my mind.
I remembered the extreme restriction and constant calorie counting. The brutal headaches due to racing thoughts about food. Wanting so badly to be able to stop obsessing.
I wanted to feel better, live my life, grow up happy and normal like the other kids.
So I tried. I went to therapy. Gliding my fingertips up my stomach to my chest, analyzing while lost in thought, I remembered the brunette with the slightly raspy voice who'd helped me break my obsession.

She'd instructed me to eat more and constantly reiterated the idea that I wouldn't gain weight from skipping even a week of exercise. Together, we worked out better habits. I still used the knowledge she taught me.

Your body needed fat, or it wouldn't function. If you didn't get enough, your menstrual cycle would stop, and you would be cold all the time.

What you saw in the mirror was not always what was there. Anxiety was warping what you saw, making you think you were bigger than you were. Making you believe you were unattractive, horrible to look at. It was lying to you.

You had to stop fixating on how other people perceived you, or you would never be happy.

That applies to Jordan, Nina.

But Jordan's seeming perfection brought some of my anxiety back.

You're pretty. I'm sure he thinks you're pretty.

I looked at the limbs I wished were a little smaller.

He might *think you're pretty.*

I took a deep breath, staring.

If he doesn't, he isn't worth it. This is who you are.

I remembered again all I'd experienced, and how it still floated through my head over a decade later.

You're healthy now, and that's what matters. Not some stranger's opinion.

I was a lot better now, but getting here was brutal. I had to heal the depression, too.

I wasn't just tired all the time, or unmotivated. I felt the opposite of the latter; I worked too hard in fear of failing. It was unhappiness. Devastation. I felt all the time like something was wrong, but I didn't know what.

I lived in that agony throughout my childhood, adolescence and early adulthood. Looking at myself in the mirror now, I remembered the face of that young girl in the pictures, the girl holding all that pain. My reflection stared back at me solemnly.

I'd gone through a dozen therapists over the years, and tried a little less than that in medications.

I blinked tiredly, remembering the exhaustion. Feeling heavy. Sometimes numb, sometimes devastated. I remembered the doctors who got kickbacks when they prescribed me drug after drug, regardless of the side effects. Another obstacle, finding doctors who cared.

Nina from those years sat tiredly at the forefront of my brain.

Overmedicated, obsessive, anxious, insecure and miserable.

It took about twenty years of life to really start living.

It's a lot better now, Nina. Be grateful, I thought to myself as I got lost in the memories.

I was. I was grateful.

A younger me would have been mortified at how she looked in the mirror. Now I was healthier, aware of myself enough to control my thinking. To identify when it was the anxiety talking, telling me I was hideous and that something was terribly wrong. I was aware that not everyone was going to like me. Aware that I couldn't constantly worry about how other people saw me.

I tried to appreciate my better assets while I stood there. Flashy muscle here and there, tan skin. Defined cheekbones, shapely lips, dark, full eyes.

I looked down to my shapely thighs. Evidence of the hundreds of miles I'd run in my life. On my ideal body, my waist would've been smaller, less love handle, more bottom. But what could I do? I loved ice cream.

I looked further. The yellow in my skin was showing this morning, glaring out from my tan.

For a Middle Easterner, I was on the lighter side. I would've loved to have tawny skin like Jordan's, which, at that moment, was about three shades darker than mine. If I'd been behaving like a good girl and not going to the tanning salon, it would have been more than those three shades.

My hair, falling all the way down to my tailbone, was dark brown, thick, silky and wavy. In the sunlight, it lightened to a milk chocolate color.

I glanced back up at my heart-shaped face, at my moderate, angular nose, dark brown eyes and long eyelashes.

I'd often wondered if I was beautiful, and I convinced myself that if I was, it was an odd beauty.

I couldn't help but hope that Jordan liked the uniqueness in me. That he was attracted to me.

My mind wandered back to him for a moment, and how I'd never done more with anyone than kiss.

I wondered if he would think I was a prude. I pursed my lips, hoping not.

We hadn't spent a lot of time together, but Jordan had me longing for closeness that I'd never had. To be held, hugged. Forehead kissed. Affection and love I deserved but was refused by the one person who was supposed to give it to me. I didn't let my brain wander further than that affection, however.

Regardless of what the world thought about it today, I'd chosen to wait until I was married to have sex. And I'd been successful so far, as hard as it was; I knew it would be harder with Jordan especially. I wondered often if he was going to apply the same pressure I'd had to learn to fight, years ago.

I chose to ignore that fear and thought about how excited I was to see him. I was in a good mood by the time I left the house.

I picked a restaurant halfway between our houses. When I arrived, he was waiting outside. I noted the punctuality. I was two minutes early.

He smiled. "Hi."

I smiled back, breathless. It was frigid. He was beautiful.

"Hi," I exhaled.

"Come on," he said, putting his hand lightly on my back. "It's cold."

I all but crumbled.

Nina, you're pathetic.

Jordan held the door open for me.

"Did you tell the hostess about a table? I'm so sorry, I forgot to make a reservation."

"Don't worry. It's okay. I made us one."

I looked up at him. "How did you know?"

He looked down at me as we followed the hostess to a booth in the back corner. "Know what?"

"That I would forget."

He laughed. "I didn't. I just figured, better safe than sorry. When you picked the restaurant, I called to get us the corner booth. You said you liked booths the day we got lunch."

I chuckled and lowered my voice. "What, you just called, and they agreed to hold a booth for you? I didn't know restaurants were so compliant."

"I'm not sure if they are. I know the owner here, and he's always very accommodating."

"Are you kidding me?"

"What?"

"You *know* the owner?"

He seemed confused. "Yeah."

Nothing else.

I sighed. He pulled my chair out for me. I'd get my answers later.

He unbuttoned his coat and hung it on his chair before sitting. His dark green sweater fit snugly on his athletic body, smoothing over the hills of biceps, triceps, deltoids, clinging to a buff chest and sliding down a tight abdomen. I wanted to touch him. Anywhere. Any way.

Before he could question my tone or face, I started talking.

"My mom interrogated the heck out of me before I left," I muttered, annoyed. I wouldn't tell her where I was going, just that I was going out with Jordan again. A restaurant I hadn't mapped yet, and that I would text the name to her when I got in the car. I lied.

She was overbearing, asking me if I *really* knew this guy. If there was something I wasn't telling her. I got irritated by the implications that I was keeping secrets and that I owed her explanations for everything I did.

I'd told her to stop being ridiculous. I knew him just fine. We'd argued anyway.

"Why?" Jordan immediately became concerned. "Was she worried?"

"Yeah," I muttered. "We argued."

He looked bothered. "Why?"

"Because she is overbearing and too protective."

He frowned. "I'm sorry. Should we have met closer to where you live?"

I shook my head, sitting back in my chair. "She doesn't even know where I went." I looked up, took a deep breath and let out a big sigh. Jordan watched me, eyebrows still knitted together.

"It doesn't take much for us to argue," I explained. "I know that doesn't sound very becoming of me, and I'm not perfect, but…" I shook my head again. "She's just…difficult."

Jordan stared at me, waiting to see if I would say more. Finally, when he realized I would offer nothing else, he murmured, "I'm sorry." I cocked my head to the side and smiled tiredly.

"Has it always been this way?" he asked quietly.

"Yeah," I sighed. "I love her, I really do. She's my mom. A great one. But she has her moments."

A waiter came by, introduced himself as Adam, left us two glasses of water and asked if we wanted anything else to drink.

"Diet Coke, please. Or Pepsi. Whatever you have, it doesn't matter."

"Diet Coke, you got it," Adam said, writing a note while I thanked him. He looked at Jordan, who said he was alright for now.

When Adam had gotten far enough away, I resumed. "But still, we've always had a strained relationship in some ways. Both headstrong, both…been through some…things."

"Explain that to me, please." Jordan sat back. "If you don't mind." I opened my eyes wider, silently inquiring about which part he wanted. "What you've been through." He hesitated, then said, "And that she has her moments."

Of course he'd picked up on those things. It seemed Jordan didn't care about breaking the ice. With Jordan, in fact, there was no ice.

I sighed again. "It's not happy stuff," I decided finally, smiling up at him. He didn't cave. "I don't only want to know the happy stuff."

That made my heart feel funny. Warm but sad.

I thought for a moment. Looked down at the table. Adam brought my diet Coke, and I took the opportunity to decide how to word my answer.

"I don't know. My parents' marriage is not good," I confessed, diverting my eyes, twirling my straw around in my Coke and watching the ice move. "My dad, he's a good man, he really is but…he's not really emotionally…present. Stunted, maybe?" I looked up to see if Jordan thought I was crazy yet. His eyes narrowed. He nodded.

"Well, I can't blame him. His parents are old-school. And he's eight years older than my mom." I glanced back at Jordan, locked eyes with him.

"She was too young to get married, I think." I hesitated. "He doesn't love her the way she deserves to be loved."

Jordan's face was serious; his intense eyes contained empathy.

I didn't say more. I didn't want to continue in fear that I was rambling, and that this had gotten too deep, too fast.

Jordan watched me for a few moments; finally, he said, "I'm sorry. For her, and for you."

I twirled my straw some more. "Why me?"

"Because witnessing your mother suffer cannot be easy for you."

Ouch.

He watched me carefully. I stared back silently.

"Or your father's inability to understand his own emotions," he continued gently. "I imagine that translated onto you and your siblings." I tried to clear my expression. I wasn't sure it worked.

"You're right about both," I said calmly, tone even.

I bit my lip. If only he knew.

"There's more," he murmured slowly, "but I don't want to press, if you don't want to discuss."

There is not an inch of ice to break. He melted it before we even ordered our food. He's pulled us into the middle of the freezing ocean already.

"Why do you want to hear it?" I smiled small, adding, "It's a bummer."

Jordan did not smile back. He seemed offended. "Because I want to know you."

I sat back, touched again.

"Okay..." I murmured. I didn't know what else to say. There were so many devastating things.

But Jordan had something in mind. "You mentioned that you and your mother both have been through things, but you've only talked about her." He narrowed his eyes. "In little detail. But now I want to hear about you. With more detail than that." He softened his voice.

"You've been through some stuff," he began for me.

This was the part that was always hard with a new person in my life. Most people couldn't handle hearing hard things and didn't know how to respond. And it was that awkward or insensitive silence that slid me into my own. I rarely mentioned any of my suffering.

But Jordan said he wanted to hear it. I would see if he knew what he was asking for. I decided I would start with the generalities.

I began in a flat, almost robotic, quiet tone. "As a child, I struggled with...some form of depression." I hated that hideous word; I made a face as I said it.

Just then, Adam came back for our orders. I hadn't even looked at the menu.

"Give us a few more minutes, please," Jordan requested politely, but there was something subtly authoritative about his words. If Jordan told you to do something, you did it. I sensed, every minute we were together, something under the surface...that thing I saw downtown, when the sleazy guy looked at me...

"Sure thing." Adam nodded eagerly and rushed to another table.

"Please, continue," Jordan said immediately, gently. His curiosity and encouragement surprised me.

I looked at his eyes now. "Um...that's the biggest thing, I think.

"But where is there room for mental health in our community?" I asked quietly.

He nodded slowly, understanding, dismay coloring his face. Historically, mental illness went unacknowledged, and the stigma was ever present globally, not just in my community.
Jordan said nothing, waiting for me to continue.
I swallowed.
It was easier to keep my face flat if I stared into his eyes and emotionally disconnected. "I've always had…social anxiety. And maybe all these things are interlinked, but the most visible thing, I think, were my eating problems." I eyed him. Waiting for the discomfort.
It never came.
"So that's the biggest bad part of my life," I added, adding some cheer to my tone, trying to seem casual.
Jordan was staring at me, the same, observant stare he always gave, but his face was clouded with more than dismay this time.
His voice was gentle. "In a nutshell," he murmured. "Those are big things."
More?
Is he asking for more?
Isn't this only our second, unofficial date?
"Yeah, that's the gist of it," I said, "and I don't think details are really dinner appropriate. I also have a feeling Adam will be back soon."
"Adam will be fine," he said.
I laughed, gesturing to the menu. "Let's order, before anything else."
"Sure. Go ahead, take your time." He sat back.
I looked at him flatly. "You're not gonna order?"
"I'll eat whatever you eat."
"Jordan, I told you I can't make decisions. Now you want me to decide for both of us." I shook my head, smiling.
"Oh, sure," he said casually, face not matching his tone. He opened his menu. "I want you to eat a burger." The words were careful, as though he didn't know what to expect in response.
"Is that what *you* want?" I asked.
"It's what I want you to eat. I don't really care what I eat."
"Why do you want me to eat a burger?" I chuckled, incredulous.
"Because," he replied casually, "I have to make sure you're properly fed. That diet Coke isn't going to satisfy your calorie requirement for the day."
Ten years ago, dread would have flooded me at the word "calorie."
"Oh, okay. Can I have chicken tenders instead?" I asked, trying to bite back a laugh.
His eyebrows went up; he was surprised, perhaps pleased.
"You can have anything you want," he said; something in those words excited me.
How 'bout you, then?
"As long as it's greasy."
I laughed. "I like chicken tenders. I don't care if it makes me look like a twelve-year-old."

"It doesn't." He looked over my shoulder, raised his eyebrows, signaling Adam over.

"Ready to order?" Adam chirped, rushing up to the table.

"Adam, I think we're going to have two orders of chicken tenders and fries," he said, looking at me. I grinned.

"Sure thing," Adam said, writing on a small notepad. "Anything else?"

"We're good for the moment, thank you." Adam nodded and power walked off.

Jordan's voice was suddenly gentle. "None of this can be easy for you. So, if you'd like to stop discussing it, that's okay. Thank you for telling me all you did."

I shook my head slightly, staring at him, "Do you really want to know this stuff, or are you just being polite?"

I watched the intensity grow in his eyes before he said, "I absolutely want to know. Everything."

The weight of the last word, the way he was looking at me, how it sounded coming out of his mouth, all made something in my chest move. I put my fingers on it.

"Okay," I said quietly. "Maybe when we're somewhere more private."

It sounded nice. Being somewhere alone with him. Telling him my secrets.

"Okay," he nodded, staring, serious. "I will make that happen."

I nearly shuddered. *WOW.*

"Tell me about your parents," I requested, playing it cool.

He nodded. "My father is Arabic, my mother, Chaldean, like you. My mother is a seamstress. My father is the director of the Arabic Community Center in East Hills."

"Oh," I said, eyes wide, nodding. "That's so cool."

"He's retired now. He used to work as an engineer. He just became a part of the community house after he stopped working, and eventually became director."

"Is your mom retired too?"

"Kind of. She used to work much more, as a partner in a laundry shop, repairing things. But now she just works from home."

I nodded. "Their names?"

"Rania and Amar."

I smiled. "I love both of those names."

"Yeah?"

"Yeah."

I thought of something. "Do you speak Arabic?"

"Yes. My parents spoke Arabic while I was growing up."

"Oh, your mom does, too?"

"Yes. She taught my dad Chaldean." The corners of his lips went up.

"That's sweet." I smiled. "Can I ask you something kinda personal?" I murmured, my tone more serious. "You don't have to answer."

He nodded. "Of course you can."

37

Cutie. "How old were you when they adopted you?"
"I was three, I believe." He sat forward, crossed his hands and put them on the table.
"Okay. Can I ask some more questions about it?"
"Yeah," he said soothingly.
"Okay...so...Were you guys here or back home?"
"Back home." He slid his eyes down my face as he spoke the next line. "They found me while they were fleeing, shortly before they found a way to get here."
"They *found* you?" My jaw fell open.
He nodded. "I was wandering around alone in Syria, near the border between it and Iraq." Before I could even contemplate asking, he said casually, "They don't know what happened to my parents. We can only guess."
I sat there in surprise. After a few moments, I murmured, "I'm sorry."
"Thank you."
"I bet your parents are lovely," I declared. "Do you have siblings?"
I got a slightly amused smile. Perhaps thankful.
"My mom was pregnant when they were trying to make their way out. They had a son right when they arrived here. My brother, Tristan."
"Oh, you mentioned him, downtown." I nodded. "How old is he?"
"Twenty-seven."
"What does he do?"
"He works for the FBI."
My jaw dropped once more. "Really?"
"Mhm." He took a drink of water. It reminded me of my Coke, and I took my first sip.
"That's awesome. Are you sure it's okay for me to ask you questions about when you were little?"
"Of course," he murmured. I was glad he didn't get annoyed.
"Do you remember meeting them?"
"When my parents found me? Not at all."
"So, they told you about it, then."
"Yes."
"Okay, so my question is," I looked at him seriously. "Did you tell them your name was Jordan, or did they give that name to you?"
He smiled, charmed.
Yes! I cheered mentally.
"They said they asked me, and I told them it was Jordan."
I shook my head. That was precious to me. I pictured a little version of the beautiful man across from me, telling two concerned strangers that his name was Jordan. I wondered if he was scared, sad, or just kind of clueless.
"I love that name," I informed him. "I bet you were adorable."
His smile grew more amused. He chuckled quietly.
Then it clicked. "Wait, so you truly don't know your nationality, do you?"

"Right." He unclasped his hands and sat back. "We can hypothesize. I was in Syria. I could be Syrian. Even Iraqi in some way. Arabic, maybe. I don't think I'm Chaldean. I've never met a Chaldean that looks like me." He smiled. "Perhaps my parents were fleeing, and I'm from a country far from Syria."

I smiled. "That's actually so cool and so infuriating."

He laughed, a real, rare, open-mouthed laugh. It was deep, matching his voice. Though it was short, it made my chest feel as though something was sucking it inward. My heart skipped.

"Why is it infuriating?" he inquired, entertained.

"Because I'm sure you want to know."

"Yeah," he sighed, shrugging. "I just don't think about it. So it doesn't frustrate me."

Yeah, yeah. Nothing bothers you. Just creepy dudes on the street.

"Well, I'll be bothered for you."

He smirked. "You're funny."

"Wait, they have those ancestry tests?"

"Yes. I'm not giving any corporation my DNA."

I grinned. "Smart man." My eyebrows shot up. "How do you know your birthday's October first?"

"I don't. My parents picked that, because it's the day they found me."

I shook my head slightly. *Found.* I didn't think I could ever process how devastating and bizarre that was.

Just then, Adam walked up with a tray of chicken tenders and French fries. Jordan looked at the tray and raised his eyebrows seductively at me, and I laughed, trying to keep it quiet so poor Adam wouldn't think we were laughing at him.

Jordan smiled a huge, fond smile at me.

It was a lovely moment, all over chicken tenders.

JORDAN

Work was miserable.

Steve, my boss, was agitated all week since our last campaign did poorly; sales were lower than expected. He sent my work back numerous times, telling me to rewrite it. I redid an article three times before he would take it.

If you hate it so much, I thought to myself, *why don't you edit the article?* Steve was controlling, despite the fact that I was beyond capable of perfecting the below-average content I received.

It was difficult to concentrate. I was frustrated with myself for not being able to come up with any ideas for the novel and wondering what this sudden lack of motivation was.

Then there was Jordan, on my mind quite often.

By the time I finished editing a piece, the last thing I wanted was for it to come right back to me and to be told, "Change this." *What do you want me to change it to?!* I wanted to scream.

When Friday came, I was thrilled. And so tired.

Sitting in my car in the parking lot after work, I called Jordan. We had agreed to meet up tonight, but we'd been busy throughout the day, missed each other's texts by hours, and had been unable to plan anything.

"Nina," he answered. His affectionate tone made my chest feel airy.

"Hi," I murmured happily.

"Hi. How are you?"

"I'm good," I exhaled. The truth was, it had been the longest Friday I'd had in a while, Steve had snapped at me twice, and I was halfway on the warpath and halfway wanting to cry. But hearing Jordan's voice made it easy for my reply to be true. "What's going on?"

"Would you meet me at a place called Lenny's? It's halfway between where you are and my house."

"Yeah, of course. Is it a restaurant?"

"It's a cigar lounge, actually." My eyes narrowed in confusion.

"I don't want to go there. I just want to pick you up. Are you interested in coming over?" he asked quietly.

I couldn't believe it. That invitation was the last thing I was expecting.

While I was smitten by Jordan, there was still my mother's voice screaming in my head to be careful, that I didn't really know him. There was that paranoid thought in my brain that, no matter how long I'd really known him, he could bring me to his house and kill me. Yes, that was the product of watching too many crime shows, the news stories my mother made sure to tell me, and her voice in my head, telling me not to go.

But he seems so genuine, I thought, and my gut told me so. *If he kills me, he kills me. Oh, well.*

It was amazing what pale blue eyes and caramel skin would make you do. Regardless, I didn't understand why he wanted to pick me up.

I finally replied, "Yeah, I'd love to. But why do you want to meet me halfway?"

"Because it's a far drive from you. I didn't want to ask you to come all this way on your own, especially since you haven't been up here before." My heart swelled. I felt warm.

"That's so sweet. Thank you. But I don't mind the drive."

"Okay," he murmured gently. "How about this time, I meet you, and next time you come up on your own, if you'd like?" *Next time*. I noted the phrase happily.

"Sure. I'll pop it into my GPS now and get goin'."

"Okay, I'll be there when you get there." I grinned. Of course he would.

"Sounds good." I hung up the phone and hit my GPS.

I'd already changed my clothes into my more comfortable long-sleeved black top, and black leggings, just wanting to feel cleaner and wipe the day off me.

As I'd spoken to Jordan on the phone, I touched up my makeup, dabbing powder where there was some shine and lifting my lashes again with some mascara. My hair was natural, long and wavy, and there wasn't much I could do about the slight frizz at the top. He would have to accept it.

I plugged my phone in to charge and played some music.

It was hard to think of anything but Jordan and my excitement.

I was curious about his house, the place where this quiet, terribly intriguing man lived, all by himself. If he didn't murder me, then this would be very enjoyable.

The drive wasn't so bad. I took the highway for most of it, and the last ten minutes of the drive took me through a cute outdoor shopping center, and then to a more industrial side of whatever city I was in, full of huge office buildings.

JORDAN

My next few turns led me to an emptier street dotted with stores considerably spaced apart. I located a large, red lit sign for *Lenny's*, the bottom of the 'y' curling around an animated, glowing cigar. I turned in, driving to the parking lot behind the building. It was an unsettling area, especially considering it was cold and dark out. I felt more and more like this was a trap, until I spotted Jordan's truck. Then my heart skipped, and I felt a rush through my body. I pulled up and parked next to it.

When he came around the front of his clean black truck, I instantly felt less spooked.

As I looked up to open the door, he was there, doing it for me.

"Thank you." I smiled. It was so nice to see him. My heart was still fluttering, but no longer from leeriness or fear, rather joy. His presence was soothing; I felt safe with him.

Hopefully tonight, after being in his own personal habitat for a few hours, he would be even less of a stranger.

He was wearing dark blue jeans and a stylish dark gray parka, hood down, so light snowflakes were settling for a moment and then wetting his dark hair, making him look more beautiful.

His outfit was less formal than before, and the youthfulness in him shined through. He truly was beautiful, his face young and fresh in contrast to his much older, much wiser aura.

He put his arm over my head to shield it from the snow so I could see. Guiding me around to the passenger side of his truck, he opened the door and stood behind me, waiting, I suspected, to make sure I didn't fall, or to give me a boost if I needed it.

If I was going to be kidnapped, I was stepping right into it.

Go with your gut.

I thanked him for holding the door.

Once I was in and seated, he made sure I was settled and then shut the door gently behind me.

Hopping in the truck, he apologized about the height. "It's okay," I assured him. I'd never been in a car with him, in neither the glossy black truck nor the black Lexus I'd seen him drive. It was odd but nice, being in such a small space together. I could smell his fabric softener and what I thought might've been his shampoo.

He started the truck, and off we went.

We had a thirty-minute drive. I had mapped the distance from Lenny's to his house, just to make sure it truly was halfway and that he wasn't giving me a ten- or fifteen-minute drive to be polite. I also wanted to prepare myself for the time alone together, in such close proximity.

I again noted how good he smelled. Clean, from his shampoo. Not just that, but I sensed the other clean scent I was inhaling came from his clothes, soft and sweet. I suspected that his skin smelled this way, and that it blended in with the smell of his hair and clothes. I shivered.

I turned to look at him. At night, I caught wind of odd sensations, different feelings for cold and warm weather. But the sensations were just as strong for both, and I wanted to call them anxiety, or thrills, but they seemed to be a combination of both.

"Are you cold?" I asked him.

"No," he replied. Then he looked at me, concerned. "Are you?"

"No." I shook my head. "You've got the heat blasting."

"I didn't want you to be cold. I personally don't mind it when I'm driving."

I smiled. "Thank you...I don't mind it either. I actually like when it's a little chilly in the car." I looked out his window. "Gives me a little rush."

He smiled a small smile to himself. Then he looked at the heat controls on the dashboard and said, "Adjust it to how you like."

I reached forward and turned the heat down. "Can we open the windows a little? Just mine and yours."

He touched his fingers to the window buttons in the middle of the dashboard. "Of course."

"Just a little," I requested.

He let them fall halfway. "Perfect." He smiled at me.

"Thank you for picking me up. You didn't have to."

Eyes on the road, he replied, "I wanted to." He ended the sentence with a glance at me. His eyes made the dark thrilling. "How was work?"

I looked up at him, surprised. Then, remembering the day, I looked down at my knees. "It was fine," I said casually, but my voice wasn't convincing. He didn't say anything for a few moments, and I listened to the sound of the engine and the wind rushing.

"What happened?"

Knowing I couldn't lie to him, I sighed. "My boss gives me anxiety."

I realized too late that that word held a lot more weight in our conversations now. I made a mental note to be more careful with my use of it. Yes, my boss gave me anxiety, but a lot of things did. I didn't want him to think something was a larger deal than it was.

Because he asked, I realized just how wiped I was. The excitement of seeing Jordan had distracted me.

"Why? What did he do?"

I sighed. "He's mad because our last campaign didn't do well, and our client was mad."

Jordan raised an eyebrow. "Who's your client?"

"Sports team."

He turned his eyes back to the road as I said it. I noticed how he only drove with his left arm.

"Your company markets sports?"

I nodded.

"Do you like sports?" I asked him.

He gave me a side glance as he replied, "I don't care for them." After a moment, he murmured, "Do you?"

I chuckled. "Not even a little."

Jordan's lips turned up at the corners. "Then why do you work for that company?"

"Copyediting jobs are not easy to come by."

His eyebrows narrowed slightly. "I can find you another one," he stated immediately.

My eyes widened as I tried to think of what to say. "No, why would you do that? And...how?"

Jordan glanced at me again, unspoken thoughts in his eyes.

Answer me, boy. And tell the truth.

"I would do that," he began slowly, "because it might make you happy. I would just call a few people and let them know I know a copy editor that they need."

Appalled by the confidence of his declaration and that he wanted to make me happy, I laughed.

"Hold on a second." I chuckled. "First of all, I appreciate that. Thank you. You don't have to do that. Second of all..." I shook my head, still smiling. "You'd call them and tell them they need a copy editor? Even if they don't?"

Jordan noticed the grin on my face and his lips turned up at the corners. "Everyone needs a copy editor."

I sat back and laughed again. "What are you *talking* about?"

"Everyone can use a copy editor. I know a couple people at different marketing companies, and I'm certain their content could be improved."

"What, and they'll just take your word for it?"

Jordan glanced at me but said nothing.

I laughed again, this time in disbelief. He sounded like a boss, in the way of unending confidence that people would do as he advised. And yet there was no arrogance. He was simply sure of himself.

I again suspected the only reason his lips turned up was because I was laughing. Before that, his face had been blank. That made me feel funny. Warm. Flattered. *You make him happy.* My heart skipped.

"Hold on a second, Jordan," I murmured, still chuckling. "Why do you even know marketers? I thought you worked in cybercrime?"

He looked at me with a relaxed smile. "Work took me to a marketing company once."

"But that's just one; you said a couple people."

A look of discomfort suddenly appeared in his eyes. "I'm sorry; I meant I know...the owner of that marketing company; there are various locations. And..." He seemed to not want to continue. "I've made a few connections through colleagues."

Owner of a restaurant, owner of a marketing company, "a few connections" who are probably more bigshots. He must be one, too.

But the discomfort in his eyes made me not want to push. I simply nodded, asking nothing further.

When Jordan noticed this, he continued, "So, there are other marketing companies who could use a copy editor."

I smiled small. "Thank you, Jordan. I think I'm okay. But I really appreciate that." I liked how he looked at me right after I said his name.

"You don't need to thank me," he murmured. "Tell me if you change your mind."

I was dazzled at his kindness. I nodded.

"So, your boss was angry," Jordan began for me again.

"Yes. And he snapped at me a couple times." I rolled my eyes. "And he kept sending my work back after I spent hours on it."

Jordan's eyes narrowed; he seemed displeased. "I'm sorry."

I shrugged, sighed. "I just have to deal with it."

"You really shouldn't have to," he said dryly. I knew he wasn't mad at me, but he did seem unhappy. Maybe by the situation? Steve?

"Yeah. My daytime job," I said, smiling. "Need it."

But his face was still focused. "I could really help you find something else, if you wanted." He looked at me seriously for a second, then turned his face back to the road. "Why go through the hassle if someone can make it easier on you?" Saying it like a statement, he turned back to me again. "And I'd like to, if you ever want."

I thought the offer was kind, almost familial. Something you'd do for a relative.

"Oh...thank you." I looked at his profile, noting how his cheekbone was prominent on his narrow face. Masculine and beautiful.

"You're welcome. Always."

My heart fluttered.

"Just let me know," he continued. "I'm sorry today was a rough day. Did something in particular happen that you want to talk about?"

"No, thank you for offering. You're very sweet," I murmured.

"You can always tell me things."

I smiled. "Same to you."

It took a moment, but slowly he smiled. "Thank you." He was in a solemn mood. I wondered if something had happened to him.

"Tell me about *your* day," I requested.

He thought for a moment, eyebrows knitting close together again. "It was laid back. I didn't go into the office."

"How come?" I asked. "Are you not feeling well?"

He shook his head slightly. "No, I just don't always go in. I can work from home. My team calls me if they need me. They can usually handle things on their own."

I remembered that I knew so little about his job. "What is it that you do, exactly?" I asked. "I know you work in cybercrime. That Deep Web stuff, the really bad stuff. But what's your official position?"

He didn't answer for a moment. "I don't have one really...I do a lot. A little of everything."

No official title? Something told me he wasn't being forthright on purpose. I tried a different route. "Okay, so explain the company to me. It's private? Not associated with the Feds or state government?"
"That's correct."
I thought, maybe when he was in this serious, unreadable mood, it was not a good time to ask about his job. I didn't think my questions were so bad, but he seemed grim. I thought I'd try a little more and see if he softened up. "Is that legal? Do you report it to authorities?" I unlaced my fingers and put my hands in front of me, speaking with them. "For example, you find a crime on the Internet. Something really horrible. What do you do? You said sometimes you track it and send the location to the cops, right? But not just that?"
"No. Well, yes, I report it. We consult for them, but....we do a majority of the work ourselves. Then a team accompanies whoever we're working with. When the criminals have been caught, we let them handle it from there." He paused. "Sometimes, we just let them know. It isn't always necessary to go with them to find a hacker who steals credit cards.
"But if the crime is of a more violent nature, we like to be there."
"Why?"
Jordan took a moment to think. "I trust…some law enforcement, but I'd rather be safe than sorry." He looked over at me. "You can never have too much help."
His tone was slightly more conversational. I was so intrigued and slightly disbelieving, but I was still hesitant to ask a question. I forced myself to. I figured, if he snapped at me, I would at least be learning something about his temperament.
"Wait," I lifted my hand up. "Your team is trained that way, too? Combat? Weapons?"
"Yes."
I was flabbergasted. Not just computer nerds, but fighters? "You work magic on computers and tote guns while you do it?"
Jordan glanced at me, and I was relieved to see his lips turn up at the corners. I'd worried he might think I wasn't taking him seriously. I smiled. "You *are* a writer."
I blinked, saying nothing so he would continue.
"To answer your question, yes. It's something like that." He thought for a moment.
"My team is well-trained. They've worked with police, FBI, some with the CIA., but not anymore. The rest of the staff are all experts in computer technology." I wondered about his pause.
"But it's those individuals who have law enforcement experience who are the investigators. My leaders." He stopped. "Our leaders." Jordan grimaced but went on. "Overall, we get the job done, together. As a team."
I shook my head, dumbfounded by his words. I was distracted by his face and the word *my* suddenly shifting to *our*.

My speculations were right. He *was* the boss.
So, when I asked you what your position was, why didn't you say you were the boss?
I put that to the side for now. I didn't want to interrogate him.
"I've never heard of anything like that before. Is it illegal to track people down the way you do?" Jordan just looked at me.
After a few moments, he said, "I have a sort of deal with the Bureau."
My eyebrows shot up. When he saw, he clarified. "The FBI."
"What? The FBI?"
He was hesitant. "Yes."
I sat back. I had so many questions.
"They appreciate our help."
Oh.
Law enforcement is grateful for you, huh? That was sexy, even though I was confused.
"So…" I struggled to gather my thoughts. "Do you get paid? Who pays you?"
He exhaled; it was a thinking sigh. "We're paid for consulting, whether for the state or the FBI. Private investors also contribute to our company, I suppose out of the goodness of their hearts."
"Who started this company? Is it relatively new?"
Jordan was looking ahead at the road. We were speeding down the highway. Traffic had cleared, and we had an open road ahead of us. Noticing it, I got chills again. Driving down the empty highway at night with a handsome stranger.
He kept his eyes ahead and face unmoving as he answered. "I did. Five years ago."
I was so taken aback by that answer that I didn't say anything for thirty seconds.
"So…." Then I just stopped for another fifteen. He waited.
"So, who funded you?"
These were questions that he was more apprehensive about answering. The pauses before were contemplative, serious, as though he was trying to decide how to answer. The rest of the time, his answers came naturally.
"I did."
I put my face into my hands and dragged my palms from the inner corner of each eyelid outward, too dumbfounded to even keep cool.
"I'm sorry," he murmured. I looked up. His tone had softened, which was what I was hoping for.
"Am I confusing you?" He looked concerned, probably that I was so slow on the uptake.
"No, no," I said, closing my eyes and shaking my head. "I've just never heard of anything like this before. I'm…perplexed. I'm just trying to process everything you said." I looked into his eyes.
More courageous due to his new softness, I piped up, "Are you okay?"

He raised one eyebrow, surprised. "Yes." He turned to look at me. "Why?"
"Because…" I struggled. "You're a bit…tense. I don't know. That's the best word I can think of."
He looked a little bothered now.
"I'm sorry," he murmured.
"No, no," I backtracked, antsy, "Don't be sorry. I just want to make sure I'm not annoying you with my questions, if you had a bad day or something."
He looked at me guiltily, still perplexed, then shook his head, opened his mouth to say something and stopped, lost for words and perhaps frustrated by it.
"I'm not annoyed with you at all," he said seriously, looking at me. I met his eyes. "I'm sorry if I've been acting in any way to make you think that. I'm happy you're here." He was firm but quiet.
"Very happy," he added.
I was anxious before, but now I was happy; the two emotions were making it difficult to focus.
I looked at my hand, trying to process how I was feeling. "Okay."
"I mean that, Nina." At the sound of my name, I looked up. We were at a red light. I hadn't even realized we'd taken an exit and pulled off the highway. We were now on a main road, driving past houses separated by large, dark trees.
He stared into my eyes intensely. "You aren't annoying me, not even a little."
I couldn't break our locked eyes, but he had to when glancing up to see if the light had changed. Just then, it turned green; the truck started up smoothly.
"Okay."
I didn't say anything for a few moments. Before he could say anything else, I asked, "Are we near your house?"
He glanced at me for as long as he could before he had to turn back to the road. I knew he was analyzing me now, looking to see if I was upset, listening to my voice, peeking at my face.
"Yes, one minute away."
I nodded. I was excited to see it. To get out of his truck, sit on his couch and talk to him. That was something I thought about the whole way to Lenny's. Something cozy like that. Hopefully, he would soften up, as I thought he was doing now.
He turned into a subdivision of large houses and many trees. It was so decorated with green that I imagined it was dark in the daytime.
He took another turn, and then another and slowed, pulling up the short driveway of the house at the end of the street. I didn't see the front. He opened the garage, and there was the Lexus. I was surprised to see he could fit the truck inside.

I was suddenly nervous. To make conversation as he parked, I asked, "Where's your key?"
Before exiting the truck, he patted his jacket pocket and smiled at me. I wasn't expecting it. It made me feel so good and so disoriented that it took me a second to remember to grab my bag and exit.
Because it took me so long to gather myself, he made it around to my side to open my door. He stood there and reached his hand out to help me down. I fell half in love.
I grabbed his hand and paid attention to how it felt to touch him. It was warm, not calloused but not as soft as mine.
Stepping down, I looked at him to lead the way.
"Right here," he guided gently, leading me to the door, quickly unlocking it with a different key and pushing it open for me. An alarm beeped out.
"Oh," I said, stepping in quickly so he could turn it off. He closed the garage with a button on the wall, not in any rush. He came in, pressed a few buttons on the touch screen alarm system, and the beeping stopped.
His house smelled cozy, like firewood and clean clothes, fresh out of the dryer.
We stepped right into his mud room. "Should I leave my shoes here?" I asked, gesturing to the rack in the closet.
He gave an unconcerned half glance at the rack, pulling his jacket off. "Wherever you'd like."
I slid off my short boots and left them neatly in front of the full rack. I stood still in my spot.
He looked at me. "Can I take your jacket, or do you want to keep wearing it?" He shook his head. "I meant to put the heat on, so it would be warm if you agreed to come over. But I forgot." He seemed frustrated with himself again. "I'll put it on right now; it should warm up soon. I'm sorry."
I shook my head, smiling. "It's okaaaay," I assured him, pulling my jacket off. "I like it cold. I'll hang my jacket up."
"Please, let me," he said, reaching for it.
I smiled. "Thank you."
As he hung it up, I looked at his dark blue jeans and black, fitted sweater, the collar coming down an inch under his collarbones. He was unbearably beautiful.
He outstretched his arm in front of him and gestured to the entrance. "Please," he encouraged.
I stepped into the foyer. Ahead was the front door, across from it a spiral staircase. The carpet in front of the door was round and beige, glowing under the large chandelier hanging from the high ceiling as Jordan flicked the lights on. The foyer led to an open room past the staircase; I assumed it was the dining room.
He gestured right, which led us to the kitchen, neighboring the family room.

JORDAN

There was a brown sectional sofa, circling the spacious room over a plush, beige carpet. In front of it sat a dark wooden coffee table, just shy of the length of the couch. Across the room was the fireplace, a beautiful display of beige and brown stone, wrapping around an unlit center and extending from ceiling to floor. Above the mantle was what I suspected to be a ninety-inch television.

"Wow," I said. "Nice."

He shook his head. "I don't watch TV. It's for my parents when they come by. My dad likes football on Sundays, and my mom likes reality TV." I smiled.

"Please, make yourself comfortable. Please," he emphasized. "Don't be shy. Go wherever you want, do whatever you want."

My eyebrows shot up, and I smiled again. "Okay. Thank you," I said sincerely. It was nice that he wanted me to feel comfortable.

"You can explore if you're interested," he added. "I don't mind at all."

"What's in that room down there?" I asked curiously, gesturing to the opposite side of the foyer.

"That's the dining room," he murmured.

I assessed the large kitchen, with its black tile and nook, boasting a black granite table with specks of white that complemented the white walls. The island a few feet away had the same black granite on top. The tall table surrounded by black wooden stools bore no flowers, no centerpiece, not even a bowl of fruit.

Parallel to it was the sink, the dishwasher, and bare granite counter space. To the right was the stove and oven, settled under a stone archway. It was cozy, just like him.

I walked back to the family room, pointing to the two doors framing the television. "What's there?"

He looked. "A bathroom and the library."

I looked at him, intrigued. "You have a library?"

He nodded. "It serves as my office as well."

I smiled. "That's so cool." The urge I always had to cross my legs and become a tight little ball came, and I sat on the floor. Jordan looked at me, confused.

"What are you doing on the floor?" he asked. I had to laugh at the look on his face.

"I'm sitting," I replied cheerily.

"Why on the floor?" He was genuinely confused.

"Because," I said matter-of-factly. "It's rude to put your feet up on somebody's couch. But I have to sit this way. I'm not comfortable any other way, really."

He looked at me, so befuddled that I had to laugh again. "What?" I asked. He was so surprised it seemed to take him a moment to think of what to say.

"Please," he said, finally. "Please don't ever think you have to sit on the floor again."

Another smile grew slowly on my face. "Okay," I said, giggling. "Don't think I'm dumb. I just want to be respectful."

He shook his head. "You're so respectful. And sweet," he added. My heart fluttered again. Then it picked up its pace as he stepped forward and reached his hand out to help me up. I smiled up at him and grabbed it; he held on until I lowered myself onto the corner of the couch.

It was a slow moment, and by the end of it, he was smiling, too.

"I got food," he said. He was quieter now.

He gestured to the counter behind the kitchen island, where there were two large brown paper bags.

"Oh," I said. I hadn't even thought of food. "Thank you."

"Of course," he said, gently unlocking his hand from mine and walking to the kitchen.

"Oh, I'll come over there."

"No, no." He wrapped his arm around one of the bags, grabbed the other by the top edges and walked towards me.

"We can eat here," he said, setting the bags down on the coffee table.

"Okay." I paused, staring at him for a moment. "That's a *lot* of food, Jordan. Do you think I'm a horse?"

"No. But I have to make sure you're well-fed. And," he added, "I don't know what else you like, besides soup, fries and chicken tenders. So," he said, pulling out two foam cups, and then two more. "I got all of those things, as well as salad and breadsticks."

I gaped. He chuckled.

"Jordan," I said, completely baffled. "You didn't have to do that. There's *no way* we're going to finish all of this food."

He laughed. "You can take it home for later."

"No, *no*," I immediately declined. "*You* can keep it for yourself." I looked up at him, a smile teasing itself at the corners of my mouth. "Since you're so large and need to eat."

His smile grew slowly again, and I got just a hint of his upper teeth, his bottom lip covering half his smile. It was murderous.

"Sit with me," I ordered, pointing to the seat across from me.

He sat and continued pulling boxes out. He opened one with chicken tenders in it and looked at me.

"I hope this isn't repetitive." But I was laughing. I reached for the box. "I think I could eat chicken tenders every weekend for a year and never be sick of them," I told him. "I don't eat much fun stuff during the week."

He nodded, taking a spoon and dipping into a cup of beef barley stew. "I've noticed," he said after swallowing.

You've what?

"You're fit," he added casually.

And like that, my thoughts jumbled.

Jordan had looked at my body and decided it was *fit*?
My whole *fit* body didn't know what to do with itself. My brain had given up.
I tried to think of something to say. "I work very hard." I wanted my modesty about my body to show. "It's not perfect; but I work out often and try to eat well most of the time."
He nodded, continuing to eat. "It shows."
A slow smile grew on my face; I couldn't help it. I never expected him to comment on my looks.
After swallowing another bite, he said, "I hope that comment wasn't inappropriate."
I shook my head. "Why would it be inappropriate?" Though it was surprising coming from him so suddenly, flirtation was certainly welcome.
"Because," he stared at me for a moment, thinking. "I don't want to make comments that could upset you. Even if I think they're complimentary. And..." he hesitated. "I don't want to make you feel degraded."
Suddenly, he seemed to regret even saying anything at all. "I apologize."
"Stop, stop," I said. "You didn't. That was nice."
He exhaled. "I don't want to be insensitive. You were honest with me the other day about your struggles, and I would like to be careful with that." His eyes were intense. "With you."
I just about sank into the cushion. I couldn't form words.
Say something, you idiot.
"Thank you," I murmured finally, looking down. "That's really sweet." I tried to sound as sincere as possible to express my gratitude. "You're so kind," I added quietly, disbelieving.
"I'm not being extra kind." I looked up at him. "You deserve respect and kindness always. I think you aren't used to it."
My eyes narrowed in confusion.
"In the car," he continued. "You thought I was angry, or annoyed with you. But I wasn't. I was unconsciously being quiet." He tilted his head to the side. "I understand why you'd think I was annoyed, but my initial thought was that you were used to a quick temper."
My father flashed through my brain. My ex-boyfriend. I didn't know what to say. *Hey, you're right. Good catch*, would sound pretty bad.
I shook my head, still unable to speak. I opened my mouth, but words didn't come out. I closed it.
"Jordan," I tried again. Still nothing.
"Jordan," I repeated finally. And instead of denying it or saying that he was very observant, I admitted quietly, "I didn't want you to snap at me."
Wow, Nina. Your daddy issues are showing.
His eyebrows crinkled together, and I knew I'd just proven him right.
"Sorry," I said right away. "I'm proving your point." I put my forehead down into my hand.
"Nina," he began quietly, looking at me with perplexed eyes.

"I would never snap at you," he said finally. "Please know that."
At this point, I felt childish.
"It's okay, it's okay," I assured. "I'm fine. I appreciate that. I'm just...I don't know why I'm so jumpy today. Maybe because of my boss," I tried to rationalize, but the truth was, Jordan was right. The only people who ever snapped at me that I'd gotten accustomed to fearing were my father and my ex-boyfriend. I didn't want to say those things. All we'd talked about were my problems; so it felt, anyway. We were *just* getting to know each other, but it seemed like he pulled them out of me without my even noticing.

His gentleness was so touching. I knew in that moment that my infatuation with him was growing beyond my control.

Take it easy, Nina.

"It's okay." His eyes were focused on me, his voice low. "You don't have to justify it. I'm sorry I made you afraid."

"It's okay. I wasn't afraid, just antsy." I left it at that. There was no point in trying to convince him he didn't. I tried not to add *I'm in love with you.*

"It's just..." I said, adjusting myself to take the pressure off my bottom leg. "Your job...the whole thing just surprised me so much."

He stared at me, understanding in his eyes. "It's not conventional."

"I just don't understand how you could have done all of that so young." *How you could afford it so young. How you could have been so smart and so skilled so young.* Where did he get his abilities? Was he lying?

I tried to be patient, to get as much information as possible, get to know him as well as I could, before I made any final judgment on his sincerity.

"How did you break into this field? I mean, you're essentially an FBI investigator. It's just that....you're not. You *sound* better than them, because they need you."

He didn't speak for a few moments, contemplating his response. "I did six months in computers with the FBI after I graduated."

I narrowed my eyes. "How did you get a job with the FBI?"

"They sought me out." He looked at me pointedly. "The FBI are recruiters. They knew *I* knew more than the typical IT student."

"How?"

"They have their ways. My assumption is that they shop schools until they find a student with abnormal abilities and potential." His face was emotionless, as if he couldn't care less about his own past.

"Your degree was computer technology, right?"

"That is one, yes."

"Okay." Then I stopped. "Wait, one? You have another degree?" I took a bite of a French fry.

"Two more."

"Three degrees?" I didn't know why I was surprised after everything I'd heard today. "Which ones?"

Straight face. "Master's in Computer science, and an undergrad in computer forensics and computer engineering each."
"Where exactly did you go again?"
"A few places. I started in Saudi Arabia. Went to China, and then came home and finished."
"You went to Saudi Arabia for school? To *China*?" He *had* told me that, I realized, but it never registered in my mind.
"Yes."
"Why?"
"The universities have great IT programs. I wrapped up my last few years in the US."
"How long did it take for you to get your master's?"
"Four years."
And I'd thought my 3.99 college grade point average was admirable.
I wanted to joke about how useless I was after hearing that, but I settled on, "Wow."
He didn't reply right away. I continued. "Do you speak Mandarin?"
"I spoke more when I lived there. Just a little now."
But the question was filler. I was trying to process everything.
I sat back and didn't say anything; he let me, waiting, eating his soup. I put my hand over my mouth and rubbed down to my chin, thinking about everything he'd said. FBI right after college? Three degrees in four years? Funding his own company? Stopping crime on the Dark Web? It was so hard to believe because of the unlikelihood, but difficult not to because of his sincerity.
Finally, without thought, I looked at him and said, "Are you messing with me?"
He tilted his head slightly and blinked. "No." He did not become befuddled, but his voice was serious; he was so believable I didn't know what to think.
I said nothing again. After a moment, he murmured, "I don't mean to seem unserious. I would take no pleasure in that."
"In what? Lying?"
His pace slowed. "Yes. Lying. So, you *do* think I'm inventing what I've told you?"
I didn't answer for a moment, expecting defensiveness. I'd never met anyone who kept their composure so well. He simply waited for me to answer, no offense taken.
"No," I murmured finally. "It's all just so...unreal. It's not anything you ever really...hear."
The thought popped into my head once more that maybe I barely knew this man. Maybe this was all fabrication. If it were, I'd never met anyone so convincing.
"I don't think you're lying to me," I reiterated.
He eyed me. "I know it's bizarre. Atypical."
"Yeah..." I said slowly. "Can I ask you something personal?"

"Yes, of course."

"How...how did you save enough money to fund a company? Like were they paying you *that much* where you worked during school?"

He shook his head. "I developed some software and sold it."

"You *developed software*?"

He nodded.

"What kind of software?"

"Application software. A web browser, to be specific."

"What's application software?" I was intrigued.

Jordan blinked his heavy lids twice, thinking for a moment. "Application software is what most people use daily, to put it simply."

My pride got in the way. I chose humility to compensate for how stupid I felt by his words and interjected. "Yes. I'm not very educated in this way."

"I didn't mean it like that," he said calmly. "I just don't want to bore you with the details."

I sat back. *Huh.*

"I'm not bored. I appreciate you putting it simply." I gestured towards him. "Please continue."

He assessed my face for a moment, as he often did, before continuing. "Application software includes things like web browsers, and things like Microsoft Office, Photoshop, Skype." I nodded.

"What's your browser like?"

"Like any, at its core." He stopped for a moment, thinking. "I had a professor who wouldn't let us use anything but Internet Explorer, just because he liked it the best. He thought it was the most developed software there was."

"No Chrome? Firefox?"

"No." I made a face. He raised his eyebrows slightly, in agreement. "Exactly. I don't personally care for it."

"Do you like any of them?"

"I like the Chrome layout."

"So, you made your own?"

Jordan nodded.

"Why? You wanted to make one better than what there was?"

He thought for a moment, crossing his arms, "I just wanted to see what I could do."

I raised my eyebrows. "That's why? It was just a personal challenge? Curiosity? No end goal in mind?"

Jordan nodded, then realized I had a point about how ridiculous that sounded.

"No. I oversimplified it. I apologize."

I shook my head before he could continue. "Don't say sorry."

He smiled small. It made my heart beat faster.

After thinking a moment, he continued. "The truth is, I thought maybe I was being overly critical; my professor told me so. Professor Harden."

Jordan shook his head slightly at the name, smiling small. It was cute, watching him reminisce.

"He said, *Developing a browser isn't as easy as you think. Don't be so arrogant.*

"He was right about the difficulty of it, and I knew that. And I wondered for a moment if maybe I *was* being arrogant. Though I never *did* say developing a browser was easy. I just didn't care for the layout of Explorer." He raised an eyebrow. "Am I boring you yet?"

Both of my eyebrows went up in sincere rejection of that statement. "Absolutely not," I told him calmly. "I think you're so interesting." At that, one corner of his lips flickered upward. It made me happy to see.

"Please continue. So, you didn't say what he accused you of...implying. I can't imagine you saying something so..."

"Arrogant?"

I nodded. He did, too.

"So I accepted that I could very well be overly *critical*. I didn't like that, either."

I smiled small. I liked his humility.

"I decided to try developing my own, just to show him what I would do differently. What I meant."

"Not to prove a point, though."

"No." He shook his head slowly as he spoke. "It wasn't easy."

Jordan sat back. "But I enjoyed it. Seeing the end result was satisfying."

"Was it very unlike the others?"

He smiled. It was so hot.

"Very different."

I nodded, returning his smile.

"What did he say when you showed him? Did he know you were doing it?"

"He didn't know. I spent all night in the computer room for nearly two years developing an average browser. The very, very basics. It took another year to finish and make it...decent."

"So did you go up to him and be like, "Hey, guess *what*.""

Jordan laughed, and I looked at him, smiling, heart skipping.

"No." He was still smiling. "I never ended up showing him."

My eyes widened. "You nev—wow." Realizing I'd leaned forward while he was talking, I sat back. "Really weren't trying to prove a point, huh."

"No," he murmured. His smile had faded into a slight upturn of one side of his lips again; he seemed happy. Not as serious as earlier.

"How old were you? When you finished it?"

"Twenty-two."

"Did you graduate then?"

"Yes, then went to the Bureau. By the time I left, I was twenty-three. That's when I sold it."

"Oh, wow. So it was good? Someone wanted to buy it, so I'm guessing so."

"It was okay, in my opinion. A tech-startup bought it with the intention that they would develop it further."
"They just didn't want to start it themselves?"
"No. It is very, very difficult, a lot of work and takes a lot of time. And they weren't particularly patient when I was trying to decide to sell it or not, so I assumed they just didn't want to take the time."
I narrowed my eyes. "So they decided to skip the hard work and just...buy it? How much did they give you?" I realized myself. "Wait, that's personal. Retracted."
Jordan shook his head a little bit. "It's okay." He paused. "Two million." He was expressionless, voice blank.
I raised my eyebrows and tilted my chin down slowly, looking at him intensely. "How could a start-up afford that?"
"They had investors."
"So...did they take off?"
Now, he shrugged. "Last I heard, the company was doing okay. The initial founders, two men—"
"The impatient ones?"
He nodded. "Sold the software and start-up a few years later. I don't keep up with it, not really. The people who took over contacted me later on and asked if I wanted to join."
"You said no?"
"Yes. They contact me every now and again somehow and ask."
I chuckled. "What ever happened to the two that initially started it?"
Jordan stared at me, not speaking.
After a few moments, I narrowed my eyes. "What? What happened? Did they die?"
"No, they didn't die." His face unmoving, he said, "They work at my company."
My jaw dropped. I couldn't help it. I sat back and laughed.
"Are you *serious*?" It was too rich to be true.
Jordan watched me, a smile growing on his face and seemingly wonder in his eyes. "Yes."
This news was hilarious to me, and impressive. I once more noted his modesty. How he didn't say, *They work for me.*
"They're very intelligent."
I shook my head. This was insane.
"So you were...twenty-three when you...found that kind of success." I crossed my arms. "There's hope yet."
He cocked his head to the side a little. "What do you mean?"
"I strive for that kind of success. But I gave myself until thirty."
"Oh." His eyes filled with understanding. "You want to be a millionaire."
The words were not judgmental or condescending. They just were.

"No, not quite. I've always wanted to be a bestseller. I didn't do it at twenty-four. I turn twenty-five in July. So unless my book suddenly goes worldwide in the next few months…"

"Book?" His eyebrows went up.

"Ah, yeah." I smiled a small smile. I never told him. "I have a book."

"What is it called?"

My lips turned up a little more. "*Brutal Intrigue*."

"That's incredible."

"Thank you."

"It was picked up?"

"By a small publisher."

Jordan sat back. "That's amazing. I'm incredibly impressed."

I looked at him skeptically, tilting my chin down again and giving him that look. "Really? You? Software engineer turned millionaire at twenty-three?" I shook my head. "I wrote an action novel."

He crinkled his eyebrows together. "You wrote a novel. Not just anyone can write a *novel*. You're *twenty-four*. I could not write a novel."

I raised an eyebrow. "I'm sure you could."

He shook his head. "I can *assure* you—"

I burst out laughing. He stopped and smiled.

"So," I continued, intrigued by him. Jordan's timeline was unlike the average person's. I wanted it. "You were…almost twenty-three when you graduated…"

"Yes."

"Huh."

He let me think for a moment as I pieced it together. The background was slowly presenting itself. "So, is that when the FBI called and was like, *Hey, come work for us, buddy*, or…?"

Jordan chuckled. "Yes. A week after graduation."

"No way."

"Yeah. I think they were waiting for it. I found it very odd when they called and then approached me."

"I imagine. I wouldn't believe it was really them."

He smiled. "I didn't."

I chuckled. "So you graduated at twenty-two and a half; then you went to the FBI for six months. You turned twenty-three then…" I looked at him for confirmation.

He nodded. "In October."

"'Kay, so you did six months, turned twenty-three, sold your software…"

What had I done since I'd graduated? Worked at a bakery making cupcakes for two years, and then worked for a marketing company the last near three. In four years, since graduating before age twenty, that was what I'd accomplished. *Don't forget the book. And that you graduated in two years.*

Something random occurred to me. "Wait, earlier you said you graduated the year you turned twenty-three, so did you start college at eighteen and a half?" He nodded.

"You graduated high school at eighteen?"

"No, seventeen."

It took me a moment to process what that meant. "You took a gap year? Or a year and a half? What did you do?"

He paused. "You're very observant."

I smiled small, waiting. He hesitated.

"I did some fight competitions for cash, and that paid for school."

"Fight competitions?" I repeated, incredulous. "Like MMA?"

"Yes," he murmured.

"Okay, where in particular? What kind of fighting?"

"All over the Middle East. Couple different kinds. Muay Thai, kickboxing, boxing, taekwondo. Others."

"*The Middle East?*" *Hold on a second...All those styles?*

Jordan nodded, expression unchanging. I wanted to kill him for being so emotionless.

"Where exactly? Like you just traveled and looked at...bulletin boards for fight competitions? And how did you learn to do all of that?"

He shook his head slightly. "Growing up, my parents put me in taekwondo, and the like. My teacher told me to try Muay Thai. I liked all of it. I started boxing when I was a teenager. At some point, my coach told me about these fights in the Middle East. He told me that, if you win, you make good money.

"Well, I was eighteen, and I had already thought about it until I graduated high school. I didn't have any money for college, and I didn't want to take out loans or take my parents'.

"So, I asked my coach if he would go with me; he's from Lebanon, so he would be the perfect guide. When he said yes, I decided I would go and see what it was all about, before the fall. Before college. In the way of where exactly, we started in Lebanon. We didn't have a plan to fight. No specific competition, no particular city. He just said that I could check out the culture, the styles. See if I was interested. He thought dynamic training made you a better fighter. Dynamic meaning you fight people who, perhaps, perform the same martial art a bit differently than you. Because they learned it differently. Because whoever taught them learned it differently than whoever taught you. And so on. Historical differences. And that's how you grow, he used to say.

"So we found a local competition. I watched one time, then I enrolled in the next. I won. I wasn't expecting to." He smiled at me. I smiled back. More unbelievable history, but I was intrigued. Oddly proud.

"We were supposed to go back home after the fight, but I wanted to stay and keep going. So I did. Eventually, my coach went back home and left me with a friend of his, someone who could train me there. I fought in

Lebanon until I heard about a different competition in the Emirates. I asked Rafiq to come with me. I was lucky that he did. This time, it was karate. And as time went on, I researched, looking for more to do in different places. I liked getting the experience."

I adjusted myself in my seat. "So it wasn't just like, the Middle Eastern Olympics. You just traveled country to country, finding small competitions?"

Jordan nodded. "Essentially. Those local competitions in different countries had nothing to do with one another." He looked at me and seemed to be debating about whether or not to proceed.

After all that, really? We were doing so well. Don't stop now.

I looked at him inquisitively. "Please, continue," I entreated. "I'm intrigued."

He regarded me for a moment more. "I won my fights." He watched me intensely. It was as though he didn't want to say it, to be boastful.

"Before I knew it, I was being invited for more, in other countries. So I spent a year or so competing. I made a lot of money and finally started school when I was nineteen, in Saudi. I fought for another year, the first year of school. Then I stopped, because I went to China."

I stared at him. "Wow," I said quietly. "You made good money then?"

He nodded. "Paid for school and invested the rest."

If Jordan was making all of this up, he was a fantastic actor and very weird for playing such an elaborate prank on a stranger. Maybe he *was* a psychopath.

Finally, I decided I should acknowledge his apprehension to say it all.

"Thank you," I murmured, "for telling me all of that. It seems a little...You seem modest," I decided. "It looked like it might have been kinda hard to say."

Jordan looked at me with curious eyes. The man could stare; he wasn't fidgety. But it wasn't just polite eye contact, either. He seemed intrigued by me. It made me nervous and humbled me at the same time.

"I don't care to share that story," he confirmed. He raised an eyebrow as he thought to himself. "My picture ended up on the Internet. I had to put in some effort to get it removed."

"What did you do? You didn't have social media?"

He shook his head. "No. Never. I didn't think too much of it at the time. I actually didn't even realize it was out there until a few years later. But when I realized it, I just put it out of my mind. I was finishing my degree. I was focused. But recently I had it taken down. In as many places as I could find it."

This man was so interesting. I couldn't stop thinking that word. *Interesting.*

"How come?" I asked gently, noting the slight distaste on his face.

At my question, his expression cleared immediately, once again becoming smooth and even.

"I value privacy."

"I do, too."
"No social media for you, then?" he asked.
"No."
"Why?"
"I hate it. It's toxic. A waste of time."
He nodded. "I agree." He adjusted himself slightly. "Tell me about your book," he murmured.
I exhaled lightly. "It's about a Middle Eastern girl."
"Oh, yeah?" He smiled small. "Is she Chaldean?"
"Oh, no, she's not. She's Arab."
Jordan tilted his head to the side. "Why didn't you make her Chaldean?"
I shrugged. "I dunno, I guess I was just afraid. People don't know us, and they'd find it hard to relate, maybe. I felt like some people in our community would just hate it."
"Why? I can't imagine that."
My community was not used to seeing itself on television, in movies or in novels. We were too small a people for us to be as widespread, read about, even known, as those of other ethnicities or races here in America. I found myself explaining to others that I was "Iraqi," not Chaldean, because it was easier and more familiar than most.
So, because of this lack of awareness, I imagined, for some Chaldeans, reading a novel that mentioned their people would be awkward. I tried to articulate this clearly.
"I think they would find it weird," I replied. "We aren't used to seeing ourselves represented, so it isn't really their fault. I think I would be just as critical or...uncomfortable, especially if the book painted me in a bad light." I thought a moment. "Or if it was so accurate that I felt exposed."
Jordan looked at me, pensive, and I thought I saw fondness. After a few moments, he said, "That makes perfect sense."
I sighed, relieved. "That's why it was so important to me to make the decision to write about an Arabic girl, because they're more well-known."
"Yet you sacrificed putting your own roots on that pedestal. And I think they should be on it," he said gently. "I think it's brave that you wrote about an ethnicity that isn't yours. But it makes me sad, too, because it could've been so much easier if you'd felt comfortable writing about *yourself*."
I thought about his words for a minute. "Yes and no," I murmured, pensive. Jordan waited, giving me his full attention. "Yes, because in some regards, writing about my people would've been easier for the obvious reason: I know my people. I *am* my people." I smiled.
"But while that's true," I spoke slowly, "writing about myself would also be hard in a different way. I'd have to be very careful not to misrepresent us, because that would ruffle feathers. And I don't want to do that. Not because I fear judgment, but because I don't want to produce something that deserves judgment."

Quicker than he usually was to respond, he said, "I imagine you'd put out an incredible novel. I can't picture you putting out anything bad. *Creating* anything bad." He was flattering me, but I thought he meant it. He wasn't flirtatious, rather serious, pensive.

"Now…" I grinned. "It's definitely happened."

Jordan smiled small. "You are so well-spoken and intelligent. I can't imagine your writing is anything short of fantastic."

I smiled, humbled. "Thank you."

It was always nice to be praised. I hadn't had much of that growing up. My parents knew I was an A-student. I never got any fondness for it, however, and there was always that little part of me that wanted their approval. I'd had teachers tell me I was fantastic at this or that. I'd had readers on my blog tell me my writing was incredible, that it touched them, but it never reached me as much as it did when I got the rare proud moment from one of my parents.

Hearing it from Jordan was pretty good, though.

He stared at me with gentle eyes. "People will always have something to say," he murmured softly. "It doesn't mean anything. Your book will be the best book ever written, and people will still talk. Can't let it stop you."

The softness of his voice and the affection in his eyes made me lightheaded. "Well…" I started, with a tiny, shy smile. "I *do* plan on making my next character Chaldean. Maybe."

Jordan's eyes lit up a little. "Really?" His voice was low, approving. Sexy.

I nodded. "Yeah."

Jordan grinned, fondness filling his eyes. I was sure of it this time. My heart skipped at the sight of it, matched by his gorgeous smile.

Always eager to please, Nina.

But for Jordan, it didn't really bother me.

KAYLA KATHAWA

JORDAN

February

I was hoping our entry into February and new campaign opportunities would lighten Steve's mood. It did not.

He gradually became more impatient. It frustrated me; we were only a month into the year and had a lot of time for improvement. But he treated every missed mark like the end of the world.

After reading a rude email from him about the editing on our last article, I grew agitated. Sitting at my desk, unwilling to look at the article he'd sent back, I rubbed my eyes and then stared at my lunch. I just couldn't eat under all this stress.

Next to the food, my phone lit up. After realizing it was a text from Jordan, I grabbed it immediately. *I miss him.*

I noticed my hands shaking as the result of the anxiety Steve's email brought me. I tried to hold them steady as I read the message, feeling a little better after seeing Jordan's name.

Hi. Do you have lunch plans?

I smiled to myself, looking at the clock. It was two minutes to twelve, my lunch hour. He knew that.

We couldn't see each other during the week; it was too hard. He lived an hour away, and we both worked full-time. By the time I'd get to his house after traffic, it would be time for me to commute back home to get to bed on time. I was an early riser; I worked out before work and had to make enough time to shower and get ready. If I went to bed late, I wouldn't be able to function properly the next day.

So we texted when we were apart. Those small interactions when we couldn't see each other continued to make him feel less like a stranger and more like a friend.

We hadn't been texting that morning, however. I hadn't heard from him since the night before, when I'd begrudgingly texted him that I was going to bed.

It was Wednesday, and I hadn't heard his voice since Friday at his house. I'd meant to text him myself, but then I got the email from Steve, shooting down my self-esteem.

I tried to calm my heart, which had picked up while I read Steve's email. I didn't want to be that version of Nina; I pictured Jordan. I wanted to be laid-back, unconcerned and definitely not anxious over a cold email my boss sent.

I texted back, saying, *No.*

He replied right away. *Are you interested in lunch with me at Don Tel?*

I couldn't wipe the smile off my face. *Yes. I can meet you there.*

I was surprised when he called. "Hi," I said happily.

"Hi," he murmured. His voice sent a chill through me. "I hope you don't find this disturbing, but I thought I would just pick you up."

"Disturbing?" I thought for a moment. "Why, are you outside?" I giggled.

"Yes." He sounded hesitant. "I thought I would surprise you."

I smiled huge, undisturbed. I was thrilled about the opportunity to see him. "I'll be right out." I hung up, grabbed my purse and hurried out.

There he was, parked right up front, leaning against the Lexus, donning black slacks, an unbuttoned, dark gray peacoat, and a sweater of a similar color.

I got a little dizzy.

Trying to prevent myself from stumbling, I noted how he carried himself, what he did that demonstrated such confidence. I liked that he didn't look down at his phone to avoid eye contact with anyone while he waited. He was comfortable just being.

He stepped forward when he saw me, a small smile on his face.

Suddenly he lifted his hands, his eyebrows shooting up and his eyes widening. "If this is creepy, I will leave right now."

But I laughed. I was so happy to see him.

"No, no," I gushed. Forcing myself to walk up to him at a normal speed, I made a split-second decision and hugged him. I hadn't done that before, but it had been almost a week, the sight of him was stirring, and all of a sudden, I wanted desperately to touch him.

He wrapped his arms around me. He smelled good. The scents of his clean clothes and skin made me lightheaded again; he was warm, and it settled my nerves.

It was a meaningful hug. He held me there for a few moments, which took me by surprise. I put my head on his chest and felt his chin tilt down and brush the top of my head.

Wow.

We faced each other after pulling back slowly. I smiled up at him again, feeling timid after the contact. "Thank you for coming."

"Of course." The fond smile on his face was heartwarming. I could've stood in the thirty-degree weather all day just looking at it. "Thank you for seeing me."

I saw a few coworkers two yards away, eyes on us. Jordan opened the passenger door for me. I slid into the car and looked directly at them. They slowed their pace and were staring with wide eyes. One woman's mouth hung open.

I snapped on my seatbelt smugly. They were always arrogant to me.

After arriving at the restaurant, Jordan requested a table in the back. I hadn't been here before. When we were seated, I picked up the long, two-sided menu, which confirmed it was the upscale brunch spot I'd guessed it was.

"Tell me what your favorite breakfast food is," he demanded.

I smiled. "Without health in mind? Pancakes or waffles. My go-to on a daily basis is usually something high protein, though, 'cause I work out in the morning. Like if I don't feel like cooking before work, I might stop at the store and grab a protein shake."

He nodded, tilting his chin down and raising his eyebrows expectantly. "But you eat more?"

"Yeah...fruits and vegetables. Don't get me wrong, I'll eat whole grain bread here and there, or natural grains at a meal. But I keep the sugar at minimum. I have the metabolism of a grandma." He smiled small.

I knew he was thinking about my eating problems, as I suspected he did every time we discussed food. It felt good that he cared, but it sucked that I was so complicated.

He decided he wouldn't push. "I think today is a day for pancakes."

I giggled quietly. "Okay."

We ordered red velvet pancakes *and* an omelet each. He said I had to have one, or he wasn't properly taking me out for brunch. I laughed. I adored him.

"How's work today?" he asked me.

"It's uh..." *Awful.* "It's alright. Just...I haven't been in the best mood." Before he could respond, I added, "I was really happy when you texted."

At that, he smiled. "Why aren't you feeling great today?"

"Steve's just being a jerk." I remembered my shaking hands and looked down at them. I was relieved to see that they'd stilled.

He studied me. "I'm sorry." I could tell he meant it. "How can I help?"

I smiled, perplexed by his constant kindness. "You already have. By asking me here." I grinned bigger. "And getting me red velvet pancakes."

He showed his teeth. *He just likes when you eat. Accept it.*

"How's work for *you*?" I asked. "Did you go in today?"

He nodded. "Yes. I was in pretty early. Left around ten and came to see you. Work was as fine as it can be."

I cocked my head to the side. "What does that mean?"

He thought for a moment. "The work we do is not the happiest. You understand." He gestured out to me. I nodded.

JORDAN

"We've come across a more difficult case."

"Do you mind my asking what's more difficult about it?"

He paused. "Tracking them down, essentially. My technology isn't working the way it usually does."

"Your technology? You developed more software?"

Jordan blinked, realizing what he'd just admitted. "Yes. Two."

I sat back. "Is that when you started the company?"

"I developed the first before and the second after."

"What are they?"

"In a nutshell, one is a hacking and tracking software that traces rerouted information and then decrypts it. The other is a security software."

"*Decrypts* it? A software that decrypts information on its own?"

He nodded.

"Is that a thing? Is there other software that does that?" I was confused.

Jordan hesitated. "The FBI bought a version of it that was...watered down."

I gaped. "And you still have it?"

"Yes. I told them I would continue to work on my other version. I developed it more over time."

"Did you give them that one?"

He shook his head slightly. "No." After a moment's thought, he murmured, "They bought the first one. I didn't give it to them. I wish I could say I was that generous, but..." Jordan seemed tired even admitting it.

"You know what I want to know. Is that bad?"

"No. It's not bad." He looked off to the side for a moment; he didn't want to tell me. Finally, he met my eyes with his intense ones and a flat face. "Nine million." He kept his voice low.

I blinked.

I was uncertain whether I wanted to gape, smile, laugh or frown. I forced myself to keep a straight face.

I'd assumed that Jordan had a couple million dollars, from the initial sale of his browser. That maybe he'd managed to maintain it by investing. I didn't think he made a large profit from his company by consulting. I presumed he didn't even make a million a year.

Let alone nine million dollars at once for software.

After forty-five seconds of silence, watching Jordan watch me with intense, waiting eyes, I asked, "How does your software work?"

Jordan exhaled through his nose. "The most utilized place for Dark Web activity is a browser called Gateway. Have you heard of it?"

I shook my head, watching him intently. A simple explanation of this software worth nine million dollars would not suffice.

"Okay. It's named ironically. A gateway lets you in. The browser makes it nearly impossible to track a person down." I narrowed my eyes.

"The browser has something like a built-in VPN—a virtual private network—which takes your requests to visit different sites or transmit information, encrypts them, meaning it takes the information and converts

it to code. *Then*, the information is rerouted, which can be done in various ways. This lets you search and post anonymously. It's always been nearly impossible to trace searches back to people on that browser. It's not like a regular VPN and rerouting technique. It's much more sophisticated."
I nodded, unspeaking.
"It's not easy for authorities to find cybercriminals. The Bureau has a whole department dedicated to it."
"Do they all have technology to do it?"
"They have technology and resources, but it's not enough. There's so much crime on the Internet, whether it's hacking and stealing credit card information or selling drugs, that it's impossible to find enough manpower to keep up. But they try.
"And they don't rely on software alone to help them. They use regular investigative work, too. They've been successful in many cases, but there are and always will be many that go unsolved, or take an extremely long time to crack."
My eyebrows crinkled together. He noticed. "Keep going," I told him.
"Groups that hack into the servers of large corporations, banks, even the FBI itself, they've been found before. Even..."
I raised my eyebrows. "Even...?"
Jordan stared at me for a while, hesitating. "This isn't breakfast material."
"It doesn't bother me."
"I'm worried you won't eat."
My eyebrows shot up in surprise. "I will, I promise. Tell me what you were gonna say. Even...?"
Jordan watched me apprehensively, seeming regretful for starting his sentence. "Pedophile rings, sex traffickers...and the like."
I kept my face smooth and nodded. Jordan's eyes were cautious.
"So, it's not like it all goes unsolved except for a case or two. But it's not easy.
"After I sold the browser, I decided to try to develop software that made it easier. I contemplated it the entire time I was with the Bureau. It was miserable to watch the cases move so slowly because we couldn't *find* somebody."
I couldn't believe the initiative I knew now that he took. The work he must have put in.
"So I left. I left because it was miserable knowing people were getting hurt, and we were barely scraping the surface for the longest time."
I realized this was the first time Jordan had admitted to feeling an overwhelming emotion. I was stunned.
"I didn't like that I left. I knew I had to, but I wasn't happy with myself. The goal was to help people, and I felt like I couldn't do it."
"It wasn't all on you, though," I murmured quietly. My heart ached for him.
He nodded. "I know. That didn't really make me feel better. I don't know why. It was infuriating to move so slowly, and I knew it was necessary, that

that was the way they'd made progress in the past. But I didn't want it to *have* to be that way.

"So I went home—"

"Wait, where were you living?"

"Headquarters."

"Oh. Gotcha. Please continue; I'm sorry I interrupted. So, you went home…"

"I found a house, bought the tools I needed, and spent years developing software that is able to decrypt on its own and get me to the source. Gateway was the most frustrating thing, technologically speaking, at the time, that I'd ever experienced. I thought I disliked Internet Explorer. But Gateway…"

"You didn't know what it was?"

He shook his head. "I did. But it wasn't until I got to the FBI that I realized how difficult it made solving crime.

"And I am an advocate for our rights to privacy. Many innocent people use that browser. But I could not accept how it enabled criminals. Criminals that hurt people to the worst extent. So I developed a software that bested the premise of that browser."

"Had that ever been done before?" I asked in disbelief.

Jordan's face was smooth, his voice level, even while speaking of his misery, frustration and groundbreaking accomplishments. They didn't reflect the words he was saying.

"No."

I ran my fingers through my hair as I thought. "What made you think of the idea?"

Jordan was pensive. "In 2013, the FBI took down hundreds of criminal sites. Part of how they did it is still unknown to the public."

My eyebrows shot up.

"I knew about it and wanted to know how, but that information was never released. Even years later, none of us in the Bureau, at least where I worked, were granted that knowledge."

"Did you ask?" I interrupted.

He nodded. "So I thought *something* was possible."

"Did you figure out what they did?"

"Not on my own."

"How?"

"When I approached them with my tracking software, I asked."

"They were happy to tell you *then*."

He returned my smile. "Yeah." He paused. "It didn't end up being technology that they did it with, but that's all they told me. My guess was that they just caught the people behind it all."

I nodded. "So you told them about the software yourself?"

He nodded. That surprised me.

"I didn't do it for the money." A hint of worry touched his eyes.

"I know," I said softly.

Jordan sat back. "I wanted to give it to them. They wouldn't allow it."

My eyebrows crinkled together once more. "Why not?"

"I suppose they didn't take donations of the sort."

"You were really just gonna give it to them?" My lips turned up at the corners. "Wow, I'm greedy."

Jordan smiled, which made my heart skip. "You're not."

I nodded. "Oh, yeah. I'm happy they paid you, because you deserve it."

He shook his head slightly.

"You just wanted to help people," I said more gently. "I know that. You prove it every day."

Jordan slightly tilted his head to the side. "How do you mean?"

"Well, you chose to live in a beautiful *house*, not a mansion. You're never arrogant or in anyone's face, flaunting what you have. You hesitate every time we even hint at anything you've accomplished, financially or not."

Jordan's face softened as I spoke, a quiet happiness encompassing him. His lips turned up slightly at the corners.

"You're modest," I murmured, lowering my voice. "It's one of the things I love about you."

I realized too late that I'd used the word *love*.

I prepared myself for the discomfort or flatness that came in response to a comment like that. But his lips turned up more at the corners; he was calm. Charmed.

"Thank you," he said quietly, leaning forward and putting his elbows on the table. Only then did I realize I'd leaned forward myself. The proximity between us made my heart skip. It was a small table.

"You're welcome," I said, smiling shyly.

After a few moments of our faces being two feet apart, I pulled back. I was hoping too much that he would come closer.

"So…" I started slowly. "You didn't give them the newer version of the software that you use?"

He nodded.

"You don't want them to have it, do you?"

He raised an eyebrow. "How'd you know?"

I shrugged. "I figure we all only partially trust the government, if at all."

Jordan smiled. "I don't want it in the wrong hands."

"It's a lot better than what you gave them, yeah?"

"Yes. Much better."

"But they still use it."

He nodded.

"And they solve more crime with it?"

"I think so." But we both knew so.

I nodded. I needed to bring this full circle.

"So, you said your software isn't working?"

Jordan's eyelids got a little heavy. "No. I don't know why."

"You've tested it a bunch, right? And it's worked a lot before? So what's different here, do you think? Wait, obviously you don't know. Sorry."
"No, no. No sorry's." I smiled. He continued. "I tested it against my own rerouter. The security software I mentioned, I mean. That's the only thing it didn't work against."
"Your tracker…can handle Gateway's rerouter…but not your own?"
He nodded.
I sat back. *No way.*
"But yours isn't a browser?"
"No, just a software installed on the computers."
"How…" I shook my head, baffled.
"I set mine up differently than theirs. And I didn't focus so much on encrypting. But please don't think I developed a magic software that can find anyone in two seconds. It doesn't work that way, and I may be making it sound like that. But it makes the process significantly easier."
"I suppose it wasn't so hard to make a software that fights against the rerouting your other one does, since you know how the other one works."
A hint of a smile teased his lips. "It was actually harder."
I shook my head slowly. "You're…unlike anything I've ever experienced. Anyone I've ever met."
Jordan's smile grew, making me itch to reach over and touch him.
"I truly hope that isn't a bad thing."
I tilted my head to the side. "It's a great thing."
Jordan showed teeth behind that smile, just when I thought my chest couldn't feel any weaker…
"That's a relief." He took a moment to assess my face, curiosity in his eyes and just a splash of wonder.
"I can most definitely say the same of you."
Why is your heart beating so fast, you nerd?
Forcing myself to stay cool, I raised my eyebrows. "Bad thing?"
He shook his head slightly. "Great thing."
"I'm glad." I looked down at my fingers, resting gently on the edge of the table. "I'm sorry work has been so hard," I murmured.
When I met his eyes, though they'd sobered, they were still full of fondness. "Don't be sorry. I'll figure it out."
"I'm sure you will. I have no doubt about it."
He smiled a small smile.
"Are they…The people you're looking for now, I mean…" I hesitated. "Are they violent?"
Jordan exhaled slowly through his nose, his face turning serious. "Yes."
I nodded slowly.
"I don't want to put more than that in your head," he said quietly.
I nodded seriously. "I understand." I paused. "Thank you."
"Don't thank me, please." He shook his head. "I would never…"
"Tell me?" I finished when he paused.

He shook his head again. "But I don't want to say that."

"Why?" I asked quietly.

He paused. "I think it would be hard to say no to you."

A thrill shot through my chest.

I didn't know what to say. It was overwhelming.

"I won't push," I said finally, quietly.

He looked at me. The waitress brought our omelets and left.

"Please eat."

So we did. I ordered a latte and tried not to imagine what he saw today at work.

JORDAN

When Jordan dropped me off at work, forcing me to take a carry-out box full of pancakes and the three-quarters of an omelet I had left, we agreed to see each other again over the weekend. Lunch was only an hour. It wasn't enough time for me. I hoped it wasn't enough time for him, either.
He asked me to dinner, and then to hang out at his house. It sounded blissful.
I told him how guilty I felt for never hosting at my parents' house; it was just too chaotic. He commanded I never worry about that, and told me I could go to his house any time I wanted.
But that's all the time, Jordan. All the time.
The week was long.
When Friday finally came and five o'clock hit, I was out. There was no working late today. *Bye, Steve,* I thought. *I won't miss you.*
Jordan had a particular restaurant in mind, and asked if he could pick me up at a store twenty minutes from my office. I didn't even argue.
"Please, please forgive me," he said, after we greeted each other.
"What?" I said, alarmed. "What's wrong?"
"Nothing. I just have to make one stop on the way to the restaurant. I apologize, sincerely."
I shook my head at him. "Jordan, don't be silly. Come on." I playfully slapped the back of his arm, but it was as weak as a tap.
He surprised me when he extended that arm out to the side, wrapped it around my shoulders and pulled me in for a hug. I wanted to crumble. He looked so good in that black peacoat. I liked that he never seemed to wear cologne but always smelled clean and fresh.
I pulled back gently and gave him a shy smile. "I'm so happy to see you," I murmured. "Wednesday feels like it was last week."

He surprised me when he said, "I agree."

I smiled bigger and stepped toward his truck, not looking away from him. He opened the door for me. When he got in, I asked him, "Where do you have to stop?"

His face became disgruntled. "My brother's apartment."

"Oh." I'd forgotten he had a brother. I racked my brain. "Tristan?"

"Yeah," he said, breathy, as he concentrated on backing out of his parking spot.

"He did something to his gun and doesn't know how to fix it." Jordan sounded annoyed, as one became when talking about their pesky little brother.

"His *gun*?" Then I remembered the only thing he'd told me about Tristan, other than his age, was that he worked for the Federal Bureau of Investigation.

"Oh wait," I said a moment later. "He's in the FBI."

"Yeah."

"And you know how to...*fix* a gun?" It was unsurprising, though I'd never thought about the fact that Jordan used guns. The image appeared in my head now. It was attractive.

He nodded. My curiosity peaked.

"So, you worked for the FBI too, but you started because of your technology skills. How did Tristan get into it?"

Jordan thought for a moment. "Well, he really wanted to do investigative work, growing up. He got a bachelor's degree in crime analysis, then went to the police academy, was a cop for four years, and then was offered a position in the FBI." Jordan turned onto a side street. "He's very good in the field." He glanced at me. "He's very good in combat, I mean. But he's also very intelligent."

"Oh, cool." I was thinking about it. I was curious to see what he looked like.

"He's been a cop for four years and is now in the FBI...please don't think I'm being insulting, but...how does he not know how to fix his gun?"

Jordan actually laughed. "Good catch."

I chuckled, heart skipping.

"It's not his work gun. It's one of his 'play' guns."

"He collects guns, doesn't he?"

Jordan nodded. I smiled. I didn't even bother asking what kind of gun it was. I'd have no clue about it, even if he said the name.

"So, does he work for a particular department at the FBI?"

"Yes, he's a special agent and works mainly in behavioral analysis."

That's so cool.

I hoped he liked me.

"Isn't he young for that position?"

Jordan nodded. "He works hard; he proved himself in his police work."

"You guys are like heroes," I murmured quietly.

JORDAN

Jordan was quiet for a moment; I looked up at him timidly. I admired him so much.

"Thank you. Tristan is a great person," he said, deflecting the attention off himself. "He works hard to help people. I think that is something we have in common. That, and we both did martial arts growing up. I think we always had the urge to protect."

I smiled at him. "I think that's amazing." He smiled.

I looked out the window. It was already dark, and snowing.

"So, he lives around here?" I looked out my window. "What city are we in?"

"He's right down the road. We're in Westborn."

"So he lives like halfway between you and your parents, huh."

"Yeah, he's closer to them than I am, physically, so I feel less bad about living so far away."

I tilted my head to the side. "Why *do* you live so far away from where you grew up? When we first met, you mentioned that work took you there, but then you told me you started your own company. Then you said that you left the FBI, found a house and started working on your software. So what made you pick there?"

Jordan spent a few moments thinking; I sensed hesitation and a shift in his energy. It was heavier.

"Truthfully, I just picked something that seemed comfortable enough. I didn't put too much thought in it."

"If you 'just picked something,' then why did you end up all the way in Cuttingham?"

This he'd left out. He paused again.

"I misspoke. I just picked something that was comfortable and far away."

I leaned back against the seat, eyes widening a little. "Away from your parents?"

Jordan glanced at me, eyes grim, the rest of his face smooth. "Yes. My family." His eyes on the road ahead of him, he added, "Everyone."

I swallowed, sad for my friend. I wanted to know what he'd been feeling back then that made Jordan want to be alone. "Why?" I asked gently.

He didn't even glance at me while he drove, the way he usually did. "I was unhappy after the Bureau," he said quietly. Picturing it made me sadder.

"You saw a lot of bad stuff," I said softly. He nodded.

"I know you were frustrated that it took so long to save people," I murmured, hoping he would say a little more.

"Yes." His voice was quiet. "I just wanted to focus."

I nodded, waiting.

"My mom and dad weren't happy. I knew they were worried about me. I didn't make many trips back down while I was developing the software."

I nodded. "I understand," I responded, sadness creeping into my tone. My chest hurt for him.

Jordan's head snapped in my direction. "Everything was okay after some time," he murmured. He was trying to give it a happy ending, but I didn't want him to stop talking about himself and how he felt.

"I'm so happy to hear that. And so sorry for what you went through."

His eyebrows went up slightly. "Don't be."

"I am. I hate the sound of you all alone because you were so unhappy."

I refused to look at him, choosing to stare out my window. I felt his eyes on me.

"I appreciate that, Nina," he said quietly. "Your concern."

I met his eyes. There was a touch of passion in them that made my fingers twitch. I wanted so badly to touch him.

"Of course. I won't keep reminding you of it, I promise, I just want to know…"

"You can ask me anything," he reiterated.

"I just don't want to take you back there. But…do you see similar things now to what you saw when you were at the Bureau?"

He nodded. "I see more of it. At the Bureau, they had me working in identity theft, terrorist tracking, other things that weren't as serious, on top of it."

"Of…of murder?" I asked quietly.

He met my eyes for what felt like longer than he should've while driving. "Yes."

I shook my head. "I'm so sorry, Jordan." I remembered he chose to do this. "You're a hero."

Jordan's face was solemn, but it softened. "Thank you for saying that."

I smiled at him now. "No thank you's."

The smile that grew on his face made me feel weak.

"I appreciate you telling me all that."

"Of course," he replied softly, matching my volume.

My heart filled up for him. Attraction aside, Jordan meant a lot to me as my friend.

He turned on to yet another side street, which was surprisingly industrial. I expected small, eerie houses. Instead, there were spaced out small businesses, and two buildings down after the turn, there was an apartment complex.

"Don't take offense to this, Jordan, but this area is kinda creepy," I commented as he turned into the parking lot of the apartment complex.

He nodded. "I'm not offended. Tristan moved here when he was in school, because it was cheap. Over time, he, of course, became more established in his career, but he wanted to continue living here. He says he doesn't mind it. He's been here so long, he just 'doesn't feel like moving.'" Jordan made air quotes with his right hand.

I chuckled. "I suppose I might personally be a creature of habit, so I don't blame him."

JORDAN

Jordan pulled into a parking spot up front. "It's much nicer on the inside," he told me.

I sat in my seat as he unbuckled. "I can just wait here, if you'd like."

He looked at me, surprised. "Oh. No, no. Please come in. It should only take five minutes." He hopped out of the truck and came to open my door. I noted the regret in his eyes. "You don't have to talk to him if you don't want to."

I laughed, though his concern was touching. "It's okay."

The night was dark and frigid. He put his hand on my back and led me towards the door. On the way there, I noticed the bushes on either side of the entrance, and the tulips that were planted in large pots in front of them. If it was much nicer inside, it started at the door.

The flowers were a brilliant contrast from the darkness of the night. They were beautiful.

"Those are so pretty," I murmured, as Jordan held the door open for me. He smiled.

We walked all the way down a dimly lit hallway. We turned right and then right again, and there was an elevator. He pushed the upward arrow and the door opened right away. We stepped inside.

When the doors closed, I chuckled. "Of course I'm gonna talk to him, silly."

We stood with our backs to the wall in the small elevator, beside one another. I tilted my head towards him, my scalp barely touching his upper arm. He turned his head a little and smiled down at me, amused at how dumb I looked, probably.

"You didn't come to meet new people. I wouldn't blame you." His blue eyes gleamed, even in the barely lit elevator.

"But I didn't want to leave you in the car," he murmured, looking down into my eyes.

"Didn't want me to get kidnapped, huh?" I smiled small.

He played along, but I knew he was serious when he said, "So long as I'm around, that will never happen."

I couldn't think of anything to say before the elevator stopped. I just remembered the cold day in the city, when that sleazy man looked at me.

"You're a hero, like I said," I murmured quietly as we exited. "I feel safe around you." I looked at his face and noted the seriousness of it.

"You should."

We stopped at the apartment door to the right of the elevator, at the end of the hall. On the white door hung the silver numbers *215*.

Jordan knocked; after a few moments, the door opened, and there was Tristan.

He was an inch taller than Jordan. Tristan's hair was black but shorter, perhaps two inches off his scalp as opposed to the fullness of Jordan's, and curlier. His skin was tan, a shade lighter than Jordan's, his eyes a pale green. His eyelids were less relaxed than his older brother's, making his

face more youthful and energetic, despite the mere three-year age difference. He had full, black eyebrows and long eyelashes. His face was chiseled and clean-shaven like Jordan's. He was lean and muscular, wearing a fitted beige sweater and black jeans. He was beautiful.
He and Jordan looked oddly alike for not being biological brothers. I was dumbfounded.
It was intimidating to be around both, but also endearing to watch. Two young, handsome, hero brothers. One coming by to fix the other's gun.
He only regarded Jordan for a second, and then his eyes were on me.
He analyzed me for a few moments; it felt like a century. I was worried that Tristan might not like me and mess up my chance with Jordan. But his face was kind, welcoming.
"Come in." His voice was smooth.
"This is Nina," Jordan said quietly as Tristan stepped aside. He was watching both Tristan and me carefully. Could he sense that I was nervous? That was embarrassing.
Tristan continued looking at me as I stopped a few steps in. "Tristan." With subtle confusion in his eyes, he said, "I'm happy to meet you," reaching for my hand.
His grip was gentle. Though he was polite and had kind eyes, I felt odd in front of him. He was watching me too long, looking too hard.
It was clear Jordan noticed it, too, and before I could reply, he said, "Where is it?" He seemed annoyed with his little brother.
Tristan looked at him, amused. Jordan was not.
Turning and gesturing to the dimly lit apartment, Tristan flicked his chin towards the living room, which greeted you when entering his apartment. Next to the entrance was a large television, situated on a mantel above a fireplace. Three sofas backed the short coffee table on which lay a huge gun I couldn't name for the life of me.
Tristan misunderstood my feigned uninterested expression as I stared at the monster weapon. He raised an eyebrow. After a moment of thought, he asked, "You guys work together?"
Jordan gritted his teeth and then unclenched them quickly. "No."
Tristan was genuinely confused about who I was.
Jordan stepped past him and lightly pushed Tristan's shoulder with his own, turning him in the direction of the table and away from me. I tried to keep my jaw from dropping and a laugh from escaping my lips.
He is so cute.
It didn't deter Tristan from watching me, but now he spoke instead of just staring. "Come in, Nina. Make yourself at home."
"Thank you." At my response, Jordan turned and looked at me, reminding me that he was right there, and that I didn't need to be uncomfortable. It was an overreaction but touched me, nonetheless. I wanted to let him know he didn't need to worry, but it was too late. "This will only take one minute,

Nina." He picked up the gun and looked pointedly at Tristan. "Then we can go."

Tristan looked even more surprised. "Why are you in a rush?" He turned back to me. "Where you guys going? If you don't mind me asking," he added.

I smiled small. "Dinner."

"Oh. Well, I apologize. I don't mean to deter your plans."

"That's okay," I assured.

"I just told Jordan that I needed his help with that." He gestured to the gun without looking away from me. "By tomorrow," he added, grinning. "But what are big brothers good for, if not fixing guns?"

Jordan looked up grimly, still working the gun. "He trapped me. I told him where we were going, and he took that opportunity to ask if I would come by and fix this, since it isn't far." He raised an annoyed eyebrow at Tristan, then looked back down at his work. I smiled.

I thought the way Tristan regarded me was interesting. His surprise that I was with Jordan. Or rather, that Jordan was with me.

"I'm sorry," Tristan said again, turning to Jordan. "I truly did not know you were with someone, or—" Jordan looked up at him, more annoyed. Before he could say anything, Tristan corrected himself, turning to me. "I *did*, he did tell me that, but I just didn't know that...I thought he might be working, or just with someone from work..."

He was trying to say anything but *Going on a date*. I tried not to giggle.

The more he talked, turning back and forth to look at us both, the more vicious Jordan's eyes got. Tristan was digging himself into a hole that Jordan was going to bury him in, if he didn't watch his words carefully. I was stunned by Jordan's behavior. He was silently but pointedly warning his brother to stop talking.

Tristan turned and looked at me only then.

"I just thought he was working," he said with finality.

I smiled. "It's okay."

And like that, I ended it. I decided to go to Jordan.

He looked at me with softer eyes as I approached. "I just want to see what you're doing," I murmured, curious.

Before Jordan could speak, Tristan defended himself. "I don't often mess up my gun; I was kidding."

Jordan went to the kitchen. "I need a drill bit."

"Top right cabinet above the stove, top shelf. What are you doing?"

Jordan opened the cabinet and reached up, pulling out a tool case and extracting a drill bit. He did something with his back to us and didn't answer.

I tried not to laugh. Before Tristan could interrogate *me*, I asked him, "If you don't mind my asking, why do you need it by tomorrow?"

Jordan glanced at me while he worked, and then at Tristan, pointedly warning him to answer politely.

Tristan looked surprised again, and then he smiled. He was so entertained by this and could barely hide it.

Before he could answer, Jordan spoke up. It seemed Tristan looked at me too long for Jordan's liking.

"He has a play date with his friends tomorrow."

My jaw nearly dropped to the floor at Jordan's completely unmasked belittling. He was so irritated.

But Tristan didn't get heated. He could tell Jordan was annoyed with him, and it seemed to amuse him more.

To stop myself from laughing in disbelief, I said, "Going shooting?"

"Yeah, actually. Yeah, I am. I think I know what's wrong with it, but Jordan is the expert in guns, and I don't want to risk ruining my antique."

His grin was hilarious. Jordan rolled his eyes, which made it even funnier. I couldn't tell if Tristan was lying, so I just nodded and smiled. Jordan could tell I didn't want to say much else.

"Here." He dropped the drill bit back in the tool case and put it away. He brought the gun back and set it on the coffee table before his brother could say anything further.

"I'm sorry. We can go now."

"Don't be sorry," I said. Jordan was ready to head out the door. "It was nice to meet you, Tristan."

He followed us to the door. "It was lovely to meet you as well."

Jordan opened the door and put his hand on my back, guiding me out gently. I turned and caught him giving Tristan an exasperated glance. Tristan grinned at him.

"Drive safe."

Jordan didn't say anything, just hit the down arrow next to the elevator. I smiled at Tristan, who was still standing in the doorway as we waited for the elevator. He smiled back, and I could tell he wanted to say something as he tapped his foot up and down and looked, amused, at Jordan.

"Goodnight," I murmured.

"Goodnight." The elevator doors opened, and we stepped in. As I moved I caught the flash of Tristan closing his door.

"I apologize if he bothered you. He doesn't mean any harm." He shook his head. "I apologize, anyway."

I laughed quietly. "He didn't bother me." I wanted to ask why Tristan was amused, but the situation seemed to unnerve Jordan.

"He's nice," I said cheerily. "Was that actually an antique?"

He rolled his eyes. "No, he just said that so he wouldn't look lazy for not trying to figure it out himself."

I giggled. They were so cute.

After we got in the car, Jordan said quietly, "He's not used to seeing me with women. That's why he was acting like an idiot."

"Oh, that's okay. I thought it was kinda funny. I didn't take any offense to it or anything," I reassured him.

I hesitated. "You haven't...dated a lot?" I backtracked. "Not saying we're dating, but he seemed to get that impression, so...that's why I ask." I squeezed my hands together, suddenly nervous.

"Are we not dating?" Jordan asked, calm but appearing worried.

I looked at him, eyes widening. "I...I mean I thought we might be." I tried to shrink myself down as much as possible in my seat. *Oh, goodness.* "I want to be." I didn't look at him.

"I do, too."

My head jerked up; I was stunned. I hadn't known how much I feared he didn't feel the same attraction as me.

A nervous, shy smile grew on my face. "Okay. So...then we are." It was a question.

"We are," he confirmed. He glanced at me. "Don't be nervous."

"Or...I know you can't help feeling nervous but...please. Let me know how I can help you not be."

Then he said quietly, "You seem unsure."

I kept trying to shrink down, suddenly jittery, feeling the cold a lot more. "I just...I didn't know if you felt the same way." I squeezed my knees together, looking at how my inner thighs curved. Anything but his eyes.

"I do." He said it with finality. Then, softer, "I do."

"Okay."

"I'm happy," I added.

"I am, too," he said gently. I felt his eyes on me as long as he could keep them before having to turn back to the road.

"You asked me something," he said. "I didn't forget."

I looked at him, trying to remember.

"I haven't dated a lot, no. Actually..." He seemed to be thinking of how to say it. "I haven't really dated at all."

I sat up and back in my seat. "You haven't?"

He shook his head.

"No serious relationships? Not...not anything even brief?"

He shook his head again.

"Not even in high school?" There was no way.

"No, not even then." I couldn't tell if he was embarrassed or not.

"I..." *Don't know what to say.* I couldn't believe it.

"Gotcha."

He narrowed his eyes. "You okay?"

I nodded, smiling. I tried to remain casual for the next few minutes. It didn't take long to get to the restaurant.

After he stopped the truck and the engine quieted down, Jordan looked at me and said, "Come on. Let's go get some food." He was watching me. He knew something was off.

I had questions in my mind I was afraid to ask him.

Jordan put his hand on my back as he guided me inside.
As we walked to the table, I tried to clear my tangled thoughts.
How do I ask him?
He pulled my chair out for me and requested two waters.
I eased into conversation; I thought I had a good way to get my answers.
"Jordan, do you practice Catholicism?"
He was looking at me with careful eyes to make sure I was okay.
"Yes, I do practice. My parents raised us Catholic, and my mom is very devout." He put his hand on the table, gripped the edge. "Do you?"
I was wearing my necklace with the cross jewel, as I usually did, tucked into my shirt. I reached up and pulled it out, held it gently between my fingers. "The same."
He nodded, looking at my cross. He reached into the collar of his shirt and pulled a small gold cross out as well. I smiled, surprised. It was attractive to see the display of devotion.
"My mother is also *very* devout," I told him. "Do you go to church?"
He nodded again. "I go on Sundays sometimes. There aren't any Arabic or Chaldean churches where I live; I make the trip down to go with my parents some weekends. It makes my mom happy."
"I think that's sweet. It also makes my mom happy when I go." I looked at the table. When Jordan mentioned his parents, it reminded me of my own. And the lack of a relationship that was there, which had been getting worse. "My dad, he...he's not devout. It makes my mother more unhappy with him." I looked up at Jordan, smiled a small smile that failed a second later. I realized I'd mentioned that out of nowhere.
Jordan didn't seem to mind. He was intent. "Do your mother and father get along at all?" he asked, staring at me intensely.
I smiled a small, sad smile. "Barely," I replied softly. I could see it more as the years passed, how unhappy my parents were. It devastated me.
Jordan looked worried. "I'm sorry," he said softly. "Do you want to tell me about it?"
"Um...I just don't think my parents are happy. Really happy." I exhaled quietly. "Neither one of my parents are perfect. But I just want them to be happy. I definitely don't want a relationship modeled after theirs, that's for sure." I laughed weakly, but he could see how bothered I'd suddenly become.
Jordan reached out and took my hand. The smile slid off my face as I looked at our fingers lacing together. It was just what I needed to snap me out of my emotional moment and focus on the present. My heart skipped.
"I'm so sorry," he said quietly, his compassion touching me once again. "You don't deserve to have to see that." I glanced at our interlaced hands while he spoke.
"I can tell their relationship has made you very unhappy." He squeezed my hand, leaning closer to me over the table. I stared at his eyes, feeling weak.
"I'm always here." His voice strengthened. "I always will be."

I nodded again. "Thank you," I said, smiling, trying for any shred of cheeriness.

"You're welcome." He squeezed my hand again.

The waiter then came to take our orders, and we gently unlinked hands. It seemed a good moment for it.

I wasn't hungry, but I ordered; I knew it would upset Jordan more if I didn't eat. I felt bad for saddening the night.

"Thank you for letting me...vent. I didn't even mean to bring that up."

"You don't have to thank me."

I couldn't argue. I just accepted his kindness.

I was brutally into him.

"So...back on the topic of religion." I hadn't gotten to the subject I wanted to discuss. "Tell me..." I stared off, wondering how to ask. "Tell me the hardest part of our religion, for you."

While he answered thoughtfully, the concern never fully left his eyes.

"When I work...I see some bad stuff. And it makes me feel closer to God, actually." His eyebrows went up. "But..."

"How?" I asked gently, interrupting.

He thought for a moment. "Well, the harder things get, the more I...seek peace in my faith."

I nodded. "I see. Please continue. You were saying you see bad stuff."

He met my eyes, and his had never looked so grave. "To stop that bad...I've done...bad." He paused, eyes haunted.

"And I can't stop. I won't. Because the bad guys have to be stopped."

He was watching me intensely as he spoke.

Is he worried what I'll think? Jordan?

"But..." His eyes flickered down to the table as he thought, then he brought them back up to mine. "I don't believe God wants violence."

"I understand." I kept my voice low.

Jordan was still watching me carefully; I kept my composure, not speaking further. I wanted him to continue.

Finally, he finished, "I won't lie to you, Nina, and say that I've never hurt anybody." He was staring so hard into my eyes it felt like his were touching my brain. "I've hurt people. To say the least."

To say the least.

So you've killed people. I saw right through the words.

"I believe you." I cocked my head to the side. "And it's alright. I admire what you do." My voice was low, serious. I was able to keep his eyes.

"I don't think it makes you a bad man. Unless you hurt people for fun."

Jordan's eyes had a flash of horror in them. "No," was all he said; it was so adamant that I reached out for his hand. He was surprised, but lifted it onto the table as we locked fingers again.

"You don't," I said gently.

"No." He shook his head, teeth gritted. "I don't." This was difficult for him to mention.

The thought ran through my head that he might be scared he would frighten me away.

I rubbed my thumb over the side of his hand and forefinger. "I believe you," I said gently.

"I'm not afraid," I added. "I'm not afraid of you, Jordan." I looked at him for a moment. "I think you're a hero."

He stared at me intensely. "I'm sure it's hard to do what you do. I imagine how conflicted it must make you. I know that if I were in your position, it would be hard for me, too." I leaned forward.

"For what it's worth, I think you're an *amazing* person. And it doesn't bother me any."

I studied his face, sensing a sadness. I imagined the words *You don't know what you're saying* running through his mind. But I remained confident.

"It doesn't?"

I shook my head and continued stroking his hand with my thumb. "No."

He continued staring at me, and I stared back, my gentleness meeting his tension.

He began nodding slowly, and then made himself snap out of it. He looked away a moment, and then looked back at me.

"Thank you," he said quietly.

"You don't have to thank me." I smiled, matching his earlier sentiment. "It's just how I feel."

I could still see the conflict in his eyes, but his face had smoothed out.

"Let's talk about you now." His voice was rough.

And although it seemed all we did was talk about me, I didn't argue. I wanted him to feel comfortable. I wanted to give him what he wanted.

"Sure," I said softly. "What would you like to know?" He had sat up and it put distance between us, so I gently pulled my hand away from his. I kept gentle, compassionate eyes on him, however, so he knew I was not shying away.

"I'd like to know what the hardest part about our religion is for you."

Here we go. I took a deep breath. "Honestly...there are a few things." He nodded.

"But one thing, in particular..." I put my pride to the side. "Sex before marriage," I exhaled.

I studied his face carefully. He studied mine. "Tell me more."

"It's hard for me, because...nowadays, it's like everybody is...you know." He nodded again.

"But...for me, I always wanted to wait. Until I was married. Because that's how I was raised. But my parents and religion aren't the only reasons."

I paused for a moment to see if he wanted to speak. He waited.

"It'll just be more meaningful to me if I wait. I can't do it casually, or...even in a relationship; it would be bad for me emotionally, you know? If we broke up." I smiled small. "I love so hard."

Jordan blinked slowly, sitting back just a little; the statement pleased him.

"But I just...I know that when I love somebody, it's hard to not want that. But I'm still trying...." I slid the statement in, nervous for his reaction. "To wait."

Jordan remained serious. "I understand."

"You do?"

He nodded. "Yeah, I do."

I wanted to ask so badly. "Do you?" The question came out much quieter than I meant it to. He knew what I was asking.

"I have been," he replied matter-of-factly but quietly.

My whole body went light with the news. I felt as if I would disintegrate through the chair, like a ghost.

I didn't know what to say for a few moments; finally I forced myself to speak. "I...wow," was what I settled for.

He tilted his head a bit. "What's the matter?" he asked gently.

"I'm not trying to be...offensive," I struggled.

He narrowed his eyes. "I'm not offended."

I nodded slowly. "Okay, I'm just...surprised. Not in a bad way. Just...you know, everyone now is...." I nodded implicatively, then looked him up and down. "And you're so...I'm just surprised...I mean...I'm *sure* you've been hit on." I looked at him, waiting for a response. I knew I was a rambling, nerdy mess.

He didn't smile or laugh.

"I was never interested."

I began to seriously question if I was conscious.

I didn't even speak.

"Nina," he said slowly. "Ask me what you want to ask me without worrying. Say what you want to say. I won't be offended," he promised.

The directness of his words was attractive and centered me a little.

Tell me what to doooooo, baby boy.

I loved it.

I shook my head. "I just...I'm happy," I declared, but I was still obviously stunned. "I just...I know I don't have a right to be..."

His eyes narrowed again. "Why not?"

"Well...because...what you've done in the past isn't my business."

"It's not abnormal to be happy someone values the same things as you." He made it sound so normal.

"Well..." I struggled. "If a guy was as happy about someone's virginity, people would call him a creep."

Jordan thought a moment. "But you're not happy about it for the same reason. It's...vile for a man to be fixated on a woman's virginity because they think it somehow...feels better. Or makes them feel like more of a man. Or thrive on the idea of taking a woman's innocence."

I nodded. He was right.

"Those aren't the reasons you care."

I tried to articulate what the reasons *were*. "I just don't like the thought...you know?" I swallowed. "Sex is such an intimate thing. When I love someone, I don't want to picture him having such intimacy with someone else. I don't want to know that he has memories of it that won't go away."

I hoped so badly he understood. "Does that make sense?"

"Of course." Jordan looked pensive, though, and I was wondering if he was thinking of it for the first time.

"Maybe I'm insecure. Or...jealous."

"Or maybe you're none of those things, and you love hard and passionately, so it's easy to be hurt by the thought of the person you love with someone else," he interjected, throwing my words back at me. "Like you said."

I couldn't speak for a moment.

You are so brutally sexy, I thought.

Finally, I said quietly, "It is so nice to be validated in how I feel."

His eyes softened. "How you feel is valid. Don't let anyone make you think otherwise. I hope this conversation made you feel at least a little better about it. You shouldn't feel guilty at all."

I smiled. "Thank you so much."

The smile he gave me in return was unbearably beautiful. After a few moments of just staring at one another, I brought everything full circle.

"So," I sat back and shrugged. "All that aside, it's hard to wait. But...I'll be okay. I'm just figuring things out as I go."

He stared at me, nodding slightly. Finally, he murmured, "Thank you for telling me all of that. I know it's very personal."

I smiled. "Thank *you*. For being honest with me. And reassuring."

"Of course," he repeated. "I always will be."

And despite my crushing difficulty to trust someone, I found solace in those words.

JORDAN

Dinner last weekend had taught me so much about Jordan and had revealed so much of me to him. And I was happy about it.

To make me even more smitten, he sent me flowers on Valentine's Day. When our receptionist brought them to my office, I looked at her, stunned. I was anxious to read the card.

"Thanks, Carmen."

When she left, and no one was looking into my office, I plucked out the small piece of cardstock. In elegant black ink was the message:

Nina,

The other night, you noticed the flowers outside of Tristan's apartment and said how pretty they were. So, I hope you like all of these. I thought roses would be fitting, since it's Valentine's Day.

I'm looking forward to seeing you again, Nina. Have a lovely day and rest of your week.

I'll talk to you soon.

Jordan

I held the note in my hand, a huge smile on my face, reading it over and over again.

Finally, I called him. He answered in the middle of the second ring.

"Nina," he murmured.

"Hi," I exhaled. "Jordan, thank you so much for this," I said immediately. "These are so beautiful. I don't even know what to say. Jordan, thank you. I feel so bad that I didn't do anything like this for you."

"No, no, no," he said soothingly, his voice gentle and low. It was so good to hear. "Don't worry about that. All I needed was for you to like them, and you do. I'm happy."

I couldn't contain the huge, nerdy smile on my face. "Jordan," I breathed. I didn't know what to say. I was over the moon.

"Yes, honey." My jaw dropped at the word.

I was sitting in my office, holding a little card in my hand, face to face with a vase of roses, cell phone to my ear, jaw hanging like an idiot.

It sounded *so good* coming out of his mouth.

"I—" What was I supposed to say? *Please come take me away from here, let's get married, call me honey every time you address me, I'm so happy at this very moment that I could die, and it's pathetic.*

"I'll get you back."

"You don't need to do a thing." I heard a smile in his gentle voice. "Nina, we can't see each other on Friday or Saturday, but I was wondering if you'd come over on Sunday for lunch." He paused. "My family's coming over."

"Oh—" I started.

"You can say no," he added.

"No, no," I shook my head to myself. As stressful as it sounded, I couldn't say no. He wanted me to meet his parents, to spend Sunday with his *family*. He'd just sent me over a dozen roses at work.

How could I say no?

"Of course I will. Thank you for inviting me." I hesitated. "Are you sure you want them to meet me?"

"Why wouldn't I?"

"Well…I don't know. Won't they question you? I feel bad. If they question you."

"It doesn't matter if they question me. They want to meet you. I want you to meet them."

My eyebrows shot up. "You told them about me?" And then I remembered. "Or did Tristan?"

"Tristan mentioned my "friend" to them the other day, and my mom called me."

Bummer. I would've been thrilled if he had told them.

"I wanted you to meet them, anyway."

Nerves and excitement crept through me.

"I'll come."

After a moment, he murmured, "Okay. Just remember what I told you. You don't have to. If it will make you anxious or uncomfortable, I want you to tell me. I won't be angry or offended."

"You're so sweet," I murmured. "No, that's okay. As long as you're there, I'll be fine." I closed my eyes and sat back in my chair. "Thank you for being so thoughtful."

"I'll be there with you the whole time," he said. "They'll be very nice, I promise."

I shook my head, smiling small to myself. "I'm sure they will be. Thank you, Jordan. You made my day so happy." I opened my eyes and ran my fingers down the vase. "I'm excited to see you Sunday."

"I am, too." I heard the smile in his low voice.

I was blissful the rest of the week.

On Saturday night, I decided I'd wear a nice orange blouse, black jeans, and short black boots for lunch the next day. I baked a large plate of chocolate chip cookies. When my mom asked why and offered to help, I confessed where he lived. After we'd argued and things settled, I promised her I'd be more honest. I didn't blame her for being concerned over my safety.

In the morning, I worked out then showered. I told Jordan I wanted to get there before his family did. I didn't want to walk into his whole family just sitting there, staring at me.

Jordan was graceful, telling me I could come whenever I wanted. I couldn't tell him that what I wanted was to wrap my arms around his waist and hide, mostly from the notion of meeting his family.

I put those thoughts out of my brain as I got in the car and set my GPS. I was slowly learning the way to his house, from all the times he'd driven me.

On the highway, my thoughts wandered. I wondered if his parents had a loving relationship. If they were madly in love when they were married. If they still were. I wondered how it affected Jordan, how he viewed relationships. Had he seen a healthy marriage growing up?

I wondered if they had accents. My parents didn't.

I wondered if they would like me. If they would think I was ugly, or an idiot. I hoped his parents thought I was good enough for their son.

I knew I was getting ahead of myself. I focused on the road and tried not to crash while daydreaming.

When I pulled into the driveway, there was already another car there. Jordan's truck was parked at the top of the driveway, in front of a small black Audi.

The garage was open, and the left space was empty. I figured Jordan had left it open for his parents. I parked behind the Audi.

I noticed a text from Jordan.

I just wanted to let you know ahead of time, Tristan is already here. He got here early. I don't know if you're driving right now; I'm assuming you are. But I wanted to let you know anyway, even if it's before you come in the house.

Then another message. *You can park in the garage. Please. The driveway is slippery.*

Ugh, Jordan. Always a perfect gentleman.

I was already parked, and I couldn't take the spot closest to the door when his older parents were coming.

I sighed and got out of the car, purse, phone and plate of cookies in hand. Jordan came outside.

"Hey," he breathed. He was wearing dark blue jeans and a loose, light gray sweater specked with little black and white dots. His natural, thick black

hair was full and riddled with tufts. He looked beautiful this Sunday morning.
Man, I wonder what it's like to wake up next to that.
He looked down at the plate of cookies.
"Hi," I murmured quietly, smiling at him. Nerves filled me. "Thanks for the heads-up."
He nodded once, still out of breath. It was cold outside.
"Of course," he sighed, dismayed. "I'm sorry, Nina. I know you wanted to get here before them."
I grabbed his forearm lightly and squeezed it. "It's okay," I assured him. "I'm not so socially awkward that I can't handle it."
"No, no. I don't think that. I just want you to be comfortable." He shook his head and stepped closer to me. "I won't let him bother you, I promise."
"He doesn't bother me," I reassured him. "I think he's really nice and kinda funny." *Man, I wanna kiss him.*
He scoffed. I'd never seen him do that before. "Yeah. Kinda."
I laughed in surprise. He smiled and looked down at the cookies again. "You didn't have to make cookies," he told me. "Thank you. Can I carry them for you?"
I smiled. "Yeah. They're for you, anyway. Come on," I said, letting go of his arm. I grabbed his waist to turn him in the direction of the house. Jordan walked beside me, hand on my back.
"Watch your step," he murmured, as I looked at the icy ground and walked slowly. "I left the garage open for you."
"I figured it was for your mom and dad," I said, still surprised. "I didn't see your text until I was already here. I'm so sorry," I said, making a face. "I don't know if you wanted me there for a reason, or…"
He shook his head. "No, no. It's okay. I just didn't want you to fall. It's icy." He looked down at the ground beneath us. "My dad doesn't like parking in driveways."
Once we'd made it inside, he set the cookies down, helped me take my jacket off and then hung it up in the closet. I slid my boots off and put them in the same spot next to the shoe rack that I always did.
As we made our way to the kitchen, I saw Tristan, dressed in black joggers and a dark green sweater, sitting on the couch in the living room; he was watching TV, his side to us as we stepped in.
He turned to us immediately. "Hi, Tristan," I said nicely, smiling.
He rotated his whole body more in our direction. "Hi, Nina," he said, and a smile, all teeth, slowly grew on his face. He instantly seemed thrilled but was trying to contain it. His amusement with our relationship amused *me*.
"How are you?" I asked.
"I'm great," he replied, smile still huge. "How are *you*?"
"I'm good. Thank you." Jordan watched the exchange, annoyed with his brother. He was searching for any sort of discomfort in me, so he could make sure to keep Tristan in line.

It was sweet.
I love him, I thought happily.
Hold up there, buddy.
Take it easy.
I forced myself to snap back to reality and sat down in one of the bar stools at the island. Jordan had held the plate of cookies in his hand throughout the whole exchange, not bothering to do anything else while he supervised. That was even funnier to me.
He set them down on the island. "Thank you, again," he said, nodding towards the cookies. I smiled.
"You don't have to thank me." I repeated his infamous line. "It's really nothing. I should've made more. I feel bad that I didn't."
His eyebrows knitted together. "No, absolutely do not feel bad. Even a little."
I couldn't argue with his commands. I wanted to kiss him instead.
"I'm serious, Nina. You went out of your way to do this."
"It's okay, I really didn't." I looked at the circular treats. "I hope they're good. I don't bake that much anymore. I used to a lot. I just don't have that much time."
He stared at me, sudden fondness on his face. After just a few moments, he said, "I bet they're incredible."
He turned towards the fridge and started pulling things out. Lemonade, different kinds of juices, and a big bowl of salad. Then he opened the oven and pulled out a couple trays. It looked like roasted chicken and a separate dish of sweet potatoes.
"I didn't know you liked to bake," he said, smiling as he set the food down in front of me.
"Yeah, I do. It's relaxing." I smiled a big, cheery smile. "I used to work in a bakery, actually."
Jordan's eyebrows went up in surprise. "Did you?"
I chuckled. "Yeah."
"When?"
"When I was twenty. For two years."
He nodded slowly, eyes full of wonder as he looked at me.
"I'll make you whatever you like."
He grinned, the full view of his teeth making my heart skip. I wondered when that would stop happening. The heart skipping.
Probably not until you're ninety. Probably never.
"That's very sweet of you."
Tristan wandered into the kitchen, staring at the cookies. I knew he'd heard the exchange. "You made these, Nina?" he asked, pointing down at them. I nodded.
"They look amaaazing."
I giggled at the goofy look on his face. "Have some."

"He'll take you up on that," Jordan said, rolling his eyes. "Have some manners," he told his brother, as Tristan unwrapped the plate and took a cookie.

"It's okay," I said, smiling at Tristan. "It makes me happy."

"In that case, I'll eat the whole plate," Tristan piped up. I laughed.

"These are *good*, Jordan," he said, chewing his first bite, eyebrows knitted together in surprise. He took another bite and looked at me. "You know, he's lucky to be able to be around you."

Before I could say anything, Jordan murmured, "Yes, I am."

All I could do was smile shyly. I glanced at Tristan, to see how he was reacting to the exchange. He looked stunned for a moment, speechless. He'd even stopped chewing. He held a cookie halfway to his mouth, frozen there as he stared. I tried not to burst out laughing.

I covered my smile. This was all too much.

I looked back at Jordan, who was still looking at me, a warm, unashamed look of fondness on his face. Then he nodded to himself, and looked up at Tristan.

"At least save some for her. She went through the trouble of making them."

I knitted my eyebrows together and shook my head quickly. "Oh, no, no. I'm not gonna eat those. Nuh-uh." I looked at Tristan. "I have the metabolism of an eighty-year old grandma."

"I doubt that." He laughed. "You're probably more ripped than this guy over here," he teased, flicking his chin in Jordan's direction. "And listen," he began, as he took another bite of a cookie, chewed and swallowed. "That guy is *pretty* ripped."

I laughed, looking at Jordan, who was giving Tristan the most exasperated, annoyed look I'd ever seen him produce.

"Stop," he told him, looking and sounding exhausted by the comment.

I grabbed his forearm. "He's just being silly," I said quietly, chuckling while trying to soothe. "I'm not laughing at you. I promise."

"I know. It isn't you who is exhausting." His voice was low. I smiled up at him, and slowly the grimness slid off his face and was replaced by something softer.

I knew Tristan was watching, but I didn't care, and Jordan didn't seem to, either.

"Man," Tristan half-whispered to himself. But he didn't say anything beyond that. I looked at him, and he just stared at me for a few moments. I raised my eyebrows at him, and a grin slowly grew on his face. I grinned back.

I liked the idea of being the person who Jordan finally fell for. The person who could make him happy, take away some of that gravity he was always drenched in.

"He's funny," I murmured, as Tristan headed back to the couch.

Just then, we heard sounds coming from the garage. Jordan's parents were here. Early.

"I'll be right back," he murmured, running his hand over mine. I nodded quickly.

"Jordan," a woman's voice with a Chaldean accent said as the noises grew closer. "Why did she park there, the garage is empty. Did you tell her?" Rania.

"She didn't know it was for her," was all he murmured.

Jordan returned, carrying a long tray in his arms, followed by his mother. Rania was a few inches shorter than me. Her olive-toned skin was lighter than my currently tan complexion, her eyes a dark brown, unlike her sons'. She was petite but full. Her hair fell down her neck, black, wavy and natural.

Jordan's father, Amar, followed her in. Five-seven in height, Amar had a stocky build, round head, black mustache and hair laced with gray, and a skin tone like Tristan's.

"Hi, honey!" Rania greeted me happily, her familiar accent making me feel more at home. *"Hi-ee hun-eee."*

"Hi," I said, smiling big at her. I didn't look at him but could feel Jordan's restless energy as he stood by my side, unable to say anything before she came up for a hug. "How are you?" I asked her politely.

"I'm good, honey, thank you."

"This is Nina," Jordan introduced. While calm, I could see he was alert.

Amar stepped up. "Hi, sweetie," he said, reaching out his hand for me to shake.

"It's nice to meet you," he continued, voice drenched in the Arabic accent so similar to that of a Chaldean.

I grasped his big hand and shook it.

"Call me Amar." He looked at his wife. "Rania."

"It's nice to meet you both." I smiled. Rania was already maneuvering around the kitchen.

"Jordan, baby, is all the food warm?" she asked as she pored over everything.

"Yes," he responded in his calm, unwavering tone.

While we made our introductions, Tristan had filled glasses of ice water and was now taking them to the dining room.

"Let me help," I murmured, following in his footsteps, grabbing two.

"Nina," Jordan started, but Rania spoke over him.

"No, honey, go sit down. You're our guest." I smiled at her as she took the glasses from my hands. This was nothing like I'd feared it would be.

"Mom," Jordan started, presumably because she took the glasses away from me.

"It's okay," I mouthed at him behind her back. He put his hand on my upper back.

"Sorry," he said quietly in my ear. The warmth of his skin ironically made me shiver.

I shook my head and smiled again.

"Let's go to the dining room," he murmured, grabbing a tray of food. Rania and Tristan had already grabbed the rest.
Amar was talking to Tristan in Arabic, and I didn't understand a word. When Tristan rapidly replied in Arabic, I was in awe.
"I wish I spoke Arabic," I murmured as we walked, his free hand on my lower back. "I have to learn."
Jordan smiled small. "I'll teach you, if you'd like."
I grinned. The thought of Jordan spewing out gorgeous Arabic the way his brother did made my heart skip. "Yes. I would love that." I kept my voice low, but the excitement leaked into it. Jordan smiled bigger.
"Anything you want," he murmured.
Jordan pulled out a chair for me at the long, brown wooden table and then sat next to me.
His family was watching me.
Jordan put me food while they served themselves. They glanced to the food one second, me the next. Tristan said a couple things to his mom quietly, and she replied back in Arabic. Even as we ate, parents and Tristan chit-chatting, their eyes always landed back on me. They regarded Jordan as well. I didn't feel judged; I could sense their curiosity, but I didn't want to eat while I was being watched.
After a minute, Jordan had had it. I was looking down at the table, trying to pretend I didn't notice his mom and dad looking at me, when Jordan said something firmly in Arabic.
I looked up, stunned. Rania put her hands up and replied back to him with wide, innocent eyes. I had no idea what she said, but her face and tone read, *What? What? What did we do?*
I was entranced while Jordan replied, clearly irritated. That Arabic sounded so beautiful coming out of his mouth.
As Tristan and Rania began discussing his job, Jordan looked at me. "I'm sorry," he murmured quietly. "I don't want to do that when you don't understand, but I figured it'd be better for you. In the moment."
He leaned closer, put his lips nearly to my ear. "I just told them to back off." I nodded. It was even sexier when he said it that way.
I couldn't help it. I loved a protector.
I looked back at them slowly. Rania was looking at me. "Nina," she began. "Jordan told me you live near us."
I nodded. "Yeah, not too far." I smiled.
"Oh good. Now when he comes down to see you, he can visit us more." She gave him a stern look. I chuckled.
"He comes every week, Rania," Amar chimed in. "He's busy, what do you want?"
I giggled quietly. Jordan looked at me and smiled such a happy smile that my heart ached.
I glanced back at Rania; she was looking at Jordan, who was still looking at me. After a minute, her lips turned up at the corners as she watched him.

JORDAN

Instead of meeting my eyes, she met Tristan's, and there was a look of pleased understanding.
They were intrigued by whatever relationship Jordan and I had. The surprise in them reiterated what Jordan had told me: he hadn't been interested in anyone before.
I looked away from Tristan and Rania quickly, not wanting them to notice I'd witnessed their moment. I knew everything I needed to know.
"Nina," Rania addressed me again. "Are you in school?"
"No," I said confidently. "I graduated already."
"Oh!" She sat back, an impressed look on her face. "How old are you, honey?"
"Twenty-four," I replied, keeping my tone light, trying to be as sweet as possible.
Again, I could feel Jordan next to me, *absorbing* the interaction. He barely tried to mask it; he was protecting me. The social anxiety conversation had stuck with him.
Amar jumped in. "What degree did you get?" Deep voice, heavy accent, asking a question typical of a Middle Eastern father from his generation. Questions in this category also included, *What school did you go to? What did you study? Where do you work?*
Etcetera.
"Bachelor's in English and Business."
I noticed Tristan's eyes on me. "When did you graduate?"
"Five years ago."
"Didn't you just say you're twenty-four?"
"Yes."
He sat back, eyebrows shooting up as his eyes widened. "You graduated college at nineteen?"
I blinked. "Yeah."
"And high school at seventeen?"
I nodded.
"Two years for a degree? A small degree," Rania justified.
"No, she said bachelor's," Tristan corrected, impressed. "Not a two-year."
"Yeah," I replied, smiling small. Tristan's face read, *Huh, would you listen to that*, as he nodded slowly. I checked Jordan's reaction, hoping too much that he would be proud.
His eyes were slightly wider than before. He was staring at me, disregarding his family's presence.
"Two?" Jordan murmured, stunned.
I turned more to him, realizing I'd never told him that. "Yeah," I said, still smiling. He stared at me, the wonder in his eyes growing.
Amar's eyebrows shot up. "How did you do the whole thing so fast?"
"By testing out, dad," Jordan said quietly, speaking up for me.
Understanding filled Amar's face for a moment as he looked at me. He turned his attention to Jordan.

"You tested out of your classes, too, right?" he asked.
Oh. Duh! I hadn't thought of that before.
"Yes."
"A lot?"
"Not as many as Nina had to."
I smiled. "How do you know that?"
"Because," he murmured, "You cut a four-year degree down to two."
"Yeah," I replied, "but you got a master's in four, not to mention your two other degrees that you got at the *same* time. So, let's not kid ourselves," I chuckled as a grin grew on his face. I glanced at Tristan, who was smiling, too. "You certainly tested out of many more."
Jordan's parents were smiling at us as well. I was relieved.
"I guess I didn't think of that," he murmured.
I chuckled. "Yes, you did." His grin grew. As I looked away, he turned towards his father.
"Nina is very driven," Jordan said.
"Well, if she did it just like you…" Amar commented. His eyebrows went up. "That means she had to be."
Being compared to Jordan was baffling. I smiled.
"Wow," Tristan said slowly. We all looked at him, confused. Finally, he added, "I didn't realize somebody as *nerdy* as Jordan existed." A grin grew on his face. I laughed.
"Tristan!" Rania scolded.
I immediately turned towards Jordan, who was giving Tristan a hard face. I imagined that, if I hadn't laughed, Jordan would've reached over and smacked him.
"I meant smart, I meant smart." He turned and winked at me, ignoring Jordan. I laughed again.
Jordan turned his head and looked down at me. I realized how close together our chairs were.
Did he move closer, and I just didn't realize it?
He stared at my eyes for a few moments. "She's smart, like our boys," Rania said to Amar; I didn't look at her, entranced in my and Jordan's moment. I could've died right there, in complete bliss.
"Keep eating," he murmured quietly. This was our conversation now; everyone else got the hint and began separate conversations.
"I'm full." I couldn't pay attention to my appetite; I was at the typical level of discomfort one was when having lunch with the family of the man they were falling for.
I also didn't like to eat in front of most people.
Jordan probably realized that, because he leaned in and whispered, "We'll get chicken tenders later."
I tried to keep myself from laughing as loudly as was provoked.

He smiled at me, pleased by my amusement. I grabbed his wrist, out of sight of the others. He looked at me like I was his favorite thing in the world.

He slid his arm back and laced fingers with me, holding my hand for the rest of the meal.

After we cleaned up the dining room, Jordan argued with Rania about washing dishes. I stood there, leaning on the counter, chin in my hand, smiling. When Jordan started off in Arabic, I made myself even more comfortable. It was a beautiful thing to watch.

Who woulda thought? A man arguing in Arabic with his mother about doing dishes, being the most beautiful thing I'd ever witnessed.

When he finally convinced Rania to go, he explained his Arabic.

"I was just telling her to go sit down and relax. What I said was more dramatic than that, but it tends to be."

"Oh, you mean when you're speaking Arabic?"

"No." He smiled. "When I'm trying to convince my mother of something."

I chuckled. "What exactly did you say?"

"That she didn't spend two decades raising and taking care of me to come to my house and clean up after me here, too."

I stared at him, wondering what the name of the angel was, who plucked this man up and set him down in front of me at the library that day.

"You…" I didn't even know what to say. "You're funny," I settled for quietly, smiling to myself. I wanted to tell him he was perfect, a gentleman, an amazing person, but I decided to chill. He looked at me with happy, lazy eyes in response.

"Look, I know you just argued with your mom about this, but…"

Jordan took the opportunity to speak when I trailed off. "Forget it."

I laughed. "Okay. No dishes. But let me help with something." He shook his head, eyebrows raised. *No, ma'am*, his lighthearted face read.

"Listen, listen," I said, as I stepped up to him at the sink. "I'm here to spend time with your family *and* you. And it's not that I'm too scared to go in there. I just want to be with you," I ended quietly, shrugging once. I looked off to the side and stepped back a little, then slowly looked up with puppy eyes. *Don't hurt me right now.*

His face was serious, his piercing blue eyes intense. Based on the wonder in them, I suspected he was charmed.

"Okay," he said easily, though his eyes were still serious. I wanted so badly to know what he was thinking. I asked him softly.

He didn't break his stare into my eyes for a second.

Finally, he said, "That I want to be with you, too."

My knees became weak.

So, he washed, and I dried. It was a happy quiet, a few comments, jokes, laughs, but no forced conversation. We were simply content, being together.

Afterwards, we sat with his family. His side was pressed against mine. I thought that if I put my head down on his arm, like I wanted, he'd put it around me. But I didn't. I'd wait a little longer.
Maybe next time.
I let our bodies touching be enough. For now.

JORDAN

It had been nearly two months of seeing each other, and Jordan I had established that we were dating. I wasn't sure if, to him, he was my boyfriend. I doubted it and thought Jordan would confirm it first.
Regardless, it had been enough time to mention to my family that I was seeing somebody. I considered that I'd met his family, and he hadn't met mine. Even though I was nervous for them to meet, I didn't want him to think he was the reason.
My mother would be sweet, especially after she realized she liked him. The Catholic part would do her in.
And it would be *terrific* to see Zana's face when she laid eyes on him.
So, I told my mom I'd like to have my friend over next Saturday for dinner.
"Is this the same Jordan you've been going out with every weekend?"
"Yeah," I said. "I had lunch with his family on Sunday, and they were really nice. I just think it would be nice to return the favor."
This was more to ask than just dinner with a friend. My family rarely ate meals together. We didn't like the same food, came home at different times, and rarely even got along. A sit-down dinner only happened on the holidays.
"Okay," she said lightly. "What do you want me to make and what time?"
"Let's do five. You're gonna love him, mom." I tried not to sound infatuated. "He's really...amazing. There's no better word for it."
"How old is he?"
Ah.
"He's thirty."
Her eyes narrowed. I looked at her red t-shirt and black pants. Her light brown hair was down past her shoulder blades. She wasn't wearing makeup, but it didn't matter. My mother was beautiful. Small, cute nose,

perfectly shaped pink lips, clean, nicely arched eyebrows, and smooth, olive-toned skin.

"Wait, didn't you tell me he's your friend from school?"

I clamped my lips together. *Ah, shoot.*

"Yeah, I lied." She looked at me with wide eyes. "Mom, you would've *flipped* if I told you I was hanging out with someone I'd just met. You want me to make friends, meet people, but when I do, it's like, 'Oh, you just met him, you can't go out alone with him. You can't trust him.' Basically, 'You shouldn't hang out with him.'" I leaned my head into my hand, elbow resting on the kitchen table. "I wanted to know him. So, we met up for coffee one day. Then dinner."

"Nina, I never say that you shouldn't go out with new people. But *everybody* knows you should go out with new people in a *group* first, until you know them a little better."

I was already defensive. Her paranoia strained our relationship more.

"We met up for coffee in a public place. I'm not stupid, mom. Can I at least tell you about him, before you worry? You're going to love him. Trust me, mom, please." She did not look happy. "Mom, please. Don't be mad about this. I'm so happy I met him, and you're going to be, too."

I could tell she wanted to believe that. As complicated as our relationship was, she did love me.

"I don't like when you lie to me."

I sighed. "I'm sorry, mom. I didn't want you to worry. There comes a point where you have to let us make our own decisions." I shook my head a little, exasperated. "I don't want to argue with you every time I go out."

"We don't have to argue, Nina. You just have to be smarter."

But we did have to argue. Every time.

I rolled my eyes and tried to keep my voice even. I attempted to turn the agitation off. "Mom, he's a *really* great guy. You're going to love him." I sat back, and when she didn't say anything for a few moments, I grinned at her. "Trust me. Just trust me. He's nothing like you're expecting."

Whew, boy. She had *no* idea.

"Oka-ay," she said. *We'll see*, her face read. She didn't hold on to her anger. "You know," she continued, "You seem pretty giddy over him for just being friends."

"He's great, mom. It's just nice to have a good friend. It's not like my other friends." I wanted to tell her about the roses. I wanted to tell her how sweet and thoughtful he was. How protective. How smart. How lethal.

I'd left the roses on my desk at work, and the rest of those details out.

"Well," she remained lighthearted. "I'm happy you made a friend, honey."

I was grateful the topic had turned, the energy lightened.

On Saturday morning, when everyone was around, I tried to nicely ask them not to be idiots.

"Hey guys, can we all be nice and respectful and not make inappropriate jokes when Jordan is here, please?"

JORDAN

My father didn't say anything, but I knew he was listening.

"Yeah, yeah. Whatever," Elijah said. "I can't wait to tell allll your secrets." He grinned.

"Sure thing, big brother. Sure thing. Anyway, guys. Dad," I looked at him, waiting for him to look back. "Please be nice to him. You're going to love him," I added. Once he knew him better, he'd be glad. He'd always "had a bad feeling" about my ex.

"We'll see about that," he said seriously. I rolled my eyes.

"Please be dressed by five, you guys," I begged. "Don't be late to dinner when you're the hosts."

I helped my mom clean all morning and afternoon, and then I showered and got dressed in a loose, comfy black shirt and leggings.

I couldn't wait to see him, but I was so nervous. Jordan handled himself well, which was comforting, but when it came to my family, I couldn't help but be anxious.

At five-oh-one, his Lexus pulled into the driveway.

Here goes nothin'. My heart skipped.

"He's here!" I called out, to warn them to be downstairs, dressed and presentable. It was dramatic, but my family needed the reminder.

Zana was downstairs, dressed and ready to go. Elijah was upstairs. My dad was watching TV.

"Dad," I panicked. "Turn the TV down. You don't have to turn it off, just down. And *be. nice.*"

I walked fast to the front door and opened it to Jordan, in his black jacket and black jeans, carrying a white box presumably filled with pastries.

"Hi," I said happily, reaching out for it as he stepped inside. I looked at him, eyes wide. "What is this?"

"Just some dessert," he murmured.

Zana and my mother were listening from the living room, dying for him to walk in.

"You can leave your shoes wherever or keep them on; it doesn't matter. Whatever you want."

He was quiet, sliding them off. I went to set the box down in the kitchen and came back quickly. "Let me have your jacket."

He smiled small. "I can hang it."

I grinned, looking him in his eyes and stepping close. His clean scent gave me chills. A thrilling reminder that he was present.

"You're at *my* house now. Gimme." He slid off his jacket and handed it to me. He wore a dark gray sweater that looked beautiful on him.

My mother met us halfway to the family room. Zana still couldn't see him. My anticipation of her reaction was overwhelming. *Come on, mom. Move!*

"Ma, this is Jordan," I introduced, standing close to his side.

"Hi," my mother smiled. I sensed surprise, but she hid it well. "I'm Bridgette."

He stuck his hand out to shake hers and smiled. "It's a pleasure," he murmured.

"Come in, please."

I grabbed his wrist. He glanced down and smiled.

He greeted my father and Zana the way he did my mother. My hand still on his wrist, knowing everyone noticed it, I turned him towards me and murmured, "Let's go in there." I nodded towards the dining room. Jordan looked at my mother at the stove, pouring food into serving dishes. Zana looked at me with wide eyes. I stifled a laugh.

"Bridgette," Jordan began, "can I help you with anything?"

"Oh, no, no; thank you. Everything's done now. I'm just gonna bring it all to the table, and we'll eat."

"We got it," I murmured to him. "Everything's ready. Thank you for coming." I kept my voice low and smiled, grateful that Zana and my mother had begun conversing. That, coupled with the low sound of the television, helped ease any awkwardness.

Elijah, the stocky beast he was, a few inches shorter than Jordan, came into the room then. When his eyes landed on us, he came up and stuck out his hand.

"Elijah."

"Jordan."

"It's nice to meet you, man."

My big brother was being nice.

"You, as well." He was softening himself because this was my family. When Jordan was around strangers, he was more reserved. Unreadable.

"Alright guys," my mother said. "Food's ready, let's eat."

We all took our seats. I sat between Jordan and Elijah, ensuring Jordan didn't have anyone on the other side of him. Zana sat across from us, to look at Jordan, I assumed. My father sat at the other end, my mom between him and Zana.

"Please, eat," my mother said.

"Tell me what you want, I'll put it for you," I told Jordan. "You know what, I changed my mind. I'll give you everything." I grinned down at him. "What do you want a lot of?"

He smiled at me. "I'll let you pick. Thank you."

I filled his plate, then I got chicken and salad for myself.

"You're not going to eat lasagna?" Jordan murmured to me. "But you love pasta."

I turned to him. I was loving the proximity. His presence was calming.

"Maybe later," I said quietly. "I honestly think I'm going to have a hard time with this."

"Why?" he asked gently, concern clouding his face.

"I'm so nervous they're going to say something embarrassing," I whispered in his ear. Everyone in my family was watching me as they spoke to one another.

JORDAN

Jordan shook his head a little, eyebrows knitting together. "Don't worry about any of that," he said, right in my ear.

I smiled small at him, picking up my fork and eating some chicken. My appetite was sparse.

Jordan followed suit, taking a bite of lasagna. "Bridgette," he said after he swallowed, surprising me. "This is great."

"Oh, thank you!" she replied, smiling and thrilled. "It's not really anything special; I should've made more."

Jordan shook his head, and gave her the same look he'd given me when I said I was nervous. "You made *plenty*. I'm very thankful to have been invited over. Thank you for having me, everyone."

He sounded so sincere, not awkward, no forced politeness. It was calm, serious Jordan, but the words coming out of his mouth were so genuine I thought my mother might melt to the floor. Zana was smiling, almost flustered.

"Of course," both women chimed at once. "Yeah, man," my brother said. My father chose to begin a different conversation with him.

"Jordan, are you Chaldean?"

"My mother is. My father is Arabic." I hoped my family was polite enough not to ask about his darker complexion.

"Were they born here?"

He responded gracefully. "No. My father in Syria, my mother in Iraq."

"Do you speak Chaldean?" my father asked him.

"Yes," Jordan replied. My parents stared, impressed.

"Please don't take offense to this, I really don't mean it in a bad way, but you don't *look* Chaldean," my mother said politely. I immediately reached out and grabbed his forearm.

"Mom," I started, appalled.

Jordan slid his arm down and locked hands with mine, squeezed. Reassuring me silently. I turned to look at him.

"I'm not."

If anyone wasn't listening to Jordan thus far, they were certainly entranced now.

My mom cocked her head to the side, confused.

"My parents adopted me."

No one knew how to respond for a few moments. I knew they wanted to ask questions like, "Well, what are you, then?" They should've been polite enough to leave it alone.

"Yes," I said, trying to decide what to say before they pushed. I squeezed his hand.

Then my father saved it. "But you speak Chaldean, anyway?"

"I didn't speak very good Chaldean growing up," Jordan confessed. "But I spent some time in Iraq some years ago, and it solidified it for me. My father doesn't speak it much. Only my mother does. Compared to Arabic, she spoke very little Chaldean to us, so my brother and I are much more fluent in Arabic."

"Oh, you have a brother?" Zana asked politely.

Yes, and you are not going to date my potential boyfriend's brother. Jordan nodded.

"How old is he?" she asked.

"He's twenty-seven."

"So you're the oldest," my father said.

"Yes."

"But your brother wasn't adopted?" It was more of a statement.

"Dad," I growled, glaring at him.

Jordan squeezed my hand again, then put his other one over it, stroking the back with his thumb. I turned to look at him, apologies clouding my eyes.

"No, he wasn't. They had him after we got here. My mother was pregnant already."

My mother's eyes widened in comprehension. "Oh, so you're from back home."

Jordan nodded. "Yes, that's where they found me." He paused. "I was a child, wandering around Syria. They were fleeing, took me along with them," he said lightly.

I looked at him with wide eyes, and he gave me a small, reassuring smile. We stared at each other long enough that I felt he might touch me. I turned away to avoid the disappointment if he didn't.

"Wow! You were all by yourself?" Though Jordan expressed no emotion about it, my mother was sad.

"Yeah. Nobody really knew why." He shrugged.

"Wait, so are you Syrian?" Zana asked. "Or you don't know?"

"Could be," he said lightly. "Could be from any one of those areas. My parents could've fled from Syria, Lebanon, anywhere, and something may have happened along the way, and then I was alone. No one knows for sure."

I couldn't believe how casual he made it sound, how inexpressive he was of his emotions when he spoke of such absurd and disturbing things.

"Wow," Zana murmured.

"Alright guys, enough," I said, grateful that Jordan was so gracious about their bluntness, and I, myself, began to be infuriated by it.

Jordan spoke his assurances this time, by leaning close to me and murmuring in my ear, "It's okay, really, honey."

"Okay, we won't ask any more questions about that," my father said. I glared at him for even saying it. He seemed confused as to why.

"What do you do for work?" he asked Jordan.

"I investigate cybercrime."

If only my family knew all the intricate, unique details about Jordan. They would be speechless.

Those details could come later, if there was a later for Jordan and me.

JORDAN

"Oh, that's cool," my mom responded cheerily. "What do you do exactly? I always found that stuff so interesting."
"We use technology to track, essentially. We consult with the police and FBI." My mom's eyes widened.
"Yup, Jordan catches all the evil people on the Internet. He makes the world a much better place," I chirped. *We're wrapping this up.*
They got the hint and stopped asking questions about his job.
After a little more conversation, I murmured softly to Jordan, "How ya feeling?" He smelled so good. Clean.
"I'm great," he murmured back, smiling small at me.
I gestured to his food with my free hand. "Eat," I whispered.
So we did. We ate with our free hands and kept our other ones linked.
"So, how did you guys even meet?" Zana asked us.
"Like nerds," I replied, grinning at Jordan. "At the library."
"Our library?" my mother asked.
"Mhm-hm," I replied cheerily.
"But you don't live around here," my dad said.
"No," Jordan replied. "I live in Cuttingham."
"I know where that is. It's north." My father leaned forward, hands clasped together and elbows on the table. He lifted his index finger to the ceiling.
"Yes." Jordan sat back a little.
"How far?" Zana asked.
"About an hour drive," Jordan murmured.
"Oh, wow," she replied.
I told them about the neighborhood, and his parents. Then, Elijah let out a long, sighing *Ahh*, and sat back. "When's dessert?"
"Is everybody done eating?" my mom asked, looking around the table.
Everyone confirmed. I grabbed Jordan's dish before he could. He looked at me with grim eyes, but he had a small smile on his face.
"*And*," I began, "you're taking food home, too." His smile grew. He looked fond. "Yup," I continued, feeding off of it. "You're just gonna have to *take* my hospitality." I grinned and giggled. He stood up, chuckling.
He leaned in for just a moment, lips right by my temple as he murmured, "You're fantastic. Thank you." I grinned even bigger up at him, his face right in front of mine, and hoped I wasn't delusional for thinking we were behaving like more than friends, and that we both wanted to be.
"You're so great. I appreciate how patient you've been."
He shook his head. "It's nothing at all," he murmured. "I take no offense to any of the questions they've asked me."
"Okay," I murmured worriedly.
After dessert, we all sat together in the family room and had much simple, unserious conversation. By the end of the night, I wasn't so stressed.
When I told Jordan that I hated that he was driving all the way home alone, he told me, "I'm gonna go to my parents' house for the night." It made me happy to think he would be nearby.

When I'd unhappily closed the door after him, Zana put her hand up.

"Okay," she started, unable to keep from grinning. "*Where* did you find him?" She let out a shaky laugh.

"Honestly, Nina," my mother interjected. "He is way too gorgeous for just meeting him casually at the library."

"I *know*!" Zana exclaimed.

Apparently pretty people don't go to the library.

"Isn't he a good guy, guys?"

"Yeah, he seems really nice. He brought desserts, he was so polite." My mother was still eyeing me. "And all this aside from the fact that you can just *tell* he's into you."

It didn't stop there. My family wanted to talk about the relationship.

"So," Zana started. "Are you guys a *couple*? Are you just dating? What is it?"

"Yeah," Elijah interjected. There was a small grin on his face. He found this comical. "Is he your boyfriend?"

"No. He isn't." I didn't look at them. My phone lit up with a message.

"Well, he sure does seem into you," my brother said skeptically, still grinning.

"Yeah. I saw you touching his arm the whole time," my mother said.

Oh. Oh well.

"I hate you," Zana chirped, and they all laughed.

I smiled, stepping into the family room, looking down at my phone and pulling up Jordan's text.

I'm at my parents' house. Thank you so very much for having me over. Your family is lovely. I enjoyed spending time with you around them. Tell Bridgette her cooking is incredible, and thank everyone again for me, please.

Another text came through a few seconds later.

I want to see you soon.

A chill went through me.

I'm so happy you came. I'm sorry again, if anything they said was too intrusive or rude or annoying. I sent another text. *I want to see you again, too.*

It wasn't. Let's go to breakfast tomorrow.

I smiled. *Aren't you going to have breakfast with them? Otherwise I would love that.*

After a minute, he said, *They sleep in. I don't. And I know you don't. So if you're up early, would you like to meet me?*

That sounded amazing.

I told him so. And when I went to bed that night, I felt so, so warm.

March

JORDAN

March came around the corner. Slowly, the air became warmer. Thirty degrees to forty, some days fifty.

The seasonal change always made me feel odd. I was both excited and anxious; summer used to come around and remind me that I was in a body I hated. I still had flashbacks to that same uneasiness.

But the joy about sunshine and anticipation of warmth brought energy and the urge to produce; writing quenched my thirst for creativity.

I put the novel aside, because, despite the surge of motivation, the ideas for the story I wanted weren't coming. I knew I couldn't force it.

So, I began posting short stories to my blog again, feeling I was taking the easy way out.

I settled for romance, which was what my readers wanted. Lord knew I had a new muse.

The weeks were long without seeing Jordan. But, as badly as I wanted to, it didn't make sense to drive so far to just spend a few hours together.

I could go there and stay late after work, but it would throw off my whole day the next day; I told myself I would not fall for him and lose myself in the process.

I'd come too far in fixing my mental health to set myself back for any relationship again.

But as Jordan and I spent more time together, I felt more strongly for him. I loved him as a person, as a friend; I loved being around him.

To lose him, the way I lost my ex-boyfriend, would be much more devastating.

And losing that other relationship was *very* devastating.

JORDAN

I wanted to talk to Jordan about what happened. I wanted him to know everything. But I also wanted to wait until he and I weren't in uncertain territory, before I told him about my former relationship.

These thoughts whirling around in my head, I stepped outside and inhaled the spring air. We were midway through the month, and it was wet with rain some days, blue skies others. Today, it was chilly, but the sky was bright and blue, dotted with a few small, scattered clouds. It was about forty degrees, and it felt amazing.

I got in my car and began the route to Jordan's house; I'd finally memorized it.

Most times we hung out, we simply talked. We watched a couple movies, but usually, we would go out to eat, or head downtown to walk around and just talk. We spent every weekend together since the night he met my family. Sometimes all weekend.

We talked about everything; he told me about Tristan, and how he used to follow him around as a child, looking up to his big brother and wanting his approval so badly. Jordan explained how he wanted to be a good influence for him, how he wanted Tristan to look at him and know the right thing to do in every situation. My heart ached, hearing this. I imagined a little Jordan, already thinking like a man, wanting to be brave and strong for his little brother to see. To feel assured. It brought tears to my eyes.

He told me how it was hard for Tristan when Jordan went to the Middle East to fight and go to school. He visited home a total of ten times in those five years, and then he went to the Bureau's headquarters for six months and didn't come home at all. Then, he found a home in Cuttingham and isolated himself for another year before he regularly went around his family again.

Jordan expressed regret at all of this. I thought of Tristan, how lighthearted and funny he was, and it made me sad for both of them that their relationship felt that strain.

I told Jordan about school, how I was a perfectionist since childhood. We discussed high school, my straight A's from first grade to my bachelor's degree. He asked me about how school was for me socially. I had to make myself numb to discuss it.

I told Jordan I was bullied throughout elementary and middle school. How kids made fun of me for being developed so quickly and "for being ugly, basically." He looked angry and appalled and said, "There's no way you were ugly. Kids are not ugly." And I shook my head and chuckled, telling him that, oh yes, they could be.

I put that out of my mind as I parked in Jordan's garage, which he'd casually started calling my spot.

The fact that I had a spot in his home was delightful.

At the door when I approached, he grabbed my hand and pulled me inside.

"Jordan." I smiled, setting my bag down. I wore a light jacket over my clothes. The chill in the air demanded it. I had chosen boots, because it was muddy outside from the rain. And I had an idea in mind.
"Can we go for a walk?" I asked.
"Of course." He wore a long-sleeved, pale red shirt and gray jeans. Jordan grabbed a light jacket and slipped on some short black rain boots. When his jacket was zipped, he said, "Let me just grab my phone, in case my parents call." He walked away briskly and called, "I wouldn't bring it otherwise."
Aw. "What about work?" I asked as he reapproached.
He shook his head. "They'll be alright."
I smiled, reaching for his hand. He took it, smiling back. It made me breathless.
There were no sidewalks near Jordan's house. He made sure I walked nearest to the houses, and he was closest to the cars that drove past.
"How has your day been?" he murmured. "Your morning."
"It's good. I love this weather. Chilly sunshine. My favorite."
He turned his head and smiled at me; he looked beautiful under the sun.
"It is beautiful today," he agreed.
"I appreciate the spring," I said. "Fall used to be my favorite season. I loved pumpkin everything. Sweaters and leggings and boots. Hot coffees. It's so cozy." I longed for autumn for a moment. "Winter is definitely my least favorite season. Dark, cold. I get depressed without sunshine."
"Let's get you a vitamin D supplement," he suggested. "It will help during these rainy months."
I smiled at him. "I'll get one. You're right, it's a great idea."
"How do you feel about summer?" he asked. The chill of the day covered my exposed face and hands; it was a lovely feeling.
"I like it. I hated it most of my teenage years, but now I love it. I can get super tan. *For free!*" I sang with glee.
Jordan chuckled and put his free hand over the one he was holding.
Do you want to touch me as much as I want to touch you? I almost asked.
"Why did you hate it?" he murmured finally.
"I was uncomfortable in my skin."
He nodded in understanding. "You have to wear less. I never considered that." He stared at my face, pensive.
"It's not something people who aren't going through it really think about. So that's okay." I noted the two-story, colonial houses in his neighborhood. It was beautiful. Hilly. Some houses were elevated, others weren't. All had large front yards. "I know most people get somewhat insecure about their bodies in the summer. That's why you always hear people talking about how they need to get their "summer bodies" back before it starts." I shrugged. "I try to just keep mine year-round."
"You're beautiful," he murmured after a moment.
I felt weak.

JORDAN

I smiled again and leaned against him, pressing our arms together. "Thank you. You're not so bad yourself." His growing grin excited me.

"Thank you, honey," he said, his relaxed eyelids and unbearably bright eyes making my chest feel airy.

I want you so bad.

"How's work going?" I asked him, squeezing his hand. He never told me much about it, but what they were working on had his attention more lately.

He thought for a moment, gazing ahead of us. A woman walking her golden retriever on the other side of the road passed us, and we smiled at her. When she was behind us, he said, "It's complicated at the moment." I noticed his apprehension.

"There is a...website...on the Dark Web. It's more like a group of people and not a website."

He saw the confusion on my face. "It's the same people running numerous websites. They make one, use it, shut it down and start again."

"How do you know it's the same people?"

"Their stamp is on it. Which is why I initially said *a* website. Because they'll restart it a hundred times, but it will always be them."

I blinked, eyebrows knitting together. "What is the stamp?"

"A little logo with their name."

I looked up at him, waiting. Jordan met my gaze intensely.

"*Right At Home* is what they call it."

"Right at home?" My eyebrows crinkled together more.

Jordan nodded. "I still don't know what it means."

I shook my head. "I...is that their way of saying that like...danger is all around us or something? That they're nearby, or...?"

I could sense his grimness, but his face remained smooth. "It's possible. That's what it sounds like to me."

"Well..." I racked my brain some more, trying to interpret the phrase. As a writer, I'd spent most of my literate years interpreting words far beyond their literal meanings. I tried to apply that here. "I mean...is there a theme to the content of their sites? Wait," I backtracked. "What is *on* these sites, exactly?"

The apprehension gleamed on Jordan's face once more.

I anticipated something gruesome. "Child pornography?" I made my voice gentle, prodding him to tell me. He shook his head slightly, trying to decide if he should answer.

"Torture?" I asked softly.

"Yes." Jordan's voice was quiet, but the regret in it rang out clearly.

I nodded, keeping my face smooth. He was worried about scaring me, and it was clear he wanted to keep his work as far away from me as possible, even in conversation. Just the words touching the air seemed to be too much for him.

Wanting to show him that I was okay, I continued thoughtfully. "So...not to get into gruesome detail, but what I said before...is there a....*theme*? Sorry, I know that's disgusting." A theme for torture. Roleplaying during a violent murder. I immediately regretted suggesting the idea.

"It's okay," he assured, squeezing my hand. This was nice, despite the topic of conversation. This walk with this person I adored. Walking with a real-life hero and holding his hand. Being under the sunshine and feeling the breeze hit my skin. Inhaling and having that funny feeling that I'd been in this wind before, and at a time when life was bad. Except this time, I was with someone whose hand I could squeeze, and I would be soothed. This time, life was good.

"There isn't a theme that I've identified." He didn't speak further.

After a few moments, I murmured, "So...these are people who call themselves, or their group or whatever, *Right At Home*. And they torture people." I kept my voice low, continuing quickly, worried he would cut the conversation off if I kept saying that. "You said they're starting sites and then shutting them down and starting again?"

Jordan nodded. "Yes." I didn't need to prod this time; I assumed he could see that I really wanted to understand, because he offered more. "It is difficult to find them."

I thought about his words. "Your software tracks, right?"

He nodded again. "When we first caught wind of this group, the software stopped working as well as it usually does. There is something about their rerouting that's making it very difficult for my software to perform."

"It's not just because they keep starting and stopping too quickly for you to pinpoint?"

Jordan cocked his head to the side just slightly. "There's that, too. But I know that the technology just isn't facing up to theirs well." I looked up at him and saw his dismay.

"Is this the first time this has happened since you finished making it?"

He glanced down at me. "Yes."

I frowned, having a hard time wrapping my head around how anyone could best Jordan. He was so smart.

"I'm sorry, Jord." The nickname fell gently off my tongue. Though I didn't mean to say it, I looked up at him and couldn't be embarrassed. His lips had turned up at the corners. His eyes were still regretful.

"Don't worry about it. There are a lot of maneuvers and other things to try."

"I know, but..." I lifted one shoulder and dropped it as I looked at the ground in front of us. "I know it's hard for you. Seeing...seeing it." I slid my eyes up to his again.

"It's okay." His voice was gentle.

I shook my head, suddenly adamant. "You're...you're quiet, Jordan," I said, keeping my own voice low. "I could be wrong, but I don't think you talk to many people about this stuff." I looked up at him to confirm or deny before I continued. He stared down at me for a few moments, and I was worried he wouldn't say anything.

Finally, he confirmed. "You're right." He was waiting, wanting to know what I was getting at.

"I think it's important to," I said gently. "So...if you ever decide you're willing, I'm here to listen."

For some reason, I couldn't shake the feeling that this was weighing on him even more than I could sense. Not because it was hard work to do, but because seeing people get hurt in heinous ways had to be his own personal torture.

"Thank you, sweetheart."

I knew he wouldn't take me up on it. "I mean it." And I did. The idea of innocent people being tortured for psychotic people to watch made me feel nauseous; if the imagination was this bad, then actually seeing it was unthinkable. My heart hurt for him.

"I can handle it." I looked up into his eyes intensely. "It's disgusting and disturbing and I hate the fact that this happens, but I can handle it."

He looked at me for a few moments, still conflicted. I squeezed his hand and covered it with my available one, stroking his skin with my thumb. I'd come back to this later.

"So," I began slowly, "These people were not around before? Or, at least, this group?"

"That's right. It's relatively new."

"And you guys find the sites pretty easy?"

"Not necessarily easily." Jordan held my hand firmly in his own. "Some sites on the Dark Web can only be found if someone wants you to find them."

"How would they tell you if they wanted you to? Would they give you a link?"

"Yes, possibly. Sometimes a person gives out a link. No one can find the site without the link. Sometimes, the sites can only be found following specific instructions. Those instructions can be written in code. If these people want their sites hidden, they can make it happen.

"We don't usually have too much issue finding them. If we can't get the links hacking into chatrooms, we can decipher the code that gives instructions on how to."

"But...these links just popped up. I have a team dedicated to searching through the Dark Web, looking for crime whose source we can track and stop. This showed up during random searches while we were working."

"So, you're trying to figure out who these people are." I met his eyes.

"Yes."

"But you're having a hard time tracing the...the...URL's or IP addresses or whatever?" I wanted to understand so badly.

"Mhm." He was gentle, watching me try to wrap my head around it. "What should have been an easy track from the first livestream has proven to be much more difficult."

"Have you tried tweaking the software?"

"I've tried a little, but there isn't a lot of time, among managing the rest of the company's work, conferring with the Bureau, police, on this matter as well as others..."

I nodded. "You guys do more than just this Dark Web stuff, right?"

"Yes. Fraud, hacking, threats to large organizations, terrorist activity. We work off the Dark Web as well. I have a few members who work on it."

I nodded again. I thought for a minute, trying to get back to the initial matter. "Didn't you tell me that your tracking software can't stand up to the rerouting software you made?"

Jordan looked down at me, a hint of befuddlement in his eyes. "Yes."

"So, you think maybe you're going up against a software similar to yours?" I looked straight ahead, worried I'd insult him.

"Yes, I..." Hearing the surprise in his voice now, I looked up. He was watching me intensely. "That's exactly it."

I again found it hard to believe that someone could create something as good as or better than Jordan's. I knew nothing about technology in this regard, hadn't the slightest clue how software worked, but I had no doubt that he was the best in his field. And if not the best, then better than most.

"It's *possible* someone made one like yours, but...." I trailed off. Jordan raised one eyebrow.

"I just find it hard to believe," I said quietly, looking away. When I dragged my eyes back up to his face, I was surprised to find a smile teasing the corners of his lips and a lightness in his eyes that wasn't there before.

I smiled small. He kept staring at me with that fond expression, and suddenly I wanted badly to stretch up and place my lips on his smooth, tan cheek.

"It is possible," he said gently. "I can never be so arrogant as to think no one can do better than I have."

His modesty combined with his frustration over his lack of progress both made my chest long for him more.

I squeezed his hand again. "I know you'll find a way." His lips turned up at the corners, eyes soft.

But with my words came the suspicion that Jordan took all the responsibility on himself, and I began to feel sad for him. "What are the Feds doing? Did they see it? Wait. What...what was it?"

Jordan looked down at me, his face serious, eyes wary.

I prompted. "What was it?" I asked him softly.

"You know," he told me, his voice low. "I don't want to put these things in your head."

"Don't worry about that." I wouldn't have pushed if not for the fact that Jordan was stuck with these nightmares all the time. All alone. "I'm okay," I told him gently. "Get it off your chest."
He shook his head slightly. "Someone preparing to hurt another person."
That was not enough of an answer for me. He wanted to give me the sugarcoated answer while he had to live with the horror in his head all by himself.
"You can tell me what it was," I prodded, even more gently. "I'm a big girl. I want you to get it off your chest," I repeated. "At least the first time. What was it the first time?"
Jordan's hesitation never strayed, and I knew I wasn't going to get much. "A young girl about to be tortured."
I forced my face to stay still. "A child?"
"No. She was around your age."
As I processed his words, Jordan squeezed my hand.
I nodded. It hit me in that moment that the violent stories I'd heard were true. The nitty gritty details, the gore. They were real. They happened. And Jordan witnessed that horrid violence often.
"That's terrible," I said quietly. "I'm so sorry." But there were more than just her.
"How...how many since?"
Jordan did not look happy.
"Two."
"How far apart?"
"Three weeks between the first two, a week between the second and third."
I looked ahead but could feel his eyes assessing me.
"Are you okay?" he asked, still worried.
I looked at him, surprised. "Yeah, yeah, I'm good." I was still holding one of his hands in both of my own. "I want you to tell me this stuff. I want to understand what you do and the things you see. You shouldn't have to...carry that stuff alone," I repeated.
The thought again occurred to me that he wouldn't take me seriously. It wouldn't stop bothering me.
I cared about him so much already.
I looked up at his blue eyes, which glittered against the sun. They were unhappy. I stopped walking and stood in front of him.
"I can take it," I said gently. He stared back into my eyes for what felt like a long time.
"Let me be your friend," I added softly.
His eyebrow shot up. He shook his head. "Friends don't burden friends with so much negativity," he said.
I blinked. "Then what kind of friend am I for constantly talking about my crappy life to you?" I felt funny suddenly. Was I a burden?
He was surprised, his eyes opening slightly. He kept his voice low.

"That's very different," he murmured. "They are not the same thing." He paused, staring at my eyes intently, then rephrased. "Friends don't burden friends by unnecessarily putting *gruesome* things into their heads. Who you are and what you've been through are not gruesome things. I want to know those things."

I lowered my pitch and tone and shook my head. "But you go through awful, awful things, too," I said adamantly, voice quiet. "I want to know those things, too. What you've gone through. Are going through."

I'd also been thinking that, if I were going to tell Jordan my most painful experiences, I wanted him to be comfortable with me, too. I didn't want there to be a flood from me while he just absorbed, hiding behind the dam he'd always had up. That made me feel like a burden.

I wanted him to trust me. I wanted him to feel safe with me, the way I felt safe with him.

"I don't know for certain that you do," he said quietly, taking me off guard.

I thought carefully for a few moments, taking my time so that I didn't sound senseless. I didn't want to stand there like an idiot and prove him right. That I didn't know what I was saying.

"Bad things happen," I said, lowering my voice even more and speaking slowly, knowing my frustration was showing. "I wish they didn't, but they do. I don't want to picture others hurting others. You're right about that. What I *want* is to understand where your head is at, and that trumps the other thing."

I did my best.

He stared down at me. Finally, after what had to be the longest twenty seconds of my life, he said, "I apologize."

My eyes widened in surprise. "For what?"

"For insinuating that you don't know what you want."

I shook my head. I'd piped up immediately to inform him that he was wrong, but I knew Jordan never intended to make me feel bad; I was just insecure.

He was just trying to protect me.

"That's okay," I murmured, looking at his eyes as they became genuinely apologetic. "I know why you said it." I shrugged a tiny bit. "You wanna protect me from it."

He nodded. "That's exactly the case."

"*I'm* sorry," I said quietly, voice rough. "I was proud just now. I'm embarrassed by it. I promise I'm not always like that. I…I can admit when I'm wrong, I just…"

"No. Don't do that." He brought his finger up and tilted my chin upward. I was in another dimension.

"You weren't," he murmured gently. He pulled his hand away from my face and took mine. "I know exactly what you mean. I'm resolute about this, maybe stubborn. I know it's frustrating. I don't mean to be. I just don't

want you to know those things, plain and simple. But..." He shook his head. "I'll try to...open up a little more."
The words were gruff, his voice low. I smiled just a little. My heart was content with that for now.
"Look," I said gently. "I know I may be small," I flattened my hand and put it on top of my head to emphasize my height. His lips turned up just a smidge. "But I'm an adult. And I know what I'm asking when I tell you to talk to me. I've heard some really bad stuff, so you probably won't surprise me, anyway."
I turned and restarted our walk, his hand in mine.
"Where should we go?" I flipped subjects for a moment, as we came to a four-way intersection. "Straight?"
"You pick," he told me, lightening his tone a bit.
I looked around. "Okay, let's go here." I pointed right, and we turned. The sun was shining even brighter, contrasting with the darkness of our conversation.
I looked at him, and he was making a regretful face. He also looked tired.
"Am I exhausting you?" I asked, suddenly worried.
His eyebrows knitted together, and he shook his head. "No. No. I just can't stand the thought of you knowing these things."
"It's okay. I just wanted you to know that I don't think a lot will surprise me beyond the "urban legends" I read online."
Jordan wrapped his arm around me, hand pressed into the curve of my oblique, pulled me into his side and kept walking.
"What's wrong?" I asked quietly. He was tense and unhappy.
He pulled me tighter to his side as we walked; I held the arm around my waist against my abdomen, gripping his wrist. The physical contact was wonderful.
His face softened. "The thought of you and the filth I have seen, in my head at the same time, leaves a bad taste in my mouth. To say the very least."
"Don't think about that," I murmured. "I understand you..." I said hesitantly. "I've been thinking. Every time you go to work, or are at work, I think of those people and the fact that you've been in physical proximity to them. And it makes me anxious."
I looked at his upset eyes. "I don't like it. At all. But let's not think about that right now." I squeezed his wrist. "I just want to know about the work. Explain it to me as though you were teaching a student," I suggested lightly.
After a few moments, he said, "Okay. What else would you like to know?"
I turned my thoughts backwards until I remembered my many questions, the conversation repeating itself in my brain.
She was around your age.
A cold feeling moved down my chest. I didn't show it.
"Do you think one person is behind all of this?"

Jordan thought for a moment. "I think two, maybe three. I think creating a shield like theirs requires the brainpower of more than one person."
It didn't for you.
"Okay. So...you're trying to track the source of the livestreams by their IP addresses, or whatever your software does exactly." I gave up trying to master the technicalities. "Are you getting any locations at all?"
"Not real ones. The streams were made to look like they were in Japan, Oregon and Romania."
"You said your software decrypts information, right?"
Jordan looked surprised by my question again. "Yes, it does. It doesn't only do that. It can follow the route of the info. It latches onto it."
I remembered about the rerouting, but I was getting lost again. "The info is what is rerouted in Gateway, right?"
He nodded. "Yes." He could tell I was struggling again, so he continued. "The data of your search, connection, activity, any part of it is all encrypted, but then it's also all moved in a bunch of directions so no one can catch it and find out where it came from. I figured out a way to take it, at the end of its journey, and follow it all the way back to its source. Following every route. Then, we decrypt it. That's what the software does." He knitted his eyebrows together. "Does that make sense, or am I confusing you?"
"No, that makes sense."
This had never been done before. It made knowing Jordan even more surreal.
I was walking with somebody who had done something, invented something, that *no one else* had.
I squeezed his wrist, hoping I was fortunate enough to continue knowing him.
"It's just not able to handle these reroutes."
I nodded. "I understand. So, when you *do* find them," I kept my words positive and encouraging, "you will give the location to the FBI?"
"Yes. Or, if I can do it faster, I will stop them."
"And by "stop" you mean physically find and put away."
He nodded. I thought some more.
"These websites that you work with, not just in this case but others, too...they can be worldwide, right?"
"Yes, they can be."
"Do you travel? Does your team travel a lot?"
"Sometimes it's necessary. But we often don't. The FBI helps us talk to the embassies and coordinate how their system will handle it. But we prepare them well, so that they don't miss them."
"Oh, so like, you tell them where to go basically, where to find them."
"Yes."
"But why do you have to go all the way there?"
"Because, sometimes, it's easier to track them down that way. We can do a physical investigation, just like the police would in their city."

I nodded. "Oh." I thought about it. "I didn't think about the fact that you'd have investigative skills from working in the FBI."
He smiled down at me. "My team has 'em, too."
That was interesting to me. "How many people are in your team? Your close team?"
"Four," he replied. "Liza, Emmett, Luke, and Eve."
"So...which of them worked for the CIA?"
"Liza and Emmett. Luke and Eve worked for the FBI."
This was bizarre to me. "Did they work for them for long? And why did they stop?"
Jordan considered my questions. "Each worked in their respective role for at least a year. Liza was in the CIA for three." He paused a few moments before answering my second question. "They didn't want to work for the government anymore. The regulations of the job bothered some of them. I think the others just didn't like the work they were doing. All of them specialized in computer technology but were of course required to be able to be in the field. So," he finished, "They fit this role perfectly."
"Okay," I said slowly, rubbing my thumb over his hand again. "What if the governments or local police force don't want to cooperate with you guys?"
He shrugged. "I'll go find them myself."
I stared at him and didn't say anything. It was attractive and startling to hear somebody's words sound so lethal.
"A real-life hero," I murmured to myself, looking away.
I felt his eyes on me, but I was lost in thought.
"Vigilante," he corrected, and when I looked up at him, he was smiling big, looking off to the side.
I laughed, thrilled to see the smile on his face. "Forget that," I said, grinning. "You're a hero." I squeezed his wrist.
"Jordan. Can I ask you, perhaps, an insensitive question?"
His lips were still upturned. "Ask me anything," he murmured.
"Have you ever been shot?" I thought better. "Sorry, I know that's blunt."
"No, that's alright. Once," he confirmed. He reached his left arm across his chest, above my head, and tapped the side of his upper right arm with two fingers. The arm that was around my waist.
"Up there?" I asked, eyes wide.
"Yes. Just grazed."
"How long ago?" I asked, incredulous.
"Years." He made a face to brush it off. "I was a few months into training in the field at the FBI."
I considered this. "Did they want you there just for your computer skills? Or did they know about the fighting?"
Jordan was pensive for a moment. "They knew about both. This isn't typical, but I didn't have to go out in the field if I didn't want to. They wanted me on computers right away. But they offered training, and I asked if I could skip the academics."

I chuckled. "Did they let you?"
"Mostly. Don't tell anyone." He grinned.
I laughed harder. "So, what, you trained in guns? That's it?"
"No, I did the academics for a little bit. Not the five months that it usually takes. I mainly trained in operational skills, and for just a few months."
"That's when you learned to use guns?"
"And how to drive like an FBI agent."
I smiled. "So, at what point did you go out into the field? To get that wound?"
"I told them to just teach me the weaponry. I already knew many types of self-defense. I just needed to know what to do with guns and what to do when one was pointed at me. That didn't take more than a week.
"But it still took about a month of *some* academic training before they let me in the field. They wanted me to know at least a little in forensic science, behavioral science, interviewing, things like that."
"Isn't that what Tristan does? Behavioral science?"
"Yes."
"Hm."
After a moment, I murmured, "I bet you could fight better than most of them already there."
"I knew more styles of martial arts than they taught. But I didn't know their protocol when it came to apprehending. I couldn't do it my way." His tone was even.
"What was your way?" I asked him.
"I, ah...I don't take care not to hurt the perpetrator." He looked at me intensely, waiting for my reaction.
"Mess 'em up, baby," was all I said, looking down and thinking. When I looked back up, he was smiling at me.
Then he said, "You're getting cold."
I assessed myself. My jaw was starting to chatter.
"I didn't think it was this cold," I shivered.
"It wasn't," he told me. "It got colder. Come on." He gently turned us down another road.
"You're not cold?" I asked. The sky was turning gray.
"Not really," he murmured. "We'll be home in a minute," he assured.
Home.
We made it to his house in two minutes. He opened the door to the house for me after we went into the garage; I grabbed my car keys.
"One sec."
I went to my car and grabbed the clothes I'd brought.
"What are those?" he asked curiously.
"Clothes," I murmured. "I just assumed we'd go for a walk, and I didn't want to smell weird when we came back."
He stared at me for a few moments, thinking.
"I'll be right back."

JORDAN

After I changed, I dropped the bag of old clothes by my boots. When I entered the kitchen, I saw Jordan in a fresh white t-shirt and black joggers, standing in front of the coffee pot. "You didn't have to change, too."
"You made a good point," he murmured.
"Coffee?"
"Yes," he murmured. "I can make you tea or cocoa, if you'd like."
"You're sweet, thank you," I said. "Coffee sounds nice."
"Let's go sit down," he murmured. "I'm going to grab blankets. I'll meet you."
I smiled to myself as I curled up on the couch. He came back and put a blanket over me gently. I brought my knees down from my chest and grabbed it. It was warm.
"Were these in the dryer?" I asked him, thrilled.
"Yes," he said. "I put them in while you were changing. Just to warm them up."
"*Thank you*," I chirped. "Come sit."
When I set my head down on the arm of the couch and lay on my side, he grabbed a pillow from the other end and set it under my head. Then, he sat down on the floor in front of me.
"Why are you on the floor?" I asked, confused.
"So I can be next to you."
My jaw dropped.
I closed my mouth quickly, sitting up. "Here, here, come up here, I'm sorry—"
"Nina," he soothed, extending his arm easily and taking mine in his hand. I stopped, and he smiled at me.
"Lie down," he murmured, dragging out the last word.
He was so cozy. I complied after a moment, lying back slowly with his hand on my arm.
"I like it here," he told me.
I laid my head on the pillow, settled in on my side. He pulled a heavy ottoman behind his back.
"How ya feelin'?" he murmured quietly. "Are you warm?"
"Getting there quick. Thank you."
We looked at each other for a moment, smiling. Then, he became pensive.
"Nina, can I ask you something?"
"Sure."
"Have you ever dated?" he asked softly.
I looked past his head, at the ground behind him, losing focus as I tried to think of how to answer.
I finally met his eyes; they were intent, waiting.
"Yeah. It ended poorly."
"Okay," he said softly. "I'm sorry to hear that. Do you mind if I ask how long?"
His gentle prodding told me he knew I was hesitant to speak of this.

"About a year. I was twenty when I met him."
I searched his face, knowing he wanted more. And the day we'd had was so comfortable and sweet, I decided to step out of that comfort for a moment and give him what he wanted. He just watched me with those same intent eyes, patient.
"You can ask me whatever you want," I said quietly.
"I'd like to know about it, if you want to tell me. At the very least, why it ended poorly," he said gently.
I nodded. I tried to picture it. Picture saying what he did to me, and what I largely suspected the reason was. It was that suspicion that embarrassed me the most.
But I wasn't thrilled to recall what he'd done, either.
I gazed past Jordan's face, remembering.
He put his hands up in front of him. "Let me explain—"
"Explain what? You've been lying." The last word cracked.
His eyebrows narrowed. "Why are you so mad? You don't have proof, other than a message from a desperate girl looking to start drama." He started towards me.
"Get away from me," I said, voice barely there. He kept moving forward. "Nin—"
Finding more power in my voice as I backed up some more, I growled, "Get away *from me."*
"Nina, just list—"
"All this time? All this time, you've been doing this? How many women? Huh?"
I didn't give him time to answer. "I spent a year with you, loyal, faithful. An entire *year. And this is what you've been doing?"*
It was clear he was trying to think of excuses. I went on.
"So, you thought you could sleep with any woman you wanted, and string your sweet little "church girl" along until you were actually ready to settle down? So you wouldn't have to worry about your wife doing all the disgusting things *you've* done to *her?"*
He was stunned. He hadn't realized how well I knew him.
He must have truly thought I was stupid.
It was clear to me that I had been.
"Nina, that's a disgusting thing to s—"
"You're a liar,*" I snarled, turning and walking out the front door.*
I turned to make sure he wasn't following me, and saw that he'd stopped on the porch.
"You're wrong for not even letting me explain!" he shouted after me. "You don't know anything about what happened!"
I ignored him, walking to my car. Entering and locking the door, I immediately began driving, tears streaming down my face.
I snapped out of the flashback to Jordan touching my hand gently, stroking it with his thumb.

"Sorry, ah—" My voice cracked. I cleared my throat and tried again. "Sorry, I was just remembering."

Jordan ditched the ottoman and scooted towards me, then rested his side against the couch where my chest was. It was blissful, having him so close.

"Don't say sorry," he said gently. Then he did something that made my heart skip, despite the memories creeping under my skin. He brushed my hair back from my forehead gently. I stared at him in wonder.

He continued to stroke my skin as he murmured, "Why don't you tell me where it all started, first?"

I pursed my lips, thinking. "Well, social media," I exhaled, chuckling. "Remember when I told you how much I hate it?" I looked at him for confirmation. He nodded, smiling small, waiting for more.

"Well, we messaged a few times. And at some point he asked if we could talk. So he video-called me. I entertained it, thinking it was interesting to talk to him. The topics. I didn't expect much to come of it. I was just bored.

"But then I found out he only lived an hour away."

I was pensive. "He was really nice. He seemed genuine. I was hesitant when he wanted to meet up, but after a few more weeks of talking, I agreed.

"So...we met up. He was cute, funny, smart. He worked a good job, which was impressive. There was something a little off about his personality at the start. There was this...arrogance I didn't really like. But it presented itself rarely. So, it was really nice for the first few months, just hanging out. He was nice to me, he complimented me all the time, he treated me like he cared about me." I rolled my eyes. I was a sucker.

I looked past his shoulder again. "I told him things about me that I'd never told anyone," I said quietly.

Jordan stopped stroking my forehead, bringing his hand down to cover mine. My palm and forearm settled on the cushion as I lay on my side. He stroked the back of my hand.

"I shouldn't have trusted him, but I did. I thought I knew what I was doing." I swallowed.

"But over time, I just...I ended up relying on him for support. Leaning on him because...I didn't have it. I never really did."

"What kind of support?" he murmured.

"Emotional. I had a few friends at the time, my same few close friends now. But my family, you know. Not the greatest sometimes. They've never said, 'Hey, I'm sorry that happened.'"

"What did they say?"

"'I told you so,' in subtle ways, sometimes not so subtle. They never liked him." I sighed. "I'm not perfect, and I've been selfish before, but I learned over time what support means. And I try to be that for them, and for my friends, and..." I shook my head. "I had that with him, but not with anyone else."

Focus.

"Anyway, as time went on, he got kind of mean. And I arguably failed myself, in wanting more than he was willing to give."

"Why do you say that?"

"I wanted him to text me when he was away for a while, for example. He wouldn't text or call me all day sometimes. I told myself it was ridiculous to worry so much. But at the end of the day…I like that contact. And with all the things like that, I failed myself by sticking around."

I looked at Jordan; he nodded in understanding.

"I just…let myself hope he'd start again. Texting and calling regularly, I mean. And I kept asking myself, *Why don't you trust him?*" I blinked, immediately shifting to another point. *Getting too close.*

"Another example, um…I wanted him to ask me how I was feeling…more." I blinked. "It was like he wanted to know everything at the beginning, so that when there was nothing else for me to tell, no other…secrets, he could stop caring? I don't know."

There's more than that. He did more than that.

I'd keep the rest to myself for now.

"I'm sorry. That he treated you that way."

"I'm just happy it's over now."

"Me too," he agreed blatantly. I chuckled.

"In what ways was he mean to you?" Jordan asked, his eyebrows crinkled together.

"Oh, well, I don't know." *You sure do.* "He made me feel needy."

"He made you feel needy?"

I shook my head. "Yeah. That's, like, my worst nightmare. Is to be needy." I glanced up at Jordan.

His face was crinkled in confusion. "You're the furthest thing from it."

Sighing, I squeezed his hand. "I didn't think I was asking for too much."

"You weren't. How can someone not text *you*, all day, every day?"

I smiled, disbelieving. "Jord. You're so cute."

"I mean that, though." He stared at me, eyebrows knitted together. He was thinking of something else, and I worried that it was the one thing I didn't want to say. I hurried on.

"I felt so stupid after I stopped talking to him," I said quietly. "It was like I'd gone through all these things, I'd felt so strongly, so unhappy, angry, *jealous*, even, over someone who…didn't even actually care about me. My wellbeing. My happiness. I feel like I was tricked. It was such a waste of energy and time."

"You shouldn't feel stupid," he told me quietly. His face was smooth, but his eyes were displeased. "I wish you never went through any of that."

My heart ached a little, not for the past but for Jordan. "I appreciate that," I said, offering him another smile.

"So, that's really the gist of it." But that was a lie. The ending was the worst part of it all; I didn't know how I would say it. Jordan noticed my sudden silence.

"Yeah?" he said gently, after a few moments.
"There are some other things, but those are deeper, and I don't really wanna get into those right now." I waved my hand in the air, as though to brush those things away.
"Okay," Jordan said seriously. "Any time you want."
I smiled small at him again. "I know you want to know stuff. I just…there's so much. And…it just felt like it was all for nothing."
"But it affected you," he mentioned. "And it's affected who you are today. I don't mean that in a bad way, not at all. I mean that it's an experience that hurt you, and," he continued, once more stroking the back of my hand with his thumb again, "I want to know all those things."
I looked at him with curious eyes, suddenly feeling softer. "Then I wanna tell you," I said quietly.
I dared to think his eyes were loving, in that moment.

KAYLA KATHAWA

April

Rain accompanied April as fast as the month flew by.

Before I knew it, I had known Jordan for four and a half months. We were mid-month, spending every weekend together, talking about any and everything, getting closer with every minute that passed.

Life stayed the same outside of that, besides a slight increase in my following on my blog. I'd been writing and posting more stories. It was a good outlet.

Work wasn't so bad. We weren't in a stressful season, so Steve wasn't putting too much pressure on me. When the boss was stressed, everyone was stressed.

"I would do that because it might make you happy. Secondly, I would just call a few people and let them know I know a copy editor that they need."

I remembered Jordan's words sometimes, his assurance that he could find me a new job in a beat. That I didn't have to stay with Steve.

But I couldn't take any chances when any day we could fall out of whatever we were in.

And I was getting antsy, wanting to know what that was.

The rain was pouring as I drove to Jordan's house after work on Friday. I'd begun staying later, much to my parents' chagrin. But the latest I'd gotten home was one a.m., and they weren't too bad about that. My dad was mad, but I rolled my eyes and told him he could kick me out if he didn't like it. Then I went to bed.

When I arrived, relieved to be off the freeway where I was barely able to see the road ahead of me, the garage was open. Jordan was standing at the door. I pulled into the spot he called mine in the garage and exited the car. It was cold but humid, and I was dying to get inside before my hair exploded.

JORDAN

When's the heat gonna come back?
Jordan pulled me in for a hug. I rested my head on his chest. It was more comfortable to touch each other in a way that was more than just friends would, like hugging a little too long, holding hands, etcetera.
"Hi," he breathed, eyebrows knitted together.
"What's wrong?" I asked him, suddenly worried.
"Nothing." He was still breathless. "I've been worried about you, driving in the rain."
I smiled a warm smile, making a shy face and putting it back into his torso. He wrapped his arms around me again.
"I'm fine," I murmured from his shirt.
He tilted his chin down and I looked up at him. "I'm so happy," he said quietly. "Come inside; it's cold."
When I'd settled into the family room, he brought me a mug of tea. My blankets were already on the couch.
"Milk and sugar, as you like," he murmured.
"Where's yours?"
"Oh! I forgot it." He hopped back up and went to the kitchen. I laughed. Jordan? Forgetting something? Maybe he really had been worried.
He came back into the room with a mug. He drank his with no milk.
"You put sugar in yours, right?" I asked. I liked learning the little things about him; every detail made us feel closer.
"Yes," he nodded. "One spoon."
"One *big* spoon or one small spoon?"
"Small." Like the smile he gave me.
"Okay," I said happily, taking a sip of mine.
"How was work?" he murmured, taking a sip of his own and putting the mug down.
"Do you want some blanket?" I said suddenly, realizing he was in a t-shirt and joggers. An atrocity on this dark, rainy night. "Sorry, I just don't want you to be cold."
Before he could even answer, I scooted over carefully, mug in my hand, and extended the blanket over to him. He smiled and took the other end of it as I faced him cross-legged.
"Your back is to nothing," he noted.
"That's okay." I smiled. "I wanna share. Work was fine. I'm happy it's the weekend. I like working, but I've been distracted lately."
"What's been on your mind?"
I hesitated, gripping the handle of the mug tighter.
"Um..." I knew I couldn't keep my mouth shut, but I didn't know how to say it. "I've just been thinking about something."
Duh, you moron. He's gonna kill you if you don't spit it out.
How did you say, without sounding like an idiot, that you were bummed he hadn't asked you to be his girlfriend?
"Tell me," he said softly, eyes intent.

"I just," I said quietly. "Can I ask you something instead?" I kept my voice down, maintaining my composure.

"Of course." He was calm, but his face had traces of worry in it.

I took a small, slow breath to calm myself. "Do you want to be my boyfriend?" I asked bluntly. There was no time like the present. I knew I shouldn't dance around it, so I stayed calm, not letting myself get worked up as I prepared for the worst.

My voice was quiet, inquisitive.

Jordan stared at me, a slight surprise in his eyes. But he didn't take the moments I thought he was going to.

"Yes," was all he said for a moment.

Yes?

I was so stunned that I sat back, eyes wide, like an idiot.

Yes!

I reached out and set my mug down on the coffee table, before my hands shook harder. And I knew they would.

"Nina," he said, realizing my uneasiness. He came forward and sat next to me, taking one of my hands in his. "What's the matter?" he asked, rubbing my hand gently between his. His voice was soft.

I was much more nervous than I thought I would be.

I looked up at his face. His chin was tilted down, and he leaned forward so his height wouldn't separate us as much.

"I was just nervous," I said quietly. I hesitated. "I still am."

"It's okay," he soothed. I met his gaze, and he looked into my eyes intently, eyebrows knitted together. Then, he said, "I do want to be your boyfriend."

I rested my head against the couch, right in front of his arm as he leaned against it.

"I want you to be my girlfriend," he told me.

Though his words made my heart skip, I stared at him, my eyebrows knitted together, lips pursed. "But...why didn't you ask? Why haven't you said anything?"

He opened his eyes more, thinking. "I didn't want to push you," he said quietly. "I wanted to make sure that was what you wanted, before I said anything." He looked like he wanted to smile a little, but he kept his face serious. "I was actually going to ask *you* the same question. Just not today."

My eyes moved down. They landed on his blue t-shirt.

"I have to tell you something."

"Okay, tell me," he encouraged gently.

"Would it be a deal-breaker if I told you I wasn't going to have sex with you?"

He blinked, surprised. "No. Deal-breaker? There are no deal-breakers." His eyebrows knitted together once more.

"I mean, not until I'm married," I said quietly.

To my surprise, he nodded. "I know, love. You told me you wanted to wait."

I blinked. *He remembered.* "Is that okay with you?"
He shook his head just a little, staring at my eyes. "Of course it is," he assured. "Why would that be a deal-breaker for me? Why did you think that?" He blinked. "Well, first, did you hear me? I said no."
I nodded.
"Okay," he said, seeming skeptical of my response but continuing. "Please tell me why you'd think that." His voice was softer.
I didn't know how to talk about this without feeling embarrassed, but I had to be honest with both him and myself and admit that it affected me. It was time to tell him what happened with my ex-boyfriend.
I stared at his shoulder. "My ex guilted me about it. He mocked me, saying I was, um…like a "church girl" or something, like it was a bad thing." I looked at Jordan for comfort as I struggled with how to say all of this.
He took my cheek in his hand, gently guiding my face upwards towards his own. I was stunned.
Jordan's eyes were narrowed. I sensed a growing anger in him that I'd never seen.
But he was gentle with me. "That's vile."
I swallowed, nodding. Before he could continue, I said, "Mhm. So…I just wanted to make sure you didn't feel the same way, ya know?" I kept my voice down, feeling raw.
He shook his head slightly, his eyes still narrowed but now appalled as well. "I feel nothing of the sort." He sat back, his eyebrows stitched together. "He called you a *church girl*? And what else did he say to you?"
"Yeah, yeah he did. Then he would apologize when I got mad. Or he could tell that I was…hurt by it. But…I knew somewhere, deep down, that he wasn't really sorry.
"He'd continue to do it, even subtly. He'd ask me…why I dressed so…modestly. He would always say, '*We're not going to church; why don't you ever wear anything fun?*'" I could feel Jordan getting heated, but I didn't look at him.
I sighed quietly. "It's not that…it's not that I'm traumatized from an insult, you know?" I finally met his eyes. "People are gonna call me a prude. They did in high school. I'm fine with it." I swallowed and closed my eyes. Before I did, I saw Jordan's fiery eyes, fixated on my faced.
I took another breath and let it out slowly. "He slept with other women. I didn't know about it until right before I broke up with him."
I finally met his eyes. The look in them was barely short of rage.
Lifting my head up and meeting his stare, I lowered my voice and added, "He kind of justified it. Or tried to, later, by saying, you know…" I made a face. "That I was holding out on him, and what was he supposed to do? But…I'd been loyal. I hadn't…even entertained anybody else. And he'd told me he was doing the same."
I shook my head. "I always told myself I'd never be with a man who didn't respect my choices. And then I stayed with him and allowed him to make

me feel guilty for it. Because I was afraid he'd leave. I was too scared to be alone." I moved my eyes away, off into space.
Before Jordan could answer, I mustered up some dignity after sharing that sad fact and continued.
"Well, I wasn't too scared to ditch him when I found out he was cheating. I just couldn't help but blame myself sometimes; feel bad about it, you know?" I swallowed.
Jordan shook his head. To my surprise, he leaned forward and kissed my forehead.
He pulled back only a little. I was in awe. I looked up at him, at the perfectly shaped lips that had just touched my skin, at his blue eyes that always reminded me of a fire, and just stared.
The rage in his eyes made the softness of his voice surprising. "I'm sorry he was so cruel to you. You deserved so much more. And you still do. Don't you ever blame yourself."
He cradled my cheek in his hand. He said the sentence slowly. "You have nothing to worry about."
"Okay," I whispered, barely audible. I felt like I was crumbling under the ferocity of his eyes.
I tried to focus as he rubbed his thumb over my temple.
"I promise, Nina. I will never do what he did. You will never have to worry about upsetting me, especially not over sex. We're on the same page."
I exhaled softly in relief.
"And I will never be with anybody else."
My heart ached all the sudden. I pursed my lips a little, trying to think of what to say. Jordan put his forehead to mine.
"I promise," he whispered.
I didn't say anything, just nodded a little. After a few moments, I opened my eyes and they landed on his lips.
I quickly brought them up to meet his eyes, our foreheads parting slightly. I glanced back down at his mouth again. I couldn't help it.
Then, suddenly, his lips were on mine. Gently, kissing me softly with my comfort in mind. Instead of taking aggressively, like what I'd known. My ex-boyfriend couldn't even kiss me nicely.
And the difference between the two made my head spin.
He pulled back a few inches and looked at my face. I felt weak.
 "Jordan," I whispered, half an exhale.
"I'm sorry. Was that too much?"
I shook my head a little bit and didn't look away from his eyes.
"No." I stared at him, pained. "No, it wasn't."
His lips were soft, and somehow the warmth of them shot chills through my body. His hand in my hair, holding my face to his, made me feel weak.
This is it. This is the temptation you chose to resist.

I never felt this desire with my ex-boyfriend. The second he started pressuring me to go further, the second I lost interest. It was his way of saying he didn't respect me. How could I want to go further with *that*?

I put my forehead to Jordan's again, and he stroked my cheek with his thumb, hand still in my hair. Then I let my face fall to his chest, and I leaned forward into him; he wrapped his arms around me, holding me tight.

After a few moments like that, he tilted his chin down and whispered, "Come here." He pulled me gently down on top of him as he lay down. He kept his arms around me, kept his hand on my head. I rested my cheek on his chest.

I basked in the comfort silently for a few minutes. It was unlike anything I'd ever known.

"I know you're scared," Jordan said quietly, surprising me. The lowness of his voice aroused and overwhelmed me with emotion at the same time. "I promise, Nina. You and me, it's going to be very different. Nothing like what you experienced before."

I turned my face into his chest. "You're very different from him," I murmured after a while.

He brushed his hand over my hair slowly.

"Good," he said gently.

Pressing my cheek down into his chest, I allowed myself to ravage my uneasy thoughts and pick the ones I could ask now.

"Jordan," I began softly, "You've never had a relationship before? Like, at all, right?"

"At all," he murmured.

"Okay." I wrapped my arm around his waist and felt the hardness of his torso. "So this is new for you, too."

"Yes, love, it is." He paused. "I have never felt this way before."

That sent a thrill through me.

"Not even a crush in college? In *high school*?"

He didn't have to think about his answer. "No, I was never interested in anyone in college. I can't remember much from high school. I'm sure I had a crush here and there. A small one."

I chuckled, narrowing my eyes. "A small one?"

"Mhm. I was always training somehow. If not training, then studying. Didn't have much focus left for girls."

My smile grew. "But *puberty*." I shook my head as I exaggerated the word. "Doesn't it force you to focus on something like that?"

He smiled. "That's a physical desire. An emotionless one. It's uncontrollable."

"But hormones race and make you emotional when you're that age. I feel like everyone definitely catches a crush or is infatuated at some point."

"Sure," he said. "I think I liked one girl. But that was only when I saw her in person. She interested me. I think I forgot about her once I left school."

I chuckled again. "Harsh."

His lips turned up again, eyes amused. "I was focused."

"You're *still* focused," I said. "I'm surprised you even have time to like *me*."

He stared at me for a little while, eyes soft and pensive. Passionate. He stroked my cheek and moved some hair off to the side.

"I didn't have a choice," he murmured softly. "Even if I had no time," he added, moving his hand to the top of my head and brushing down to the base of my skull. It felt good.

"I still wouldn't have a choice," he finished. "And I'd have to make time. But there is no question about it: I have to have you around."

The deepness of his voice again radiated through me. His words gave me sensations that I couldn't identify.

"I have to have *you*," I murmured, my smile fading.

The look in his eyes intensified. He was less calm. I sat up a little, and he brought his head forward so his lips could touch mine.

The more we kissed, the more I wanted. *Heat of the moment*, my mother used to warn me about.

It was unbearable. I put my hands in his hair and kissed him a few seconds longer.

I pulled back and exhaled, breathless. "Jordan."

He held my cheek in his hand; his eyes looked a way I'd never seen before. Wanting. He was breathing slightly harder.

"I'm sorry," I breathed. "I'm...I still have to figure out our limits. How to control myself." I sat up and moved to his side, lying back down on mine. His couch was as wide as an extra large twin bed. There was enough room to lie on our sides, facing one another. We both propped our heads up with our hands, elbows sinking into the cushion.

He brushed my hair back. "It's okay," he murmured softly.

"I just..."

"You don't have to justify it. It's your choice. If you want to explain more to me at any point, I want to know. But you aren't obligated. I'm not mad at you, or disappointed."

I chuckled weakly. "Yeah. You're a grown man that acts like one. I guess I'm not used to seeing that."

He smiled, staring at me for a moment. It faded as he said, "I'm sorry anyone made you feel bad about your choice."

"Aw. Thank you. It makes me feel better to hear that."

"I mean it. Don't let anyone make you feel ashamed, Nina."

I shook my head. "Oh no. The only person whose opinion on it I ever let myself feel concerned over is the love of my life." I didn't meet his eyes. I hadn't told him he was the love of my life, but I was hoping he would just get it.

He did. "Well." He paused, smiling. "If that's me, then you have nothing to worry about."

A huge smile grew on my face. My heart was beating faster just at his words. I looked down at the cushion, nervous.

"I mean…" I struggled to figure out what to say. *Screw it.*

"I'd be lying if I said I didn't love you." It took me a moment to drag my eyes up to his.

His face had softened even more, the smile having shrunk but still resting on his face. He looked affectionate.

As he ran his hand up and down my cheek, he murmured, "I'd be lying, too." I looked down again, trying to process his words, slightly dizzy. Heart pounding. He touched my cheek gently, so I'd meet his eyes.

"I love you."

It felt like my heart stopped beating for five seconds.

I dredged in some air and quietly replied, "You do?"

His lips turned up some more. "Make no mistake. I absolutely do."

I wondered if I was going to pass out.

By the grace of God, I was able to think clearly enough to reach up, cup his cheek in my hand and say, "I love you, too."

The joy that filled his eyes made me even weaker. I just smiled small. There was nothing else to say. The moment was perfect as it was.

I was tired all of a sudden. I had the strong urge to lay my head down on him and go to sleep, wrapped in his arms.

"I'm tired," I murmured, content with ending the conversation there.

As he continued stroking my face, Jordan said, "Do you want to go to sleep?"

Those were beautiful words.

I hesitated. "No, that would be selfish. What would you do?"

"I would stay right here with you. Maybe read, maybe sleep."

"Where would you sit? Would you stay here?"

He nodded. "Keep you in my arms the whole time."

I smiled shyly. "Okay. Can we...are you sure?"

"I'm positive." His voice was mostly a whisper, low, masculine. Perfection.

I nodded.

"Yeah?"

I nodded again. "Yeah."

Jordan turned to lie on his back, but before he could pull me to him, I swung my leg over him and stood up. "I want to get you a pillow."

He smiled. "I can get them, honey."

I shook my head, already heading towards the closet. "They're by the blankets, right?"

His smile was fond. "Yes."

I grabbed a big, soft pillow and another huge blanket. I was such a sucker for coziness.

I was excited to lie down with him, wrapped in his arms, under a big blanket, and close my eyes. The thought was so thrilling and warm that I was scared I'd wake up. It was right at a moment like this, in which I got so close to that comfort and joy that I always wanted, that my eyes opened, and suddenly I was awake, in my bed and alone.

I hurried back to him. I didn't want to wake up.

But he was there where I left him, now sitting up. Beautiful as ever. I looked at his whole body, at how his arms were long but muscular, how I could see the narrowing of his waist through his shirt, though the fabric wasn't tight. I glanced at his long legs and torso. All six-foot-three of him sitting down on the couch made him look so big. It made me even more excited to be touched by him. To be held.

Everything about him was safe. Jordan always had a calming presence to me. It was kind of backwards.

If you were with the most lethal person in the room, you were the safest. And I was certain Jordan could be lethal.

"Here you go," I said cheerily, setting the pillow down.

He put his hands on the outside of both of my thighs and looked up at me. "Do you want to go sleep in bed?"

He took a moment to watch me, and then added, "I have multiple bedrooms. It doesn't have to be mine. Whatever you're comfortable with."

"Oh...no, this is okay," I said, speaking and smiling shyly. I gave a breathless and nervous chuckle.

"Next time. If I get in a bed right now, I won't get up until morning, and my parents will kill me."

His lips turned up, and he nodded.

Smiling, he pulled my hips with him as he slid back into his seat. Once my head was settled on his chest, he fanned one blanket over me, then the other. I noticed that he hadn't grabbed a book.

"Are you gonna read?"

"I don't think so," he whispered, stroking my hair.

"Are you tired?"

"A little bit."

I felt myself already getting drowsy with his fingers moving through my long hair.

"Will you be bored?" I asked softly.

"No." I heard a smile in his voice. "This is right where I want to be."

I continued to smile, happy. "I'm right where I want to be, too." I snuggled my cheek into his upper abdomen. "You make me feel safe." I wasn't sure if I sounded childish.

He tilted his chin down and kissed my head.

"You are." He kept his mouth in my hair.

And after that sentence processed in my brain, I drifted off completely.

JORDAN

May

"Happy birthday, brother," I cheered, setting the cake down in front of him. My big brother was twenty-seven years old.

My sister, parents and I commenced in song, singing "Happy Birthday" to Elijah while he tried not to smile.

After he blew out the candles, I cut pieces of cake for everyone.

"It sucks that my birthday is on a Thursday," he complained.

"Just go out this weekend!" I piped. "It's better than a Monday."

"Yeah, yeah," he said. He was tired. His salary was good, but he was overworked.

Everyone ate a slice of cake. I had a few bites and took the opportunity to talk to them all at once.

It was rare that we all gathered in one place.

"Jordan and I are a couple," I said casually, looking at the cake on the plate in front of me as I played with it using my fork.

"What?" my mom gasped; I glanced up. A smile was growing large on her face.

"Yeah, yeah, we know," Elijah said, though I could sense some surprise in him. He went on. "You're only with him every second of your life."

I looked at my dad, but he had already turned away and gone to the couch.

He would say nothing, as though he didn't care, then he would contemplate all the things he wanted to say and ask me and attack me later.

I wasn't worried; I knew he wanted me to get married and move out *eventually*. I figured he just wished I could do it without dating first.

"I *knew* it," Zana exclaimed. "You lucky…*how* did you land him? I hate you."

My siblings laughed; my mom said, "Hey, stop it," but even she was grinning. I didn't say anything.

"How long have you known him again?" my mom inquired, thinking as she washed dishes.

"Since January," I replied. They didn't know we'd already been together for about a month.

"When did this happen?" Zana asked, still feigning, maybe only in part, outrage.

"Um. A few weeks ago."

I looked for my mom's reaction, and she turned her head to look at me as she scrubbed a pot.

"Why didn't you tell me?"

"Umm...I just...wanted to keep it to myself for a while. Wanted to have time with him without discussing it."

"But why?"

"I just...after everything that happened before, you know...last time, I just didn't feel like sharing anymore."

"Are you talking about with—"

But before she could say his name, I cut her off. "Yes. I'm talking about him. Please. Let's not talk about him."

"Please," I entreated, less emphatic this time, so as not to be rude. "I just don't want to think about him anymore."

"Okay," my mother replied innocently. "We're happy for you, Nene," she said.

"Speak for yourself!" Zana piped up, and everyone laughed.

I grinned. "Hater."

"Yeah, you're right, I do hate you."

I chuckled. "I'm going over to his house tomorrow after work," I mentioned to my parents.

My mother sighed. "I'm really happy for you, Nene, but I hate that you drive that far so much."

"Mom," I began. "I only drive out there on the weekends. It's not that big of a deal." I stood up to walk away. "I can't bring him here. It's too crowded and loud."

"Why not?" she interrogated, though I'd just said why. "Are you doing stuff you shouldn't be doing?" And though my back was to her, I could *hear* one of her eyebrows go up.

I turned around and rolled my eyes to make sure she could see. "Will you not do that, mom," I snapped, exasperated. I lowered my voice. "In front of *him*, no less," I gritted my teeth together, gesturing towards the rocking chair, where my father was seated, back to us. "You're gonna put ideas in his head, and he *already* gives me a hard time about driving there. Stop."

I could tell she felt bad then. I was sure she would rather be the only one nagging me. She knew my father's temper and was unsure how he would react.

"I hate that you said that, too," I said at my normal volume, "because I was just about to say it makes more sense for me to spend the night there on Fridays."

Before they could argue, I reasoned, "I fall asleep almost every night I'm there. It just doesn't make any sense to drive home that late just to go back to see him in the morning or whenever. We'd prefer it that way, anyway. We never see each other," I muttered.

"If you fall asleep, then why do you even go?" my mom asked.

"Mom, I fall asleep when it gets late, after we've hung out for hours. I'd rather just keep sleeping than have to drive home almost an hour when I'm already sleepy." I looked at her. "You know I'm right. But you guys are hellbent on the idea of me having sex with him, which is gross, by the way," I added, "so you don't want me to stay there."

Before they could give more ridiculous reasoning, I said, "Look. I'm not gonna argue with you guys right now. It's Elijah's birthday, it's late, I'm tired. I just wanted to let you know about us dating. I'm not concerned about spending the night at his house. I'll see him either way. Even if I have to make the drive home every time," I threw in for good measure.

My mom began to speak again, but I just tuned her out. When she was done, I said, "Goodnight, guys. Love you, brother," then headed to my room.

After I got in bed, the weight of the day hit me. I was happier lately, having Jordan around, even on the phone and via text, but I was trying so hard to fill my life up elsewhere. Outside of work, I was posting to my blog all the time. Building up a group of connections on social media so that I could market my book. I was reading more, trying to stimulate my brain for writing.

But my brain was tired now.

I plugged my phone in to charge and then went to text Jordan goodnight. His new message said, *Can I pick you up tomorrow after work instead of you driving?*

As if he'd heard the conversation I just had.

I texted him back, *Don't worry about that, love. I'm gonna come there right after work. Should we do something?*

After a few moments, he said, *Yes. We're going to dinner. Do you want to do anything else?*

Well, I began. *There is this scary movie I want to see, but I don't want to subject you to it.*

It wasn't that Jordan hated scary movies; he didn't watch TV at all. I never wanted to ask to watch violent or disturbing things with him, because I knew he saw enough of that at work. I always tried to pick a mystery and something less gory.

He texted back right away. *What is it called? I'll find a showing. Dinner before or after?*

I smiled and decided to call him. He picked up on the first ring.

"Hi," I murmured.

"Hi," he replied, and I heard a smile in his voice, too.
"What are you doing?"
"Lying in bed," he murmured affectionately.
"Me too." I smiled. "Listen, we don't have to go to the movie. I realized after I said it that it would be a selfish activity."
"Why is it selfish?" Confusion clouded his tone.
"Because, you don't really watch stuff like that, or anything at all really, that's number one. Number two is…" I hesitated. "I just don't think you need to see any more disturbing stuff. It's probably not your idea of fun."
Jordan paused for a moment before he said, "No, honey. It doesn't bother me. I mean it. I'll be happy if we are doing something you enjoy doing."
I sighed. "I know, but when are we going to do something *you* like?"
I heard a smile in his voice again. "I don't do anything for fun."
I laughed loudly.
"Jordan." I chuckled again.
"I mean it. Let's go to the movies. Would you like to get dinner before or after?" he asked again.
I sighed once more. "Okay. After. So we can decompress after the disturbance."
He gave an amused "Hm." I smiled.
"Okay," I said. "Get some sleep. I won't keep you up, as much as I want to."
"You're never keeping me," he murmured. "You ready for bed?"
"Mhm," I answered sleepily, feeling soothed by his voice. Everything was always better when he was there. The bed felt more comfortable, even though he was only on the phone.
"Okay," he said softly, matching my volume. "Goodnight, lovely. Sleep well."
"Goodnight," I said happily. "I'll see you tomorrow."
"See you then, baby."
My eyes opened wide at 'baby.' I grinned to myself like a nerd as I hung up.
"I love you," I said out loud, to myself.
I picked up my phone to text him the words. I wasn't brave enough to say it out loud as often as I wanted to.
After a few moments, he texted back,
I love you, too. Don't ever forget.
And those words danced in my head until I drifted off to sleep.

The next day, I'd taken care to blow-dry my hair in the morning, which I didn't do often. In my office, I glanced at my reflection in the black screen of my phone. It looked pretty good.

"Nina," Steve called from his office next door to mine.

"Here I come."

When I got to him, he handed me a couple sheets of paper. "Can you make copies of these for the meeting?"

Sure, Steve. Because not only am I your slave-copy editor, I'm also your assistant.

"Yeah. How many do you think we'll need? Fifty?"

This was an office-wide meeting. Everyone, including our graphic design team, our writers, our advertisers and our sales teams would be there.

"Uh, yeah," he said, finally looking up from his computer. "Will you remind the managers?"

"Of course."

I used the opportunity to stretch my legs, walking around to their offices. "Hey," I said to each manager. "Meeting at noon, don't forget. Then late lunch."

When that was done, I quickly made the copies, stapled each packet together and headed to our large conference room. I silenced my phone, so it wouldn't ring during the meeting. Sitting with my notebook and pen, I prepared to write down any concerns the copywriters had. I was already antsy to leave and thought about Jordan, wanting the workday to be over.

When it *finally* was, I headed to the restroom and changed my clothes. As I slid my seatbelt on, I called Jordan.

"Hi, honey," he greeted. "How are you?"

"I'm good." *Man,* it was good to hear his voice. "How about you?"

He sounded less relaxed than the night before.

"I'm good, too. Thank you. I'm running a little bit late. I'm so sorry. You might get to my house before me."

"Oh," I said, surprised. Jordan was never late, but I didn't mind. "That's okay. Don't worry about it. Where are you now?"

He released a frustrated exhale before he spoke. "I'm in Senton."

"Where is that?"

"It's about an hour and a half north from my house."

"Okay," I said lightly, confused and concerned by his tone. I heard the aggravation in it I could tell he was trying to hide.

"Is it work?" I asked.

"Yes," he replied. "I'm so sorry."

"It's okay," I assured him.

"How far are you now, do you think?" he asked. He was unnerved and upset that he would be late. He hated the idea of letting me down, or not keeping his promises, but I wasn't upset. He was beating himself up for nothing.

"I haven't even started driving yet. You know what, I'll head home really quick and take a shower. That way, I'll get there closer to when you will."

"Okay," he agreed. "I really hate this. I'm sorry, Nina."

"Jordan," I began, pulling out of the parking lot. "It's *okay*. It's fine, honey, don't worry. Don't worry."

I barely heard another small, frustrated exhale. "Will you please call me when you leave your house?"

"Of course I will."

"Thank you," he murmured. "I don't want you to get home before I do and have to wait in the car."

I blinked, realizing he meant *his* house when he said *home*. I was breathless.

"It's okay, love," I soothed, still confused by his distress. "That's not that big of a deal. I'll call you when I get out of the shower, and if you want me to wait at home until you're close enough, I will. How 'bout that?"

"It's whatever you prefer," he said, his voice lower and clouded with guilt.

"Okay. It's okay, Jordan," I repeated gently. "Don't be upset. I'm not mad or anything like that; it's not a big deal." I kept my tone soft and soothing.

"Okay, baby. Call me when you leave, okay?"

What is going on? Why is he so worried? I couldn't make sense of it, or of the fact that he didn't seem to want to be apart for a minute. He'd never behaved this way before.

"Okay." I hesitated. "I love you. I'll talk to you soon."

I was stunned when his voice weakened. "I love you, too."

After I hung up, I tried to think of what could be running through his head. Maybe that case at work was getting bad. Maybe they were close to cracking it.

Maybe someone had gotten killed. Maybe he was at a crime scene.

I'd wait until I saw him to ask.

After I arrived home, showered and dressed, I grabbed some extra clothes and my toothbrush. I hadn't decided that I was going to spend the night, but something had been nagging me to do it, just in case.

Before I started driving, I dialed Jordan's number.

"Hi, baby." He sounded less tense now, though there was still an edge to his voice.

"Hi, babe. I'm leaving my house now."

"Okay," he said calmly. "That's good. I'm closer to home now. I should get there before you. I'm sorry again, to keep you waiting."

"Jordan, stop apologizing. You didn't. I got to shower and get all clean."

"I feel bad," he said quietly. "We'll have to push the movie to another showtime. There's one at seven-thirty. Is that too late? You're probably hungry. Should we get dinner first?"

"No, that's okay. I'll eat popcorn. Then we can have dinner like we planned."

"Okay," he said, sounding relieved. "Definitely popcorn."

I smiled. I had to eat, or he wasn't happy. "Yeah. Don't let me eat too much, or I'll ruin my appetite." I was trying to get his mind off of whatever was bothering him.

"I will never stop you from eating," he said, and his voice was so low and serious that I laughed out loud.

"Okay," I replied, still giggling to myself. Despite my worry, I was excited to see him.

"I'll let you drive," he murmured, and he sounded happier now, likely because I was laughing like an idiot. "Please be careful."

"Okay, I will."

As I drove, my mind wandered. Maybe Jordan had seen something brutal today. Maybe killers from the Dark Web were up in Senton. I shuddered at the thought of him being around criminals, around violence.

I told myself not to jump to conclusions.

When I arrived at his house, the garage was open, and he was waiting for me. I hopped out of the car, grabbing my purse, phone and keys. I left the overnight stuff in the car, because I didn't want him to think I was inviting myself over. I didn't even know my own intentions.

Jordan let me step inside before he pulled me into his arms and held me tight. He didn't say a word.

I wrapped my arms around his waist and squeezed his back, which was hard as rock. The hug felt heavy. Desperate.

When we finally pulled back a little, he kissed my lips with no prompt. Though his energy was slightly aggressive, he kissed me gently, putting one hand on the back of my head and holding me to his face. I was stunned. And thrilled.

When he let go, I pulled back to see his expression. I took his cheeks in both of my hands and let the fingertips on one fall down to his jaw, the thumb on my other hand stroking his temple. I stared at him, trying to decipher his emotions.

His eyes had small bags and a purple tint under them that weren't there on Sunday. He looked tired, but his energy didn't match. I felt an uneasy tension from him.

As I stroked his temple, I sensed some of that negative energy lighten. Seeing the weight in his eyes, a tiredness I'd never seen before, made my heart ache. He was always so collected, secure. Unbothered. To see him this way, though he was hiding it, unnerved me.

"What's wrong?" I murmured softly, feeling my eyebrows knitting together.

"Nothing is wrong," he murmured back. "Work was difficult today."

I was relieved he admitted it. I brushed my fingers over the side of his head, smoothing over his thick hair. "Do you want to talk about it?" I asked quietly. I anticipated a quick *No*.

Instead, Jordan stared at me for a few moments. Finally, he softly replied, "Not right now." His hands on my waist, he moved them slowly up my down back. He'd never touched me that way before. It lifted my shirt up a little.

"Thank you," he murmured softly, putting his forehead to mine. For a moment, I thought he was giving in to his emotions, leaning on me for support. But then he lifted his head back up, said "Let's go to the movie," and kissed my temple.

I was amazed at how well and how quickly he hid what he was feeling.

He'd allowed himself a few moments in which he didn't completely conceal the desperation that baffled me.

I continued to watch him as we stepped back out to his truck. I assumed our showtime was now.

He stood behind me as I hopped in the truck. He'd gotten into the habit of asking me which car I wanted to take. Suspecting that he preferred the truck—big man liked big things—I always picked it.

Once we were both in, I continued watching for any emotion slipping through the cracks. A slight wince, a twitch of the lips, eyes zoning out or a flash within them, a tremble in his hand, a heavy sigh.

Absolutely nothing. He somehow seemed less tired than before.

It made me happy that he'd opened up earlier and came to me for comfort, even subtly. It devastated me that he retreated so quickly and hid it all again.

He drove with his left hand. I grabbed his right. He looked at me as he turned onto the main road.

"Jordan," I murmured.

He turned his head and glanced quickly at me before turning back to the road. His eyes were brighter.

"Yes, lovely."

"Are you okay?" I asked quietly, sounding childlike as I made myself small. I couldn't help it. I didn't want him to become upset with me for prodding. Perhaps I had a slight trauma from my past relationship, from being snapped at for talking too much.

I watched his face immediately crinkle with concern at my tone. "Yes, sweetheart," he replied gently, kindly. "What's wrong?" He kept looking back at me and then the road.

"You just seem off today. Something bad happened. And...I don't want to push you to talk about it. But I'm just worried about you. About how you're feeling."

I was so relieved he wasn't annoyed with me. He shook his head, his expression softening. "You've nothing to worry about, my love."

I was trying to wrap my head around how he dodged the discussion and also that he'd called me his love.

I slid my hand under his black jacket, running my fingertips over as much of his forearm as I could reach by fitting my hand underneath. I didn't want to keep pushing. "Okay," I said quietly. "Hey, listen. I won't be upset if we don't see the movie."

He shook his head. "We're seeing the movie."

I looked down at our hands. "I kinda don't want to anymore."

"No?" he said, surprised. I shook my head, feeling like a kid again.

"Why not, sweetheart?"

"Sorry," I said guiltily, ignoring his question. "I don't know where we were supposed to eat, if it's nearby or if we're heading in the opposite direction."

"No, no, the restaurant isn't out of the way."

I let go of his hand then, having an inkling that I should. He lifted it up and wrapped it around my shoulders; I leaned into his side.

"Tell me what changed," he murmured softly.

"Um..." I didn't know how I wanted to explain it. "I don't know. I just don't want to anymore. I want to talk to you instead. Not be quiet for two hours." In reality, I was worried that something awful had happened today and didn't want to subject him to more violence.

"Did I upset you?" he asked softly, despite my answer.

"No, no. I just missed you." I paused a moment, looking past the dashboard at the road ahead. Then, I turned my head to the right and kissed the hand he had around my shoulder. I slid out from under his arm and took his hand in my lap again.

"I missed you, too," he murmured.

When we got to the restaurant, I felt calmer. It was warm inside, dimly lit, and I knew I could look at him directly.

But something changed when we stepped inside. Suddenly, it wasn't just us. There were people all around, and I sensed his energy shift. His face stayed smooth, but there was something in his eyes that wasn't there before. He was on guard.

Suddenly, he was hard and cold towards everyone around us, and gentle with me. Nobody had even done or said anything.

After the waitress brought us waters, I reached out for his hand. I noticed how he paid her no mind. She was pretty, blue eyes, blonde hair pulled back in a little ponytail, not a lot of makeup.

He didn't look twice. He thanked her for the waters with half a glance and turned his eyes back to me, his face smooth. "What do you feel like eating, honey?" he asked.

"Umm," I broke my stare from him and looked at the menu. I was thirsty. "Lemonade," I responded, and he smiled small. "Strawberry lemonade."

"And I don't know about food. What about you?" I asked, wanting to give him some normalcy.

He broke out of his stare and glanced at the menu for a moment, then looked up and said, "I'll get pasta."

"You don't eat pasta often," I said, suspicious.

"Well," he said, rubbing his thumb over my hand, "if I don't like it, you can eat it." He smiled a small, sweet smile.

"Ohhh," I said lightly, trying not to grin. "That's the plan, huh?"

He nodded. "Yes."

"You better eat it," I warned him, smiling.

He grinned and gestured to the menu. "You have to be hungry."

I looked at him for a moment, then nodded. "Are you?" I asked. "When's the last time you ate?"

He thought for a moment. "Around one."

My eyes widened, though it was the same for me. But Jordan was bigger. And also a man. And he burned calories like a fourteen year old boy.

"Jordan," I exclaimed as quietly as possible. "That's so long."

He smiled small, eyes tired again. "I've been distracted." Then he looked at my menu. "You're right, though. We shouldn't go so long without eating."

His eyes turned up to my face, suddenly concerned. "When did you last eat?"

I didn't want to answer. "Ummm," I murmured lightly. "Around the same time." And before he could hit me back with my hypocrisy, I added quickly, "You're big, I'm not, so it's not so bad if I go a little while."

He shook his head. "Small people need to eat especially. How will they grow?"

I burst out laughing at his joke, and only then did he grin. I didn't know how he said the most ridiculous things with a straight face.

"Okay, okay," I said. "We're gonna eat."

I looked at the menu. "I want a burger," I announced. Tonight was off so far. I thought I might as well throw it off a little more and do something unusual.

A grin grew slowly on Jordan's face. I didn't know why it pleased him so much when I ate, but it was endearing and made me feel cared about. I chuckled.

"Fries, too, yeah?" he asked, eyebrows shooting up. I had to laugh at his face.

I bit my lip. "Yeah."

His eyes lightened genuinely for the first time that night. He seemed happier.

"Tell me about your day," he requested; it was kind, welcoming.

"It was alright," I murmured. "I was excited for it to be over. So I could see you." I smiled. "And get strawberry lemonade."

He grinned. "I'll only ever pick restaurants that have it."

Once I'd taken a deep breath and laughed enough, I told him, "Tell me about your day."

The smile dissipated off his face slowly. "It was very busy. Very long." He paused, thinking. Then, he seemed to decide to be honest. "It was hard."

I grabbed his hand and gripped it tight. "What happened?" I murmured.

He stared at me for what felt like a long time. "There have been four more livestreams."

My eyes widened. "When?"

"Two last month. One a week ago and one today."

I gaped. "Why didn't you tell me?" He'd seen *four* people being tortured and said *nothing*.

He blinked, his face still expressionless except for the stress around the edges he couldn't hide.

"I don't want to worry you, sweetheart."

His gentleness made me even more frustrated. Devastated me even more.

"You've *suffered* through those awful videos," I whispered. I wanted to get up and wrap my arms around him and squeeze him, but we were in the middle of a crowded restaurant. "Jord, you have to *tell me* these things." His eyes softened. "*Please*. Please."

I couldn't believe he had been watching more girls get tortured, and I had no idea. As far as I'd known, there were the two girls from before Jordan told me about the case in March. I didn't know it had gotten worse.

He was conflicted and unspeaking as he thought of how to respond, so I went on. "Jordan, I'm so sorry. I'm so sorry for what you saw."

He squeezed my hand. "It's okay, honey," he said softly. "We're gonna find them. Don't worry about me." He hesitated. "I've been doing this for a long time. I know how to handle it." His eyebrows knitted together slightly.

"But you don't have to do it alone," I said quietly, heartbroken. When he didn't speak or agree, I pushed. "Tell me what happened today," I said gently.

He took a deep breath. "The video streamed. Then, forty minutes later, we got an email at the office with a picture of the warehouse where it happened, and the location was in the subject line."
My eyes widened. "Is that what was in Senton? It was here? They tortured the girl here?"
Jordan stroked my hand with his thumb. "Yes, honey," he said gently.
I stared at him hard. "Was her body there?" I asked finally.
He shook his head. "No, but...there was blood."
I shivered a little, hoping he didn't notice. I felt cold. The people behind *Right At Home* were...right at home.
"Jordan," I said, my eyes widening. "*Right At Home?*"
"Yes."
"But..." I shook my head. "I always assumed the streams were all over the country, all over the world even. But now I'm wondering...are they all here? What are the odds they call themselves right at home all over the place? And I just remembered, you told me you thought it might be two people doing this."
He stared at me intently, his eyebrows knitting together in concentration. He was a little surprised. After a few moments, he murmured, "I don't think that's likely anymore."
"Why?"
He looked away for a moment, which made me suspicious. "I just...I've been wondering if it's more of a network than two people. These people...they don't enjoy these things on their own. Two people don't livestream for themselves."
I nodded, eyes opening up more. "It's a cult." I swallowed. "Yet they're taunting *you*."
"They could be taunting everyone looking for them."
"Who's looking for them? Other than you?"
Jordan stared at me more intensely now, but he wasn't angry with me. He just wasn't expecting me to question so much. To demand so many details. Normally, I was apprehensive to push. But Jordan had been hiding things from me. The more I found out too late, the more desperate I was to find out what he was hiding *now*.
"Police. FBI."
I shook my head. "Wait...how? I just thought about this: are bodies being found? They can't be, or you'd have so much more to go off."
Now his eyebrows went up. He was still serious, but impressed.
"You're right. No bodies were ever recovered."
I exhaled, thinking. I had the feeling that these people *were* closer to home than our theories. And it worried me. Worried me that at least a few of the people in this cult were nearby, and that Jordan was going to crime scenes.
"So you don't know who the girl is yet."
"No."

I shook my head, confused. "You said they could be taunting everyone. Did they, now? Did the police get the email, too? Or just your office?"
He hesitated. "Just mine."
"*Why?*"
"I'm not entirely certain, my love. Perhaps they assumed we would just get it to the police or FBI. And we did."
I shook my head. No, they would have given it to the police if they wanted the police to have it.
"It sounds like they wanted you guys to have it," I observed, voice low.
Jordan stared at me for a while. "Could be. I'm not entirely certain."
"Was there any text in the email?"
"No. Just the location in the subject line."
I shook my head, disturbed. Someone sent a message revealing the location of a livestream, declaring they were not concerned about being caught. What was more unsettling was that it seemed Jordan wasn't telling me everything.
"Okay," I said slowly, nodding. I wished he would tell me the things he was thinking. I immediately wanted to tell him anything that came to mind in any situation. It bothered me to think he didn't care to share as well. That maybe he didn't trust me.
I tried to convince myself he wanted to spare me the horror, but it didn't make me feel better.
I didn't speak for a while. He studied my face, even as the waiter came and took his order for pasta. I snapped back to attention in order to request my burger.
I laced my fingers through his.
"What are you thinking?" he murmured quietly.
I wanted to keep talking, to say what I was thinking, but I kept it to myself. To do what he was doing and not say everything on my mind. Not to be petty, but because I felt I was pushing my luck with the interrogation. I still feared he would become angry with me at some point.
"Just about what you told me," I said quietly. I met his eyes. "I'm so sorry work was hard today, Jord. I really am."
He squeezed my hand a little tighter. "Thank you, love. Don't be. I feel better now."
But, as much as I wanted to, I didn't believe him.

JORDAN

After that conversation, dinner went by quietly and even cozily. He asked me about my day, about Elijah's birthday. We ate without saying much, and it was oddly comfortable for me to be eating a burger in front of him. He made me try his pasta.

When we got to his house, he pulled me into the family room.

"You're tired," he murmured.

I smiled small. "Yeah, thank goodness we didn't go to the movies. I'd be dead by the time we got home." And then I caught myself, realized I'd said *home* instead of *here* or *back*. But it wasn't my home, and I felt the exhausting need to ensure I was never imposing, or trying to take what wasn't mine.

"By the time we got back," I corrected myself, sitting down so I didn't have to look at him.

I peeked up finally; he'd cocked his head to the side little. "Why did you say it twice?"

I looked up at him innocently. He knew why.

"Well, just...you know. It's your house," I said quietly.

Jordan sat down next to me, never once breaking eye contact. He put his hand on my lower back and grabbed mine with his other. "It's yours, too."

The deepness and seriousness of his voice was so heavy that I could not argue. I just sat there silently.

I didn't know what to do. I wrapped my arms around his neck and kissed him.

Just softly. I didn't mean for it to get too intense, but slowly the kisses got deeper. He held onto my waist as I lifted myself and shifted onto my knees; he turned his body onto the couch more, so that one leg was up on the cushion, the other still on the ground.

Jordan kissed me deeply. He was never rough. Just slow and romantic. I began getting too hot and knew then that I had to stop.

I pulled back breathlessly and looked at him. He stared back into my eyes, and the feeling was overwhelming.

"I'm sorry," I whispered, feeling guilty. I knew he would reassure me that everything was okay, but there was the constant fear in me that at some point, he would become frustrated that we didn't go further.

"Don't be," he whispered back.

"I feel like at some point, this is going to get old for you."

His eyebrows crinkled together, and then I felt bad for assuming.

"Sorry," I said quickly. "I don't mean to be…"

He shook his head. "You're not being anything but honest, and that's what I want. It's a good thing." He kissed my temple. "It's not going to get old. I'm committed to you. I'm not with you for sex and nothing else."

"Okay," I replied quietly.

He kissed my lips softly. "I love you," he murmured.

The words made me dizzy.

He lay back and pulled me with him, wrapping his arms around me.

"I love you, too. It's been a rough day for you, Jordy. Why don't you get some rest?"

"As long as you stay with me."

I smiled, cheek against his chest. "Of course."

I didn't think I'd sleep more than an hour or two before waking up. As we lay there, I drifted off to the sound of his breathing.

I opened my eyes slowly. It took me a few seconds to realize where I was. Jordan's family room. I'd never been in here when it was dark.
I rolled my head back, and as my eyes adjusted to the darkness, I saw Jordan's sleeping face, a few inches from mine. His body was warm underneath me. I set my head back down on his chest gently, but then a wave of anxiety shot through me.
What time is it?
I sat up slowly, not wanting to wake Jordan. Sliding off the couch very gently, I felt around for my phone. When I felt the hardness of it under my fingers, I picked it up, anxiety running through my chest. There were ten missed calls from *each* of my parents, five from Zana, and two from Elijah. There were multiple text messages.
It was four in the morning.
I'd forgotten to turn the ringer back on after my meeting.
I knew that if I read the messages, the anger, the angst, the panic, and the threats would all unnerve me more. I dialed my mom and jogged to the foyer.
"Nina?" she answered on the second ring.
I swallowed. "Mom, I'm sorry. Don't be mad at me. I fell asleep."
"Nina," her voice was low, the way it got when she was too angry to yell. "We've been *terrified*. You weren't answering your phone, your texts, *anything*. We thought he'd hurt you or done something to you. We've been calling nonstop. Your father almost drove up there to find you. He almost called the police. *Why* didn't you answer your phone?"
"Mom, I'm sorry. I fell asleep. We had a meeting at work today, and I forgot to put my ringer back on when I left. I'm sorry, I swear I wasn't

purposely ignoring you." I had to keep my voice down, so as not to wake Jordan. Going home was going to be hell.
I heard a small sound and then saw the lights in the family room go on.
"Just get home *now*," she growled. "Be careful." She hung up the phone.
Wow. My mother never hung up the phone without saying *I love you*, and most definitely did not just hang up the phone without saying *goodbye*.
I was in for a battle.
I heard a sound behind me and, turning, saw Jordan coming into the foyer. He was sleepy, but then concern clouded his face when he saw mine.
"What's wrong?" he asked, walking up and brushing my hair back from my face.
"Nothing, nothing. I'm sorry I woke you. Go back to sleep, baby."
I didn't want him to hear this; it wasn't his problem. This was embarrassing and frustrating.
"Tell me, love," he murmured softly.
I shook my head. "It's okay. I just...I have to go home now."
Jordan's eyes opened more with understanding. "I'm sorry; I forgot. Are your parents upset with you for falling asleep?"
I frowned. I couldn't lie to him, but I also couldn't bring myself to admit the extent to which they felt they could control me.
Because I'd been letting them for years.
"I think so; I'm just gonna go talk to them, maybe spend some time with them to get them to cool down...if...if they really are upset. I'm not sure."
I was downplaying what I knew to be true, and I hated doing that to him.
Jordan brought his other hand up and rubbed his thumb over my temple.
"Who was that on the phone?" he asked gently.
"It was my mom."
"What did she say?"
"That they were worried; I told her everything was good, though," I said, feigning lightheartedness.
He lifted an eyebrow. "Are you sure?"
"Yeah, yeah. Don't worry," I replied casually. I couldn't look him in the eyes.
Turning, I went to grab my purse. I couldn't be around him much longer, or I'd cave and tell him what hell I knew was waiting for me at home.
Jordan paused for a few more moments before he said, "Can you wash up here first? Or do you need to leave right away?"
With my back to him, I grimaced with sadness. He didn't want me to leave. Before I could respond, he said, "Can I come with you?"
Oh, shoot.
I racked my brain for what to say. I didn't know how to reject him.
"Oh, Jordy, I can't." It was such a scary thought, of how they would react, even if Jordan were there. They'd likely spent the last eight or nine hours thinking he'd abducted and murdered me.

"They might go off on you, or something." I tried to keep my nerves out of my voice; the thought of that mortified me more.

I forced myself to swallow the aching desire to stay with him. I was tired and cold and being forced to leave this new bliss to go home to rage.

"I'll be fine," I sighed, wiping my face of emotion as best as I could, leaving a weak smile. "Um, would you be annoyed if like…I came back after?"

I wanted to spend the whole weekend with him. I was embarrassed once more to even ask him, but I couldn't soothe myself any other way than to look forward to coming back.

He pulled me towards him again, tilting my chin up to his face.

"Of *course* you can." He paused. "Are you sure, though, Nina? Are you sure you're parents aren't going to try to argue with you?"

"Yes, I'm sure, love. I'm sure." I had to turn away again. Now I was lying to him, and I hated every second of it.

"Okay," he murmured. "Let's wash up first."

I couldn't say no. I was feeling so bad for lying, and for telling him he couldn't come with me, that denying him again would be grueling.

"Okay," I said softly.

Jordan grabbed my hand. "Come on, let's go wash up." He gently pulled me towards the staircase. Once I realized where we were going, my heart skipped. I'd never been upstairs.

I complied, walking by his side. The stairway curved with its cream wooden banister, and we followed its path, hand in hand.

We stepped into the large loft; to the left were a few cream sofas, and a few feet further were what I assumed were two bedrooms.

We continued straight, to his bedroom door, in the corner of the loft. To the left were three more doors.

He caught me looking. "My room." He gestured over the threshold we were about to cross. "This door is a bathroom, the one next to it and the one at the end are bedrooms. Those," he turned slightly and pointed at the two rooms running parallel to the banister, "are a bedroom and another bath."

I nodded. The house was much bigger on the inside than it looked out.

His bedroom was large, covered in a soft, plush cream carpet, like the one in his family room. To the left of the doorway was a large closet, and next to that was an open door. I could see part of a frosted shower door. The master bath.

The king-sized bed was in the center of the room, framed by two nightstands. I looked to the right side of the room, noticing the large wooden armoire.

The bed was covered with white comforters and a large frame made of wood that matched the chests next to it.

Jordan let me gaze around for a moment, and I looked back at him quickly, trying not to get lost. I had somewhere I dreadfully had to be.

JORDAN

He led me to the bathroom. "Oh, shoot," I said, remembering. "I have a toothbrush in my car, and clean clothes. I forgot." When he looked at me, I immediately felt the need to explain, but clamped my lips together. I tended to embarrass myself the more I spoke.

Jordan's eyes lightened, however. "It's okay," he murmured. "I have new ones."

"Oh," I said, surprised. "You just...keep new toothbrushes?"

He nodded. "Yes. Sometimes my parents decide to stay the night. Not often, but they do."

As he spoke, we stepped into the spacious bathroom. Across from the shower was a light gray granite counter with two sinks. To the right of the counter was the toilet, and a few feet away, next to the shower door, was a long ceramic bathtub.

Jordan opened the cabinet under the sink and pulled out a pack of toothbrushes.

He extended the box to me. "Is this okay?"

I smiled shyly and nodded, pulling one from the pack. "Thank you."

He smiled back, noticing how I was feeling. Then he opened the long drawer in the center of the counter, exposing various unopened boxes of toothpaste. He grabbed the only open tube.

"Take whichever you want. I'll be out there."

"Where are you going?" I asked, confused.

"To give you time to wash up. I'll head to the other bathroom."

I shook my head. Despite there having been two sinks in this bathroom, I appreciated the offer of privacy.

"Jordan, let me use the other one. This is *yours*. Why did you bring me in yours for you to go to the other one?"

He smiled small. "This one is bigger." He stepped up and kissed my head before I could argue, then walked out and said, "Take your time."

I stood there, smiling to myself, watching him walk away. He was so perfect.

"Sexy," I said under my breath. I closed the door gently and washed up, looking at myself in the mirror above the sinks. My eyes were clouded, mascara having left a little bit of a shadow smudged beneath them.

I stepped out holding my toothbrush. Jordan had just entered the bedroom. "What should I do with this?" I asked.

"You can leave it in there. There's a little case for toothbrushes in the drawer to the right."

I didn't know how to respond to being told to leave a toothbrush at his house. Having one in a little case.

It felt funny leaving mine next to what I assumed was his; he was alone, and then suddenly, he wasn't. It was like leaving my presence around, even though I didn't live here.

I stepped out of the bathroom shyly. Jordan was changing his shirt a few feet away. I watched the muscles of his bare back move as he slid on a new, long-sleeved gray shirt. He was so beautiful; it made me ache.

When he turned around, I stepped towards the door. "I'm gonna run home and come back right after," I chuckled casually, still embarrassed by it but testing him to see if he still wanted me to return.

He frowned slightly; I knew he didn't want me to leave, or go alone, at least. "Okay, babe...do you want a new shirt?"

I smiled. "No, thank you though. That's really sweet. If I come home wearing your clothes, they're *definitely* going to think we had sex." I sighed. Jordan nodded. I thought he would follow, but it didn't seem like he was going to.

"Nina," he grabbed my arm gently. "The code is four-six-nine-eight-one. Hit that, then hit enter. Then you'll have to enter a second one. I'll call it down to you."

I was shocked, so it took me a moment to respond. "I—okay." I smiled again. "Four-six-nine-eight-one. Got it."

When I made it to the door, I did his first code.

"Okay, Jord!" I called.

But when I turned, he was right there. He still let me do it. "Five-two-eight-one-eight." I smiled as he came up behind me and put his hand on my back. I should've known he would always walk me out.

"Can I grab you something to eat before you go?" he asked softly. "Something small, even?"

"No, no," I said, shaking my head. "Don't. Thank you, baby."

With all this anxiety, I'll just be nauseous after. "It's a little early to eat for me."

Jordan's eyebrows furrowed together. He brushed his hand down the back of my hair slowly. "Okay," he murmured.

"Maybe after I get back, we can go out to eat. If you want."

He nodded. "Yes, that sounds lovely." He kissed my cheek. I wrapped my arms around his neck. He put his own around my waist, and he did something he'd never done before. He put his lips to my neck, kept his face there.

He kissed it one time, enough to get me heated. He turned his cheek so that it was touching my neck as he held me, and then he pulled back slowly, face disturbed.

"Nina," he murmured, concern clouding his voice. He lifted his hand and put all of his fingers except his thumb to the right side of my neck, just under my jaw.

"Your heart is beating fast," he whispered. He pulled my face close to his and looked at my eyes intensely.

Shoot.

"Yeah, I just..." *What do I say?!*

"My heart always beats faster when you touch me," I said breathlessly.

He stared at me, and I knew he wasn't convinced. But he also knew that I didn't want him to come with me. I just hoped he understood why. That it wasn't him, but my embarrassing family.
"Okay, sweetie." He kissed my lips softly. I smiled small, then forced myself to turn around and go.
"I'll be back," I murmured. I bit my lip and turned back.
"I love you."
"I love you, too. I'll see you soon. Drive carefully."
The drive home was miserable. I sank into a dreadful mood. I knew this was going to be a fight. And I'd lied to Jordan about it, which didn't make me feel any better.
I tried to reconcile the idea that I may leave here homeless, and forced to ask Jordan if I could stay with him.
The idea was mortifying, but at the same time, I didn't know if I'd rather that or submit to my parents' abusive tendencies to just keep the peace. And my bed at their house.
As I pulled into the driveway, I swallowed, undecided about how to behave. I was going to go with the moment.
I opened the garage and went inside, sliding off my shoes. I met eyes with my mom in the kitchen. She was an early riser, but on Saturdays she was up around seven. It was just turning six when I walked in.
"Hi," I said quietly.
She turned from mixing her coffee towards me. Her face was blank, but I recognized the anger in her eyes.
She wasn't speaking, so I went on. "I'm sorry, mom. I had a meeting at work. I turned my ringer off, and I forgot to turn it back. You know how my memory is. It was a long day, I was tired, and I just didn't think to put it back on. You know I would never ignore you guys on purpose. Especially not with *that* many calls coming in. I fell asleep." I kept my voice quiet.
"You *terrified* us, Nina. What do you think is going to happen to us when our daughter isn't answering her phone all night? *Knowing* that she was with a man we barely knew? When you *always* answer?"
"Exactly! I always answer. So why wouldn't I this time if not for forgetting?"
"Because you were *murdered*!" she snapped, her eyes wide with rage. She was angrier than I expected.
I forced myself to stay calm. "Mom, I'm truly, truly sorry. I understand why you would be afraid."
"We weren't just *afraid*, Nina. Your sister had a panic attack, and your father could barely stand still. Your brother was a nervous wreck all night. I finally got them to go to sleep."
I swallowed. Guilt was already building in me.
"Mom, how many times do you want me to say I'm sorry and that I didn't do it on purpose?"

"It doesn't *matter* if it was on purpose or *not*! Your lack of responsibility is what caused this. And until you can get it together, you're not going out with him anymore."

I blinked, stunned.

Did she really think she could stop me from being with him?

I knew she would be angry. Furious, even. But I hadn't expected her to tell me I couldn't see him.

I breathed slowly. Finally, I said, "Listen. I apologized. I am genuinely sorry. Genuinely. But remember that I'm twenty-four years old, and that—"

"I don't care how old you are. You live here, you follow our rules. Until you move out, you do what we tell you to."

I gritted my teeth, trying so hard not to raise my voice. I wanted to go off on her, but I knew it would go nowhere. I was so tired.

Before I could say anything, the floor creaked in the foyer. A moment later, my dad walked into the kitchen. He stopped when he saw me and just glared.

I knew that look. A look I'd hated all my life.

"Look, dad," I said, throwing my hand up. I would not show them fear or pain. "I just told mom. I'm sorry. I didn't purposely ignore you. I fell asleep, and my ringer was off. I am really, really sorry." I hoped I could appeal to his soft spot for me.

But he shook his head. "No, no, sorry isn't good enough." He pointed his finger at me. "You are not to see him again."

My eyebrows shot up. I couldn't believe it. That was the final straw for me. I was enraged, frustrated, and miserable.

I wanted to yell. I wanted to cry. I hated upsetting them; I hated knowing they were angry with me, that they would ignore me for days, and that if I tried to speak with them, they would snap at me, again and again.

I hated being in this house, miserable. Hated being away from the love of my life, where I was happiest. I was so tired.

Tired of the emotional abuse. Of being told all my mental health problems were in my head. Tired of the constant yelling, constant fighting.

My hands shaking, I lowered my voice.

"Fine," I said quietly, more to myself than anyone. I headed upstairs to my room, ignoring my father as I passed him. I closed the door and glanced over to my backpack. I stared at it for a split second, so angry and frustrated, before deciding.

I moved to my dresser and began pulling out everything in its drawers, shoving into my tall backpack as many clothes as possible. I went to the bathroom, grabbed my toiletries and a plastic bag to put my shoes in. I'd buy the rest of what I needed later. Socks, shampoo, conditioner.

I was so heated.

Things had been so difficult lately. Work, money, not getting to be with Jordan as much as I wanted to be, the heat, not sleeping enough. All of it was making it harder to cope with this moment than it typically would've been.

But it didn't matter. No one deserved to live this way.

Amidst constant arguing, shouting, a loveless marriage that devastated and frustrated you at the same time. Anger issues and the inability to cope with anxiety that rubbed off on all your kids.

I pulled out whatever clothes I had left and threw those in my only suitcase, then packed up any paperwork I had, any books, my laptop, anything else I could find, in the single storage bin I had in my closet.

When it seemed I had nothing left in my small bedroom, I went out to the car from the front door, so as to avoid seeing my parents again, with my backpack on my shoulders, suitcase handle in one hand, dragging the bin with the other.

I opened my trunk, put the bin and the suitcase inside, and then set my backpack in the front seat.

My mother, now standing in the doorway next to my father, snapped, "So, you're just going to leave?" The notion made her mad and, I assumed, helpless, because when my mother didn't know what to do, when she didn't have control, she got angry. The anger flew out with her words. "Go ahead. Go running off to a man you barely know, and when he kicks you out onto the streets, don't come begging me to help you."

I couldn't believe my ears.

Taking cheap shots just to hurt me. Or scare me. Or both.

She's trying to intimidate you to stop you from leaving. She's trying to make you think you have no place with Jordan, that you'll end up on the streets if you trust him.

To keep you dependent on her.

The fury managed to spread to every corner of my body. I watched my fingers twitch as I moved and also felt anxiety spreading, worsened by the uneasiness and frustration already coursing through me. I clamped my lips together and didn't say anything.

I didn't like hearing those things said of Jordan, regardless of what he'd proven.

He would never do that to me.

But the fear, that little part of me that always worried he would fall out of love with me, that things wouldn't last, that I couldn't trust anyone, made it harder to do what I was doing. My heartbeat picked up.

You have to take that chance if you want to find happiness in love.

"Nina," my dad said sharply.

I looked back at him, saying nothing.

"Where are you going? What are you doing?" His eyebrows were knitted together in anger.

"I'm leaving," I answered, my voice low. Then, I turned away and got in my car.

"Oh, okay," he said passively. Then everything shifted from his feigned casual attitude.

"If you walk out that door, don't you ever come back!" The expletives made the sentence even more disgusting.

"And who's gonna pay your bills?"

I couldn't keep my voice down as I snapped, "I pay all my own bills."

"Yeah, except rent or a mortgage. Good luck affording somewhere to live when the two of you break up," my mother commented rudely.

I didn't respond to the comment but pursed my lips, not letting any words come through them as I slammed the car door shut.

Nice to know how my parents look at me. A dependent, helpless little girl who can't do anything for herself. All bark, no bite.

It bothered me that I feared they were right. I repeated in my mind that Jordan would never leave me on the streets.

I wasn't as convinced as I wanted to be.

The idea that had been plaguing me every day crushed me now. I needed a higher salary.

I would figure out how to make this work. I made enough money for cheap rent somewhere, if I ever ended up on my own. I would have no money to spare after bills, but I thought I could manage it.

I would be fine.

I made a mental note to look for other jobs, regardless.

At the first red light, I picked up my phone to text Jordan that I was on my way back. Before I could type anything, I stopped myself.

Setting the phone back down in the cupholder, I told myself to just drive. I wasn't thinking straight.

I tried to concentrate on the road. It felt like forever. I'd never wanted to get to my destination so bad as right then. My mind wandered to the worst once more. I couldn't rid the dread from my chest.

My hands were shaking. I squeezed the steering wheel tight, trying to keep my focus just as strong.

I couldn't handle the panic that accompanied even the thought of being out of a home and having to desperately figure something out.

Twenty minutes into the drive, my phone rang.

I glanced down to see Jordan's name light up the screen. My heart skipped. *Don't answer. Just talk to him face to face. You can't drive and figure out what to say at the same time.*

For the first time, I let Jordan's call ring.

When the ringing stopped, my phone locked and then the screen brightened up again. I glanced quickly to see a text from Jordan pop up. I didn't read it. I stared ahead of me and forced myself not to pick up my phone.

As the panic and stress moved through me, tears filled my eyes. I didn't know what to do. I would be so embarrassed if I didn't get myself together before I saw him.

I forced myself to keep it in. The ache stayed in my throat, tears still running down my face.

My immediate response to those tears was to catch them before they ruined my makeup. But I was only wearing day-old mascara that was now leaving gray streaks down my cheeks. I looked awful.

So I'm losing my parents and *my boyfriend on the same day.*

I forced myself to breathe. The depression was building. It was after the flood of intense, negative emotions that things began to feel worthless. I began to feel worthless.

My parents always seemed to have that effect on me. I took a deep breath, thought of Jordan, and was comforted a little. I wasn't going to the dog pound.

I was going to my love. But the heaviness still settled on me, as I pushed the anxiety away and depression took its place.

I would have to see if Jordan really loved me, smudged makeup or not.

I gripped the steering wheel, trying to focus on the road. Jordan called two more times. I didn't answer.

It was forty-five minutes of torture.

When I got to Jordan's street and saw his house, my heartbeat picked up. I was so embarrassed at the thought of his seeing all my belongings in my car.

I pulled in; the garage was already open. My car was halfway in when Jordan appeared at the door, in black sweatpants and a black t-shirt. My heart ached as I looked at him.

He ran outside and opened my door for me, pulled me out of the car and into his arms for a moment, then took my face in his hands.

"I've been so worried," he whispered. "Tell me what happened. What happened?" But I was shaky, exhausted and on edge. I shook my head and set it down on his chest. He wrapped his arms around me tightly as I fought the urge to bawl like a toddler.

I didn't let go until I felt like I could stay steady. I had no idea what I was going to say to him. How I was going to ask him.

I didn't think too long. I swallowed, inhaled deeply through my nose and pulled back.

"Um," I said, voice shaking. "Do you mind if I stay with you for a little while?"

I sounded pathetic, voice weak and trembling.

Reluctantly, I looked up at his face.

There was no apprehension. No hesitation.

Just slight surprise. "Of course you can. Of course you can."

I figured the question told him all he needed to know about what happened. "I'm so sorry for imposing this way, I just…I need to find an apartment or something."

He shook his head. "Don't ever say that again. You are not imposing. I told you that you can come here any time." The words were firm, but his voice was gentle.

I swallowed, trying to balance the overwhelming comfort and nerves he gave me, at the same time.

"Let's go inside," he murmured softly. "What do you have that I can help you bring in?" I looked up at him right away, thought for a moment and then shook my head.

"No, no. Let's leave it. I'll just grab some clothes and my phone charger and stuff. That's all I need." My quiet voice quavered. Anyone could tell I'd been crying, even if they weren't looking at me. I was embarrassed by it.

"Is that all you brought?" he asked gently.

I hesitated. "No, I…I packed all my stuff up and threw it in my car." I blinked and then met his eyes. "I don't plan to go back."

He nodded, kissing my forehead. "Let's get the rest of it, then."

"I put what I need for now in my backpack." To humor him, I added, "Maybe we can bring some other stuff in later."

I still felt like I was imposing. I couldn't help it. I didn't want him to look inside my trunk and see all my stuff.

I went to the front passenger seat and dragged my heavy backpack over my arm. Jordan immediately slid it off my shoulder and carried it from the top handle.

"It's okay," I said, my voice shaky.

He didn't respond, just waited patiently while I grabbed my purse and phone from the car and shut the door.

"Come on," he murmured, putting his free arm around me. I felt like the backpack might break from the weight if he didn't support it from the bottom. That thing was heavy.

Only a few steps into the house, I felt calmer. Even a little sprinkle of joy. And just as fast as it came, that flash of joy vanished, and the emptiness surfaced. It was the emptiness that came until my mind remembered what was wrong, and then brought back the anxiety and depression.

Jordan led us to the family room. I really wanted to curl up and sleep.

He set down my backpack gently and then sat me on the couch. I instinctively turned inward to face him as he sat down.

I looked at my phone and noticed the text message icon at the top. Zana and Elijah had both texted me.

I started with Zana's.

Listen. I know you and mom and dad don't agree on everything, but this is not the right way to do things. I know you love Jordan, but you haven't known him that long. You don't know if things will last. I'm not trying to sound negative, but you just need to be careful. I think you should come home.

JORDAN

I ignored her. Then came my brother, unconcerned what my parents or Zana had to say. He was going to get his own answers.
Where are you
I knew that if I didn't text him back, he would blow up my phone. I replied, telling him I was at Jordan's house and why I didn't answer their calls last night. Then I locked my phone and put it on the couch next to me.
"Tell me what happened," he murmured, after waiting patiently for me to go through my messages.
I shook my head. "They were livid. I'm sorry I downplayed their behavior earlier. I just didn't want you to worry. I mean, I knew they'd be mad, but I didn't think they were gonna yell and curse at me the way they did." I couldn't look at him as I rambled. "They told me I 'wasn't allowed' to see you again. I was so mad. My mom said that stupid, 'You live under my roof, it's my rules' thing. So I went to pack my stuff. My dad told me not to 'come back', just not as nicely. So I threw all my stuff in my car and came here." I shook my head. "I have to find an apartment," I said, staring down at the cushion.
Jordan didn't speak for a moment. I willed myself to look up at him; he was staring at me, thinking intently. Then he said quietly, "Did they hit you?"
I stared back at him numbly for a moment. I was stunned, unable to open my mouth and respond right away.
Shaking my head, eyes wide, I replied, "No, no. No, they didn't hit me." I swallowed. My voice sounded more normal.
Jordan nodded right away, a gentle look on his face. "Okay," he said softly. He kissed my forehead. "You're not getting an apartment. You're living here with me," he said into my hair.
For the first time that day, I felt relief.
I leaned into him for a moment. My eyelids began to get heavy, and I knew my eyes themselves looked exhausted. As they sank into the fatigue on my face, I bet I looked like a zombie. I pulled back and looked at his face.
"I'm sorry for—" I wanted to say *imposing*, but I knew he would be upset. "—for springing this on you, like...we didn't plan for it or anything."
Jordan shook his head slightly and put his forehead to mine, brought his hand up to cup my cheek and stroked it with his thumb. "No, my love. I've been waiting for you."
I chose to believe him. I chose to give in to his comfort and just take the chance. Maybe things wouldn't work out between us in the long run. I'd have to figure that out when the time came.
But we were together now, and it felt like such a waste to be beside all his love and continue to fear the worst. I looked down at my quaking hands, willing them to stop.
"Let's go to breakfast," he whispered. I nodded once, and we stood up at the same time. He kept his eyes on me.
I changed, and in the car I relaxed some. Jordan held my hand, stroking it with his thumb. I sighed.

"We'll get you adjusted, I promise." He was gentle.

I shook my head. "No, no…you're so sweet. I just know it's gonna be hard…the drive. That's all."

"To work?"

"Yeah. I need more time now. I'm usually up early, anyway. To work out, you know?" I sighed again.

"Ah," I groaned quietly, before I could stop myself. "I don't even have my treadmill." I frowned.

"We'll buy one today," Jordan said immediately.

I looked up at him, stunned. "Jordan," was all I said.

"Yes, love."

"No." I didn't know what else to say.

"We will," he murmured. "We can put it wherever you want it."

I shook my head, unable to wrap my head around his willingness to not only welcome my moving in on a whim, but immediately begin spoiling me. "If you have space for one, I'll buy it." I hesitated. "But you can't be around. I would die if you saw me all sweaty and gross."

Jordan didn't smile or tease me. He kissed my temple, seeming to understand. "I will always leave you to your privacy, my love."

That soothed me only a little.

"You will not buy anything," he continued softly. "The room next to the library is empty."

I shook my head. I wouldn't argue about buying it, but I did need one; we could fight over that later. "That's too close to where you work. What about the basement?" I'd never been down there.

"Sure," he murmured. "It's a little cold down there, though. That's my only hesitation."

I knew he was saying that for my sake, but even the slightest resistance on his part to anything I said made me retreat. I could not ask for anything more than he was willing to give.

"Okay, whatever you want," I said quickly. "Any time you're hesitant, we won't do it."

Jordan was very calm in contrast to my antsy behavior. "No, sweetie," he said gently. "We can put it down there if you like. I have a lot of room. We can feel it out when we get home, and you can tell me what you think, okay?" He stopped at a red light and kissed my temple.

I just said, "I love you."

He blinked slowly, his lips turning up. "I love you, too," he whispered.

I rested my head against his arm for the rest of the drive, wondering if my parents would ever speak to me again.

JORDAN

June

JORDAN

The Monday after I moved in was June first, perfectly symbolic of my new beginning with Jordan. The day was hard. Waking up early to be sure I'd arrive in time. I needed to learn new discipline in order to have enough time to work out, shower, get ready and drive an hour to work.

Being in Jordan's arms made getting up to get ready miserable. I'd have to become accustomed to leaving him every day.

He woke up as soon as I shifted to stop my alarm clock, sitting up and kissing my temple as I tried to rub the drowsiness out of my eyes. I told him to go back to sleep, instantly worried that my presence would make him sleep even less.

Jordan was a six a.m. kind of guy. Maybe five, depending on what was going on at work. I was a four a.m. kind of woman, and I hated subjecting Jordan to it. I told him repeatedly that I would sleep in another room so my alarm didn't wake him, but he said it didn't bother him; he told me that he could fall asleep as easily as he'd woken. He just preferred to be awake when I was.

I didn't believe him. I asked him a hundred times if he was sure it was okay. That morning, I'd gone to the basement to try out my new treadmill.

Jordan had meant it when he said we were getting one on Saturday. I teared up on the way home, disbelieving his generosity.

After I worked out the first time at his house, I chose to shower in the other bathroom, so as not to wake him. I didn't want to risk his seeing me looking gross and sweaty, anyway.

When I came back into the bedroom to get dressed, however, he was awake, standing by the nightstand. He glanced quickly down at me in my towel; I immediately felt shy, rushing over to the dresser to get clothes.

JORDAN

Jordan came up to me, pulled me gently to him and asked why I didn't use our shower. I told him I didn't want to disturb him, and he pulled me closer and kissed my lips, wrapping his arms around me. He was so warm, and I was freezing. He told me not to worry about that, and that he was already awake by that time, anyway.

Once I was ready for work, I found him in the kitchen. He'd brewed me coffee, made me breakfast and prepared me lunch for the day.

I was overwhelmed with emotion; I started to feel weak. I wanted to collapse against him and never let go.

Jordan put his hand through my hair, though it was wet, and kissed my head. After telling me three times to call him if I needed anything, he watched with worried eyes as I backed out of the driveway.

After work, I suffered a miserable drive in traffic; the thought of Jordan waiting for me got me through it. When I finally arrived, he greeted me at the door, pulled me in for a hug, kissed my head and asked how work was. The next day, after my workout, I came to the bedroom to a warm shower waiting for me, folded towels, and brand new shampoo, conditioner and body wash sitting on the counter. Jordan was sitting up in bed, which was already made, sleepy and beautiful as ever. He told me the shower was ready for me. I wanted to crawl back into bed with him and kiss him again and again, tell him I was quitting my job and never going back.

That was every day.

I knew he wanted to make me feel comfortable, and at first, his kind gestures did the opposite. I felt bad, thinking he was going out of his way to do nice things for me. I wasn't used to being treated that way, especially not all the time.

But after a little while, I learned that this was just who he was. He would always have my showers ready, always make sure I was fed, always open doors for me, help me into the car, take my bags or anything I was holding so I wouldn't have to, carry me to bed from the couch if I fell asleep, buy me anything I wanted or needed. If my car were close to empty on gas, the next day, the tank would be full.

I was spoiled beyond belief, but if it made him happy, I wouldn't fight it.

My mom called me on Tuesday, apologizing for the way she and my father spoke to me. He called me a few days later, and I got a rare apology from him as well. They both told me they wanted me to come home, but neither pushed. We'd hung up on peaceful terms. After that, I regularly texted them to see how they were doing, and vice versa.

By the end of the month, I was happier than I'd ever been. With Jordan around, I didn't think I would ever be depressed again.

JORDAN

July

JORDAN

As the days got hotter, they got harder.
We were well into July, and the heat meant the need to wear less clothing. It was easier now than it had ever been to live in my skin, but there were still days I was uncomfortable in it.
I was pretty lean. I worked out six mornings out of the week. I ate relatively well, except for when Jordan was feeding me chicken tenders or pasta. Which he liked to do. Often.
I needed some new clothes, particularly a dress for my birthday, since Jordan told me we were going out somewhere nice. So I went shopping on the morning of the second Saturday in July, a week before my birthday. Summer was present; there was no time to waste. I needed a dress and couldn't sweat my days out in long-sleeved clothes at work.
I liked outlet stores. They had a variety of good clothes that didn't cost me hundreds of dollars.
Including shoes. My favorite.
I wanted a new pair of those for our birthday date, too.
I browsed the racks and texted Jordan while I did so, letting him know I was shopping. The night before, he'd kissed me to sleep and said he'd be at the office early today. When I asked him why he was working on a Saturday, he was apologetic, telling me there were just a few things that needed to get done, and he wouldn't be there long.
True to his word, he was out of the house at five a.m. this morning. Shortly after, I got up, looked up what clothing stores were open at seven a.m. and headed out myself.
I thought about his gorgeous face now, as I searched for short-sleeved shirts that were nice enough for work. Jordan responded quickly, saying,
Are you shopping alone?

JORDAN

The question was what my parents asked me often and immediately made me hesitant to respond. I felt like I was in trouble.

But I replied with the truth, because I never had to be afraid of Jordan. I was actually curious to see what he would say. I'd been noticing his growing protectiveness as the days went by.

He asked me where. I was about thirty minutes from the house.

I didn't want him to worry. When he texted back, *Is it busy over there?* I called him.

"Hi, sweetheart," I murmured, pushing through shirts on a circular rack. There was a red one that caught my eye.

"Hi, baby." I heard a little surprise in his voice.

I pictured him standing there, and wondered if he was trying to remain rational about my being alone. After all these years of seeing the things he saw at his job, he had to force himself to not assume everyone was going to torture and kill the people he loved.

"Hi, my love," I murmured cheerily. "How ya feelin'?"

Despite how seriously I believed he was worried, and how devastated it made me to think he was scared something would happen to me, I was so happy to hear his voice.

"I'm doing alright," he said lightly. "I'm sorry I left this morning before you woke up."

Aw. "That's okay, babe. I know you have work to do."

"We're going to spend the whole day together." I smiled. "How's shopping? Have you found anything you like?"

"A couple things, but I haven't tried anything on yet. You know, I often go into the dressing room with a hundred things and come out with zero. It is *not* easy for me to find clothes I like."

"Really? Hm." Jordan paused for a moment, and I anticipated he had more to say, so I waited. "I bet you look amazing in everything you try on, though."

That made me cheeky. "Thank you."

"What are you looking for?"

He was fishing for things he could buy me later on. *I know your game, boy.* "Well, I need some new shirts and pants. Also looking for a dress and new shoes for our date."

"Oh," he murmured, surprised. "You want to buy something new?"

"Yeah, I don't have much that's very exciting, and….I like taking the opportunity to shop."

He paused for a brief moment. When he spoke again, there was a smile in his voice. "Oh, honey. You don't need to do that...I didn't know you wanted something new. Let me get them for you."

A smile grew on my face. "No."

"Nina, it's your birthday. I can't live with myself, knowing you bought your own dress and shoes for our date when it's *your birthday.* I didn't even think you might do that. Let me."

My smile got even bigger. "No, love. Taking me out to who knows where and what it'll cost is more than enough." I immediately regretted sounding so ungracious and unappreciative. "Sorry, that was rude. You just do too much for me already."

"I do absolutely nothing."

I had to chuckle at the seriousness of his tone, because that was an outright lie.

"Jordan, come on."

"Nina, money is the least important thing in the world. It is nothing. You, however, you are everything. And you hardly let me do anything for you. Definitely not too much. It could never be too much."

"Now you're just spoiling me." I was cheesing it up like an idiot.

"Not even a little bit."

"You're so cute. And I love you so much. But I'm here right now, and I'm gonna get my stuff. I don't want you to worry about it. Okay?" I hesitated. "I don't want you to see my outfit until the day of."

After another brief pause, he murmured, "You got it, my love." And his voice was filled with adoration that made me feel full. "You're gonna look as amazing as you always do."

"Hopefully better." I chuckled. Before he could argue, I continued. "Anyway, I, uh, I just wanted to call you and see how you were doing."

"I'm doing well, baby," he said. "I wish I was with you, though."

Hm.

"How come?" I murmured. "Is it 'cause you miss me so much?" I smiled, but I was wondering if he would give me a full, honest answer.

"Yes," he replied right away. He didn't say anything about being sure I was safe, but instead repeated his earlier question. "Is it busy over there? You didn't say if you were with anyone."

"Yeah, pretty busy," I told him. "And no, I came by myself. I wish you were here, too."

"Do you want me to come?"

My eyebrows shot up in surprise. I didn't think he'd offer.

"Aw," I said. "I'd love that. But you're working, babe. Don't break out of your focus. You'll finish up and then we can hang out later."

"Yes." He sounded disgruntled. "Have you been there for a while?"

"No, I just got here a few minutes ago."

I figured he wasn't happy about that, though his voice was light when he said, "Okay. I want you to enjoy yourself. Take your time. Just do me a favor, honey, please."

"Yeah?"

"Call me when you walk out."

Ah. My suspicions were confirmed.

"Oh. Sure!" I kept my tone light. "Anything you want." I didn't question it.

I didn't want to make him feel he had to explain himself, but he did anyway. "I want to make sure you make it home safe."
I smiled small. "I know," I told him. "And I appreciate it. And I love you. So much." I kept my voice quiet.
"I love you, too," he said immediately.
"I'll talk to you soon," I told him. "Oh! Hey, what are we doing today?"
"Whatever you want to do."
"I just want to be with you. You know I'll pick staying home, and that has to get boring for you."
"It never does. I want to be with you, too. That's all I care about."
I smiled to myself. "Okay," I murmured shyly. He always put me in this shy, nerdy little mood with just about anything he said.
"What time you think you'll get home?"
"Twelve," he told me. "No later."
"How is work going?" I asked. I'd go home when he was free.
Jordan hesitated briefly, and then he said, "It's busy. Your call was the first break I've taken."
"Oh. I'm sorry I interrupted, Jord. But you have to take some breaks. Have you eaten?"
He paused. "Not yet. I will soon," he promised
"You have to, love," I said quietly. "Call me when you're on your way home so I can make sure I'm ready to do whatever we do. And be safe," I added.
I was nervous when Jordan went to work. I still suspected at least part of this cult remained nearby. He wasn't telling me much.
"I will."
I let him go, instantly missing him. I tried to focus on shopping, but the sudden edge in his voice when I mentioned work stressed me.
I tried to focus on filling my basket with different colored clothes and not so much black. Had to keep my mind off it until I got to him.
I found a couple of dresses that I was excited and apprehensive about. I'd never worn a dress in front of Jordan. He'd always asked if I wanted to go somewhere more upscale, and I told him upscale wasn't my style. So there was never a need to get this dressed up.
And it had been a long time since I'd worn a dress and heels. I hadn't seen what my body looked like in one in a while.
First, I tried on shirts and pants. I put a couple I liked to the side. Victory one.
When I finally got to the dresses, I was excited. I'd chosen five.
The first three were duds. One was blue but didn't fit right, another was long-sleeved and black but looked more granny-like than I anticipated, and the third was tan and showed every single line on my body.
No, thank you.

The fourth dress was nice, a long-sleeved, navy blue dress with thin fabric. It was just fitted enough that it showed my shape, hanging down to my knees. It was classy, with a crew neck and no cut-outs.

But the fifth one gave it a run for its money. This one was crimson, similar style, still form-fitting enough that I didn't look like a slob

It went down to my knees, which I always preferred. Anything too short wasn't my style.

I liked how they were both modest, but the crimson brought an even more elegant touch.

I stared at myself in the mirror for a long time, wondering what Jordan would think if he saw me in this.

Jordan was a modest man. I didn't know what *he'd* wear, and I made a mental note to ask him. But he told me that a dress would be fitting for this restaurant. When I inquired, he asked me again if I was sure I was comfortable with that dress code. I told him yes, that I was excited for the change of scenery. Excited to be surprised, and so grateful for him.

So it was at that point that he knew I would wear a dress. He didn't ask or tell me what style; when I asked him how modest I should be, he told me to wear whatever I wanted and not worry about that. I supposed he trusted that I wouldn't come in something closer to a bikini than a dress, since he knew me.

But I wasn't sure if he would see me and think I looked boring. I was worried.

I loved the dress though. Seeing myself in it made me realize I liked where my body was. I hadn't been paying much attention to it before.

I'd never worn anything skimpy around him, because I never did that at all. There was a nagging feeling somewhere that again made me wonder if I bored him.

I was uncertain sometimes that he thought I was attractive, because of how polite and respectful he was. I had to remind myself of how passionate he was the times when we'd kissed, the way he looked at me with those intense, wanting eyes, and that Jordan was just a reserved man.

I hoped wearing this dress would show me that he thought I was beautiful, not lame and too old-fashioned.

I swallowed, sad at the thought.

I wanted the dress. I made myself buy it. I had a long-sleeved, blue dress at home that would suffice in case I changed my mind.

Then, I gave myself the luxury of browsing the shoe racks, looking for some matching heels. It was definitely what I considered a good time. When I found some red pumps about three inches in height, nearly the same color as the dress and in *my size*, I fell in love.

I called Jordan on my way out.

"Jordy, I love shoes," I said immediately.

He chuckled. "Do you, love?"

"Yes. So much. There were so many."

"Did you get all the ones you liked?"
I sighed. "No. But I got one that I did."
"Travesty that you didn't let me get them all."
I laughed.
When I got home, three new shirts, a pair of leggings, dark red heels and a pretty, crimson dress in tow, I fell back onto our bed and let my thoughts wander.
Changing in the fitting room, after slipping off the dress, made me wonder even more if I was attractive to Jordan.
I didn't know generally what men liked. I didn't know if the truth was that most men liked curvy women, or skinny women, or if there were no "most" and that it depended on the man.
Logically, Nina.
But I grew up looking at thin women in magazines and on TV. Showing more skin than I ever had the courage to.
I went downstairs, settled into the family room, opened my laptop and wrote a short horror story, trying to wipe my insecurities out of my mind. A few minutes into writing, I thought to text my mom and dad.
Separately, because they wouldn't be honest with me about how they were doing, in the same chat.
After asking how they were, my mother responded,
Okay. How are you, my love?
and my father,
I'm good. How r u baby
I responded that I was good, and asked my mom why she was just "okay."
I completely lost the will to keep typing after reading her response.
Your father is being a menace today, as usual.
I was bummed. I asked her why.
It was the usual. She told me that he was snapping at everyone, in one of his bitter moods, and leaving her behind again to go out with his friends. Eventually, she decided she was being irresponsible.
I shouldn't even be telling you these things. I'm sorry, my love
I responded, *It's okay. You know you can tell me anything.*
When I finally heard the garage open, my heartbeat picked up. I stood and stretched and then went to greet Jordan at the door. I wanted to be close to him.
I noticed he was standing in the driveway and leaning against the truck, talking on his cellphone. Just the sight of him soothed me. I stood at the door for a few moments, waiting for him to finish up. I didn't want to be overbearing.
He looked at me in the doorway while listening to the person on the other end and moved in my direction, which made me braver. I went outside and wrapped my arms around his waist, unspeaking. I looked up at his face; his eyes were tired. His expression made me think for the second time that day

that he might be stressed out, though he smiled small at me and mouthed, "I'm sorry."

"Analyze the footage. We're done with the software for now."

Jordan hung up the phone. It was attractive to hear him give orders. But I put that thought aside, because his seriousness was worrying me.

"Is everything okay?" I asked softly, putting my hands on his cheeks. He leaned down and kissed me slowly. His lips were cold, despite the seventy-five degree weather.

When he pulled back, he murmured, "Yes." He took my face in his hands and put his forehead to mine.

When we finally pulled back, I assessed his eyes. Something was certainly bothering him.

"Let's go inside," I murmured. He nodded and grabbed my hand, leading the way.

"I was going to offer to go for a walk, since it's so beautiful outside, but my dumb self showered before you came home."

"You're not dumb," Jordan said.

I shrugged, feeling odd. The happiness from seeing him clashed strangely with the dejected feeling I had from knowing my parents were fighting, and that my mom was unhappy.

"I dunno. Hey, can we go to the store? I kinda want some pop. Maybe we can cook lunch."

The tiredness on Jordan's face cracked a little; he smiled small, seeming amused and charmed. "Of course we can."

His grin improved my funky mood a little bit.

"How's your day been?" he murmured. He put his arm around my waist and kissed my temple.

"It was good. I bought the things I needed at the store, which is good."

He nodded, opening the passenger door for me. "How about after?"

I shrugged again, still thinking of the texts with my parents, which seemed to have tainted my afternoon. "It was okay. I wrote for a little while. Just chilled a little."

Jordan eyed me, not closing my door. "How are you feeling, love?" he asked softly.

"I'm fine, how are you?"

He shook his head. "I'm good. You sure you're okay?" he murmured, reaching up and stroking my cheek.

I nodded. "Come in the car. We'll talk."

So he made his way around to the driver's side and hopped in, looking at me immediately and taking my hand.

"Is something wrong?" His face crinkled just slightly.

Those blue eyes were so hauntingly beautiful.

I admired them as I spoke. "No, I just...I'm kind of annoyed. I texted to check in on my parents, and my mom told me that they'd been fighting again." I rolled my eyes, trying to brush it off and be honest at the same time. "But I'm super happy now that you're here."

Jordan didn't seem convinced by my smile. He leaned in, gently kissed my lips and then my forehead.

"Do you want to tell me about it?"

"Nah, it was dumb." But I knew his worry was greater than he would show; he wouldn't press regardless. "They were just arguing, 'cause my dad is going out tonight, and he never hangs out with my mom."

I looked away. I couldn't trust myself to say the next part with a straight face.

"It makes me sad for her," I said quietly. The words alone flooded me with emotion. I swallowed and looked at my hand for a moment, trying to focus on gathering myself.

It wasn't fair that I was here, showered with love, and she was at home, unhappy and lonely.

Jordan put his hand on my cheek, and once I felt sure I wasn't at risk of crying, I looked at him.

His eyes were filled with concern, which I didn't want. He kissed my temple, keeping his face close to mine.

"I'm sorry, love," he said gently. "I'm sad for her, too."

I blinked, surprised. "Thanks for saying that."

He shook his head slightly. "I mean it. I don't wish those feelings on anyone."

I stared into his eyes for a few moments, happy he understood. Cared.

"Yeah." I let my mind space out to keep from getting sad again. "Me neither." I grabbed his hand, kissed the back of it, and reached for my seatbelt.

I took a deep breath as Jordan mimicked my movements, and it seemed he could tell I was done discussing it.

"It's okay," I exhaled. "Let's go get some pop."

His lips turned up slightly at the corners. He leaned in to kiss my lips softly before he started the car.

On the way to the store, I decided to poke around and see if he would tell me about work, concerned about the stress he wore.

"So, what was going on today at work?" I asked casually. "How is everything going? Are you busy?"

Jordan paused briefly. His face was serious, eyes getting a little far away. "It's very busy. This is such a complex case."

"Complex how? Apart from what I know?"

There were pauses before his replies. He thought, even only briefly, each time he spoke. "Many players in this game, we realized. We're trying to find the head honcho."

"So...are you close? How's...how's the software? Have you been working on it still?"

He shook his head a little. "Not really." He sighed. "We're making progress every day, but it's not fast enough. The software isn't getting better."
Not fast enough. It reminded me of the time he told me how he felt working for the FBI. Not moving fast enough. "Are they….have more girls gotten hurt?" I asked quietly.
Jordan looked at me, face slightly bleak. "Not yet."
But there was more. There was something he wasn't saying.
I didn't know how to ask *what* though, without directly accusing him. So I didn't. It was hard to keep pushing the issue, because he seemed so unhappy about it. And though I believed Jordan would never snap at me, I didn't want to take the risk of pressing until he wanted to.
At the store, I picked up a couple bottles of diet soda, different flavors, not sure which one I wanted.
"You don't want anything?" I asked him.
Jordan looked to his left at the stuff on the shelf and said, "No, I think I'm good."
"Did you eat?" I asked him.
He shook his head. "We need to get food. I'm assuming you didn't, either."
I wanted to frown, because he'd said he would eat and I didn't want him to make himself sick. But I couldn't be upset with him; he was busy and stressed and certainly just forgot.
I didn't respond to his assumption, because he worried I never ate enough, anyway.
"We're gonna cook!" I said sweetly, suddenly determined not to let the heavy things in our lives weigh us down today. Jordan smiled small.
"What do you wanna eat?"
I shrugged. "I dunno." I bounced away, looking up and down different shelves, trying to get ideas. I was determined to be cute enough to make him smile.
"What do *you* wanna eat, baby?" I asked lightly, smiling big.
He smiled back now, and I knew my charm was working. "I don't have a preference."
"Joooordaaan," I whined, turning back to the shelves and tried to think.
"Let's be healthy and have chicken and vegetables and whole wheat pasta."
I looked at him with my eyebrows up, waiting to see what he thought. He smiled.
"Sure."
"Does that sound good or are you just agreeing because you always agree?" I gave him a stern look that wouldn't frighten even a little puppy.
He chuckled. "It sounds good to me." He grabbed my hand. I smiled at his little laugh and then led us through the store to get what we needed.
I took all the bottles of soda, the vegetables, the whole wheat pasta and chicken breast to the counter and pulled out my wallet, but Jordan wrapped his arm around my shoulder, kissed my head and murmured, "Put that away."

I smiled. It was cute when he casually took over the situation, and me. He didn't get worked up or serious. Didn't move fast or aggressively. Just said to stop and slid his card out of his wallet, not in any rush, not panicking to stop me. I didn't even bother to argue. It was wildly attractive when he stepped in and took over.

When we got home, I got the chicken in the pan and Jordan moved it around as it cooked. I washed fresh vegetables and threw them in a roasting pan. Cooking together in the kitchen, quietly, peacefully, felt nice. I wondered if this were what it would be like if we were married. Cooking dinner together all the time.

Once the pasta was boiling, the chicken was cooking on the stove on low heat, and the vegetables were in the oven, we sat down in the nook to stay close to all of it. We held hands and looked at each other.

"I love you," I murmured suddenly, the words coming out of their own accord.

Jordan's lips turned up a little at the corners, and it only made him look more tired. He was not himself today. "I love you more."

It was killing me to see him so out of it. I got up from the kitchen chair and sat in his lap. *Risky, Nina.*

Oh well.

He wrapped his arms around my waist, and I wrapped mine around his neck as he tilted his head back to look at my face. I kissed his nose and got another small smile out of him

"Would you tell me if something was wrong?" I asked him quietly.

Jordan's smile slowly faded as his face turned serious. He finally said, "How do you mean?"

"If something was wrong. In life. At work. Between us. Would you tell me?"

He nodded, hesitating only a second before responding. "Of course. Is something wrong?"

I shook my head. "No. But you seem so tired today. And I'm sure you are; you've been working so hard. But you seem *wiped*. Like something is draining you mentally, too." I spoke quietly.

Jordan looked at me for a few moments, eyebrows slightly knitting together as he thought of how to respond.

"It's really just that the case is very difficult."

"Difficult how? Just in the tracking, or...?" I asked slowly. "Is there something in particular about this case that is unlike the rest?"

Jordan hesitated. "Yes."

I tilted my head to the side, waiting for more.

After a few more beats, Jordan murmured, "I think all of them are here. I just don't know where."

My eyes widened. I was right.

So it isn't just the software.

I thought of the day Jordan was late to our plans because he had to drive north to a crime scene. The blood.

"But it's okay," he murmured right away. "You're safe. Everything will be okay."

My eyes opened up a little. I wasn't even thinking about my safety. "I was more worried about you."

He shook his head a little, rubbing his hand up my back. "I'm okay, my love."

But I wasn't convinced. This solidified my fears from earlier, my anxiety, thinking of Jordan in danger. I felt a new uneasiness about going out alone. *No wonder he was so nervous this morning!*

I chose not to press further, putting my cheek down on his shoulder, wanting the contact badly. He continued moving his hand up and down my back and used the other to run his hand over my hair. The moment was nice.

We sat that way for a little while, commenting back and forth about little things. What exactly did I buy at the store today, the birthday outfit is a surprise, hopefully we don't burn the food, should we get up and check the pasta.

Eventually, we got up to see how everything was cooking. It took a little while, but we finally sat down to eat. I looked at Jordan, not saying anything as we ate.

I took in his beauty. As the sun set slowly, the light from outside burned through the window above the kitchen sink and gave his caramel skin a warmer tint. It contrasted beautifully with his casual, pastel blue long-sleeved shirt. His pale blue eyes gleamed past his low eyelids that never seemed to open up too much. His black hair, thick as ever, stuck out far, some tufts pointing their own way while the rest aimed upward.

He just looked so good.

Jordan asked me how work was going; I told him I wanted a raise, and that I was still looking for something else, in case my boss didn't agree to increase my pay.

"I already have things lined up for you, if you do leave," he told me.

"Jordan," I replied, surprised. "I told you, you didn't have to do that."

"You don't have to entertain any of them, but they are always available if you want them."

Oddly, I didn't know what to say. It was always like me to immediately deny help, but I didn't really feel like talking about it. I played with a piece of broccoli with my fork for a moment and muttered, "I want *you*," the words falling out of my mouth quietly.

After a moment, I lifted my eyes to his face, which brightened, eyes widening slightly. His lips turned up at the corners.

"Do you?" he murmured. His voice was calm, confident and *unbearably* attractive.

I clamped my lips together and just nodded, keeping my face serious.

JORDAN

Jordan smiled now. He didn't say anything for a moment, so I stood up and lifted my dish. He hadn't touched his food in five minutes.

"Are you done?" I asked quietly. He nodded, standing up and grabbing his own plate.

"I got it, Jord," I told him, grasping his dish in my hand and pulling it away from him. He let me. It was nice to do something for the gentleman for once, as little as it was.

He watched me begin to wash the plates.

"You don't have to," he started, but I immediately said, "How about you pack up the food and I do the dishes?"

Jordan raised an eyebrow. "Those aren't equal tasks."

I smiled a small smile. "You're ridiculous." I turned my face back to the sink.

After a moment, I felt him behind me, sliding his hand across my stomach to the left side of my waist.

Oh boy. My heart beat a little faster.

I stopped scrubbing for a moment and looked back and up to smile at him. He kissed my lips. My smile grew against his mouth.

He murmured, "I'll put the food away." Then, after lingering a moment, he walked away and pulled out containers to pack up the food. We worked in silence, but tension had filled the air.

Come on, Nina.

When the stuff was put away, I began washing the roasting and frying pans, and the pot. Jordan dried. We did this in silence as well.

Finally, when everything was finished, he grabbed my hand and led me into the family room.

"What do you wanna do?" he murmured, sitting down on the couch, lifting his feet up and then pulling me down onto him.

"Movie?" I suggested. We were both in quiet moods, and I thought that something mindless might be good for us.

And with the desire in the air, I wasn't quite sure what would happen next. We needed a distraction.

Jordan turned on the TV and scrolled through the horror movies. I was picky about which ones I chose. But after Jordan scrolled a few times, I picked something randomly. "That one," I told him, and he selected it, watching me, *knowing* my decision was much too quick.

He was right. I couldn't stop thinking about the way he came up behind me in the kitchen, wrapped his arm around me, stood up against me and kissed my lips. It wasn't like him.

And neither was the way he was looking at me since. Not with his usual smooth expression and assessing blue eyes.

Lustfully.

The movie started playing, but I turned my face towards his. I hadn't set my head down on his chest as I normally would've; I was too restless. I

looked at his eyes, he looked back, and then down at his lips a couple times. I couldn't stop myself. We leaned in and touched lips.
Slowly. As the moments passed, I lost more control.
Jordan pulled back suddenly and gently whispered, "Let's watch."
I exhaled hard, thanking God silently for blessing me with a man with more self-control than I had.
Despite having to fight the desire for him, I was happier. Initially, because I was realizing more and more that he *was* attracted to me. And then I realized, for the first time, I had a partner whose values aligned with mine. One who loved me enough to stop me when he knew we were getting into something I would regret.
"Thank you," I said, stroking his cheek. "I just want to say thank you."
He smiled back. "Why, love? I've done nothing."
"No, you keep us in check. And it's really, *really* helpful. I know it takes a lot of self-control. At least it does for me."
He nodded, chuckling. "It does take a lot of self-control. But for you, it's worth it."
I smiled bigger. "I just love you so much." He kissed my cheek and brought my head to his chest.
"I love you more."
I rubbed my hand up and down his torso, just happy to be touching him. To be close to him.
"That is so impossible that it's not even funny."
Later that night, my mom texted me about my birthday plans for next Saturday.
So I know you and Jordan are going on a date Saturday. Are you spending the whole day with him, are you gonna spend time with us at all...?
I'll be with you guys until mid-afternoon. Then I gotta go home and get ready for dinner.
Where are you guys going to eat again? she asked, and I was happy she was interested.
I truthfully do not know. He said it's a surprise.
Is it fancy? she asked. *I thought that's what you said.*
Yeah, I bought a dress. I hadn't sent a picture to her and Zana yet.
And new heels, I added.
What did you buy? Let me see.
I'm too tired to try it on now, but I promise I'll send a pic before we leave for dinner. Give you enough time to tell me if you hate it or not. I sent a laughing emoji, but I really did need her opinion. I was still worried about what Jordan would think.
And if my *mother* told me I looked boring, then I'd know for certain that I did.

JORDAN

On my birthday, I woke up at six a.m., unable to sleep. My plan was to run on the treadmill for thirty minutes, take a quick shower, throw on some comfy clothes and light makeup, and head to my parent's house.
But not before Jordan started my day, drowning me in love.
Rolling over in bed and squinting in the darkness, looking for even a shred of a sign that he was there, I found nothing. I reached over on either side of me, but no Jordan in sight.
Good. I decided to get up and brush my teeth as quickly as possible. I knew once he heard me, wherever he was, he would come up. I was certain his plan was to be there when I opened my eyes.
Oh well, Jordy. You're just gonna have to kiss me when my teeth are clean.
Just as I was rinsing, I heard movement in the bedroom. But instead of storming in the bathroom to greet me, he let me finish.
I love you, you perfect man.
I exited into the bedroom, workout clothes on.
To my surprise, he was waiting on the edge of the bed, facing the bathroom door. Doing nothing but sitting there, hands in his lap, waiting.
I wanted to tackle him, as lovingly as possible.
He probably wouldn't even move an inch.
A small smile grew slowly on his face as he caught sight of me.
"Hi," I said, feeling shy already, knowing his affection would be through the roof, more than it normally was.
"Hi, my love. Happy birthday," he said, and his sweet tone had me feeling weak already.
"Thank you." I walked up to him as he stood and approached me. Wrapping my arms around his waist, I tilted my face up for the kiss I'd been waiting for.

He didn't disappoint, taking my face in his hands and kissing me deeply. When he pulled back gently, keeping his face close to mine, he murmured, "How long have you been up?"

"I got up at six."

He looked up at the ceiling and sighed, the frustration with himself finally showing. But he was at ease.

"I was supposed to be right here when you woke up. I'm so sorry."

I smiled. "Stop. Don't be. It gave me a minute to freshen up before you saw me."

He raised an eyebrow, grinning. "You must not know how beautiful you are when you wake up."

I chuckled, because I didn't know what else to do. How did you respond to such a thing, when the person who says it is so sincere?

"Why didn't you sleep in a little, love?" His low, gentle voice made me want to crumble.

"Umm. Well, you know I'm going to my parents' house, but I wanted to do a quick workout first."

He shook his head. "Do you ever rest?"

I chuckled. "No."

His laugh was even sweeter. He was not expecting the honesty.

"Okay," he sighed, smiling beautifully. "When do you want your coffee?"

"After, my love." I rubbed my hands up and down his back.

I frowned suddenly. "I wish you could come to my parents' with me."

He kissed my forehead gently. "You're going to spend time with them, and then I get to have you the rest of the night. As much as I loathe it," he said, grinning, "I'll deal with it. It's only fair."

That made me feel a little better. I did miss my parents and siblings, and we had plans.

Before I made it to the basement, he stopped me on the first floor with gorgeous flowers and a box of chocolates.

"I'm assuming you won't eat a single chocolate now, will you?"

I threw my head back and laughed. "No, but I'll let you feed me one when I come back up." I raised an eyebrow seductively, desperate for another laugh from him. The sound and sight of it was just addictive.

He fed my addiction and laughed right back at me. "You better believe I will."

After I worked out, he called out to me from the library. He didn't approach me, because he knew I hated when he saw me sweaty.

What a guy.

"Hey baby," he called.

"Yeah?"

"Shower's running."

My smile was uncontrollable, even as I caught my breath.

When I stepped into the bathroom, my jaw dropped.

JORDAN

The normally clear vanity was loaded with expensive hair products. I noticed the two gallons of shampoo and conditioner, remembering telling him, a few weeks ago, that I needed so much conditioner to keep my hair from looking like a monster. "Two feet long." I'd chuckled. "I buy a new bottle every week."

I thought my face would get stuck in a smile, since it never seemed to go back to normal with Jordan around.

I wanted to go downstairs right away and tackle him with a hug, but I figured he would be happier to hear me rave about how good the shampoo and conditioner smelled.

And they did. The scent was sweet. After I finished showering and dried off, I could still smell it in my hair.

I dressed quickly, put on light makeup bounded down the stairs, finding Jordan waiting for me in the kitchen.

I didn't even say anything, just walked up to his smiling face and hugged him.

"Can you smell it?" I giggled.

"Smell what?" I pulled back and just looked at him. "Your hair? It smells amazing."

"Yeah, that would be because my boyfriend spoils me."

"Not nearly enough," he murmured, kissing my forehead. He reached behind him and grabbed two small boxes off the counter. Putting them in my hands, he said, "These are for you. There will be more later," he informed me, kissing my temple.

I took the boxes gently. "Jordan..." One was clearly the chocolates he mentioned earlier.

"What is this?" I finally spit out.

"You love chocolate," he murmured.

"And you want me to eat all the calories in the world," I commented, looking at the box of gourmet chocolates. I'd never heard of the brand.

He chuckled. "I hope you like them."

"I've never heard of this company. It looks *so* good."

"It's a store not too far away," he told me.

"A chocolate store?" I said in wonder. Some of my favorite things included bakeries, candy stores, and coffee shops, and Jordan knew this. He thought it was endearing. Especially the candy store.

"Mhm. I picked them out; there are different flavors. I know how you feel about variety."

He did. I *loved* it.

"You picked them out?" I asked, incredulous. My heart felt like it was going to burst as I pictured Jordan in a little gourmet chocolate shop, pointing to different flavored truffles and discussing what each one was like with a small, polite, middle-aged man behind the counter. Jordan would take as much care doing something like that as he would picking out a wedding ring.

Just the chocolates alone made me melt.

"You're so sweet. Jordan, I love this so much. Jordan," I repeated, unable to form any more normal sentences.

"Good," he said, his lips turning up at the corners and making me ache.

I leaned up and kissed his lips.

He kissed me back gently. When I pulled away, I lifted up the rectangular box. "What is this?" I asked quietly, turning solemn.

"A present," he told me, being coy in his quiet way.

I shook my head. I had to take it, regardless of my fear of what it was. I was so scared it was going to be something expensive, and considering it was in what looked like a necklace box, I was almost sure.

Opening the wrapping paper carefully and noting the black velvet box, I glanced up at him. "Jordan."

"Yes, angel," he said softly.

"I don't…" *Know what to say.* So I lifted the lid off the box and saw what looked like a diamond necklace with a cross.

"Jordan, what is this…Jordan.

"What…?" I shook my head, eyes wide. "This is so beautiful."

I wasn't crazy about jewelry, but the idea that he bought me a cross in respect of my faith touched my heart.

"These…please tell me these aren't…" I didn't want to say *real* and sound ungrateful, or even imply that he would buy fake diamonds. I didn't know if he would be offended.

But he knew. "They're diamonds," he said quietly. "I didn't know if you preferred those or gold, so I just hoped—"

"Jordan," I repeated for what felt like the hundredth time. "I cannot believe you bought…Jordan, this is too much, I…"

He took my cheek in his hand. "Remember what I always tell you about money?"

I knew if I didn't stop myself, I would start crying.

I leaned up and kissed his lips deeply. He kissed me back, and I felt so full. I didn't want to leave him.

I thanked him ten more times and ended up sinking myself into full-blown sadness at the thought of leaving him.

He turned and finished mixing my drink. I watched, still trying to believe that he was actually making me a latte.

He'd caught me hunting for an espresso machine on my phone one night, when my head was in his lap. He was supposed to be reading, but he noticed and asked me what I was looking for. Oblivious, I told him I wanted an espresso machine so I could make my own drinks and not buy them.

Two days later, I came down in the morning to Jordan setting up a giant espresso machine on the kitchen counter. It fit perfectly up against the wall, under the cabinets.

My jaw had dropped. I didn't know how I hadn't realized he would pull something like that.

We'd learned how to use it together. Then, he asked me to show him how I'd make my own lattes in the morning. Once I did that, he started making them for me. He loved doing it himself. I could tell by the way he grinned at my giddy face. It made me want to cry every time he handed me one, every time I caught him making it. I would never get used to his generosity, his selflessness.

He could barely finish this time, however, because I was all over him. Arms around his waist, stroking his cheek, grabbing his hands. He laughed at my affection and returned it.

I was procrastinating. I really, *really* did not want to leave him.

Finally, heading for the door, holding the latte he made me, I suddenly had an idea. I turned around.

"Hey, Jordy?" I started, setting my latte down on the counter.

He looked up, surprised. "Yeah, baby?"

I pursed my lips, considering it a little more.

Yeah. Solid idea. I nodded to myself.

"Is the restaurant closer to our house or my parents'?"

He blinked, wondering what I was getting at. "It's close to neither, but closer to your parents' house. We'll be heading that way when we go." Before I could even respond, he approached me, saying, "Do you want to go to dinner straight from your parents' house?"

I smiled. "You mind reader." I ran my hand over his hair. "If you don't mind dropping me off right now? I don't want you to go out of your way to take me if you have other things to do. It'll just save time." *And also, I'll get to spend nearly an hour more with you, in the car.*

He smiled. "No, that actually saves you driving time, and if you prefer it, then so do I."

I shook my head. *Always spoiling me. He'd let me get away with murder.* And staring up at his beautiful eyes, I had no doubt I'd do the same.

We arrived at eight. Only my mother was awake.
"Happy birthday, my love!" she said in her gushing tone, smiling hugely. Her cheeks were so cute when she smiled that way. She noticed Jordan behind me and gave him a hug as well.
"Thanks, ma," I told her as she leaned in to kiss my cheek, hold me tight, and say her infamous birthday line: "I can't believe my youngest is twenty-five."
I chuckled. "You say that on all our birthdays, you nerd."
"No, you're twenty-five. How is my daughter twenty-five when I'm only twenty-three?" She grinned.
I laughed again. "Oh, yeah?"
"Mhm. I didn't know Jordan was coming. I would've gotten you coffee, too." She frowned, looking at him.
He smiled. "No, don't worry about that. I'm only dropping her off for her family time."
"Why don't you stay?" she asked.
"Because I hog her all day long."
I grinned, remembering his earlier words. "He says it's only fair I come home and spend time with you guys." I rushed to add, "And obviously, I want to."
Jordan nodded and pulled me close. "I'll be back at five," he whispered, kissing my forehead.
After we'd said goodbye, I stared out the window, watching him drive away. I missed him already.
My mom saw me frowning a little. "The way you two love each other is precious."
My eyebrows rose in surprise. "What makes you say that?"

"How sad you are when he leaves," she chuckled.
I smiled. "Yeah, you're right."
"Why did he drop you off?"
"I asked him to, under the guise of saving driving time. The restaurant is closer to here than our house, so he agreed to bring me."
She raised an eyebrow. "Why did you really ask him to?"
I giggled. "Because I'm extra."
"What do you mean?" She smiled.
"Before we left, I ran upstairs and grabbed all my stuff to get ready here. I just...kind of want him to be surprised when he sees me all dolled up, you know? Maybe that's corny. Or vain."
First, she nodded in understanding, and then she shook her head. "It's not corny or vain. Do you guys not go to high-end restaurants?"
I shook my head. "I'm not into it. You know that."
She nodded again. "I see. Well, that was sneaky and not a bad idea."
I chuckled. "I just hope he didn't catch on. You might not think I'm corny or self-absorbed, but maybe he will."
"Oh, Nina," she said, snorting. "You have no idea how that man looks at you. It's like you could do no wrong in his eyes."
My eyes widened. "I *know*! He seriously spoils me, mom."
We entered the kitchen, and I noticed that the table in the nook was clean and cleared except for a frozen coffee from Marinette's and a bouquet of flowers. She'd had the coffee drenched in caramel, the way I liked.
"Those are for youuuu," she informed me happily.
I addressed the coffee first. "Oh, mom, no," I whined, grinning. I didn't know how I could consume that much sugar in the morning when I had a fitted dress to wear later.
"You know I can't resist these, and I'm going to be wearing a dress later; it's going to make me feel so fat."
She shook her head. "That's ridiculous. Just drink it and live a little. You hardly eat, anyway. You're not going to get fat off of a frozen coffee," she said, in her *Duh* tone.
I frowned, staring at it. The dilemma of lingering eating issues and a mouthwatering, sugary, caffeinated drink in the morning.
"I had them put extra espresso in it, so you'd at least have the extra energy, the way you like."
I rarely ever got just plain vanilla drinks, hot chocolate or anything decaf. I couldn't justify drinking so much sugar if there wasn't at least the benefit of the energy from the caffeine.
On my birthday, however, I indulged. There was no way around it. I was a fiend for sugary coffee drinks.
But sugar tended to weigh me down, mentally, more than anything, and that made me sluggish.
"Okay, I'll drink as much as I can. Jordan *did* already make me a latte." I grabbed the flowers.

"These are gorgeous. I love them!"
I wanted her to feel good about the gifts, and hoped she hadn't gone out and bought me something more expensive, as she usually did. "Thank you so much."
"You're welcome, my love. Did you just say Jordan *made* you a latte?"
I laughed.
Sitting at the table and sipping the cold drink, I confessed, "I'm so antsy for this date."
"Why are you antsy, honey? You're gonna have so much fun. Jordan wants to take you out and treat you to a nice dinner. Let him. Go, enjoy yourself. You deserve to be spoiled a little, and treated well."
My face fell. Her words made me more sad than happy.
I wished my dad did those things for her.
"I appreciate that, mom."
I didn't want to tell her the thoughts running through my head and make her sad. She would tell me not to worry about it, that she was used to it. And that would just make me feel worse.
"He's just so nice to me," I admitted, and I knew that would make her feel good. "I meant it when I said he spoils me. Did you know, basically from day one, he told me his home was mine?" I shook my head.
"Aw. That's so sweet. I'm not surprised, though. Anyone could see how into you he was back when he came over."
I smiled at the memory, wondering how things could have changed so much since then.
Again, I thought about the dress and wanted to put it on. I looked up at her, pondering about if I should do my hair before or after breakfast.
"I'm really happy you found someone like him," she said seriously.
I smiled. "Me too. You'll never believe what he gave me already."
I told her about the chocolates, hair products, and the diamond cross.
"A *diamond* cross?"
"Yeah." I stared off, thinking about him. "I'll show it to you. I have it with me."
About an hour passed before Zana came down. Finally, my father, with Elijah trailing behind a few minutes later.
It was eleven by the time everyone was together.
My father wrapped his arm around me and kissed my cheek, and they all said their 'Happy Birthday's.'
"Thanks, guys."
"So, is everyone ready to go?" my mother asked, now that everyone was in the room. We were going to breakfast.
"You seem like you're in a rush, mom," Zana said. "How come?"
"Nina has a date with Jordan, remember? And you guys still have your nail appointment."
Understanding filled her face. "Ohh. You're right."

"She has to be ready by five. We want to give her...what do you think Nina, an hour to get ready?"

"Uh," I thought for a moment. "No, I need at least two."

Elijah rolled his eyes. "Where are you going?"

"Out to eat," my mother answered for me. I'd begun to think that she was more excited for me than I realized. Our chatting about all he did and said to and for me seemed to have persuaded her I hit the jackpot.

She must have already known that, Nina. Look at him.

"At McDonald's?" Elijah joked, grinning.

"Aw, yeah, for sure," I told him, rolling my eyes and smiling. "Let's get out of here."

When we arrived at the restaurant, each one of them asked me what I was going to eat.

"I don't know, guys," I chuckled. "Something light."

"Enjoy yourself, Neen," my mom said.

"*Live* a little!" Elijah scolded. I laughed.

But none of them pushed me too hard, or complained when I ordered an omelet instead of pancakes or something sweet. They knew how I was when it came to food. It could affect my mood.

Breakfast was lovely. Everyone seemed happy today, getting along and teasing one another. They prodded for some details about Jordan, Zana in particular, but I whispered to her that I would tell her everything at the salon.

We went back to the house, and Zana and I immediately left for the salon. She drove.

I was happy to do my nails for once, usually not wasting the time or money on it just to go through the annoyance of the nail polish chipping off.

But tonight, I wanted to feel extra good.

I decided to get a pedicure and a manicure and went for a simple, light pink polish.

"So," Zana began, sitting next to me as we got our nails fixed up. "How are things with you and Jordan?"

"Things are good," I told her happily. "I'm really excited for later."

"Yeah," she said, looking at her hands as the nail technician worked. Then she surprised me. "I'm happy one of us gets to go on a special date."

"You'll meet someone, too, Zane. In God's time."

"Yeah, you're right." She glanced over at my nails then eyed me sideways.

"What?" I looked at her suspiciously.

"Well, there *is* this cute guy that started working next to my office..." She grinned.

My eyes widened. "Are you serious? Why didn't you tell me? Have you talked to him?"

We chit chatted about how things were going for her at work, this new guy she met, and how things were at the house.

Then, she asked me, "Are you nervous for later?"

"Yeah," I admitted. "I hope he likes the look and everything. I don't really go to fancy restaurants, and I wanted to be sure it was appropriate. But like...Jordan would *never* tell me to not wear something. So if, for example, I had too much cleavage and he was embarrassed, he wouldn't say it, you know what I mean?"

"Well, *is* there too much cleavage?"

I shook my head. "No, no. Just an example. Actually, I've been kinda worried he thinks I'm boring," I said, trying to keep my tone lighthearted.

She blinked. "Why? Has he said something to you?"

She was ready to fight in a heartbeat.

I smiled. "No, no, he hasn't. You know I'm just, like...I cover up."

She wasn't having that as an answer. "Does he not kiss you or anything?"

I shook my head again. "No, he does; he definitely does. The...chemistry is there. I'm just insecure."

"Honestly, Neen. Jordan seems like the kind of person who *prefers* somebody dresses more...modestly."

I nodded. "Yeah, I'm sure you're right. But as I said, he wouldn't ever tell me what to or not to wear."

"What did you buy?"

"It's a fitted, dark red dress. It's really, really pretty. It goes down to my knees."

"Does it have a sweetheart neckline? Is it short-sleeved?" she asked.

"No, it's like a crewneck. And it's long-sleeved. You'll see later."

"I'm sure you're gonna look really good," Zana said. "Mom was telling me on the way home how in love with you he is."

I laughed. We'd taken two separate cars to the restaurant. I'd ridden in the car with Elijah and my dad.

"That's so cute. Yeah, he definitely loves me. Not sure why," I half-joked.

She rolled her eyes. "Stop it. You gotta stop putting yourself down."

I raised my eyebrows in surprise. "I don't, really."

"Okay, good. But I mean...with the attraction thing. You said you're worried he thinks you're boring. Stop thinking like that, too. It's not just *saying* it that's detrimental to you. *Thinking* it is bad, too."

"Yeah, you're one-hundred percent right."

She nodded. "So, what do you guys *do* when you hang out? Like, you're together all the time. But what do you *do*? Do you watch TV, do you play games, what?"

I chuckled at the thought of Jordan and I playing games.

"We literally just talk. We'll watch movies and stuff. When we don't go out to eat."

"Yeah, I mean when you're at his house."

"We talk, watch movies. Last Saturday, we cooked lunch together; we went shopping for the ingredients and everything. Then we ate and cleaned up together. Then we went to sleep."

My nails were painted, the technician sliding on the top coat. Zana's were done, too, so we stood and went to the UV drying station, in the center of the salon, to let them dry. Our toes were already done.
"That's it?" Zana said, her voice flat. "You just fell asleep?"
"Yes. He put on a movie, but we didn't watch it. We were tired. He was *so* tired," I murmured, staring at my hands, purple under the ultraviolet light in the table.
"Work is hard for him right now."
"Why, what's going on? What does he do again? Internet crime?"
"Yeah. Cybercrime. His company is full of super smart people who are good with technology. Computers. They hunt down criminals."
"So what's going on, then?"
"Well," I hesitated, not wanting to put his business out there. I figured the generalities were innocent. "They're just having a hard time on a case. That's all. And he was so tired." My face went soft, my eyebrows knitting together slightly. "It made me so sad."
"That he was tired?"
"Yeah, 'cause Jord isn't usually. He's always just...fine. I'm not trying to make him seem like a robot, but literally nothing is ever wrong with him. So he's either super good at hiding his emotions, or things just don't really bother him. I know it's usually the latter. Or maybe both?
"But he can't hide the tiredness on his face, you know?" I asked, staring off across the room. Eventually, I broke out of my trance and turned to Zana. "So he was really tired. He fell asleep so easily."
I smiled. "It was so cute."
"Do you sleep in his bed?" she asked curiously.
"Yeah, I do. Nothing freaky, though," I smiled.
She couldn't help but grin. "I wanted to ask, but didn't want to ask."
I laughed quietly. "No, no. You know I'm not."
"Well," she replied, tilting her head to the side. "The reason I was wondering was because of what you said earlier. Like, you're worried he thinks you're boring."
I nodded, seeing what she was implying.
The same question I'd had. Was he even really attracted to me?
"I got you. Yeah, no. He is into me that way. I can tell just by kissing him. If you know what I mean."
She thought for a moment, then nodded. "So stop worrying about it, then," she repeated.
Zana's words helped with that insecurity a little bit. It made me less worried and more excited to go home and get ready.
When our nails were dry, I felt even better. The pink on my little nails and skinny fingers looked nice.
After we went home, she asked, "Why did you decide to get ready here?"
I informed her of my intentions, and she nodded. "Well, let me help you with your makeup."

I took a quick shower. When that was done, I grabbed the blow dryer and dried my hair completely before straightening it with a flat iron. I was pleased to see it fell down to my tailbone.

Then, Zana helped me with my makeup. As simple as it could be for a formal outing, with foundation, blush, and the lightest tan eyeshadow, accented with mascara. I preferred it that way. Simple.

The time finally came to get dressed. I glanced at the clock. It was four-forty.

I took a deep breath and exhaled hard, then slid on the red dress. I couldn't wear Spanx, in fear Jordan would somehow see them.

I was happy with the way my body looked in the fitted dress and no Spanx. Relief flooded through me. I had been so worried I would hate how I looked in it after a week, thinking maybe my makeup would look off, or my hair, and that would change how I felt about the dress. Or how I looked altogether.

I slid on my new red heels and assessed myself. Then, I grabbed the final touch out of my bag and hooked it around my neck. It looked beautiful, the bright silver standing out against the deep red of my dress.

Taking one last deep breath, I grabbed my phone and my bag. It was four fifty-five by the time I'd stopped assessing myself in the mirror.

I opened the door to the bathroom where I'd gotten dressed, heels clanking against the foyer tile. I walked quickly to the kitchen, not wanting to be near the front windows when he pulled in.

"How does it look?" I asked my mom.

Her eyes widened, and I knew she was being half dramatic and half serious. "Wow, Nina. You look beautiful!" She and the rest of my family all eyed me up and down. To my great surprise, my father was smiling.

"You look good, girl!" He beamed, and I laughed in complete disbelief.

"Thanks, dad," I told him, squeezing his arm for a second. Then I quickly walked back to the foyer. I would wait there.

My sister and mother followed, and even Elijah came over. They continued assessing me in awe. It made me feel good, though I was so nervous for Jordan to see me. None of them even stepped forward to adjust anything on me, so I knew I'd done a good job.

"He's here," Elijah said, looking out the window. "Man, I thought you said he had a truck."

I chuckled nervously. "He knows I'll be in heels. Okay, guys, I'll see you later."

"Don't you wanna wait for him to come to the door?" my mom asked.

"I'll meet him on the porch." I grinned, pulling open the front door. I knew they would watch, but I didn't want them to be in such close proximity when Jordan first saw me. They could stay inside.

Jordan was halfway up the walkway to the door when I stepped out. I'd forgotten to ask him what he was going to wear, and it made seeing him even better.

He donned a well-fitted, white dress shirt, a black blazer and black slacks. Not a full-blown tuxedo, but very sharp.
He looked so good I nearly toppled over.
Slowing his pace as his eyes landed on me, I watched them grow wider as they took me in, his face stunned.
Jordan's mouth was slightly open, his eyes intense. His awestruck reaction was sincere; I would've been embarrassed if it was fake. He looked me up and down.
"Nina," he said softly, his voice full of awe as I stepped down from the porch and he took my hand to help me. He shook his head slightly.
"You look…" He kept his voice low. "You are so beautiful."
I smiled shyly, so relieved.
"You are absolutely breathtaking," he breathed, leaning down and gently kissing my lips.
"Is it rude for me to touch?" he asked quietly, lifting one hand up to my hair. My eyes opened up in surprise.
"No, of course not," I told him softly.
So he gently touched a strand of my hair, running his fingers all the way down to the tips.
"I've never seen your hair straight," he murmured.
"Yeah, I don't do it too often." I hesitated. "Do you like it? I prefer to keep it natural, but…"
"Then why don't you?" he asked gently.
I shook my head. "I like both, but sometimes I just wanna do this, you know?"
He nodded. "I love it, baby. It's beautiful. Both ways."
He continued looking at me in wonder. "You're wearing the necklace," he noticed, his voice even softer, pitch getting higher with joy. The happiness that filled his face made me ache. I knew putting on the cross he'd bought me was the perfect way to show him how much I loved it.
"I love it so much," I told him quietly.
The sincerity of his smile was thrilling. I wrapped my arms around his neck and kissed him.
He pulled back as my family stood around the door, trying not to congregate. Zana just peeked out from the sides.
"Hi, everyone," he said, glancing up rather quickly to address them. He brought his slightly amused eyes back down.
"Hi, Jordan," my mother said from the doorway, smiling. I could tell this moment pleased her.
"Let me know if she gives you trouble," she teased.
He glanced back up. "She's never trouble," he said kindly, smiling at her, kissing my temple.
My father surprised me again by coming to the doorway.
Ah, shoot. I was hoping he didn't say something embarrassing.
This wasn't prom, and their curiosity was already too much.

"Just keep her safe," he said quietly to Jordan.//
I exhaled. That wasn't too bad.//
"I will," Jordan assured him quietly, confidently, his face and eyes calm but serious. Never overcompensating. He locked eyes with my father as he spoke slowly. "Always."//
I turned to see my dad nod, and then I grabbed Jordan's hand.//
"Are you ready, my love?" he murmured.//
I nodded. "Mhm. Bye, guys," I said to my family.//
"Bye!"//
Jordan opened the door to the Lexus so I could slide in. "Thank you," I murmured shyly.//
When he got in, he leaned towards me and kissed my lips gently. "No thank you's."//
I smiled. "You look absolutely…perfect," I told him.//
His lips turned up. "Thank you, my love." He shook his head as he backed out of the driveway. "But you are the stunning one. You are unbelievably gorgeous, Nina."//
My smile grew as big as it possibly could. "Thank you," I repeated shyly, breaking his rule. I took his hand and kissed the back of it. "I'm always gonna thank you," I added.//
He just smiled, lacing his fingers through mine. I noticed him glance at my nails.//
"Yeah," I said, suddenly a little embarrassed. "I know I don't usually do my nails, but Zana wanted to go, and I just wanted to be as nice as possible for this…" I hesitated, the corner of my lips turning up on one side. "For you."//
His face softened again. "Honey, you are the most beautiful thing I've ever laid eyes on."//
I looked down, unable to meet his eyes after his kind words.//
"Have you eaten?" he asked me.//
"Yeah, at breakfast."//
His eyes widened some. "Nothing since then? What time was that?"//
"Maybe…ten-thirty?"//
"Oh, love. We've gotta get some food in you."//
I nodded, not wanting to disappoint him.//
We drove for about an hour and fifteen minutes, Jordan apologizing that it was so far, telling me he wished he'd picked something closer so I could eat sooner. I told him not to worry.//
I was surprised by the fact that we were surrounded by trees, driving on a narrow road in a place I'd never been. I was so curious as to where we were going. It was getting dark, which made the vibe better for me. I liked the thrill of being in a new place at night with him.//
He was safe.//
We turned onto a slightly winding, steep, one-way road surrounded by grass. There were no houses or buildings nearby.

JORDAN

The road was long. Eventually, I spotted the shape of a large building. As we got closer, I noticed that the road that was more like a trail, with only room for one car coming one way, continued past the side of the building. My jaw dropped.

Settled on grass, its walls were made of different colored stone. The building itself was short except for the two towers that stuck up out of it. Steep, first-floor overhang in various sections made the building's height dynamic captivating. It grew in height as the second story further back came to view. The dark gray shingles contrasted the stone, making the place look more rustic.

On the far left was a beautiful garden, bordered by a stone gate. It was breathtaking.

Perhaps the loveliest part to me were the scattered walls covered in moss, accenting the building.

We were on the driveway to what looked like a giant, gorgeous, rustic restaurant on a farm.

Jordan slowed down on the path as I absorbed the sight in front of me.

After he parked, he moved quickly around the car to open my door, holding his hand out for me to take as we stood next to the forest that bordered the driveway. After he gently helped me out, we walked towards the front door of the beautiful rustic building.

"Jordan...what—?" For the second time that day, I was speechless. He held my hand and gently guided me around the car, where I noticed a walkway. The path took us to the center of the building, whose front doors were like sliding, wooden barn doors. The gorgeous bushes that lined the walls, the flowers that grew down the path, were breathtaking.

"Jordan, oh my goodness," I murmured quietly in awe.

His lips turned up at the corners, his heavy eyelids hanging over those gorgeous blue eyes.

"What do you think?" he asked me softly.

"It's...I don't even know what to say yet. Just give me a minute." I chuckled breathlessly.

He released such a happy, quiet laugh, and the genuine smile on his face on top of it made my knees nearly buckle.

I still couldn't believe how happy he was to see me happy.

Opening the door for me, Jordan followed me inside and put his hand lightly on my lower back as we walked through a stunning, elegant inside.

I was surprised to see the white tablecloth-covered tables empty.

"Where is everybody?" I asked in wonder.

"It's ours for the night." He smiled.

My jaw dropped. "Jordan, you're not actually serious, are you?"

He just kept smiling at me, the tiniest bit of amusement in his eyes, drowning in the fondness he often had when he looked at me.

"Oh my goodness," I burst.

"Welcome," a calm voice said. I looked to our left and met the eyes of an older man dressed in a dark blue suit.

"Hi, Lenard," Jordan said. I tried to keep my jaw closed, but it wanted to drop again.

Jordan just *knew* the people at this fancy restaurant, in the middle of nowhere, stunning and rustic and probably costing thousands of dollars for its guests each time they had a meal here.

"This is Nina," he introduced. "Nina, Lenard is the owner of this restaurant," he told me, barely sparing the man a glance. He didn't seem to care at all *what* Lenard was.

"It's nice to meet you," I said, trying to contain my wonder. I didn't extend my hand.

"And you as well," the man said, his voice low. "Right this way."

"Jordan," he said, as he guided us through the dimly lit restaurant. "Did you decide on seating?"

"Nina," Jordan murmured, instead of responding to Lenard. "Is eating outside alright?"

My eyes widened. "Of course it is. That sounds lovely."

After we rounded a corner, Lenard led us to an exit.

I couldn't believe my eyes.

The stone pathway broke apart when it hit the edge of the grass. It continued in large, asymmetrical circles.

Large candles bordered the trail every few feet, lighting up the patio gorgeously. It led us to a canopy standing on white pillars. Underneath was a small, dark wooden table and two wooden chairs with soft, plush seats.

String lights draped from the ceiling, as well as two huge flower baskets with warm pink geraniums poking out of the leaves. Surrounding the canopy were large stones that stood at the height of the hill where the forest trees began, a few yards back.

All around us was a garden.

"Gerard will be out shortly," Lenard told us, saying no more before retreating into the building.

Once he was gone, Jordan held my hand until I was seated comfortably. Then, he sat across from me.

"This might be the most beautiful thing I've ever seen in my life," I told him breathlessly.

The smile that grew on his face definitely made that statement untrue.

"That's what I've been thinking ever since I saw you," he murmured. It didn't even sound like a corny, stupid compliment. He was completely serious, and it made my heart skip.

"I mean that," he murmured. "Except not 'might.' I know."

I smiled slowly. "I was taking it back in my head when you smiled."

And he did, again. The flirting made me feel light.

"Jordan, I don't know how to thank you for this."

"Good. I don't want you to."

JORDAN

I laughed breathlessly, and in turn he chuckled.
He reached across the table and laced his fingers through mine on one hand, gesturing to the menu in front of me with the other.
"What would you like to eat, my love?"
I shook my head, finally feeling hunger hit me. "Umm," I glanced down.
I expected there to be steak and fancy raw fish dishes that I didn't want to eat, but the list of options was surprisingly appetizing.
Right in the center of the menu was my favorite food.
"Pasta," I said, grinning. Jordan hadn't stopped smiling, I presumed, waiting for me to notice, and it made my heart feel so full.
"Perfect."
Another older man came down the path, dressed in wait staff attire more formal than I was used to seeing.
"Hello," the man I presumed was Gerard said politely.
"Hi, Gerard," Jordan replied, barely sparing him a glance. The smile never left his face.
"Hi," I said politely.
Gerard set down two waters in deep wine glasses. "What can I get for you two to start?"
"My love?" Jordan murmured, his affection making me dizzy.
"This water is fine," I said quietly, smiling.
"Gerard, we'll both have pasta," he told him. I smiled.
Our polite waiter nodded. "It will be out, fresh, soon."
When he walked away, I could stare at Jordan in peace.
The jacket was sharp, his tawny skin looked extra beautiful under the lights, and his pale blue eyes were making me lightheaded again.
I felt elegant in my dress, and the way he was looking at me made me feel beautiful, too.
"Nina," he began, "I'm so happy you agreed to come here with me."
I shook my head. "*You* are? Jordan, this is all incredible. You have made my day amazing." I squeezed his hand.
His smile grew. "That's the best thing you could've said," he murmured quietly, rubbing his thumb across my own.
I brought his hand to my lips and kissed it. "I love you."
Jordan's eyes lit up. "I love you more."
I stared at him lovingly. This moment was incredible.
Unfortunately, the lightheadedness was getting worse. I blinked a couple times, trying to make the feeling go away.
"Are you alright, my love?" he asked, concern filling his eyes.
"Yeah, yeah, I'm okay," I assured him. "Just….a little lightheaded." I knew he was going to get worried, but I'd be fine once I had some food in me.
"Oh, no, honey. Are you okay?" He started to get up.
"No, no, Jord, I'm okay, I swear. I just went a little too long without eating."
"I'm going to tell them to put a rush on it."

I shook my head. "No, please, please. It's okay. I'm just gonna sip some water. That's definitely part of it. I'm probably dehydrated."

"What have you eaten today?" He was so worried; it made me feel bad.

"I had half that drink and an omelet." His eyes widened when I stopped after that. I grimaced. "Don't be mad at me; I just couldn't eat."

"Why would I be mad at you, honey?" He leaned over the table and kissed my forehead. "I'm just worried about you, never mad."

He tilted his forehead down to mine. "You gotta eat now, okay?" I nodded. "I know," I told him softly.

His concern was truly touching.

"Why did you eat so little, my love?" he asked me gently as he sat back down.

"Because I didn't have much of an appetite." I hesitated. "And...I just...it's hard for me to eat before an event. Especially when I know I'm gonna be wearing something nice," I confessed.

Jordan's eyebrows were knitted together. "Why, honey?"

"It's...it's just one of those psychological things. I...if I eat sweets, for example, I feel gross sometimes. Bigger. It's mental; it's not reality. I obviously know that I don't gain weight immediately after I eat something sugary, or carbs, but it's just what happens. I start to feel bad.

"So..." I struggled to think of how to say it. "I didn't want to eat something, or eat too much, because I knew it might make it hard to put this dress on." I finished my explanation quietly. I knew he was going to feel bad for it.

"Nina," he started.

"But it's not too bad," I insisted. "I'm so happy to be here, and to wear this, like I've been so excited to dress up and go out with you, and—"

"I don't want you to not eat," he said gently, though his voice was adamant.

I sighed. "I know, but it isn't because of this," I gestured around us. "It's my own personal...issue." I tapped my head. "It's a body thing."

He brought my hand to his lips once more. He looked so beautiful, sitting there in his sharp outfit, his hair as thick as ever but smoother tonight, not as many tufts sticking out.

"A body thing, meaning one of your struggles with your appearance," he clarified, his voice gentle still. I nodded.

"I understand." He reached across the table this time and stroked my cheek with the backs of his fingers. "I need you to tell me how I can help you," he said. "I don't ever want you not to eat because it's going to make you feel bad about yourself. If I'd known that wearing a dress was that hard for you, I would've told you not to." He sounded regretful, frustrated with himself.

"No, love, no." I shook my head. "It's okay. It's...how I've always been. I'm a lot better now," I assured him. "It's just...today I was extra excited, and my appetite truly wasn't there. That was the bigger thing, I promise. If I was hungry, I would've eaten. I'm not nearly as bad as I used to be. I would've been able to put those thoughts to the side and gotten dressed

anyway. It just might've been a teeny bit harder. But I think today...today I was all over the place and didn't want to risk messing up my mindset."
"All over the place?" His eyebrows were still knitted together slightly. "Do you mean emotionally?"
I nodded. "Yeah, like...I was just...I've just been so excited, and..." I looked off to the side, sighing. "This night is really special to me. I don't...I don't know how to say this without feeling so embarrassed."
Jordan was confused, his eyes widening. "What do you mean? Talk to me, love. Don't be embarrassed."
I looked at our hands. "I've never really had a date like this." I flicked my eyes past his shoulder. "My ex never brought me out to places like this. He could afford it, but for some reason he never did. And..."
He tightened his grip on our laced fingers. His eyes were encouraging.
"I don't know." I closed my eyes slowly, pausing just a moment to conjure up the strength to say this. "I don't know if...I think the insecure part of me always wondered if it was because I wasn't...sexy enough for him. Like he didn't want to show me off. Rather, hide me...I guess."
"Oh, my love," he murmured, kissing my hand again. I finally met his eyes. Gentle with me, angry at my words.
"That can't have been the case. He must have had other idiotic reasons, but it couldn't have been that. How could you think that? Do you think you're not beautiful?"
I shrugged a little. "No, no. I just...he cheated on me. I figured I bored him. I wondered if maybe...I was worried the way I dressed would bore you." I grimaced again.
Jordan's eyebrows smoothed out and went up in a silent anger that you could only see in his eyes.
"*Never*. You couldn't possibly bore anyone," he began, voice low. "The person you used to date just so happens to be a *vile* one. That doesn't make you boring. He didn't know what to do when he couldn't have you, so he sought out satisfaction somewhere else."
I swallowed.
"And I promise you, Nina," he said, eyes burning into me. He was *serious*. "He didn't find it."
My jaw dropped a little. The seriousness in me dissolved slowly. I actually smiled.
"You..." I began. "You are the sweetest...I just—"
My quiet laugh was breathless. I couldn't say anymore.
"You're so beautiful, Nina." His expression lightened. "I'm never gonna let you forget it."
My grin was at its peak. He went on.
"It means so much to me to be the first person to do this." His smile was sincere and gentle.
I looked down shyly, unable to meet his eyes again.
"I hope I'm the last."

My head snapped up.
What?!
I swallowed. I didn't know what else to say other than, "Me, too." My voice was weak.
"Yeah?"
"Yeah."
His smile made me dizzier.
The rest of dinner went by beautifully. Our conversations about my body issues, insecurities and ex-boyfriend didn't throw us off even a little. After his comment about wanting to be my last love, we went right back to our flirting, our laughing, our incessant smiling. The joy from the night couldn't be tainted.
The pasta was divine. I knew I was hungry, but I could tell despite that. When I sat back and told him I was absolutely stuffed and beyond satisfied, he smiled. I didn't know how he signaled to Gerald to bring out an adorable mini cake with a single candle in it.
"I'm not much of a singer." He grinned. "But if you asked me to—"
"No, I love you so much, you don't have to." I took his hand and kissed it, unable to conceal my joy as I laughed.
He chuckled. "I figured I wouldn't embarrass you."
"You could never. I bet you can sing happy birthday in ten languages."
"No, not ten." He grinned.
"Not, *feliz cumpleaños*, no *bon anniversaire*?" The grin slid off his face.
"You know French and Spanish?" he asked, stunned.
I smiled. "It's not that impressive. I studied romance languages for a long time. English was my major, but I have a serious thing for foreign languages."
Jordan's smile was fond, his eyes enchanted. "I didn't know that. That's incredible. Do you *speak* any…?"
"A lot of Spanish, half as much French and Italian. I always planned on studying them when I had more time. Arabic, too."
"I can help you with that one." His smile was beautiful. I thought of how melodic he sounded when he spoke in Arabic. I almost shivered.
"You'll have to help me with French," he murmured. "When we go to France."
My eyebrows shot up. "You wanna go to France?"
"Yes. Of course, only if you do. There's a quiet little village there I think you'll like."
"You've been, I'm assuming?"
He smiled. "Twice."
I smiled back, not knowing what to say. I pictured holding Jordan's hand and shopping in a quiet village in France, ordering for us at the café. It was a lovely thought.

"There are more places I'd like to go with you," he said quietly. "If you're interested in traveling. You...told me at the library that there aren't many places you've been. I'd like to change that."

I couldn't wipe the smile off my face, even if I tried. I remembered that day at the library and was touched that he did too, down to the little parts of our conversation. "How come?"

"Because you told me you like new places. And even if you hadn't, you have such a curious mind, so my assumption would have been the same."

It couldn't just be for me. "But do you want to travel?"

He tilted his head to the side slightly. "I find new places interesting, but have never really cared enough to go alone. With you, however, is a different story entirely." He blinked his heavy lids slowly. "It sounds incredible."

As though he hadn't made my heart ache enough.

"Jordan, that's..." I shook my head, unable to fully articulate my feelings. "That sounds incredible. To be somewhere, anywhere, with you. It would be so fun." I grinned. I pictured the fancy hotel room he would get us.

The joy on his face was thrilling.

Because I didn't know what else to say, I commented, "I should probably blow this out," gesturing down at the candle. He smiled.

"Please do, my love." He ran his thumb along my hand. "Happy birthday."

I blew the candle out, smiling. *"Merci beaucoup."*

When it was finally time to go home, I was thrilled. I wanted to be lying down with Jordan, nice and comfortable, not doing anything.
I felt bad for him, because he had to drive. I was sleepy and wouldn't have wanted to, but that was what big, protective men were for.
"How long is the drive, babe?"
"Back home? Around two hours." He held my hand as he pulled onto the main road. "Look in the back seat."
I raised an eyebrow, stretching around my seat to see what he was talking about. There were blankets and a pillow. My grin grew slowly.
"What…"
"If you're tired, you can sleep, my love. I anticipated after a long day, you might get sleepy. And it's a long drive."
I couldn't stop smiling. I leaned across the cupholders and put my head on his arm. He lifted it to wrap around me.
"I just wanna hug you, but I can't, 'cause you're driving."
He ran his hand up and down my arm. Eventually, I sat back in my seat and reached for the blankets.
"I'm just gonna cover. I'm not gonna sleep."
"Why not?" His voice was always so gentle that I constantly had my guard down.
"I don't want to leave you alone."
"I'm okay, honey. You don't have to worry."
I held his hand and stayed quiet for the drive, except for a little conversation and the hundred times I thanked him.
When we finally got home, Jordan asked, "You ready for bed, love?"
"Umm." I wanted to go upstairs and hang out. Cuddle. Resist all the temptation I knew I would face.

JORDAN

"I wanna change, I think. Then, I don't know. We can hang out."
I stepped forward and grabbed his hand. "Sounds perfect to me, honey," he murmured.
I pulled him to the stairs. When we got up to the bedroom, he stopped at the doorway.
"I'll give you some privacy to change, my love."
I smiled a small, timid smile. "Thank you."
I threw on a white, cropped crewneck sweater and matching sweatpants. I ran to the bathroom and washed my face quickly.
"Jordan, come back," I called.
He strolled in, still in his evening clothes.
"Put on jammies." I grinned. "I'm a sucker for cozy."
He laughed.
"Give me one moment, my love."
He headed to the tall dresser in between the nightstand and the bathroom. I then noticed the boxes on top that I'd missed when I first walked in. There were three, two the size of an average shoebox, one a little bigger, all wrapped in dark red wrapping paper.
Oh my goodness.
He grabbed all three, stacked on top of one another, and set them down on the bed.
"I want you to open these," he murmured.
I sat down next to them, softly saying, "I...oh, Jordan. What is this?"
He leaned down and kissed my forehead, smiling.
"Presents."
I chuckled, not even bothering to argue. I gently tore off the wrapping paper. Sure enough, a shoebox.
I opened it to a gorgeous pair of nude heels. I rolled my eyes back into my head and fell backward onto the pillow. But I couldn't wipe the grin off my face.
Jordan laughed. The sound was invigorating.
I sat back up and pulled one pointy-toed heel out, examining it. *They were my size.*
"Jordan," I whined. "Why do you do this to me? You know I'm weak for these."
"It's absolutely thrilling."
I laughed, gently setting the shoe back into the box. "You knew my size. How?"
His grin was the most beautiful smile in the world. "I investigate for a living."
I threw my head back and laughed, harder than before. I shook my head, not even responding.
He handed me the other box, and I opened it to a pair of red pumps. I covered my mouth with my hand.
"No way." Jordan's eyes lit up brighter than I'd ever seen them.

I leaned forward and pulled his face to mine, kissing him deeply, keeping his cheeks in my hands as I murmured, "You didn't have to do this."

"This is one of the happiest moments I've ever had."

I wished I could sink and disappear into the mattress to physically match the melting feeling inside.

"Goodness, I love you so much."

He tapped the other box, longer than the other two, and these were the icing on the little cake from dinner.

Tall, cream, glossy heeled boots.

"Jordan—Jordan, I—"

I was *weak*.

I looked up at him, my voice low and serious. "Did you know heeled boots are one of God's greatest creations?"

His laugh was delicious.

I reached forward and wrapped my arms around his body, quaking with his laughter. He did the same, chuckling into my collarbones.

"I love you so much," I said quietly, suddenly feeling emotional. "And not because of the boots, either."

"I love you more, honey."

When I pulled away and closed the boxes, he put them on the dresser. Then, he changed into sweatpants and a sweatshirt, like me. I patted the spot on the bed next to me.

As he slid in, I said, "Thank you. Thank you, Jordan."

He pulled me close. "You don't have to thank me. Ever."

I settled my face against his chest, and he pulled the blanket up around my shoulders.

"You're safe," he whispered suddenly.

And after twenty-five years, I finally felt like it.

August

Our last full month of summer brought a change in Jordan.
He wasn't cold or distant. But he was different.
He was more reserved with every day that passed. Jordan was a quiet man in general, but now, he said even less. Most things I said or did got minimal verbal reaction. If I were trying to be cute, trying to cheer him up, he would smile small but would say nothing. Beyond that, during some of those moments, there'd be adoration in his eyes and suddenly, a flash of something hot. I couldn't identify it. It was intense, definitely like anger, protectiveness, determination.
Something was very off.
While he was quieter than usual, and I couldn't get the greatest reactions out of him, he was actually more loving. His passion for me seemed to grow even stronger than it was, which I didn't think was possible. But it made my heart ache. It felt too good to be true, all the time.
He would hold me tighter, kiss me harder, pull me to him the second he saw me. He wouldn't let go if he didn't have to.
If we were out in public, he'd hold my hand or have his arm around me the whole time. It didn't bother me; it made me feel protected, loved, and safe. But it concerned me that he was so worried about my safety, and I wondered if more girls had been killed, or if he'd proven that the killers were nearby.
I humored his every request, allowing him to keep me close. My only grievance was that he wouldn't talk to me about it.
Jordan never complained. He never said something was wrong, rarely said he was anything other than content or happy. He never said his head was hurting, or that he felt anxious; he never showed any anger, or snapped. He was the most reserved person I'd ever met in my life.

JORDAN

He always found ways to help me deal with whatever struggles I had. We talked through solutions, and, by the end, I felt better. He always made me feel like everything was going to be okay.

It broke my heart that I couldn't do that for him. That he wouldn't give me the opportunity. I feared the most that even if he did, I wouldn't be able to. But I still wanted the chance, wanted him to know that I was there. It made me feel awful, that he was amazing at comforting me, while never showing me that he needed me the same way. I didn't like to need. I definitely didn't like to need and not be needed in return.

I just hoped that he knew there wasn't anything I wouldn't do for him.

Jordan started working onsite five days a week. Normally, he would work from home at least three. He worked late nights before I moved in, but he cut those short to spend time with me. Or he would do both. Sometimes, I'd write, and he'd work, and we would just be together. He made time to be with me.

Yet I still missed him when we were apart, without fail.

Midway through August, on a hot, sunny Friday, that longing for him drove me to do something I'd never done.

I was entirely disconnected from my work that day, more bored and restless than usual. It was a slow day, there wasn't much for me to do, and I missed Jordan. Steve had gone on a trip with his wife.

I texted him that all the work was done. When he responded that I should go home early and enjoy my weekend, I was surprised but thrilled. It was only eleven. I could go home and be there when Jordan got home, which almost never happened.

Jordan promised me he wouldn't work late nights how he used to. We would at least spend our evenings together during the week.

Sometimes, I'd get home around seven instead of six, and sometimes, he would as well. But never later than seven, because I went to bed early. He'd usually join me, which was lovely, but sometimes he would work after I turned in for the night, and come up a little later. But however it happened, we spent at least part of the night together, usually all of it.

It was rare that he ever got home *after* me. Perhaps he always wanted to be there when I got home, and his drive wasn't as long as mine.

Today, I could go home, clean up, cook a nice dinner; I could go to the store for what I needed. Perhaps I could plan a romantic night, a nice weekend together.

Then, on the drive home, I thought about taking him lunch.

I missed him badly, and having the day free felt odd. I spent most of my free time with Jordan. We still saw our families; we just did it together or while the other was busy. Neither Jordan nor I were exactly extroverts. We had friends, but it was never a habit for either of us to be with them all the time. It was just family or being alone. We were compatible in that way, except now, all the time that we used to spend alone, we spent with one another.

So, as I drove down the highway, enjoying the beautiful sunshine and clear skies, I decided I'd be brave and take him some food.

I stopped at a nice restaurant we liked. After picking up the food, I put the address of his building into my GPS. I'd never been there, though he gave me the address a while back.

I was nervous. I thought he might get mad at me for showing up to his office, especially at a time when he was so stressed because of work and my safety. I knew Jordan didn't want me anywhere near the work he did.

But I took that chance, because I missed him, and I wanted to make his day a little better. Something in me was surer that he would be happy than he would be mad. I was hoping.

When I got there, I got anxious. There was a security gate.

Shoot.

I wanted to at least be in the parking lot before I called him.

I stopped at the gate, embarrassed. There was definitely a camera somewhere, and a bunch of professional investigators looking at me, saying, "Who the heck is *that*?" The screen to the left of me had no writing, and I assumed it required a key card.

I dialed Jordan. As the phone rang, my pulse picked up.

"Baby," Jordan said into the phone. "Are you okay?"

"Yeah, I'm actually here...at your building. I didn't know there was a gate."

"You're here?" he asked, surprise coloring his voice. I immediately heard shuffling as he began walking. "Hold on just a second, honey." I waited a moment, and then the gate suddenly lifted.

"Pull in," he said, and I heard him still walking.

"Did you have someone do it?"

"I did it from my phone."

Huh. Techy and smart and cool. I was the girlfriend of a rich genius and suddenly felt small.

As I drove in, I assessed the building. The parking lot was huge, wrapped around the tall, multistory facility, which was dark and round. I liked it. It was sleek, professional, and screamed *"We have the latest and greatest technology."*

"Okay, I'm stopping by the two doors right where you pull in."

"That's perfect. I'll be right there."

As I hopped out to grab the food from the passenger seat, my heart was still beating fast. Jordan didn't sound mad when I told him I was there, but I was still worried.

As I shut the car door, Jordan pushed through the entrance of the building and, spotting me, came quickly. I walked at a normal pace towards him, swinging the bag a little, trying to pretend I wasn't nervous. He wore black slacks and a long-sleeved, black shirt. And looked really good in them.

"Nina," he breathed as he pulled me to him, kissing my head. I smiled up at him. The area under his eyes was a little puffier underneath than usual. I tried to stop myself from frowning. His fatigue broke my heart.

His eyes themselves were alert. I could tell he'd been having a stressful day, but I immediately felt the love coming from him. No anger in sight.

"Hi," I said quietly. "I'm sorry to bother you at work; my boss isn't in, you know, so he sent me home early, and I just wanted to bring you lunch." I lifted the bag of food.

He reached for it. "Don't be sorry. You brought me lunch?"

I smiled shyly. "Yeah, I thought I would, since I had the opportunity to for once." Jordan stared down at me for a moment, and then put his fingers under my chin and gently brought my face to his, so he could kiss me deeply.

I pulled back slightly. "I'm sorry to just show up. I know you're busy, and things are tough right now, and that's why I wanted to bring you something—"

"Don't apologize, please," he begged. He brushed his free hand over my hair as he stared into my eyes. "I love you," he said intensely. "You can always come here."

I shook my head a little. "I love you, too. I just thought you might not want me here, because you don't like work and me mingling…"

"You're always safe here. Always. Anywhere I am, you're safe." Kissing my forehead, he murmured, "Come on. Let's go inside."

"I'll leave you to work, Jordy. It's okay. I just wanted to bring that by."

Jordan took my hand and gently laced his fingers through mine. "I want you to come eat with me," he murmured.

I smiled up at him shyly again. I thought of being around all these professionals and became nervous. Jordan was extremely private, and he never let anyone know about his personal life. He was close to his immediate team, but all I could think of was Tristan's initial reaction to me. What would his *employees* think? The boss, the unbeatable man behind the operation, the person to whom they all reported, was with a woman. They would definitely be curious.

As we walked, I murmured, "This is a big building."

Jordan looked down at me. "Yeah. We've got operations on each floor. There's a couple research floors, a couple development floors, analysis floors. Up above, near my office, they do the digging." It took me a moment to understand that he meant the search for the more heinous crimes. "And there's a floor for food and off-time."

We entered the large, open lobby. There were two sitting areas on either side of the entrance, with turquoise couches, ottomans, and glass coffee tables. Directly ahead was an elevator. The halls on either side were decorated with offices. The lobby was abandoned.

"This is where administration works," he murmured.

As we stepped into an elevator, he kissed my head again. "Where do you work?" I asked, amazed.

He smiled small. "Top floor."

My eyes were wide as I processed his words. The building was exceptionally larger than I'd thought it would be.

"The floor I have to stop in is crowded. Do you want to wait in the elevator? I just have to go grab something quickly." He kissed my temple as we ascended. "I don't want you to be uncomfortable."

I smiled a half-smile. "That's okay." I would most definitely not part from his side, not even to wait in the little box alone.

We exited the elevator, face to face with a huge floor of computers, tablets, various other devices, and a lot of people, just as he'd said. Initially, everyone was focused on what they were doing, some staring intensely at screens, reading and assessing, some in heated conversations about things too technological for me to understand; they didn't even look up when the elevator opened.

When they did notice, the air in the room shifted slightly.

The boss was here.

So the room changed. The volume went down slightly, eyes that were focused moments before were now distracted, shifting up towards Jordan and away quickly as the staff tried to pretend they didn't notice him walk in. I saw awe in eyes, curiosity, sudden determination, even excitement. I saw a few women eye him with more than that on their faces.

There was an air of admiration. Of respect. I felt it instantly.

That energy did not prevent the curiosity and shock that came with the sight of me, however.

A woman's jaw dropped slightly, and when she noticed me noticing her, she quickly closed it and turned to the side, still eyeing me a little.

Oh, boy.

"This isn't the top floor?" I clarified. It was shocking to think there were more floors to go after we'd come so high already.

"No," he murmured, keeping me close by his side, arm around my waist for anyone to see. "I just need to grab something."

As we maneuvered through the many circular tables with desktops, the long rectangular one bordered with laptops, and the high tables with propped up tablets and tall stools, more people noticed. I kept my eyes in front of me, or turned to look towards Jordan. It was strange, being the odd one out after having done absolutely nothing but exist.

We moved towards a closed door on the opposite side of the room. There were a few men around one of the circular tables in the back, near the office we were going to. They were young, late twenties. Thin and white, one taller than the other. One was a redhead with freckles, the other a shorter brunette who was not as thin but still lanky. The two of them were simply staring in awe for a moment, standing close to one another. Then, one made a comment to the other, inaudible to me and, I thought, to Jordan. A smile grew slowly on one's face, and then the other's.

"Ryan, Donovan," Jordan said as we passed, his voice low. He did not yell or snap, but there was finality around the edges of his tone. I was stunned. I looked up at him immediately; his face was blank, but there was a coldness in his eyes that almost made *me* shiver. The smile vanished off both men's faces.

Stopping at the door and keeping himself between me and them, he asked, "Do you have any news for me?" Jordan's tone was as flat and cold as his eyes.

Ryan, the redhead, cleared his throat and replied, "No. Not yet." He kept his voice light for his own good, but his eyes were unhappy. His friend, Donovan, seemed more uneasy than Ryan did. He only nodded in agreement.

"Get me something." Jordan's voice could've cut shapes out of the air.

Ryan simply nodded, ever so slightly, and turned back to his screen. His buddy did the same.

Jordan waited until both of their eyes were off us before he turned to the keypad on the door, pressed a few numbers and opened the door. Then, he turned his eyes back to them to ensure they didn't look back. They didn't.

Jordan gestured for me to enter, following close behind me. It was a large office with bookshelves and cabinets everywhere. On the single large desk in the center of the room, there were multiple folders, files, books and binders.

"Sorry, honey," he murmured, closing the door behind us. "I just need to grab something." Moving to the bookshelf up against the back wall, he perused one shelf for a few seconds, sliding his fingers down the line until he found the file he wanted. They were all labeled.

The memory of Jordan at the library the first time I ever saw him flashed through my mind.

As he slid the file off the shelf and turned to me, I stared at him in awe. I couldn't believe how far we'd come since then. I was so stunned I lost the ability to speak.

How the reality of time passing just hit you at certain points...

Jordan came up to me and, looking down at my face, he asked, "Are you okay?"

I forced myself to snap out of it. Nodding, I murmured, "Yeah," trying to keep my tone light. I put on a small smile.

The truth was, I was anxious in that building. I felt insecure, being around all of these genius people, who were exceptional in one thing or another.

"Come on," Jordan murmured, putting the file under his arm and the other arm around me. As we exited the office, I saw Ryan and his buddy quickly look away from the door. Jordan's face immediately turned cold again as he blatantly stared at them, silently daring them to look again.

Whew! It was nice *having such a* sexy *man protect you.* I tried not to laugh from the thrill. And the surprise.

We got more looks than before. Every face turned away just as fast as it had looked.

We stepped back into the small elevator, and as I slid against the side wall so no one could see me, Jordan stood in front of the entrance until the door closed, blocking anyone's sight.

I loved him endlessly.

Jordan hit the button *10—Sheesh, ten floors!*—and off we went. We were on the fifth. I hadn't noticed that on the way up.

When the elevator stopped moving, and the doors slid open, we stepped out into a small hallway. There was only one door. Jordan pressed a couple numbers on the keypad, tapped a few times on the small, square screen above it, and the door opened.

We stepped into a large, modern office. The desk in the center of the room was all black, a silver computer monitor, mouse and keyboard in the middle, bordered by neatly stacked files, a few thin books, and a tall silver lamp. There was a large black desk chair on the opposite side. Next to his desk was another black desk, identical to the first except half the length. It was big enough to fit three large monitors. I stepped behind the desk to see what they showed.

Each screen held various shots of rooms in the building and a couple of the parking lot. I could see what I presumed to be everyone. I didn't know how Jordan could look at this and not get overwhelmed. But I figured it made sense that the creator and head of a company so heavily centered on technology utilized it carefully himself.

I looked around the room some more. A few feet from his desk, close to a wall of windows, were a large coffee table and four light turquoise armchairs.

The windows showed the rest of the street, lined with plazas filled with small store fronts, and bigger restaurants. It was a beautiful view.

I didn't remember being able to see into an office. "People can see into here?"

He shook his head. "No. Windows are tinted." I nodded, relieved. I didn't like the thought of anyone watching him.

The walls were white, which made the room bright. This office was in much less disarray than the one with all the files and books; there was also a full bookshelf here, directly behind Jordan's desk.

Opposite the window was a restroom, and from the cracked door, I could see a black countertop and stylish faucet, even in the dark.

Overall, the office was clean, sleek, and modern. Simple, but nice. Jordan deserved nice things, in my opinion. He worked hard his whole life and had earned and continued to earn everything he had.

He grabbed my hand and pulled me to sit down next to him on one of the large armchairs.

"I got you good stuff," I murmured happily, trying to keep the awe off of my face and knowing I was failing miserably.
Jordan smiled a small smile and kissed my forehead. "Eat with me."
I shook my head. "I'm not really hungry." I reached into the bag, because he hadn't. I opened his food and set it in front of him. Looking around, I spotted, in the corner of the office, a fridge and a microwave.
"Perfect!" I hopped up and took the grilled chicken, rice and soup to the microwave, leaving the salad there for him to start with. I saw him look after me regretfully.
"Honey, you don't have to do that." As he started to stand, I turned back and stuck my hand out.
"Uh-uh! Sit. Eat." I kept my voice sharp, and then I smiled at him sweetly. A grin slowly grew on his beautiful face.
As I set the microwave, I said, "This is a very, very beautiful building, Jordan." I shook my head to myself. "I can't believe it."
"What can't you believe?" he asked, not eating his salad.
"Jordy, eaaaaaaaat."
He didn't move. "Not until you're sitting next to me and eating, too."
I couldn't help but smile. I loved him so much.
I took the chicken and rice out of the microwave, put the soup in, and walked over to the table with the hot food before going back for the creamy potato concoction. Cheesy and topped with bacon. I loved feeding him calories as much as he did me.
"I can't believe how big this place is," I said, answering his question. "When I pictured your building, I really just thought of like, one big room full of computers and a bunch of smart computer geniuses, maybe, like, a meeting room for you and your team, and then your office. I had *no* idea that it was like *this*."
Jordan's facial expression didn't change much. As often as I doted on and complimented him, he only ever seemed humbled. I waited, *waited* every time for that arrogance to show, or that pride, *something* akin to the narcissism of my ex-boyfriend. It never came.
"I needed the room," he murmured. "I was fortunate enough to build such a large company of people. It wasn't always this big," he informed me.
"No?" The microwave beeped, and I grabbed the soup and walked slowly over to him, so it wouldn't spill. Setting it down on the table in front of him, I said, "I'm so proud of you."
Jordan's lips turned up at the corners. He patted the spot right next to him. I knew that if I didn't sit down, he was going to stand up any second and carry me to the chair. Jordan did not care to be serviced by me. I thought it was cute, because I was going to do it anyway, in any possible manner I could.
I went around the table and sat next to him. He silently handed me a spoon and fork from the bag. I didn't argue. I took a spoon of rice and ate it in

solidarity. Jordan smiled a proud smile, lips together, and then ate some chicken.

I chuckled to myself, still in complete shock. "This is wild."

Jordan laughed. I leaned in and kissed his cheek. He brushed his hand over my head and down my hair.

After a few moments of gazing lovingly at each other, he murmured, "Thank you so much for lunch, baby. This was lovely of you."

I smiled a big, happy smile. "You don't need to thank me." I was cheesing it up, thrilled to see him happy. "I missed you so bad," I said suddenly. I quickly added, "I wanted to come see you and feed you."

Jordan's smile was fond. He leaned in and kissed my forehead, then took his fork, cut off some chicken and held it to my mouth. I laughed, biting it off the fork.

"So this is what we've resorted to? Feeding me like a child?" I chuckled.

His smile grew. "It is very satisfying to me when you eat. Very comforting."

I laughed again. "It's comforting to *you* when *I* eat?"

Jordan nodded. "Yes. I know you're healthy, then."

His words sobered me, and I looked at him longingly, feeling full of love.

We ate, took our time, laughing and smiling in his big, chic, modern office. It was so nice to see him smile, so nice to hear that gorgeous laugh radiate from him. I missed seeing him happy. While I could still see the tiredness on his face, I knew he felt good then.

When we got done eating, Jordan recycled the cartons. "There's a few people I want you to meet."

My eyebrows shot up in surprise. "Your team?"

He nodded. I took a deep breath.

As I stood up and he took my hand, I asked, "Like Liza and Emmett and them?" Jordan nodded again, smiling small.

"You remembered," he murmured.

"Of course I did." I smiled. "I think about your work all the time." I looked ahead but felt his eyes on me.

"Do you?" he asked, and I could hear in his tone that he was trying to keep it light.

I nodded, reaching out for the button with the down arrow at the elevator and looking at him for approval. He nodded.

We went down a single floor. The elevator doors opened to a large room with white walls and white tile. There were five large desks spread around, each with three or more computer monitors and a few laptops. Some had tablets, books, folders, food, and other small things.

Seated at one desk, clicking away at something on one of the computers, was a thin, pale woman with fuchsia lipstick, black, square-rimmed glasses, and short, sandy brown hair pulled back into a ponytail. She wore gray dress pants and a simple black button-down top. She was perhaps in her mid-thirties, her narrow face and sharp cheekbones making her look fierce, in conjunction with her intense, assessing gaze. Initially, her eyes were unwelcoming. For just a brief moment.

At another desk was a tall, bulky and muscular man, with short, smooth, dark brown hair and a clean-shaven, youthful face that hardly matched his physique. He was even paler than the woman. Though he was sitting, I could tell he was at least six-foot-six.

Holy crap.

Both were looking at me, but the woman quickly turned her attention to Jordan. "Well, look who decided to show up to the party." Her voice was low and a little raspy.

"I didn't even know you were here," the man rumbled, the depth of his voice contrasting his youthful face.

Another woman in the back of the room stood up and walked over. I hadn't noticed her or the other man in the room until then. She was pretty, petite, even shorter than me, and Indian. Her straight, silky black hair swept her shoulders, her curvy lips and small, cute nose complimented her big, dark, kind eyes, and her voice was rich and pleasant when she said, "Hi, Jordan." She smiled warmly at me.

"This is Nina," Jordan said, looking at her and then the others. The man from the back approached us; he was of similar age to the others, with a light brown beard and hair, gelled back. He was of average complexion. His serious brown eyes made his face solemn as he respectfully waited for Jordan to finish his introductions.

Jordan looked down at me and gently said, referring to the Indian woman, "This is Eve. That," he said, looking up at the other woman, "is Liza. This is Luke, and that's Emmett." He tilted his head to the man with light brown hair and then the giant, respectively.

I was nervous and intimidated. These were ex-FBI and CIA agents, but if Jordan trusted them, I had to. I didn't think there were that many people that Jordan trusted.

"Hi, Nina," Eve said brightly, smiling at me beautifully and extending her small hand for me to shake.

As I took it, Liza spoke, smiling. "It's nice to meet you." I was pleased to see her face brighten up.

Emmett moved his chair in half-circles, almost smiling but mostly looking at me in awe. "Hi," he said, so enthusiastically I stifled a laugh.

Luke was more serious, but he extended his hand out for me to shake as well. "It's a pleasure," he murmured respectfully, then he looked at Jordan. "I have something to show you."

I looked up at Jordan and smiled a small smile. "I'll wait," I told him softly, planting my feet by the elevator door.

But he took my hand and said, "It's okay." Looking back at Luke, he murmured, "Give me a little bit." Luke stared at him for a moment, nodded, and then, without looking at me, turned and walked back to his desk.

Jordan gently guided me over to the two empty chairs next to Liza. With the exception of Luke, all eyes were on me.

Jordan had me sit, but I already felt I was interrupting important work. I didn't want it to get to the point where I was told I should leave, though I knew logically Jordan would never do that. I still didn't want to get those vibes from anyone, so I told him softly, "I'll go, so you can get back to work."

He shook his head, sitting down next to me. "You don't have to." I could feel that he didn't want me to leave, which warmed my heart. He was in a good mood the entire time I was there. Liza was watching us, and, though I wasn't looking, I was sure the others were as well. I kept my eyes on Jordan, then followed his gaze to Liza.

As he laced his fingers with mine, he said, "Have you eaten?"

"No," Emmett replied for her. "Can't decide."

"Let's just get Chinese," Luke muttered.

"No, way too heavy and greasy." Liza's thin frame suggested she ate healthier, and less, than the rest of us.

Jordan cut in. "I'll have Elizabeth put in an order for sandwiches."

After contemplating, they all shrugged and nodded at their own pace.

"Have *you* two eaten?" Liza asked, looking at Jordan and me.

"Yes," he murmured. Liza flicked her eyes down at our hands. There still seemed to be shock floating around the room. "Nina eats healthier than any one of you. She's a much better influence."

Liza raised an eyebrow, but everyone, including her, smiled. Emmett cackled. Jordan's face barely moved, which was the funniest part about it.

"I could use an influence like you, Nina," Eve said, with that sweet smile still on her face. I smiled back.

"Hey, me too," Emmett piped up, patting his big stomach, which was clearly void of fat and loaded with muscle, since it sounded hard as rock. "Can you make me a meal plan?" He grinned at me.

"Don't agree to that," Luke called from the back. "Not unless you're prepared to plan out four thousand plus calories of food each day."

I chuckled. At that, Jordan smiled.

I could feel his protection reign over me. It was a similar feeling to meeting his family for the first time. He wouldn't let anyone make me uncomfortable.

And I couldn't be. I thought being in a room with such incredible people would make me uncomfortable, but the vibe was laid-back. Everyone was more welcoming than it seemed initially, and conversation had barely been had.

I could see how these were the people Jordan trusted the most. They didn't need to say much. It was an energy.

We sat there for a little while. Liza, Eve and Emmett asked me a bunch of questions: Where was I from, what did I do for a living, when Jordan and I met, what were my plans for the night, which was awkward, because Jordan

JORDAN

hadn't directly said I was his girlfriend; I didn't know if they knew. The conversation was nice, and I didn't feel so intimidated by the end of it. Jordan stayed quiet while we spoke, listening carefully, only chiming in when spoken to or when he sensed I didn't know what to say.

It was good to finally know who he worked with, to not feel so intimidated by how intelligent he and his team were.

I couldn't keep off my mind his earlier response to Luke, when he'd wanted to show Jordan something. I had the feeling Jordan didn't want me to see anything they had going on.

Which was for my protection, but it still made me feel small.

I leaned close to him so the others wouldn't hear. Thankfully, they were speaking to each other.

"I'm gonna go," I murmured. "Clean up, get dinner ready, all that. We can spend the night hanging out, all cozy." I knew he was going to argue about my leaving, so I tried to keep a light face.

"You don't have to rush out of here," he half-whispered into my ear.

I smiled small at him. "I'll let you get back to work, and I'll see you at home." I stood up, knowing that I had to act, or he would keep me there. Jordan stood up as well and gently put his hand on my lower back. His team snapped to attention.

"You're leaving?" Liza asked, surprised.

"Yeah." I smiled small at her. "I know you guys are busy; I wanna let him get back to work," I said politely, looking towards Jordan.

"I'd rather have you than him!" Emmett called. I smiled, looking at Jordan, who returned it.

"Come back soon," Eve murmured in her lovely voice, hitting the elevator door button for us. I smiled and thanked her.

When the elevator doors closed, I waited a beat and then asked Jordan, "Do they know I'm your girlfriend?" I looked at him. "Was that a stupid question?"

He put his lips in my hair. "No, my love. It wasn't. They do know. Just them, however. The rest of my staff do not."

I nodded. "So...I'm guessing the rest of them thought I might be, though. A lot of them seemed pretty surprised. Like, 'Dang, look at the boss man's girlfriend.'" I grinned up at him.

He smiled back. "They may have thought you were a consultant for something."

I chuckled. "Ha! Yeah right. Look at me. Do I look like a consultant for the kind of work you do?" I gestured down to my "business casual" outfit.

"You look perfect." Jordan kissed my temple. "Regardless, though, they know to mind their business."

Jordan walked me to my car. I rolled down the window once situated and said, "I love you. I'll see you soon." He leaned in and kissed my lips.

"Drive safe, my love. I'll be home around four today. No later."

I smiled. He was going to leave early.

I was in a good mood, having missed him all morning, only to get the pleasant surprise of being able to see him.

When I got home, I did a deep cleaning. Around one, I started dinner. I got bold and made bread rolls from scratch, so I needed to let them rise while I prepared chicken, pasta and roasted vegetables.

Around three-thirty, the rolls were cooling on the counter, round, smooth and fluffy. I was thrilled. I had just pulled the chicken out of the oven. The pasta and sauce were cooked, staying warm on the stove. The veggies were still roasting. I headed up for a quick shower.

As I got dressed, I looked at my makeup-less face in the mirror then grabbed my mascara and put some on. It added a light, pretty touch.

I wanted a nice night with Jordan. I wanted to make him feel special, taken care of and romanced, and I wanted to look pretty while I did it. I'd been in a good mood since the morning, which motivated me fiercely. That, paired with my unending desire to please him had me fast on my feet, smiling to myself, giddy for him to come home.

It was three fifty-five when the garage opened. I set the table while waiting for him to come inside, putting everything in serving dishes. By the time he'd settled in, the vegetables would be done. I'd made it in perfect timing.

I went to the garage door just as he was stepping in.

"Hi." I smiled big. It had only been a few hours, but it felt like days. Wrapping my arms around his neck, I leaned in to kiss his lips. He kissed me back deeply, and then his lips curled up against my mouth.

"Hi, lovely," he murmured. I pulled him into the kitchen after he took his shoes off. "It smells amazing in here."

I smiled, thrilled. "I made dinner. Are you hungry?"

Jordan's lips turned up slowly. "Yes." He took my face in his hands and kissed me slowly. His tongue teased mine, sending heat through me. I almost moaned. "You are precious."

The words made me giddy. "No, you." I grinned. "Come on. Have a seat. I just gotta pull the veggies out."

"Let me help," he said, standing over me. "Let me get them."

"It's okay," I told him, oven mitt on and tray in hand. "I'm just gonna pour 'em….in heeere," I spoke as I worked. Jordan waited, then walked by my side as I took the hot tray to the table.

As we sat down and began to eat, Jordan continued to look at me with love in his eyes, a tiny curve at the corner of one side of his mouth showing me that I'd done well. It made my heart throb.

"I hope it's good," I told him.

"It's incredible."

I hadn't stopped smiling since he walked in. I ate happily, barely hungry and just wanting to be done so I could wrap my arms around him and not let go. My want for him today was strong.

"Thank you again for lunch, and thank you for this," he murmured, eyes, full of wonder, flicking down to his dish.

"No thank you's." I smiled. The pure joy and adoration that filled his face as he grinned made me feel weak. When we finished eating, I took the dishes to the sink.
"I'm washing," he said.
"Nuh-uh," I argued. "I am."
"You cooked." He raised an eyebrow. "And you cleaned. You made the house look flawless." He shook his head.
"Yeah, I wanted to. And I want to wash these up. Why don't you go take a shower and get comfy? It'll only take me five minutes." He began to object, but I told him, "Please, Jordy. Let me. I showered already. You deserve to feel comfy, too. Plus, you know me. I like to lie down until we're sleepy and then go to bed. If you get up to shower, I'm gonna be sad." I pouted, making him chuckle.
"I don't like this," he stated, but he was conceding. I smiled.
"Go shower," I murmured, wrapping my arms around his neck and kissing his lips slowly. Desire poured through me. I was in a great mood, I loved him desperately, and he was so, *so* handsome.
After kissing me back and staring into my eyes for a moment, he nodded.
"I'll be right back," he murmured into my cheek.
As he went upstairs, I turned to quickly wash the dishes, pots and pans that I'd used. I finished before he was done and, not being able to help myself, went upstairs. Jordan was in the bedroom, hair wet, wearing black sweatpants but no shirt, searching for one in his big dresser. He turned his head when I walked in.
His naked upper body made my fingers twitch. My goodness, he looked *perfect*.
The cut muscles looked like they were drawn on. His long torso was so defined, and his skin was that perfect, dark caramel color that made me dizzy.
"Hi," I said, smiling shyly, not wanting to be overbearing.
"Hi," he replied, and his loving smile made me feel less worried about being clingy.
I walked up to him before he found a shirt.
Bad idea.
Putting my hands on his bare hips, I smiled up at him. The feeling of his warm skin against my small hands, the bare body of the thing most precious to me, the charmed, passionate look in his eyes that was getting more intense by the moment, all made me feel weaker.
Bad, bad idea, Nina.
He returned my smile, assessing my face. Looking at his lips, I felt my smile fade. I stood up on the balls of my feet and put my mouth on his.
Jordan wrapped his arms around my waist, and I lifted mine around his neck as he kissed me deeper.
After a minute or so, unable to bear it any longer, I stepped backwards towards the bed and sat down.

"Hmph." I exhaled hard through my nose. "I'm sorry."
He shook his head, then walked up to stroke my cheek. "Don't be."
"No, I am. I gotta stop…initiating this stuff. I'm just making it harder on you. I'm sorry."
"And it's not hard for you?"
I blinked. "No, that's not what I meant—"
"Exactly," he said gently. He put his forehead down against mine. "It's not all about me. And it's okay. I think we're doing pretty well."
I chuckled, feeling better, less frustrated. "Yeah, I think so." I held his cheeks in my hands and kissed the tip of his nose. Then I told him to grab a shirt and stop tempting me. He grinned, turning around and doing as I jokingly ordered. Then I pulled him back in bed with me, covering us with the blanket.
We both read for a little while, letting the evening settle in peacefully. Then, I held him against me as sleep crept up to my eyes and fell asleep to the sound of his slowing breath, feeling more content than I'd ever been.

September

I snapped into consciousness at the sound of my alarm and reached for it immediately. I never wanted it to wake Jordan. It usually did, but trying to prevent that was enough to snap me out of my exhaustion. I glanced at my phone; the brightness was all the way down, yet it still hurt my eyes.
Four a.m. The first Monday of September.
I dismissed the alarm, then plopped the phone back down on the nightstand. I prepared to get up and get some coffee before my workout, but then I felt something around my wrist.
I looked over; Jordan was slowly coming to, holding on to my arm.
I looked at him curiously. He hadn't slept well the night before. He came to bed around nine pm, worked on his laptop for a few hours and didn't try to sleep until one in the morning. And even then, though he tried to keep still in order not to wake me, I could feel his adjusting and turning often.
So, I thought he'd certainly be knocked out, but he wasn't. He pulled just slightly at my arm to indicate he wanted me to come back down.
He did this sometimes, pulling me close to him in the morning so I wouldn't go. I'd sleep an extra twenty, thirty minutes, sometimes an hour, because I was so tired, and so in love, that I couldn't resist.
Though I knew I shouldn't, because skipping a workout, despite how far I'd come from my days of obsessive calorie counting and excessive workout sessions, still made me feel guilty sometimes.
Rarely would I skip my workout altogether and sleep in with him. Jordan was always careful not to keep me too long, because he didn't want to throw off my morning routine. He knew that my workouts meant a lot to me, that they helped my mood and self-esteem, and that I liked to have time to dilly dally in the morning. He told me once, "You would benefit from more

sleep, so I like to keep you with me for a little longer. But I won't hold you back from your morning routine, my love. Just get you a little extra rest."
This morning, I sank back down, and, while I thought he was nearly asleep and would drift off, he pulled me against him and wrapped his arms around me, kissing my temple. My heart felt full; I melted against his body.
"Stay," he whispered, sleepy. "Don't go."
I wrapped my arm around his waist. In all my drowsiness, I noticed that this time, he didn't feel playful. I could sense something heavy in him.
"Okay," I whispered groggily, resting my head against his chest. I had another alarm at five and another at five-thirty. I fell back asleep and opened my eyes to my five o'clock alarm. Jordan woke up, too. He lifted his arm to let me reach for my phone and silence it. As I was contemplating sleeping another half-hour, he pulled me back against him.
"Jordy," I murmured, sliding my hand under his shirt and up his side. His skin was warm, torso solid with muscle. I didn't get up.
Something didn't seem right. I turned off my five-thirty alarm and decided to sleep until six. If I got up right at six, chugged my coffee black and flew through my workout, then I could make it to work on time.
When six came around, however, I realized my gut was right.
I sat up, then heard, "Nina." Jordan's voice was rough and groggy with sleep. But there was something else in it that immediately sent uneasiness through me. I turned to look at him and, seeing his expression, slid back down.
The tiredness on his face could not hide the pure unhappiness that shaped it. His eyes were sad, he was frowning as though he'd just endured something horrible, perhaps a nightmare, and I couldn't bear the sight of it.
"It's okay, baby," I whispered, unsure why he was acting this way but aching because of it. I stroked his hair and cheek with my hand and kissed the top of his head.
He put his arm around my waist and his face against my chest. To see and feel Jordan rest himself against me instead of the other way around made me weak.
While I'd held him before, it never felt this way. Before, I always pulled him against me, and he just complied. Now, he came to me of his own accord, somewhat desperately.
I didn't know why I was comforting him, just that he needed it.
I wanted him to go back to sleep. I couldn't bear the sight of him so upset without knowing why, but I couldn't ask him what was wrong; he was too tired. So I continued whispering in his ear and running my hand over his face and hair.
"I don't want you to go," he whispered against me, voice so low that the deepness of it contrasted with its emotional intensity in a way that made my chest feel funny.
"Okay. Okay," I soothed in a whisper. "I'm gonna stay."
What is going on?

I comforted him in this way until he fell back asleep, wrapped in my arms. Even while asleep, his arm stayed around my waist tightly.
I drifted in and out until seven, too stunned to relax completely. When my next alarm hit and I reached for it, he moved in my arms, lifting his head.
"I'm sorry, my love," I whispered. "I have to get up now."
He blinked a couple times and then started to sit up, so I retracted my arms from around him.
"I'm sorry," he apologized, his voice deep and rough with sleep. I moved in and kissed his cheek, then put my face in his neck.
"You have nothing to be sorry for," I whispered.
"I shouldn't have asked you to stay; I kept you from your morning."
I kissed him on his neck then pulled back to look at him.
"I wanted to stay," I murmured, stroking his cheek with my fingers. "I'm gonna go shower. You lie down and get some more sleep."
He shook his head once and replied, "I'm getting up, too."
I frowned a little. "How come? You didn't sleep well last night," I responded softly. "You need to rest. You've been working so much lately."
I was hoping today he would sleep in, work from home, and then we could spend the night close together.
"I'm okay," he murmured, his voice still rough. "I'm going in today, too."
I didn't argue, because I didn't want to try and keep him from the work he cared so much about. Especially at a time when he was this stressed.
"Okay," I said quietly.
I stroked his cheek once more and got up to shower.
When I came out, dressed for the day and drying my hair, I found him doing the same. I hadn't realized he was going to shower, too.
"Oh, I'm sorry, love. I didn't know—"
He interrupted, knowing what I was going to say. "Don't do that," he murmured softly, coming up to me and kissing my forehead.
Jordan brushed his hand over my hair and pulled back to look at me. I looked up at him and saw the love in his eyes that I was feeling in my heart. I just stared at him for a few moments. "Selfish."
He shook his head, smiling slowly. "You are not."
"One day I'll get you in that shower with me."
The full grin on his face made my heartbeat pick up. It was such a relief to see something other than exhaustion and stress on his face.
"Come on," I murmured, knowing I had to go.
As I gathered my things to go, he called me over for breakfast.
"Where's yours?" I asked him, as he handed me a bagel lathered with cream cheese.
"I'll get something when I get there," he murmured, pouring milk into the espresso he'd made me. "I'm not hungry right now."
I watched him put a lid on a paper coffee cup and frowned, unhappy that he wasn't eating. I could tell he was telling the truth, so I didn't want to

push. He seemed tired; I sensed the stress had returned under his cool exterior. But there was warmth on his face when he regarded me.
I kissed his cheek and grabbed my purse, thanking him for the coffee and the food.
"I love you more than anything," I murmured, looking into his eyes. They were intense suddenly as he replied.
"I love you." His voice was deeper than usual. "So much."
Lately, he'd been acting as if one of us were dying. As though we would inevitably be apart soon.
I swallowed. I would ask him later if there were something he wasn't telling me.

The work day passed much too slowly. I dreaded it being this way all week. I was aching to be with Jordan. The emotion he'd shown this morning in bed, the way his eyes looked when I sat up to leave, the way he'd held me and told me he loved me before we parted, were all overwhelming and replayed in my head. I needed to be with him.

When the day finally ended, and I walked to my car, I admired the lovely weather. For some reason, it made me even happier to go home to my Jordan.

Fall had approached beautifully, sunshine cascading around the trees as they turned orange, red, even yellow. The slight chill in the air slowly turned cold as the days passed. I loved autumn.

I thought about the pumpkin desserts, the switch to warm coffee, the cozy sweaters and scary movies and enjoying all of it with Jordan as I walked. Just as I was wrapping my hand around the handle of the driver's door, a chill brushed against the back of my neck, making the hair there stand up.

Turning sharply, I assessed the entire area around me. It was breezy that day; I liked it. I liked being able to wear sweaters while it was still sunny. What touched me just then didn't feel like wind, however.

Like the coolness that on my skin, I brushed the sudden uneasiness off. The emotions of the day were getting to me, and I always had an odd wave of anxiety in certain weather. I got in the car quickly and locked the doors, because that was what I always did.

I thought about the morning for the entire drive. I felt nothing but love coursing through me, and I was anxious to get home. I forgot all about the odd feeling I'd had in the parking lot.

JORDAN

I felt the same way all week. Unhappy leaving him and dying to get back to him. Full of that same love, want, protectiveness and need to care for him.

Nothing was directly said about it, but Jordan did not like parting from me; knowing that it was becoming increasingly difficult for him made it harder for me. His energy started to make me nervous. Because if Jordan was worried, I knew I most definitely should've been, too.

Leaving in the mornings all week consisted of the same routine. He would hold me in his arms for a long time while we stood in the garage, and then he—looking miserable—would watch me drive away.

Friday morning, it seemed it had become impossible for him.

"How would you feel if I took you to work?" he asked me, as I poured some warm milk over the espresso in my paper cup.

"What do you mean? Drive me all the way there and then come all the way back?"

He shrugged slightly. "Not necessarily. I can work nearby until you get done. I like being over there. I can go see my mom and dad, as well."

I narrowed my eyes a little bit. "Jordan," I said quietly after a moment. I went up to him as he leaned against the counter, watching me. Wrapping my arms around his waist and looking up at him, I softly asked, "What's going on, my love?"

The conflict in his eyes was overwhelming, and every second that passed increased my anxiety. It felt like a long time before he finally responded. Jordan let out a hard exhale. Standing against him, I felt his abdomen pull in with the release of air.

"This case," he said quietly. "Someone is targeting my team, and I don't know who it is."

It took me a second to comprehend his words. When the meaning finally hit me, my heart sank.

"What...what's...what do you me—how do you know?" I could barely speak. My voice came out low. Jordan held me close to him.

"They've left us messages in their livestreams."

A chill went through me. "Saying what?"

"Saying that this is our fault. That they're doing it 'just for us.'"

"Killing people?" My voice was desperate.

He swallowed, his eyes burning into mine. He was adamantly against telling me any of this. He nodded slowly, taking my cheek in his hand.

"And...and...they're leaving little messages for you?"

"Yes," he replied, voice barely there.

The dread started in the center of my chest. I had not considered this as a possibility.

"Did they say your name directly?"

Jordan didn't say anything, just looked at me with intense eyes.

"Jordan," I said, feeling the dread well up even higher.

Finally, he replied quietly, "Yes. Mine, Liza's, Emmett's, Luke's and Eve's."

A realization hit me. "It's *your* company." I struggled to speak; my voice was coming out pitchy. The fear for him was building in me fast. I'd never been this afraid for anyone I loved. "Are they really after you?"

Jordan ran his hand down my hair, his eyes serious but voice gentle. "Yes, my love."

It was getting harder to breathe. The thought of my Jordan being targeted, in danger, terrified me. It made me furious.

I felt like the biggest idiot for not realizing this.

"Why didn't you tell me?" My voice cracked, rose in pitch. Jordan brought my face close to his and touched our foreheads together.

"I don't want you to worry," he said firmly. "I will never let anything happen to you."

"Jordan, I'm not worried about *me*, I'm worried about you!" My voice shook.

He pulled my head to his chest and wrapped his arms around me. I was weak, my head getting light.

I understood then how our parting was unbearable for him.

"I'm gonna be just fine, sweetheart," he whispered into my hair. "And so are you."

I brought my face back a little to look at him. "Do you think they know about me?"

Jordan's face filled with regret. "I don't know for certain. They've said nothing about you. They know who I am—"

JORDAN

"But how? You specifically? Someone who knows you personally, someone whose buddies you stopped or something? But even then, how did they know you helped the cops?" I shook my head slightly, rambling as I tried to make sense of this mystery. This nightmare.

"As much as I loathe it, I have made a name for myself, amongst not only law enforcement, but the people on the other side, as well." He stroked my cheek with his thumb. "But all that matters is that nothing is going to happen to you. I'll make sure of it." His voice was gentle, but there was a sharpness to the words themselves.

I swallowed, then a memory jumped to the forefront of my mind suddenly. "That day, when you went to that crime scene—." I stopped when Jordan's eyes turned worried.

I had to know. "The email...they...they sent it to *you* guys, and...and you said you didn't know why—" *He lied?*

Jordan exhaled through his nose and looked at me for a few moments. Finally, voice quiet and full of regret, he said, "I didn't want to scare you."

I didn't know what to say. The words *You lied* were lurking in the back of my throat, but he'd kept it from me so I wouldn't be afraid. That made it hard to be angry but not hard to panic at the idea that he was okay with hiding things from me.

"Jordan..." I started slowly. "You can't...you can't keep things from me..."

"I know, my love. I'm sorry. I regret it immensely but could not convince myself to bring you this kind of worry. I wanted to deal with it quickly, but...it's proven to be more difficult than I thought it would be." He brought his face closer to mine. "I wanted to tell you," he whispered.

"You should've." I could barely give sound to the words. "I'm an adult, and I can handle it, Jord. I *need* you to let me be here for you, even when your safety *isn't* on the line. And *especially* when it is!"

My insides felt like they were being torn up at the idea that he felt he couldn't tell me something so important. I tried telling myself that he was just worried about scaring me, but I knew that I couldn't even get him to talk about how he felt in general. Let alone when something this deranged was happening. That made me feel desperate. Like I was a helpless little kid, and he was the only one who could deal with any big problems. The sound of it was so lonely and made me terribly sad for him. How alone in it he must have felt.

"I know, my love. I am truly sorry. I didn't want it to get to this point," he whispered.

And at what point were we? Jordan's life was in danger. Crazy, sick people were looking to hurt him and decided they would taunt him first, by torturing and killing other people.

He already blamed himself for not being able to save everyone. Now, they were saying it was his fault. My lips trembled at how he must have been feeling. Jordan pulled me tightly against him.

"Don't be sorry. Just tell me, just tell me. Just talk to me, please. Please."

He kissed my temple firmly. "I will. I will tell you everything."

That barely settled me. "What other messages have they sent?"

Jordan exhaled hard through his nose, thinking for a moment. "Since May," he said, clearly unhappy that he was telling me, "there have been three more livestreams." My stomach dropped, but I kept my face smooth. Jordan watched it like a hawk, taking in my expression and every twitch, blink, movement. He would stop talking the second I seemed uncomfortable. "And on the website, the little advertisement for the show was always something along the lines of *Just for Jordan* or *Do it for Jordan, everyone. Bid your money, tell us what to do.*"

I felt sick. And enraged.

How could they torture him by torturing others in his name? How could people hate him so much? A man who did so much good?

But I knew. Of course they could. The good he was doing was stopping evil like them.

There had been ten girls now. Since March.

"Do...do to the girl?"

He grimaced. "Yes." His voice was low.

I took a deep breath, wrapping my arms around his waist to be close to him. After a moment of thought, I continued with my questions.

"Are you guys taking extra measures to be safe?"

He nodded. "Yes. I have our doors locked, extra security onsite every day." He paused. "I have people watching my family. And yours."

My eyes widened.

"Don't worry," he said quickly. "It's preemptive, my love. My point *especially* is that *you* are safe. I have no reason to believe they know about you. And that means they know nothing of your family, so I'm only doing this as an extra measure. For all of us."

The faces of each member in my family flashed through my mind. *Not them.*

"Jordan." I looked at him intensely. "Are you *sure*?"

I'd never questioned him before. But that same confidence in him that he'd instilled in me told me that I *should* worry, because *he* chose to set up security for my family. Didn't that mean he thought something was going to happen? How could it mean the opposite?

The expression on his face fought my fears. He was deathly serious, his voice grave. "Yes. I am positive that they will be just fine. I would never allow the risk of danger for any of them."

His confidence settled over me, and the security he always gave me resurfaced.

Then I realized that all of that would disappear if something happened to him. What hurt and terrified me further was the idea that there was no one giving *him* that same security. Tears filled my eyes. I *hated* the thought of him vulnerable and in a terrible struggle, physical or emotional, alone. I gripped his shirt in my hands.

"Jordan," I said, my pitch low, voice quivering. I looked up at him. He brushed my hair back soothingly, staring into my eyes.

"Please..." I didn't know what I wanted to ask him. *Please don't go to work. Don't leave. Stay in the house with me. Lock the doors and let your team handle it.*

He saw the wetness of my eyes and held onto me tighter, kissing my temple. "Shh," he soothed. "It's okay. You don't have to worry."

But I was terrified. Not for myself, but for Jordan. I couldn't bear the thought of his being hurt. Being prey. Lethal as he was, as unlikely as it was, I couldn't keep the thought of him being vulnerable, injured, tortured, brutalized, out of my mind.

I needed to be better than these tears. Needed to grow up and soothe *him*, and he wouldn't let me if I didn't get it together. I looked down at our torsos for a second, took a deep breath, swallowed and looked back up at him.

"What can I do to help?"

Jordan was slightly appalled for a moment, and then his face softened.

"Just be as careful as you possibly can be. I'll tell you how," he assured me. "It's just as a precaution. I won't let anything happen to you," he repeated.

"What should I do?" I asked, ready.

Jordan looked at me for a moment, focused. "I don't want to make you feel suffocated," he said carefully. "What I would *like* is to have somebody with you at all times."

I shook my head a little. That would end up being overwhelming, since I was an introvert and needed time alone, when I knew no one was watching. It was illogical, because it would be better for security to watch me than to risk some violent criminal spying, just because I wanted to be alone. But I couldn't help the face I made.

"I know," he said, acknowledging my look. "So, would you please do me the favor of calling me whenever you're out? Staying on the phone with me when you're at the store, when you're walking to and from the car, at work, at your parents' house, it doesn't matter. I know shopping might be difficult in that way."

I half-scoffed, half-chuckled. As though it mattered to me to be shopping.

"I'll go with you when you shop. I will be invading your personal space a little bit, and it will be annoying calling me every time you leave, but I just need us to be careful. I'm sorry." He frowned, and I knew he did not like having to ask this of me.

I wrapped my arms around his waist. "It's okay. I don't mind. I'm not too worried about shopping at the moment."

Jordan kissed my forehead, and then my lips hard. "I will *never, ever* let *anything* happen to you." His words were firm, and his voice had gotten rough.

I swallowed, looking into his eyes. "I know."

After a few moments, I reached my hands up to hold his face gently in my hands. I couldn't bear the thought of someone or something hurting him. It made the air in my throat stop moving.

"You be careful," I said fiercely, looking straight into his eyes, mine wide and serious. "Do not let anything happen to my baby. I'll go crazy, Jordan," I added in a whisper, feeling my face soften then crumple.

Jordan wrapped his arms around me again and murmured softly,

"I will."

October

JORDAN

Amidst trying to cope with the stress of Jordan's chaotic case at work, I was unsure and terribly stressed about how to make his birthday as lovely as he'd made mine.
What could I buy him? What did you buy somebody that had everything they wanted?
It had to be meaningful. Jordan had bought me three pairs of expensive shoes, a diamond necklace, flowers and gourmet chocolates. Then, he took me to the most beautiful restaurant I'd ever seen, had it closed to other guests for the night—which had to have cost at least a years's worth of American college courses—and bought me Lord knew how expensive a dinner.
"Is there anything in particular you'd like to do for your birthday?" I'd asked him about two weeks prior.
He'd glanced at me thoughtfully, blinked and then murmured, "Just be with you."
I'd smiled, having already known his answer would be useless.
Thus, the planning began. Step one was dinner. Jordan didn't have a favorite food or restaurant. His food intake before I'd moved in had consisted of various fruits and raw vegetables throughout the day, chicken, fish, brown rice and a few other things. Sometimes he ordered food from the nearby Greek or Arabic restaurants when he didn't want to cook. "I learned young that I wouldn't fight or do anything my best if I didn't eat well or enough." He knew how to cook and made time to do it, which, to me, was impressive for a single, busy man who lived alone. I found it endearing.
But now, it took away my option of picking something that would be special to him. We could go anywhere, and he would find something to eat.

JORDAN

I resigned myself to the fact that I'd just have to pick anything nice. He wouldn't care regardless. I chose a top-floor dinner downtown in one of the tallest buildings in the state; it overlooked a beautiful river.

Then, I had to plan the day. His birthday fell on a Thursday, so I took that and Friday off work and asked him to do the same, so we could sleep in both days and be together. A long weekend for us both. I knew it might've been hard for him, considering our current situation and his desperation to solve this case, but he complied with no complaint. His face softened when I explained that all I wanted was some time for him to rest.

I thought of what Jordan liked. The first things that came to mind were working with computers, reading, and professional martial arts. I began my research, sorting our day out.

I couldn't go anywhere without him, so I'd ordered some gifts online and made sure to be home when they arrived. I snatched the boxes and ran upstairs to one of our guest rooms, where I hid everything in the weeks before his birthday.

Wednesday was long; I was so excited, thinking he'd genuinely like everything. I wanted to spoil him from morning to night.

I woke up Thursday morning to his beautiful, sleeping face. He seemed content, and though it was a rare occurrence, I hoped I could sneak out of bed and get ready before he woke up.

Creeping out of bed, I kept my eyes glued to him to ensure he didn't wake. Fortunately, his eyelids stayed closed, his soft breathing steady. I stared at him for a few moments, admiring his beauty, my heart filling with love for my now thirty-one-year-old sweetheart. I wanted to kiss his cheek, but I feared I would wake him. Sighing quietly, I headed off to the bathroom to brush my teeth.

When I'd washed up and put makeup on and found he was still asleep, I changed and went back to the bathroom to straighten my hair. Jordan knew I only did that for special occasions. He would wake up and see it and know that today was important to me.

Odd what a hairstyle could do.

We were going to his parents' house for breakfast, so that eliminated my need to do something in the morning. I'd told him I needed our schedule clear at three, so we could make it to our plans at four. He looked at me, his lips turning up at the corners.

"Plans?"

I nodded, smiling sweetly. "Yup!" I kissed his cheek and skipped off before he could protest.

When my hair was sufficiently smooth—and burned—I crept back into the bedroom. It was still early, two and a half hours before we were supposed to be at his parents' house, which meant he didn't need to get up for another hour or so and get ready.

I sat down next to him, stroking his cheek lightly with my hand, then brushed over his hair. I stayed there for a while, content to just be with him. My birthday man.

Eventually, he stirred, my thumb stroking his forehead. He opened his eyes slowly and met mine. I smiled.

"Hi, angel," I murmured softly, leaning down and kissing his cheek. "Happy birthday."

I pulled back to a gorgeous growing smile that had my heart skipping. He pulled me back to put his lips to my cheek.

"Thank you, m'love," he murmured into my skin, his voice thick with sleep. I ached.

"Have you been awake long?" he wondered, observing my makeup and taking my straight hair in his fingers gingerly.

"Just a little while. I wanted to sneak around and get ready, so I'd be good to go by the time you got up."

"Why, love?"

"So we could leave on time. I take longer than you, so I figured we'd have more time together before we left, if I was done early."

"We'll stop for coffee."

"Yeah, and we can get you somethin' sweet." I grinned. "Since it's your birthday."

He sat up, smiling happily. "I won't be long."

"Take your time. Have a nice, relaxing shower. We have plenty of time."

As we stood, he leaned down and kissed my cheek again. "I'll kiss those lips when my teeth are brushed."

My eyes widened at his flirtation; I laughed in surprise.

"Sounds like a plan to me, sugar."

As he headed to shower, I snuck off to the guest room to look at his presents, wrapped up in shiny green and blue wrapping paper. I was excited to give them to him tonight. There was one I needed now.

I picked up the small box, smiling as I headed down the stairs.

A few minutes later, Jordan came into the kitchen donning dark blue jeans and a loosely fitted beige sweater. His hair was still damp.

"Is this an okay outfit for our plans?" he asked, glancing down at himself.

Adorable.

I grinned. "Yes, baby."

I approached him, small box in hand, and kissed his lips, fulfilling his promise for him. He kissed me back deeply.

I pulled back some, smiling against his mouth.

I gently put the box in his hand. His eyebrows shot up.

"Nina," he began.

"This is for you, baby. There will be more later," I told him, grinning as I repeated his words from my birthday.

His lips turned up. "Thank you, honey," he said quietly, and the joy in his voice thrilled me more. I was ecstatic that he didn't fight me.

He gently peeled the blue wrapping paper off of the small, rectangular box. I bit my lip as he tenderly lifted the lid off the box.

"Nina," he said, the smile wiping off his face, his eyes widening as he pulled out the small gold cross.

"I'm not a copycat." I grinned. "I just wanted you to have a new one, too." I took his cheeks gently in my hands. "I love to see you wearing these."

He leaned forward and kissed my lips hard, wrapping his arms around me. "My love," he murmured, sincerely touched. I felt full. "This is beautiful. Thank you. Thank you, my love."

"No thank you's," I reminded him.

"Will you help me put it on?"

I wanted to jump up and down from the glee.

We headed out shortly after that. I drove, because he wasn't allowed to know ahead of time where we were going in the afternoon.

The long drive together was nice. The sun was out, the sky clear on this chilly October day. October first.

"We'll go home before dinner, right?"

I nodded. "Yes, m'love."

We'd been over to Rania and Amar's house only a few times, but it was comfortable for me now. Tristan's car was already in the driveway when we arrived.

"Look, my bestie is here."

Jordan smiled. "Biggest idiot there is."

I laughed.

Rania pulled us into the house, hugging and kissing both of us, squeezing Jordan as she wished her eldest a happy birthday. She clutched his cheeks as her eyes watered.

"Mom," Jordan said, shaking his head, eyes wide. "Don't cry." Then he whipped the Arabic out, and I sighed quietly to myself.

I stepped into the house and rounded the corner just to be face to face with Amar.

"Oh!" I chirped. He smiled, which was not a common sight.

"Hi, honey," he said in his thick accent.

"Hi, Amar," I greeted, hugging him. I spotted Tristan behind him, in the kitchen. I grinned slowly as I stepped aside to let Amar go greet his son.

"Well, hello there, gorgeous," he said, grinning. "Happy you decided to come visit your real boyfriend."

I laughed. "Shut up and go say happy birthday to your brother." I hugged all six feet and four inches of him. He looked good in his fitted black shirt and jeans.

He did as instructed, teasing Jordan for a minute before turning serious and hugging him.

"Hey, Nina!" he called, strolling towards me in the kitchen as I helped Rania put food in serving dishes. "Your boyfriend is getting old."

"If Jordan is old," I said, smiling, "then you're gonna be old pretty soon yourself."

"Hey, I got three years until that age, punk." I laughed. Jordan shoved his head lightly.

"Watch it." But he was smiling at me as I laughed.

"Jordan," his father said. I saw him flick his head towards the other room. Jordan turned and kissed my temple.

"Be right back."

I wondered if something serious was going on. I blinked, trying to keep my face smooth, but Tristan could tell I was beginning to worry.

"He's just going to give Jordan his annual, *I'm proud of you* speech," he informed me. A smile grew slowly on my face.

"Aw." It was a sweet notion to me, a father telling his son how proud of him he was. I couldn't remember a time when my father had said anything of the sort to my brother. That sobered me, the smile slipping off my face.

"You okay?" Tristan asked quietly. I nodded quickly.

"Yeah! Yeah. I just think it's really nice."

Tristan eyed the pancake batter his mother was mixing. "Rania, let me help with those," I suggested.

She smiled. "Okay, honey."

I turned to Tristan. "Make yourself useful, handsome, and grab us a spatula."

His eyebrows shot up. I laughed. "I'm just kidding," I told him, revealing the one from behind me that he hadn't seen.

He came around the kitchen counter and leaned down to speak low into my ear. "If you don't shape up, I'm gonna give that to Jordan and tell him to—"

"Stop!" I cut him off, worried Rania would hear, laughing too hard to even reply.

Rania said something in Arabic to Tristan, who leaned down and kissed her cheek. "You got it, ma," he replied, pulling white ceramic dishes out of the cabinet above my head and heading to the dining room. But not before he leaned down and said, "Put chocolate chips in mine, punk."

I giggled. "You're such a child."

He shrugged. "Least I'm not an old man, like your boyfriend."

I raised an eyebrow, grinning as I lowered my voice and told him, "You know how I like 'em."

"Old and wrinkly?"

I chuckled. "Ain't no wrinkles on your brother, baby. Anywhere." I winked, flipping a pancake in the pan as Rania pulled glasses out of another cabinet a few feet away.

His eyes widened. "My innocent ears," he burst, but he was laughing hard as he headed out of the room.

Rania smiled at me, watching Tristan and I laugh, unaware of what was said.

I returned it, looking down at the small woman as we worked next to each other.

"I can't believe he's thirty-one." She shook her head, her heavy accent coating each word. She looked up at me. "I'm so happy he found you, Nina."

I blinked, touched by her words. "I'm so happy he did, too." I looked down at the pancake I was waiting to flip. The edges were still wet. "I love him so much."

"I know," she said quietly, smiling. "Jordan, he…"

I looked up to see her shaking her head. Curiosity filled me.

"He never dated," she said finally, meeting my eyes.

"I've been telling him for a long time I wanted him to find someone, but he…he never even dated. He told me, 'In time, mom.'" We both chuckled at her impersonation. I was captivated by her words.

"But he just wouldn't date. He was always working. I was *worried*. I thought maybe he didn't like anyone. Like maybe he would never get married."

Frowning, she continued. "Jordan likes to be alone. He was happy that way, I think," she said, dismayed. "It made me worried," she repeated. "I wanted him to have a family."

I swallowed.

"But he didn't date. The girls, you know," she said, her eyes serious, "they were always looking at him. Always, Nina."

"They still do," I murmured, thinking of all the times we'd been out. Women looked Jordan's way for a *little* too long.

"So you know what I mean." She gestured out to me as she cut up some fruit. "But before, he never even looked at them. I'd tell him, 'Honey, at least look and see if you think they're *pretty*,' but he wouldn't look!" Her pitch rose; she was flabbergasted. "He just didn't care. He was always *working*. There was a time, *years*, Nina, that he didn't even come home. After that FBI," she said, shaking her head and clicking her tongue. "I never wanted him to go there."

I frowned a little. "I know what you're talking about."

She nodded. "I think that made it worse. He didn't want to be around people. I couldn't push him more, because I saw he was having a hard time. But I thought maybe it would help him to have a wife to be there. Not living all alone, far away from his family!" She hunched her shoulders up, her eyes wide, innocent and upset as she relayed the memory.

I nodded sympathetically. "It was very hard for him," I said, keeping my voice quiet. I would hate for Jordan to hear us discussing this. He'd be upset with his mother for mentioning it to me.

"It was." She put the full plate of blueberries, strawberries, cantaloupe and oranges off to the side as she pulled the teapot off the hot burner and onto a cool one. "My baby," she said to herself, thinking of her son and no doubt the pain he suffered.

After a moment, she looked up at me. "But he found you," she said, finally smiling again. "I couldn't believe it. Tristan came over and told me and his father. Jordan was with a girl. I didn't believe him, Nina," she repeated adamantly. "I thought, 'Okay, it's for work, right?' But Tristan said Jordan was acting funny. Not like him. He said, 'She's pretty, too, mom. *Cute.*'" I chuckled, flattered.

"I called him the next day. He wasn't happy that Tristan told us, but I told him I was just happy for him; he didn't have to bring you around if he wasn't ready. But I wanted to meet you, Nina." Her eyes were wide as she smiled, shaking her head still as she recalled her anticipation of meeting Jordan's first love interest.

"He didn't want to talk about it too much, but he said he was going to ask you over for lunch with us. Amar and I couldn't wait, Nina, we couldn't wait."

I chuckled, happy. It was so relieving to know that they weren't worried about him anymore. I felt funny, knowing I was the one Jordan chose, the one who finally took his isolation from him. And that he was happy about it.

My heart ached.

"I was excited to meet you guys, too." We were leaning against the counter now, facing each other as we spoke in low voices. The food was ready. I turned the burner off under the pan and pulled it off the stove. Rania took it from me and set it in the sink, running cold water over it. A sizzling noise sounded as steam rose.

"Oh, Nina, when we saw you, we were so happy. I didn't know! I wondered for a long time who Jordan would finally pick."

I smiled shyly, trying to hide how hard her words were hitting me. I felt more blessed with every syllable that came out of her mouth.

He picked me.

He didn't know it, didn't agree about it, but I was so fortunate that he did.

"I said, 'She's so pretteeeeeey,'" she buzzed.

"Thank you, Rania," I said, laughing but humbled.

"He really loves you," she told me, her face sobering. "I've never seen Jordan this way, Nina. I'm so happy." Her voice cracked on the last word.

I pulled her in for a hug. "Aw. That makes *me* happy."

She hugged me and then pulled back, gathering herself so she wouldn't cry.

After a moment, she asked, "Do you know what he told me?"

My heart skipped. I sure didn't.

"He said, 'Mom, she's my baby.'" Rania smiled proudly, thrilled by her own words.

"No he didn't." My jaw dropped, eyes widening. *Jordan? Jordan* said that? She grinned. "He did. I couldn't believe it. I thanked God, Nina." She flicked her eyes up to the ceiling.

I thanked Him, too.

JORDAN

We heard Amar and Jordan heading in our direction. I swallowed, smiling at her before I turned towards the entrance. Jordan walked in just then, his eyes searching. When they landed on me, he smiled. He slid his arm around my waist. I put my face into his chest, wanting the contact badly.

"You okay, baby?" he murmured. "Sorry, that took longer than I thought it would." His voice was quiet as he pulled me away from the kitchen. I grabbed the plate of pancakes on the way, and Jordan took the dishes with sausage, bacon and fruit. Rania brought scrambled eggs, which Tristan, who strolled into the kitchen just then, took from her, as well as the teapot.

"It's okay," I told him as we set the plates down on the dining room table. "I was helping Rania."

He smiled, kissing my cheek. We all sat down to eat, Tristan already teasing Jordan.

"Eat up, old man," he told him. "We've got a big day ahead of us."

"We?" Jordan raised an eyebrow.

I smiled up at him. "Tristan's coming with us after."

Jordan was confused, but he smiled down at me, curiosity touching his eyes. I knew he couldn't picture what I'd picked for the afternoon, since Tristan was coming. That made me giddy. I'd worried I would never surprise him.

"I figured it'd be nice to spend time together, you and him."

"Just pretend like you agree," Tristan told him, before he could respond. I laughed, setting my head on Jordan's arm.

"I agree," Jordan said calmly. I leaned up and quickly kissed his cheek.

We ate and spent some time with his parents before we had to head out. Our venue was an hour south.

"Thank you so much for breakfast," I told Rania, hugging her and Amar.

"Thank you for helping me." We locked eyes, both recalling the conversation we'd had.

When we stepped outside, Jordan looked at Tristan curiously. "You driving separately?"

He nodded. "Y'all got plans after. I'm not invited to the fancy restaurant."

I chuckled. "You wanna come, bad boy?" I asked, looking at his leather jacket.

Tristan grinned, opening the door to his black Audi. "Can you imagine," he laughed, "me third-wheeling your romantic dinner?"

It was a hilarious thought.

As I drove, Jordan put his hand on my knee. "Thank you for coming. I hope you feel at home when you're around them."

I smiled. "I sure do, baby. Did you have a good talk with your dad?"

"Yeah. He was just telling me how proud of me he is. He says it every year."

"You don't have to tell me what you talked about," I said quickly. "It's not my business. I just wanted to know if everything was good."

"It's okay, baby." He stroked my cheek as I stared at the road ahead. "Everything is good." When he went quiet for a few moments, I glanced at him. He was looking out through the windshield, thinking. Finally, he murmured, "He told me about Turkey, though. He hasn't really ever mentioned that."

My eyebrows shot up out of curiosity. "Yeah?"

In my peripheral vision I saw him blink and turn his head towards me. "Yeah. He said he was sad when he saw me." I looked at him again, trying to glance as often as possible. Jordan's face was sober.

"Sad?" My eyebrows knitted together.

"Yes. Because I was alone. And scared."

My eyebrows smoothed out in understanding, my heart breaking. "Oh, no."

"I don't remember."

"That breaks my heart." I picked his hand up without looking and kissed the back of it. "I understand why he was sad."

Jordan kissed my hand now, murmuring, "That's because you're the sweetest person there is." I smiled. After a moment, he went on. "He told me bringing me home was one of the best decisions he's ever made."

"*Awwwwwwwww.*"

Jordan smiled small. "That was a nice thing for him to say."

Ah. My quiet, thoughtful boyfriend, showing some emotion. I could tell he was touched. My heart skipped, seeing him that way.

"Yes, it was." I kissed his hand again.

I felt his eyes on me again as I drove. "He also said that he's very happy I met you. That I deserve you and deserve to be happy with you. And he's thankful for you. That such a good girl loves me."

My jaw dropped. "No way." First Rania, then Amar?

"His words exactly." I sensed the smile in his voice and glanced at him, stunned.

I smiled for the rest of the drive.

When we pulled into the lot, Jordan stared at the large building, assessing. I knew he was confused, trying to figure out why we were at an arena. I'd assumed he would realize right away why we were there. He didn't.

I parked, then took his hand, smiling, as Tristan hopped out of his car and approached us.

"What's here?" he murmured, smiling down at me.

"You'll see." Tristan grinned.

We headed inside the crowded building, Tristan looking around until he met eyes with a tall, bald man, who flicked his head so we would approach. We walked around large groups of people and to a door at the end of the floor. The bald man unlocked it, he and Tristan murmuring to each other ahead of us. We followed them in.

Jordan looked down at me curiously, not asking me questions, knowing I wouldn't answer them.

JORDAN

We walked down a long, empty white hallway. Tristan glanced back at us, grinning.

"Get excited, Jordy boy!"

"Why?" His eyebrow went up.

Tristan laughed and turned back, not responding. I leaned up and kissed Jordan's cheek as our bald guide pushed open heavy doors and ripped the quiet away.

Loud screams and cheers filled the air around us as we stepped into the arena.

When Jordan spotted the ring in the center of the huge floor, circled by thousands of seats climbing up high, understanding filled his eyes. He looked down at me.

"Who's fighting?" he asked, putting his lips to my ear, smiling.

"I dunno." I giggled. "I don't know who they are; I just thought you'd like to watch. Since it's been a long time since you've done anything like this."

Jordan's smile was proud and affectionate as he stared down at me. We followed Tristan and our guide as they strode down the steps towards the center of the room and to our front-row seats. The fight was starting in just a few minutes.

We sat, Jordan's eyes still a little disbelieving. He kept looking at me. "Was this your idea?"

I smiled coyly. "Yeah."

Jordan shook his head, his smile big and beautiful. He leaned in and kissed my forehead, then my lips. "I love you."

"I love you more." It thrilled me that he was happy. I'd worried he'd think it was stupid.

When the idea initially came to mind, I decided to call Tristan; I didn't know how to navigate events like this, at big arenas with lots of people. I was out of my element. Tristan, on the other hand, was not.

"Oh, yeah," he'd said. I could hear the smile in his voice. "A few years after he came home, we started going to fights all the time. We just haven't gone much in the last few years. I think this is the perfect idea. You're brilliant."

I was thrilled.

So, he helped me plan the trip. Tristan apparently knew "a few people here and there," and that was how we were able to skip the line and head straight to the front row. I tried paying him for our seats, but he wouldn't take it.

"Come on, Nina. You think we're paying for any of this?" He laughed. "The things people will do for your humble boyfriend are ridiculous." I had been stunned, but I'd shrugged as I wondered how many people really knew Jordan's name.

It was odd watching the fight, but I could see the allure of it, the thrill of watching two people trying to best each other.

Jordan checked on me a few times, when blood splattered, or somebody got hit maybe a little too hard. I just smiled up at him to show him I was fine. That he didn't need to baby me. I held onto his arm the whole time as we watched. I could see the look of intrigue in his eyes as he focused on the fight. I'd never seen him so engaged in something that was made for entertainment. The only time he looked away was to check on me and to assess the area around us.

I knew that he would do that, because I knew having me out in public stressed him. That was another reason I liked having Tristan there. I figured it might put Jordan at ease, knowing that I was surrounded by two fighters myself.

He still skimmed the room many times during the two hours we were there.

When the fight ended, people stuck around. I wasn't entirely sure if there would be another one, but Tristan and Jordan both stood up.

"The rookies hop in the ring now," Tristan told me. "We don't watch those."

I chuckled. "I used to watch them all the time," Jordan told me. He kissed my temple for the millionth time.

"Yes, your humble old man used to watch anyone fight."

I laughed.

When we got out to our cars, I thanked Tristan for all his help.

"Ain't no thang, sugar." He pulled me in for a hug, then looked up at his brother. "Happy birthday. Be nice to her," he instructed, tilting his chin down towards me. "She planned all of this."

I shook my head. "Stop it." I nearly blushed with joy.

Jordan wrapped his arms around me, kissing my head.

"Always," he said.

We watched Tristan drive off and then slid into my car.

"I hope that was fun for you," I confessed hesitantly.

"Oh, baby," he said, leaning towards me and taking my face in his hand. I noticed his big body then, his masculinity hitting my nerves as he touched me. I nearly shuddered.

As he kissed me, I pictured Jordan winning a fight. Every fight.

I smiled.

"I loved it," he said softly. "That was incredibly thoughtful of you. Thank you so very much."

"Tristan helped a *lot*," I informed him.

He shook his head. "I don't care about that idiot." I laughed. "It was your idea, not his."

"He did help, though."

"Good. You would've gone through unnecessary trouble if you did this by yourself. He knows enough people."

"Yeah, he said you guys used to come to these all the time."

"Yeah, we did. We haven't in a long time, though. That made this really special," he added quietly.

"It was really nice having him there, right?"

He nodded. "It was."

"Just like old times." I grinned.
Jordan rested his head of big black hair against his headrest, sitting back. "Better."
We drove home, Jordan's big hand on my thigh the whole time, stroking it with his thumb.
He was quiet for most of it, except for when he was telling me how much he loved me and thanking me for being so thoughtful. I couldn't stop smiling.
Part One: Success.
When we stepped into the house, it was nearly six. Our reservation was for eight.
"I'm gonna go take a quick shower in the hallway bath; you go in ours."
"No, love. Go in our bathroom."
I shook my head. "No arguing. It's your birthday." I took his hand and guided him up the stairs.
He complied, and we both showered quickly. I didn't get my hair wet, just freshened up and washed my face so I could re-do my makeup.
Afterwards, I padded to the guest room for the bag with my garments for the night and brought it back to the bathroom.
I slid on the long-sleeved and fitted, navy blue dress that came down to my knees.
I assessed myself in the mirror, nodding slowly. *Not bad.*
I slipped on the blue heels I'd ordered to match my dress and walked carefully down the steps. Jordan was already in the kitchen, in a long-sleeve, black button-down and dark gray slacks. The top few buttons undone revealed just two inches of skin under his collarbones. The black fabric looked beautiful on his tan complexion.
My knees nearly buckled, and not due to the new heels.
He stared at me for a long time.
"You are so beautiful, Nina," he finally murmured.
I walked up and wrapped my arms around his neck, kissing him slowly.
"Honey, are you going to be okay driving in heels? Do you want me to drive?"
I shook my head. "No, I can do it. It's actually not that hard."
The drive downtown was also long. We sat there peacefully, Jordan looking over at me repeatedly, staring at me with a loving look on his face that made me feel good.
We arrived at the tall building in which the five-star restaurant was situated. As we exited the car, Jordan spoke briefly with the valet, taking charge, even on his own special day. We held hands as we entered, making our way to the elevator and finally, the top floor.
I didn't have enough money to rent out the restaurant, but I did invest in the best table they had.

When Jordan saw the restaurant as we entered, his eyes widened slightly. After I'd murmured quietly to the hostess who I was and he saw our table, his shock became blatant.

The view of the river was stunning. I looked up at Jordan as he pulled out my chair for me and stared at the water simultaneously. I followed his gaze. It was nearly dark now, and the sky and water were both a rich blue. The river was calm, the water gently swaying as the tiny waves sounded up to us. Across the way, we could see the tall, lit-up buildings on the other side. It was beautiful. Jordan seemed to think so, too, and when he looked down at me, his eyes, just a little wider than usual, were full of wonder.

"I love you, Nina. I love you."

I smiled, stretching up and kissing his lips softly.

"I love you more. Come sit."

He waited until I was comfortably seated before he settled.

"What do you feel like eating, baby? We haven't had anything since breakfast." I was worried about his giant self and ridiculously fast metabolism.

Jordan skimmed the menu for just a few seconds before looking up at me. "I'm uncertain."

I smiled. "You didn't even look."

"I don't want to look at it. I want to look at you."

I chuckled, feeling special. "I understand that completely. You're the most gorgeous thing that's ever existed," I stated casually. His lips turned up. "But I need to get some food in you, big guy."

Now Jordan was grinning, a shiny white smile that gleamed against the night. "Okay. Salmon?" He raised an eyebrow.

"Whatever you want, lovely. Sounds good to me."

"What would you like to eat?"

"Crab cakes." I smiled.

"That's it?"

I nodded. "They're filling. So," I began, before he could argue. "Tell me. How are you feeling right now?"

He blinked, his face soft. "I feel amazing, my love. You've made today so incredible."

I smiled. "It's not over." I assessed his heavy lids, and the purple underneath his bottom lashes. "You tired, sweetie?" I asked gently.

"No, I feel wide awake."

I reached forward and gently caressed his cheek with the backs of my fingers. "You've been working so hard," I said softly. "I'm so happy you took the day off to relax with me."

His lips turned up at the corners. "It was too irresistible a thought."

"Aw. My baby." I frowned a little. "You *are* tired, my love. I can tell." Though his eyes were invigorated, having had a fiery intrigue since the fight this afternoon, his energy was low. "And I know it couldn't have been easy for you to take off work. I want you to know it means so much to me that you did." I took his hand and kissed the back of it.

Just then, our tall, thin waiter approached. I'd made sure to ask them to pick someone to serve us while I made the reservation. I wanted to know as much as I could coming into this date, after feeling so clueless at the arena while Tristan led the way. Knowing our waiter made me feel more in control. Kind of like Jordan, in any situation he handled.

"Rick," I murmured. The hostess had pointed him out to me, so I knew exactly who to expect.

The tall, young man smiled. "Ms. Nina."

"You can just call me Nina." I was glad he was even told my name.

"Of course. What can I get the two of you to drink?"

"I'd like this berry cocktail, but Rick." I smiled. "I need you to put half the amount of vodka in it. I'm only drinking for the taste, and," I winked at Jordan, "I'm driving."

Rick smiled. "Absolutely."

Jordan was grinning, his eyebrows up high. He was surprised, because I didn't drink. "If you'd like to have a drink, my love, I will absolutely drive home."

I giggled a little. "No, you're drinking, too."

Now he raised just one eyebrow. "Am I?" The smile on his face was delicious.

"Mhm. At least a beer." Jordan didn't drink either, but that didn't mean he hadn't had anything his whole life.

"He'll nurse a beer if you give it to him," Tristan had told me, after I'd asked if I should buy us a bottle. "Don't buy him a bottle. He's been to many upscale events where he didn't even touch a glass. A beer will suffice. He kind of likes them. He doesn't care to drink anything else at all. You two nerds are perfect for each other."

Jordan smiled, unable to say no to me. "Sure, love." He looked at Rick. "Any one you have." Rick nodded, taking notes.

"Any appetizers for the two of you?"

Jordan looked at me. "Beet salads, tomato bisque. Please."

As he wrote and nodded, Rick said, "I will bring fresh bread as well."

After he walked away, Jordan took my hand. "You're adorable."

I grinned. "Why? Because I have to cut my vodka in half?"

"No, because you planned a perfect, perfect day, went out of your way to do such amazing, thoughtful things, and I would've been thrilled to just be at home with you. You've made this day incredible, my love. And leaving work wasn't so hard. I knew my whole weekend would be with you, and that made it very easy, actually. Don't worry about that." He kissed the back of my hand. His words made my heart feel full.

Rick brought out Jordan's beer and my cocktail, which was sweet and fruity and didn't taste like vodka at all. Perfect.

Jordan nursed his beer the way Tristan had said he would. We ordered our meals when Rick brought us our drinks, and it didn't take long for them to come out.

As we ate, Jordan looked down at my dish. "Share with me."

I shook my head. "I'm already getting full."

"You're so little, baby." His eyebrows knitted together. "I'm worried you're not eating enough."

I blinked. "Is this dress that flattering?"

Jordan shook his head slightly. "It's not the dress. You just are."

I pursed my lips, thoughtful. I didn't think I'd lost weight.

"Okay," I told him, trying not to be delighted by his words. *Thinner isn't always better.* "I'll try to eat more." I wanted to make him feel good on his birthday.

He cut a piece of salmon and extended his fork to me. When I bit it off, he smiled. His relief was obvious, and it touched my heart.

We spent a few hours sitting there, laughing and talking. He held my hand for most of it, never quite losing the wonder in his eyes.

I was thrilled he'd enjoyed his day so far. But I could tell he was tired. It showed in his eyes.

I wanted to get him home and in bed, resting. I remembered his sleeping face in the morning, how peaceful and relaxed he was, as his body was able to shut down for a little while. I didn't think he slept enough when he was working on intense cases, and this one was clearly keeping him up more than I realized.

When we were ready to leave, Jordan asked Rick for the check right in front of me. He probably assumed I would protest but did it anyway.

"There is nothing for you to pay," I murmured before Rick could respond. Jordan's eyes narrowed slightly.

"Rick," I told him, looking up at him and smiling as I stood. Jordan followed suit. "Thank you so much for everything tonight."

"Thank *you*, for your generosity, Nina." He smiled, wished us a good night, and went off.

I met Jordan's incredulous eyes. "You paid ahead of time?" He was disgruntled; I could see it.

"Yes, m'love," I told him lightly. "It's your birthday. I get to treat you for once."

But I'd broken a code. Jordan *always* paid for food.

"Listen, you gotta let me do this for you, at the very least, today," I said softly, taking his cheek in my hand. He blinked his lowered eyelids, the mild flatness that had taken over his face dissipating now.

"You tipped him, too."

I almost laughed. He spoke as though it was the ultimate betrayal.

I sighed instead. "Did you hear what I just said?"

He nodded once, putting his hands on my waist. "You didn't have to do any of this, my love." He wouldn't say it, but he didn't like my spending money on him. Because I earned far less than he did. Far, far less.

"I wanted to." I kissed his cheek and took his hand. His eyes were still stunned.

On the drive home, he again held onto me in any way he could. Whether his hand was on my thigh or stroking my hair or cheek, he never lost contact. I could feel the love emanating from him.

When we arrived, Jordan kissed my temple as we stepped inside the house.

"Come on, my sweet love," he murmured. "Let's go up to bed."

I took his hand. "In just a sec." I grabbed his hand and pulled him to the kitchen.

In the middle of the island, just where Tristan had told me he'd left it, was a beautiful, three-tiered, round birthday cake covered in white chocolate shavings. There was one candle in the center, and Tristan had left a lighter right next to the cake for me.

I smiled as I lit the candle, meeting Jordan's once again surprised eyes and charmed smile.

"That cake wasn't there when we left?" He walked up and kissed my forehead, the smile never leaving his lips.

"I gave Tristan my key. He'll give it back tomorrow or Saturday."

Jordan just stared at me, that same look of wonder, having nearly manifested into awe, in his eyes.

"Now, I'm no vocalist myself, so I'm hoping you don't want me to sing, but…"

He chuckled. "No, sweetheart." Kissing my forehead again, he wrapped his arms around me. "You are the sweetest, most precious person that has ever existed."

He blew out his candle, and we cut a single slice for us to share. We both took a couple bites, Jordan feeding me off his own spoon, as he seemed to like to do. I giggled shyly every time.

I put the lid on the cake and stuck it in the fridge. I promised Tristan he could have some the next day. I just couldn't let Jordan come home to a cake with a missing slice.

"Okay, now we can go to bed."

I slipped off my heels and followed him upstairs to our room. As we climbed the stairs, he spotted the red indentations the shoes had left in my foot.

"Baby," he half-gasped, half-whispered, "those shoes did that to you?" He sat me on the bed and, to my complete shock, took my foot gently in his hands and rubbed his thumb over the lines.

"It's okay, honey," I told him. "They're new. And when you don't wear certain shoes a lot, they mess up your feet a lil'. It's okay."

Jordan continued gently massaging one foot, then the other, his eyebrows knitted together as he assessed the red marks. I smiled.

The man really did have a soft spot for me.

"They'll go away in a little bit." I was so happy to finally have those shoes off. Nothing better than taking off a pair of heels and hopping into bed.

"Would you like to take another shower, my love?" I asked, trying to distract him.

"I think I'm good for the night. How about you?"

I thought for a moment. "Yeah, just to wash this makeup off. I'll be out in two minutes."

True to my word, I stepped out of the bathroom just a few minutes later, only my hair was wet. I couldn't stop myself. I had to wash it.

Jordan, who now wore blue joggers and a big, long-sleeved white shirt, was sitting up in bed, a book in his hand. He looked so cozy. I wanted to crawl in next to him and go to sleep, but there was something else I had to do first. Seeing him read made me think this was the perfect time.

"I'll be right back," I told him, smiling. I felt his eyes on me as I exited and headed to the guest room. I came back with a stack of boxes in my hands. His eyes were wide as I set them down on the bed in front of him.

"Nina, you bought more presents?"

"I told you I did." I was already grinning. I knew I wouldn't be able to stop. I was so excited to give him things; I rarely ever got the opportunity. The day had gone so well thus far, and I figured this would top it off nicely.

"Baby." His voice was soft. I handed him the first one.

I'd individually wrapped five designer shirts, two of them sweaters, one a dress shirt, two casual for the house, and a new pair of winter boots.

If there was one person I wanted to break the bank for, it was him.

Every time I handed him another one, his face was even more stunned. After the shoes, I handed him his last box.

It was heavier than the others. Jordan gently peeled off the wrapping paper and lifted the lid to the sturdy box.

As he pulled out each of the four different books, his face softened even more. The shock on his face eased up as his lips turned up at the corners.

I'd researched numerous books on computer technology, trying to find newer ones that were already highly rated. I didn't want to risk buying him one he already had, so I went for books released just this year.

"Nina," he uttered. "This is so thoughtful."

"I just wanted to get you stuff you could use. I know there aren't many things you typically like to shop for, or..."

"Honey, this is incredible. I love every single thing you bought me. I'm wearing that sweater to work on Monday," he said, pointing at the light beige fabric next to me. I grinned. "And I am thrilled to read these."

"I was worried I'd get you something you'd already read."

He shook his head. "I've never seen these before. I know of this author," he stated, gesturing to one of the glossy covers, "but haven't read this one."

"They were all released this year." Jordan met my eyes. "I wasn't taking any chances."

He stared at me, smiling, for a few moments. I reached forward and took his cheek in my hand so I could stroke his temple with my thumb, and he took my face in his palm as well, leaning in to kiss me softly. I pulled back and brushed my fingers over his hair gently. His eyes were more tired up close.

I wanted badly to get him some rest.

"What would you like to do right now, my love?" I asked him, my voice soft. "You ready to sleep?"

Jordan stared into my eyes for a few moments. "Yeah, with you." He touched the spot next to him. "If you're ready."

I nodded. Suspicions confirmed.

"I sure am." I smiled, kissing his cheek.

After I stacked all his new clothes on the dresser to be washed tomorrow, set his boots by the doorway, and he piled his books on the nightstand next to him, we settled into bed together.

Jordan wrapped his arms around me tightly, kissing my head over and over again.

"Thank you for such a special day," he whispered. "You have made me the happiest I have ever been. It was so thoughtful of you to take me to a fight. I hadn't been to one in a while. I can't believe you thought of it without even knowing Tristan and I used to go." I shrugged against him, thrilled by his words.

"Dinner was phenomenal. Breakfast was, too. It was even better having it with you there this year."

I smiled against his chest.

"This is by far the best birthday I have ever had," he whispered into my hair. I tightened my arm around his waist, kissing his abdomen.

"I just wanted to make you happy."

"You did. And you do. Every second of every day."

It was Jordan's idea to have our families meet for the first time at our house. I woke up at six in the morning that Saturday. We needed to go to the store, which excited me. I loved to plan and prepare for parties and gatherings, so this part would be fun.
"Would you have come if you weren't worried about my safety?" I asked when we were in the truck.
He looked at me, surprised. "Of course I would. What made you say that?"
I shrugged. "I dunno. Guess I just want to make sure you actually like spending time with me." I bit my lip to hide a smile, but I was only half-joking.
Jordan put his hand on my thigh and glanced at me for a second at a time while he drove.
"I love spending time with you." He picked my hand up and brought it to his mouth, kissing the back of it. "It's my favorite thing to do."
I smiled shyly. Once more, I felt so blessed to have him.
Every time I feared I would lose him, the thought flickered through my brain that God put him right in front of me because he wanted us to be together. I held his hand while he drove.
When we arrived at the large grocery store, I grabbed a shopping cart. We began perusing the aisles, taking our time. That was the benefit of waking up early. I didn't have to rush.
I filled up the basket, thinking hard to make sure I didn't forget anything and looking at every shelf to see if there was something else we would benefit from buying.
I was going to cook, and then I changed my mind. It would be so much easier to get a couple trays of food and use up all my planning creativity baking a couple of desserts. I would stress myself out trying to cook enough

food for everyone. Jordan agreed, though he told me that if I wanted to do it, he would help me.

"Maybe another time," I'd told him. We'd pick up the food together later.

When we got to the register, I tried to pay, as I did every now and again. But Jordan was already there, wallet in hand. I sighed.

As we walked away with our groceries bagged up neatly in the cart, I murmured, "You gotta let me feel useful sometimes."

He kissed my head as we walked. "You are useful, and hardworking, and perfect, and all I want to do is pay your bills, and you won't let me." I looked up at him in disbelief, laughing. He was grinning. I held onto his arm as he pushed the cart, thrilled by his silly mood.

On the way home, I played some music; we didn't speak much. While we were out, I'd forgotten about the situation we were in, being extra cautious about our safety while Jordan worked this case. It was nice.

When we pulled into the driveway, I quietly asked, "Are you still having people watch our families?"

Jordan put the car in park and turned to look at me. "Yes, my love," he said, voice low and soft, the deepness of it as beautiful as ever.

As we met around to the trunk to get the groceries, he said, "Why do you ask that?"

I shrugged. "I don't know." I paused for a moment, thinking. "I worry about them."

Jordan nodded. "They'll be okay. I've got people watching your family nonstop."

"Yours, too," I murmured.

He nodded again. "Tristan has a couple guys, but he mostly spends a lot of time with them himself nowadays. This case has him extra worried."

I sighed. *Me too.*

"Don't you think those people you send to look out for them get bored?" I asked; we each picked up a bunch of bags and walked inside.

"I don't think so. They're very focused individuals, so they know that the job means more than sitting around all day, doing nothing. They're on high alert." As we set the groceries on the counter, he added, "That's what they get paid for."

I smiled a little to myself, going back to get more groceries. It was unbearably attractive when he talked like the boss.

"I'm really excited to see Tristan tonight," I told him. "It's so fun hanging out with him."

"Yeah?" Jordan replied, smiling small. "I'm glad." Then out of nowhere he said, "He's an idiot."

I burst out laughing. When I looked back at him, he was smiling, just watching me laugh.

Oh, my love. My heart couldn't take it.

I walked up to him and kissed his cheek, smiling big.

"I love you," I said cheerily. He grinned even bigger.

"I love *you*." He pulled my face in for a kiss.

Joy flashed through me; the fatigue from this morning subsided. I loved the good mood we were both in; though things were stressful, today felt laid-back. We would be with our families, all of us safe at home, together. The thought was cozy to me.

"You're so cozy, Jordy," I murmured against his cheek. "And you know how much I love cozy."

I played music, and we cleaned for a while, straightening up certain rooms, wiping down others. We could've been married. We were certainly a team, a family. I felt full.

Around one, the cleaning was all done. I had a marble cake in the oven and had just taken the sugar cookies out. The cake was nearly done. As I waited for the timer to drop its last sixty seconds, I turned to look at Jordan.

While I baked, he worked on his laptop, sitting at the kitchen island nearby. He initially offered to help me, and I took him up on the sugar cookies, because I hated shaping the dough. I did the cake on my own, though; it was easier, and I knew he had better things to do. It was nice to just have him there while I worked. Sometimes, I looked up and he was just watching me as I maneuvered through the kitchen, cracking eggs, pouring oil, weighing flour, pouring batter, setting the timer, sticking a knife in to see how the cake was baking. Sometimes, when I looked at him, the beauty he radiated would stun me for a moment, and I would wonder, *How did I get this blessed? How did a man like* that *fall in love with me?* I would smile shyly and look back to my work, still feeling his eyes on me.

I walked up to him now, draping my arms over his shoulders, forcing him to turn away from his laptop and the kitchen island to face me.

Jordan smiled up at me, and I leaned down and kissed him.

Softly at first, but then the kisses got deeper. Jordan wrapped his big hands around my waist and opened his knees, so he could pull me against him.

The timer went off.

Jordan kept kissing me in spite of it, and I didn't fight him.

A few extra seconds wouldn't burn anything.

Finally, I pulled back.

"The cake is gonna burn," I breathed.

He kissed my neck, and I turned to grab it from the oven.

In time, Nina. In time.

When the desserts were complete, I went upstairs to shower. He went to the library to check in at work. When I finished and entered the bedroom, there he was, pulling off his shirt.

I walked up and kissed his cheek. He pulled out a pale yellow sweater and a gray one and asked which he should wear.

"Yellow," I told him, smiling small. I asked if I should get dressy.

"Be comfortable."

When we were dressed, he took my hand, walking with me down the stairs. Everyone was supposed to arrive at six and, knowing my family and the fifty-ish minute drive they had, they'd probably be late. A little before five, Jordan's phone pinged.

After reading something, his face turned the slightest bit frustrated.

"What's the matter?" I asked him, hating the shift in his mood. I wrapped my arms around his waist and looked up at him, eyes concerned.

"My dad's car stopped running yesterday. He didn't tell me."

"Why not?" *Oh, Amar.*

"He thought he would have it fixed by now, but the shop is taking too long, he said." Jordan sighed and looked down at me. "I'm going to go pick them up. I'm sorry, love. Do you want to come with me?"

I shook my head. "Why are you sorry?"

"Because it's the last minute, and I'm leaving."

"It's okay, honey." But my eyebrows knitted together.

I didn't want him to leave, but I couldn't go with him. I had to get the food. He would be gone nearly an hour and a half, at the quickest. I considered texting my mom and telling her to aim to get here around seven and not six.

"I'm really so sorry, my love." Jordan grabbed his keys and came over and kissed my head. "I shouldn't be too long. My mom just texted me that my aunt will bring them halfway, so the drive should be roughly the same amount of time as going one way."

"Oh, that's good. Otherwise you would have been gone for almost two hours. But that's okay." I shrugged. "Seven is not too late to start an evening."

Jordan frowned. "When your other company is over, it is."

I smiled up at him, not liking that frown on his face. "It's okay; you guys will get back around the same time, and everything is pretty much done." I looked around at the clean house, glanced into the kitchen to assess. We had soda, drinks and desserts. I just had to go pick up the food.

"I'm gonna leave now, too." I went to grab my jacket.

"Oh," I heard him mutter to himself and then exhale through his nose in frustration.

"What's wrong?" I said, alarmed, coming back into the room. I thought maybe he'd gotten another unfortunate text. Hopefully, Tristan didn't bail.

"I completely forgot about the food." His face was upset, his eyes suddenly tired. I went up to him again and cupped his cheek in my hand.

"It's *okay*," I soothed, unsure why he was so bothered by it. I knew it scared him when I went out alone, but I had been calling him every single time I walked to and from my car, on the phone with him before I even opened my door to get out. Nighttime was harder for him, though we both knew that daytime could be just as dangerous.

"It's okay," I whispered again, into his neck. I wanted to wrap my arms around him, but I knew I wouldn't want to let go once I did.

"Come on," I said, keeping my tone light. "Let's walk out together."

As he opened my car door for me, I smiled. "Why don't you tell your aunt to come, too?" Jordan's mom only had one sister, with whom she was very close.

"Nada is not as social as my mother. And she's not much of a late-night person. By the time we actually sit down to eat, she'll be ready to go home."

"Sounds like me."

Jordan smiled, leaning down to kiss my head. "Be careful," he murmured into my hair. "Call me."

I nodded, eyes serious as I looked at him. I waited to drive until he got into his car, and then I backed out and headed to the restaurant.

The Arabic restaurant was only fifteen minutes from the house. When I arrived, I went inside the small restaurant and told the hostess I had a carry-out order for Jordan. He, of course, had already paid for it.

"Only one tray is ready," the young Arabic woman behind the cash register said, her accent dripping off of her words.

"Oh," I said lightly. "Will the other one be long?"

The woman made a face that said *Ehh. Yeah, probably*.

"I don't know for sure. I know they are taking the food off the grill and putting it right in. Everything is fresh," she added.

"Okay," I breathed. "That's okay. I'll take this one to the car now."

The silver tray was large, and I would have needed to make two trips, anyway. Hopefully, Jordan hadn't thought of the fact that it would be a lot to carry. *He would have a conniption, thinking of me doing it alone.* I chuckled to myself as I walked the first tray out to my car.

The night had already settled in. It was nearly dark, and there was a chill to the air. I didn't park far. Halfway there, I suddenly had an off-putting feeling, but I didn't know what it was. I turned around sharply, as though someone would be there. There was no one.

I sped up towards the car, stepping around to the trunk, lifting the door and setting the tray down quickly. I'd forgotten to call Jordan when I exited the car and when I came back out.

You idiot!

I slammed the trunk shut, slid my phone out of my jacket pocket and dialed him immediately, quickly walking back inside. I couldn't shake the odd feeling that someone was watching me. I thought at any second, someone would pop out.

"Hi, baby," Jordan said before the second ring.

"Hi," I said breathlessly.

"Are you okay?" he asked, his voice immediately hardening.

"Yeah, yeah," I assured him, not letting any angst slip into my voice. "I'm just going inside now." I wouldn't yet tell him about that feeling I'd just had as I walked to the car. He might panic.

"Okay," he said, sounding unconvinced. "It's already paid for."

"I know, baby." I bit my lip, opening the door to the restaurant once more and heading inside. "I forgot to call you the first time I went in. This is the second trip, 'cause I couldn't carry both trays at once. I'm sorry." I made a face, bracing myself for his reaction.

"Don't be mad at me," I blurted nervously. Jordan had never gotten angry with me before, but with all of the tension he was feeling because of work, I wouldn't have put it past him. He'd asked me for one simple thing.

"I'm not mad at you, baby," he said seriously. "Just as long as you have me now."

I made eye contact with the hostess. No, the second tray wasn't done yet.

"Um, I'm still waiting on the second tray. I guess it's still being made," I said quietly into the phone. I hoped it wouldn't be long. It was already five-thirty.

"That's okay," he murmured. "Keep me on the phone, I don't mind."

As I sat down on the bench for people waiting for tables or carry-out orders, I asked, "Where are you?" I tried to calm my sudden nerves from the parking lot, now that he was on the phone with me. There was no one in this area, except for the hostess a few feet away. I glanced through the windows, scanning the parking lot but seeing nothing. It was creepy, nonetheless.

"I'm almost to my parents. My aunt brought them a little more than halfway, which was nice of her. She didn't have to do that."

"Invite her," I murmured. "Hey, baby?"

"Yes, my love."

But then something flashed through my brain, and I didn't respond.

I remembered what happened that Monday after work a month prior, on the way to my car. How I'd felt the hair on the back of my neck stand, how I'd brushed it off, chalking it up to anxiety over Jordan and the things that were going on. How I'd forgotten about it just a few minutes after it happened.

The connection between what I'd learned about the case a month prior and that uncomfortable feeling in the parking lot then *and* now hit me, and I shivered. Hard.

I was an idiot.

I knew I would be horror-movie-stupid if I didn't tell Jordan this time.

"Nina?" he asked, his deep voice snapping me out of my thoughts.

"Hi, sorry," I breathed. "I just got distracted, I'm so sorry."

He was most assuredly going to be suspicious now.

"Are you okay?"

"Yeah, I'm good. I'm good." I exhaled hard, wondering when my breathing would go back to normal.

"You were gonna ask me something?"

"Oh, I..." I couldn't remember. *What* was *I going to ask him?* I thought it might have been something to do with the food...

"I can't remember, I'm sorry."

Jordan didn't speak for a moment. Finally, he murmured anxiously, "Are you sure you're okay, baby?"

I nodded, knowing he couldn't see me. "Yeah, sorry. I'm just a little out of it, I guess." *Shoot, what was I gonna ask him?*

"I don't think I'll make it there before you. It's taking longer than I thought."

"It's okay, honey. Just keep me on the phone."

"Okay." I tapped my foot restlessly. I was unnerved at the idea of being away from him.

I sat there for a few more minutes. Jordan didn't say much until he met up with his parents.

"I'll call you when the food comes out," I told him, wanting him to be free to talk to his mom and dad. "No use in bugging you when I'm just sitting here."

"It's okay, honey."

"Don't worry," I murmured. "I'll call you right back. Soon as it's done." I got off the phone with him, after he gave me a concerned "Okay."

I waited fifteen more minutes, feeling I was going mad. I knew what it was like to go from feeling fine to suddenly feeling as if everything was wrong, even if nothing was. It hadn't happened in a while. This shift in my mood was bothering me.

Finally, the second large tray of food was brought out.

I dialed Jordan immediately, ready to get to my car. "Okay," I said determinedly, "The food's here."

I exhaled, balancing the phone between my head and shoulder as I grabbed the other tray.

I couldn't rid myself of my discomfort. I looked around me as I walked quickly to the car. All I saw was a Middle Eastern couple with two small toddler girls, walking towards the restaurant entrance. The parking lot was full, but it wasn't large. There were about forty cars.

I slammed the trunk shut and went to the driver's door quickly. Even with Jordan on the phone, I was still uneasy.

"I'm in the car now," I murmured, still breathless from the cold and walking fast. I heard Amar and Rania speaking in Arabic in the background.

"Okay, my love. Thank you for calling me," he said.

"Of course."

When I *finally* got home, I saw my parents' car in the driveway. My chest sank inward. I was late and had missed the introductions.

Everyone except Jordan cheered when I walked in, holding only one tray of food. Tristan hadn't yet arrived. I chuckled tiredly.

"Hi, guys." Jordan took the tray out of my hands and set it down in the kitchen.

I smiled at and hugged everyone. Jordan headed outside to get the other tray.

I looked at my mom. "You met Rania and Amar?" They both turned towards us and said yes. Rania was smiling.
I tried to keep my face light. Tristan walked in behind Jordan, who carried the second tray of food. A flash of joy shot through me, watching him enter in his black jacket and jeans, looking like a stud. Oh, the giddiness I felt, thinking about Zana's reaction.
"Tristan," I called happily, meeting his eyes and smiling at him. He smiled back and said, "Hey, cutie pie." I turned to look at Zana, who was smiling politely and looking at him. When Tristan smiled at her and turned away to hang up his jacket, I saw her look at my mother, trying not to grin, her eyes widening. I smiled.
While Tristan made his introductions and everyone seemed comfortable, I approached Jordan in the kitchen. He had opened both trays. All the different meats, including chicken and beef kabobs, shawarma, tikka, cream chop, and more, sitting over yellow rice. It was steaming.
"Hey, Jord?" I murmured, stepping close to him. Everyone was just a few feet away in the family room. He looked down at me with calm but attentive eyes.
"Can I talk to you for a sec?" I had to get it off my chest.
He immediately became alert.
"Of course," he said quietly, taking my hand.
As we went into the foyer and stopped next to the front door, he gently asked, "What is it, my love? What's wrong?" He watched my eyebrows crinkle together, worry clouding his expression and tone. He stroked my hair.
I tried not to let my swallow be so obvious. "I have to tell you something," I said quietly, looking into his eyes, trying not to let mine show my anxiety.
"Tell me." He was focused.
I started speaking quickly. "When I was walking to and from the car at the restaurant, with the food, I...I had this weird feeling," I said, my voice getting pitchy and breathy. "Just like...uncomfortable instinct. I don't know. I felt...uneasy."
Jordan's gaze became more intense as I spoke, his eyebrows knitted together in concentration. "What was your first thought?" he asked me suddenly. "What was the first thing that popped into your head when you got that feeling?"
And, not having a choice but to do what he asked, because I loved him, because I could never, ever lie to him or deny him again, I blurted, "That someone was watching me."
That was when I saw the side of Jordan he had only ever teased, the side that peeked out from around the edges and called out to my intuition. Reiterating my suspicion that Jordan was a lethal man, if need be.
A rage like I had never seen before filled Jordan's eyes that made my knees weak. They buckled, and Jordan caught me. He put his hands around my

waist and pulled me close to him, our torsos touching, making sure he could still see my face.

Still holding onto me firmly, he asked, "Did you see anyone? Who was around? Everyone you can think of." There was not a trace of lightheartedness in his tone; he was all business.

"Just a family going into the restaurant the second time."

Then I blurted, "And there's something else." I forced myself to look at him, though the sharp seriousness on his face made me uncomfortable.

"I thought nothing of it at the time, I really didn't, or I would've told you; but I remembered today. About a month ago, it was a Monday, I think."

I swallowed. "When I was getting into my car after work, I...I got a chill, just randomly. On the back of my neck."

"What was your first thought?" he asked me again. "Really think about what first popped into your head. What your gut said."

"Same thing," I said quietly, feeling helpless. "Like someone was watching me."

"And then, was there anyone around?" Jordan's face was hard as stone.

I swallowed, trying to focus. "Most of our staff stays later than me. No one was outside. I looked around, but I didn't see anyone. Though I was expecting to." I blinked, trying hard to remember. "I even looked at the plaza across the street. I think I saw a couple getting into their car. I don't think the weird vibe came from there, though. The discomfort was coming from my parking lot, if that makes any sense."

Jordan stared at me intensely. "You're sure you didn't see anyone outside? Not a coworker, not anyone from the building next door? The store in front?"

"I don't think so, Jordy. I looked around for a solid ten seconds, then got freaked out and got in my car."

"You did the right thing," he murmured. "What about tonight? You're sure there wasn't anyone else?"

I nodded, eyes wide. "I looked around when I got in my car, as I drove off. I didn't see anyone."

"No people?"

"No. Everyone was inside." I felt like a disappointment. I wished so badly that I had an answer for him. A description of a person standing across the parking lot, staring at me. A height, hair color, male or female, bird or human. *Anything*. Anything to give him some answers.

After looking at me for a few moments, Jordan lifted his head and nodded.

"I'm taking you to and from work." There was finality in his voice. I had no desire to argue.

Jordan's face focused. "If I absolutely have to be somewhere else, then I will have someone follow and stay with you while you're there. Don't go anywhere without me. No stops on the way home, on the way to work, if I'm not with you."

I swallowed. The extremity of the situation was hitting me hard.

"Okay." I put my head down on his chest. I never wanted to part from him again.

Jordan wrapped his arms around me and kissed my head. He held me for a while, and then spoke into my hair, the sharpness of his voice fading away. "You just go to work and not worry about a thing, okay? And if you want lunch, or to go out to lunch, call me, and we'll go together. Please don't go alone. If you need something from your car, call me, and I'll come right away and get it for you. Please don't walk out of the building." He kissed my head. "I don't want to take any chances. Wait for me inside at the end of the day. I'll be there, right at five."

The picture of Jordan being the barrier between me and any potential danger came to mind. The reality that he would be the one to stop the violence, to put himself at risk, made me ache.

"Who's gonna protect you?" My voice cracked. If I felt this way, like I was the target, when we both knew that *he* was, how must he have felt?

"Don't worry about me, baby," he soothed gently. "No one can get me."

I knew he was right. I was certain there was nothing that could stop or get the best of him.

Yet my terror would not cease.

Not knowing what to say, I reached up and took his cheek into my hand, then I kissed his lips hard. I pulled back quickly in case someone came into the hallway and saw. I looked in the direction of the family room, where everyone was congregated, unaware of the grave situation we were in.

"Let's go back," Jordan whispered, keeping his arm around my waist as he turned towards the kitchen. He waited until I nodded before walking. "Enjoy yourself tonight. We'll talk about it when everyone is gone, okay? I'm sure you have more questions."

I tried to keep my face blank as I nodded. He kissed my temple as we made our way back.

"Hi, guys." I smiled, trying not to sound weak. Rania looked at me for a second, turned away, and then snapped her head back and stared.

Evidently, I wasn't doing a good job pretending.

"Let's get some food, guys," I told everyone, smiling at Rania and heading quickly to the kitchen.

"Help yourselves; dishes are right here. Then we can go into the dining room."

I lost my appetite. As I debated pouring some cranberry juice into a cup, Tristan approached me.

"So," he began, quietly enough so no one around us could hear. "Taking my brother into the hallway to make out when your families are fifteen feet away, huh?" I laughed. He grinned.

It was nice to relieve some of the tension I felt. Of course, Tristan would do just that.

But he knew. He was the only person in the room besides Jordan and me that knew what was going on. I appreciated his attempt to lighten things up.
I shook my head. "Shut your cute self up."
Tristan laughed. I asked him, "Do you want something to drink?"
He shook his head. "Not anything on this counter," he said, gesturing to the counter covered in two liters of soda and red cups. I chuckled.
"We have beer and wine coolers in the fridge, bottom drawer." I raised an eyebrow. "No vodka until later. Then everyone can go nuts."
He rolled his eyes. "If you really loved me, you'd give me somethin' good *now*." He set his forearms down on the counter, leaning towards me. "Matter 'a fact, give Jordan somethin'. Loosen him up a little."
Now I was the one rolling my eyes, grinning.
"Do whatever you do before you take him to bed," he said quietly, so Jordan wouldn't hear. If he had, he would've slapped him.
A loud laugh escaped my lips. Tristan laughed, too.
"Leave him be," I told him, still chuckling.
I grabbed my drink and we headed towards the dining room. Tristan stepped in front of me before I took four steps.
"Is everything okay?" he asked quietly, no trace of teasing left.
I took a breath. "Yeah. Yeah. Everything's good." I didn't know if Jordan would want him to know. I'd have to ask him later.
"Let's talk later," I suggested. He nodded in understanding. Not around the family. He put his free arm around my shoulders, the other hand carrying his food, and we walked through the family room together.
I sat next to Jordan, of course, and Tristan on the other side of me. It just so happened that Tristan ended up next to Zana. Despite the stress Jordan and I were feeling, I was ready to sit back and watch her drool. Cute guy at work or not.
Our parents spoke in Chaldean. I didn't know what they were talking about. I leaned my head a few inches closer to Jordan's and asked.
"It started with where they were all from, who their parents are. Now they're talking about you and me." He kept his voice quiet.
My eyebrows shot up. "Will you tell me later?"
He nodded. I took his hand. "Eat," I commanded. I needed him to stay healthy and strong, so I'd loaded a plate of food for him, despite his protests.
He picked up his fork and murmured, "You, too, please."
I nodded, mimicking his motion with my fork and taking small bites of chicken. I had no appetite.
"So," I began, speaking louder, "Zana, Elijah, did you guys meet Tristan?" Elijah nodded. "Yeah."
"No." Zana smiled. "I'm Zana."
I assumed the few inches between Zana and Tristan had her sweating bullets.

"Nice to meet you." He smiled, taking a huge bite of food like an animal. I chuckled.
"Whatchu laughin' at?" he said after he swallowed.
I shrugged. "You're funny."
He looked down at Zana, and I knew his gorgeous, tan face, big eyes, muscular body in that fitted green shirt had her going crazy.
"She loves me more than Jordan," he said, so smugly that everyone except Amar and Jordan started laughing.
I chuckled. "You wish." I leaned over again and put my head down on Jordan's arm. He kissed my head.
"No kissing at the dinner table, you slobs."
By the way she and everyone else were laughing, I knew Tristan would have my sister weak by the end of the night. Or by the end of dinner.
I turned and smiled up at Jordan. I felt Tristan's eyes on us.
I disregarded everyone else for a moment and assessed Jordan's expression. The worry was drowning him. It made my heart hurt.
I wished I hadn't had to tell him about the feeling I had, but I knew for my own good that I did.
All night, Tristan watched us carefully, pretending he wasn't. I could feel his eyes on me and caught him staring at Jordan, too.
After dinner, everyone returned to the family room while Jordan and I cleaned up the kitchen, packing up the food. I went to wipe the table in the dining room and when I came back, Tristan and Jordan were alone in the kitchen, speaking quietly. Each deserved time to speak with his brother, so I stood, dirty wipe in my hand, next to my mother, Zana and Rania seated on the couch.
"Isn't it a beautiful house?" I murmured.
"It is," she agreed, smiling up at me. "I hope you're keeping it clean."
"Of course I am. He's so gracious to me," I added quietly. "He'd let me destroy the place if I wanted to. I could never."
I glanced back up at him, and he was blatantly staring at me as he spoke to his brother. He said something to Tristan and then called my name.
I walked over to the kitchen and threw the wipe away.
"I didn't want to interrupt," I said, smiling.
Jordan put his arm around my waist. "You wouldn't have been." He kissed my head. "Tristan and I were just talking about the case," he said quietly.
"I appreciate the consideration, though," Tristan added. "Jordan doesn't wanna keep anything from you, and I think that's wise. You're levelheaded. You're also close to Jordan." Tristan was honest and straightforward; the federal agent in him showed. "You need to know the risk you're at, so you know how to approach it."
A thought occurred to me. "Was someone watching me tonight? When I went to get the food?" I turned to Jordan.
His face filled with regret quickly. "I didn't have anybody here, no." His voice was low and full of guilt. "I was supposed to go with you."

"It's okay," I whispered, putting my arm around his waist and looking up into his eyes. "I was just wondering if maybe that's what I felt." I worried about the blaze in his eyes, and how badly he was beating himself up.

"No." He swallowed; his face was grim. "I thought keeping you on the phone would be good, since you weren't so far from home, and we've had cops surveilling the area." I watched his hand ball into a fist, and he nearly growled, "I was wrong."

My chest started to ache in a way it never had before. "It's okay," I whispered again. "I'm fine."

"And we're just going to be more careful, now," Tristan cut in, and I knew he could see what was happening to his brother. What he was doing to himself. The agony he was feeling. Tristan seemed alarmed by it but was trying to remain cool to soothe us.

"I've got teams working on this, Nina," he informed me, cutting short the conversation about my drive to the restaurant. "The FBI knows. They're helping, however they can. We can," he corrected, but I knew that, when it came down to it, Tristan was more on Jordan's team than he was the Bureau's. He worked for the FBI, but he lived for his family. Would do anything for his brother. That love nearly brought tears to my eyes.

So would I.

I nodded. He continued. "We'll keep you guys posted. I've been talkin' to Jordan a lot, but I want you to know." His eyes were serious but tired. The tired eyes of a cop. "We've got the city cops on the ground, making sure everything over here is clear, everything by Jordan's building as well. While Jordan and the team pin these people down."

I squeezed Jordan's side. He turned and kissed my head.

"Okay," I replied quietly. "Thank you. For everything you're doing. For telling me, too."

He nodded. "Just listen to what Jordan tells you, because he *knows* what it takes to keep you safe. And if you ever need anything, just call me," he instructed. "Jordan already knows to."

Again, I nodded. "Thank you. Tell me if there's anything I can do to help, too. Use me as bait if you need to," I said sincerely. Jordan stiffened.

"Never." His voice was a growl now, coming from gritted teeth. I felt bad.

"We don't need that," Tristan said, much more gently. "You're the best, though." He smiled, trying to make me feel better, knowing his brother was not himself.

Rania walked up then, deciding that her boys weren't allowed to keep secrets from her.

"What's going on?" she asked loudly, her accent coating her words. "You're all too *cool* to be with your family?" It was cute.

Tristan and I smiled, and he put his arm around her. Jordan's face did not change.

JORDAN

"No, mom, we're not. We're coming right now." He kissed her head and turned to guide her to the family room, looking back at us with concerned eyes. Rania wasn't having it.

"Jordan, baby, what's wrong?" she asked, noticing the upset look on Jordan's usually smooth face, the rage melding with the fiery pale blue of his irises. Rania's eyes were worried, eyebrows knitted together as she, in all her Middle Eastern fierceness, prepared to leap upon anything that was bothering her baby.

"Nothing, mom," he said quietly, his voice surprisingly clear and smooth in contrast to what it had just sounded like. He said a few words in Arabic to her. She studied his face.

"Okay," she said, her accent heavy. Tristan, his arm still around her, guided her to the family room. She looked back, and Jordan and I followed them.

"I told her I didn't sleep well last night," he murmured. I nodded.

As we came to the family room, I noticed my father and Amar talking. They seemed to be getting along well.

"Nina," my father called from across the room. As I walked over to him, I heard my mother and Rania discussing how they make one of our Chaldean dishes. I smiled.

"Hi," I murmured, smiling at my father and Amar. "Hi, Amar, how are you doing? Can I get you guys something to drink?"

Amar shook his head.

"I'm fine for now," my father agreed. He paused for a moment. "I like this house."

I smiled bigger. "Isn't it nice?"

"Yeah. Did he renovate?"

"That's a good question. Let's ask him." I called Jordan over.

He walked up and put his hand on my lower back. "Hey, did you renovate the house at all when you moved in?" I, of course, knew that he'd left most of it as is but did put carpet in the family room.

My man. Made the house cozy, like he knew I was coming later on.

It was a nice thought, untrue as it was.

"Not too much. The carpet, painted the walls in the library and got new shelves." He looked at my father as he spoke. Then, he murmured to me, "Let's sit down, honey."

Jordan pulled me down at the same time as him, and I was happy and nervous to see that he chose the spot next to my father.

"I like it," my father repeated to Jordan, referring to the house.

"Thank you."

"You know, as headstrong as she is, I'm surprised Nina didn't come in here and change everything around. You know, she really loves designing and decorating?"

"I know that she likes to decorate. She told me she wanted to put up holiday decorations in our front yard." He looked down at me and gave me a small smile that melted my heart.

I nodded. "You know I like to do that stuff, dad." I looked at Jordan and then at Amar. "You should've seen our house last Christmas. Hundreds and hundreds of dollars." Amar smiled.

"It was worth it. Some cars slowed down in front of the house, and I realized parents were showing their kids the decorations. It was lovely."

Jordan was smiling down at me fondly.

"I bet it was amazing," he murmured. My father always seemed to be watching every sweet moment Jordan and I had.

"Nina can change anything she wants around here," Jordan told my dad. "I don't care. It's just as much her house as it is mine."

I smiled small. My dad watched my face, and I couldn't tell what was going through his mind.

What I did know was that the rest of the room heard Jordan's words. I glanced up to Zana and saw that everyone was watching us.

"Pardon my eavesdropping and interrupting," Tristan began, leaning over the top of the couch where his mother sat, "But I think you meant that it's *hers* now, Jordan. Nina's stronger than you, and she takes what she wants." I grinned slowly as he sounded more and more like an idiot. "She took one step inside, looked around and said *That's it. It's mine.*" He turned to Zana. "Same thing she did when she saw Jordan for the first time."

Everyone in the room besides Jordan laughed, including my parents. I chuckled, looking up at him. Jordan smiled down at me again. My chest ached.

Despite what Tristan said, I was Jordan's. The first time I saw him, I was his.

My whole heart belonged to him.

JORDAN

Saturday night, once we'd hugged and kissed everyone goodnight, Jordan silently locked up and set the house alarm.

I stood at the doorway, assessing the room to see if there was anything left I should pick up. Jordan came back into the room and said, "I'll be back in just a second," then headed to the library.

A moment later, he returned, holding a cell phone out to me.

"Use this. My number is in it. You can program your family's, your boss's, your coworkers right now with your phone."

Slowly, I looked from his eyes to the phone and silently took it into my hands. I walked over to my own phone and immediately began copying all the important phone numbers into the new one.

I looked up at him when I was done. "What do I do with this?" I asked, holding up my own cell phone.

"I'll take it," he said. I handed it to him.

"This is temporary, until we completely stop the filth that's giving us trouble."

I blinked. His mood had gone flat.

"It's okay," I said. "I don't care. I don't need that." I tilted my chin in the direction of the phone.

The anxiety from earlier, that I'd brushed off while we were with our families, came and settled back onto my shoulders and chest. My face became solemn, the joy gone; watching Jordan feel this way hurt me.

He pulled me close to him and kissed my head. "Let me just put this away," he murmured, referring to the cell phone, "and then we'll go to bed." I nodded, not saying a word.

Once he'd returned from the library, he took my hand and we headed for the stairs. When we finally settled into bed for the night, I was exhausted, my eyelids already heavy but the uneasy feelings kept my mind awake.
I knew it was worse for Jordan.
Without a word, I pulled him down and put his head on my chest, wrapping my arms around him before he could do the same with me. I wouldn't let him soothe me, as much as I wanted him to. I would care for him.
He looked at me with alert eyes for a moment, and then his eyelids lowered. Keeping his face turned up towards mine, he stared into my eyes and said, "I love you more than anything. Do you know that?" It took me a moment to process the heaviness in his voice, the gravity his words held.
"I love you, too, baby," I murmured, my voice low. I kissed his forehead. "Everything's gonna be okay."
"Yes. It will be." He crossed his arm over my chest and brought his hand up to my cheek. "I don't want you to be afraid. You have nothing to fear."
I tried to keep my face smooth as I whispered, "Okay. Okay, baby."
Jordan stared into my eyes for a few more moments and then finally turned and laid his head my chest. I put my hand on his cheek this time and kissed his bed of thick black hair.
His eyes stayed wide open. As I stroked it with my fingers, I soothed him. "It's okay. It's okay," I kept telling him gently. When he realized I was trying to help him sleep, he closed his eyes and didn't open them, giving in to my comfort and trying his best to settle down. After about forty minutes, he was asleep.
Baby boy, I thought in my head, feeling so much love in every cell of my body, as I watched him sleep and listened to his slow, quiet breathing. *An angel.*
Eventually, I drifted off, too. I dreamed about being grabbed and shoved into a car by a stranger in the parking lot after work.

JORDAN

On Monday, we went to work together. I wanted to ask him more questions on the car ride there, but my anxiety silenced me. Irrationally, I felt it was unsafe to talk about it unless we were at home. Besides, I couldn't seem to deduce what exactly I wanted to know.
He was trying to be lighthearted. He kissed my temple again. "It's a good thing there's a coffee shop next door."
"You're really not gonna leave?" I asked him. Standing at the entryway to my office, it hit me that Jordan would be just a few meters away at all times, should he really stay. "I thought you would go to your mom's or something."
He didn't move, and his face didn't change. He just replied, "No, my love. I won't leave you."
The conflict inside me ran rampant. I didn't want his being here with me to affect his progress at work. The sooner this whole thing was over, the better.
I toyed with the idea all morning. Then finally, at lunch, I asked Steve if I could talk to him. He nodded and gestured to the door. I closed it behind me.
"I have something quite odd to tell you, and a request that's difficult to make." I wanted to be as honest as was safe to do.
"What's up?" My forty-one-year-old boss, maybe five foot nine, not thin but not quite stocky, sat back in his chair with curious brown eyes. His short brown hair looked like milk chocolate against his pale skin. In his blue button-down and gray slacks, he was a decently attractive man that carried himself well.
"Well...in a nutshell, I'm in danger."
Steve's eyes widened slightly, filling with confusion.

"My boyfriend works in crime. There's somewhat of a personal case, and...he's incredibly worried that I'm a target. And I think I might be." I kept my face smooth as I watched Steve's reaction through careful eyes.
"What kind of danger are you in? What does your boyfriend do?"
I had his attention.
I wasn't going to give details. "He's an investigator." To make this sound as serious as it was, though this had nothing to do with it, I added, "He used to work for the FBI.
"And...bad danger. These are very bad people." I hoped my eyes would do the talking.
"Okay..." Steven said slowly. "Are the police involved?" I nodded.
"I'm not really supposed to talk about it," I said quietly. "So, please keep this between me and you."
He stared at me for a long moment, and then said, "Okay. What do you need?"
I took a deep breath and let it out quietly. "I need to work from home." When his face didn't change, I added, "Either that or take a leave."
"How long do you anticipate this will be?" I noted that he didn't immediately say no.
"I'm not sure. They're working the case day and night, but this has been going on all year, maybe longer." I narrowed my eyes. "I can work from my laptop or desktop. Just send me what you need me to do, and I'll get it done. And you can call me anytime. Oh, but...I have to use a new cell phone for the time being. I'll text you from it so you know it's me."
I assumed that made him believe me more. I was worried he'd ask for a note from the local police department or something.
After a long pause, he said, "Okay. Well, is your Internet connection good at home?"
"My boyfriend works in computer technology. It's good."
"Okay. Well...I suppose it should be fine. I'd rather have you working from home than taking a leave, but...would it better for you to just take the leave?"
I shook my head. "Absolutely not. It would just be better to stay home. Less risk." I couldn't go indefinitely without income.
"Okay. So, how long should we plan this for?"
I sighed, frowned. "I don't know, Steve. I wish I did. It's indefinite. It's been so long. And worse." I swallowed. "This wasn't a worry until recently. I'd say let's plan for a month and take it from there. If that's alright with you."
He nodded a couple times, thinking to himself. "Alright," he said finally. "That's fine. It doesn't make that much of a difference, anyway, where you work. And your safety is obviously more important."
I was stunned.
"I'll call you. Send you stuff through email. Text me from that new number." He paused. "Do you need to leave now?"

I shook my head. "No. My boyfriend's in the area, so I'm good for the rest of the day."

"Okay."

"Thank you, Steve," I said quietly, standing to head back to my desk.

"Nina."

I turned, met his eyes.

"I have to head out early today. So...stay safe. I'll talk to you tomorrow, on the phone."

I smiled a small smile. Though I had resented Steve for steering clear of paying me more, there were moments I did like him.

"Thank you. I will." I quietly turned and headed out of the office.

When five o'clock came around, I called Jordan.

"Hi, baby," he answered on the second ring. "I'm outside."

I exhaled hard. I knew he would be.

Walking to the glass doors, I saw him waiting for me a few feet away. When we locked eyes, I smiled at him.

He opened the door to the Lexus for me. It was his car of choice nowadays, it seemed.

When he shut the door behind himself, I said quietly, "I have something to tell you."

His head snapped towards me. "What is it?" He kept his voice gentle, but his eyes were sharp.

"Nothing bad. I...I talked to my boss today and asked him if I could work from home." I fiddled with my hands in my lap, nervous that Jordan wouldn't have wanted me to say anything. Maybe Steve was one of the psychopaths that lingered on the Dark Web. "He said yes."

Jordan stared at me for a moment, the sharpness in his eyes dulling a little. "Why did you do that?"

I fiddled some more. Jordan noticed. "Because I thought it would be easier for you if I was at home, as opposed to you driving here every day with a laptop. You'd be closer to me if you went to work, and..."

"I'd stay home with you." He was pensive, and didn't seem angry.

"Yeah." I shrugged. "I just thought it would be easier if you didn't have to drive all this way. And you have more stuff to work with at home," I said quietly. I looked down at my hands.

After a moment, Jordan spoke. "Baby," he whispered.

I looked up at him just as his fingers met my cheek gently. His face had softened, and his voice was much weaker than I expected.

"I don't want to disrupt your life," he said quietly. "That's the last thing I want." His voice was sad.

"No, no," I said quickly. I grabbed his hand from my cheek and held it in mine. "It's okay. If it's easier for you, then it's easier for me. And Steve, Steve was much more open to it than I thought. I didn't tell him much," I said quickly. "Just that you were an investigator, and that a case at work had kinda turned personal, and that you were worried about my safety.

"Oh, and I mentioned that you worked in computer technology, but that's it. I didn't say more," I added, nervous.

Jordan stroked the back of my hand with his thumb, thinking. "That's okay," he murmured. "That's okay." After thinking for a few moments, he lifted my hand up to his lips and kissed it. Then he said, his voice still so low, "Thank you. For being so thoughtful." His eyelids lowered as he looked at me passionately. "I love you. You didn't have to do that. I would've driven here every single day. It doesn't matter. Your safety is the most important thing. The most important thing," he repeated intensely, articulating each word.

"It's okay," I whispered. "We can be together more. I think that's helpful for us...because of all the stress." I tried to fight the tears that threatened coming.

He nodded. "Yes." He took a deep breath and exhaled slowly. "I want you close to me."

"I'm right here." My voice was low, barely a whisper as I met his intense gaze with equal intensity.

When we got home, I went straight to the kitchen and cooked. Jordan was looking thinner, enough to make me ache.

I choose pasta. Lots of calories.

The next day, waking up, opening my laptop and getting right to work was odd. I went from my workout to the shower to the island in the kitchen. No makeup, no work clothes.

It worked well. Steve emailed me what he needed, and I got it done. There wasn't much outside of my digital work that I did for him, anyway. It was typically editing content, reports, presentations, and, as he kind of used me as an assistant as well, making him lists, keeping an eye on everyone's production. I could do that through our portal on my laptop. Plus, I saved gas money.

Around eleven, I jumped up and went to the library. Jordan had left me to my work, so as not to bother me. I could tell he felt bad about my decision to work from home, so he was trying to leave me alone as much as possible.

Well, he'd succeeded. I missed him, even though he was only in the other room.

I didn't want to disturb him, either, but I needed a change of scenery. My back was starting to hurt from sitting on the kitchen stool.

Wandering into the library with my laptop and a glass of ice water for Jordan, I set it on the desk next to him as he looked up at me. He had two laptops open in front of him, next to three computer monitors, all spread out on his huge desk. He wasn't sitting. His desk elevated, so he could stand while he worked.

"Hi, baby," he said, surprised. "Is this for me?"

I nodded. "Drink." He complied, taking a couple gulps until the glass was nearly empty. Like the weak woman I felt I was, it made me emotional to see that he was thirsty. That he didn't eat or drink when he was so wrapped up in his work, so stressed. I didn't want his health to suffer. He never thought of himself. He was probably thirsty for hours and didn't know it, or did and just ignored it in favor of not stopping his work.

"Thank you," he murmured. I didn't want to linger. I had to figure out where I was going to sit next.

"Are you okay?" he asked, coming around the desk and standing in front of me, tilting my chin up to look at him. I assessed his face as he assessed mine.

His eyes were tired but focused. They'd sunken into his face a little and were more purple underneath than usual. His face had even thinned out.

Why hadn't I noticed all of this this morning?

My eyebrows crinkled together, and I knew my eyes filled with horror. "Jordan," I whispered.

His eyes widened. "What's wrong?"

I set my laptop down and took his face in my hands. "Did you sleep last night?"

Jordan's eyes filled with understanding. He didn't say anything for a few moments.

"For a few hours."

"Jordan," I breathed. He'd been awake when I fell asleep.

That wouldn't happen again.

He wasn't sleeping, he was barely eating, forgetting to do simple things like drink water.

I made a vow to stay up until he fell asleep, and to bring him breakfast, lunch and dinner, on the days he worked late. Juice, just to get extra calories in. It was getting cold. He liked tea. I'd make him some of that with extra sugar.

As these thoughts raced through my mind, he murmured, "I know I probably don't look too great," which made me feel horrible. "But I'm okay. I promise." He offered a small smile.

"You're perfect," I said, pitch rising. I kissed his lips. "Please don't say that. That's not what I was thinking." I kissed him once more.

"I won't bother you," I said quietly, though I was going to get him more water and something to eat and bring them back. "I just wanted to bring you some water and see how you were doing. And I have to find another spot to work. The stool was hurting my back."

His eyes focused some more as a thought came to mind. "I'll buy you an office chair. We'll get a new desk. Do you want to work in here? I have that desk over there," he pointed to the shorter, dark mahogany desk on the other side of the library, "and you can have my chair. I'm not using it."

I shook my head. "You're so sweet, but that's okay. I don't want to distract you."

"You won't," he replied immediately. "Come sit in here."

I hesitated. He wanted me to. And I didn't know why that surprised me.

"I don't know, Jordy." I thought for a moment. "Here, how about this. I might come in now and again. I think it's good for me to change scenery. How's that?"

He nodded. "Whatever you want to do, m'love. You're more than welcome to anything in here, but you already know that."

I smiled. "Thank you, honey." I walked to the desk on the far side of the room, with its back to one of five huge bookshelves, and set my laptop down.

"There's a chair right here?" I didn't understand why he offered his.

"Yes, but this one is more comfortable," he replied, gesturing to his own.

I shook my head as I headed towards the door. "You spoil me. I'll be right back."

I went to the kitchen and warmed up some pasta, cut an apple, washed a bunch of grapes, then sliced some carrots and cucumbers. I took it all back to the library.

His eyes widened. "What is all this?"

"It's your lunch. Eat," I ordered. "I'll be right back."

I headed to the kitchen for the glass of orange juice I poured for him. Setting it down on his desk, I murmured, "I don't want to hear anything about too much sugar. It's fruit."

Jordan stared at me for a moment, blinked a couple times, then his lips crept up at the corners. He walked up to me once more, this time bringing his arms all the way around me and pulling me against him. Then he tilted my chin up with one finger and kissed my lips slowly.

"I love you, so, so very much." He touched his forehead to mine. "Thank you."

"No thank you's. You'd do it for me."

He smiled small. "Eat this with me or I'm going to do the same thing for you."

"No, no. I'm not really hungry at the moment, but when I am, I promise I'll go get something."

"Tell me. I'll get it."

To humor him, I smiled and said, "Maybe." I reached up to kiss his cheek and, resisting the urge to wrap my arms around his shoulders and hold him, walked over to the other desk.

He watched me for a moment, a small smile still on his face when I turned around to glance back at him; it made me feel warm. Then he went back around his desk to view his screens.

Every now and again, I'd look up and watch him work. In his white t-shirt and black jeans, shuffling side to side as he moved from screen to screen, his youthfulness stood out more. Smooth skin, bright eyes, no facial hair. His face was chiseled but not rugged.

He was beautiful as ever, and even though I was impressed by just about everything he did, I was enamored watching him work, especially now. His intense concentration on the screens, a couple books open in front of him that he would glance down at every now and again, how he would jump on a call here and there, take down some information, give instructions and then get off again.

I didn't know how I ended up with a mogul, a genius, a fighter, perfection, but I did. It made the copyediting I was doing feel small.

I mentally shrugged. We all had our own path in life.

The books, the books, Nina! You have more books to write. But I shrugged that off, using the stressful situation we were in as an excuse to ignore my lack of ideas.

At around two o'clock, midway through rewriting an article, I heard, "You haven't eaten anything."

I looked up; Jordan was making his way towards me, regarding me with curious and fond eyes.

"Oh, I, uh...yeah. I'm just trying to finish this article."

He rounded the corner of the desk and stood beside me, looking down at my laptop.

"May I?" he asked, gesturing to my laptop.

"You...you wanna read it?" He nodded.

"Oh, well...it's not done, but sure."

As I started to scooch my chair over, he said, "No, no. You don't have to move. I'd rather you keep writing."

I looked up at him with narrowed eyes. "You want to watch me write?"

He nodded.

"Why?"

"Well, if you are concentrating, then it'd be like a front-row seat into your brain," he said quietly. "I could watch the thoughts as they came to you."

I was amazed by the thought as he said it.

It was odd how he could say the most genius things, things that I, as a writer, should've already thought of but hadn't. To me, that was a brilliant notion.

And a very romantic and thoughtful one.

To want to be inside someone's mind...to care about them enough to want to see their thoughts and to view that as a privilege...that was love.

I smiled up at him. "That's a very interesting point." I looked back at my screen. "By all means. Just know I'm not supposed to be writing this. I'm supposed to be editing it. They did such a bad job that I'm having to do it all over again."

I willed myself to focus on the article, trying not to be insecure as he read through all the new words, watched all the backspaces and typos. When I'd write two or three sentences and then delete all of them after a moment of thought and go in again. Eventually, I forgot that he was there.

I thought he was bluffing, and that he would stand there for twenty seconds, murmur, "Nice," and then walk away. My ex wouldn't even have done that.

But Jordan stood there for five straight minutes, reading as I slowly pieced together an article about the star of a famous basketball team.

Then, he murmured, "Wow."

I finished typing my sentence and then turned to look at him. "What?"

"It's amazing to watch your thoughts as they come." His deep voice was low, which emphasized his sincerity. "And I just thought again about what you said. You're a copy editor, and yet Steve uses you as a writer. You're brilliant, Nina."

He was flattering me. "Come oooooooon," I replied, smiling.

"I'm serious," he said, and he was. I could see it on his face. "You do their job for them, because they're just not as good as you." He smiled. "That's impressive."

I smiled, knowing he was flattering me but appreciating it, nonetheless. I didn't think Jordan ever lied to me, but I was still trying to tell if he truly meant it.

"It's really not." But my teeth were showing.

He ran his fingers through my hair, still looking at the screen. Re-reading.

"It is." His eyes didn't move from the laptop.

"Jord." I chuckled.

"Do you know you're an incredible writer? You have to know, right? You publish books, stories."

"Yes, I know I'm a good writer. But, just so you know, anyone could publish a book. And it could be garbage. So that's not the best deciding factor." I raised my eyebrows.

"The drive it takes to do what you do...I've read your book. It's as good as a published book should be. You're not just anyone," he added quietly.

"You read my book?" I couldn't believe it. My romantic action thriller. The one I'd mentioned when I first met him.

"Yes. And it was phenomenally written."

"I'm...actually so embarrassed."

"What? Why?" He crouched down now, all six feet and three inches of him, and turned my chair towards him, putting his hands on my thighs as he looked up at my face.

"Because you read my...romance." I smiled. To someone who didn't read fiction at all, it must have made him cringe.

Oh, no. No, no, no.

"It must have been corny to you."

He shook his head. "No, romance can be good, *or* it can be corny. Your writing is good. By the end of it, I was impressed. It wasn't fully about the romance, though," he added. "The female assassin aspect of it was very creative. I loved the fact that she was Middle Eastern," he said gently.

I tried not to smile like an idiot, but I couldn't help it. I thought this whole time that it was a fact I'd mentioned once, one that we then both forgot about. I was stunned and so flattered that he liked the premise.

"When did you even read it?" I asked, shaking my head.

"I bought it the day you told me your last name."

I grinned and shook my head again. This sneak.

"As if you needed my last name to find out who I was." I chuckled. I wrapped my arms around his neck and hugged him tight, feeling his arms come around my back.

"I love you so much," I told him, unable to resist the delight filling me. He could've just been saying that to make me feel good about myself, but his sincerity was incredibly humbling.

I pulled back. "Did you eat what I brought you?"

He nodded. "Now it's your turn."

"Let me finish this article and we'll go grab something together, yeah?"

"Sounds like a plan." He kissed my temple and went off.

I continued smiling to myself as I forced my concentration. When I finished the article, I just about danced to his side, took his hand and led him to the kitchen.

KAYLA KATHAWA

November

Steve seemed to trust me to work from home. A few weeks of it had taken us into November. Some of my coworkers texted me, asking if I was alright.

Steve didn't call me much, just sent emails and text messages. He didn't need to worry about my dedication to the job, or that I was slacking off. I appreciated the trust. I was surprised when he asked about me personally.

How's everything? The case?

"Well, that was nice," I murmured, looking up at Jordan, who was assessing something on one of his desktop screens. He glanced at me.

"What was?"

"Steve texted me and asked how things were going. With the case." I set my phone down and grabbed my laptop; break time was over.

Seated in Jordan's library and office on the maroon couch opposite the desk I'd taken as my own, I was closer to him. His standing desk was in the center of the long room with high ceilings.

"He's a rather indifferent man. Sometimes I think he's self-absorbed. So this was surprising," I added, rubbing my eyes. I'd been fixing a three-page article about the rise in appreciation for soccer, and I wanted to claw my eyes out. *I really had to pick a company that marketed sports.*

Editing is editing, I'd told myself at the time. *Toughen up.*

I was an idiot.

"That's nice of him," Jordan replied. He was wearing dark-rimmed reading glasses. I hadn't known he needed them until I walked into the office this morning and saw him.

My knees nearly buckled.

He was a *sight*. He looked so good with those glasses on, so sophisticated and beautiful. It was unreal.

"You okay, baby?" he asked, watching me rub my eyes.
"Yeaaah, I'm okay. How about you? How you doin'?" I'd been bringing him snacks and meals as I'd planned, but getting him to eat was hard. He was absorbed in his work, and I was certain didn't have much of an appetite. He'd go hours without touching what I brought him if I weren't in the room.
I didn't personally feel snubbed. I just wanted him to be healthy.
He wasn't sleeping well. In his sleep, he pulled me to him randomly and held on tight. I knew this case was getting to him.
"I'm okay, love," he said absentmindedly, clicking away at something. Then he looked at me. "Thank you."
I nodded. I wasn't tiptoeing around him, because Jordan would never allow me to be afraid or nervous. But I didn't want to risk being snapped at or rejected for the first time. I also worried I would disturb him when he had important work to do. So, I made a deliberate effort to keep to myself and let him concentrate.
Glancing back down at my computer and cutting the chit chat short, I was surprised when he walked over and sat next to me. Rubbing his hand on my lower back and kissing my temple, he said, "How's work?"
I looked at him, confused. *Like he read my mind.*
"It's good, baby," I said lightly, quietly.
He brushed my hair back from the side of my face, regarding me for a moment.
"Are you sure you're okay?" he murmured, echoing his earlier question.
My eyes widened in confusion. "Yeah. How come?"
After a moment, he said, "You've been quiet lately."
So, he noticed. I thought it was good to stay out of the way, something he'd appreciate and use to his advantage, not having to worry about paying me enough attention.
I shrugged lightly. "I just don't want to disturb you while you work."
His eyebrows knitted together slightly. "You're never disturbing me."
I smiled small. "I know. I try."
He shook his head. "You don't have to be quiet, love." He tilted my chin up and softly kissed my lips. Then, in a much quieter voice he murmured, "I miss your voice."
I nearly melted into the couch.
He kissed me again, a little more deeply. When I pulled back, I smiled shyly and looked down. This was incredibly refreshing after feeling so worried I'd bother him.
I brought my eyes back up to his and, after a moment, brought my fingers up to caress his cheek.
"I miss yours, too," I said quietly. He smiled small.
"Let's go to dinner tonight," he suggested softly.
It was funny that I didn't know how badly I wanted that until he said it.

We'd been cooped up in the house for weeks, working quietly, only leaving together to go to the store. He worked all day. Sometimes he'd stop around five and come join me on the couch when I was doing my own personal writing or reading, just to be with me. We had a mutual understanding that work was better when we were at least side by side.

There was nobody else I'd rather be with. But I missed him. I missed seeing him smile a big, real smile.

I smiled. "You want to?"

He smiled back, a little bigger. "Yeah, I do baby." He kissed my lips again. "We haven't left. Don't think it hasn't dawned on me. I could stay in the house for weeks working until something is done. I'm depriving you." The story of how Jordan isolated himself for a year after leaving the FBI, so he could work on his software, popped into my brain.

He brushed his fingers over my hair again. "And you haven't complained once, though you should."

I shook my head. "That would be awful. To complain when you're just protecting me."

His eyes softened and he kissed my forehead, letting his lips linger there. I felt weak for him.

"You shouldn't be stuck here," he said firmly. "We're gonna go to dinner in an hour. How's that sound?"

A thought occurred to me. I frowned. "Do you actually want to go, or are you just doing this to make me happy? Because you feel bad?"

He shook his head, his eyes serious. "I want to. I want to be with you. Just you. You and me."

My heart fluttered. "Okay," I said softly. "You wanna work for one more hour?"

"No. I want to go shower and freshen up and be nice and presentable for you."

My jaw dropped, and I forced myself to close it. I grinned in disbelief.

"You aren't serious." When he didn't crack a smile, I continued. "Jordan, come *on,* babe." I sat up a little more and kissed his temple. "You're perfect."

He shook his head again. "You're dressed and beautiful. I haven't showered since last night and have been wearing the same clothes I woke up in. It's unacceptable."

I laughed. I couldn't help it. I was stunned.

What was this nonsense? When did I ever care if it had been less than a day since Jordan washed his hair? When did he care? I couldn't believe this.

It touched my heart nonetheless that he wanted to look nice for me.

"You're the cutest thing I've ever seen in my entire *life*," I crooned, wrapping my arms around his neck. He hugged me back, and when he pulled his head away he was smiling.

I'd gotten a good reaction out of him, instantly putting me in a better mood.

"You're perfect," I told him. "But if you want to go shower and change, by all means. It will probably make you feel a little better, too. Forget about me. I just want you to feel good."

He stared down at me, his eyes bright under his normally lazy lids. Almost devious. I grinned.

"I won't be long." He kissed my head.

"Take your time."

I spent some time going hard on the article. I wanted Jordan to take his time and have a nice relaxing shower. He needed it.

My heart broke every time I looked at his frustrated face. It was horrible to see him feel helpless.

He blamed himself for all of those deaths. The cult taunted him, telling him it was his fault people were dying. It infuriated me..

I loved him so much. I couldn't bear to see him suffer.

I considered all of this, and I began to want to hug and kiss him, tell him I loved him so much, I believed in him wholeheartedly, and I knew he would figure this out.

I finished the article and was touching it up when my thoughts completely strayed to Jord. This would suffice.

As I was waiting for my laptop to shut down, I heard a quiet clanking noise. My head snapped up immediately, eyes searching for the source of the disturbance. The room had just been silent.

I stood up, setting my laptop down on the couch and moving to the entrance of the library to see Jordan. *He finished fast.*

When I got to the doorway, however, no one was there. I walked through the house; once I got to the staircase, I decided to go up. Maybe I'd heard him shuffling through his drawers.

But halfway up the stairs, I heard the shower running. He wasn't done.

I pursed my lips and headed back to the library. *Maybe it was the wind against the house, or a branch hitting it.*

When I returned to the library, there was more noise. More clanking.

Then it clicked. It was digital audio, coming from Jordan's computer.

I quickly moved around to see the screens. I wondered if he had received a video call.

But he wasn't here to answer it, so how did the line connect?

I shifted my eyes back and forth quickly and pinpointed that the video was on the far right monitor.

The second my eyes landed on it, I knew what I was seeing. A loud gasp escaped me.

An unconscious young woman, strung upside down by rope, tied around her ankles and hooked to something out of sight of the camera.

The clanking was a person adjusting the camera. Then, the noise stopped, and an individual in all black, wearing a ski mask, stepped into the frame. My eyes widened in horror.

He walked up to the woman and, using both hands, he pulled her shirt down and over her head. She was left in her bra and pants.

Stepping away for a moment, the man returned with a knife in his hands.

"Oh, no, no, no, no," I whined to myself quietly, unable to look away but already praying to God to end this nightmare.

He lifted the waistband of her pants, using the knife to cut them off.

The knife in such close proximity to her bare skin brought a harsh wave of nausea to my throat.

Suddenly, the person slapped the girl's face. He did it again and again. When she finally came to, her eyes widened.

And that was when the screaming started.

I backed away from the computer, running into the bookshelf behind me, tears in my eyes. When the man took the knife and brought it to her stomach, I ran.

I sprinted up the stairs, screaming Jordan's name.

He met me at the doorway, his eyes huge, alarmed and simultaneously full of rage.

He was dressed, his hair was wet; I crashed into him and felt a few drops of water fall onto my forehead.

"Jordan, Jordan," I cried. He tried to take my face in his hands, a desperate worry on his, but I pulled him by both of his hands towards the staircase.

"Something came up on your computer," I informed him through my tears. I felt out of control. Panicked. I couldn't believe I was seeing it in real time.

"A livestream or something!" I turned to him and saw a horrified shock in his eyes. We made it to the family room, and he could hear the screaming. Another wave of nausea moved through me.

"Jordan." I wouldn't let myself sob. He would *never* let me in again, never tell me anything about the case or what he'd seen.

"I don't want you to look at it," I said breathlessly. Desperately.

But we entered the library just then, and he rounded the corner of his desk, eyebrows knitted in concentration. I followed him around too fast for him to stop me.

"No, don't look," he said sharply, but I was already there. I turned my head away so I didn't see, holding onto his upper arm with both hands and putting my face in it. The screaming was making my head spin.

I peeked so all I could see were Jordan's hands, typing on one of his keyboards so fast I couldn't distinguish his fingers from one another. After a few seconds, the screaming stopped.

Immediately, he pulled me close and held me tightly. I wouldn't let myself sob, but the tears kept coming, one after another, warming my face as they fell. I put my head against his chest, sniveling.

Jordan brushed his hand down my hair again and again to soothe me, and used the other hand to click away at his computer. He stopped for a moment to grab his cell phone off the desk and dial. As it rang, he spoke into my hair.

"I'm sorry," he whispered. "I'm so sorry."

"It's okay," I told him, voice shaking. I didn't look up. "Just find her."

Someone picked up the line. "Emmett, get the police out to Senton and surrounding areas and tell them there's another one."

Emmett spoke loudly on the other end, but I couldn't distinguish what he was saying.

After a moment, Jordan replied, "I'm not coming to this one. One of you can go with the cops. I'd rather have all the brainpower on the computers."

I was stunned. Jordan was passing up a search for the criminals nearby? Perhaps the most difficult case of his career, and he was staying home?

Jordan hung up the phone and took his other hand from my hair so he could type; his arms stuck out above my shoulders as I put my head on his chest. When I tried to walk away and let him work, he pulled me back in front of him, my back to the screen.

"Don't go," he said softly, kissing my forehead. "I'm gonna try to trace this IP address." As he spoke, he moved his hand back to the keyboard. "I don't think I'll have much success, but the team is trying, too."

I tilted my head back to look at this face. He glanced down and met my eyes but continued typing.

"It will only take me a few minutes, and then we'll leave." He looked back up at the screen, eyebrows knitted together in concentration.

"It's okay," I repeated. "That girl is more important."

He glanced down at me for a second and studied my face. Before he looked back at the screen, he kissed my forehead again.

I wrapped my arms around his waist and set my head down on his chest.

After a few minutes of typing, he pulled his hands back and took my face in them.

"Anything?" I asked him, knowing my eyes must have looked as lifeless as I suddenly felt.

His eyes were intense as they burned into mine, as though the answer to my question was in the back of his mind and not his main concern. "The IP was rerouted. Made it look like the stream was happening in Arizona."

"Could it have been?"

"No." His voice was quiet. "Well, yes, it could have been. I can't trace it, of course. But it's not likely."

No, it wasn't. They were here.

Police were searching, desperate to find this girl.

I didn't speak for a moment. Finally, I willed myself to quietly ask, "Is she dead?"

Jordan just stared at me for a long time. My heart sank.

"Did you see it happen?" My pitch rose with desperation.

"No, my love," he whispered, being gentle after my horrified response. "I turned it off. Eve and Luke are assessing the footage right now for any evidence or indicator of where they are. The police are out, searching Senton and nearby areas. The FBI has been alerted."

I frowned. I hated that so many people in authority were working this to no avail.

How my poor, sweet Jordan must have felt. All these years. Since twenty-two, when he got his first look into this disgusting other world.

"So the stream is over."

"Yes."

I shook my head. "How did they get onto your home computer?" I was frightened. Did they hack into our own network? Could they find *us*?

"I'm logged into a portal, the one we use at work. They didn't actually access my computer. And I was in a browser searching. Waiting for results to pop up. I didn't think they would."

I exhaled hard. "Are you sure you don't want to go back and look? Study it, see if there's any evidence, any information?" I didn't know what he'd be looking for, but if his search results came up with something, he should look into it.

"I'm sure, my love." His voice was low, soft.

"Are those the people you're looking for, for sure?" I asked quietly. I didn't see anything on the site around the video saying his name.

"Yes," he said hesitantly.

I nodded again and looked around the room. I didn't know what to do.

Did we just move on like nothing had happened? Was anyone going to find that girl?

Oh, that girl. That poor, poor girl.

I looked up to the ceiling and asked God to please give her peace now, after she'd suffered so brutally.

I pulled away from Jordan slowly.

I'd told him, months prior, that I could handle this.

"Nina—" he started. He was unhappy, watching me move this way; my face was wrecked, my eyes blank, lips trembling and eyebrows crinkling every few seconds.

"I'm fine," I told him, wiping the tears away and clearing my throat. "It took me off guard." My hands were shaking.

I turned and walked to the couch and sat down next to my laptop. I didn't want him to comfort me. I felt odd, like I didn't want to be held or hugged. Didn't want to *be*.

An unbearable moment in which I didn't know what to do with myself to make the discomfort go away.

I was trying to process that what I'd just seen was real. My mind and body were rejecting the idea, and I was trying to force myself to accept it.

I didn't want to be. I felt that heavy wave of desire to curl up and dissipate into nothing. The desire I used to sometimes feel I was drowning in. I didn't want to be. To be.

I sat down cross-legged and pulled my knees halfway up my chest, linking my fingers around them. Locking myself in.

JORDAN

Jordan sat next to me and rubbed my lower back. I sensed hesitance to touch me, after I'd walked away from his comfort.
I took a deep breath and held it until I was steady.
That poor girl just suffered so much agony for no reason. And now she was dead. Her life was gone. The people who loved her were void of her presence forever. For absolutely no reason.
My stomach sank each time I had the thought.
He watched my face with pained, worried eyes. He would beat himself up about it forever.
"I'm sorry," he whispered again. "I'm so sorry, my love. I didn't ever want you to see something like that. I should have shut my computer off." He was angry with himself. "I'm so sorry, Nina."
I blinked, clearing my face of any emotion as best I could. *Now would be a good time to disconnect emotionally*, I thought to myself, *so that he doesn't worry.*
"It's okay," I told him again, blinking as I tried to maintain eye contact.
"Let's get out of this room," he suggested softly.
I complied without a word, standing and letting him take my hand. He brought me into the family room but didn't sit down. He tried once more to take my face in his hands. I let him.
"Everything is going to be okay," he told me, his words suddenly firm. "I am going to *find* these people, and I'm going to stop them from what they're doing, and I promise you, I *promise* you, I will never, *ever* let anything happen to you."
I felt tears coming. I brought my hands up to his wrists and gently brought them down. I didn't want him staring at my face in case I started crying.
I looked down at my empty hands. After a few deep breaths, I felt stronger but still separate from him. As I stared downward, I desperately tried to think of why I suddenly wasn't comforted by his touch or his words. What changed in me in the last thirty minutes?
Seeing that poor girl hanging upside down, stripped so that her skin was nearly all exposed, terrified...
This is what Jordan does for work every day.
This was what he saw, what I'd known about but never actually had to see. How could he bear any of it?
I realized how much pain he must have suffered over the course of his career, trying to save people and at times failing, those failures gruesome and unspeakable.
He'd told me about the pain, not calling it that but informing me how, because of it, all he'd wanted to do was isolate himself from the people he loved. He'd told me, but the agony I knew he felt fully registered in my mind and body now.
It hurt so badly to think of the weight he carried.
Maybe that was why he was such a solemn man. Maybe that was why he said so little and observed so intently.

He saw too much horror for small, trivial things to faze him. That horror made him realize being insecure was a waste of time; how you looked or what people thought of you didn't matter when others were suffering so immensely because of crooked, sick people in the world. All over the world.

Then the thought danced through my mind that this man, who'd never loved anyone but family, this hero who'd been hardened without a choice, this person who carried so much weight in his heart, in his soul, saw me one day and felt something soft. Something warm.

He saw me and suddenly, despite all the evil that he had to swallow in order to help people, despite the way it made him so numb at times, he saw me and had room for love.

He loved me. *Me.*

He loved me enough to take away some of his security and strength. Jordan, the person always sure of himself, the person who always made me feel steady and safe, couldn't always win. The hero couldn't always win, couldn't save the poor girl who'd lost her life in agony for simply no reason at all.

I at least had enough time to drop my face into my hands before I burst into tears.

I cried for him, for all he'd been through, for all the times he'd hated himself for not being able to save those victims. I cried for those victims, for the girl in the livestream.

And just as quickly as the discomfort by Jordan's touch and love had come, it vanished. After I realized why I'd felt discomforted by Jordan, the hurt for how he'd suffered flooded me. I was full of love and suddenly wanted to be close to him again.

Jordan pulled us to the couch, laying us down then holding me in his arms. "It's okay," he whispered. "It's okay. It's gonna be okay, I promise."

I lifted my head, shaking it for the first time, revealing my tear-stricken face.

"I'm sorry." I couldn't stop hurting for him.

His eyes widened in alarm and confusion. "Why are you sorry, baby?" He brushed my hair away from my tear-streaked face. "Why are you sorry?"

"Because of all of this that you see," I cried quietly, gesturing towards the library. "You've been seeing it for so many years, and you still *endure* it to save people."

I sniffed as I breathed short, hard breaths. "It's mental torture," I wept. I put my hand on his face but couldn't see it through my tears.

So much for showing him I could handle it.

"Honey, honey," he soothed, and I could detect the distress and heartbreak coming from him, too. I was hurting him even more. I wanted to tell him to just ignore me, I was being a baby, but he would never do that. And I was the most blessed individual on the planet for it.

"Don't be sorry, baby, I'm okay," he said softly. "I'm okay; everything will be okay." He spoke to me gently with his face close to mine. I dropped my head down finally, giving in to my weakness, and he brought his lips to my hair.

I caught my voice immediately after a sob. "No, no. You've s-s-seen too much," I cried. I lifted my head again and took his face in both of my hands, struggling to clear my eyes to see him. Jordan brought his hands up over mine and held them to his face.

"It's okay, lovely. I'm just fine. I'm just fine, my sweet, sweet girl."

He held me, whispering soothing words while I wept for what he'd been through, and because I could probably never comfort him in the same way. Not for lack of trying, but after all he'd seen, I knew it would be hard. Even though he loved me.

"I don't want you to hurt," I told him, my voice thick. "I just don't want you to have to see that stuff."

He stroked my hair. "No, lovely. I'm not hurting."

"But you do," I argued, lifting up. "You are. I know it kills you to watch people suffer." His bright blue eyes seemed to dim with my words.

Then he did something he'd never done. He took my hand and put it to his cheek. It surprised me the same way it did when he pulled me back to bed that morning and put his head down on my chest.

I blinked, sniffled.

"You are an angel," he said; the sound of his words just barely caressed the air.

I shook my head slightly.

He nodded. "You are an angel," he repeated louder.

"I have never had that kind of concern for me. You are the sweetest, most loving, and selfless person I've met. And my mother is pretty great." He smiled a tiny smile.

"Your mom has the same concern for you, I'm sure. And Amar and Tristan, too." I sniffed again.

"You're different," he murmured. "You're not related to me. You are not bound to love me the way family typically is. You could rid yourself of any concern and sadness for me and walk out that door." He gestured slightly with his chin in the direction of the garage. "But you feel it, anyway. You stay." His hand was warm over my own. His cheek was, too.

"I love you, Nina." His words were full of compassion and adamance. "I will not stop until you and I are both rid of this hell."

And there was his verbal confirmation that this was hell for him. I felt another surge of sadness and slowly leaned forward, wrapping my arms around his neck and setting my cheek on his shoulder.

We stayed there for a while. I pored over the things I'd seen and heard all night.

We stayed in for the night, but Jordan insisted we would go to dinner tomorrow night, or breakfast, or both. I didn't have much appetite.

Before we went to bed, Jordan went into the library and came out with a much smaller laptop than he usually used.

"What's that?" I asked, my voice almost back to normal. I was still a little congested from crying, but most of it had cleared up. We'd spent the night watching a mystery film, and I blew my nose for the first half of it.

"It's one of my other laptops," he told me. "The keyboard is quieter than on my other one, and I'll be working tonight."

Yes. I anticipated that.

"The other one doesn't bother me." For someone as sensitive to noise as I was, this was true. Jordan made it a point to type lightly on the keyboard.

"I want to make sure," he murmured, coming up beside me and putting his hand on my lower back as we walked to the staircase.

"It's so tiny," I commented. "And thank you, babe. The other one really doesn't bother me."

He kissed my temple as we went up to our room.

A thought occurred to me as we stepped in. "Do you anticipate not sleeping all night?" I asked, voice flat.

He simply shook his head slightly.

"You have to rest, Jord," I told him, as I pulled the comforters back and slid into bed. I waited on my side, watching him as he slid in next to me. When he was settled, he pulled the blankets up over my shoulders. He stayed sitting up, putting the small laptop on his thighs.

"I will," he murmured. "I just want to work until I've made *some* sort of progress."

I accepted this, knowing I couldn't stop him. "That's such a tiny laptop," I repeated. "I've never seen it before."

He smiled a small smile. "I've just had it put away."

I started to get sleepy as the soft mattress molded around me. "Does it have your software on it?"

He nodded, typing away already. "I put it on all my computers."

"Oh." I yawned.

Jordan ran his hand over my cheek as I lay by his side, facing him. Then he ran his fingers all the way down my hair to the ends.

"Sleep, my love. I'll be right here if you need me."

I tried, closing my eyes and breathing as slowly as I could. But I anticipated nightmares, and my mind stayed alert.

After about twenty minutes, I opened my eyes again. Jordan glanced over. "What's the matter, honey? Is the screen bothering you? The keyboard?"

"No," I told him, yawning again. "My mind is just still on."

He frowned. "How can I help you sleep?"

I actually chuckled. I suspected the events of the day and being tired were getting to me.

"You're the one who's gonna stay up all night." I slid closer to him and put my head against the side of his thigh, facing it. He brought his hand to my

hair immediately, and as I closed my eyes to try and sleep once more, I noticed the sound of Jordan rapidly pressing against the keyboard.
Not because it was annoying, but because one of his hands was in my hair. I lifted my head up and was appalled to see him typing away on the keyboard with *one hand.*
"Are you serious right now." It wasn't a question.
His eyes were confused, then upset. "It's loud? I'm sorry, I'll go—"
"No!" I felt bad, realizing then how I'd sounded. "No, no, I'm not talking about that. Sorry. I meant the fact that you're typing with one hand. How…?" I just shook my head slowly, not even bothering to finish.
"I learned to do it while working on two computers at once."
"Wait...that means you literally are thinking and typing two different things on two different keyboards at the same time...that's not even possible."
He smiled a small smile. "No, it's not really at the exact same time. I'm usually typing code, and I'll do it on one computer and then immediately on the other. I'll be working on one thing," he explained, "but doing two different tests for it. So, I'll use one computer for one test and the other for a different one. It saves time."
I was amazed. "And like…the thoughts are coming at you fast? Like you'll think, oh, this, this and this for your one test, and then immediately something for the other pops up."
"Exactly."
"That's craaazy," I said, my voice low, drawing out the word and dropping my head back onto the mattress suddenly. Jordan chuckled. It was a nice sound.
He continued to play with my hair, which was a foolproof way to put me to sleep. Eventually, I dozed off.
My eyes snapped open to Jordan, leaning down in front of me with his hand on my cheek, saying my name. His face was gentle when I looked at him, but his eyes were unsettlingly alert. He was trying to wake me, which he'd never done.
"What's wrong? What's wrong?" I asked groggily, sitting up.
"Nothing is wrong, honey." I heard the slight restlessness in his voice. "I think I figured out the problem." My eyes widened.
"Wait, like...you found them? Like what you've been trying to do this whole time?"
He nodded. "Not yet. But I think I will be able to now. So, I have to go into the office. It's going to require more than one person."
"You're leaving?"
Jordan had put on his socks and was about to stand. He stopped dead in his tracks and turned to me.
"I have to, my love. And I want you to come with me," he said softly, "but I don't want to disturb your sleep. And if I know you're safe at home, then there's no reason for me to do that." He paused, hesitant. I didn't think he believed himself. "Luke is going to come stay with you."

I frowned. "Don't you need him there?"

"They need me more than they need Luke," he said, and it sounded harsh, but I knew it was true. "And I don't trust anyone other than the four of them to stay with you." He leaned in and kissed my forehead. "I'll wait until he gets here before I leave."

"What time is it?"

"Two-thirty."

Two-thirty in the morning. I sat back. I wanted to go with him but didn't want to insist. I didn't want to be in the way. I was scared, however, and worried for him.

My heart started beating faster. "Jordan—" I grabbed his face in my hands desperately. "What if something happens to you? I'll lose my mind—"

He grabbed onto my wrists and held them tight. "I will be okay, I promise you. We will stop this, and I will come home, and it will finally be over. Then it'll just be you and me."

At this point, my pulse was beating hard, and my chest started aching at the thought. I wanted that to be happening *right now*. I wanted to skip the part where he left, and I panicked the whole time. My face crumpled. I tried to hold back the tears.

"No, no, no, my love," Jordan whispered. "Shh, shh, shh." He kissed my head and wrapped his arms around me. "It shouldn't take long. I will call you and text you as much as I possibly can, okay? And I will let you know when we find them and head there." Tilting my chin up, he kissed my lips gently.

"I love you."

I tried not to cry. "I love you so much."

Jordan kissed me again. "I'll wait until Luke gets here to be with you while I'm gone. Just to be safe."

I shook my head, needing this to be over with. "Just go. I'll be okay in the time being."

Jordan looked at me and only thought for a moment before he said, "No. It's a forty-minute drive."

"It's okay. I'll keep the doors locked."

I exhaled hard. It was a shaky sound. Jordan held me steady. "It's okay. I'll be fine."

I knew how urgent the matter was, because Jordan began considering it. The struggle was obvious on his face, but he needed to go before they lost the success they'd been working so hard to obtain, however he'd obtained it. He needed to go before someone else got hurt. So they could end this madness that was slowly driving us insane.

And where was I safer than in Jordan's house?

He looked at me intently for a few moments, then finally said, "Okay." He made an angry, frustrated face. He was not happy with what he was about to do. "Okay." Steadying himself, he took a breath and exhaled before he spoke again.

JORDAN

Coming close to me and bringing his face directly an inch in front of mine, he said, "I'll make sure everything is locked, and I'll set the alarm from my car. If you get up, do not open the door for anyone. *Anyone*. Luke will stay outside, surveilling. You don't even have to see him or talk to him. He's gonna call me when he gets here." Jordan looked down at his phone. "He's speeding. It shouldn't be more than thirty minutes."

Staring intensely into my eyes, Jordan said, "I will be home soon. You just stay here, don't go anywhere. I'll be home soon." His voice was fierce. "*Call me* if you need *anything*. Even if you're just scared." His voice became soft.

I *was* scared. My hands were shaking, but I knew he wouldn't leave if he saw. And he needed to go. I clasped my hands together.

"Go." My voice was not as intense as his, but still sharp. "I'll be waiting." Reaching up and taking his face in my hands, I kissed him hard. "Be *careful*. Do *not* let anything happen to my baby."

My voice softened to a whisper. "I can't live without you." I couldn't help the crack in it, and the tears that started forming in my eyes. I forced myself to calm down enough to stop them from coming all the way.

Jordan kissed me this time, the same way I did him. "I will be home before morning; I promise. I promise. Everything is going to be okay. I promise." He kissed my forehead. "Just lie back, relax, and sleep. When you wake up, I'll be here." Gently he guided me down. He stroked my forehead, but I couldn't get sleepy. I told him I was okay, and that he could go. I'd fall asleep eventually. Jordan pulled his gun from the little container he kept, in between our bed and the nightstand.

And with that, he was gone.

I'd never been so terrified for someone I loved in my life.

These people were crazy. *Crazy.*

I'd seen it firsthand. I'd seen that poor girl...

I knew what they were capable of, what they *liked* to do. I knew how much they hated Jordan.

The self-hatred in me screamed that if I were stronger, knew more, was better, I would have been able to go with him.

If one of them got the best of my Jordan...and though it seemed impossible...if it happened...

A sob escaped my mouth.

I rocked back and forth; I had never had anxiety like this in my life.

I remained that way for just a few minutes, then eventually stopped moving and crying. Just lay there, staring off into our bathroom.

I wasn't sure how long I stayed that way. Maybe five minutes, but it felt like forty. I couldn't sleep, though I wanted to. Because when Jordan suggested something, it was normally the best thing to do.

But sleep wasn't an option. I got dressed and went downstairs.

I decided to make some tea. Maybe that with some milk and sugar would help me. I'd watch TV or something, until Jordan came back.

I opened the kitchen cabinet next to the sink and stuck my hand into the box of tea bags, pulling a few out. I'd make a whole pot.
I grabbed the teapot from the stove and turned to the sink to fill it with water. As my eyes landed on the faucet, I felt something sharp on the back of my head.
The last thing I heard was the steel teapot crash onto the floor.

JORDAN

Jordan was nearly to the office, his heart beating faster in anticipation of getting the answers he was waiting for.
He didn't understand how it took him so long to think of something so simple.
He raged inside.
Sitting next to Nina as she slept, some hours after she'd dozed off, Jordan rearranged numbers a hundred different ways, scanning through his own software a million times, trying to figure out a way to make it better.
Nina's intrigue in his small laptop floated through his brain the whole time. Her innocence soothed his frustration over their stagnant position in this case, and the fact that she'd seen something so horrible.
All over a laptop, he'd thought. *So adorable over a laptop.*
This laptop was indeed small, smaller than the ones he had at work. Why had he chosen larger laptops for the office when he set up the layout? He'd picked average fifteen-inch laptops to utilize beside his numerous desktops, because he liked everything to be large and in front of him. He could see what was being worked on, and he also knew that staring at small screens was not efficient for his teams. Plus, they didn't need to be mobile-friendly. The laptops never left the building. No technology did.
Jordan's head snapped up at the thought, away from the algorithm he was exhaustedly working on. He stared at the bedroom wall directly across from where he sat, Nina's soft breathing sounding from beside him.
The laptops never left the building.
No. The laptops were *supposed* to never leave the building.
A rush surged through him. He picked up his phone, eyes wide, and dialed Liza.
"I need you and everyone else at the office as fast as possible. Please."

"We never left."

Relief flooded Jordan. "Listen to me very carefully. I need you to count laptop inventory. Put me on speaker."

"You already are."

"I need an exact count of all of the laptops on all floors and all the ones in storage." Another thought crossed his mind. "Make sure they're all company computers and not fakes."

Emmett's eyebrows had knitted together in confusion. Eve looked at Liza, ideas piecing themselves together in their minds. A surge of excitement flashed through all of them. Jordan had figured something out.

He had gotten off the phone with them and slid out of bed, feeling terribly guilty for what he was about to do as he knelt down to wake Nina.

As he drove, he pored over how such an obvious possibility could have escaped him, that and Nina taking turns at the forefront of his mind.

She was so afraid when he left, so worried for him. It made him ache.

But he knew he had to go, because if his suspicions were correct, he was the only person that could break down the steel barrier these murderers were using.

Just a few minutes before he arrived, Liza called him.

"There are one-hundred twenty-five."

He cursed to himself. That was the amount he was supposed to have in inventory. He didn't get discouraged.

"Are they all ours?"

"We have to power them all on to find out?" Eve knew there had to be another way. Jordan wouldn't stock just any generic laptop.

She was right. He realized he'd never told them.

"No. Pull out the tray from the CD drive completely; I don't care if it damages the laptop. On the back of the tray there's a blue logo."

"We're going through each one now."

"Check the ones in storage and the spares that no one has used in a while. The spares in the locked shelf on the top computer floor. Check those first. Don't turn any of them on. I'll be inside in a minute."

He pulled in as he heard Liza moving; he grabbed his phone and little laptop and ran inside.

When he made it to the top floor, he found Emmett and Liza staring at a single laptop.

"These are not ours," Emmett told him, voice grave and eyes wide. He held the backs of two CD trays up to Jordan.

The blue logos were missing.

"Where is Eve?"

"Eve—" The elevator doors opened as Liza finished. "—is right there. From the next floor."

Petite Eve in her soft beige sweater carried another laptop.

"This is not ours," she told Jordan, alarm in her eyes.

Jordan was right.

Some of his laptops were missing.

Why had it taken him so long to *think* of this?

"I just find it hard to believe." That was what Nina had said when he suggested, months prior, that somebody had developed a better rerouting software than his.

It had humbled and also saddened him. He'd wished he lived up to her expectations. At that moment, her look of disbelief had sent a flash of fierce determination through him. To get better than who had gotten better than him, if only to live up to her idea of him. If only to not disappoint her.

She was right. No one made a rerouting software like his, a software that could reroute searches and data so no one could track it. No one had mimicked this software he'd created in order to protect his company and his company's work from being hacked and obliterated. The software he'd created so no one could trace his company's work back to him or his team. In order to keep them safe.

No one had done anything like it. Nina was right.

His was taken.

Right At Home.

The murderers were right at home. In his and everyone else's faces. Taunting him.

Jordan began racking his brain, poring over the list of his two-hundred and some employees, trying to pinpoint those who seemed the most likely.

"I have to go to my office. Emmett, check every console. Eve, check for the mark on every laptop. Liza, turn on only one laptop and call me."

"Tablets? Phones?"

"Don't worry about those."

The rerouter wasn't on them.

Jordan ran to the elevator. When he finally made it to his office, he sprinted to his center screen, turning on his main console that controlled every device that belonged to the company.

He blinked as he clicked, swallowing at the idea of what he was about to do.

His phone rang.

"What do you want us to do now?" Liza asked.

Jordan exhaled through his nose, eyes fierce as they focused on his screen. "In a minute," he said slowly, "I'm going to disable the rerouter on all of our computers."

The women's eyes widened.

That would leave them with a few firewalls. Firewalls that the FBI would've used, but nothing compared to what Jordan had created.

Not even Jordan's own tracking software could bypass his rerouter.

All of their confidential information would be at an exponentially greater risk.

"I need you to tell me how long the alert stays on the computer."

"Which alert?"

"It'll say, *Warning: Your Device Is Unprotected.*"

Liza crinkled her eyebrows together. "Okay."

Jordan exhaled hard again. He hovered the cursor over the *Disable* button.

He could find the laptops without even his software. He had basic trackers in them.

If there were streams that weren't affiliated with one of his laptops, then he'd use his software to track them.

He clicked. The red alert popped up on the screen, and he hit the exit button. "Alert was only on the screen for three seconds."

He exhaled through his nose hard a third time, hoping that whoever had stolen his laptops had not realized what he'd just done.

"Liza, shut that laptop off and trace each stream as fast as possible on a tablet. I'm doing the one from tonight. Emmett and Eve, go through the laptops as fast as you can and find the fakes. *Break them if it means going faster.* Make sure not a single one is on." He located the livestream from tonight and everything Liza and Eve had logged about it.

Then, using his software the way they always had, he began to track the IP address. In one minute and twenty-three seconds, he found that the girl was in the Lankin area, the most southern part of the state, right near the border.

"Call Lankin police, please."

Emmett flew through the laptops faster than Eve. She called.

Jordan's heart was beating fast. That was one out of eleven girls.

While his team worked, he typed in an IP address and stared at the map that popped up. More specifically, the little flashing blue dots. There were four.

"Did you figure out how many laptops were fakes?"

"Almost done checking," Emmett responded. "There are seven so far."

He cursed.

That meant three of the stolen laptops were shut down.

He needed to find all of them. One of the missing laptops was in Lankin; he pinpointed the exact location with the laptop's tracker, and there it was. Right in Lankin.

Now, he was down to three more missing, active laptops.

And three shut down. *It doesn't matter.* They could trace the streams.

Jordan exhaled hard.

The three other active laptops were also in the state. Adlin City was two hours north, Westlake three. Oak Ridge was an hour and a half east. He logged all of the coordinates in case the laptops were shut down and immediately sent them to his team and Tristan. Those areas needed to be raided, and he told them so.

Jordan's heart was beating so hard it distracted him for a second. He was trying to control the disbelief pouring through him over the months wasted on this case alone.

He wasn't sure what else was moving through him, but it was becoming overwhelming.

He needed to call Nina.

He needed to hear her voice. They might have been so close to finishing this, as he'd hoped and prayed. For her sake. So she could be safe again. So she didn't have to be afraid, for herself, for him, for her family.

His heart was longing for her. He hung up with the team as he headed to their floor and called Nina.

No answer.

He called again. Still nothing.

His heartbeat picked up faster as he dialed again. He *had* told her to get some more sleep...

Jordan called five more times, all with no answer.

Instead of floor six, he hit floor one in the elevator. He was going home to get her.

Just as he pressed the green call button to reach Luke, his phone lit up with an incoming call from him. Jordan hit the talk button before the ring in his earpiece could even sound.

"Jordan, I'm here, and she's gone! She's gone. She's not at the house. The front door is wide open. She's gone. I didn't make it in time."

Jordan's heart sank harder than it ever had before.

When the elevator doors opened to the lobby, he flew out and sprinted to his car.

"I don't know what happened. I'm so sorry. I'm inside, I'm looking around. Nothing seems to be disturbed except the teapot. It's on the floor by the sink." His voice was in a panic.

"Luke," Jordan ground his teeth in order to keep from screaming as he sped out of the parking lot and hit the main road, heading north, pressing down on the gas pedal. It was necessary to stay calm, or one reduced their chances of finding a solution exponentially. He knew that. "Trace the phones. Her number, and the one I gave you." Jordan called off both cell phone numbers.

She'd been taken. He was sure of it.

Nina would not leave. She would not ignore his calls.

But who?

Someone in the company.

It didn't matter who right now. He just had to know *where*.

They'd likely destroyed the phones. If they were smart enough to work for him, then they would.

How did they get into his home? There were two possibilities.

One, Nina opened the door.

Two, they disabled the alarm themselves. The more likely scenario.

No average person could hack that alarm system.

Those who did it were intelligent and skilled. And evil.

And now they had Nina.

Jordan added Liza to the call. She put Jordan on speaker for Emmett and Eve.

"Where are you?" she demanded. "What happened?"

"Nina's gone. *Whoever* has a tablet, type in this IP address," he demanded sharply, calling off digits and numerals quickly.

"Hold, on, hold on, we're going to the car," Emmett said, breathless as the three of them ran to their cars.

Jordan tried not to scream while he waited. "Take two; don't all drive together. I need you in different locations, and I need Eve on the tablet."

He heard car doors slamming. He'd take his opportunity to begin hitting the places he knew to start with. The reason he chose to drive north. His instinct told him that these psychopaths stuck together.

Which meant there would be more up north.

"Luke, I need you to head up to the coordinates in Westlake that I sent you. The cops should all be there or be on their way. They have our laptops and I have one tracked up there." Luke plugged in the coordinates as he sped.

"Emmett, go to Oak Ridge and Liza, Adlin City. Did you trace all the streams? Were any in Oak, Adlin or Westlake?"

"Yes. One in Oak, one in Adlin, and one in Marsh Hills, but that's right next to Westlake," Liza replied sharply. "We found three laptops for three streams."

"Okay, give me the IP." Eve waited for the numbers and his next instructions. As he called them out, her fingers flew on the little keyboard connected to her tablet. Finally, she was looking at a map with four single blue dots. It was clear she was looking at their missing laptops.

"Call Tristan and put him on." He prayed to God Tristan wasn't sleeping and had missed Jordan's message with coordinates and instructions to get police and FBI agents to them.

Liza dialed Tristan, who *had* been awake and in contact with the Bureau and police, filled him in in under ten seconds so he would approach his brother calmly, and a few seconds later, Tristan's voice rang in everyone's ears.

"Jordan—"

"I need police at each location. Now, Tristan. All three cities. Are the cops out in those areas yet? They need to go *now*, Tristan."

"Yes, they were sent once I briefed my director, a few minutes ago. I'm heading to you right now."

"No, wait. There may be other places to go. I need you to be ready to make more calls. Get the Bureau on standby."

"They already are. I'm going to tell the director about Nina." Tristan put them on hold.

The Bureau was going to be a racing madhouse when it found out there was another missing girl in one night, and that she was Jordan Asad's girlfriend. Jordan was thankful for that loyalty, somewhere in the back of his mind.

"How many coordinates on the screen, Eve?"

"Still four."

Jordan cursed out loud.

Eve blinked in surprise. "What is it?" She tried to keep her voice as soothing as possible.

"There are at least seven missing laptops. I need the other three locations. They'll only show once the laptops are on."

Understanding flooded each member of his team.

"The Lankin location is still there? Tristan, did Lankin police find anything?"

"Yes, they raided and found two men with the laptop, they just left it on. They're questioning onsite. No Nina."

Jordan tried to push away the frustration; there hadn't been enough time for them to take Nina hours away. She had to be close.

Forget the laptops. "Where did other streams take place?" That was where they'd go next. Jordan's voice was flat through gritted teeth. It alarmed his brother and his team. They'd never heard him that way.

They'd heard him frustrated or angry in his quiet, vicious manner. Never this way. His voice was flat, empty, and there was a sharpness to his words that cut through the air. Eve and Emmett looked at one another with wide eyes.

"One more was in Lankin, and the rest were also in-state: *four* in Lyson, and the other two were in Senton and Bayview."

Eleven livestreams. Seven missing laptops. Jordan and the team sorted it out in their heads.

One laptop in Lankin, two livestreams.

One in Adlin, one livestream.

One laptop in Oak Ridge, one livestream.

One laptop in Westlake, one livestream in Marsh Hills, its neighboring city. Though they could not verify if the remaining three laptops were currently in the livestream locations, they logically assumed so.

One laptop in Lyson, four livestreams.

One laptop in Senton, one livestream.

One laptop in Bayview, one livestream.

The streams could all be accounted for with that many computers. And he had three more places to check now.

Their odds at finding Nina sooner than later were a little better.

Lyson was north, and closest to Jordan's house and his office. He was now thirty minutes away.

Lankin was checked. No Nina. His team was heading to Westlake, Oak Ridge and Adlin.

No search relied on a team member to arrive. There were police in every city.

"Tristan, cops out in all of those cities. Every single one. We are not close enough." But Tristan had already phoned his director, who had the six-way call on speaker in front of Tristan's fellow agents. Jordan realized it then.

"Now," Jordan growled to Tristan's boss. He had only met the man once, through Tristan at a conference, long after he'd left the Bureau and a year after Tristan joined. Jordan had never worked with the man. He could hear the muffled voices of Tristan's team at the Bureau.

"Jordan, she could have left on her own," Luke tried to rationalize.

"Not likely," he replied through clenched teeth. "I told her not to. Did you get anything with the cell phones, Luke."

"I didn't come up with anything." Luke's voice was filled with regret. He'd sped faster than he ever had on his way to Jordan's house. The GPS could barely keep up with him.

Jordan's fingernails dug into the steering wheel.

He knew his tracking software could not get precise locations. It would pinpoint one area, and rarely would that area be exactly where the source was. If the laptops were on, it would be more helpful. But they weren't. So he would go to every city, starting with Lyson, and run around the streets and into every building until he found her.

"Eve, use your tablet and go through our company records to see if anyone lives in any of these areas. I have no one that travels out of state for work." Jordan tried to think of anyone off the top of his head, but he couldn't. All he could think of was Nina.

"Jordan," Tristan said, his voice sharp. "Police in Adlin, Oak Ridge, and Westlake found the killers and laptops, but Nina isn't with any of them."

Jordan cursed loudly.

Tristan bit his lip, uneasy for his brother but with good news.

"Police are on their way to Lyson. The others are *scouring* Senton and Bayv—." He could not finish before Emmett interjected.

"*Wait.* Oh, no."

"*What?*" Jordan's voice could've snapped all of their phones in half.

"There's a livestream, Jordan," Eve said quietly. "It's Nina."

Jordan's heart fell into his stomach. He couldn't breathe.

He thanked God for Eve's next words. "*New coordinates popped up in Lyson!* I'm sending them to *everyone*. Hold on, hold on, hold on." Jordan wanted to scream. He could not hold on.

Nina could not hold on.

"Tristan, get those to me *now*," the director told him.

"Are Lyson police on the ground yet?" he hollered to Tristan and the other agents. Then came a new dread as he remembered Lyson police were known for their incompetence and corruption.

No wonder four happened in Lyson, and no one knew.

"No, they were only alerted a minute ago, finding things out as we are," the director said, speaking to Jordan more calmly than he did his brother. It was deeply personal for the Bureau's former agent. "They're on their way out now."

Jordan got the coordinates and told his phone to take him there.

"I'm forty minutes away," Luke said, horrified by what he was hearing.

Eve stared at the laptop screen intensely. "We are an hour and ten."

"I'm the same," Liza said.

None of it meant anything to Jordan. He was twenty.
He'd known. Something in him had put him in the direction of Lyson and not any of the other locations.
Twenty minutes was too long. He didn't know what they were going to do to Nina.
He had ideas in his head, from the previous livestreams that took place.
The raping, stabbing, sawing, shooting, skinning.
Jordan stifled a scream and forced himself to think of other things.
He didn't think it was likely they'd kill her right off the bat. He tried to admit to himself that they would torture her if he didn't get there in time.
They'd set up cameras, chat screens, all of it. That meant that they didn't know he was coming.
They would take their time.
And that meant he had more time to find her.
He just prayed to God that they didn't hurt her. That they didn't touch her before he got to her.
He pressed down on the pedal harder. The speedometer crawled up to one-ninety.
Jordan made himself ignore the aching in his chest for his girl. His love.
"Jordan," Eve said calmly, "It looks like she's in an abandoned hospital—"
"What are they doing to her?" he interrupted.
"It doesn't look like they've hurt her, but they've stripped her down to just her underwear and have her hanging by her arms in chains." Emmett swallowed, glancing at the screen as he drove.
Jordan felt like his skin was going to go up in flames.
With every second that passed, it was harder for him to breathe.
He sped faster still, praying that Nina remained unscathed.
Tristan didn't speak for a few moments, and then he cursed.
"The cops haven't hit the location yet."
Jordan grit his teeth. "*Why*? They should be the closest." He tried to maintain his volume, but his voice was rising.
"They'll get there. The helicopter is out." Tristan's words did not soothe Jordan even slightly.
A new call suddenly came into Jordan's earpiece.
He didn't look at the caller ID. He just answered.

Nina

Ping!
I woke up, drowsy, in a dimly lit place, to a repeated ***Ping!*** sound. It reminded me of the noise of a phone notification.
The first thing I noticed were the tripods set up around me.
As I opened my eyes wider, trying to fight the drowsiness, I spotted two familiar men and remembered at the exact same time what had happened.
My stomach sank. I pushed back against the drowsiness harder.
My head fell against the tiredness. My arms were in the air above me. I looked up and saw that there were chains wrapped around my wrists, tied to a pipe, below which ceiling tiles had been ripped out.
It looked like we were in the center of a hospital floor.
I blinked, assessing the two men in front of me. They looked familiar, but my eyes were still foggy.
The air was cold and felt like it was pressing into me. As a chill brushed over my skin, and then another one, I realized I was wearing only my underwear and bra.
Looking in front of me again, I saw a forty-inch TV, propped up on its own stand. It looked like some sort of chat room. I could barely make out the words on the screen. They got clearer as my vision came into focus.
My eyes fell onto the long white table near which the men were standing. Spread out on it sat the various blades of different shapes and sizes. There were drills. There were saws. The high-pitched sound kept dinging.
Ping! Ping! Ping! Ping!

I swallowed and tried to breathe, but I felt like I couldn't.
This was going to be everything my mother and father warned me about.
This was going to be worse.
This was going to be as awful as what I'd seen and hadn't seen on Jordan's computer a few hours prior.
How quickly I took that poor girl's place.
My mouth felt dry as I tried to get air in.
"Good morning," one of the two men sneered. "We were waiting for you to wake up, princess."
I knew that voice from somewhere, but I couldn't remember where. "Let me go." My voice came out low and rough from sleep. I tried to raise it. "Let me go."
He smirked. "That would ruin all the fun."
My stomach sank. I thought of Jordan, and my chest hurt so badly it made it more difficult to breathe. I wanted to sob immediately.
I forced myself to hold it in. They wanted to see it. They wanted to see fear.
I knew I was pale. I knew I looked weak and innocent at that moment. But I would not let them see me cry, if I could help it.
"There are a lot of people who have been waiting for this, Nina, sweetheart," he continued, patronizing. He looked at the TV screen; I followed his gaze and realized where the pinging was coming from.

Ping! 4zzone: Come on!!! We've been dying for this
Ping! notrack3: what are you waiting for. cut her open
Ping! blazenking: is this really his girl?
Ping! theinquisitor: You're wasting time. Kill her before he gets there.
Ping! dodgeman87: yeah, this'll be the best one yet. the best one.
Ping! thuheat44: HURRY UP MAN.
Ping! fangsnally: he won't find them if they were smart with their vpn's.
Ping! justwait4it: this is risky. doing it so close to him
Ping! justwait4it: you think a vpn is gonna stop him? do u remember what rtech told us?
Ping! justwait4it: the software they have there is ridiculous. they know more than we do
Ping! 4zzone: justwait4it don't be a child. he has the same thing JA has. he took it. have you been living under a rock
Ping! 4zzone: kill her
Ping! amintheprince: cut her legs off 1st
Ping! justwait4it: 4zzone ur the kid if u think we arent all at risk now.
Ping! becoming52: wut i wanna kno is how rtech managed 2 hide this from him 4 so long

The chat went on more explicitly. Horror filled every cell in my body. These abominable people, hiding behind random usernames and computer screens, were cheering him on. Reminiscing on the other times they watched innocent people die. They were waiting for this, waiting to see me, anyone Jordan loved, or Jordan himself die slowly, in agony.

I teetered between trying to anticipate and accept my own torture and death, and praying Jordan and his team, the police, the FBI, *someone* found me before they touched me.

I prayed.

JORDAN

"Jordan, Jordan, Jordan," a familiar male voice taunted.
Jordan knew he was talking to the person standing in front of Nina. He was sure of it.
"Let her go," he growled, voice so low and fierce that Nina's captor felt a quick wave of hesitation. He forced himself to push that intimidation aside.
Jordan would not find them. They made it impossible for them. Impossible. He would not let this bastard intimidate him. They had the upper hand now.
"Jordan?" Liza asked, driving her own car to the site. They were all confused. Was he talking to...?
"Do not touch her," Jordan went on. Nina's captor had to force a straight face. He wanted to wince. Years of hatred, envy and fear of this man did not make this moment as sweet as he wanted it to be. He had doubts.
He found his voice, however, reminding himself that he had the advantage. Remembering that there were hundreds watching him, having waited for this. He couldn't disappoint.
He would be the king of the Underground.
"Now, now, boss," he said, and he grinned slowly at the word, the word that finally brought him excitement at what was taking place.
Finally, *finally*, the bastard would be stripped of his power and control.
Everyone acted as though he was untouchable, undefeatable. As though you couldn't hurt Jordan Asad.
But he crushed that idea in his mind as he thought that no amount of money, authority, experience or brains could save him from the pain he was about to feel.
Pain for acting as though he was better than all of them. For having that nerve after he sabotaged them so he could get to where he was now.

Jordan had set them up for failure. He'd done it on purpose. They should've realized that Jordan not caring about their success was a lie. Everyone was greedy. Everyone wanted to see their competition fail.

And Jordan's current net worth proved that he was just as greedy as them all.

Jordan would feel pain for ripping into the place he and his online colleagues had built for themselves, tearing down their hideaways, one by one, ruining their fun for no good reason. Pain for selling them something useless, leaving them unable to create the new Underground they'd been planning on building for years. They just needed a base, someone to do the difficult construction, so they could turn it into something even better than Gateway, something that every average person couldn't get into. It was supposed to be for them. For the people on Gateway, watching him right now. A more private place so that bastards like Jordan couldn't cut into it. Jordan was supposed to set himself up to fail by giving it to them.

He set them up instead.

Why did he *care* what they did in their free time?

They were nobodies. Nobodies. Jordan spent all his time, all his energy and money saving *nobodies*. Worthless lives.

Now, they would take his.

"Listen, boss," Nina's captor repeated the word cheerily. "I have to touch her. I just have to." He feigned sincere adamance.

And he told himself Jordan could do nothing.

Nothing.

JORDAN

The second time Jordan heard the word *boss*, it hit him.
It was Ryan.
How did Jordan not *know*? How did he not know the simplest explanation for what was taking place? Had he doubted himself that much, so as to never consider that his own creation could be used against him? If not for the fact that Ryan was blatantly envious, with his superficial respect and constant eyerolling that he thought Jordan didn't see, or the permanent attitude he had with everybody else, females especially?
Jordan wanted to punch himself.
If not for all of that, how did he not know when he looked at Nina the way he did, so sleazily, hideously? And there was something in that look that Jordan had not been able to put his finger on; he chalked it up to Ryan just being obnoxious. Looking down on her because she was with him.
No. It wasn't just sleazy.
It was sinister.
Jordan's nails dug into the steering wheel.
He should've known.
Jordan and everyone else just thought the enemy had gotten better.
They hadn't. They couldn't do anything for themselves, the same way they couldn't do anything with his browser six years prior.
They, his own team members. His own employees.
Right at home.
Jordan felt stupider than he ever had. And so full of regret and fury that he had to remind himself to inhale. This was his fault.
He brought Nina around them. If not for the stop on that floor at the office, they wouldn't have even known Nina existed.

"Ryan," Jordan fumed, his voice low, "Don't you dare lay a finger on her. Don't you *dare*." His voice was quiet. Deadly.

"Hey, Nina, listen. It's your boy toy on the phone," Ryan chirped.

Suddenly, Jordan heard her.

"Jordan," Nina wept.

His heart stopped. He suddenly forgot how to breathe.

Then he heard nothing.

She was reigning it in, like she always did. She was being strong.

Finally, he dredged some air in. He had to.

"Nina." Jordan's voice was drenched with pain. "Nina, I'm right here, baby."

The speedometer inched up to 195 miles per hour.

Ryan laughed on the other end. "Except he's not."

"I am, Nina." Jordan made his voice strong and firm. It felt like his chest was being ripped apart from the inside. "I'm right here, and I'm coming. I'm coming."

"No, he's not, Nina. He's gotta tell you that. To make you think you're walking out of here alive. To convince himself he hasn't failed. Hasn't killed you."

"Ryan—" Jordan growled.

"I don't know if you've realized this yet, but Jordy boy, the big, smart boss man, lies. That's what all greedy, arrogant bastards do. They lie.

"Let me tell you a little story about your boy toy."

Jordan wanted to tell him to shut his filthy mouth before he ripped it off his head, but he didn't want Ryan to get worked up. He might hurt Nina.

"Years ago, Donovan and I, we approached Jordan for a browser he'd made. We thought it might be a nice base for something greater, so we paid him a pretty penny for it. He probably told you about it, didn't he? Probably made it sound like God's handcrafted Internet Explorer."

Nina was breathing hard, trying to follow along, trying to understand while she clung to Jordan's presence, as minimal as it was.

Ryan's voice turned flat. "He failed to mention how many flaws the software had."

Jordan exhaled hard through his nose, disbelieving what he was hearing.

"We gave a couple million dollars to your arrogant *prick* of a boyfriend, just to find out he was selling us a dream while *he* built something even greater, something that would make him a practical billion. *Billion.* Your boy toy is sitting on some pennies, baby. And he thinks he's better than all of us because of it."

"The browser he gave us was a piece of garbage. It forced us to lose out on millions. Not only did our business plan fail because of the garbage he sold us, but we lost ties to important investors that are *still* after us for their money back." Ryan's voice became angrier, as Jordan grew more appalled.

No, Jordan's browser software wasn't flawless. But as he recalled it, the conversation went differently.

335

JORDAN

"It isn't perfect," Jordan told a much lankier Ryan and more boyish-looking Donovan. *"It needs much more work."*

"We got it, Jordy boy," Ryan's arrogant voice drawled. Jordan gave Ryan a menacing look, wiping the condescension out of Ryan's tone. Ryan put his hands up. Even at twenty-three, Jordan was a threat, and Ryan and Donovan knew it.

Lowering his volume, Ryan said, *"We can improve it, buddy. Don't worry. Just take the money and let us work it out. Make your work even better. You'll be so proud, knowing you were the one who made it all happen."* Ryan was schmoozing. Jordan knew what he was thinking. *"Yeah, right, pretty boy. You can have your couple million now. In a few years, you'll be looking at the next billionaire, toting your amateur work that we perfected."*

Jordan wondered how Ryan could possibly have twisted the initial dialogue so much in his head. He'd practically begged Jordan for the browser, trying to convince him it would be the next billion-dollar Chrome. Jordan had hoped it would be, for their sake. He wished them well and moved on. He never claimed the browser to be perfect or sold them a dream the way Ryan alleged.

And now, because of Ryan's inability to take responsibility for his own failure, Nina would suffer.

"You understand, don't you, Nina?" Ryan gave her wide, puppy dog eyes. "Being a little broke girl, just barely makin' it. You know what it's like to need money you don't have."

Jordan's skin was blazing. "Ryan—"

"Oh yes, we did our research on you, baby. We know all about you and the boring little life you've lived. Unfortunately, it's going to end soon.

"And what's even more unfortunate is that you have to die, knowing your boyfriend is a liar. Realizing all he's probably lied to you about."

"Nina," Jordan started. Ryan went on over him.

"Can you imagine, Nina? Can you imagine all the people he's killed, maybe all the things he's stolen, even? Can you imagine all the other skinny, pretty girls he's—"

"Nina, don't listen to him, baby, listen to me—" Jordan tried to get her attention, but Ryan carried on as if he didn't hear him.

"—while you were working your poor little self to exhaustion? Or in therapy, crying about how you couldn't be as skinny as them?"

The hair on Jordan's arms shot up. His skin became cold as Ryan spoke, the fury unlike anything he'd ever felt.

He'd never wanted to kill somebody so badly.

"Ryan, shut your mouth," he growled viciously, squeezing the steering wheel so tightly his knuckles turned white.

"But maybe that's not it, sweetheart," Ryan continued. "Maybe he isn't lying. He probably *thinks* he's coming. I wouldn't doubt it. Your boy toy is an arrogant man. Thinks he's unstoppable." He was fuming now. He had worked himself into a growing fit of rage, and Jordan could hear it. Nina could see it. Ryan was a thin man with too many freckles and mean eyes, the eyes of the angry bully who didn't have enough strength to back his nasty attitude.

"But we got *juuuust* a little too good for you this time, boss." Ryan's anger was suddenly replaced with smugness.

Jordan did not want to inform Ryan about how wrong he was. But he needed Nina to know he was coming.

His GPS said nine minutes.

"Never thought your own boy scout software would be used against you, now did ya?" Ryan beamed. "Never thought *you'd* be responsible for so many ugly, *violent* deaths."

"Stop," Nina said weakly as she breathed hard. Even tied up, terrified, hurting, she was protecting Jordan, protecting his heart in one of the spots she knew was most vulnerable. It bled inside Jordan as he heard her speak in his defense. His throat was aching hard. "Shut your mouth."

She mustered up all her energy just to say those words. He could hear it.

"Oh, shut up, you dumb whore." All of Ryan's theatrics vanished. "Just as worthless as the rest of them. Thought you were special, didn't you, walking into boss man's office like a little special trophy wife."

Jordan's rage was rabid. If he were there, he would've snapped Ryan's neck before he ever said Nina's name.

"Get away from her, you miserable, disgusting—" Jordan growled, but Ryan cut him off loudly.

"No, no. Actually, Jordy boy, I'm gonna touch your little whore of a girlfriend in every way you could possibly imagine."

"No," Eve gasped.

Nina screamed.

"Get away from her!" Jordan snarled, expletives flying out of his mouth like they never had. He addressed Eve. *"What is he doing to her?"*

"Her leg Jordan, he's burning her leg, her—"

Nina screamed again. *"No!"* And Jordan nearly ripped the steering wheel off the dashboard. The speedometer hit two hundred.

Jordan's voice got low, fast and intense. "I swear on everything, Ryan, I will rip you apart, limb by limb. I will *snap* every single bone in your body—"

A sudden silence.

"Jordan," Nina whimpered.

The pain that shot through Jordan's body again made it hard for him to breathe.

His voice shifted and filled with love and assurance. "I'm coming, baby. I'm coming. I promise you, I'm coming."

Nina continued sobbing his name. Jordan's GPS read five minutes.

Nobody had gotten there yet. Not one cop.

Then, "You'll never see her alive again." Ryan's voice oozed with confidence.

"I love you, Jordan," Nina whimpered.

Jordan felt like something was ripping the organs in his body apart from the inside.

"I love you so much," he promised adamantly. He tried to keep his voice calm and soothing. "I'll be right there, I promise. Just stay strong, like you always are. I'm coming, baby."

And then his voice turned into a menacing growl, so venomous that it brought Ryan down from his high for a moment and sent a wave of trepidation through him. He was shaken by the cursing, the growls, the screaming at them that Jordan had never done.

The words were slow and articulate.

"Do not touch her again, Ryan. I will make your death the worst possible torture you could ever imagine."

Three minutes. Jordan blew through three red lights.

He could see the buildings in the quiet area ahead. He spotted the three-story, decrepit hospital.

"Gotta go, boss," Ryan said cheerily into the phone, though the threat made him swallow.

"Say goodbye to your little dime. You know, I must say, she is pretty cute, Jordy boy. Maybe we'll have some fun with her before we kill her." The phone disconnected.

"Nina." He could barely say the word. She was gone.

One minute.

"*Is she alive?*" he hollered.

"She is, she is, he burned her leg, she's okay. He's not touching her right now."

"Burned her with *what*?"

"Hot iron, I think." Eve's voice was regretful as she watched the poor, sweet girl she knew was pure, as pure as they came. Because Jordan fell for her.

Jordan's heart was beating so fast that he had to force himself to ignore it. It was getting even more difficult to concentrate after hearing Nina scream out in pain.

It was his worst nightmare.

But he knew he had to focus. He knew he had to concentrate. The hospital entrance came into sight.

No one would touch her again.

Nina

The pain was excruciating.
Just as I'd heard Jordan's voice, heard him say my name, tell me he was coming, after discovering who Ryan and Donovan really were, Ryan slammed burning iron into my flesh.
First I screamed, and then the air in my airways stopped moving. It was unbearable. I was dizzy from the agony of it.
Then, I heard Jordan threaten him in a voice and with words I had never heard from him before, and it snapped me back into focus and gave me a newfound energy.
I didn't know if it would kill me. I was so horrified for when the next one would come, but I knew that if I was still alive, it was a good thing.
I just needed to endure long enough for Jordan to get here.
And he had to be coming.
He had to.
No, Nina. Accept it. Accept it. They're going to rape you, cut your limbs off, saw you in half. You're just going to have to take it.
God, please *help me.*
I was terrified that, at any moment, Ryan would pick up a blade and stick it into my abdomen and kill me on the spot. Or that he would slit my throat. Use a chainsaw and cut me apart. Skin me alive. Set me on fire. The horrific thoughts flooded me.
I watched his every move.
When he came back a second time, as I felt the searing pain, I forced myself to listen for Jordan. I knew I would hear him. I knew it would make the agony more tolerable.

Jordan threatened to rip Ryan's body apart; I made myself picture it as the iron seared my skin.

I cried but forced myself to think of him. When Ryan ripped the burning rod off and I caught my breath, returning to the present, I told Jordan I loved him. I didn't know if it would be the last time. I cried harder at the thought.

Ryan taunted Jordan a few moments more and then hung up the phone, and I was alone with him again. Jordan was gone. I wanted to be dead.

Suddenly, Ryan walked towards me fast. Instinctively, I squeezed my eyes shut. I heard something clank to my left and felt something cold against my wrist.

Just as I opened my eyes to see what he was doing, my arm fell out of the cuff on the chain. Then the other, and I slammed into the ground. The pain from the burns took my breath away.

"Come on out, boys and girls!" Ryan called, as enthusiastic as a late-night talk show host, announcing his guest for the evening. I saw the large key in his hand.

Then, creeping in through the far end of the corridor, were multiple figures, dressed in all black, that I could barely see. They moved slowly towards us, menacingly. I could tell they were wearing gas masks. And holding weapons.

Ryan looked at me, excitement on his face. His eyebrows shot up as he lowered his voice and sneered, "Run."

We were in the center of the four corridors. They were further down the abandoned building, seemingly at the end of one corridor, perhaps one-hundred-fifty yards away. It was enough of a distance that I thought I had a chance at escaping.

I had to think that.

Prepare yourself for it to be like the dreams. They'll catch you.

I stood up, ignoring the pain that tore through my wounds, the pain in my limbs from falling, the aching in my arms from being held up for so long, and I ran. It was difficult, so difficult, to get my legs to move straight. I focused on balancing, centering myself so I could run as fast as I could. I was lightheaded.

"Wow, Nina!" Ryan called, patronizing. "I didn't think you'd be able to move so fast!"

I didn't, either.

I ran down the corridor opposite from where the masked men were coming.

This is a hospital.

My earlier guess had been right; the realization hit me as I ran. I hoped the corridors were as maze-like as possible.

I made it halfway down the corridor before I turned right. I continued running, passing different rooms, storage closets, little corners with large pipes moving up to the ceiling, but I couldn't find anywhere to hide. The closets that I passed were too empty to hide in. A couple rooms only had tables and shelves in them. The hospital was clearly abandoned. It seemed like the first floor. I was terrified it was the basement.

How am I gonna get out of here?

There would certainly be one of the masked people waiting for me at a staircase or elevator, if I found either.

Are there exits in the basement?

I decided to put as much distance as possible between them and me, searching for an exit, though the whole time, I never really anticipated finding one. But I thought the more corners I turned—left here, left again, right there, left again—the more likely they'd lose sight of me. Somewhere in the back of my mind, I was thankful that the hospital was huge. I forced myself to stop crying, because I knew I needed the breath to move as fast as possible.

The pain I was feeling, physically and emotionally, tore through me, so hot and merciless as I begged God to save me. *Help me. Please, please help me.*

I rounded a corner and heard footsteps echoing. They were getting closer. I kept turning corners, trying to bury myself enough until I found somewhere to hide.

"Just stay strong, like you always are. I'm coming, baby."

And for him, I would be.

You need to get away.

Think, Nina.

As my legs flew faster than I thought I was capable of, I had an idea.

Holding my breath, I pressed my hand against the bleeding on my thighs, stumbling as I continued to run. The pain was brutal, but I ignored it.

Hoping I had enough blood on my hands, I stopped running for ten seconds to spread it onto the bottoms of both feet. I pressed into my thigh for more. It was agony, but I knew I would be wasting precious seconds if I didn't do this right.

Once I couldn't scrounge up anymore, I walked quickly around another corner, pressing my feet into the ground to leave footprints on the dirty, once-white hospital floor. Once they left no more marks, I turned around, dodging the bloody footprints and running in the opposite direction. The sounds of people running got closer.

Please let this work.

I picked up my speed as much as possible and made a few turns. When my eyes landed on the unlit *Exit* sign, my heart soared in my chest.

We *were* on the first floor.

I prayed no one was waiting outside as I pushed it open as quietly as possible. I didn't hear any more running.

It was dark out, but the glow of the streetlights gave me enough sight to not crash into things. My eyes scanned the area around me as I ran, looking for more masked people. The night was quiet. I needed to get away from this building.

As the frigid air assaulted my bare skin, I ran toward the rear of the hospital, away from the streets where these killers could be waiting, and cut across the backs of two huge buildings.

My exhaustion and the agony all over my body were catching up to me. My lungs were screaming for air.

Keep going. You've gotten this far.

I can't. I can't. I wanted to sob but I had no air.

I had no choice but to dip into an alley past the third building and find somewhere to hide.

I crashed into a corner where the building would shield me from the street. I was losing the mental capacity to be strong. My head was spinning, my thighs were screaming in pain, and I wanted to give up, to just pray someone stopped them before they found me. I was so tired.

I thought of Jordan and how badly I wanted to be with him again. How devastating and joyous and comforting that reunion would be. All the years we'd spend together after. If only he came. If only he was really on his way. I brought my knees to my chest, trembling viciously. I sobbed, missing him so badly and drowning in the thought that I would never see him again. No pain in my life was as paralyzing as this.

The cruel burning in my thighs hurt worse with each passing second, along with the dry aching in all my limbs. A searing pain was spreading through my head.

It grew until I began to panic.

I can't run anymore.

They'll find me.

I rocked back and forth, my thoughts melting into each other until I could no longer think or see, just feel myself quake. I didn't know if I was imagining the faint sound of gunshots, cutting through the roaring in my ears.

Jordan forced himself to initially take it easy on the brakes as he drove towards the hospital entrance. If he slammed on them, he risked flipping the car over. He was trying to focus on easing it down low enough so he could finally stomp without risking killing himself. As it slid down to fifty miles per hour, he hit the brakes harder, shoved the car into park and flew out, drew his gun and heard Eve's voice ringing from his earpiece as he sprinted inside.
"They're chasing her," she breathed, the words loud. "People with weapons." Jordan ran so fast his feet barely touched the ground.
He could hear the sound of the world flying past the car Eve and Emmett were in as they sped to him. "I've counted twelve so far, Jordan. The cameras are facing where she ran." Alarm shot through his body. "She had a head start." Eve wanted Jordan to know Nina's odds were better than they sounded.
It didn't make him feel any better. It didn't slow his pace.
Eve's voice continued. "You're looking for gas masks and lots of weapons. I didn't see guns, but prepare for them. We'll be there in less than ten."
Jordan didn't think the police would arrive for at least another ten minutes either.
It didn't matter. He was there now.
As he ran to the emergency room sliding doors, which looked stuck in place, he heard clanking and shuffling in the distance, heard a high-pitched dinging sound over and over again. He spotted, through the dysfunctional sliding doors, Ryan and Donovan.
Two on the inside of his company. There were two.
Jordan spotted the chains on the floor, the tripods, the television. The table with knives and saws and other weapons. He did not have enough time to

process the reality of finally finding the miserable pieces of filth who had given him and everyone he loved hell, the reality that he was in their physical presence, in the presence of the weapons he'd watched torture innocent people. The reality that he finally found them only for Nina to be the last victim they had brutalized.

And she didn't have much time.

"GO!" Ryan screamed, eyes wide in disbelief as they landed on Jordan. He and Donovan both reached for the guns on their waists as Jordan pulled the sliding doors apart with the little gap between them. There wasn't much resistance.

Ryan was more apt with his gun, but it was still evident to Jordan and everyone watching that neither had any experience or skill with the weapon.

Jordan aimed and pulled four times, hitting each with every shot, as he ran. Then, he continued running towards the sounds down the corridors. The watching members of the chatroom were stunned by Jordan's presence as well as his precision.

Ping! *justwait4it: i **TOLD** you!*

They watched Jordan fly down the corridor through which his girlfriend had chosen to run, praying the members chosen to participate in Nina's torture would kill him.

Most of them knew if he did not die, Jordan would find them.

The **Ping!** sounds lessened in frequency as the cult members retreated in fear. Those remaining were too gripped by their shock to look away.

As Jordan moved through the seemingly never-ending corridors towards the sounds he was hearing, he became more and more frustrated at all of the empty rooms. He screamed out for Nina. The noises he heard became louder, but he did not hear Nina's voice.

Then, he saw the first one.

Immediately, Jordan aimed and shot at the figure donning a gas mask and holding a chainsaw. He was miserable, the thought flickering through his mind at how terrified Nina must have been.

If they hadn't already killed her.

He was in agony. And full of rage.

No.

Jordan had gotten there faster than anyone expected. He'd found her. They'd figured it all out just in time.

He would not lose her now.

He ran faster to catch up, and they started popping up, seeming to have paused their hunt to eliminate the threat. This was good. It took their attention off Nina.

Jordan aimed and hit each, missing a few before landing the bullets where he needed them. There were five, then six. Far behind him, Jordan heard the shouts of police officers and agents, calling out to each other. They arrived faster than he'd thought.

Seven, eight. Each went down immediately as the bullet pierced either their unprotected hearts or the gas masks on their faces.

Suddenly, a masked man jumped out of a storage room past which Jordan was running and shoved him against the wall. He had a long blade in his hand. Jordan kicked him in the gut and shot him in the head.

Jordan ran through hall after hall, dipping into each room for seconds, searching. His eyes landed on bloody footsteps and his heart, as fast as it was beating, skipped a few. He followed them and then heard running. Down the hall across from him, two masked individuals rounded the corner and spotted Jordan. One began running towards him while the other reached for something on his waist. Jordan didn't know what. He just shot and killed them both.

Just as he began to run in the direction of their dead bodies, thinking they might have had Nina before they tried to kill him, he heard a faint sound behind him. Somewhere in the opposite direction of where he was heading. He kept sprinting towards the two dead bodies, about a hundred feet, praying he wouldn't find her lying there around the corner.

But she wasn't there. He didn't know if he should continue down one of those halls, or go back to the sound he'd just heard. There were no more footprints to guide him.

He stopped his search, conflicted. He called her name but heard no response from either end of the corridor. He headed back in the direction of the noise, unsure of himself, praying he wasn't making a mistake.

"Eve, you said there were twelve?" he yelled into his earpiece. "Has anyone gotten the last one?"

"Yeah, twelve," she responded. After a moment, she added, "No one has found any of them alive. There's one more?"

Jordan didn't answer. "Have they surrounded the building? Southeast corner?"

Another pause, then, "No, they just started scaling the perimeter. Why, Jordan?" She was breathless, running along with the others to join him.

He ignored her question again. He was trying to decide if he should keep running toward the noise, or go back to the corridor to which the bloody footprints led. If there were really only one person left chasing Nina, and the teams hadn't reached that area of the building, then the noise he'd heard was either her or the one left. Or both. And they'd caught her.

But what if Eve had miscounted, and the noise he heard was only one of numerous masked men left? The others still chasing Nina where the footprints led?

"Have you seen her in the camera again?" he yelled.

After a moment, Eve responded breathlessly, "No. She hasn't come back in that direction."

She might not have known they were there. Of course she wouldn't run back to where she thought Ryan and Donovan were.

JORDAN

The hospital was huge, anyway. Jordan had been trying to keep track of each corridor and the room numbers, to make sure he wasn't running in a circle and missing something.

Now, he didn't know if he was doing the right thing. It didn't make sense not to follow the footsteps, but what about that noise? He couldn't think about it any longer.

He kept running.

Following the sound, he ran down the hall, turning a corner. But when the sound became faint again, he doubled back. It grew louder as he sprinted. Suddenly, he felt a cold rush of air just as he rounded the last corner. A dead end.

And an open exit.

He bolted out into the empty lot, praying his love had escaped. Praying the last murderer hadn't found her. He screamed her name, sprinting towards the back of the building, thankful this was not the side with the parking garage.

"There's an open exit at the southeast corner of the building," he yelled into his earpiece. "Either she or he or both are outside. Split up between the rooms inside and the outside of the building. Check the higher floors. Does anybody see her or him up front?" He decided to run to the back of the building. If everyone else was just arriving, there would be no one to find her in the back.

After a few moments of silence, he heard Liza.

"Eve just added us to the call, Jordan. What did you say?"

He tried not to grit his teeth. Eve spoke.

"Does anyone see Nina or a masked person up front?"

"I'm up front," Emmett said breathlessly. "No sight." Jordan heard him yell at everyone to search that area.

"Why am I having them do that?"

Jordan just sprinted as Eve explained the open door and last murderer standing. He rounded the corner and faced the back lot of the hospital. Completely empty. All he saw was a dumpster. No sight of Nina or anyone else. He screamed her name. Spinning around, scanning his surroundings and finding nothing, he turned to run to the next building. Out of the corner of his eye, he spotted movement where he'd just seen nothing. He turned back and sprinted towards it.

Halfway down the hospital was another open exit. Jordan entered and rounded a few corners. And there he was.

The last masked man, unable to find a way out, backed into a corner, Jordan here, cops on every other side.

As the man lifted his knife, Jordan shot him in the knees. The blade clattered to the ground, and Jordan grabbed him by his collar, ripping off the mask to see the face of a scruffy man with bloodshot eyes.

"Where is she?" Jordan screamed in his face as the man grunted and groaned in pain.

"You'll never find her, you piece of—" he sputtered, unable to finish, seeming to have accepted his fate. Jordan wrapped his hand around the man's throat and squeezed. He grasped at Jordan's hands.

"*Where is she?*" he repeated. Jordan loosened his grip on the choking man's neck so he could reply.

"I don't know," he gasped, hatred and panic taking turns clouding his eyes. Jordan assessed the man furiously but found no blood anywhere other than his knees. Maybe he was telling the truth, and Nina was still out there.

He prayed so.

Jordan pointed his gun at the man's forehead.

"One last chance. Everyone else is dead. Where is she?"

The man blinked hard a few times, still gasping with Jordan's free hand on his throat.

"No one found her, huh?" he choked out, managing a slight smirk. "That's too bad."

Jordan pulled the trigger without a thought.

She's out there, he thought as he exited, unconcerned with the members of his team hearing what just happened.

"No sign of her yet," Liza said, running.

"Grab Ryan and Donovan and find out if they know where she is. Torture them if you have to."

If anyone was surprised by the order, they said nothing about it.

"Scour the area and surrounding buildings to the east," he continued as he approached the next, pulling at locked doors.

"No one is seeing her in the streets."

Helicopter lights beamed down, moving around the strip of buildings. Flashlights and headlights gleamed from the street. The faint glow helped him see.

"No sight of her in the hospital," Liza announced breathlessly, frustrated.

Jordan reached the opposite side of the office building and saw police across the alley, breaking in. He sprinted past the next building and stopped in the alley, scouring and trying to catch his breath at the same time. He kept moving, the love of his life in the front of his mind, his lungs in the back.

His eyes landed on the covered porch at the side entrance of the next building, just as he heard labored sobbing.

His girl.

"Nina?" he yelled, flying across the alley. As he approached, he saw her, crouched in the corner next to the door.

The relief that flooded him nearly knocked him off his feet.

She sat, in bra and underwear only, knees up to her chest, arms wrapped around her legs, rocking back and forth, sobbing.

"I got her!" he bellowed breathlessly. "Side entrance of the third building east. Send the ambulance!"

JORDAN

As he pulled his jacket off and wrapped it around her, he scanned her shins, ankles, and knees but didn't see wounds. He didn't know where she was hurt, but he knew she was, somewhere on her legs. He wrapped his arms around her quivering body and held her tightly against him. The back of his hand brushed her knee; her skin was so cold against his, despite the running she'd done.

"I'm so sorry, I'm so sorry, I'm so sorry," Jordan repeated, rocking her. He felt the urge to cry grow, but he knew he still needed to concentrate. He shoved the feeling back as Nina shook in his arms.

He pulled back just enough to look at her face and assess her body, looking for wounds. Her calves and feet were dirty from running barefoot. Her long hair had dust in it. He saw small scratches on her lower legs, from sliding against things as she ran. Bruises covered her legs and were forming in different spots on her arms. There was a particularly large one near her shoulder.

"Where are you hurt, baby? Where are you hurt?" Jordan looked at her, eyes wide, desperate for a response.

The sobs had stopped. Nina shook, inhaling short, sharp breaths. Her eyes were wide with terror. Small sounds escaped the back of her throat as she trembled. Jordan didn't think she was processing his words as she stared at him.

He turned away from her as voices neared and yelled, "*I need clothes!*" She jerked at the noise, but he didn't see.

Facing Nina once more, he told her, "We're gonna get you some clothes, baby. We're gonna get you warm. The ambulance is coming, they're gonna help you feel better. I need you to show me where you're hurt. I need to see up here." He slid his hands over her knees and pointed down to her upper thighs.

Nina shivered, not speaking. Agony shot through Jordan, again and again in large waves as he watched her shake, pain, shock and horror having crumpled her face. He thought she might be hyperventilating.

As Liza ran down the alley, Jordan kissed Nina's forehead, lacing his hand gently through her hair at the roots as he leaned in. When he pulled it away, there was blood on his fingers. His eyes widened.

"I've got them!" she shouted, sprinting up and handing Jordan sweatpants and a sweater. She screamed into her transceiver, "I *need* an ambulance *now!*"

Jordan was going to explode if help did not get here fast.

"Her head is bleeding," he said through grit teeth to Liza. *They must have hit her, and that was what knocked her unconscious in order for them to take her.* He gently moved some hair out of the way to see if it went deeper, his heart beating even harder. He was trying not to become overwhelmed as his head raced between the blood on her head and what he couldn't see on her legs.

Jordan took the clothes and moved slightly to kneel in front of Nina.

"Where are the wounds?" he growled.

"Her thighs," Liza breathed. She turned away and snapped into her receiver that the EMT's needed to pick up the pace.

He wrapped the hoodie around Nina's back and over his jacket, but she wouldn't unlock her hands to slide her arms in. "Okay, baby," he told her, as he settled the sweater over her hunched shoulders. "I have to see your legs, honey, I have to see your legs."

Jordan talked to her gently, soothingly, eyes wide and serious but just as gentle as his voice as he looked into hers, trying to get her to understand or at least react. She did not until Jordan tried to gently pry her hands apart and move them from around her legs.

Nina locked her fingers together, leaned back away from Jordan and shook her head vehemently. Jordan's eyebrows knitted together in distress.

"*Now!*" Liza shouted into the radio once more. Nina flinched at the sound. Jordan jerked his head towards Liza with fire in his eyes. He turned back.

"Let me see, baby, let me see," he said softly, and finally he was able to gently unlock her hands. As he started to pull her legs forward, wrapping his hands around her ankles in the same, gentle manner, whimpers and whines vibrated from the back of her throat. Jordan was terrified that he was hurting her. Every sound she made cut through him.

"Jordan," Liza started.

But Nina let him slide her knees down slowly; before he could bring them all the way down, he spotted the blood on her inner thighs.

Her knees split apart a little. Jordan's eyes widened at the bleeding, swelling welt at the top of her inner thigh and, when her legs suddenly split open more, the one just next to her genitals.

Liza turned and ran, hollering, "*I need a paramedic, NOW!* What is taking so long?!" It was worse than it looked on camera.

She was halfway down the alley when two paramedics rounded the corner with a stretcher. She turned back.

Horror morphed into rage within Jordan, then turned back into horror.

Eve had said her leg. Not her groin. Not right next to her genitals.

Her underwear was covering her. He didn't know if Ryan had burned her more than this.

"Liza," he snarled. "Did he go further? Underneath...?" Though he hesitated to ask in front of Nina, his voice was sharp.

"Eve said he didn't move her...didn't move them out of place, but it has to be checked, just in case." Her face was regretful as she approached again. "The cameras weren't close enough to be sure."

Heat like he had never known exploded all over Jordan's body.

He couldn't see straight for a moment. The rage and agony were too much. There was a lot of blood. Those burns had to be torturous. Not deep enough to numb but not shallow enough for the pain to die down with a little time. Looking at her broken face and thinking of how those welts must have felt, he crumpled with sympathy for the love of his life. He ached for her.

"It's okay, baby," he whispered. "We're gonna get you all better."

He turned to see the stretcher roll up, followed by two paramedics.

Jordan slid his arms under Nina and carefully lifted her up.

"I got you, baby," he said gently. "I got you."

He lowered her onto the stretcher, but she'd just barely touched it before she locked her arms around his neck.

"No, no, no," she whimpered desperately, as Liza informed the paramedics about the burns.

Jordan held her tightly against him as he set her down. "I'm right here, baby, I'm right here. I'm not going anywhere, my love."

Nina didn't seem to process the words as she cried and begged, "Don't go. Don't leave me," her voice forced. She was shivering hard, squeezing his arms tight as he bent to stay close to her.

Her face, her voice, the words. It was too much.

Jordan felt like his heart was snapping in half.

She looked broken. She looked like she was in agony, still terrified. The physical wounds on top of it all were certainly making her head spin. The soreness and aching from those bruises. How did she get those bruises? Did Ryan hit her? Kick her? Eve said nothing about that. But they were purple and yellow and spotted up and down her body.

He grit his teeth for a few moments, rage coursing through him, taking turns with his agony. He looked at Nina's desperate, tormented face, and he softened. Once more, the urge to cry welled up in him. She had been so strong, running through the pain. His poor, sweet love.

She was so scared he would leave her alone.

"I'm not gonna leave you, baby, I'm not gonna leave you. I promise, I'm not going anywhere. I'm gonna stay right here. Right here." He kissed her temple over and over again.

The paramedic looked at him. "We need to get her lying flat," she said gently.

Jordan looked into Nina's eyes. "Okay, baby, let's lie down," he told her softly.

But she shook her head and clung to him.

"You don't want to lie down?" Nina trembled and shook her head quickly.

"Okay, baby, that's okay." Jordan looked up at the paramedics. "Let's lift the seat. She doesn't want to lie flat." They nodded and one of them elevated the seat.

"Okay, honey, can we sit back? We don't have to lie down, let's just sit back." He gently guided her back against the seat, keeping his hands on her. Nina complied slowly, letting him guide her. As he did it, he looked up and spoke sharply to the paramedics.

"The wounds, I don't know if..." He didn't want to finish the question with Nina listening, but he didn't know how bad they were or if they extended beneath her underwear.

The female paramedic quickly pushed the stretcher alongside her male counterpart. "We're gonna check. We need to get her calmed down first," she told Jordan. She looked at Nina's trembling body and terrified face. "Let's get her to the truck."

"She's bleeding on the back of the head," he said, standing tall just long enough to bring his face close to the female EMT so Nina couldn't hear. She was crying and shaking too hard to notice, squeezing Jordan's forearms so he wouldn't move away from her.

The paramedic nodded, gently touching the back of Nina's skull as they moved. Nina didn't notice at first, but when she did, she jerked away and into Jordan. He came even closer to her face to keep her focused on him.

"She was hit by something hard. It may require stitches," the EMT said to herself. She turned her attention to Jordan. "A full assessment will be done at the hospital."

Jordan swallowed, desperate to know how bad the burns were, how hard the hit to her head was, and if Nina was hurting even worse than it seemed. He kissed her head as they moved.

"I'm right here," he whispered. "I'm right here."

He continued soothing her as they wheeled her quickly down the alley. Jordan pulled her face to his chest. As they moved out onto the street, he held her tightly, so she didn't see all the people around and become more frightened.

Tristan and Eve were standing next to the ambulance that was waiting for Nina. Jordan yelled sharply to Tristan, whose face, as his eyes landed on Nina, was horrified.

"Call Dev!"

Then they rolled a shaking and crying Nina into the ambulance, and they were gone, sirens blaring once more.

JORDAN

As the ambulance took off, small sounds of pain escaped Nina's throat as she breathed hard against the agony all over her body.

In her distress and pain, she didn't notice the look of understanding between Jordan and the female paramedic as they carefully leaned her seat down until she was just slightly elevated.

She noticed the IV, however.

"No, no," she fought, writhing against the pain and trying to sit up.

Jordan, right by her side, put his hands on her arms to keep her still as the paramedic quickly administered a mild sedative into her thigh. When she felt and saw it, she screamed.

"No!"

Jordan held onto her as she cried. "Nina, Nina, baby, it's okay." He kept his voice soft and gentle, wanting to soothe and not scare her more. He didn't want to hold her down, didn't like allowing them to do something she didn't want them to do, but he didn't want her to hurt herself more. They needed to see if the burns touched past her groin, and he wanted the paramedics to get the welts cleaned and covered as soon as possible.

He wanted to ease her fear and panic and wondered if she thought she was still captive to the men who hurt her.

"You're safe, love, you're safe." Struggling to meet her eyes as she cried, he tried to bring her to the present and make her aware of her surroundings. The paramedic quickly and carefully slid the needle for the IV into her wrist. As the seconds passed and the painkillers and sedative moved through Nina, she stilled. He locked eyes with her finally and she cried, "I don't want to go to sleep."

As the aching for her moved through him, he swallowed hard.

"It's okay, baby, they're just gonna give you some medicine so it doesn't hurt anymore, and they can take care of these burns." He spoke carefully and gently.

But Nina didn't seem to agree. "No," she cried, her energy dissipating. "I don't want you to go. Please don't go. Please don't leave me." The agony in her voice as she lost the ability to fight made his throat ache hard.

What's more, the realization that she did not want to sleep, because she feared he would leave her when she closed her eyes, sent his own agony through him, like when he heard her screaming out for him, as Ryan slammed a scorching iron rod against her flesh.

She was afraid he would leave her again.

Again. Second to when he left her hours before and allowed her to be taken, tortured and reduced to the unbearable pain she was in.

"I will not leave your side for one millisecond," he said forcefully, voice low. His eyes were filled with love and compassion for the woman he would die for. He had killed for. "I am *right* here. I'm not going anywhere, my sweet girl. I'm not going anywhere."

He moved his hands from her arms, gently took her palm with one and used the other to cradle her cheek.

"I'll be by your side the whole time. Even if you fall asleep. And I'll be right here when you wake up. I promise." The same promise he'd made earlier. The one he'd broken. He wouldn't blame her for not trusting him again.

But his voice nearly shook as the ferocity of his promise trembled through him: "I promise, I will not let *anybody* hurt you ever again." He needed to make her see.

Nina was still breathing hard, quiet cries catching in her throat every few seconds, but she had stopped fighting. As Jordan moved his hand from her cheek to stroke her hair, she rested her head back against the headrest on the stretcher.

"It's okay to rest," he whispered.

As her eyelids drooped and her blinks got slower, Jordan whispered, "I love you. I love you. I love you." As he did, her eyes finally shut completely.

The female paramedic put her gloved hands between Nina's thighs and gently separated them. "We need to check underneath."

She edged her fingers into Nina's cotton underwear next to her groin, careful not to touch the burn in between it and her leg.

He watched her every move to ensure she was being as gentle and careful as she could.

Jordan stared, his heart pounding harder as she exposed Nina's body to reveal that Ryan had not burned her genitals. The paramedic gently set the fabric back into place.

"She's not burned beyond the spot on the groin."

When he saw the evidence and heard the words, relief flooded Jordan so hard he felt weak.

But there was nothing to celebrate. He looked up at the paramedics and asked, his voice suddenly rough and flat, "The burns, how bad are they?"

"It's hard to say for sure, but they look second degree." When Jordan continued staring at the male paramedic, a slight, crazed desperation in his eyes, the man continued. "They penetrate the first and second layers of the skin." Jordan bristled, looking at the two wet marks, different shades of red, blistering and swelling on Nina's body.

"I'm almost positive they didn't get deep enough to affect her muscles. We will know more when we get to the unit."

He tried to take a deep breath as the relief pushed through him. It made him more restless that he wouldn't know the extent of the damage until they got to the hospital.

"It's just a sedative, right?" he asked the female, worried she'd lost consciousness because of the blow to her head. She nodded, monitoring Nina's vitals.

"Why did she fall asleep so quickly, then?"

The young woman, perhaps in her mid-thirties, didn't look up at him as she continued monitoring Nina's vitals. "She definitely has a concussion, but she's also exhausted, dehydrated, in pain and in shock. The sedatives helped calm her system down, and the painkillers are in her now. It's natural that she falls asleep." She continued listening to Nina's heartbeat as she added, "We'll be at the hospital in just a few minutes."

Jordan closed his eyes and exhaled through his nose. God was watching over them. They could have done so much worse to her. What they had done was torture enough, for both of them.

Jordan looked up to the ceiling of the ambulance as though it was the sky and thanked God, from whom he was simultaneously begging for forgiveness.

He asked Him, as he'd done a million times before, *Is it wrong to kill evil to protect the innocent? When there's a knife to their throat, a gun to their head?*

Blazing iron slammed into her flesh?

That couldn't be wrong.

It couldn't be.

When they arrived at the hospital, they took Nina to the burn unit to assess her wounds, and then to Radiology for an MRI.
She slept the entire time, Jordan watching her like a hawk.
The hospital staff tried to keep Jordan out of the way but learned quickly it wouldn't happen.
Dev Jain, an old friend of Jordan's and an accredited doctor in the state, stepped in and let the nurses know that Jordan could stay. Dev or not, it wouldn't have made any difference.
Jordan was staying.
Before his phone lit up with the name *Tristan Asad*, Dev had heard from a friend in the police force that a huge search was happening in Lyson and a few other cities, but he couldn't give details yet. Dev didn't know that the only victim would be the girlfriend of his longtime, quiet friend, the same Jordan who never looked twice at a girl in all the years he'd known him. After speaking with Tristan, Dev had run to his car and sped off to Mercy Lake Hospital, the one closest to Lyson.
Jordan watched as Dev examined the four-inch burn on her thigh. As he pulled an unconscious Nina's legs open more to see the one on her groin, Dev thought Jordan was going to break something. The tension emanating from him made Dev think he might explode. The agony and simultaneous rage in Jordan's eyes as he looked at the burns were unlike anything Dev had ever seen in his friend.
Jordan held her hand the entire time. As Dev cleaned then bandaged her burns, he murmured to Jordan, "They are second degree. My greatest concern is the one on her groin."

Jordan's fingers twitched. He swallowed and cleared his throat. His voice was flat. "How will it affect her?"

"We just need to keep them clean, and prevent infection. Apart from that, it will be painful for her to walk. It will be painful for her in general, so I want to give her some painkillers for a little while, maybe a few weeks. And some antibiotic ointment. Cool water over them might feel good once they seal over," he told Jordan gently.

Jordan said nothing, just watched as Dev finished covering the wounds completely.

"We'll take her to a different room now." Dev hesitated. "Would you like me to call her parents?"

Jordan continued staring at Nina's bandaged wounds as he replied, "No. I will." He glanced up. "Not yet."

Nina was admitted and transferred to another room outside of the burn unit. Jordan asked why she hadn't woken since she fell asleep in the ambulance.

"She's exhausted. She's also incredibly dehydrated and on heavy painkillers and antibiotics. Her body is working to fight infection. It's also trying to heal itself from the physical and mental trauma. She has a few serious burns. And on top of that, what she's gone through has drained her. She will need time to rest and regain her strength."

Dev hated saying these things to him, knowing it all made his friend feel worse. Jordan absorbed every word, making mental notes and planning how he would care for her.

"I recommend therapy as well," Dev added quietly.

"She's already seeing one," Jordan said, his face blank as he stared at her sleeping face. "Will she need a specialist?"

"Maybe, maybe not. It depends on what her counselor specializes in. It's good that she already has one, regardless. It eliminates having to start something new during a difficult time. She'll be just fine." He kept his voice gentle still, sad for his miserable friend.

Jordan prayed that was true. He stayed as positive as he could, knowing how resilient his girl was.

When they'd settled into a large room with a TV, armchairs, and a bath, Nina was laid on a more comfortable bed. Then Jordan called Liza.

"Jordan," she answered on the first ring, worried about him.

"Liza." Jordan was so exhausted that he could barely think to be friendly. He knew his team, Tristan, Dev, the police, contacts and old friends in the Bureau were all doing whatever they could to help. "Please send somebody here to the hospital with a tablet. Transfer the stream onto it first, as a file."

Liza's eyes widened; Emmett and Luke stared at her, knowing she was talking to Jordan, worried there was more bad news.

She knew she couldn't argue. When Jordan wanted something, he got it. Even if what he wanted was to torture himself.

That wouldn't stop her from voicing her opinion. "Okay. I'll bring it."

"No, send Carter or James. I need you to help with questioning, and I need the research on the users in the chat to begin as soon as possible." Jordan stopped for a moment. "No. Let the Bureau work on it now. You guys go home and get some sleep. All of you."

As much as they wanted to stay and keep working, they would do what he requested. Because, even while feeling tormented, exhausted and distressed, Jordan was looking after them. They owed it to him to at least comply.

"Okay. We will. I'll send Carter."

Jordan was about to hang up when Liza quickly added, "But Jordan, I don't think it's a good idea." Her face was like steel as she waited. Liza was hard, smart, and unafraid of anything. Her bravery was one of the things Jordan liked most about her.

But he couldn't care less what anyone else thought right now. "An officer will meet him downstairs and bring it up to me." He hung up the phone.

Dev returned to the room thirty minutes later. "MRI show no internal injury. Just a cut to the head from whatever was used. She'll be okay."

Another wave of relief flooded Jordan.

"Concussion?"

"We'll only be able to look for symptoms of that when she wakes up." Again, Jordan had to wait, which was torture; he needed to know if she was okay.

After that, Jordan instructed everyone to stay out of the room, and all complied, giving him time alone with his girl. No one dared try. Jordan looked like a ticking time bomb, even to a stranger. He had never exploded the way he did on his way to Nina.

Everyone who knew him knew that it was over for anyone who he perceived to be even a mild threat.

So they stayed away. Jordan would wait a little while to call her parents. He didn't want them there this soon.

He put his hand on Nina's face and stroked her cheek with his thumb, aching for her.

His baby. The love of his life.

He hoped she wasn't having nightmares. The thought had him leaning in, kissing her face over and over again. Eventually, he settled his cheek on her chest, closing his eyes, the only place in the world he wanted to be. She was the only place he felt calm. He breathed in her soft scent, her warmth and innocence throbbing through him, the pain making him tired.

Not too tired to stop the grief from rising up his chest and making his jaw ache.

Gripping the sheets around her, he wished with every cell in his body that he that suffered in her place.

He sobbed, for the first time in years.

JORDAN

A tall, young Officer Duncan brought the five-inch tablet to the elevator on the first floor when Federal Agent Tristan Asad jogged up behind him and said, "I'll take that up. You go ahead and get back to the station. They need you, brother."

Officer Duncan nodded with respect for the reputable agent and headed to the exit, monitoring the hospital floor, as they'd all been doing. Though local killers were being apprehended, Jordan wouldn't take any chances. He ordered supervision.

As the elevator doors closed, encasing Tristan in the little space by himself, he considered trying to wipe the stream from the tablet before he got up to his brother.

He knew he wouldn't be able to keep it from Jordan, that his brother would find it somehow, but he considered trying regardless, knowing that what Jordan was going to do would kill him even more than he was already killing himself.

Tristan felt a heavy sense of dread as he entered Nina's hospital room.

"Jordan," he said quietly, alerting him of his entrance.

Jordan turned, reaching his hand out for the tablet before Tristan even rounded the corner of the small bathroom to Jordan's left. When he saw Jordan's outstretched hand, he inhaled deeply through his nose.

"Are you sure?" he asked his brother slowly, voice low.

Jordan stared at him with empty eyes, waiting for Tristan to hand it over. He would not snatch it out of his hands. Jordan was better than that. Or he was trying to be, at least.

As Tristan unwillingly passed him the tablet, he became devastated at the redness of his brother's eyes, and how they were sinking into his face.

Jordan unlocked the tablet and opened the file.

No one but his team had access to this. He'd provided it to the Bureau temporarily for their investigation, but they were not to transfer it to any of their devices.

Jordan would not allow this footage to remain out in the world. Eve and Luke had scoured the Internet, the Dark Web, Gateway, searching for any copied footage, even a still of the video.

Every single person in that chatroom would be found and would pay for their participation in Nina's torture. That was the only reason the footage had not been erased. The chatroom was directly linked to the stream.

Tristan stood there, watching his brother stare at the screen as it loaded. Jordan, feeling his gaze, tried to keep his aggravation under control.

"Thank you," Jordan said, trying not to grit his teeth. "You can go."

Tristan leaned back against the wall directly across from Nina. "I'm not leaving."

Jordan looked at his brother now, and the rage in his eyes made Tristan more unwilling to leave. He didn't know how Jordan would react to what he saw, but he knew it would kill him. He would not leave his brother in pain, though Jordan would have preferred that.

Jordan stared at his brother for a few moments, frustrated; he didn't want anyone ever again to see Nina brutalized. But his brother was adamant, and he didn't want to argue with him. He wanted to get this over with, didn't want to waste any more time not knowing what she went through. The longer he waited, the longer she went through it completely alone.

"I want you to tell me this stuff. I want to understand what you do and the things you see. You shouldn't have to...carry that stuff alone."

"You've suffered. Jord, you have to tell me these things, honey. Please. Please."

"But you don't have to do it alone. Tell me what happened today."

"I need you to let me be here for you, even when your safety isn't on the line. And especially when it is!"

"You've been seeing it for so many years, and you still endure it to save people. It's mental torture."

"You've s-s-seen too much."

"I don't want you to hurt. I just don't want you to have to see that stuff. You've seen too much of it already."

She'd begged him, time and time again, to let her suffer with the same horrible knowledge he did. Now, she'd endured worse than he ever had. He would suffer with her now.

Jordan settled himself with the knowledge that Tristan would not be able to hear. He slid his wireless earbuds into his ears and connected them to the tablet via Bluetooth. He turned his back to the wall across from Tristan, so that the screen would not be in his line of sight at all.

He stayed by Nina's side, gripping her wrist in his hand to be close to her while he watched, to remind himself that she was safe with him now.

JORDAN

After moments of loading, the video popped up on the screen. The still was of Nina's strung up body. Jordan immediately stiffened as heat coursed through his body. He pressed play.

At first it was quiet, except for a repeated, high-pitched pinging. Nina was unconscious, strung up in rusted chains to ceiling pipes. Jordan exhaled hard, forcing the air out of his nose.

Across the room, Tristan shifted his weight to his other foot, itching to take the tablet away from him.

Distress flooded Jordan as Nina rolled her head to the side, waking up. When she blinked drowsily, looking around her and realizing her surroundings, her eyebrows crinkled together a little bit. Her face was still a little blank as she tried to wake herself up, but he could see the terror fill her eyes as they widened slightly.

Jordan squeezed her wrist, reminding himself she was right there with him. That this had already happened, and was over.

Except it wasn't. Nina would relive this again and again, tormented by the memory. And that was why he watched. He would not leave her alone with her agony.

"Good morning. We were waiting for you to wake up, princess."

Ryan's voice taunting Jordan's poor, sweet girl had him gripping the tablet so hard his knuckles turned white. The rage that was coursing through him, fighting a breathtaking agony for his attention, were both making him nauseous already.

"Let me go." Nina's voice scratched the air, low, quiet and strained. It cut through Jordan's chest.

She raised it, using whatever strength she could muster. *"Let me go."*

Still not in the frame, Ryan answered. *"That would ruin all the fun."*

Nina's face crinkled, the pain on it clear as day. Jordan leaned closer to her sleeping face, putting his lips to her temple, not breaking his gaze from the screen.

He watched his girl clamp her lips together as she forced herself to stay calm.

Jordan found it immensely difficult to do the same.

Nina's head rolled slightly as her eyes landed on something then filled with horror. As hard as she was trying to hide it, pain crumpled her face once more. It was agonizing for him to see.

The pinging continued.

"What do you say we call your boy toy up and let him know how you're doing?" Just then, Ryan's lanky body entered the frame as he stepped up to her. Jordan looked for something in his hands, tense to the point of trembling, knowing that he would put something to Nina's skin to burn her. Ryan held nothing but a cell phone. *"He must be very worried about you,"* he told her, feigning seriousness, the taunting edge in his voice making Jordan's body twitch.

Tristan sensed his brother losing control.

"Jordan, Jordan, Jordan."

His rage worsened as the seconds passed.

"Now, now boss," Ryan taunted him. He sneered at the word. As he went on, Jordan remembered the words Ryan had said before Nina screamed. He braced himself for them.

"Hey, Nina, listen. It's your boy toy on the phone."

Nina's face immediately crumpled as Ryan pulled the phone away from his ear and hit a button on it. She couldn't hold it in anymore. *"Jordan,"* Nina cried for him.

The same agony that had initially flooded him that night poured over him again now.

He could just barely hear his own voice on speakerphone, telling Nina he was on his way.

"I'm right here, and I'm coming. I'm coming." He burned as he recalled his promise to her, a promise he didn't fulfill before they hurt her.

While Ryan recalled to Nina how Jordan had allegedly conned him, he stood next to her; her arms, suspended in the air, were likely burning from the steady pulling of her limbs. Every inch Ryan stepped towards her took Jordan closer to exploding.

Then, he walked out of the frame. Jordan stiffened even harder, listening to Ryan relay his story and work himself into a rage. Nina blinked, her face pained.

Jordan heard his own useless interruptions, feeling the same helplessness he'd felt at the time this happened, unable to rip Ryan's tongue out the way he'd wanted to.

"Can you imagine, Nina? Can you imagine all the people he's killed, maybe all the things he's stolen, even? Can you imagine all the other skinny, pretty girls he's—"

Jordan watched Nina's jaw tremble, as he heard himself try to cut Ryan off.

"—while you were working your poor little self to exhaustion? Or in therapy, crying about how you couldn't be as skinny as them?"

The rage in him was rabid. If Nina hadn't been beside him, he might've punched something.

He was burning.

"Ryan, shut your mouth."

The growing anger in Ryan's voice had Jordan grinding his teeth harder, knowing he was going to take it out on Nina at any second.

"Never thought your own boy scout software would be used against you, now did ya? Never thought you'd be responsible for so many ugly, violent deaths."

Suddenly, Nina rolled her head to the left and spoke. *"Stop."* She inhaled but could barely get the breath in. *"Shut your mouth."*

Jordan bit his lip so hard it began to bleed.

"Oh, shut up, you dumb whore. Just as worthless as the rest of them. Thought you were special, didn't you, walking into boss man's office like a little special trophy wife."
The words with which Jordan threatened him on the phone were not dirty enough for how he felt, hearing those things said about her again.
Ryan stepped back into the camera frame with an iron rod in his hand.
"No, no. Actually, Jordy boy, I'm gonna touch your girlfriend every way you could possibly imagine."
He grabbed Nina's knee, as her eyes widened and filled with terror, and slammed the rod into her thigh. Her scream was brutal.
Jordan gripped the tablet so hard Tristan heard it crack.
"Jordan—" he started.
But Jordan couldn't hear him. His skin was burning all over as he heard himself scream his threats to Ryan, feeling the exact rage he could hear in his voice. The same agony he'd felt inside.
No, it was worse. Somehow, it was worse.
He recalled Eve telling him how Nina was being tortured.
Watching it was undoubtedly worse.
Ryan jerked her leg open more and stuck it against her groin. Nina screamed harder this time.
"Nooo!" she begged in a blood curdling shriek.
Jordan's voice sounded through the video fast; halfway through his vicious threat, Ryan pulled the rod away, and Nina's scream died down. Her head fell forward as she tried to catch her breath from the pain. As she struggled to inhale, she whimpered Jordan's name.
He ripped his gaze from the screen and put his mouth to Nina's temple, wrapping his arm around her shoulder to bring her closer to him. He squeezed his eyes shut for a few seconds, trying to calm down. The warmth of her skin just barely soothed him as the sound of her sobbing continued in his ears.
He opened his eyes and looked at her sleeping face desperately, telling himself over and over again that she was here now, that they weren't hurting her.
It did not ease the torture inside him.
"You'll never see her alive again."
Jordan pressed his lips into her temple harder.
"I love you, Jordan."
He squeezed the pillow next to her shoulder so hard his nails dug through the material and cut into his palm.
"Just stay strong, like you always are. I'm coming, baby."
He wished so badly as tears filled his eyes that he'd been able to keep that promise sooner.
"Say goodbye to your little dime. You know, I must say, she is pretty cute, Jordy boy. Maybe we'll have some fun with her before we kill her."

Jordan's fury burned through him; he struggled to see straight. He dragged his eyes back down to the screen just in time to see Ryan press a button on the phone. Then, he stepped out of the frame. Nina hung there limply, weeping. The sound and sight took Jordan's breath away once more.

Ryan came back into the frame with a large key in his hands. Jordan watched intensely as Nina squeezed her eyes closed, and Ryan unlocked one cuff around her wrist, then the other. When she slammed into the ground, Jordan winced.

That would be where so many of those bruises were from.

When her eyes widened in pain from the fall and no doubt the pressure against her burns, he grimaced, gritting his teeth so hard his jaw hurt.

Nina looked up, then the camera moved, rotating towards the opposite end of the corridor. *"Come on out, boys and girls!"*

And there were the twelve masked individuals creeping towards the camera, wielding their blades, saws, machetes.

Jordan's head was spinning.

The camera turned back in Nina and Ryan's direction in just enough time to catch Ryan raising his eyebrows and excitedly instructing Nina to *"Run."*

Nina's eyes were full of horror as she stared at them, and a second later, Jordan watched her struggle to stand as she moved off in the opposite direction, away from the cameras. It started as a limp, and then she managed to break into a run. She moved faster than Jordan would have ever expected anyone to with those burns.

And where they were on her body.

He tried to picture the agony she felt, sprinting away with those welts. The pain of her movements pulling the burned and bleeding skin on her groin as her legs flew, one after the other. The hot scraping she must've felt as her thighs collided while she ran, trying to keep her balance.

Nina disappeared as she rounded the first corner. Twenty-five seconds later, the twelve others entered the frame, running, beginning their chase.

Jordan was thankful for whatever angel that forced them to give her a head start.

It was only a minute later that he heard Ryan scream, *"GO!"* and the gunshots he remembered unleashing.

Ryan's voice did not sound any longer.

He stopped the video and held the tablet up to Tristan. He turned his face into Nina's skin once more. Tristan practically leapt the twelve feet between them. Once he took it, Jordan wrapped his free arm across her chest, meeting his other hand and holding her tight. Then, he pulled her head to his neck, leaning back only enough to kiss her temple.

Tristan watched his brother with anguished eyes, wishing he could've prevented Jordan from seeing any of it.

But Tristan knew, somehow, Jordan would've felt more agony not knowing.

After a few moments of contemplating what to say, feeling certain that nothing would offer Jordan any solace, he turned to exit. On the way out, he dredged in some air and murmured, "Call me if you need me." Jordan said nothing, barely processing his brother's statement.

Alone with Nina, he pulled the earbuds out of his ears, shoved them in his pocket and again settled his head against her, burying his face in her neck. But he couldn't cry anymore. The pain left him breathless. All he could do was lie there, holding his love, eyes wide as the pain, disturbing, potent, seeped through him.

Nina's parents did not react well, as was to be expected. Her father especially.

Jordan hated to have to make the phone call, but he couldn't pass it onto anyone else. And he wouldn't. It was his responsibility.

So, after he'd spent the night with her, not sleeping, as the video had made him even more tense and on guard, he dialed Elias and asked if he could speak with her and Bridgette.

Initially, he'd just said she was hurt and that they were at a hospital in Lyson. When they'd asked what they were doing all the way there, Jordan asked them to please come, and he would explain everything in person.

When they initially got into the room, Bridgette began crying. A near-crazed rage flooded Elias's eyes. Zana was horrified, shocked, and Elijah didn't know what to do with himself.

After Jordan explained everything, Elias had shoved his way forward and tried to punch him in the face.

Jordan anticipated this, and had caught his fist and knocked his arm down to stop him. Elias kept coming, and Jordan kept carefully knocking his attempts away.

Elias was a hard, strong man in his fifties. He wasn't as tall, at five foot nine, as Jordan, but he was ferocious.

Jordan still had the upper hand, as he usually did in a fight. He was careful not to hurt Elias in dodging his hits, calmly telling him, even as he swiped away more punches and attempted grabs, that he would hurt Nina if he didn't stop, as they were standing just a foot away from her bed, and anything could've happened. What if Jordan fell back?

Tristan, Elijah, Bridgette and Zana had all jumped in his face to stop him. Elijah had considered behaving the same way his father did, but his

JORDAN

rationale caught up to him before Elias's did. He was livid, regardless. His little sister was tortured because of this man.

Elias screamed at Jordan that he never wanted to see him again, and that if he came near his daughter one more time, he would kill him. But Jordan told him, calmly again, that he would not leave her.

The Executive Assistant Director of the Criminal, Cyber, Response, and Services Branch, Kelly Spencer, Jordan's former superior when he was just twenty-two years old, had accompanied Tristan to the hospital.

He'd flown out immediately when he heard the news that one of the largest, web-based criminal rings had been penetrated.

And of course, Jordan Asad was the one to do it. He was unsurprised. The man, hardly a man when he'd served the Bureau, was one of the smartest people, if not *the* smartest person he'd ever met. But apart from that, Jordan Asad held a will unlike any other. He accomplished what he wanted to accomplish. He made breaks in technology that changed the way even the Bureau operated.

Kelly calmly asked if Elias and Bridgette would speak with him. Tristan knew they might not listen to his own rationalizing, because he was Jordan's brother. Thus he quickly asked Kelly to help him.

When they went out into the hall, Zana and Elijah following, Tristan stayed in the room with Jordan.

Kelly told them about Jordan's company, how he'd assisted the FBI for years, finding and stopping some of the most heinous criminals to exist. He told them things they didn't know, how Jordan was once a federal agent, for example.

"I know that this is very difficult," he told them gently but sternly. "But I need you to understand something. Jordan was not home when Nina was taken. If he was, you better believe she wouldn't have been.

"He left her alone for the first time in a month, probably more, because of the break in the case. He sent his team member to stay with her, but he didn't make it in time. Jordan would never tell you this, so as to prevent you from thinking he was making excuses.

"Cases like this are timely. That's the only reason Jordan left before Luke arrived. Now, of course, he made sure to lock the doors and set the alarm. But the person who took Nina was an ex-staff member of Jordan's company. Anyone who works at Jordan's company has to be able to break into an alarm system. Even one as good as Jordan's."

"They just happened to know when Jordan was leaving?" Elijah snapped. *FBI or not,* he thought. This was his baby sister.

"We aren't sure. They had needles and drugs that could hypothetically knock a person out, in the car." His lips flattened. "I'm sure they knew they couldn't win a fight against Jordan. It's possible they'd been hiding out, waiting for Jordan to leave her alone."

"So you're telling me it's *not his fault* that this happened? *He* said they were after *him*. And that they did this to hurt *him*. And *my daughter got the worst of it*," Elias unleashed in the hospital hall.

"These criminals have had a vendetta for not only Jordan, but the whole company *and* the FBI, for a long time. Ryan got close by coming to work for the company. The goal of this network of people was to hurt Jordan, his whole company, and even us." He gestured to his badge. "I think they saw Nina and ran with it. But that's not Jordan's fault. He has done everything he could to protect her. If he had known they would be breaking into his home, he, of course, would *never* have left."

"Did his brother tell you to say all of this?" Elijah asked skeptically.

Kelly's eyes narrowed. "I don't take orders from agents, especially not from those who aren't even in my division. Tristan is a decorated agent, but I've known Jordan longer. And I assure you," he looked into Elijah's eyes intensely, and then Elias's, "Jordan would never ask me to speak for him. Jordan has barely said two words to me since I arrived. Tristan wanted to talk to you himself, but I told him it might be a better idea that he stays with his brother."

Kelly looked at each member of Nina's family as he spoke firmly. "Jordan is devastated. He hasn't left her side for a second. And I want you to know," he lowered his voice, "that he got there before any of us could. I think that man was doing over two times the highway limit. And he took out every single person in that hospital by himself. Every. Single. One."

"How many were there?" Bridgette asked, horrified.

The fifty-six-year-old breathed deeply and sighed. "There were Ryan and Donovan, the two behind it all. Then there were twelve other people."

"That were chasing her?" Zana's voice shook as she asked for confirmation.

Instead of answering that, he murmured, "Jordan got there in good timing, in the way of those people chasing her, at least. She made it out—she's tough—" he added sincerely, "—and she hid a few buildings down. Jordan handled all of them until he found her."

"Are they dead?" Elijah asked. Elias's eyes burned into Kelly.

He nodded once.

"He killed them all?" Elijah couldn't believe his ears. "There were no cops?"

"No. They arrived as Jordan was running through the hospital. It all happened rather quickly." Seeing the family's disbelieving eyes, he explained Jordan's combat and weaponry training.

After a moment of silence, Zana murmured, "I didn't know he used to fight professionally."

Kelly nodded again, then lifted a finger and jabbed it in the direction of Nina's hospital room, where Jordan was sitting. He looked between Elias and Bridgette's eyes.

"That man has done nothing but work hard his whole life. Everything he has done, he has given a hundred percent of his time and dedication. He has done the same thing for Nina. I'm telling you, Elias, Bridgette, family, he loves that girl more than he has ever loved anything. I can see it on his face. He's killing himself over this."

The girls frowned. Elias pursed his lips, and Elijah huffed and exhaled hard through his nose, trying to decide if he believed it. But the sight of Jordan corroborated everything Kelly was saying. The bags under his eyes were deep and purple. He had lost at least fifteen pounds since October, and it showed on his face especially. And his eyes were horrible. Lifeless one moment, then filled with a just barely glossed over rage the next. Even as angry as Elijah was with him, he didn't dare get in his face about it, the way his father had.

Everyone had to accept what happened and be civil.

When Elias finally calmed down, everyone decided it was best to keep him and Bridgette on the other side of the bed as Jordan.

Nina

Quiet, incomprehensible murmurs coming from the right of me were the first things I registered.

My eyelids were heavy, too heavy. I wanted to open them, but it was much less strain to leave them closed. My head was throbbing hard, feeling heavy as a brick. I felt a mental exhaustion blanketing me; the sweet drowsiness was tempting. If I made my brain settle just enough, I'd be in the comforting blackness again.

But why?

Then, my body slowly returned to me as consciousness did. It felt heavy, too.

My arms were limp against my sides, my back feeling glued to the soft thing I was lying on. I didn't know what it was. Too uncomfortable to be our couch, or our bed.

There was the same limpness in my legs, except there was a burning pain in one of my thighs and part of my groin just above.

What *happened*?

Open your eyes, Nina.

A sudden dread, an anxiety—*something is wrong, but* what?—grew in me. I was afraid. I didn't want to remember.

As consciousness spread throughout my body, my mind picked up a little too. My eyelids became lighter.

My eyes cracked open just slightly, but the light hurt too much. I closed them.

The dread became too much, then. With the light came the realization that I would have to face whatever bad thing was plaguing me, hiding in my memory and waiting to pounce.

A small, low groan vibrated in my throat. The sound woke me even more. Then: "Nina?"

Jordan.

A wave of comfort washed over me immediately.

When did I leave him? I couldn't remember...

I tried to open my eyes again, and it took a couple of blinks before I got them halfway there.

"Nina, baby," Jordan's voice came again. I couldn't see him clearly, but I could feel his warmth right in front of my face.

The murmuring picked up. "Nina? Honey?"

"Nina?"

My mom and dad.

Oh, no.

Oh, no, what happened?

After a couple more blinks, my vision cleared enough for me to see my mother's face directly ahead of me. I felt a warm hand stroking my head slowly.

"Nina!" Was she crying? Her eyes were red.

I could see my father behind her. "Nina, honey?" He looked wiped out. As though he'd had a long, long day.

After turning my head to the left, I saw Jordan, then realized I was in a hospital.

And then I remembered.

Ryan. The chains. The cameras. The screen, the chat. The burning iron. The people with gas masks. The machetes, knives, and saws. Hiding in the alley.

I couldn't tell if it was a dream or not. But lying down, groggy, waking to my mother, father, Jordan and—oh, my siblings standing behind my seated parents—being in the hospital told me it was real.

Oh, no, no.

The masks.

The echoes of the people running behind me, searching, toting machetes, blades and chainsaws, the certainty I felt that Jordan would find me, missing at least one limb. The worst terror and anxiety of my life as I watched them run toward me. How I had begged God to kill me before I felt the agony. How my heart beat so hard, staring at all those weapons, that my chest hurt.

It took me a few moments to realize that my breath was stuck in my throat. I tried hard to suck in some air, but it didn't work. My eyes widened as the realization hit me, and the gas masks and weapons slid from the front of my mind as I struggled to breathe.

"Get a doctor, she can't breathe!" my mom screamed. "Elias, get a doctor!"

Then came Jordan's level, firm voice with an edge of panic as he took my face in his hands, looked at me with calm eyes that held just a twinge of terror and willed me to focus.

"Nina, Nina, baby, breathe, breathe. Look at me, just breathe, breathe, it's okay."

Looking into the near whiteness of his pale, crystal blue eyes took me into a trance. I felt air finally move into my throat.

"There you go, just breathe, baby. That's it." Jordan's eyelids went slightly less wide, but his eyes were still alarmed.

A doctor and a nurse rushed in as he spoke, moving to the opposite side of the bed as Jordan. I noticed the IV there.

"She's okay," he murmured, kissing my forehead and then putting his to it. He stroked my cheek for a moment, then moved his lips to the side of my head and left them there.

As the doctor put his stethoscope on my chest and asked me to take a deep breath, Jordan stiffened.

I tried to take a deep breath but was still catching my normal pace after wheezing.

I was distracted by Jordan moving his face right in front of me, nearly eye to eye with the doctor. His face was locked, smooth as he watched him. His eyes were so cold, yet they could've burned a hole in the doctor's white coat.

"Dev Jain has been tending to her. Has he returned?" The flatness in Jordan's quiet voice cut through the air. Behind him, against the far wall across from me, Elijah's and Zana's eyes widened in surprise. My parents' eyebrows shot up.

The middle-aged doctor met Jordan's glance and said, "I'm uncertain. I'm Dr. Roberts. I've been briefed on Nina's condition and am the official doctor assigned to her in case Dr. Jain has to step out."

But Jordan didn't seem to care. As the doctor spoke, he dialed a number on his phone and brought it to his ear. Instead of replying to the doctor, he spoke into the phone, "Dev. She's awake."

A voice began speaking on the other end, but I couldn't hear what he was saying. After a few moments, he hung up the phone without saying another word.

I wondered why Jordan was so distrusting of this doctor, who continued on as though nothing had happened. I zoned out as he tightened a cuff around my arm to take my blood pressure.

Gas masks flashed through my brain. A filthy old hospital, nothing like this one, trapping me.

I pushed the thoughts away before I started suffocating again. I was desperate for answers.

Where are we? Where are all those people who chased me? Where is Ryan, where's his partner? Did they shut everything down, finally?

JORDAN

Do my parents know everything? How long have I been asleep? What are my injuries?

I remembered blazing iron pressed into my legs. I rolled my head to look at Jordan and distract myself.

"Jordan," I said, startled to hear my rough voice.

His eyes widened slightly as he looked into mine; he was surprised I'd spoken, and alert.

"Yes, my love," he responded, taking my cheek in his hand. As far as Jordan was concerned, the doctor and anyone else were no longer in the room.

"I'm alive, right?" The words fell out of my mouth unintentionally, as I realized I wasn't sure.

Did they kill me, and I just don't remember? Is this some sort of dream? Am I still in the hospital, half-dead, just dreaming that I'm here with him?

Jordan's face fell; he was so sad, even desperate. It made me think I might actually be dead, and that this was God's way of saying so. Or telling me to wake up and run again.

But then Jordan said, "Yes, my love. You're alive. You're safe." His throat caught, and the last word was barely audible. "You're safe," he repeated, voice stronger.

"Do you remember anything, honey?" my mom asked softly. Jordan stiffened again but did not turn around to look at her. I did.

I kept my face blank; I knew I looked like a zombie.

"Yes."

She swallowed. My brother quietly asked, "What do you remember?"

Jordan's eyes slowly moved up; he was trying not to roll them, and trying to control himself. He grit his teeth for a second, let them go and looked at me with dead eyes. When he realized I was watching him, his face softened, and he leaned closer.

I was stunned, but too weak to assure him it was okay. Jordan had never been so obviously agitated.

"I remember everything."

Though his face had softened, he watched me intensely, devastated by my answer before I'd even said it. When I spoke, his face became pained. He swallowed but did not look away.

Nobody said anything for a few moments.

Finally, Jordan leaned in closer, kissed my forehead and whispered, "You're safe now."

I watched my father. He was stiff. Angry.

Watching Jordan.

"Dad," I said. My voice was *rough*.

His face softened immediately. "Yes, sweetie?"

I didn't know what I wanted to say. I just wanted his attention on me and not whatever was making him mad.

Finally, I croaked, "Are you okay?"

Everyone's eyes perked up; my father's widened in surprise.

"I...yes, honey, I'm fine. How...how are you?" He cleared his throat. "How are you feeling?"

My head felt strained, as though I was holding it up and wanted to collapse it back against the hospital bed pillow. But it was already flat against it.

"I'm tired." I decided to be honest. Jordan's eyes were burning into me. "My leg is hurting. So is my head." If the room wasn't still before, it was now. As though time stopped. I looked at the doctor, who was writing notes.

Just then, a young, handsome Indian man with silky black hair, perhaps in his mid-thirties, wearing rectangular glasses with thin black rims, sped into the room. He wore a light blue button-down and khaki-colored slacks. My first thought was that Zana would very much be into it.

Maybe I would be alright.

"Hi, all," the man greeted the room in a light, kind voice. He looked at me immediately.

"Hi, Nina," he said gently. He noticed Dr. Roberts and extended his hand. "Dev Jain."

Dr. Roberts took his hand. "James Roberts. It's nice to meet you, Dr. Jain." He was a *doctor*? He was so youthful.

"From Sitren Hospital, correct?" Dr. Roberts asked.

Dr. Jain nodded. "I'll be working with Nina." He turned to smile at me, then added, glancing at Jordan, "I had to run to Sitren for a few hours. Thank you for assuming my position." He smiled respectfully.

"Sure thing." Dr. Roberts looked at my parents and said, "Please have the desk call me if you need anything." He turned to Dr. Jain and nodded, then left.

"Hi, Nina," the handsome doctor repeated. "I'm Dev."

Jordan spoke up quietly. His voice had gotten rough. "Dev is an old friend of mine. He's been taking care of you."

Dev smiled again. "Yes. I apologize that I wasn't here when you woke up. We've all been waiting." His voice was very kind. *If I had to leave a review, I'd let everyone know that he had a great bedside manner.*

I might have been slightly delirious, because, for a split second, I wanted to chuckle at my own thought. My face didn't move.

"That's okay," I told him with my scratchy voice. "It's only been a few minutes."

"Well," he exhaled, putting on the stethoscope he had hanging on his neck and listening to my heartbeat, "How have you been feeling these last few minutes? Did I hear you say your leg hurts? And your head?" His voice was gentle as he leaned in to assess my eyes, then moved the stethoscope to my back and listened. He smelled clean. I looked at Zana but forgot why a second later; she probably wondered why I was staring at her.

"Yeah," I told Dev. "They hurt." I rolled my head to the right slightly and looked at his face. His brown skin and slight five o'clock shadow surrounded large eyes of a deep brown, and a wide smile with straight, white teeth.

"Okay," Dev said lightly. "Well, first, I'd like to do a couple things to check on your head."

He asked me questions, like where I lived, who the president was, what year we were in. I answered correctly.

Jordan quietly and regretfully said, "She said she remembers everything, Dev."

Dev stared at him for a few moments, then looked back to me. "You do?" he asked me gently.

I swallowed. "Yeah. Just...just not the house. But I remember being...there," I said, referring to the hospital. He knew what I meant.

He nodded. "That's good. Do you feel pressure in your head?"

"A little. It's hurting really bad."

Jordan's eyebrows crinkled together. It broke my heart that he was distressed. He leaned in and kissed my forehead.

"Okay. We'll get some medicine for that, okay? Do you feel any nausea?"

I thought for a moment. "Not really."

He nodded. "Okay." He looked at me, Jordan, my parents, then back to me again. "You have a mild concussion. Because of your leg, it would be hard to do a balance test right now. Later, I'll have to do a reflex test at the very minimum." My parents both nodded, and Jordan exhaled quietly. I pictured trying to swing my legs over the edge of the bed so he could snap a hammer on my knee to check my reflex. I suddenly felt even more exhausted.

I blinked. Waiting for more.

"Now, you said your leg is hurting."

"Yeah, it's stinging. Worse. It feels hot." I grimaced. My inner thigh and groin seemed to sting more with my words.

"Well, you have a couple of pretty bad burns on it," he said gently. "I'd like to take a look at it, make sure it's healing okay." He met my eyes. "Is that okay?"

I realized why he was asking. There was a burn on my groin.

I didn't even know if I had clothes on.

All I could see was the hospital gown which, halfway down my stomach, was covered by a few blankets.

They were keeping me warm; I didn't want anyone to lift them for me to see the damage. I was terrified.

I felt Jordan's eyes on me. I didn't know what to do; I met his glance.

"It's okay, baby," he murmured gently, keeping his voice down. "Do you want everyone to leave?"

I knew my parents wouldn't take kindly to being asked to leave while Jordan stayed.

"Um," I said, and my voice sounded nearly childlike, even in all its roughness.

"We'll go," Zana offered, looking at Elijah. "Come on." Elijah looked hesitant. He was stubborn. He'd force himself to see the damage, as bad as it might've been.

"Go, Eli," my mom said quietly.

The two of them exited. My mom looked at me, waiting for me to say something. My dad looked uncomfortable. I knew he assumed I wanted him to leave, but, as a father, he didn't want to go.

"Mom, Dad," I said quietly.

"I'm not leaving," my mom said. Jordan stiffened.

I exhaled through my nose, too weak to argue but frustrated by her response. I couldn't help it; my eyes filled with tears.

"Bridgette," my dad said quietly, his voice rough.

Jordan cupped my cheek in his hand and turned to say something to my mom. I spoke up quickly.

"No, no, I don't want you to see them. I just don't want you to see them." I swallowed the urge to cry and forced my voice to be normal.

"I'll be fine, honey," she said. I knew she would fight.

"Bridgette," Jordan said quietly, and the tension I sensed earlier in the room got heavier.

I didn't want him to say anything, because my parents, especially my father, would be furious that Jordan would stay and they could not.

As though Jordan decided it and was controlling me.

"Mom," I said quickly, before Jordan even got her name out fully. "Just a few minutes so he can look, please." My voice was pathetic. Weak, scratchy, and half gone.

"It *will* only take just a few minutes," Dev said kindly.

Her face heated up, but after a few moments, she stood.

"Call me if you need me," she said firmly to me.

"I'll be okay," I reassured her. "Just a minute. Don't worry. I just don't want you to see them. I...I don't want you to get sick."

"I wouldn't, honey," she replied, her voice softer than before. She was still angry, but she and my father walked out.

"Would you like me to go as well?" Jordan asked quietly. I knew my parents weren't out of the room yet and heard him. *Okay. Good.* They knew he didn't think he was the exception.

I waited a few moments until they were out, just staring at him. I decided to say nothing, shaking my head slightly. He nodded.

Dev gently pulled the blankets off. I was wearing no pants, but there was something wrapped around my upper thigh and groin, looped up to my waist.

"Um..." I sounded like a scared little kid. I didn't think I was wearing underwear.

I was so embarrassed.

Dev looked up. I shook my head.

"You okay?" he asked gently.

I nodded, looking at Jordan, who was watching Dev and my face alternatively.

He saw that I wanted to say something but wouldn't. He came closer to me immediately, his face now right in front of mine. Dev couldn't see my face.

"It's okay, baby," he said in a quiet, soft voice, eyes inquiring.

"Am I dressed?" I whispered, barely audible. The room was quiet, but the sound of Dev's unwrapping the gauze made me think he couldn't hear me. He nodded. I exhaled hard.

"It's okay," he whispered. He pulled back as Dev unwrapped the gauze that looped around my thigh, then up and around my hips to cover my groin. Gradually, I felt more of my skin exposed. When he finished, I glanced down to see that I was wearing underwear.

I was. I barely noticed it.

As Dev gently pulled my legs apart, I could see the top of the thick burn, starting on my right inner thigh. It was dark red in the center where it had begun to scab, and bright red on the edges. I got lightheaded.

Dev pulled my legs apart more, and I could see how the welt trailed downward; this also exposed the burn on my groin, between my legs.

My head started spinning.

Even as I sat back and dropped my head against the pillow, I could still see it. Jordan came up in front of me again, blocking my view. He could see what was happening to me.

"It's okay," he whispered, rubbing his fingers gently down my face again and again, alternating between them and the side of his hand. He kissed my head and blocked my sight of the burns.

The air on my open wounds felt sharp; on the uninjured skin around them, it was cold. I waited for pain, for pressure, for Dev to touch with his gloved fingers or some cold metal tool, but I felt nothing.

"Okay," Dev murmured. "They're healing well."

"Do you have to clean them?" I tried not to grit my teeth. I anticipated a touch at any moment.

"No, we cleaned them quite a bit while you were asleep. At this point, they've begun to scab over. I'd just like to let your skin heal. I'll check it a few more times before you go home."

The sound of that made me ache. I wanted to go home. I wanted to go home and get in bed and sleep forever.

I didn't respond, just felt a heavy sadness settle over me at the thought of home. My face must have changed, because Jordan put his forehead to mine and whispered, "It's okay. We're gonna go home soon. It's okay."

I wasn't sure how he knew what I was feeling. Maybe he didn't. Maybe he just assumed it was all bad.

Dev wrapped my legs once more, switching the gauze out for a new one. Then he pulled my gown down and grabbed the blankets. Jordan took them from him and covered me, making sure my legs and feet were underneath. Then he pulled one up to my shoulders.

"You're looking good, Nina," Dev said gently. "We're going to get you home in no time. Just take it easy for now. Do you feel hungry?"
I didn't know if I was hungry, but I had no appetite. I shook my head. I felt numb.
He nodded slowly. "Okay. Well, let's try to get some food in you at some point, okay? Even if you don't feel too hungry. And something to drink as well." He looked at Jordan, who had turned to glance at him. He nodded.
"We'll get something," he murmured, looking back at me.
"I'm going to go make a couple calls. Call me if you need anything, okay?" Jordan nodded.
"Please don't go far."
Dev nodded seriously. "I won't. I'm staying now. I'll send the family back in. I might suggest they get something to eat." I nodded. That sounded like a good idea. Dev smiled at me and then headed out.
Jordan began stroking my cheek with his thumb. "Rest, my love. You can rest now."
I shook my head. I wanted to ask him questions before my family came back.
"Is it over?" My voice was low, emotionless.
Jordan kissed my forehead. "Yes, my love. It's over."
"You got them all?"
He paused. Briefly, but I noticed it.
"Everyone is handled," he said quietly, staring into my eyes. "I got them, baby."
Jordan brushed his fingers over my temple, sliding my hair away from my face. "I got them." Relief settled over my chest. They were gone. Ryan, the rest of them.
I sat back, realizing I'd leaned forward in anticipation to the answers to my questions.
Jordan continued caressing my skin, and I stared at his beautiful face until I got sleepy, comforted by his touch. As my family came back into the room, I began to doze off.
The last thing I heard was Jordan quietly say, "She's going to sleep now."

JORDAN

Shortly after Jordan's confrontation with Nina's parents, she woke up for the first time since her sleep in the ambulance.

When she moaned in what he assumed was pain, his heartbeat soared. Emotion flooded him. He wanted to pull her close to him and not let her go. He didn't want her to remember what had happened. He wished he could take it all away.

When she stopped breathing, Jordan was flooded with so much terror and panic he nearly forgot how to keep his composure.

After she finally caught her breath, she said his name, her voice hoarse. The sound of it made his heart skip.

When she asked him if she was alive, it made him wish he weren't.

Nothing would have happened to this sweet, sweet girl if he had just left her alone.

Or if he had at least protected her.

Now, she was lying in a hospitable bed, remembering what happened and wondering if they'd killed her.

He assured her she was alive and safe. Dev finally returned from his primary hospital and checked her wounds again. Seeing how embarrassed and frightened Nina was made him feel more terrible.

As she slept now, Jordan thought of the anxiety Nina already suffered from, and how that multiplied exponentially when she was taken. How it must have been so bad that it would scar her forever. He burned inside, all over his body, thinking of her so afraid.

He thought of Nina's body image issues, how she must have felt being strung up, nearly naked, in front of cameras, knowing people were watching. How she felt when she was so vulnerable and Ryan mocked her

378

struggles, implied she wasn't skinny, revealed she went to therapy, and tried to convince her Jordan had repeatedly cheated on her.

He thought of how her body issues might flare up from all of this. She'd already lost so much weight.

He imagined how the scars would worsen the moments she was already feeling self-conscious, unconfident. How he would love her for the rest of his life, and how hard it would be to convince her that those scars meant nothing to him. Jordan ached at the idea of Nina unhappy, hating herself, because of what she feared he thought of her.

He thought of the depression she already had. He was terrified of how it would worsen, so devastated that, at a time when she was doing so well, was happy, she was brutalized, traumatized, and thrown into relapse.

He prayed to God to have mercy on her. On his love.

Jordan tried to control his rage, but he didn't know how.

In his entire life, he had never felt anything like it. It ripped through him every second of the day that he wasn't looking at or aching for her.

There was a constant flipping between those feelings. Agony for her suffering, and then rage for it.

And he didn't think either would ever go away.

JORDAN

Nina

I was with Ryan.
It was just the two of us alone, in the hospital. Us and the *ping, ping, ping, ping* of the chat on the TV screen.
My arms were no longer strung up; I was curled up on the floor, dizzy. I wanted to get up, but I was too drowsy. I willed my limbs to move, willed my arms to retract from around my knees, for my body to lift itself up and run. I couldn't do it.
I was stuck.
Though I was on the floor, I could see the shine of the weapons on the table next to which Ryan stood, perusing each blade, each saw, each drill, trying to decide what he wanted to use.
Move, Nina! Move!
I was paralyzed with fear as Ryan picked up a long, iron rod.
Somehow, my knees split apart without my command, only for me to see that there were no burns on my inner thigh. And that was how I knew he was coming for me, that I still had to endure his violence.
As he moved towards me, I fought with all my will to get up, to crawl, but all I could do was put my arms up to stop the blow. Just as he lifted the hot rod, inches from my skin, I screamed.
"Nina, Nina!" Jordan's voice suddenly appeared. I still had my arms above my head, blocking my face. I felt no pain and wondered if Ryan was still standing over me. Something crowded me. I didn't know what it was, if it wasn't him.
"*Jordan!*" I let out a bloodcurdling scream for him. I hoped he would make it in time.

Though I felt no pain, I was terrified. It would come any moment now. Where was Jordan?

They were gonna kill me. Oh, how I wanted to see his face, his beautiful face, one last time before I died. I began to sob, my face in between my knees. As I looked towards the floor, all I saw was black, all I heard were my sobs.

"Nina!"

Then I felt something touching me.

No, some*one*.

I lifted my head and tried to hit whatever it was as hard as I could. Just as strong hands grabbed my arms to still them, my eyes opened.

"Nina, honey, look at me, look at me."

Jordan let go of my forearms and took my face in his hands, his worried eyes staring into mine. Someone was holding onto my right arm still. My eyes flickered to the right to see my mother and father, both with hands on my arm. They looked heartbroken.

After just a split second of that, I moved my horrified eyes back to Jordan's. My heart was pounding.

I was awake. In the hospital. Right. It was a dream.

Despite this positive realization, I began sobbing.

I couldn't contain the grief in me. Couldn't get Ryan's face or the rod out of my head.

Jordan brought my head to his chest as he stood over me. "It's okay, baby, it's okay." He spoke quickly, concern and devastation in his voice as he tried to calm me.

"It's okay, my love, we're right here," my mother told me, pain distorting her voice as well as she stroked my forearm.

I knew everything was okay now. I knew I was safe, and that the network of people that caused all of this was being shut down. Ryan and Donovan were dead. I was alive and would heal from my injuries. Everything was okay.

So why did it feel like the exact opposite?

They're dead. Ryan and Donovan are dead.

Eventually, the aching, the brutal sadness glazed over. It was still under the surface, but it had numbed enough for me to stop crying.

I sniffled into Jordan's chest as he kissed my head. Finally, I pulled back. "Can I have a tissue?" My voice, thick, congested and weepy, was hideous.

I didn't want to be here. I didn't want to *be*.

Everything felt wrong.

Jordan handed me a couple tissues, and I shamelessly blew my nose so I could breathe again. He reached his hand out to take the dirty tissues, and I had enough dignity left to deny him.

"No," I said, in my nasally voice, shaking my head. "Where's the garbage?"

"Here, honey." My mom snatched a plastic bag from somewhere behind her and held it open for me.
"Thanks, mom." I sounded pitiful.
Jordan leaned in and kissed my forehead, then stroked his thumb across it, looking into my eyes. I sniffled again, resting my head back on the pillow. His hand followed; he never broke his connection with me.
"It's okay," he whispered, looking intently into my eyes.
I breathed slowly, the quick sound of the air moving at the end of every inhale. It sounded like the hiccups, courtesy of the crying. Jordan's eyebrows crinkled together, his eyes so, so sad.
"Sorry." My voice definitely was.
His face was horrified. "What are you sorry for? What are you sorry for? No, no, no, no."
"You have nothing to be sorry for," my mother and father echoed.
Jordan kissed my forehead again. I felt bad for how he was feeling, but my apology was not what he wanted.
He wanted me to be happy. I knew that.
It disappointed me to disappoint him.
I tried to think of ways to alleviate some of the pain compounding inside of me.
I suffered from depression and an anxiety disorder. I already had some coping mechanisms for when they returned.
First, I reminded myself that everything was okay. *Everything is okay.*
Then, I told myself it was just the depression making me feel this way. *Everything is okay.*
After that, I would try and do something that might make me feel better. I looked around the hospital room, at my worried siblings, parents, boyfriend. I saw the TV, but it looked as appealing to me as going back to the abandoned hospital.
My head felt heavy, but I did not want to go back to sleep. I'd had enough nightmares for the moment.
I might write, or read. A lot of the time, I'd curl up on Jordan's chest and do something mindless, like stare at the TV, though I never really wanted to watch. Just being there was joyous enough.
"I want to go home," I mumbled, and it was half a whimper, the words just tumbling out of my mouth. *Breathe, everything is okay.*
Jordan exhaled hard; he was fighting off pain. "We're going to soon, my love." He stayed close to me, never losing contact.
"How long have I been here?"
"A day and a half," he murmured.
"I miss my bed." My voice was sad. "I just want my bed."
He leaned a little closer and whispered, "I know, honey. We're gonna go home soon. Let me just talk to Dev and see what else he wants to look at."
He dialed a number and lifted his cell phone to his ear.
"Where is he?" I asked.

"He had to go back to his hospital. Dr. Roberts has been checking on you," my mom informed me.

"Dev," Jordan said quietly into the phone. "When will you be back? I want you to check everything before we go home."

After a moment, Jordan said, "Yes. She wants to go home, and if there's no reason to keep her here, then we aren't going to." He looked up into my eyes.

He listened as Dev spoke, and a minute later said, "Okay. See you then."

As he pulled his phone away from his ear, none other than Tristan Asad passed the corner of the bathroom wall and into view, holding two full coffee carriers of drinks from Marinette's. A second later, a nurse came in with two more. I stared at them in surprise.

"Coffee delivery," he said, cheery, looking at me. He set the drinks down and came up to me right away, kissing my forehead.

He stood over me, taking my hand. "How ya feelin'?" he asked softly, his face turning serious.

I stared at him for a moment. "I'm fine." I didn't want to talk about how I felt. I looked at the coffees. "Why did you get so many?"

Tristan glanced at them. "Because I didn't know what everybody liked," he replied, turning and smiling small at my family, telling them to take anything they'd like. "They're labeled. I don't drink all the fancy sugary stuff, so I told them to mark them. But," he said, grabbing a frozen vanilla bean drink and coming back. "I was told that you like these watery milkshakes." He grinned, putting it in my hand. I was pleased to see I was strong enough to at least grasp it in my hand. "But Jordan said no caffeine for you, and I agreed, so I got you vanilla."

The *watery milkshakes* got me. I let out an amused *Hm*, as my entire family chuckled. Jordan had never stopped staring at me, and as I glanced at him, I noticed his face soften at my noise. My mom told Tristan he didn't have to do that. We all took a moment to process his ridiculous generosity.

Suddenly, my family all turned their heads in the direction of the door, and a few moments later, Rania and Amar walked in. Rania's face was fiercely worried, and Amar was serious, seeming stunned as they both looked at me.

"Oh, Nina," she said, rushing up to me, past Jordan. I thought she wanted to hug me but was afraid to hurt me, so she just stroked my cheek instead. Amar went up to my father who, to my surprise, stood up and gave him a hug. My mother did the same, and they kissed each other on the cheek.

It was a relief to see them all kind of acting like a family. As though Jordan and I were married. The thought helped me escape my misery for a moment.

"How are you feeling?" Rania asked me.

"I'm okay." Amar looked at me and listened. I said no more.

"They taking care of you?" I nodded.

She looked at my parents and began speaking Chaldean.

JORDAN

"Oh, no, no Rania, you don't have to do that," my mother said. Then they began going back and forth in the language I didn't understand.

"I think we should try to eat something soon," Jordan murmured, leaning in past his mom as she stepped around the bed closer to my parents to speak to them.

I nodded. "I was right. She was talking about food."

Jordan paused for a second, registering my words. He looked exhausted. After that brief pause, he nodded. "Yes, my love." He looked at the cold drink in my hand. "Do you want to drink?"

I did. I nodded. My arm felt weak, but I was able to lift the cup and bring the straw to my lips. I was thirsty, and the rush of sugar felt good. As the cold spread through my head, I began to feel a little more awake.

When I was done sipping, I set the cup right in front of my chest, holding it with two hands, the way a young child held their sippy cup. Jordan kissed my forehead.

"I don't want to eat," I told him. "I'll try when we get home." There was no prodding needed. I knew I would have to eat, but there was no way I was doing it in a hospital bed.

"Dev will be here soon," he murmured. "If we have to stay, will you please try something here?"

I blinked a couple times, trying not to let emotion show on my face. The idea of putting any food in my mouth was nauseating. The drink felt like enough sustenance for the moment.

I nodded anyway. I could never say no to him.

To those sweet, worried eyes. To his exhausted face. He was miserable, and I knew it was because of me. And I wanted to take it away, take away all the guilt and pain I knew he was feeling.

"Jordy," I said suddenly, my voice quiet. I was so sad for him. I didn't know what I wanted to say, but I just wanted him.

When I didn't continue, he leaned in. "What is it, my love?" he whispered. His face close to mine was exactly what I wanted. I lifted my hand up and touched his face, holding it in my hand. He stilled with the realization that I didn't want anything, just him. He turned his face into my hand just slightly, bringing his up to hold it there.

Love coursed through me as I looked at his beautiful face and those worn, devastated blue eyes.

I leaned towards him as best I could, and he moved in an inch or two more so that I could kiss his forehead. His eyebrows crinkled together slightly, lips twitching once. I thought he might cry, and my heart started pounding. But he didn't. His face then turned somewhat lifeless, as it had been.

Rania and Amar stayed and spoke with my parents. Tristan came to my side and made jokes that got a few smiles out of me. My siblings laughed a lot, which was nice to see. Everyone loved Tristan.

Before he left, he looked at Jordan with serious, concerned eyes; he wanted to say something but couldn't. So he turned back to me.

"I won't be far," he told me. "If you need anything, anything at all, just call me, or have this guy call me." He pointed to Jordan. "I'll bring you a million more watery milkshakes if that's what you want." He leaned down to kiss my forehead as I chuckled. He stopped in front of my face so I could smell his shampoo. His eyes got serious.
"I mean it. Anything you need." I nodded.
"Thank you," I said quietly. He nodded, pulling away and saying something similar to my family, then left. After staying an hour and talking to my parents, Rania and Amar left as well. They were there to support them as much as they were there to support me. They said they would be back, and if we left the hospital, they would come to our house.
When Dev returned, I felt a jolt of anticipation. I was hoping hard that he would say I could leave.
He checked my vitals, asked me how I was feeling. I told him that I was tired, my head felt heavy and kind of ached, my body was sore, and my thighs were burning. Same deal as before.
Speaking to both Jordan and me, he finally said, "You can go home. But you have to clean the wounds a little more. If they start to look worse, or if your head continues hurting badly or you begin to feel nausea, more pressure, you gotta come see me." I nodded. "Or I can come to the house." I felt my chest sink. I didn't feel deserving of the special treatment that came with Jordan territory.
"Let's do a quick reflex test. Nina, do you think you can bring your legs off the bed, so your knee is bent?"
I started to sit up. "Hold on just a second, honey," Jordan said softly, standing up quickly and putting his hand on my back as I managed to lift myself to a sitting position. I hunched over.
"You okay?" Jordan asked me, bending over and looking into my eyes. I lost my breath just from the small movement.
"Yeah," I breathed.
He helped me gently turn so I could let my legs bend over the edge of the bed. Dev was quick to flick his hammer under my knee. It jerked.
"Perfect," he murmured. I sighed.
"Now, I can show you how to wrap your leg back up," he said, but Jordan shook his head.
"I know how."
My heart skipped then, at the thought of Jordan unwrapping my gauze, checking my wounds and re-wrapping them for me. There hadn't been any doubt in my mind that he would take care of me, but I couldn't imagine even being without pants in front of him. The thought made me feel funny, that he would be doing this for me. As if he were my husband, and he would take care of it. I was used to doing things for myself.
Dev nodded. "That's right. Let me go talk to the desk out there and let them know you need discharge papers. And to have your file transferred over to my hospital." He headed out.

"We'll get you a wheelchair," Jordan murmured.
I figured. I didn't think I could walk just yet.
"Or, I can carry you. It's up to you, my love."
I looked at him with wide eyes. "You can't carry me," I told him. "I'm too heavy. I bet we're on a high floor."
Jordan's face didn't change. "You aren't too heavy. We'll do whatever's comfortable for you." He kissed my cheek.
I chose the wheelchair, knowing well that Jordan would have carried me if I asked him to. He would never bluff. He probably would've preferred it.
My mother helped me use the restroom before we left. I was mortified at the thought of Jordan helping me do that, though he offered. When that was done, I felt a lot better. I'd been worried about how I would keep him away long enough to do that.
Finally, we left.
I looked around me as Jordan wheeled me to the elevator, and then throughout the first floor to the hospital exit. This was an unfamiliar hospital, a bunch of unfamiliar faces, and I wanted to get out of there fast. My family followed alongside us.
Valet had brought the car around.
"The truck?" My voice was scratchy. The cold November air touched my skin. It felt nice for a moment, after being in the stuffy hospital room, but it also sent that uneasy chill through me. Only now, I had a reason.
I was afraid.
We were outside, in a public place where any member of the cult could be. I took a deep breath and focused on what we were doing, pushing the thought away. My stomach felt funny.
Jordan stopped a few feet away from the open passenger door and crouched down in front of me.
"Yes, my love. There's more space," he assured me. "I'm gonna carry you, baby." He stuck one arm under my knees and another behind my back. I sat forward as much as I could.
"Just lean back against my arm, baby. I got you," he murmured. I did as I was told, wrapping my arm around his shoulders as well. Then his voice got even quieter, and he suddenly sounded stressed. His face was close to mine. "You have to tell me if I hurt you."
I nodded quickly, wanting to assure him. I knew that was one of his biggest fears.
He moved slowly as he lifted me. A flash of pain moved through my thigh, and I put my face in his neck so he couldn't see me wince. My parents stood behind with their hands out, as though Jordan might fall back and drop me. He stepped up on the running board and gently put me down. There were soft pillows on the seat, which was leaned back some.
"Lie back, sweetie," he whispered, brushing my hair back as I put my head down. Then, he pulled the seatbelt across my shoulder and clicked it in place. He moved to the back door, and I turned my head as much as I could

to see what he was doing. He came back a second later with blankets. They felt good, shielding me from the cold that was making me shiver already.

After I was sufficiently covered, Jordan stepped back, moving to the outside of the door and holding onto the handle. He gave my parents a moment to say goodbye.

My mom and dad kissed my cheek. My mom stroked my hair for a few moments. They were both deeply unhappy.

"We're coming by in the morning," my mom said.

I nodded, my cheek still against the headrest. "Okay," I exhaled. She kissed my forehead again, then looked towards Jordan.

"Jordan, call me if you need anything tonight," she told him, while my dad kissed my head.

He nodded. "We'll be okay. You guys drive safe."

"You too," she told him seriously. I didn't know if it was the worry that suddenly softened them, but my mom leaned in for a hug. Jordan's face didn't change except for the slight surprise in his eyes. *I* was surprised, especially when my father pulled him in for a hug as well. I thought they would certainly blame and resent him for all of this.

Jordan gently shut the door and walked quickly around to the driver's side. His inability to be apart from me was comforting and saddening at the same time.

I hated that he was so stressed and worried. His eyes were exhausted, sinking into his face. I rolled my head to the left as he jumped into the car. As he slammed the door shut behind him, he met my gaze.

His face softened. "Hey, baby," he said quietly. "How ya feelin'?" Brushing my hair back, he assessed my face.

"I'm okay. I'm tired." He nodded, eyes sympathetic.

"It's a bit of a drive, my love, so please tell me how else I can make you comfortable."

I shook my head as much as I could. "I'm okay. Thank you for the blankets and pillows." My eyelids were getting heavier.

"Of course, my love," he whispered. His affection was so strong; it soothed me, the way it was supposed to. "Rest. You can rest now, baby." He kissed my forehead and stroked it with his thumb. Sitting in the car was as comfortable as it could be, but the entire discharge process had exhausted me even more. So I drifted off, wishing I could lay my head back more.

JORDAN

I awoke to Jordan pulling my door open. We were in the driveway. At home. Finally at home.

"Hi, my love," he whispered. He smiled the tiniest smile, and though I could tell it was the most he could give, it was sincere.

"Let's get you outta here, okay?" I nodded, lifting my arms up weakly. Immediately he slid his arm behind my back, and I wrapped my arm around his neck, falling into him as he picked me up.

When we walked around the car and into the garage, I noticed that he'd already opened the door.

As he headed up the few steps, the bump of the movement hurt my sore back. I didn't show it.

When we got to our bedroom, he pulled the covers back and set me down.

"Would you like a bath, my love?" he murmured quietly.

I was still tired. I didn't want to sit in a bathtub and get even drowsier, but I did want to get clean. The bed was so comfortable, however, making the idea even more dreadful.

"Can I even do that?" I squinted, trying to open my tired eyes wider.

"Yes," he murmured. "We can keep your leg wrapped."

Interesting. "Okay, can I just shower?"

He did say anything for a moment, face unmoving. Then, he murmured, "Of course."

"Maybe I can just sit in the tub, actually. And wash myself that way, with a little sponge. But no bath."

"I think a bath might be relaxing, no?" he murmured, cupping my cheek in his hand. His beauty radiated, even while his eyes were so exhausted.

"I don't really like baths in general. I get bored. I just want to be clean, though." I frowned. "I feel gross."

He kissed my forehead. "No, baby, we're gonna get you all clean."

Jordan grabbed a couple bath towels from our closet, then went to start the water in the tub. Then, he came back and helped me slide off the huge sweatpants we'd put on over my gauze. "I'll keep my underwear on," I told him quietly. "I'll...take this off when I get in there," I said, pinching the loose t-shirt I was wearing, no bra underneath. He watched me carefully, then nodded.

"Let's leave this on," he said carefully, touching the gauze around my thigh and groin just lightly with his finger, "throughout the shower. Then, at the end, we'll take it off, clean the wound real light, then wrap it up again."

"Okay."

He carried me to the tub, setting me down gently. Then, he grabbed a tiny towel and set a couple other ones on the edge of the tub.

"Um..." I started quietly. "Do you mind if I just wash up real quick..." I was about to say, "on my own" and hesitated when his eyes widened a little and he said,

"Alone? Of course," he nodded quickly. Then he stopped, looking at me hesitantly. "I'll be right outside. You just call me when you're done, or if you need help. Okay?" He looked at me with wide eyes, waiting for confirmation.

"Yeah, I will," I said quietly, nodding to reassure him.

His eyebrows crinkled together a little. "Do you think you'll need help cleaning the wound?" he asked softly. I assumed he meant, *"Do you think you'll be able to actually look at it?"*

I nodded. "I'll be okay. I'll call you if I can't." He stared at me for a long moment, and then nodded.

"Okay. I'll be right outside," he repeated quietly.

I could tell he did not want to go, but if he didn't think there was a great chance I'd get hurt badly, he wouldn't fight me on it. I knew he wanted me to be as comfortable as possible, and it made me ache, how sweet and helpful he was being.

I was kinda nervous to take off my shirt, knowing he could come in at any time out of concern. I felt insecure and was terrified he would see me naked.

Forcing myself to strip, I put some soap on the towel, got it wet and scrubbed at my skin. I washed my hair lazily; it would take forever to rinse out the shampoo and conditioner in just a bath, so I barely put anything in. I washed my whole body then unwrapped the gauze. It took me a minute, and when I finally got it off, I swallowed hard before looking.

The burns were worse than they looked in the hospital bed. One deep mark, no longer a swollen welt, on my inner thigh, and one in between that and my underwear. That was where it hurt worst. I got slightly nauseous but forced myself to gently scrub around it.

"Hey, baby?" Jordan called gently through the door. I pictured him standing there, nervous, not knowing what to do with his hands. With himself.

"Yeah?" I called.

"How ya doin'?" he asked, trying to keep his tone light, but the concern in it was heavy.

"I'm okay, I'm almost done."

"Take your time, honey. I'm right here."

I was antsy to be done myself, to get back to him.

My underwear were soaked, but I would not strip completely. If I did, I would be completely naked under my towel when Jordan came back in. I couldn't wait to get outside to get dry clothes.

After turning off the water and grabbing the towel hanging on the tub, I wrapped it around my chest. I tightened it as much as possible. I knew he was going to carry me out, and I was so afraid it would open.

"Jordan?"

"Baby, you ready?" he answered immediately. He hadn't moved from right outside the door.

"Yeah," I called. It seemed he was in the bathroom before the word was out of my mouth.

He was two steps into the bathroom, clothes in his hands, when his eyes landed on me, and he froze in his tracks.

I looked at him, my eyebrows crinkled together. Before I could ask what was wrong, he moved towards me.

There was something off about his eyes. He looked a little disturbed. But when he knelt down, his eyes were gentler. That flicker of horror—*was that it?*—disappeared, replaced with compassion.

"Um..." I said quietly. "If you pick me up, I'm gonna get you all wet." I'd turned the faucet off and opened the drain back up, but the tub and I were still soaked.

"That's okay, my love," he murmured, grabbing a towel from the counter behind him. As he spoke, he squeezed my hair with it gently, getting rid of any excess water. "Are you cold? I'm gonna get you out of here right now. I just wanted to dry your hair a little bit so it's not dripping on you."

I was too tired to smile, but I would've otherwise. Because he was so sweet. So loving.

"It's okay. It's warm in here. It will be cold out there." I jerked my head towards the bedroom.

"I'm gonna put the heat on when you're dressed. Let's put your clothes on in here so it's not too cold when we go out. Hang on just one sec." He went back into the bedroom for a moment.

When he came back in, he set a pillow on the closed toilet seat lid. I tried to grab the gauze from the tub, but he told me no.

"I'll get that, baby." He didn't give me a chance to grab it.

He came and gently lifted me out of the tub, in my towel. I used one hand to grip my towel closed tightly as best I could. My heart was beating fast. Thankfully, it only took a few seconds to get me seated.

Once settled, I ignored Jordan's eyes on me; he'd noticed how scared I was that he might see too much of me. That embarrassed me more.

I took one of the towels off the counter next to me and began drying off the exposed parts of my body. Jordan dried my hair a little more. When he pulled away, I took the opportunity to slide forward, lift myself up and try to pull my underwear out from under my towel without exposing myself.

"Baby, what are you trying to..." He stopped, understanding. Immediately he knelt down to figure out a way to help.

"I just want to take these off and put new ones on." I lifted myself up again just slightly, but it hurt my leg and groin. I wasn't holding on to anything. I grunted in frustration. If he went outside, then I could just take my towel off and not have to lean forward and pull from the bottom.

"Let me help you," he suggested quietly instead. "I won't look; I'll just pull 'em down."

I hesitated, wishing I could just do it myself. But I didn't want to ask him to leave again. I knew it hurt him. It wasn't like anything I'd ever done. And though he knew it wasn't rejection, that I was just embarrassed, it still hurt him. I could tell. I suspected it made him feel bad, as though it was suddenly his fault that I wasn't comfortable enough to be naked around him.

These were my suspicions, and if they were true, I couldn't further upset him. He wouldn't ever admit it, so as not to make me feel bad for what I wanted, and that made it even worse. So I agreed.

"Okay," I said quietly, sounding like a child again. Feeling this vulnerable was beginning to grate on my nerves. I was too independent at heart to be this reliant. I didn't like *needing* help. The reality was, however, that I was *terrified* he'd see too much.

Looking up at me, Jordan slid his hands up my thighs, under the towel, very gently, being careful not to roll the towel up with them. I felt his fingers lock underneath the waistband of my underwear by my sides.

"Ready?" he asked softly. His eyebrows crinkled. He looked worried. "I just need you to lift for three seconds. If that's gonna hurt, then we can do this another way..."

"No. Go ahead." I started to lift. "Wait, um..." I looked next to me at the counter, wondering if holding on with one hand would be enough support.

"Hold onto me, baby. Hold onto me." I looked at him for a moment. I felt so stupid and weak, leaning forward and grabbing onto his shoulders. As I lifted myself up, I focused on the shape of them, the little dips in hard muscle as he moved his arms, sliding my underwear towards him. I did not want to be.

It bothered me more than I expected that I couldn't do it myself. Jordan got them down my legs and around my feet quickly, then reached for the clean pair that he'd gotten me.

"Are these okay?" he asked, holding up the pink, cotton bottoms. It was odd seeing his holding my underwear. There was nothing perverse in this situation, and yet I didn't know how to feel. He was seeing more of me than he ever had. I nodded quickly, just wanting them on.

He held them open for me to slide my feet in. When he got them to my knees, we had to do it all over again. I frowned, frustrated.

When the entirely too long process of getting my underwear on was done, I reached for the form-fitting long-sleeved shirt he'd brought me.

I'd always been more comfortable in loose clothing. Though I'd been feeling secure with my body before being taken, I now felt icky and depressed. And when I felt depressed, I felt huge and ugly. Hospitals also had a way of making me feel unkempt and gross.

"Um…" I felt dumb asking this, but I suddenly wanted it so bad. "Can I wear something else?" My voice was pitchy. I didn't like asking Jordan for things; I made myself small when I did.

His eyes widened. I also didn't want to make him feel bad for what he picked, and at a time like this, I knew he would, as silly as it was. "Of course you can!" His voice was soft but adamant. "What would you like, my love, I'll go—"

"Let's find something in the room," I told him. "Can we wrap my leg in there, too?"

"Of course, honey." He looked at me a moment, assessing if there was anything else we needed to do in there, I assumed.

"Do you want to use the restroom?" he asked me gently. I thought about it and shook my head. I had already gone while we were at the hospital, with my mom's help. The irrational side of me was thinking maybe I'd be able to do it without help by the time I had to go again.

But the truth was, I couldn't walk yet. The pain in my leg and groin from the gashes was too bad. Apart from that, I was sore. I had bruises everywhere. My bottom and back and legs were all sore, probably from when the chains were set loose and I fell. My arms, shoulders, elbows and wrists still ached from being held by the chains. I didn't know how they handled me when I was unconscious. I assumed they were rough. My body was exhausted.

I swallowed my pride and tried not to think of it. I reached forward and put my arms around his neck, and he lifted me, knowing I was ready to go.

After setting me down gently on the edge of the bed, he murmured, "What shirt would you like, baby?" He got up and started towards the dresser I used.

"Um, wait," I said, my voice small. "Can I…wear one of your shirts?" It sounded so nice, to be lost in one of his big sweaters.

Jordan's eyes widened slightly. Quickly, I added, "I just feel like...I want to be in something loose." And we knew his shirts were huge on me, lean as he was. I was much shorter than him, and some of his sweaters were like blankets with sleeves on me.

"Of course. Of course." He turned and fast walked to his dresser, opening drawers. "Which one would you like, baby? You tell me."

"Um, just a big sweater, it doesn't matter which one." Still, he held out a couple, letting me choose. I pointed to a large, white crew neck.

"That one." He glanced at it, then shoved the other ones in the drawer and hurried back to me. I reached for it. My arms, sore and tired as they were, worked just fine.

"Thank you," I murmured, pulling it over my head. It swallowed me whole.

Perfect.

Jordan assessed me for a moment, different emotions flickering through his eyes. What I thought I could decipher were sadness, adoration, pity and love.

"You're welcome, my love." His voice was so low and soft that it made me shiver. His eyes widened, and he put his hands on my arms.

"Are you okay, baby?" he half-whispered, worry clouding his beautiful, beautiful face. "I'm gonna go put on the heat."

"No, no," I told him. "I'm gonna get hot in the sweater. That's why I like it cold."

"Then why don't you wear a t-shirt?"

I looked down. Finally, I said, "Because I just feel like...hiding. Just...this is just more comfortable." I met his eyes. "It's just a body thing." His face filled with understanding, his eyebrows smoothing out. I wished then that I'd lied and said something more subtle, however, because his eyes got even sadder.

"It's okay," I told him. "I love this sweater. It's perfect. Thank you. Just don't put on the heat, or I'll die of heat stroke."

Shoot.

Word choice, Nina, word choice!

"I'm just kidding," I told him when his face turned hard.

He looked at me for a moment, and the emotion faded. Just like that. Suddenly, he was the smooth-faced, unreadable Jordan again.

What happened?

Grief filled me. He was hiding it all again.

"Jord," I said softly, my voice sad. I felt my eyebrows crinkle together.

"What's wrong?" he asked gently, and all that was there was the slight crinkle of his own brows, the worry he always showed when something wasn't quite right. The exhaustion, uneasiness, and unhappiness were all masked away.

"Just..." I frowned. "It's okay."

He stared at me, trying to understand.

I sighed a little. I would work on it later.

"Let's um...let's do the gauze," I said. The heat from the water had made me even more tired, and I wanted to get this done so I could lie down.

Jordan nodded. "I'll be back in under twenty seconds," he told me.

I snorted lightly, the sound breathy. I smiled small.

At that, his lips too curled up slowly as he stared at me, wonder touching his eyes.

It made my heart jump, seeing that smile.

"Take your time," I told him softly.

He looked at me lovingly for a few more moments, then jumped up and walked quickly out of the room. I'd never seen someone's walk look like flying before.

Jordan was true to his word. A few moments later, he shuffled back in with a black duffel bag in his hand.

Setting it next to the bed, he knelt down in front of me and pulled out a roll of white gauze from it.

"Let's get this wrapped up," he murmured determinedly.

The little moment we'd had made me feel a little better. "Okay," I said softly, a small smile still touching my lips.

I unwrapped my towel for him. Now that I was in a shirt and underwear, I would be okay with the rest showing. My legs were small and muscular enough for my body insecurities to not paralyze me. I was okay with his seeing them, apart from the hideous burns. Those, I didn't want anyone to look at.

I slid forward to the edge of the bed, closer to him. He looked up, unrolling some gauze as he stared at me. He glanced down at the burns and was careful not to make a face before his eyes flicked back to the white material in his hands.

"Okay," he said quietly. "The best way to do it is to have you stand with your legs apart. You can try and lift them up while you sit. If you stand, you can hold onto me," he promised. I hadn't stood on my own much; Jordan had lifted me in and out of chairs. They'd wheeled me to the bathroom.

"I'm sure I can handle standing," I told him. "Just tell me when you're ready."

"Okay, come on." He was careful, staying knelt down but wrapping his hands around the side of my thighs as I held onto his shoulders and stood slowly. Every time I bent and straightened my legs, it hurt, particularly in my groin. But I'd been doing that, so I was fine with it. The pressure of pressing into the floor and supporting myself, however, sent a different pain through my muscles. I winced.

"Let's do it differently," he said quickly, but I shook my head fast.

"No, it's okay, it's okay." I slowly stepped my legs apart a few inches, feeling the tug of the dry burn on my groin and trying my best to ignore it. I pressed my weight into the foot of my unburned leg and balanced by holding onto Jordan. He watched my face worriedly, and some of that fear and anxiety returned to his own. Somehow, the emotion fading in and out—one moment he was able to hide it, one moment he couldn't—felt worse than either or.

I stepped apart some more, wanting so badly to show him I was making progress.

"Is this enough space?" I asked him, slightly out of breath. There were five or so inches between my thighs.

"Yeah, I think I can get it, baby. You're doing great." He couldn't hide his worry.

He began wrapping, starting in the middle of my burned thigh and working his way up. Once he got to the very top of my inner thigh, he brought the gauze around again and then crossed my waist in the front, brought it back around and then down under my groin and up again, sealing it.

He taped the end in place, and we were done. He did it so smoothly and quickly, it seemed like he'd been doing it his whole life.

"Okay, honey, you can sit." He guided my hips down gently. "What pants do you wanna wear?"

"Um...none, I don't think." The blankets would suffice.

He frowned slightly. "Are you sure? I think you'll be cold."

"No, I got the blankets and stuff," I told him. "When we go downstairs, I'll put some on, but...can I sleep now?" I asked him, ending the sentence quietly. "I'm a little tired." A *lot* tired.

"Of course you can," he told me softly, his eyes wide and full of love and surprise. "You don't have to ask me, baby. We're gonna get you some rest, okay? We're only gonna do what you're ready for." I nodded.

He pulled the covers back even more and helped me ease back on to the bed as I slowly straightened my legs and lifted them. I winced.

Jordan's eyebrows crinkled. "I'm sorry, I'm sorry."

"It's not you," I said breathlessly. "It's not you."

When I was finally in, Jordan pulled the cool covers over me. They felt good on my bare skin. The bed was so soft and comfortable compared to the hospital bed. My eyelids immediately got heavy.

Jordan leaned down and kissed my forehead gently, keeping his face in front of mine and stroking my forehead with his thumb.

"Are you gonna sleep, too?" I asked him softly.

He kept his voice quiet, as his face was inches from mine. "I'm not sure, my love. I'm going to be right here with you, though."

I frowned. "When's the last time you slept?"

He stared at me for a moment. "I think I dozed off for forty-five minutes or so yesterday."

My eyes widened. "Jordan! Jordy, you have to sleep." My eyebrows knitted together. "Please sleep with me. Please."

Jordan cupped my cheek in his hand. "Don't worry about me, love. I will rest."

"Do you wanna go shower? You can go, Jordy, I'll be okay."

He thought about it, hesitant. "I should, before I get in bed with you. But only if you're comfortable with it. I'll only be two minutes. Just enough time to get clean."

"No, baby, I'll be fine. You go shower, take your time, relax, and then come back to me." I touched the hand he had on my face. "Go," I whispered, knowing this was difficult for him.

He nodded, pulling away slowly. He went and grabbed a towel from the closet, clothes from the drawer and then looked back at me hesitantly, conflicted.

"I'm okay," I told him softly. "I'm perfect. Don't worry," I encouraged.

After a moment, he nodded, his face still hesitant. He rushed into the bathroom and didn't even close the door, in case I needed him.

I couldn't see into the shower, and he got in before he undressed. Again, I was touched by his concern.

I willed my eyelids to stay open until he came out. I tried to tell myself that everything was okay, but the anxiety I was feeling wouldn't go away. The heavy anxiety that mingled with depression, where everything just felt wrong.

They're dead. They're gone. You're fine.
Everything is okay.

I blinked and turned away from the bathroom door so he could come out and get dressed. When the water turned off, after maybe three minutes, I called to him and said I wasn't looking.

"That's okay, love," I heard. A moment later, he was closer, and I heard the bathroom light flick off.

I turned, seeing my boy with wet hair, donning nothing but black sweatpants. Though still buff and cut, he had definitely shrunk down some. He ran the towel over his head as he dug in the drawer.

Pulling out a white, long-sleeved shirt, he looked at me.

"Are you alright, honey? How are you feeling?" he asked, as he slid the shirt over his head and approached.

I scooched over for him to come in before he could object. He crawled beside me, smelling clean and fresh.

Thinking of his thinner body, I felt the heaviness of all the grief he'd been feeling and was so terribly worried about him. I opened my arms, longing to hold him. He leaned towards my chest hesitantly.

"I don't want to hurt you in my sleep," he whispered.

"You won't," I assured him. "I would sleep on *you*, but I have to lie on my back right now." *And I need to be close to you.*

He looked up at me for a moment, considering. Then he nodded slightly, put his cheek down and wrapped his arm around my waist.

Stroking his hair, I murmured, "Thank you for taking care of me."

Though his head was down, he shook it a bit. "No thank you's. Please, my love. You don't have to thank me for anything."

I leaned down and kissed his head, saying nothing further. Eventually, with Jordan in my arms, I drifted off to sleep.
Entering my dreams, the first thing I heard was a loud *Ping!*

December

December first. One week after the night in the abandoned hospital.

When the month rolled around, it was difficult to accept that I was still feeling so strongly the effects of what was done to me.
It was difficult to be apart from Jordan. I noticed that about myself and was trying hard to eliminate that dependence. I didn't feel safe if he wasn't nearby.
He'd told me that the case was cracked but not closed.
"But at this stage of it, you are safe. There is no longer a threat to you." To any of them.
They still had work to do, still had people to find and stop. So when we were out, I couldn't help but wonder which of the many people around us was one of them. The guy in line behind us at Marinette's. The old man sitting in an armchair at the library, book in his lap, not reading, just watching. The flat-faced hostess at the restaurant. Anyone could've been a part of the evil underground world.
I even considered my coworkers. When Jordan let me know that he'd contacted Steve and informed him what happened, it occurred to me just how possible it was for him to be as sick as the rest of them. I didn't know him that well. I edited his projects, made copies and organized his meetings for him; I knew he was married to a blonde woman named Lisa, knew he had no kids and that he liked Mexican food for lunch, but I didn't know him well enough to know he wasn't a sick man who, for fun, watched people get tortured and killed.
Fortunately, Jordan had informed him I would need a leave, at least for a month. Apparently, Steve took no issue with that. I wondered, if Steve had said no, Jordan would've told him I'd be quitting. I didn't think so, but at a

time like this, Jordan would do anything he thought was necessary to help me heal. Regardless, I didn't need to see any of my coworkers for a while. Steve did call me, and I spoke to him briefly. He asked how I was feeling, even if there were anything I needed, but I made the call short, unable to keep a sinister version of him out of my head. Even after he told me to take all the time I needed, and that my spot would be available when I came back. I told myself to be relieved. I couldn't be.

For the first week after we returned home, I didn't want to get out of bed. After that, I could walk. Slowly, more like waddling, but still, I could move on my own. I only got a few feet before wanting to stop. Maybe I could've gone more. But the frustration of moving so slowly and stupidly made me want to quit.

If the burns had been in most any other place, they wouldn't have affected my walking so much. The soreness and bruises eventually faded, though some yellow and purple marks still stained the skin along my arms, legs and back. But the aching in my muscles and bones wasn't holding me back anymore. It was just the dryness and stinging of the burns. The cream Dev gave me didn't soothe them much.

Jordan told me it would take time for them to heal, and to try to be as patient with my body as I could.

"It's not your fault. It's not that you aren't strong enough. They're just some really bad burns, baby. Let yourself heal; it takes time."

He was right, of course. I knew all I could do was wait.

That was a week ago. Now, we were two weeks into December, and Jordan decided that it was time for me to consider going back to therapy.

He wouldn't force the issue, because he knew I'd eventually come around and accept that I had to go back. But he would gently push until I did.

I hadn't had a session in over three months. I'd been doing well before the incident. My therapist, Dr. Marshall, agreed that it was okay to take a break.

Now, I called and told her that I'd been hurt, and that things were really bad. She told me I must come in and see her.

"Can Jordan come with me?" I asked her quietly. He sat right next to me on the couch, arm around my shoulders.

"Well, sure!" Her just barely quivery, high-pitched voice replied. Elizabeth Marshall was in her early seventies, but she was still sharp and observant as ever. "Bring him with you."

I didn't give her details over the phone about my injuries. She met Jordan and me in the waiting room, after Jordan told the receptionist in his polite but authoritative way to please get Dr. Marshall, so that I wouldn't have to sit and stand repeatedly. My doctor was surprised to see me limp slowly, Jordan's arm around my waist, into the hall and down to her office. The few people in the waiting room stared.

As bad as things were, I was still proud to introduce her to Jordan. She was polite, of course, as was he. In her way, my small, pale doctor with sandy brown hair and fuchsia lipstick on her thin and long lips, observed Jordan as much as she did me, listening carefully as he spoke. I wondered if she was pleased to see his lovingness. Describing it could only do so much. She could, of course, see in my other sessions that I was in love with him, and I didn't blame her if she assumed all my gushing may be about someone average, someone who didn't treat me as well as I stated. I did, after all, as my brother would say, "date a heathen."

I was surprised and relieved when Jordan asked to speak with Dr. Marshall in the hall alone for a minute.

She looked at me for approval, eyes showing just the slightest bit of surprise. I nodded.

"I'd just like to explain to Dr. Marshall what happened."

They were outside for ten minutes; I couldn't hear anything, as they'd closed the door. Jordan popped his head in halfway through to see how I was doing and informed me that it would only be a few more minutes.

When they returned, Dr. Marshall's big blue eyes were horrified and full of sympathy.

"Well, it seems you've been through something very, very horrible," she began. Dr. Marshall sat at her desk a few feet away. She turned her back to it to face us.

I nodded silently as Jordan settled next to me, wrapped his arm around my waist and held my hand with his other.

Our sides stayed pressed together at all times. Dr. Marshall noted this with a quick glance.

"Jordan told me what happened," she said slowly, carefully. "That you were kidnapped from your home and hurt by a few men. On camera." She nodded slowly as she relayed the details, waiting for my nods of confirmation.

"And then you were chased," she finished. "Of course, that is the gist of it. I know there is much, much more to discuss."

"Did Jordan tell you how it all started?" I asked quietly, speaking for the first time.

Dr. Marshall nodded. "Jordan told me what he does for a living, and that there were some bad people that had it out for him, so they targeted *you* to hurt him."

At the very last line of her recap, I squeezed Jordan's hand. He didn't move, his face smooth, but I knew that her words had to have burned him inside. He most definitely had taken the blame while explaining it to her.

"Did I get it right?" she asked considerately.

"Yeah. It wasn't his fault," I said, looking at him. He looked down at me with the same intense eyes he'd always had, just heavier since the incident. His face may have been smooth, but it was not light. Anyone could see he was unhappy.

"No, it wasn't."

"It wasn't anyone's fault but theirs," I insisted. I turned my cheek into the front of his arm a little bit, then looked back at her.

She observed us for a moment. "That sounds right to me. How are you feeling?" She gestured to my loose sweatpants that draped around the bandages on my legs. "I hear your leg is hurt pretty bad."

"Yeah. A big burn on my inner thigh and one up higher that makes it hard to walk. Other than that, I'm fine."

Dr. Marshall and Jordan continued observing me. Jordan was watching like a hawk, making sure I was okay.

"I know this is deeply personal for you," he'd murmured to me in the car before we arrived. "And if, at any point, you want to stop or want me to leave, you just say so." I'd nodded and told him I would be fine.

"Okay," Dr. Marshall replied to me. "How are you feeling emotionally?"

I cleared my face of emotion, voice falling flat. "Depressed." It burned me to be this honest in front of Jordan, but I knew I had to. "Anxious."

I didn't meet his eyes right above me.

"What do those things look like? What is being depressed? I know we've talked about it as being tired all the time, lack of motivation. How does it show now?"

I thought for a moment. "Those same things. I don't want to do anything because I'm scared," I admitted. "I'm scared, and I feel like I'll be scared and on the lookout for the rest of my life, and that's depressing. It makes me not..." *Want to be alive.* "...want to do anything.

"And I'm sad. Then, I think about what happened and get so anxious and scared again. Sometimes, I remember and get nauseous, or dizzy." I swallowed. "I've been getting dizzy a lot."

Jordan, unconcerned with Dr. Marshall's presence, kissed my temple firmly, bringing the hand around my waist up to that side of my head and brushing his fingertips over my hair.

I glanced up at him. His face was unmoving, but his eyes were serious, watching me intently. I could feel his love and protection as he kept me close to him.

"Have you been eating?" Dr. Marshall asked me.

"Here and there," I admitted. "Jordan's been trying to help me eat more, but I don't have much of an appetite. I'm trying to drink more water to at least stay hydrated, but..." I lost the will to do that as well.

Dr. Marshall thought for a moment. "When you get scared, what happens? Are you eating lunch, watching TV, reading, when a memory occurs to you?"

"I remember all day long," I said quietly.

She nodded. "A memory comes into your mind. What happens after that? You start to feel...."

"A flash of something bad. That anxiety that doesn't make your heart beat fast or make it hard to breathe but that sits there and makes you feel...bad. Sometimes, I can't tell if that's the depression or the anxiety, or both. But

I think it's both, because something feels wrong. Which must be anxiety. It's…" I stopped.

"It's what?"

I swallowed. "It's pain."

She stared at me. Jordan had brought his hand down from my hair and wrapped his arm around my waist once more. I held onto his wrist. He was not speaking. He wouldn't, unless directly asked. It was my session, and he was there for moral support, he'd told me. He wouldn't infringe on that. It wasn't about him.

But I knew it must have been hard, because if I'd said something like that to him, he would've pulled me into his arms immediately and held me there for a while, gently asking more questions and soothing me. He couldn't do that now.

"What does that pain feel like?" Dr. Marshall finally said.

"I don't know," I told her, a little frustrated. "I feel sad. I feel unhappy. I feel like something is wrong and there's nothing I can do."

After a moment, she continued. "It's difficult for you to move around right now. What have you been doing during the day?"

"Reading. Watching TV. Sleeping. Lying with Jordan. Looking at Christmas decorations online and getting sad I can't put them up." I could see Jordan frown the tiniest bit in my peripheral vision.

"Because they require standing and walking."

"Yeah," I said flatly.

"Jordan," Dr. Marshall addressed him. "Would you be willing to help Nina put up her decorations?" she shamelessly interrogated, though he was not her patient.

"Of course," he murmured immediately.

"Would that make you feel a bit better about the decorations?"

This was what Dr. Marshall did. She looked for resolutions, not for just the big issues, but for little things as well. One by one, we solved problems, found solutions. Made things feel a little better. Right now, I wasn't feeling it.

"It wouldn't be the same." I let go of his wrist and used that hand to hold his in both of mine. "I appreciate everything he does for me. And that would be so kind for him to do. But it's not the same as doing the work yourself. So I'm bummed about it. It is what it is." I tried to take the edge out of my voice. This was the most I'd spoken in a week. This was the most I'd spoken about my feelings in a while, *especially* my depression.

This was the most depressed I'd felt in years.

Jordan kissed my temple.

"Now, I feel worse than I have in so long, and I can't do anything to alleviate it."

"Well, that's not true," Dr. Marshall interjected in her lilting voice. "There are things you can do. We just have to figure out what those things are."

Of course. Strategies. Good habits.

I didn't feel like doing any of them.

"I don't know," I rebutted. "I don't know if I'd even have the energy for it, if I could walk." Maybe I was being difficult, but I felt low, irritable, and on edge. It ironically gave me anxiety to be feeling this way again. Anxious and depressed that I was anxious and depressed. A never-ending, tumbling drop.

"How have you been sleeping?"

I sighed. "I sleep through the night some nights, and others I don't sleep well. I toss and turn. I have nightmares almost every time I go to sleep. I don't have them as much when I nap. Maybe it's nighttime or something that gets me."

"What are your nightmares about?"

I swallowed. "The hospital."

"Where you were taken?" she clarified.

"Yeah." I knew she was going to ask for more. "He's in my dream. The guy who took me. The men with masks." Dr. Marshall made a confused face. I assumed Jordan hadn't mentioned that.

"The people who chased me were wearing gas masks," I clarified. My voice was dry, low. I felt tired. "I see them. I see the weapons. There's always bloody footprints. And an iron rod."

"Why those two things, do you think?" These were the details Jordan may not have gotten to.

"Because he branded me with a burning rod." My voice fell flat, saturated with bitterness, the sentence filled with expletives of which I was too exhausted to be ashamed. Dr. Marshall was surprised by my cursing, Jordan alarmed.

Saying the words suddenly brought a wave of anxiety to the surface. I had not recalled the details of that night to anyone, not even Jordan.

"Sorry," I said quietly. Jordan began shaking his head but didn't speak as I went on. "Then," I swallowed. "I shoved my hand into the big burn and put blood all over my feet so I could leave footprints in the opposite direction of where I went." Jordan's eyes widened, understanding filling them. He must have seen the footprints.

Remembering made the sudden anguish worse.

It wasn't just the lurking anxiety or dread that appeared. My heart started beating faster, my lips quivered, and my voice cracked every few words. I tried desperately not to let tears come to the surface, feeling a sob in my throat. Jordan would not sit still. As though we weren't already pressed together tightly, he pulled me closer with the arm around my waist. Again, he kissed my temple. "It's okay," he whispered.

Dr. Marshall shook her head, disgusted. "I'm sorry about this, Nina." She had to say it eventually.

I just nodded. Jordan kept his lips to my temple.

"So, you see those things in your nightmares," she prodded gently. "An iron rod and bloody footprints. Your own."

I swallowed again, forcing control over my voice. No crying.
"I see them in my head during the day, too."
"How often?"
I tried to think. "A lot, I guess. Sometimes I think I'm seeing footprints on the floor." I stared at the arm of her couch as I thought about it. "It's hard to look at the fireplace. And the teapot."
I froze. Jordan didn't know any of that.
Finally, I looked at his face. His eyes were disturbed. Though his face did not move apart from his eyebrows knitting together, I could sense rage.
"Why the teapot?"
I swallowed. I couldn't stop now. "They told me the teapot was on the floor when they got to the house. I can't really remember when I think about it, but when I go in that part of the kitchen or see the teapot, my heart starts beating fast."
She nodded, thinking. "And the fireplace, it reminds you of that night?" she asked, waiting for more. Jordan's eyes burned into me.
"Y-yeah. Because...because of those...those rods, the...the iron ones. I just think of when he burned me." I shook my head, looking at the floor. I knew I was upsetting Jordan, which brought me more pain.
They were waiting for more. I knew that if I stopped there, Jordan would feel worse, wondering about all these things. "My leg throbs," I said quietly. "Like when you're watching a movie, and someone's arm gets cut off, and you immediately grab yours, because it starts to feel sore. You know what I mean."
Dr. Marshall nodded. "What do you do when that happens?"
"I look away, and then get depressed that this is happening."
She stared at me. *We have a lot of work to do,* I imagined she was thinking. After a moment of thought, she recapped. "So, you aren't eating very much. You aren't sleeping too well. You have nightmares when you sleep and have flashbacks during the day. These things make you depressed."
I made a disgusted face at how awful it all sounded.
"It sounds rough," she said gently, "because it *is* rough. But the good news is, we can find ways to make these things better."
I hoped so.

JORDAN

After a few more minutes of therapy, I told Jordan and Dr. Marshall I was done for the day.

We scheduled another appointment via video call for the next week, so we wouldn't have to travel all that way.

On the way home, I asked Jordan what he thought of her.

"She's a nice woman," he said quietly.

I laid my head back. I wanted a nap. This was the first time we'd left the house since coming home from the hospital, and it took a lot out of me. I figured my body still needed time to recover, even though the soreness had eased.

I said nothing more, just looked out the window. The snow had been light throughout November, but now, as though by default in December, it covered the streets.

"Nina," Jordan murmured.

I turned to look at him. Before he said anything, I remembered what I'd wanted to say to him. What I'd thought of throughout the session but had already forgotten.

"Sorry you had to hear all that," I told him quietly. "I don't want you to have to hear those things."

He frowned. "Please don't say that."

"Why?"

"Because I want to know everything," he told me, as he had, long ago. He took my hand in his.

"I love you more than anything," he murmured, and his voice, deep, rough and full of emotion, stunned me. "And I promise, we're going to get you feeling better."

I swallowed. My jaw was aching all of a sudden, my throat feeling full. My eyes watered, despite my efforts to stop them.

"Is that what you were going to say?" My voice cracked, lips trembling.

Hell.

His eyes filled with that uneasy concern. "Yes, my love," he told me, anxious that he couldn't face me directly as he glanced between me and the road. "It's okay. It's okay," he soothed as I fought my crying. No sobbing, though.

An accomplishment.

"I'm just tired," I lied, voice weepy. I *was* tired, but I was also full of grief. "Thank you, Jord. Thank you for everything."

"Don't thank me," he whispered, stroking my cheek with his fingers as he drove. "You did so great today. When we get home, you're gonna rest, okay?"

True to Jordan's word, we went upstairs and he tucked me in.

"What are you gonna do?" I asked him.

"Stay right here."

"I just need a short nap." I felt guilty. Though it made me feel safe and secure, I didn't want him sitting around waiting for me to wake up. He insisted that that wasn't the case but never had a book with him. The laptop on the nightstand soothed my guilt slightly.

"You rest as long as you need," he told me, kissing my head and then crawling in next to me. Instead of grabbing his laptop, he pulled me to his chest.

"Are you gonna work?" I asked him.

"In a little bit, maybe. I want you to get to sleep first, so the typing doesn't bother you."

So he'd noticed.

My noise sensitivity was bad lately and got worse when I was agitated. I never directly said that, but when I asked my visiting family to please not chew gum, he noticed.

I wrapped my arm around his waist. There would never be anything I loved as much as lying in his arms. No matter what happened.

"Thank you, but it's okay," I lied.

He kissed my head, ignoring me. "Get some rest."

I drifted off to sleep, and when I woke up, he was gone.

"Jord?" I called out groggily.

I was numb for a few moments, confused. Then dread crept into my chest. The thought registered to me that I was alone. What if he had left? And I was at home, all by myself? Why would he do that? *Why would he do that?*

He wouldn't.

Would he?

What if something serious and unexpected happened at work, and he had to go?

No. Jordan would never do that again. *And Ryan and Donovan are dead, Nina. They aren't here in the house. They can't get you again. You're fine.* But I didn't believe myself. My phone was downstairs somewhere, so I couldn't call him to reach him faster than I could by searching the house. I looked around me for a note as I called out again, my chest beginning to hurt and tears filling my eyes.

"Jordan?" Panic and desperation built in my chest and voice. "Jordan?" I slid to the edge of the bed. It took forever. I was hot. The room felt stuffy. Then I heard a quiet, indistinguishable voice and footsteps coming up the stairs fast. I froze. My heart began racing. Gas masks, rods and saws flashed through my head.

Jordan appeared in the doorway, a water bottle in one hand and the other holding his cell phone to his ear.

His eyes widened when he saw me. "I'll call you later." He threw the phone and water lightly on the edge of the bed as he ran to me.

"Hey, baby, where are you goin'?" he asked softly. It made him nervous to see me halfway out of bed by myself. "Do you have to go to the bathroom?" Then he saw the tears in my eyes.

"Where were you?" I asked, so relieved to see him and unable to keep the fear out of my shaking, high-pitched voice. It wouldn't have mattered if I did. The wetness of my lids, my crinkled eyebrows, slightly labored breathing, trembling hands and sheen of sweat all told him I was terrified and panicking.

He pulled me close and held me tightly against him; my heart slowed down gradually, the pain in my chest easing as I felt his warmth and strong arms around me.

"I'm so sorry, my love. I just went into the hall to take a call, and then thought I'd go grab you some water real fast. I meant to be back before you woke up. That was bad timing." He kissed my head firmly and lowered his voice to a whisper. "It's okay. I'm right here. I would never leave you again. I won't. I promise."

His words soothed me greatly, but I was frustrated that I was terrified just waking up alone.

You are ridiculous, Nina. Acting like a child.

I hated this dependence that I'd developed. It made me feel a strong need to begin doing things on my own, as much as some of them scared me. I'd have to figure out a way to get him to leave me and go downstairs when I slept, so I could deal by myself with the fear I'd just experienced.

But it was just like before, when I'd gone downstairs. All alone. Then suddenly I wasn't, and the next thing I knew I was waking up in a filthy, abandoned hospital, chained up and nearly naked. Staring at blades, guns, saws, and rods while various torture scenarios flickered through my mind.

It's over. They're dead. Case cracked, problem solved. You're fine.

"It's okay." I pulled back. My heart was still beating too fast. "I'm gonna go to the bathroom."

"I'll help you."

I shook my head. "No, I'm okay."

Jordan looked at me with concerned eyes. He didn't seem comfortable with my going alone. As I'd gotten more mobile, he'd at least walked me into the bathroom.

He helped me stand, and I waddled away. I anticipated he would come up behind me, but he didn't. He watched me walk the fifteen feet slowly.

I turned around at the door. "Be right out," I told him breathlessly.

"I'm right here," he called out as I closed the door.

I thanked him. It took me a few minutes to get through the whole process. As I washed my hands, I assessed myself in the mirror.

I'd lost weight. Maybe ten, fifteen pounds. It showed on me because I wasn't tall.

My skin was pale, my eyes surrounded by purple bags and heavy eyelids. I'd worn no makeup to my appointment.

I felt withered. I looked even tinier, hiding away in Jordan's big clothes.

I dried my hands and turned to walk out, just as Jordan called for me.

He was right there at the door, and he put his hand on my back as I exited. Holding it there lightly, he allowed me to make my way a few feet forward.

"Hey, I wanna try the stairs," I told him.

Jordan stared at me hard. If he could've carried me everywhere for the rest of his life, healed or not, he probably would've.

"Okay," he said quietly, coming up beside me. "I'll be right by you, though."

I nodded. I wasn't sure if the movement would hurt too badly.

We made it to the top step, and I slowly brought down my unscathed leg. I felt a slight twinge in my groin that continued as I brought my other one down. I made a barely audible sound in my throat, but Jordan's eyebrows crinkled. He kept his hand on my back and didn't say anything, though, just watched me carefully.

I made it all the way down to the bottom and managed to waddle to the kitchen.

"What would you like to eat, my love?"

I was thirsty. "I kinda want some juice," I told him, heading slowly to the fridge.

I noticed the teapot was gone, but I didn't say anything. I glanced over at the fireplace. The iron tools were no longer on their stand. The whole thing was gone.

I was touched once again at how he cared for me.

As I closed the fridge behind me, bottle of cranberry juice in my hand, I looked at him. I knew he was watching me but wasn't expecting the look on his face.

There was pride and some relief. It made me happy to see. Despite everything, I smiled a small smile at him and turned to get glasses.

I poured us both juice. I hadn't forgotten that Jordan was thinner as well. Turning his way and leaning back against the counter, I extended the glass to him. He rushed forward to take it.

"Thank you, my love." He smiled, kissing my forehead.

"You're welcome," I murmured, feeling as good as I could in that moment. I gulped it all down at once. Jordan grabbed the bottle and immediately put me more. I smiled, finishing it again.

He topped me off three times. I laughed when I was done with the fourth one.

"I guess I was dehydrated." I chuckled. He smiled a real smile that made me feel good. I felt cuddly all of a sudden. I reached my arms out, and he brought me in happily, maybe desperately.

I needed that closeness, too. He held me there for a while.

"I'm sorry this has been so difficult," he whispered into my hair. I pressed my cheek into his chest.

"It's okay," I assured him in a moment of unusual positivity. Going down the stairs had made me feel a little better. "We'll be okay."

Jordan kissed my head.

"Yes, we will."

Jordan had never felt so emotionally exhausted in his life. He didn't think, in all his years of doing the disturbing work no one wanted to do, he'd ever experienced the extreme grief, anxiety and guilt that he felt now.

Every time he looked at her, he ached.

When Nina had woken up, terrified and sobbing, at the hospital, his chest hurt so badly he could barely breathe. He wanted to wrap his arms around her and keep her inside them forever, drown her in his love. Do something so she could feel it.

The first time she smiled and laughed since she'd woken up, it made his heart skip. Yet he ached more, seeing that flicker of joy that he missed watching her have. The joy she deserved. He considered asking Tristan to stay longer, but Nina needed to rest.

In the car on the way home from Lyson, when she'd fallen asleep just a few minutes into the ride, she'd looked so exhausted, as though the trip from the eighth floor, down the elevator and out to the car, had wiped her out. He'd known being awake for too long, amidst all the physical pain and the emotional whirlwind she was in, would do that to her.

She'd looked so innocent as she slept. So vulnerable. It hurt his chest.

He'd carried her inside and up to bed, the way he'd been dying to do the entire drive. Carry her in his arms.

When they got upstairs, she asked to bathe by herself. He felt mixed feelings in response.

He was relieved. Proud. She was trying to do things on her own. She was regaining strength. This was his weakest emotion.

Secondly, he felt terribly sad. She didn't want him to see her naked, or see her wounds. She wanted to be alone; she didn't want his help or comfort. That cut into him.

Thirdly, he was scared. He wanted her to be able to be independent the way he *knew* she was dying to be, and he would give her the privacy she asked for. Unless he really thought she would get hurt.
But he was afraid that she might be pushing too hard. He was always afraid, from the beginning of her recovery, that she would push too hard to get better fast. He couldn't be sure unless he was in the bathroom with her. Would she throw up at the sight of her burns? Would she faint? Would it hurt her to touch them? If water touched them? Would being seated in the tub hurt? Of course it did. She was burned and sore, and it was hard porcelain. But did it hurt more than he thought it would? More than she made it seem?
Would she try to get up on her own without telling him? What if she slipped and hit her head?
He was scared and nervous and aware of his constant need to hover; he tried hard to reign it in. It wasn't easy.
When she was finally done, he'd rushed in, relieved. But he forgot that feeling of relief when he saw her.
She was sitting, nearly naked, with her knees to her chest, arms around her legs. The same way she sat in the freezing cold when he found her hiding that night, rocking herself, terrified, shaking, sobbing.
The image had flashed through his mind and made him want to pull her to his chest the same way he had that night. He wanted to cry.
He'd seen the terror and agony in her eyes when he returned upstairs with water in his hand and Tristan talking in his ear. The terror in her eyes in that split second when he appeared in the doorway, before recognition hit. He realized he hadn't been imagining the faint sound of her calling out for him. She was crying, her cheeks pink and face crumpled. He could feel her pulse racing when he pulled her close, her skin burning. Her voice shook along with her hands as she asked where he had gone.
He instantly regretted even stepping out into the hall to take the phone call, knowing she'd woken up alone and afraid. He felt horrible. She couldn't convince herself that he wouldn't leave her again. She didn't believe his promises.
It was unbearable for him.
Jordan would never forgive himself. He didn't think, even the slightest bit, that Nina should either.
The possibility terrified him still.

Nina

Dr. Marshall handed me off to someone else. She told me that of course she would still see me, but for the time being, she wanted me to see someone who had the expertise that she didn't.
Her name was Dr. Amy Rodriguez, and she was a trauma specialist.
I had a video session with her a week after my first with Dr. Marshall, and Jordan left me alone in our bedroom for that hour, door closed, to speak with my new therapist privately.
After our introductions, we recalled the night once more, except in full this time.
She asked me to walk her through it. I didn't feel confident. In the moments before even speaking, I began trembling.
Forcing myself to open my mouth and concentrate, I started with the livestream that appeared on Jordan's computer.
Dr. Rodriguez stopped me so she could write some notes. After that, I told her about Jordan's small laptop and his leaving. Then it got fuzzy.
Tea?
Tea, right?
"I got out of bed. I couldn't sleep, so I think I just decided to go downstairs. I don't remember the last thing I was doing. I guess I was making tea, because they said the teapot was on the floor."
"You can't remember?"
"No."
"And when you woke up?"

I swallowed, recalled the chains, my arms up above me. Seeing Ryan, Donovan. The table with weapons, the television screen and the tripods around me.

"And there was this dinging noise from the chatroom. It went off every time a new message popped up on the screen," I told her. My fist clenched. "I hear it all the time."

Dr. Rodriguez observed me through the laptop screen. Jordan's laptops and Internet speed were exceptional. The picture was clear, and there was no lag. It made the experience less unpleasant.

"You think you hear it?"

I nodded.

"Okay. Tell me what happened after you noticed the chat room. Could you read what the people were typing?"

I said nothing for a while, just staring at her.

Finally, I willed myself to nod.

"Okay," she repeated, her voice more careful. "Do you remember what you read?"

I was hoping she wouldn't ask me that.

Swallowing, I closed my eyes and thought back to the place I hated to go to in my mind.

"Things like, *Kill her,* and *Rip her apart*, or *Cut her* or something like that. Some of them were surprised that it was really 'Jordan's girl.'" I made air quotes. "Some were warning Ryan that he was putting himself in danger, and the rest of them, too."

"Because the police would find them."

"Because *Jordan* would find them," I corrected.

Dr. Rodriguez paused. "What did *you* think?" she asked gently.

"About what?" I swallowed again. I couldn't keep the saliva from forming in my mouth. It irritated me. "The police coming?"

"Yes. The police, or Jordan, or both."

"I didn't know." Suddenly, the grief hit me, and my throat got sore. "I wanted to believe it so bad." My voice cracked.

Tears filled my eyes. "I didn't know if he would make it. I thought they were gonna kill me."

That was it. I brought my hand to my mouth to catch the sob as it escaped. Dr. Rodriguez waited, giving me time to feel what flooded me.

I caught my breath and sniffled as I forced myself to stop crying. Waiting for Dr. Rodriguez to say something, I reached over to our nightstand for a tissue.

"But they didn't kill you."

"Yeah." I sniffed, my voice thick and nasally.

"You're still afraid."

I stared hard into the screen, losing concentration on her and thinking of what she said.

I *was* still afraid. I knew they wouldn't kill me, knew that they were dead, but I still felt that fear.
Or maybe that wasn't it.
"I feel anxiety all the time. That something is wrong. And I think what I feel is wrong is that they could've killed me, they were so close, but they didn't. I think…" I swallowed hard against the ache in my throat. "I think it bothers me how close they got. How possible it was.
"Of course that bothers me," I added, struggling to articulate my revelation. "But it's like...it doesn't make me feel better that they *didn't* kill me, when I think about it. I just keep thinking of how close they were to killing me. How Ryan could have done *anything* to kill me. Anything. He could've started torturing me sooner and not stopped. In the livestream, that person took the girls clothes off and immediately started...cutting her, I think. He had a knife. I expected it would start sooner. Ryan could've just started with any of those weapons, but he went slow, and that's what saved me.
"Or those guys with the masks could've caught up to me, grabbed me, and tortured me. I'd guess that I'd just barely made it to the next building over when someone found the door I left from. I found a hiding spot quickly enough, but any longer than when Jordan got there, they might have found me. They probably would have. Jordan was literally there *just* in time. It's so hard for me to believe. I think it's hard for me to accept. I don't know." I gave up, defeated.
My new therapist thought for a moment, then said,
"Do you feel guilty?"
I blinked.
Guilty?
I thought hard. Was it guilt that made it hard for me to move past what happened? To accept it? Or was I just scared that it would happen again?
I didn't think it was so much the latter. Yes, I would flinch at a small sound and couldn't *stand* to be touched by anyone other than Jordan. And yes, going out in public did make me anxious. Scared, even. And I, of course, suspected anyone could be one of the monsters that hurt people the way Ryan hurt me.
But, as difficult as it was to cope with, that fear wasn't so bad as the constant obsessing over the fact that I was so close to dying. To being killed.
I should've died. It almost didn't make sense that I didn't.
"I don't know," I said finally, frustrated. "Is that guilt?"
"It could be," she said, her tone light. Then, her face smooth, eyes serious, she asked "Do you feel like you shouldn't be alive right now?"
I looked down. "I…"
Wait. Do I?
I was trying so hard to understand my own emotions. "Yeah, I guess. I guess so, because it's so hard to accept that they didn't kill me," I repeated. "It's almost like in movies, when the hero comes just in time. I felt so much

grief at the time, when I was tied up, when he was burning me, when they were chasing me. I kept thinking, *I'm not gonna make it.*

"*It won't be like the movies,*" I continued, meeting her eyes. "The entire time, I felt like I was gonna die. At least, I kept telling myself that, because my instinct was to hope and pray that Jordan would come to me. And I forced myself to think that it wasn't going to happen. I tried to accept that they would...brutalize me, torture me and kill me. I tried to make myself prepare for the pain that was coming. That's how I spent the whole night. Until he got there.

"But then he came. He actually came. It was like a dream. You don't die in a dream. Like every time a person runs at me with a knife or comes to attack me, I wake up before they do. Or in a movie, or a show, they're usually saved right in time. You know?"

Dr. Rodriguez nodded. "Yes. Real, traumatic situations like this tend to be unlike television."

"Exactly." I sat back against the headboard, realizing I'd leaned forward in the heat of my explanation. My back was getting sore. "*Exactly.* But this *was.* So...it just *won't register* in my mind that I actually lived. Like I should've died. I should've died," I said with more finality.

Then the weight of my words hit me. I stared off at the wall, wondering where Jordan was. How he would react to that statement.

"Do you want to be alive?" Dr. Rodriguez asked me gently, and I snapped out of my daze just to be hit with another wave of grief.

"I don't know," I told her, shaking my head fast as my eyes watered once more and my voice became weepy. "I don't know."

"I just want to forget what happened, but I know that I never will and it's so *frustrating,*" I said through clenched teeth. "I don't know if I'll ever be able to move past it, or accept it." I began to cry quietly into my hand, lifting my face out of view of the laptop camera.

"You will," Dr. Rodriguez said gently. "You will."

After I'd calmed down, I decided I wanted to be done with this. I'd had enough. I quickly ran through the rest of the night, trying so hard to disconnect from myself so I didn't have to feel any more pain.

I mentioned the phone call with Jordan, and though she tried to stop me and ask me more questions about it, I told her no.

I couldn't go back there. I wasn't strong enough. Not yet.

Just remembering his voice on the phone, the sound of it through the crackly speaker, brought tears to my eyes, and I immediately wanted to sob.

Hearing my love, my safety, my family, right in front of me but in reality, so far away—how far away, I didn't know, though I'd assumed the worst—was agony.

I'd never wanted him so badly. He'd always made me feel safe and secure. Then, suddenly, I was the opposite, and Ryan dangled him in front of me,

as though to say, *Look. When you need him most, he isn't here. And he won't be coming, either.*
That was worse torture than the iron rod scorching my flesh.
I continued on, not allowing those thoughts to come to the front of my mind, instead telling her of the people with gas masks, how I ran, looking for a hiding spot. How panicked I was that I couldn't find one, and my idea to leave bloody footprints on the floor. How I'd made it outside without running into any of those monsters, and made it a few buildings down before I had to stop. How I heard gunshots, wondering if Jordan was there, and then completely losing focus from the pain and fear.
She cornered me there with another question.
"How did you feel when you heard the gunshots?"
I frowned. "It was brief. I wasn't sure I was hearing them. My whole body was in agony, my head especially. It was pounding. I thought I'd been imagining it. But the small part of me that focused on the idea was hopeful. Then, even though I was barely...mentally present in that moment, I tried to convince myself not to be excited. Or relieved. To expect the worst. That it wasn't Jordan, and they were just being psycho and shooting guns to scare me."
Dr. Rodriguez nodded, regarding me.
I looked at the time, relieved that it had been fifty-five minutes already. She watched me do it.
"Nina, you went through something horrific. It's going to be difficult to move on from it, I will be honest with you. But you *will*. You *will* move on, and you *will* accept what happened. It *is* possible, and we are going to work on it until you do. And then we'll keep working, so we can stay on top of it.
"You're doing great already. You've been very open with me, and just the fact that you were willing to see me and do that is great. You've already made excellent progress from your situation. Okay?"
I stared at her, unmoving.
"That said, I think we should speak at least twice a week."
A groan built in my throat, but I quickly stopped the noise from escaping.
"Okay." I swallowed.
"Through video," I told her. It would have to be. She was even further out than Dr. Marshall.
She nodded. "Yes. Though I think it might be good for you to get out of the house, if possible, and move around a bit."
I said nothing once more.
"Let's do an hour in the mornings. What days work for you?"
I sighed. No days.
"Which days make the most sense in terms of frequency?" I asked flatly.
We decided on Tuesdays and Saturdays. She told me we could switch them up if I didn't like that arrangement.
How kind of you to make your schedule flexible for me.

Stop, Nina.
I tried to accept that this was necessary as I shut Jordan's laptop screen. I swung my legs over the edge of the bed, and as I stood up slowly, I called out to him.

"Hey, Jord?"

A few moments later, he was pushing open the door. I walked in his direction, but he met me quickly, beating me ten times in pace.

I was moving much better now but still going slowly. It looked like I had a limp, because I kept my legs spread apart some as I stepped and led with my uninjured leg, dragging the burned one behind.

"How'd it go?" he asked gently, putting his hand on the side of my face and caressing my cheek with his thumb. I knew he saw the redness of my eyes, because his own filled with sadness and concern.

"It was hard," I confessed, voice still thick. "But at least I did it."

Jordan nodded. "You did a great job. I'm so proud of you." He pulled me to him. A wave of comfort settled over me. After a moment, he leaned back and said, "Come on. Let's go get you something to eat."

That was another struggle. My appetite was in and out. But so were my good moods.

There were some parts of the day in which I felt okay. But my mood dipped fast, dragging me down into that same depression I'd fought for so long, only this time, it was coupled with crippling anxiety.

I nodded anyway. I was trying to make progress.

"You *will* move on," Dr. Rodriguez had told me.

And I prayed all day long, all the time, that that was true.

As the days went on, Nina came around to allowing Jordan to put up her Christmas decorations. Because she wasn't walking well, they'd also sat together on the couch, shopping for more on his laptop.
It was one of her favorite activities.
And she actually let him order whatever she wanted. He asked her what she liked, and she'd point at different things, her eyes lighting up. She smiled a couple times, talking about them as they looked through the sites. It was enough to make his head spin with joy.
He ordered a few hundred dollars' worth of decorations. It was the happiest he'd ever been while shopping.
When they came in, they bundled up and went outside. Jordan bought a porch swing with a pillow on it, so she could sit comfortably, covered in blankets, and direct him where to put everything. Jordan's front yard was wide, no breaks for a driveway. It was entirely grass and not steep. Nina thought it was perfect.
He was blissful as she contemplated, asking him his opinions. Should all the tall statues stay together, or should they be scattered? Should Rudolph be next to Santa? His heart skipped at her excitement when she thought they'd done a good job. He happily rearranged them seven times.
After all of the decorations were set up, Jordan helped her down to the street to look at their work. Her smile was huge as she giggled in excitement.
His heart felt so full it ached.
Nina thanked him five times. He begged her not to. He wanted her to see how willing he was to do anything that would make her feel better.
He would help her do anything *she* had to do to feel better. She would speak to Dr. Rodriguez twice a week, and he prayed that would also help her move forward.

JORDAN

Jordan wanted badly to be in her sessions with her, but he knew he had to give her time alone with her doctor. It was important for her recovery for her to be independent and deal with her emotions on her own. She knew that as well.

But when she came out after that hour, her eyes red and throat thick every time, it made him want to insist he be there the next. He hated leaving her alone, knowing she was crying, in pain, facing the thing that he should be facing with her.

Tristan said Jordan should consider therapy as well, to which Jordan said "Goodbye, Tristan" and hung up the phone.

Somewhere in his mind, he thought it made sense. He was feeling pain like he had never felt before, loving in a way he'd never loved before, and he didn't feel in control of himself the way he always did.

But now was definitely not the time to think of himself. He only cared about Nina.

And she did make progress. He knew she was depressed, but as the days went by, she had more moments of joy, more smiles here and there.

The flashbacks continued, of course, and so did the nightmares. The depressive bouts as well. Often, he'd catch her staring off into space, looking desolate and empty. Her voice sounded that way sometimes, too. He would go up to her immediately, trying to break her out of the spell so she wouldn't feel the pain he knew was spreading through her. But he wanted her to have the ability to fight it on her own and not require his distracting, so he'd suggest she do something that made her feel better. He'd ask her if she wanted to read, or write, or watch a movie, and could he get her a book and some tea? Would she like to go for a walk?

And she *was* making progress. She knew what her brain could do to her, the lies it told her. She was aware of the power it had, but that the power she had to control it was greater. She told him this.

She'd been through hell before, and she'd survived. Jordan knew she'd be okay.

It didn't make it less difficult when she broke down. When she woke up screaming, crying. When she sat, looking somewhere, eyes lost, seeming broken. Empty.

When he saw her burns, as he helped her change or into the shower. Though she was able to move better with each passing day, he still aided her in any way he could. She shielded the burns from his sight when she could, but he still saw them. Seeing her in physical pain was brutal as well. Seeing how much weight she'd lost, watching her struggle to eat.

It was a constant battle internally. Jordan had to remind himself that she would get better. He, himself, may have been struggling with a depression he'd never known before. But he wasn't sure. He wasn't sure of anything he was feeling.

The only thing he was sure of was that he'd protect her. That this would never happen again.

And that the people who hurt her did not get away with it.

JORDAN

Nina

We weren't sure what we would do for Christmas. Jordan asked what I wanted to do, but as I contemplated our options, nothing felt right.
Rania and Amar would have us. My parents, of course, wanted us to come over.
The solution would be to go both places, or have everyone over our house. I didn't think I was up for that, emotionally or physically, but I mentioned it.
"Maybe it will be fun," I said, trying to keep my voice light as I stared off, considering it.
Jordan nodded slowly. "We could absolutely do that. But only if you feel up to it."
I frowned. "That's the thing. I don't want to agree and then at the last minute want to back out."
He tilted his head to the side a little bit. "They'd be fine."
I shook my head. "No, that's rude. If we decide to invite them, we have to stick with it." I looked past him once more, thinking. It *would* be nice to sit with Tristan and my siblings and have a good laugh. And that was bound to happen in that company.
"We have a few weeks until then," Jordan said gently. "Why don't you take some time to think about it?" He knelt in front of me as I relaxed on the couch.
"I think we should do it here," I decided, disregarding his suggestion. I met his glance.
He stared into mine for a few moments, then asked, "Are you sure, baby?" His eyes were soft.

I nodded. "Yeah, let's do it here. That way I don't have to get up and walk around during the night. Just have to clean beforehand. We can tell everyone to bring food. It's not like they weren't going to, anyway." I rolled my eyes, unsure why I was feeling irritable suddenly.

"You won't be cleaning," Jordan said immediately. "You'll just be relaxing. Nothing to worry about."

It was true. Jordan had been cleaning the whole house on his own. We never made much of a mess in the first place, spending most of our time in the family room, kitchen, library or our bedroom.

But whatever cleaning there *was* to do, he did. He vacuumed, mopped, washed the dishes, wiped things down, picked things up. We usually both did those things. We had no set schedule. Whoever got to the sink first did the dishes. Whoever grabbed the vacuum or mop did it. Sometimes it was me, sometimes it was him.

I hadn't done anything since the incident, however, and I felt guilty the whole time.

"Jord, I gotta start cleaning again," I told him, frowning. "This is making me lazy."

Jordan raised an eyebrow. "Lazy? Recovering is not lazy."

"But I can walk now," I insisted. "There's no reason I should be lounging around all day, doing nothing." I frowned. "I'm gonna get fat." I missed the treadmill.

That made his eyebrows knit together in concern, which left me feeling guilty. He worried about my eating issues more than I did.

"You are not going to get fat," he said softly, taking my cheek in his hand. As he stared into my eyes, I wondered once more how his could be so bright. They glimmered.

I continued staring, getting lost in the whitish blue around his tiny pupils, underneath his heavy lids.

"How are you feeling?" he whispered, staring right back.

We had not discussed the night of the incident on our own since the hospital. I'd avoided it, worried about upsetting him, and I was sure it was the same for him.

Now, I chose honesty. "Kind of agitated," I said quietly. "I might just be anxious."

Jordan's thumb moved across my cheek. "How can I help?" His voice was still a whisper, eyes sympathetic and worried.

"I'm just happy you're here," I told him, voice barely there. I offered a weak smile.

He didn't say anything for a few moments. Then, finally, he murmured, "I'm happy to be here." His eyes were careful. "Nina, you know you have to tell me if there's anything you need, right? Anything you want?"

His seriousness overwhelmed me. All that love he'd always given. The same Jordan.

JORDAN

I put my arms on his shoulders and laced my fingers through the back of his hair as I looked down at his face, inches from mine. He noted the touch, his eyes following my hands.

"Thank you, my love." Suddenly, I wanted to be wrapped in him. Just Jordan. No more Christmas plans, no more thinking of that awful night that continued to plague my thoughts. Just Jordan.

"I mean it," he insisted quietly. "And if you ever want to talk about anything, anything from that night or anything else, you can."

I nodded, then slowly leaned my forehead into his. He brought both of his hands to the sides of my head now and held me there. I carefully dropped my lips to his, kissing him softly.

I was worried he would be resistant, assuming he was in no mood to do anything of the sort.

I just wanted his lips. To be close to him.

But he kissed me back gently. Didn't go stiff, like I thought he would. Didn't pull away, even after I kissed him a little deeper. Not wanting to push my luck, I pulled back and stared at him. He smiled a small smile; there was passion in his eyes, but he looked so tired.

"Baby," I whispered. I turned to look at my phone. It was seven p.m. "Is it too early to go to bed?" I asked.

"Are you tired? It's not too early." He put his arms out past my waist. "Let me carry you."

But I put my hands on his shoulders and stood. "No, it's okay. I wanna walk. Thank you, though, my love," I said, my voice low. I took his hand. "Are you tired?"

"A bit."

I nodded, guiding him to the stairs.

He walked patiently beside me as I moved up each step, letting me move up first each time so he could monitor behind me. He always did that, even though I was getting better. He never let me walk up the stairs by myself. Even if he was just at the landing, watching. I had to ask him to stay there. If I didn't, he would walk by my side, every time.

When we finally got to our room, I told him, "I want you to sleep. To really sleep."

"What about you?" He was confused. "You're not tired?"

I shook my head. "It's not that. I am, a little bit. But I want you to sleep, too. Not just me."

He stared. Finally, he murmured, "Okay."

No fight at all. Good.

But he was all talk, it seemed. When we got in bed, he lay on his side and stared at me. This time, I didn't close my eyes and drift off, though I was tired. It had been so easy for me to fall asleep. I was more tired than usual since the incident, my body feeling much weaker and head too heavy to keep up for long. My mind constantly racing didn't make being awake much easier. Neither did the crippling depression.

Tonight, however, I would not sleep. I would wait until he did.

"Come here," I instructed, opening my arms. He looked so beautiful, lying there on his side, black hair pressed against the pillow. He hadn't had it cut in a few months. As he crawled into my arms, I ran my hands over it. Then, I kissed the top of his head, over and over throughout the night, brushing my fingers through his hair, over his cheeks lightly, touching him gently, just enough to soothe.

"I'm okay, honey," he murmured, but despite this protest to my comfort, he was humoring me.

Little did he know, I wouldn't stop until he actually did fall asleep.

"I know," I said, so as not to argue. Though he looked far from okay. "But I just want you close."

I continued touching him, kissing him, and said nothing more. It seemed he decided he really would just sleep for the night. Eventually, he dozed off.

I was reminded of the morning Jordan had pulled me down and said he didn't want me to get up for the morning. He was unhappy. He needed me for once. And even if he wouldn't admit it, I thought he did now, too.

Seeing his innocent, sleeping face against my chest made me feel full. I kept my arms around him tight, feeling protective and full of love. I would never let anything hurt him. Not even me.

Jordan couldn't let Christmas come and go without doing what he considered wrapping up the situation.

For the first time since the night she was taken, Jordan left Nina.

"I have to go do something for work," he murmured. "Do you think you'd like to spend some time with your family?" He caressed her cheek, hating this but forcing himself to think of all the pain she'd endured. All the pain they'd caused her.

She frowned, which immediately made him reconsider going. "Can I just stay home?"

He exhaled slowly. "I'd rather you be with someone, honey. If you don't feel like leaving, I can have Tristan come by. Or ask Zana. I want you to have company." He kissed her forehead. "I'll be gone four hours at the very longest."

Her eyes were unhappy. "Are you going to the office?" Jordan knew she was calculating time, trying to decipher if four hours was really enough for whatever work he had to do.

It was.

"Yeah, I have to go and work a couple things out. It's about the case," he added in a quieter voice. "It won't take me very long, I promise."

"When?"

"Tomorrow."

She'd agreed, not seeming happy about it. Jordan forced himself not to let that sway him.

This had to be done. He couldn't sleep at night, thinking about it.

This was for her.

The next day, he dropped her off at her parents' house and walked her inside. She'd called ahead of time, asking if it was alright. Jordan had picked a Saturday, because everyone in her family would be home.

"Hi, honey," her mother greeted her warmly, pulling her in for a hug. It'd been a few days since she'd come by to see Nina, and Jordan knew she had been extremely worried about her daughter. Nina insisted they not constantly make the drive.

They could also tell that Nina didn't really care for company, as best as she tried to hide it.

"Hi, Jord," Bridgette greeted him. He couldn't offer a smile, but he did lean in for a kiss on the cheek.

He followed Nina inside. It had been nearly a month since the night in the abandoned hospital. She was walking much better, but he still worried about her in every way. A million thoughts raced through his mind.

What if her leg started bothering her, the burns started aching? He wouldn't be there to give her painkillers. What if she got tired and wanted to take a nap? Her family was loud and not usually considerate. They weren't always nice, which is what propelled Nina to finally move in with him. He didn't know if, at a time like this, they would make an exception. He hoped so. The thought otherwise made him angry.

What if she had a flashback? Or just got so depressed that she started crying? What if she got agitated, what if one of them bothered her, and she wanted to leave but couldn't?

Four hours, he told himself. *No more than four hours*.

He forced himself to stop worrying, by providing logical answers to his concerns. If her burns ached, her mother could give her painkillers. If she wanted to nap, he was sure they would take her to her old bed and let her sleep in peace. Put the fan on. They hadn't had the heart to turn her bedroom into something else, holding onto the hope that she would come back home. If she got depressed, she would call him, and he would stop whatever he was doing and speed back to her.

That was the only solution he had for that.

"Baby," he murmured as he knelt in front of her. She'd settled on the opposite end of the couch as Zana. "If you need anything while I'm gone," he lowered his voice, "if you start to feel bad and you wanna go home, just call me, okay? I'll come back sooner." He stared at her with wide eyes, waiting for her agreement.

She nodded. "Don't rush," she said quietly, though she didn't want him to go. "Take your time." Jordan could feel Zana's eyes on them, could sense that Bridgette and Elijah were listening. He didn't care if anyone heard.

"Four hours max. It could very well be less than that, but not a minute past four hours." Nina knew he wasn't lying. He sounded pedantic, but he would not break his promise to her. And he would not be gone for more than the set amount of time he'd given himself.

He didn't want to go, but he did at the same time. He tried to make sense of it. What he wanted most was to stay with her. But he also wanted to get this done. He felt the need to.

Forcing himself to stand and move away from her, knowing that if he knelt there too long, he would never leave, he asked Bridgette if he could speak with her a moment. Nina heard but pretended not to care. She did. She knew he would be talking about her.

"Please call me if she needs anything. If you guys need anything. *Anything*," he told her quietly. "If she begins to get upset..." Bridgette nodded.

"It's okay, Jordan," she told him, sensing his uneasiness and unwillingness to leave her. She smiled gently. "She'll be okay." She wanted to say, *I raised her for two decades. I think she'll be okay for a few hours with her mom.* But she knew it wasn't so much that Jordan doubted her parenting abilities as it was his fear of leaving her alone. But Bridgette would never let anything happen to her. Neither would Elias. And she told him so.

Hesitating, Jordan nodded. Lowering his voice so that Nina couldn't hear, he murmured, "She had therapy this morning. That's really hard for her, and usually after she's a little out of sorts." He stared at Bridgette hard, making sure she took in this piece of information. "Please make sure that everyone is sensitive to her," he said bluntly.

He wouldn't beat around the bush when it came to Nina, not even with her family. Especially since they were not always the most functional group. He didn't want to step on Bridgette's toes or insult her as a parent, but he would not risk anyone upsetting Nina when she was in this state. And from the way Nina described their dynamic, her family could be incredibly insensitive. And harsh. And inconsiderate.

Jordan was really beginning to rethink his plans.

"I will," Bridgette said quietly, surprisingly taking his request well. "I know she's struggling; she's my daughter. I can see it, plain as day. I won't let anyone upset her."

Jordan exhaled hard through his nose. "It upsets her when other people fight, even if she's not involved. If they argue. She jumps at loud noises," he added, not wanting Bridgette to feel personally targeted. They were a family known for arguing. "I'm not implying that you all will be insensitive to her, I just don't want her to panic."

Even if Bridgette had gotten annoyed or offended by his comments, she no longer would have been by the end of Jordan's statements. His eyes were so worried and frightened that she felt bad for *him*, wondering if Nina had been a terror unintentionally. Was she doing *that* poorly? *He must just really love her*, she thought. Something that had become obvious to her over time.

She nodded again. "It's okay, honey," she told him. She'd never seen Jordan so unconfident or hesitant before. "I'll make sure no one upsets her." She lowered her voice even more. "I already warned them."

This soothed Jordan little, but he made himself accept it as truth. Nodding, he turned to leave. He stopped only to say, "Do not hesitate to call me," before he turned and strode out, jumped in his car and made himself drive off.

Just a minute alone, just sixty seconds away from her, made Jordan uneasy. He realized that he'd developed a separation anxiety or something of the sort. He didn't know what to call it. He didn't think it was dependence. Maybe fear. Anxiety.

He had not left her once since she was taken. Not once.

In the back of his mind, he'd known eventually they would be apart. Eventually, she would return to work, she would go out with her friends, Zana, visit her parents, go shopping, go for coffee, all without him. But he hadn't accepted the thought, always pushing it away under the irrational mantra, "I will never leave her side." But he told himself if that were the only way to protect her, he would do it.

Somehow, however, the situation sprung on him. It was his doing, leaving her, but he felt dragged into it, almost against his will, and suddenly he was going against his word that he wouldn't leave her alone.

After this, he wouldn't part from her side for months. He didn't care if he was hovering, or dependent, or needy, or whatever any professional called it.

He swallowed as he drove and noticed his shaking hands.

It must have been separation anxiety.

Was he afraid she would get hurt? He knew in his mind that his team, the police and the FBI had tracked and found every cult member nearby and put them away. Short of someone breaking into the house for a random murder or robbery, no one would come to hurt her.

He had to remind himself of this, over and over again. He nearly called Tristan and asked him to go by, but his brother was also needed where he was, so he couldn't. Jordan was anxious, worried.

Afraid.

Jordan had rarely ever felt fear in his life. Even facing death, even with a gun pointed towards him, he'd felt calm. As long as he did what he was supposed to do, as long as he stayed focused and performed proper procedure, as long as he stayed smart, he would be fine. And if he died, it would be for a good reason. Saving people.

Fear had rarely touched Jordan in his thirty-one years of life. But now, it plagued him.

He tried not to press too hard on the gas pedal.

The further he drove, the hotter it felt in the car. The rage grew, the closer he got. He slid off his jacket at a red light, despite the ten-degree weather.

The forty-minute drive to his office should've taken close to two hours, especially in the snow.

But he couldn't help himself. Maybe he could've, but he didn't care to.

JORDAN

Jordan pulled into the lot and reached into the backseat to grab the white sweater he'd thrown in there the night before, prior to taking Nina up to bed. He parked smoothly, hopped out of the truck and walked fast to his building, meeting the eyes of the federal agents who had delivered what he needed. They'd wait in the parking lot.

As he all but ran into the building, dropping the sweater on one of the couches in the lobby and heading straight for the stairs that led to the basement, Jordan's skin turned hotter. With each step, he was reminded of the night at the abandoned hospital, when he'd flown down corridors, looking for his love. The poor, brutalized and terrified love of his life.

A few feet further was a door with an alarm pad on it. He punched in his code and slammed it open.

Just steps into the giant, open basement, his eyes met theirs. The second he saw them, his skin crawled. It felt as if it would go up in flames.

Tristan, Emmett and Luke stood there, watching him, but Jordan hardly noticed them.

On the far left side of the basement were three detention cells, caging them in with vertical bars three inches apart. Holding cells for the criminals Jordan didn't wait for cops to apprehend, a place to keep them until they or the FBI showed up.

Two of them were occupied. Ryan was in one, Donovan in the other. Fear in their eyes.

He had not seen them since the night they took Nina against her will and tortured her.

Finally, he snapped his head in the direction of the three men closest to him. As they met his glance, his eyes flickered towards the door and back to them. Emmett and Luke nodded hesitantly, faces serious, eyes wide. They slowly headed to the door and Jordan's eyes flicked towards the cells again.

Tristan remained unmoving, eyes narrowed and intense, watching his brother.

Jordan turned his head back, trying not to get agitated with his brother but unable to reign in his rage.

"Go." His voice was low, deeper than usual. A growl, if Tristan had ever heard one. Commanding.

Tristan stared harder at his brother. After a moment of intense eye contact, Tristan said,

"Don't do something you'll regret."

His voice was surprisingly soft, in contrast to his somber face.

Jordan looked back at him, saying nothing. After a few moments, Tristan turned and exited the room. The steel door clicked shut behind him.

When he heard the sound, Jordan turned back to the cells. Every time his eyes landed on Ryan, his fingers twitched. He was flooded with a fury he had never known before.

He walked towards Ryan, whose knees were still wrapped, just like Donovan's. Ryan backed into the corner of his cell as Jordan unlocked it with his key. He ripped rather than slid the gate open.

"Jordan—" Ryan's voice rang quickly, weak with fear. Unlike how it was that night, when he arrogantly taunted Jordan on the phone, as though he was unstoppable, untouchable. No worry for his own safety.

Too confident.

Jordan didn't give him a chance to finish, grabbing him by the throat with one hand and slamming him against the wall. Ryan was four inches shorter than Jordan, his frame lanky. He had no fight in him.

Which was why he had to hit an unsuspecting woman in the back of the head, knocking her unconscious, so he could take her. Why he had to chain a five-foot-four female up to ceiling pipes in order to hurt her.

Jordan landed a hard kick to each of Ryan's knees, then kicked him in the side hard as he fell to the ground. Ryan grunted in pain with each blow to his injured joints, healing from gunshots to both knees, then groaned as he tried to crawl away on the floor.

He sputtered foul expletives, but he was so breathless from the pain that the words barely sounded.

Somehow, he'd thought he wouldn't get caught.

Idiot! he thought miserably to himself as Jordan wrapped his hand around one of his injured ankles, squeezed and jerked his arm back so Ryan would flip over. He shouted in pain.

Jordan put the tip of his shoe on Ryan's chest and pulled his shoulder out of place with one swift pull. Ryan shouted once more as the agony ripped through his arm.

"*Jordan,*" Nina had wept over the phone. Her sobbing voice rang in his ears as he tore the other shoulder out of place.

A few feet away, in his own cell, Donovan cowered in the corner, awaiting his own fate.

"*I love you,*" she'd wept, no doubt believing she would never say it to his face again.

Jordan pressed one knee into Ryan's torso, lifted his arm straight up and snapped it back against his thigh, breaking it. Ryan screamed.

The image of Nina cowering in the corner of the building porch, stripped down to nearly nothing in the freezing cold, flashed through his mind. The image of her screaming in agony from the pain of scorching iron against her skin. The image of her terrified eyes as twelve psychopaths yielding weapons prepared to chase her and murder her brutally. The images he'd been pushing away all these weeks. He let them come.

And snapped Ryan's other arm.

Again and again, Jordan pulled, snapped, twisted, broke, until Ryan was in so much pain he couldn't cry.

Weakly, wheezing hard through the agony, Ryan stared up at Jordan. His eyes were like fire—pale blue flames. He expected Jordan to look crazed, disturbed. He did not.

His eyes were perfectly sane.

Fiery, but calm. Jordan did not take pleasure in breaking or crushing Ryan's bones. He simply could not do anything but, as the picture of Nina, terrified, in agony, the sounds of her crying voice, the sight of her blood, all flashed through his brain.

He'd told them he would rip them apart. They tortured Nina anyway.

"You think you're God," Ryan sputtered over his wheezes, barely able to get the words out. Though the pain in his body was excruciating, he managed to express his hatred for Jordan.

"You aren't," he spat, blood falling out of his mouth alongside the words. "And we'll get you one day," he said, breathing hard. Then, suddenly, a rush of energy and adrenaline flashed through him and he raised his voice. *"They'll get you one day!"*

Jordan stepped behind Ryan and lifted him up by his head. Ryan's body was too broken to struggle.

"You'll burn in hell, you bastard," Ryan forced the words out of his mouth, adrenaline pumping. The pain had gotten so bad he couldn't see straight. Yet somehow, the words kept coming.

"You'll die!" he screamed. "They'll kill you! *They'll kill y-*"

With one swift twist of his arms, Jordan snapped Ryan's neck.

And that was it. He stood, not even out of breath. Stepping over Ryan's dead body, he exited this cell and moved to the next.

The anger in him was running rampant, yet he stayed calm as he snapped Donovan's bones apart, and killed him in the same manner he did Ryan, simply for being an accomplice. Complacent, enjoying himself while Nina was tortured.

Then, without having said anything at all, Jordan exited the jail cell and walked towards the basement exit.

Pulling open the door, he regarded Emmett, Luke and Tristan for just a second as they took him in uneasily.

Jordan's hair had barely moved from its position. He wasn't breathing hard. There was no sweat on his body. Just the slightest bit of blood on the arm of his long-sleeved green shirt. His face was empty as he brushed past them and up the stairs.

The three men knew, though it still stunned them to their cores, that both men in jail cells were dead. They hadn't been able to hear through the door or walls, but they knew.

"On the record?" Tristan asked, just loud enough for Jordan to hear as he climbed the stairs quickly.

Jordan didn't look back as he responded. "They escaped." His voice, flat and low, was just as empty as his face.

Tristan met the eyes of the two men he considered friends and nodded. The three of them entered the room, all inhaling deeply before letting their eyes touch the bodies that, less than ten minutes prior, were living.

As he approached them, he was only slightly surprised by their broken bones, their twisted limbs.

He'd wondered if Jordan would actually do it. He'd even warned him against it, calling to inform him that the FBI wanted to indict Ryan and Donovan. Jordan had actually taken a minute to answer his call, stepping out into the hallway while Nina slept in bed.

"Listen," Tristan had said carefully, "I don't know what you're planning on doing to them, Jordan. But no good standing with the Bureau will justify murder when suspects are in custody."

"Who said anything about murder?"

The coldness in his brother's quiet voice had sent a chill through Tristan. Jordan was not himself after what happened.

"Jordan…" Tristan began slowly. Jordan was silent, waiting.

"I don't think this is something they will cover for you. Whatever you plan on doing."

"I don't need cover." Then, Tristan had heard his brother move quickly, as Jordan descended the stairs.

Tristan didn't know what to say. He knew Jordan had killed before. They both had. Sometimes, they killed the bad guys, in a time of capture. Bullets flying, people running at them with knives.

Jordan consulted for the cops, the FBI. At one time, he'd worked for the Bureau himself. He'd gone on his own hunts and caught a psychopath or two on his own. Jordan had seen his fair share of bloodshed, and righteously.

But as far as Tristan knew, Jordan had never killed when not in defense of himself or another. He hadn't known for certain if that would change.

His suspicions that it might grew when he arrived at the abandoned hospital to find Ryan Clayton and Donovan Rivera shot in the legs, alive.

When he saw that they were still breathing, he realized the possibility of what Jordan might do.

He, Liza, Emmett, Luke and Eve all knew that if Jordan had wanted them dead, they would be.

Jordan didn't have to say it. They'd known. Tristan had known.

And though he'd been uncertain if Jordan would actually do it, he knew now that when he said he would rip them apart, limb by limb, he meant it.

Staring at the mangled bodies of two men, for whom he couldn't bring himself to feel any sympathy, he just hoped his older brother would finally sleep peacefully after this.

JORDAN

As Jordan walked through the lobby and made his way towards the restroom halfway down one of the administration halls, he slid off his slightly bloodied, forest-green shirt. Once inside, he assessed himself in the mirror quickly.

He glanced at his face to make sure there was no blood. He assessed both arms to ensure there were no cuts where Ryan and Donovan had grasped uselessly, trying to fight their way to survival.

His skin was smooth, except for the little bit of their blood on his hands.

His jeans were black, but no blood had touched them anyway. His hair was just slightly disheveled. He brushed it back into place with his hands, after he washed them, scrubbing hard to get the blood off, to get *them* off. He couldn't touch Nina with such filthy fingers.

When he was clean, he exited the restroom quickly, green shirt in hand, and walked through the lobby, grabbing the white sweater as he walked by. He slid it on before he pushed open the door to the entrance of his building and exited into the cold December air.

He dropped the green shirt on Tristan's car, knowing he would handle it for him.

As he drove, he felt anxiety crawl through him. He wanted to be back with Nina so badly, but he felt agitated, slightly nauseous, and guilty.

He flicked his eyes up towards the sky and asked God to forgive him. Then he remembered Nina on the cold porch of that office building, in the freezing night, rocking herself back and forth in terror, in agony, and didn't know what else he felt.

The guilt he certainly felt was for going back to Nina after doing something so dirty, so heinous. For constantly telling God he only killed when it was to help people, and he'd done it now, premeditated, when Ryan and Donovan were not a physical threat to anyone.

But it would torture Nina every day if she knew they were still alive. And what they'd done to her could very well take away her peace of mind for good.

If they were dead, at least she would not fear their touching her ever again.

I'm sorry, he told God. *I'm sorry.*

The only consequences to his actions in this life would be his own guilt and the stain on his soul.

Even confessing to a priest wasn't going to make the feeling go away. Only time could make it numb out a little.

But right now, he was feeling it. Maybe it felt stronger as it mingled with the agitation and anxiety. But he felt guilty, dirty and undeserving to go back to her, despite his pure desperation to.

How could he touch her with such filthy hands? He'd washed them of Ryan's and Donovan's blood, their skin, the lint on their clothes, but what he'd done, he could not so easily wipe off.

It made all of him dirty.

God wasn't the only one he needed forgiveness from.

He would have to tell Nina, or he would never sleep again.

At least one person in every FBI building throughout the country knew Jordan Asad's name.
There were, of course, rumors, invented reputations that aligned with whatever an agent or cop wanted to believe. But even the people directly involved in this situation, who knew him better than the rest, were unfamiliar with the love he had for that girl.
When Kelly Spencer had seen him, before the family had arrived, he could barely get a word out of the boy. Jordan hardly even looked at him. He only had eyes for Nina.
And those eyes were worse than Kelly had ever seen Jordan don. While Jordan was only with him at the Bureau for six months, they'd run into each other a lot over the years, working the same cases. Jordan consulted, and sometimes the Bureau aided him. That was just how it went with Jordan Asad.
So, he'd been around Jordan long enough to know that he was not well.
The rage was evident from the first look Kelly took. His usually smooth face was stiff, lips flat, eyes hard. They were full of so much restlessness and pain that he almost looked crazed. And he radiated rage.
The purple underneath his eye sockets and the weight he'd lost made it evident that Jordan was not handling this situation well internally.
Which signaled to Kelly that Jordan was wholeheartedly in love with this girl.
And when Kelly had seen the poor, innocent thing, lying in her hospital bed, exhaustion showing even in her sleep, the gauze around her thighs and up her groin, he swallowed hard. *How could it have happened to her, of all people? Jordan's girlfriend, OF ALL PEOPLE*, he asked himself.

He'd been told, over the phone, that she was taken. At that time, the FBI didn't have access to the livestream. Jordan's team had not sent it over by the time Kelly had gotten on the flight, and then it was too late. He couldn't watch a livestream of a girl being tortured while on a flight.

He got notice before he landed that the girl was safe.

He'd immediately gone to the crime scene, then back to Jordan's facility, where he finally watched the footage himself. Watched this girl he did not know scream in agony, weep for his former agent, one he had not known to ever involve himself with a woman.

He couldn't imagine how Jordan was feeling.

Kelly knew Jordan was a good kid. A good man with a good heart. That was why he chose to save people for a living.

Jordan had made a lot of money, more money than Kelly would probably ever see in his life. Jordan didn't need to work. He could've lounged around for the rest of his life and been just fine.

Instead, he chose to help people, to use his skills and the money he'd earned and save lives. Kelly had always known his intentions were pure.

But when he saw the way Jordan looked at this girl, however, he began to wonder how pure those intentions would be if he got his hands on the oddly still living Ryan and Donovan.

After Tristan called and informed him, tense and as implicit as possible, that Ryan and Donovan escaped, Kelly could only think of the good he'd always seen in Jordan.

And that the only thing that could've brought him to the lethal state that Kelly had always sensed was in him was an excruciating amount of pain.

Nina

"Hey, Jordan's back, Nina," Zana informed me. My heartbeat picked up slightly.
I looked at the clock. It was 3:22.
Less than four hours.
It may have only been a couple hours with my family, but I'd gotten restless rather quickly, missing Jordan and wishing he was around.
I was working on removing my dependence on him, however, and would not let myself call him, unless it was horribly urgent and necessary.
I didn't even text him. I wanted to, to at least see how work was going and make sure he was okay, because I had no idea what he was doing. I didn't bother him. I let him do what he had to do, forcing myself to be patient. I wanted to show him that it was okay to leave me on my own.
Sitting with my family as we talked to each other, I zoned out for a little bit. I wondered how I would've felt if Jordan had let me stay home by myself. The thought alone made my heartbeat pick up.
I wasn't ready for that yet. I wasn't ready to be alone in the house, to be in the same situation I was in before I was hit on the head and taken.
Today was proof that I could be without him. It sucked, but I did it. I just didn't know if I could be by myself yet.
One thing at a time, Nina.
I stood up slowly, pressing my palm into the arm of the couch for support. This was how I always stood. The burns didn't sting as much if I straightened my legs slowly. I only needed the support because I'd been sitting for so long, and standing made me lightheaded.

But my family didn't know that. My brother, Zana, and my mother rushed to help me. My father watched with wide eyes.

"I'm fine, guys," I told them lightly, smiling as much as I could. Being with them had been nice, and I was in a lighter mood than I thought I'd be, despite being without Jordan.

"Can someone let Jordan in, please?"

Zana turned and headed towards the front door as I convinced my brother and mother to give me some space, assuring them I was fine. I rounded the corner of the living room and headed towards the front door, just a few yards away. Jordan was just stepping in.

"Hi, baby," I said, smiling at him as I limped over to the door. The cold air landed on my skin.

Jordan's eyes touched my face, and the look in them was abnormal.

His face was smooth, except his eyebrows were knitted together slightly, as though something was wrong. Kind of like when he got bad news about a case.

Except he seemed uneasy; he was stressed out and unable to conceal it.

His voice reflected the idea as well. "Hi, my love," he said, offering me a smile, which, though small, seemed genuine, even surrounded by the angst he emanated. He wrapped his arms around me, and I felt them flex against my back.

I pulled back just enough to look up at him, touching his cheek gently.

"Is everything okay?" I asked him.

"Yes, my love," he said, voice low. He certainly wasn't in a good mood; not angry, but rather simply unhappy, stressed.

"How are you?" he murmured, touching my face lightly.

"I'm okay." It was true. Though I'd missed him, I felt oddly calm. I chalked it up to being in the house that would always be my home, the safe place of my childhood. Here, what had happened to me wasn't possible. I assumed that was the reason for my emotions' unusual stillness. The thought of leaving the warmth here made me a little sad.

"Yeah?" Jordan assessed my face, but his eyes seemed far away. He was thinking of something else.

I wanted to ask him about work but decided to wait until we were alone.

"Let me grab my jacket and we'll go."

"You're gonna leave so soon?" my mom asked, surprise and sadness in her voice.

Sad as that made me, I wanted to go home, wanted to talk to Jordan until the distress in his eyes was gone.

"Yeah, ma, but we'll come back soon." I told myself that I meant that as I hugged her.

Then, as I limped over to the door, my mom by my side, Jordan kissed her cheek and said goodbye to everyone else with me.

"Bye, guys," they chorused.

Jordan held on to my arm as we stepped over the snow and ice on the walkway.

When we made it to the truck, Jordan opened the passenger door for me. I stepped up on the running board, but the step into the vehicle itself was higher and it hurt me to try it. So Jordan gave me a boost every time.

As he stepped around the front of the truck to get to his side, I thought something was off about him; I couldn't put my finger on what.

Jordan hopped into the car and started it immediately. He was far away.

"How did everything go?" I asked him lightly. I watched his face carefully.

He looked at his mirrors as he reversed the truck into the street. When the car was in drive again, he responded, "It went as planned."

"What did you do? Was there, like, paperwork or something? Was it tracking stuff, or…?"

Jordan glanced over at me and kept his voice smooth and low. "How about I tell you about it when we get home? I want to know how your day went."

I felt my eyebrows crinkle together slightly.

Jordan had never denied me an answer to a question.

"I missed you, my love."

Though the added sentence sounded sincere, I couldn't help but wonder if he'd said it because he knew his response was odd.

"I missed you, too," I said carefully, knowing my face was skeptical at this point. But I didn't speak on it further.

Jordan noted my expression, and I could sense him get restless. He didn't want me to wonder, but he also didn't want to tell me what he was thinking.

He was hiding something. Jordan was hiding something from me.

The revelation hit me hard and suddenly made me feel extremely uneasy.

"How did it go?" he asked calmly. I stared at him hard.

"It went fine." I was beginning to feel the anxiety creep into my chest. I wanted to know what was wrong, but if he wanted to wait until we got home, I wouldn't push.

"Were they nice to you?"

"Yeah, they were." I didn't say anything further. Every time I answered a question, I wanted to ask one of my own.

Jordan glanced at me again, and by now there was unhappiness in his eyes. He didn't speak for a few more moments, and the energy in the car made me slightly nauseous. I'd never felt this far away from him. It happened so suddenly, with just a few sentences.

I leaned onto my door and put my head against it. The discomfort made me want to curl up and go to sleep. I missed our bed.

"Are you tired, honey?" Jordan asked softly, and the sudden softening of his voice brought a little normalcy back. Was I just being sensitive? Was what happened to my nerves and mental health finally affecting our relationship?

"Yeah, a little," I told him quietly. I turned my eyes to the passing stores out the window and observed the snow everywhere. A small pawn shop

JORDAN

called *Rickey's* had a thick layer of white covering its old-school, red LED sign.

"Why don't you take a nap? Before you know it, we'll be home."

I shook my head. "No, I don't really feel like I can sleep right now."

"How come?" he asked gently. The deepness of his voice soothed me a bit.

"I dunno." I shook my head again, feeling childlike for some reason. I felt vulnerable. Like anyone, including Jordan, could get the best of and do whatever they wanted to me, and I'd put up no fight.

It had to be the effects of that night making me feel this way. It had to be.

We spent most of the drive home in silence, and observing Jordan's uneasy, slightly agitated demeanor, hard as he tried to hide it, made me more and more antsy.

I was so grateful when we finally made it home. As we stepped inside and took off our jackets and shoes, my courage came back. I set all my bad feelings aside, grabbed his hand and brought him to the family room.

As he sat next to me on the couch and looked at my face, I realized what looked different about him.

He'd changed. Before he'd left, he was wearing a dark, forest-green shirt that I liked. I thought it complimented his skin and hair.

But now, he was wearing a soft, loose white sweater. When had he even grabbed that before we left? Did he have it in the car?

"You changed," I observed. He nodded, as though he was waiting for the question.

That didn't matter as much to me as what had happened at work. However odd it was.

"What happened today?" I asked. "You're acting weird and it's making me nervous." I chose honesty, figuring it was the best route. I wanted to wipe out this uncomfortable air around us as quickly as possible.

Jordan stared at me with intense eyes. I stared back, not shrinking underneath the weight as some might. Waiting.

Finally, he exhaled quietly through his nose. "There is something I need to tell you," he confessed, his voice low.

Instantly, my pulse picked up its pace.

"Okay," I said, my voice rising, along with the anxiety. "Tell me. Please. Tell me fast. I'm getting nervous."

Jordan's eyes widened as he realized how uncomfortable I was becoming. He quickly took my hand and slid closer so that our bodies were pressed together.

"It's okay," he murmured quietly, but the words didn't touch his eyes. I didn't respond, just looked at him with wide, nervous eyes.

"Nina," he began quietly, "Ryan and Donovan did not die that night at the hospital."

He paused for only a moment. Before I could even process his first words, he added, "They were alive until today." Jordan's face and body were calm, but I could see the fear in his eyes. He couldn't hide it.

What was he afraid of? Was he afraid I'd panic? That I would be mad at him? Was I mad at him? What had he said a second ago? Ryan and Donovan…

They were alive.

Ryan and Donovan were alive.

This entire time, since being tortured at the old hospital, I'd thought they were dead.

That was how I slept at night. By telling myself that the people who'd hurt me were gone.

Hadn't Jordan told me they were dead? Hadn't he…?

I struggled to remember our conversations in the hospital room. Though we hadn't discussed the night since we returned home, we spoke of it there. What was it he'd said?

"I got them, baby."

"You said…you said…" My head was spinning. I pulled away from Jordan, easing my hand back and sliding down the couch a few inches. I stared at him with wide eyes.

"You said you got them." My voice was gravely low. "You told me you got them."

Jordan's eyes were intense and worried as he watched me. He inched closer to me to bring me back next to him, but I pulled back some more.

"No, no." I looked at him with terrified eyes.

Jordan's eyes widened, stunned, his eyebrows knitting together in devastation. I shook my head, my own words throwing me into an even deeper dizzy spell. I'd never rejected Jordan. I couldn't think straight, didn't know what I was feeling enough to consciously choose my words. Was I overreacting?

I stood up and limped towards the hallway, heading for the stairs.

I didn't know where I was going, didn't know what I wanted to do, but I just moved numbly away from him as I tried to process the emotions coursing through me.

"Nina," he said, his voice filled with an aching worry, with devastation, as he followed me. He did not touch me, though he easily met my pace and could have.

I was lightheaded, not just feeling off from the anxiety. I grabbed onto the banister at the bottom of the stairs and forced my way up the seven steps to the circular landing. Instead of continuing, I grabbed onto the wall and slid down to sit. There was no way I could make the entire trip upstairs.

Jordan brought his hands out to catch me, but I slid down slowly so he didn't have to. He exhaled hard through his nose in frustration. I barely heard it; just on the outskirts of my consciousness did the sound register.

Knees up to my chest, I gripped both sides of my head and tried to get my mind together, tried to get the grainy warmth and spinning in my brain to stop. If I focused hard enough, maybe it would.

Except I couldn't think of the physical sensation that long. I just kept thinking, over and over again, that they were alive.
Ryan and Donovan were alive.
They were alive.
I rocked myself back and forth just slightly. I didn't understand what was happening to me physically, and again I wondered if I was overreacting. It was hard to be present in that moment. Emotions were racing underneath the shock.
Eventually, they overflowed. Nausea filled my throat as anxiety soared inside me, and grief made my face hot and eyes wet. A sob built in my throat, and my body trembled. They could've taken me again. Could've been watching us outside of our house. The irrational thoughts flooded me. "They've been alive this whole time," I muttered to myself. "This whole time." I continued to rock myself, lost in the terror, then realized a warmth that wasn't from my body. I turned my head.
It was Jordan. Jordan. He'd been here the whole time. He'd sat next to me and was staring at me with desperate, horrified eyes.
"Nina," he said, and it sounded as though he was aching. "Nina, honey. I'm sorry."
Sorry. He's sorry. Why is he sorry?
"Where are they?" I cried. *Where are they? How close are they? Where—*
"They were alive until today."
"Until today?" I cried, meeting his eyes. I felt the horror on my face morph into shock, noticing it because it paralleled how I felt. I stopped rocking, still trembling. I stopped crying and stared at him.
"You killed them."
"You killed them," I repeated quietly, staring at him. Jordan's eyes were full of grief, but his face read as though he anticipated this.
I was still so confused. Ryan and Donovan were alive this whole time, and today they died. Today, they died because Jordan took me to my parents' house and went and killed them.
How would I explain that to Dr. Rodriguez?
I wouldn't. In that moment, the thought of keeping a secret like that was overwhelming. I put it out of my brain as my mind flickered elsewhere. Racing.
"Did you shoot them?" The words barely came out.
He shook his head, staring at me regretfully. Loathing every second of this.
"How?" I mouthed.
Jordan looked at me with sorrow in his eyes, shame knitting his eyebrows together and keeping them there.
"I don't want to tell you," he said gently, quietly.
I couldn't bear it. The sobs began to shake me again.
But I wasn't sad that they were dead. I hadn't even fully processed that they were alive after that night.

I just couldn't wrap my head around the fact that he'd left me to go take two people's lives.

Was I mad at him?

Was I disgusted with him?

Afraid of him?

I shook my head at my own thoughts, realizing that none of those things were true. I wanted the shock overwhelming me to go away so I could know with certainty how I felt. Did I love him still? Did I know him? Did I really know him?

As I rocked myself once more, I repeated the words over and over again in my brain. *Jordan killed them today. Jordan killed them today. Jordan killed them today.*

I looked over at him. Suddenly, I was desperate. Desperate to come to terms with this and be done with it.

Is it such a bad thing? I asked myself. I knew he'd killed people before, because they were the bad guys. But this was premeditated. It had to be.

It had to be.

So what?

As the words came to the front of my mind, they squashed every other thought, fear and worry. *So what?*

I stilled once more and stared at Jordan. Feeling the shock ease slowly. Letting myself accept what happened. I was shaken still, but trying to focus.

Of course you still love him.

For reasons I couldn't articulate, even to myself, I felt so much grief. I put my head down, slid my legs forward and leaned into him.

He immediately wrapped his arms around me. Comfort came and settled all around as I cried quietly.

"I'm sorry," he whispered. "Shh. Shh. I got you. I love you," he soothed amidst his apologies.

My heart ached. I held on for a while.

I wanted him to feel me, too. I felt sorry for not letting him touch me, for rejecting him; he probably thought I was afraid of him.

This had to be hard for my love. Jordan was not a killer.

This I was sure of. Jordan did not kill people for pleasure.

Of course I knew him and still loved him.

He did it for me.

Maybe not entirely, because I knew the fury he felt towards Ryan and Donovan after what they did. To me and all those people. The way they flipped our lives upside down.

But I knew the rage he felt over what they'd done to me. I'd heard it with my own ears, on the phone as Ryan tortured me.

After contemplating what I wanted to say first, I leaned back just enough to keep his arms around my body, touching me.

I sniffed, looking into his sorrowful eyes. Even at a time like this, his pain still brought me so much of my own.

"Don't say that. Don't say sorry." My voice was thick and nasally. His eyes were full of grief.

I held onto his waist to have some part of him to hold in our odd position. Unable to keep still, I scrunched his shirt on either side, over and over again, just to have something to do with my restless hands.

I could see he was full of so much pain. And now, I could tell that he was also anxious, which broke my heart all over again.

My baby, the calmest, most secure person I'd ever met. Anxious. Unhappy. Scared, even.

Of himself? Of me? Of my reaction? Of God?

Likely all of those things. It made me ache to see him suffer.

It was so quickly that I pushed away my own shock and fear, accepted what had happened and was ready to comfort him however he needed, as though I'd needed any more certainty that this man was my soulmate.

I wanted him to make peace with it, too.

"You should be disgusted with me, I think," he said quietly.

My eyes widened with horror. Though I'd asked myself a similar question earlier, it pained me to know he was aware of the possibility, the *probability*, and that he believed he deserved it.

Shaking my head, I leaned forward to bring our bodies closer together. His warmth was comforting. This was still my Jordan. Nothing had changed.

"No, I shouldn't be." Tears slid down my face. "I know you did it for the right reasons. Reasons that weren't evil."

"I killed." It was a slow whisper. "Despite my reasons, I still killed, not in self-defense or defense of anyone at that moment."

He blinked, his eyelids heavy. "But I would do it again. And again, and again. I'll kill anyone that tries to hurt you, *tries*, because no one ever, *ever* will again. I'll do it all over again. If that makes me *evil*..."

His voice returned slightly on those last words, aggressive still but sad as all hell.

"It doesn't," I cut in. "It does not." I brought my hand out from under his arm and took his cheek in it. I couldn't bear to hear him say these things about himself.

"You did it for me." My voice cracked on the last word. "You are *nothing* like them," I whispered viciously. "They are *evil*. You are so pure." I had to prove it. Had to make him prove it to himself.

"Did it make you happy?"

"Not even a little," he said immediately, and his exhausted voice demonstrated his sincerity. He stared into my eyes, and his were worn.

"I love you," I told him.

"I love you, too." He was aching. I could hear it in his words.

"Do you wish, even a little bit, that you hadn't done it?" I stroked his cheek with my thumb.

"No."

Jordan squeezed his arm around my waist. "I'm sorry I didn't tell you they were alive." He swallowed, face full of regret.

"I need you to know, Nina," he began, the deepness of his quiet voice cutting through the air with its intensity, "the reason I didn't tell you is that I didn't want you to be scared."

He paused in between sentences. "And to think that you weren't safe. Not because I ever intended to keep what I did today from you.

"And if what I did makes you want to be apart from me, now, or at any time, I will go." His words softened into a whisper. "Or I can take you to your mom and dad, or help you find another place to live. But I will go. You don't have to be okay with it because of what they did to you."

His eyes watered.

I couldn't breathe.

"Jordan, stop," I said, the words barely there as more tears fell from my eyes. "Stop, stop, stop."

I took his face in both of my hands now and inhaled sharply. "No. No," I said viciously, even as I cried. "Please. Please. Please don't leave." He nodded quickly, his eyes softening. He blinked away the tears.

The thought of Jordan leaving for good, temporarily, even, made me nauseous again, made my throat, jaw, and chest hurt.

"Okay, okay," he whispered soothingly, but I spoke over him.

"I love you," I begged in my pitchy, crying voice. "I know you didn't want me to be scared. I know. I'm not mad at you. I'm not mad."

I didn't think he was selfish for making me deal with the knowledge that my boyfriend had killed, and on my behalf.

Jordan's honesty meant more to me than any of that. He wanted me to know who he really was, the things he did, the things he was capable of, and his reasoning for it. He told me, fully aware that I could be horrified, disgusted. That I could leave him, after he'd put his soul on the line for me. That I might tell someone. He knew what he was risking.

He told me, anyway.

I loved him regardless of what he'd done.

"I don't want you to be sad," I told him. "I know this is hard for you. I know. You aren't a killer."

"Don't worry about me," he murmured right away. "Don't worry about comforting me. That's not your responsibility."

"Yes, it is!"

"No, I knew what I was doing. I don't deserve any comfort. You don't have to tell me what I did was okay." His eyelids went low.

"But that's how I feel," I told him. "It doesn't matter to you how I feel?"

"It doe—"

I shook my head. "Of course it doesn't," I muttered to myself. I met his eyes. "It's not all about me. I'm sorry. That was dumb."

"It matters to me what you think of me more than anything in the world." His words were clear and fast, his voice hard.

"I just don't deserve your comfort, and you don't need to give it to me."
My body was starting to ache. The grief of this whole situation was taking over me.
"I love you," I repeated, voice as firm as his was. "You don't deserve to feel guilty.
"I'm not justifying murder," I whispered. "But this wasn't evil. It wasn't evil. You have a pure heart, Jordan. Nothing can convince me otherwise. You spend your life helping people when you don't have to. You don't have to work, you don't have to employ people, you don't have to save people's lives. You could sell your technology and make more money, but you keep it, because you don't want it to get into the wrong hands. So you use it for good.
"You saved my life," I went on in a whisper. "You saved me and got rid of them, of that *filth*, so I could sleep at night. So what if you were angry? So what? So what if you're happy they're gone? I'm happy they're gone."
"I broke their bones," Jordan said quietly. "I tortured them."
His eyes were exhausted, as though the guilt had settled into his cells and was weighing on him too heavily for him to bear. The pain in them was agonizing.
This piece of news was startling but didn't disturb me. My face didn't change.
"I don't care," I whispered. "I just don't care." I stared into his eyes, unflinching, unmoving.
He shook his head slightly, not breaking his tormented eyes from mine. "Nina." His voice was barely there. "I'm so sorry." His devastated eyes, heavy eyelids, and his defeated, empty face made my lips tremble and chest ache.
"No, no, why? Why, baby?"
"What I did to them will never take away what they did to you." His voice was lower than I'd ever heard it. It was as though something was bearing down on him.
"Wha—no, love, I..." I didn't know what to say. "I can sleep at night, Jord," I whispered intensely.
"But it's not going to take it away, Nina, and I'd do anything to make it go away. I told you I would protect you, and I left you." His deep voice cracked throughout the sentence.
I blinked, realizing what I'd been missing.
The image of twenty-three-year-old Jordan, leaving his position at the FBI after six months, defeated, buying a house an hour away from his parents and isolating himself from the people he loved and the people who loved him, flashed through my mind.
Because he felt so guilty for the lost lives they didn't save in time. For the people who were only saved after they were brutalized.
I remembered just a few weeks before, sobbing for him in his arms over the pain he must have felt after seeing all of the horrible things he'd seen.

He'd told me I was an angel for caring. He'd told me he wasn't hurting, but I knew he was.

They'd tortured people for months and told Jordan it was his fault, that everything they were doing, all the people they were killing, was because of him. When he already blamed himself for not getting to the lost victims in time, the cruel people of this cult told him it was blood on his hands. I truly didn't realize to what extent he was hurting. But he was.

And he *still* was, worse than ever now, because it was me that he didn't get to in time. Before they hurt me. Because, to him, he'd broken his promise. I knew he hadn't, that he didn't *let* them, that it happened because he needed to go and no one anticipated they were outside our home. That he didn't know what was going to happen and never would've left if he had. But to Jordan, it was a broken promise, the gravest promise he'd ever made.

"Jordan," I began, eyes wide. I put my hand over my mouth, tears forming. *What he must be feeling...*

"I never should have left you, Nina." He shook his head, his face crumpling. "They did it because of m—"

"Because they're evil," I interrupted, taking his face in my hands. "They did it because they're evil. It is not your fault. *Not* your fault." The guilt on his face, in his sad eyes, was making me feel weaker still. Brought me a worse version of the aching that possessed me that day in his arms, after the horrible livestream and the reality hit me that he'd seen it, countless times. Too many times. He was hurting so much more than I'd imagined. My jaw trembled.

He stared at me, not saying what I knew he was thinking. That it *was* his fault. That he was in so much pain he couldn't speak.

I sat up on my knees quickly and wrapped my arms around his neck, holding him tight. He brought his arms around my waist and held on.

"I'm sorry," he whispered. "I'm sorry I did this to you. Everything I did to you. I'm so sorry."

That took me over the edge. Hot tears poured down my cheeks fast, one after the other.

"Jordan," I managed. "Stop, baby, don't say that. You didn't do anything to me."

I pulled back, sucking in as much air as I could and taking his face in my hands.

"I know what you're doing to yourself," I told him. "I know."

The pain in his eyes was too much to bear. I wanted to rip it out of him. I pulled him right back to me. He settled his cheek on my shoulder, leaned on me; I wanted him to seep into my body.

"I know you're killing yourself," I told him, steadying my voice as I whispered intensely into his temple. "I know you're killing yourself, baby. You have to stop.

"You have to let that guilt go." Tears poured down my cheeks, but I continued whispering into his skin as he turned his head, cheek on my shoulder looking out, then face back into my neck then back again, unable to settle.

"It's not your fault, baby. What they did to me, it's not your fault. What they did to those people and said was because of you, for you, it wasn't your fault either. Those people you worked so hard to help when you were at the Bureau, it wasn't your fault."

Jordan inhaled sharply, but the air seemed to cut off fast. As it did when you were trying not to sob. His body shook slightly against me.

The grief was unbearable; I could hardly breathe as I felt him lose control. I continued to soothe him, maintaining myself as best as I could. I tightened my arms around him, and he tightened his around me.

"It's not your fault, Jordan. You have to let go of that guilt. I know you're killing yourself," I repeated. "I need you to stop, Jord, I need you to stop doing that to yourself."

I felt his tears against my skin; he released short, quaking breaths into my neck.

"I love you," I whispered. "It's okay, my love. It's okay."

He was feeling it. What he was always hiding, stifling, had gotten to be too much. Jordan was in so much pain that he couldn't hide from me anymore.

"It's okay. It's okay, baby. It's okay to cry," I assured him, knowing he was fighting it.

"It's not your fault. It's *not*. It never was," I reiterated, again and again, needing him to hear it enough times that he would consider it.

"I know it's so hard to let go of all that guilt, all that pain. I know. I love you so much. I need you to try.

"I need you to stop torturing yourself."

Jordan cried into my shoulder, my neck, though barely any sound came from his voice. It was hard for him to breathe; I could hear it.

I kept his head against me, running my hand over his hair, turning to kiss his temple, again and again, as I whispered soothing words to him, promising him it was okay, telling him I loved him.

Eventually, he stilled in my arms, sniffling once or twice before all I heard was his breathing.

I continued holding him against me, eventually shifting from my position on my knees and sitting down, pulling him with me.

Jordan pulled his face back, then.

His eyes and cheeks were wet, the gleam of the tears against his diamond blue eyes, the red around the edges both so foreign. They had sunken in slightly, the bags underneath them prominent, worse after crying.

It hurt too much watching and feeling him cry to even acknowledge how stunned by it I was.

He watched me for a few moments, the most vulnerable I'd ever seen him. I simply looked back with gentle eyes, stroking his temple with my thumb, holding his cheek in my hand.

"I love you so much," I whispered.

He blinked slowly, his eyelids heavy as his face smoothed into the expressionless look I knew him for. Not hiding, just blanking out with exhaustion.

After a few moments, though I thought he would say nothing, he replied, "I love you, too." His voice was rough, scratchy, cracking on every word. But he had to make sure I knew. Always loving, caring for me, making sure I knew he loved me.

After a few moments of staring at his beautiful, exhausted face, I told him softly, "We're gonna go to church."

Jordan kept his eyes locked on mine. He nodded slowly, and nearly inaudibly said, "Thank you."

I pulled him in, wrapping my arms around his neck as he wrapped his own around my waist. We held each other tightly.

"You don't have to comfort me," he whispered slowly. He didn't have enough strength to speak louder. I held him tighter. "But you are, anyway. Thank you."

He was never so vulnerable with me. I felt open, as though my chest was split apart and love was flooding in.

"We're comforting each other," I whispered back. "That's how it's supposed to be."

I pressed my cheek into his shoulder and held on for a while. We rocked slightly. His warmth calmed my own restless nerves.

"We're gonna be okay," I murmured finally.

Jordan pulled back. Now, his eyes were calmer. His face smooth, dry. The grief seemed to have eased.

"Yes," he told me, looking in my eyes. Confidence rang through his quiet words, settled on his face. His security was showing once more. "We are."

JORDAN

We had Christmas at our house.
The news Jordan had told me about Ryan and Donovan did not eventually disgust me, or make me fear him.
Instead, I felt calmer. It was as though, up until that day, there was a restlessness that disappeared when he told me they were gone. As though my body and mind knew, somewhere.
I felt more secure. The anxiety and depression were still a struggle, but I worked on it. I talked to Dr. Rodriguez twice a week. I didn't tell her that Jordan killed them. I just told her that knowing they were dead made me feel better. She was unsurprised.
Jordan and I went to church the day after he told me, and again a few days later, and then made it a mission to begin going regularly on Sunday.
I was happy we were defeating our demons together.
The flashbacks continued, but as the days passed, they lessoned. I limped less and less. The wounds were scarred over, and I could wear regular leggings without any bandages. It was nice.
I even wore a red dress, nice and long, down to my knees, on Christmas. A dress Jordan and I went shopping for together. I let him buy it.
Jordan made most of the arrangements for the evening. I was able to host without much issue. I still became tired easily, but Jordan bought me a frozen coffee the morning of; it helped the tiredness and my mood. I texted a picture of myself with it in my hands to Tristan, whose response made me laugh for five minutes.
WATERY MILKSHAKES, BABY

I'll bring five later and we can get caffeine high, rob Jordan and run away together

Jordan could not stop smiling throughout my laughing fit. Because I showed him what Tristan said, I thought he would playfully smack him later. Instead, he hugged him, then looked at me, speaking inaudibly. I wondered if he thanked him for making me laugh, or if I was just self-absorbed. Later that night, their eye contact every time I laughed made me think I wasn't.

That morning, I woke up to presents all over the floor around our Christmas tree. Big, small. Some covered with plain, colored wrapping paper, some with snowflakes, one with Santa, and many more. They were everywhere.

"What is this?" I gaped, my eyes huge.

Jordan smiled a small smile. "They're presents," he said casually.

I turned to him. "For your family, right? And mine?"

"No. Those are in the car. These are yours."

"Jordan." I didn't know what else to say. "Jordan."

I'd bought him presents too, of course. It was hard. What did you buy a wealthy man who could afford anything he wanted? What did you buy a person who hardly wanted anything?

It had to be the thought that counted. I knew he would like anything I got, but I was still nervous. I went back to my birthday planning and reconsidered.

I'd ended up ordering him a couple designer sweaters and t-shirts, a couple pairs of jeans, and a few other things. They only shipped to the store, and Jordan and I weren't going anywhere without one another lately, so I asked Zana to pick them up for me.

I also bought him another small, diamond cross. Jordan was not interested in anything flashy. If he were, I would've drained my savings.

When he opened the small, long box and saw it, he stared for a while. It made me so happy to see that he liked it, that it meant something to him. He finally looked up at me, wonder in his eyes. It made me feel full.

As he opened the last large box, I said, "This one isn't entirely selfless, because I'm sure I'll use it at some point, so I feel kind of bummy even gifting it."

When Jordan pulled out the box with the glass teapot inside, his eyes widened with understanding, then his face became solemn.

"My love," he began.

"We need one," I said quietly. "You drink a lot of tea."

He looked up at me, the affection emanating from him. He gently set the box down, took my face in his hands and kissed me. I smiled small against his mouth.

"Will this bother you at all?" he asked softly. "Even a little bit? Please tell me."

I shook my head. "I don't think so. I wasn't bothered by it when I saw it for the first time." I shrugged. "It's new. It's glass. Different."

"I love it." He kissed me again. "But we have to move it if it starts to bother you…"

"It won't." This I felt sure of. Oddly enough, the fact that it was glass eliminated the dreadful feeling I had when I'd looked at the steel one we had before. "It's really cool," I murmured. "It's stovetop compatible. And I like the way it looks, actually."

Jordan's lips turned up. "I do, too. Thank you, my love."

It took me a while to open all his presents. I couldn't help but feel guilty for all of it, and I told him so. He insisted I not allow myself to feel that way, that this made him so happy to do.

"I ordered most of it," he admitted. "I couldn't take you shopping for your own presents."

"Oh." I frowned. "I'm sorry. You could've gone; I would've been alright."

He shook his head. "I didn't want to. I ordered most of it while you were asleep."

I nodded, turning back to the presents.

I sat on the floor, wearing leggings and one of his loose sweaters to be comfortable for the morning. Jordan told me I had to be. He sat next to me. It was cozy as ever.

I'd unwrapped new white gold earring studs, which were more my style than hoops or anything long. A thin ring that looped around itself at the top, lined with tiny diamonds. A couple sweaters that I would later discover fit exactly right. A new pair of black boots. Pointy-toed, black pumps amongst a *load* of other heels. New running shoes.

Even a new laptop. "I don't know why I didn't get you your own months ago. I only realized that yours was slow when you asked to use one of mine for your sessions. Not my brightest move." There were still boxes on boxes left to open.

I shook my head, stunned, and thanked him. For the fifteenth time.

"I wanna show you something," he murmured.

He helped me up and led me to the library. As he guided me towards what had become my desk on the far side of the room, the desk I sat at with my laptop, I saw two long computer monitors facing away from me.

"Jordan, what's this?" I asked him, stunned once more. I rounded the corner and saw a small computer modem plugged in under the desk. The brand new, much longer and dark red wooden desk was covered with the new screens, a brand new keyboard and mouse, and a bunch of ink pens, markers, pencils, colored pencils, highlighters, all bundled up in their own holders. There was also a lamp on the far right side, perhaps to light up my end of the dimly lit room. He slid open the deep drawer on the left side of the desk, and it was filled with elegant notebooks of various sizes.

"Jordan." I could not believe my eyes.

"There's a printer," he murmured, pointing to the right. Sure enough, on a shorter extension of the desk was a printer that looked expensive. "And a scanner on top, in case you ever want to scan something in.

"This computer has a great processor; it's faster than even I thought it would be. And I figured you'd like having a place to write and see your writing on bigger screens."

"Jordan," I repeated, still unable to form other words. There was even a new office chair that looked comfortable enough to sleep in.

I turned to him, unable to lower my eyelids to a normal level. I wrapped my arms around his waist in disbelief.

"You didn't have to do this," I whispered, still gaping slightly, leaning back to see his face.

"I wanted to," he said softly back, smiling. It was small, but it was the most beautiful smile I'd ever seen.

"I love you so much," I told him, unable to comprehend the thousands of dollars he'd spent on this setup alone. "Jordan," I repeated.

"Thank you. *So* much."

He shook his head. "No thank you's."

"Oh, I'm gonna thank you," I told him. "I'm gonna thank you until Christmas ten years down the line."

He chuckled, pulling me in tighter.

"I barely got you anything!" I frowned, distraught.

"Nina, please, please." His face was gentle, eyes sincere. "Please don't worry about that, love. You got me gifts, and you didn't have to. I wasn't anticipating it."

"You thought I wasn't gonna get you anything?" I groaned. "That's even worse."

"No, no, listen to me. Your gifts mean so much to me," he whispered. "I am *so* happy."

I stared into his eyes and realized he meant it.

"Jordan," I told him, choking up a little at his generosity and the fact that he liked his gifts. "Thank you." Then tears streamed down my face.

I still couldn't believe he loved me so much.

"Don't be sad, my love," he whispered, wiping a tear away with his thumb. "I didn't mean to make you sad."

I shook my head. "I'm not sad. I'm happy. I could never thank you enough for all of this. Every single thing you've done for me. You *took me in*, you—"

"Woah, woah. I didn't 'take you in.' You moved in with me. We live together. You weren't a stray puppy." He caressed my cheek.

I frowned. It was worth a shot. "Then let me contribute to the mortgage payment."

Jordan threw his head back and laughed, a real, genuine laugh that was so lovely I couldn't be mad at him for it.

"Don't laugh at me." But I was chuckling too. His laughter was contagious.

He shook his head. "I'm not laughing at you." His eyes turned serious. "I would never."

He kissed my forehead then chuckled again. "I just wasn't expecting you to say that."

Jordan put his hands on either side of my face. "You're so funny; I know you weren't meaning to be, and I *know* you can afford it, so please don't think I was laughing at you."

I shrugged one shoulder. "Weeeeeellll. I knew you wouldn't let me, so it did sound funny." I smiled.

He kissed my lips gently. "You aren't paying *one* bill," he told me, as though I'd asked to pay them all and not half of one. And though he was serious, his smile was huge. I laughed, wrapping my arms around his waist.

"It's so good to hear you laugh," I whispered after a few moments. "And to see you smile."

He kissed my head. "I feel exactly the same way about you."

KAYLA KATHAWA

The New Year

Everyone always talked about what they wanted to change or accomplish during the New Year. Come January, people were filling gyms, training for marathons, starting educational courses, learning new skills. Setting goals. I avoided this mindset, always of the belief that it was better to set goals and work to better myself year-round.
But when the discussions began parading around, I thought of the novel that I'd left alone, due to my inability to conjure up ideas. Then I met Jordan, and my year took an unexpected turn. So I left it alone, choosing to spend every minute of free time I had with the love of my life.
After everything that happened in November, he thought I should stay home throughout January, give myself a little more time to recover, physically and emotionally. Part of me was relieved by the idea and thought of calling Steve, who had been gracious enough, after Jordan somehow delivered the news, to tell me to take as much time as I needed.
I worried, despite the patience my boss had shown thus far, that eventually, he'd want to permanently replace me. And I was beginning to feel lazy at home.
"You're recovering from something traumatic, my love," Jordan had told me. "You're the furthest thing from lazy. You need rest in order to recover. Physically and mentally."
He'd stroked my cheek and brushed my hair back from my face, lowering his voice to a whisper. "You've always been so hard on yourself, angel." His words made me feel soft, as he glided the back of his hand gently over my face. "Let's go easy until you're back at full strength. Please, my love."
I told him I'd take two weeks out during January and reconsider after that. After Christmas, I spoke to Steve myself for the first time since the

incident. Jordan had done the communicating or had someone else send emails for him.

Steve had asked me how I was feeling, his voice hesitant and much kinder than he'd ever sounded. He told me that the company was busy as ever, and that everyone missed me and was sending love and well wishes.

"I know I've been gone long," I'd said quietly, feeling Jordan's eyes on me from the kitchen. "And I know you've been having Elise fill in as an editor." I swallowed. "I know you want someone editing full-time, and that having Elise doing two jobs isn't sustainable." I took a deep breath. "So...if you want to find someone else, I understand."

"Well, Nina," Steve's voice was calm. My heart sank in anticipation of his agreement, but I knew my options were limited.

If I went back to work too soon, I would be unable to concentrate. Therapy was intensive, and my leg was much better, but the weight of the night in the old hospital and all Jordan and I had been through was still very much upon me. Upon us. Those two weeks in January were probably more necessary than I wanted them to be.

"I don't want to find anybody else. You've been with us a while now, and while Elise isn't having the easiest time, I'd rather wait for you to come back than to find somebody new.

"A couple-month leave isn't so abnormal. Now, I couldn't keep Elise doing this until *April*, but she's alright for now. What do you think about maybe starting back up from home? Less hours as well? And Nina," he added. "You can continue to work from home. Permanently, if you'd like."

I couldn't believe what I was hearing. I was certain he would agree that I was taking too much time and had to go. It wasn't his job to work with me, to help me integrate myself back in. He had a business to run. I wasn't expecting this kind of patience or kindness.

"I—wow. I think that might be good. Thank you..."

My voice trailed off. I was tired and surprised and couldn't think of what else to say.

"Of course." Steve's voice was kind. "When do you think you want to start back up?"

I turned my head in Jordan's direction but didn't make eye contact, forcing myself to decide on my own.

"I think I should take at least two weeks in January and then consider it from there. Jordan and my family think I should take longer, but I don't know..." I hesitated. "I think I should be okay at that point. I'm just really, really tired still."

"Listen, if you want to start back up in February, I can have Mary help Elise. Together, they'll be just fine going over everything. Now, do they have your attention to detail, or your eye for great writing? No, not really." I could hear the grin in his voice. I chuckled, flattered. "But they'll be fine."

"Thank you, Steve." I exhaled hard, feeling good. "I'm gonna call you in a few weeks. I really appreciate everything. I'm sorry to leave you for so long."

"Don't apologize," he instructed. "Just get better, and let me know if you need anything. Oh, and Nina?"

"Yeah?"

"I'm giving you a three-dollar raise."

My jaw dropped.

"Wha—well, thank you, Steve, but...what made you decide that?"

Pity?

"When you were gone, I realized just how much you do for me, and you deserve more. And the company didn't cover all of your leave. I fought for it, but you know how corporate is."

I was stunned. "I...wow. Thank you so much. That's so considerate."

When I got off the phone with him, my mouth stayed open as I sat there in awe.

After telling Jordan the news, his lips turned up.

"You deserve more than twice the entire rate, but that was still nice of him."

I shook my head, laughing.

Dr. Rodriguez thought it was *better* I go back to work sooner. And I agreed that it was the only way I would make progress easing back into my life again.

I didn't want to be a hermit, doing nothing all day long. I'd had social anxiety keep me on the brink of that for far too long.

I'd come too far in my life to let this thing that happened to me drag me back down now.

I wouldn't let it control me.

Jordan still insisted I take more time. I suspected this was in part because he was worried about being apart from me. And I didn't blame him for that fear. He'd been through hell, too. I thought he needed me just as much as I needed him.

Dr. Rodriguez could wait.

I agreed to take two more weeks off come January. Then, I'd log back into our portal from home and get started again.

Thinking of the two weeks in January that I knew I would be off made me feel refreshed. As I felt better, little by little, my itch to create came back.

It was funny to me how that happened after such a traumatic experience. But I didn't want to sit around and do nothing. Jordan and I would go out and spend time together, but every second of the day could not be spent glued at the hip. He had business to attend to, even in the other room.

And I had a brand new desk and computer.

In the afternoon on New Year's Eve, I sat down at my new, sleek desk and reconsidered the novel I wanted to write, for the first time in nearly a year.

JORDAN

As the screen flickered on and the computer lit up even faster than what I used at work, a flash of excitement pushed through me. I hadn't written in a long time.

I thought back to my Chaldean girl, the girl I never read about in fiction books. The Middle Eastern girl that twenty-something-year-olds, like myself, could relate to. The girl that women even younger and older, Middle Eastern or not, could connect with.

But how? What made a reader connect with a character besides in age, gender or ethnicity?

Their shared experiences. Emotions. Thoughts. Their fears, their joy, their pleasure.

Okaaay, I thought the word out slowly in my head, contemplating.

How would crime fit in? How would mystery? Romance?

I would have to balance it out and give the reader a divide between the girl's mind, her experiences, the things the reader could relate to, and the crime and romance.

But what crime? And with whom did she fall in love?

Is she a cop? Is she a victim? Does she fall in love with a cop? With a killer? Does she fall in love with the victim?

Is she unaffiliated with the police? Is she a federal agent? Is she the sister of a criminal?

I pondered these things for hours, typing out a bulleted list of all the possibilities. I thought back to a year prior when I couldn't even come up with one thing to put on the list.

I had fourteen pages full of ideas by the time Jordan stepped into the library. I glanced at the time. It was shortly after five, time for our evening together. I'd had a few hours of brainstorming, and he'd been doing something of which I was unaware, not in the library. When he stepped in, I saved my document and shut the computer down.

We'd decided to stay in for the New Year. Our parents wanted us to come over to each of their houses, but I didn't want to be around a lot of people. Even the ones I loved.

Jordan proposed going out, if I wanted. I contemplated getting dinner, even going to a movie, just getting out and being together. But, in the least depressed way possible, I just wanted to stay home. To be with him, and be cozy.

Especially after we'd taken hours apart, hours apart that we weren't used to.

It was easy to miss him, even when he was in the other room.

Standing, I took in his lovely smile.

"It makes me so happy to see you writing," he murmured, as I stepped up and took his cheek in my hand.

"It makes me happy, too," I said quietly. I reached up and kissed his lips softly.

When we stepped out into the family room, I smelled food.

"I ordered carry-out," he began slowly. "And I wanted to know how you would like to spend the evening. Maybe watch a movie, or just relax. I can run a bath..." He trailed off.

"I just want to get out of these clothes," I said quietly, feeling happy because of his gentle tone and at the prospect of getting comfortable for our night in. The leggings and sweater I'd been in all day needed to be retired.

"Mkay," he murmured, kissing my cheek. "Why don't you go take a nice warm shower and wear something comfy, and come back down and we'll eat?" His voice was soft, nearly a whisper. I wanted to wrap my arms around him and never let go.

"Will you come upstairs with me?" I asked quietly. "I won't be long in there; I just wanna get clean—"

"Of course I will, honey," he murmured, his lips in my hair. "I just have a couple things I want to get done before our night together, and then I'll be up there.

"You take your time," he murmured. "I'll be right there when you're done." He kissed my lips gently. "Can you pick out one of your sweaters for me?" I asked quietly. The hint of a smile that was lingering on his face since he came into the library grew.

"Yes, baby. I will." I hugged him a little longer and then went up to shower. When I got upstairs, I went straight to the bathroom and ran the water. Stripping down, I pulled my hair out of its ponytail and let it fall down my back.

As I showered, my mind wandered to the night we'd have together, and then back to the book.

I thought over the list I'd created so far of possible plots, characters, and themes, trying to listen to what my gut liked best. I wanted my story not to just entertain, but to touch people's hearts. And I knew I had a way of making people feel. They'd told me so over the years, as I blogged.

Taking my time to give Jordan a chance to do whatever he needed to do, I brushed through my hair in the shower and tried to think of stuff we could do besides sit together and talk.

Jordan typically didn't have much of a preference; he would be helpful in giving suggestions, but it seemed there were only so many options when we stayed in the house.

Maybe we would just sit together, eat and talk. We hadn't done much conversing in the last month or so. I'd tried to keep my feelings to myself, not let him see when I was in pain and how the night still ran through my mind at times.

But it was also hard for him to tell me things, because he worried so much about upsetting me. All he wanted to do, I assumed, was try and uplift me. And that was what he had done. He hadn't told me anything about him and how he was doing. Nothing about work and what was going on in the office.

How everyone was handling things. If he'd talked to Tristan and had seen how the FBI was working the case after what happened.

How he was feeling about the day he left me and went to Ryan and Donovan. How he was doing with God. We'd been going to church, but I never asked him what he was thinking or what he prayed for. That was personal, vulnerable, but I wondered if he would offer it up when the subject was broached.

I wanted him to start fighting again, to get in the ring or call up his trainers and once more begin practicing the arts he'd excelled in years ago.

I wanted to suggest that he take on another big venture outside of work, the way he'd created and designed his own web browser in his early twenties.

I wondered if he liked the idea of creating something new, the same way I did, after a year of not writing.

We could discuss all those things, maybe keep the heavy stuff out for the night. I thought it would be good to conjure up new ways to enrich our lives and get us out of the dark hole we'd fallen into. The hole out of which we were slowly rising, together.

Jordan and I were strong as a pair. It could've been so easy, after all that had happened, for one of us to want to leave the other, despite the love we shared. Something so traumatic could either bring two people closer or rip them apart. I tried to keep that out of my mind before fear got the best of me.

Jordan and I loved each other ferociously, unceasingly. This horrible situation managed to bring us even closer, bound us to one another.

Unless one or both of us fell out of love, which was unlikely, there wasn't anything more from this that seemed to stand a chance.

After maybe twenty minutes of contemplation, I began to get lightheaded. I hadn't eaten or drunk much, and the hot water wasn't helping. I'd spent enough time in the heat.

After I stepped out of the shower, I caught sight of myself in the mirror. I'd been so depressed for so long that I hadn't allowed myself to look, knowing it ripped me apart to do so when I felt this way.

But now, feeling warm and excited for the night with my love, I thought I would handle it better.

I assessed myself for a moment in the mirror. I'd put on a little bit of my normal weight, so I didn't look as sickly as I'd begun to. It may have been the first time in my life I didn't panic about gaining weight. Especially since Jordan had been pining for it, worried for my health.

My eyes were still so tired, sinking in more than they ever had, but the bags were smaller since I stopped crying as much. They were still more purple underneath than usual, but that was okay. My skin was oddly clear, missing even a single red spot. My dark hair had somehow thrived over the last few stressful months and grown two inches longer, touching my hip bone.

As my eyes trailed down lower, I noted that the burn on my leg was scarring up hideously. I'd been seeing it when I looked down in the shower and when I changed, but I hadn't looked at myself in the mirror and seen what they looked like on me overall.

The rectangular, swollen scar on my thigh was four inches long and half an inch wide. It was still red, and hadn't turned into that pinkish white that scars typically did with time. It moved horizontally from the inner edge of my thigh and outward.

The burn on my groin was not noticeable as I stood. I separated my legs apart a little and turned my knee outward. This burn was perhaps an inch and a half long and still red like the other.

They looked worse than I imagined.

I tried not to get sad, looking at them, but the disgust and unhappiness flooded through me anyway. The truth was Jordan hadn't ever seen me fully naked. The thought flashed through my mind that these burns on my body might be too repulsive for him to see and ever want to touch me.

I told myself repeatedly that that was not the case and never would be.

You know Jordan. You know how much he loves you.

But I couldn't quite shake the idea that, no matter how much he loved me, he wouldn't be able to ignore them enough to touch me. I remembered the times lust filled the air so strongly, the ravenous look in his eyes all the times we had to stop ourselves from going too far. Tears filled my eyes, and my throat began to close from those memories alone.

I worried he would never look at me that way again.

I thought of how my skin used to be so smooth. How my body was normal, scarless, before I was taken. He would never see me like that.

Seeing myself visibly frown as my throat ached, I forced myself to take deep breaths. I didn't want to ruin New Year's Eve with my love over this.

But what if this night is in vain, because the first time he sees your body, he decides he doesn't want you anymore?

The soreness in my throat and jaw got worse, and the tears overflowed down my cheeks, which had darkened slightly from the heat in the shower.

I slid on the silky panties I liked to wear sometimes.

The underwear looked wrong on me now. I looked abused. I looked like a victim who had no control over herself, who was being crushed under the weight of what was done to her.

I took a shaky breath.

No.

I would not allow it.

I decided I had to be brave and see for myself. I braced myself for his face to get solemn as he tried to hide his disgust, his agreement that my body did, in fact, look terrible. Undesirable.

Just tell him how you feel. He's always begging you to.

My jaw was trembling as I wrapped a towel around my nearly naked body, throat thick. I was sad that I was hurting on what was supposed to be our special night, celebrating nearly a year together.

JORDAN

I stepped out of the steamy bathroom and spotted Jordan laying out a sweater next to a few others on the bed. When he turned and saw me, his eyes landing on my face and then widening, he walked up quickly.
"What's wrong, my love? Is something hurting?" I shook my head.
"Is the water not getting warm—"
I kept shaking my head as he spoke and felt the sadness build up even more. Looking at him made it hurt worse. The idea that he wouldn't want me anymore. Tears welled up in my eyes.
"Nina, what's wrong?" He looked terrified and so concerned over what could be wrong.
"Jordan." I tried to speak as he took me in his arms. I sniveled, trying to think of what to say.
"What is it, my love?" He didn't bother to mask the horror and distress in his voice. We'd been good. I hadn't had any sort of episode in over a week. No flashbacks or nightmares that he knew of. I hadn't cried. I'd been okay.
"They look h-h-horrible." My voice cracked and wavered throughout the sentence. It was awful.
"What does, honey? What looks horrible?" But I could tell by the sadness in his eyes that he knew, or at least suspected, what I meant.
"My burns," I cried quietly. "They're gross. I-I-I looked at them for the first time in the mirror, a-and they're so bad, Jord, they're so bad."
I looked directly into his eyes, the despair possessing me. "You're never gonna wanna touch me." The onslaught of hot tears blocked my vision of his face. But not before it filled with devastation.
"Oh, honey," he whispered, and his voice was heartbroken. He pulled me against his chest and squeezed me, despite my wet hair soaking his shirt. After he kissed my head over and over, he pulled back just enough to take my face in his hands. He looked me directly in the eyes.
"Listen to me," he said firmly. "Listen to me. That is the furthest thing from the truth."
He kissed my lips hard. "Nina, I *love* you. I love you. No matter *what* changes about you over time, I will *always* love you." I cried harder, trying so hard to process the comfort from his words while balancing it with my misery.
"A couple scars will not and never would make me want and love you any less." His eyes were heartbroken, but his words were resolute. "*Nothing* could."
"You are my *love*, Nina. You are the great love of my life," he told me more softly, but his voice was clear. "I'm going to spend all my days wanting to touch you.
"You are just as beautiful as you've always been," he whispered fiercely. "And you still make my heart beat fast, every time I look at you."
I wept at his words. "But you haven't seen them," I cried. "You haven't seen what they look like now."

Jordan kissed my lips once more, starting off firmly and then gentler and deeper. I felt my weeping die down as I adjusted to the sudden love I was flooded with.

He pulled back and whispered, "I *have* seen them, at the beginning and a couple times since then. And it changed nothing, baby. It changed nothing."

I sniveled. After a few more kisses to my face and head, he pulled back and, looking into my eyes, whispered, "It's okay. It's okay," until I was just sniffling.

The short speech made me feel a little better, and though the heaviness lingered, I was stunned.

"Thank you for saying that," I told him, voice thick and sullen. "I love you."

"I love you, too," he said softly. "So much." I felt his soft lips against my temple.

"Come on," he told me, putting his hand on my back and guiding me to the bed. "I brought out some sweaters, and if you don't like any of them, I'll get some more."

But I spotted a large black crew neck with huge sleeves fitted at the wrists and picked it up. I loved those.

"No, I like this one," I told him quietly, trying to clear my voice so I didn't sound like I'd just been crying. "Thank you so much."

"Of course, honey," he whispered. "I'll wait outside while you change, if you'd like."

I shook my head. "No, that's okay." Sitting on the edge of the bed, I pulled the sweater over my head and down over the towel; then I reached over for the leggings I'd pulled out of the drawer before I showered and slid them up to my knees, standing to pull them all the way up, lifting the towel carefully with them so Jordan saw little to no skin.

He was watching me with gentle eyes. I went to the bathroom to get some tissue, blow my nose and dry my face, and once I'd made myself look somewhat normal, I went out and took Jordan's extended hand.

"Are you hungry?" he murmured as we made our way down the stairs.

I shrugged. "A little." I didn't have much of an appetite, but I wanted to make him happy.

"Okay." He kept his voice gentle. "Does anything in particular sound good?"

"I thought you already got food."

"I did," he said, stopping on the landing. The foyer was dark. I noticed that there wasn't much light coming from the family room or kitchen. "But if there's something you have in mind that I didn't get, I'll order it."

I shook my head. Always trying to spoil me.

I couldn't help but smile. "No, that's okay. What did you get?" I asked as we walked through the entryway and into the family room. I didn't hear his response as I absorbed what was in front of me.

The room was dark, and there were candles lit all over the house. In the kitchen, on the family room tables and stands, on the brick ledge under the TV. A fire was burning in the fireplace down beneath it. The curtains were closed, and the TV was on but muted. He'd piled a bunch of blankets and a couple pillows on the couch. On the center table, there was a bottle of wine and two wine glasses.

It was such a lovely ambience. My favorite kind. Warm, relaxed, cozy. I was taken off guard.

"Jordan—" I started, realizing we'd never had candles or had even lit a fire in the fireplace. We'd been so distracted in our first full winter together that we didn't think of it. It made this moment more special.

My mouth hanging open slightly, I turned my head in his direction slowly as he put his arm around my waist and kissed my temple. "What is all this? It's lovely," I said softly in wonder.

"You said to me earlier that you just wanted a cozy night in, you and me," he murmured. "I wanted to make the New Year as happy and comfortable as possible for you. As cozy as possible."

I tried not to tear up again as I held his hand and walked slowly into the family room.

"I love this," I whispered. It felt so warm, so comfortable.

Jordan was watching my face intently, lips slightly turned up at the corners. He seemed happy.

"Is there something you thought you might like to do tonight?" he murmured. "Even if you changed your mind about going out."

I knitted my eyebrows together. "No, no. This is perfect," I told him, feigning offense. "My boyfriend went through all this trouble to make the house amazing. Don't be rude."

His smile grew as he pulled me in for a gentle kiss. "It was no trouble at all," he murmured.

As he pulled me to the couch, he said, "Sit. I'm gonna grab the food, okay?"

I complied, still looking around the room slowly. "You never said how you felt about what I got," he said from the kitchen. "I'm bringing everything over."

"I'm sorry," I said calmly, feeling soothed by the environment he'd created. "I didn't hear you."

Jordan came over with dishes of food. He carried three things at once. A dish with chicken tenders, one with fries, and a bowl of salad. A grin grew slowly on my face as he walked fast back to the kitchen and came back with a bowl of soup and a plate of breadsticks. He left once more and came back with two plates and forks and spoons.

Seeing my face, he grinned.

I laughed happily, unable to control myself. What he'd done to the house, the food he'd gotten, the *look* on his face, were all too lovely for me to stay sad. I felt lighter.

I remembered the first night I ever came to his house, almost a year prior, when he'd bought the same huge assortment of food, because he didn't know what I liked besides chicken tenders, soup and fries. I had been so stunned by it I laughed.

Jordan sat down and put two blankets over me, then asked me what I wanted, so he could serve it.

I couldn't stop smiling as I shyly told him, "A little bit of everything, please." His smile grew so big that his almond-shaped, diamond blue eyes narrowed.

When he'd made us both a plate of food, he sat down right next to me. Though I felt a lot happier, my appetite still wasn't really there. I nibbled on everything he put me, watching him eat and forcing myself to do the same.

Numerous times throughout the night, he leaned forward and kissed my head, temple or cheek. After he did that now, he murmured, "I got wine, even though you don't really drink it. I thought it added to the ambience, and in case you wanted to sip it."

I didn't drink, as he said, but after everything he'd done, because it was New Year's Eve, and because our lives had been flipped upside down and everything was crazy, anyway, I poured us some white wine and we sipped it together. It wasn't so bad.

"Never were the biggest partiers, were we?" I said quietly, smiling as I sipped. Jordan's grin grew slowly. I lifted the glass. "Well, they can't call us nerds now." We laughed, and he leaned in with that fond look on his beautiful face and kissed my cheek again.

When we were done eating, he cleaned up and refused to let me help. When the food was all put away and he came back for the final time, he had two mugs in his hand.

"What are those?" I laughed as he handed one to me.

"Hot chocolate. It's better than wine." His smile was contagious. "I figured I couldn't get you to eat any other dessert."

In that moment, joy spread through me in a way it hadn't in a long while.

He put his arm around me and pulled me against him, covering us with blankets. I put my head down on his side.

Though I didn't really care for it, I asked Jordan to put on one of the parades but keep the TV muted. Glancing up at the screen every now and again as we spoke, seeing all the people in the cold night, crowded together, smiling and laughing, made the night feel like New Year's Eve as I'd known it to be.

Cuddling up next to him amidst the fire and candles was incredibly cozy. I felt warm and relaxed.

We talked, and I wondered why I'd ever doubted how just being in one another's presence would be enough. I was content. Happy.

I asked him about martial arts and if he would ever train again, to which he thought for a moment.

"I'm not sure," he murmured. "Maybe."

He looked down at me curiously. "What makes you ask, love?"

"I don't know." I shrugged up against his heavy arm. "I think after all this stress, it might make you happy."

"I am happy," he said softly.

I put my hand on the blanket in his lap. "I know, but...I think it might bring you more joy. More fulfillment. You haven't practiced in a long time."

Jordan was pensive, still looking at me with surprise in his eyes.

He nodded. "Eleven years."

I shook my head a little against his side. "Wow. Can you imagine what it would be like for you now? I'm sure you still remember everything."

"I'd be very rusty in everything." We chuckled.

"You've had experience over the years though," I told him, smiling. "You've still fought for work."

"You're right, baby. Though there is much more to practice than what that's required."

"Never done no cool karate jump kicks when catchin' a bad guy, huh?" Jordan threw his head back against the couch and laughed.

"No, never, baby." He chuckled, kissing my temple.

Rubbing my hand over his lower stomach, I murmured, "Well, I think you might have some fun, even if you go back to just one thing. Karaaaate, Taekwondooooo...what's that one with weapons? Hapkido?"

I could hear a smile and fondness in Jordan's voice as he said, "Yes, my love. Hapkido."

He kissed my head. "Would you wanna learn something?" he asked gently.

I was surprised. "Oh, I don't know. I...that would be cool. A cool skill to have. But I don't have much coordination and...I think training would be really embarrassing." A body thing. Working out in front of other people.

"No, no, baby," he half-whispered. "It's not. I know quite a few people that would love to teach you, and they would never, ever judge you. I've trained with a lot of good fighters who are also good people."

I smiled to myself. "That sounds cool," I replied quietly. "Maybe." I gave it some thought.

"It might make you feel a little safer, too."

I nodded, my smile fading. "Probably."

Jordan kissed my temple again. "I think it *would* be fulfilling to start it," he told me. "That's a great idea, my love. Thank you for thinking of me that way."

That made me happy. "Of course," I said softly. "And hey, I was also thinking that it might be nice for you if you started designing some more software...or creating something, you know?"

He leaned back a little to look at me, the surprise on his face clear now.

"Wow. It might be." He shook his head, eyes wondrous. "I haven't thought of that. Of doing that."

After a moment, he murmured, "I would like to perfect the tracking software...get us precise locations..." His eyes were pensive.

"Yeah, baby," I told him softly. "Now that you're not under so much stress. Maybe take a break from that now and try something new. Maybe you'll have fresh ideas when you come back later." I kissed his chin. He nodded in agreement.

He matched my volume. "What made you think of these things?"

I shrugged. "I just...want you to be happy."

Jordan's eyes softened and filled with love. "As long as I have you," he whispered, "I'm happy. I want you to be happy, too. It's all I want."

And I believed him. I looked down, smiling.

"Hey, baby," he murmured. "Look." He tilted his chin up to the TV.

On the screen, the time ticked down as everyone at the parade counted. There were fifty seconds until midnight.

"No way," I murmured, turning back to Jordan, smiling. We'd talked for hours.

It hit me then that I'd known Jordan for nearly a year. A beautiful, unexpected, terrifying year. A year that was more incredible than any of the bad.

I stared in wonder at the man who walked into my life all those months ago and completely changed it. The man who made me look at love differently. Who showed me what love really was. Who brought me so much joy, pleasure, and knowledge. Who enriched my life. Who saved it.

His eyes were filled with wonder, too. With love.

"We're gonna have a better year next year," he whispered, staring into my eyes with those pale blue diamonds that still amazed me.

I nodded. "This year was amazing, too."

"I agree." He kissed my cheek, his lips lingering there. "Because I met you, it was the best year of my life."

My heart skipped. "Me too," I whispered back.

Jordan's eyes turned towards the TV, and mine followed. Two seconds later, it was the New Year.

My eyes flickered back to Jordan. He brought his lips to mine and kissed me slowly, deeply.

I took his cheek in my hand. Jordan pulled back and looked into my eyes for a few seconds before he kissed my lips again. The crystal blue was filled with love.

Glancing down into my lap, he brought his hand down and traced his fingertips up my thigh, over my lowest scar.

Meeting my eyes, he whispered, "I will always love you. Don't ever forget that."

I swallowed, taking the hand on my thigh and lacing mine through it.

"I love you," I whispered.

He blinked slowly to reveal a gleam in his eyes I'd never seen, followed by the whispered words, "I want to marry you."

My lips parted in surprise. No jaw drop, no words.

Oh, thank you, God. For answering my prayers.

My hand began shaking, and he squeezed it. Tears filled my eyes.

"Me too." I could barely make my voice heard.

He smiled so beautifully I all but crumbled. "Plan on it," he told me, his deep, quiet voice back.

I nodded, smiling so big that the tear from each eye landed perfectly on my upturned cheek.

We had time, but I knew one day, perhaps sooner than I thought, we'd take our vows.

And I'd be ready.

Jordan slid back and lay on the pillows at the end of the couch, gently pulling me with him. When I was lying on his chest, he put a couple blankets over us and held me tightly.

We lay there for a few minutes before he whispered,

"Happy New Year, my love."

And lying there, wrapped in him, feeling warm and happy, my mind, tired and nearly high with joy, wandered to an idea.

An idea for a novel that fit everything I wanted mine to be. A story with atypical crime and a twist that I didn't think anyone would expect. I was surprised that I had finally thought of something I considered to be unique, intriguing. I told myself not to be, to have more faith in myself this year. The story crept through my brain.

It took all that time to finally have an idea, all that love, fear and pain that I'd experienced with Jordan, to come up with something different. Something new. Something raw.

I guess love and pain really do inspire the best art.

I would go into the New Year with the idea in mind, the story brimming from my fingertips, itching and ready, finally ready, for the keyboard.

I would take all the facets of it that came to me as I lay there in the arms of the thing I loved most, and I would put them together into a new novel that I could say I was proud of. It would be a novel about real life, real pain, and the dangers of the world. It would be a novel not just about surviving, but about living. Loving.

I would call it *Jordan*.

KAYLA KATHAWA

About The Author

Kayla Kathawa is an author and poet. She has two published collections of poetry, *If You Don't Hear From Me* and *Heavy Things*.

Made in the USA
Columbia, SC
02 April 2023